E.E. STAR

THE
VIOLET
RAVEN

Content Advisory

The Violet Raven is a nonstop, thrilling historical fantasy set in the Celtic lands of 1823. During this time, areas in both Ireland and Scotland were reeling under the weight of systemic oppression. In the wake of failed uprisings and brutal land seizures, entire communities faced starvation, forced displacement, and cultural erasure.

Within these pages, you'll encounter elements including: colonial violence, cultural suppression, political conflict, death, grief, loss of family, mentions of suicide, mentions of wrongful execution, intense physical violence on page, decapitation on page (of a bad guy), attempted sexual assault, mentions of attempted sexual assault, and consensual sexual activities that are shown on page. Readers who may be sensitive to these topics, please proceed with caution. If you need clarification, I welcome you to reach out directly.

But for those who are ready... steel your heart, raise your blade, and prepare to stand among the Raven Queen's warriors.

Name/ Pronunciation	Type	Accent
Alexander "Alex" Mumford	Side Character	American
Amelia Curran	Side Character	Irish
Bran Mumford	Side Character	American
Caitríona "Triona" Sinclair/ Ka-TREE-nah	Main Character	Scottish
Callan Sinclair	Side Character	Scottish
Casey Sinclair	Side Character	Scottish
Colina Sutherland	Side Character	Scottish
Dana/ DAH-nuh	Side Character	Irish
Dealla Johen/ Dee-luh Yo-hen	Side Character	Received Pronunciation (RP)/ British
Deidre Wallis/ Day-druh	Side Character	Received Pronunciation (RP)/ British
Eamon Agassey/ AY-mun ah-GASS-ee	Side Character	Irish
Ellen Sinclair	Side Character	Scottish

Name/ Pronunciation	**Type**	**Accent**
Finnis "Finn" MacGregor	Main Character	Scottish
Henry Charles Sirr	Side Character	Received Pronunciation (RP)/ British
Indech/ In-deh	Side Character	Irish
James Sinclair	Side Character	Scottish
Mannie	Side Character	Irish
Marcus Murray	Side Character	Received Pronunciation (RP)/ British
Saoirse Agassey/ SUR-sha ah-GASS-ee	Side Character	Irish

To those who fight battles no one sees, to the survivors rising from the ashes, and to every woman who has been told she's too much or not enough—I see you.

I know what it's like to be overlooked, dismissed, and told to stay silent while your soul screams to be heard. But listen to me: your fire was never meant to be extinguished. It was meant to blaze.

Queens are not born—they are forged in fire, tempered by trials, and crowned by their own unyielding will. And every single one of you carries that crown within.

So stop waiting for permission. Smash the walls, break the chains, and unleash that unstoppable, untamed force inside you. It's time to rise. To own every scar, every strength, every piece of who you are. To claim the life that's been waiting for you to seize it.

I write this story for you.

Acknowledgements

Writing this book has been a journey—one filled with long nights, countless cups of tea (or something stronger), and an ever-growing stack of scribbled notes. But through it all, I was never alone.

To my family—Thank you for always believing in me, even when I doubted myself. Your unwavering support, love, and encouragement have been the foundation upon which this book was built. To my husband (the inspiration for Casey), who sacrificed time with me so I could lose myself in this story, and to my kids, who graciously gave me "quiet time" when I needed it most. To my entire family, who made sure that even if no one else bought this book, it would still have a place of honor on their shelves—you have my deepest gratitude.

To my friends—both old and new—you were my sounding boards, my cheerleaders, my sources of inspiration. This book would not exist without your guidance. Whether you listened to me ramble about plot twists, screamed over character angst with me, or simply reminded me to take a break and breathe, I am endlessly grateful for each of you. Kerri, whose unwavering support over the past 20-plus years has made her my Samwise Gamgee. Emily, Cat, Ashley, and Michelle, who patiently listened to my romance-novel ramblings and never once judged my obsession with fictional men. Kenzi, Jen, and Lauryn, who became fast friends and pushed me forward on the days when doubt threatened to consume me. My attic ladies, who turned this book community into a true family. And to Teri, whose words of encouragement always seemed to find me exactly when I needed them—I'm honored to call you a friend.

To my writing community—fellow authors, narrators, influencers, and those who offered advice and encouragement—thank you for your honesty and insight. Your belief in my words has meant more than I can express.

To my editor—Nicole, you ensured this novel was worth reading. You were the first person to experience the full story from start to finish, and your notes throughout the editing process reignited my confidence.

To my sensitivity readers—Catherine and Claire… your insights helped me ensure I was honoring the people and histories woven into these pages with the respect they deserve. Your guidance was not only invaluable—it was deeply grounding.

To my beta readers—After staring at 180,000+ words repeatedly, I was going cross-eyed. You helped make sure no detail was overlooked and that this story was in its absolute best shape.

And last, to the readers—thank you for picking up this book, for stepping into this world with me, and for allowing these characters to take up space in your heart. This story is truly for you.

With all my love and gratitude, **E. E. Star**

Special Note About Mumford & Sons

They are a constant source of inspiration.

Music fuels my very being—it is my compass in the dark, my calm in the storm. It offers comfort when nothing else can, so it would feel wrong not to acknowledge the band that carried me through countless hours of writing.

When I felt trapped in my thoughts, unable to move forward, their lyrics stirred something in me. Their melodies took my mind on a journey, awakening emotion when I had none left to give.

This hopeless wanderer found solace in their sound, and for that, I am forever grateful.

"Well, I know I had it all on the line, but don't just sit with folded hands and become blind. 'Cause even when there is no star in sight, you'll always be my only guiding light."—Mumford & Sons

Author's Note

This book is interwoven with threads of historical reality and imagination. Throughout its pages, you'll encounter real historical figures alongside beings drawn from the rich tapestry of mythology. Some elements have been adapted or altered to serve the narrative, but are not placed there to distort or disrespect historical truth.

For readers who, like me, are passionate about uncovering the layers of the past, I invite you to dig deeper into your own ancestry—and explore the discoveries that helped shape this story.

The inception of this book stemmed from a curiosity that gripped me years ago:

What would Ireland and Scotland look like if the Great Potato Famine had never occurred?

We'll get to the meat and potatoes of that question as the story unfolds.

Driven by an unquenchable thirst for knowledge—and, admittedly, bouts of insomnia and the ability to hyper-focus for months on end—I embarked on a journey that has culminated in this work.

This book strives to honor historical integrity while acknowledging the importance of filling in historical gaps. Oral traditions, while invaluable, can only tell us so much. Irish mythology is no exception—its narratives have been fragmented, reimagined, and often misrepresented, largely due to the systematic suppression of the Irish and Scottish Gaelic languages.

This is not intended as a scolding. Rather, it is a call for greater awareness. Cultural appropriation often begins with good intentions but can lead to erasure when stories are stripped of their roots. We are part of a generation with unprecedented access to knowledge—it's our responsibility to use it wisely, and with respect.

Researching the near-erasure of entire languages, cultures, and ways of life gave me a new perspective. It challenged me to ask difficult questions, to stay curious, and to unlearn reflexive defensiveness. I encourage others to do the same.

This story holds deep personal meaning for me—it is tied to the lands of my ancestors, to family history both spoken and unspoken. I'm honored, and deeply grateful, that you've chosen to read this fusion of thrilling action and heartfelt, steamy romance—two of my favorite things brought together. At its heart, this is a hero's journey, inspired by the timeless classics we so often return to.

My greatest hope is that this blend of fantasy and historical fiction honors the legacy of those who shaped history—often at great personal cost—and who stood in defiance of the powerful and self-serving. While we cannot undo the injustices of the past, we *can* learn from them. And where it is still within our power—we can do better.

Love you to pieces, and I hope you love this story as much as I do.

"I am confident that there truly is such a thing as living again, that the living spring from the dead, and that the souls of the dead are in existence."- Socrates.

PROPHECY

In whispering woods where shadows play, a life unfolds with grief's first day.

Some souls in solemn vigil bend, their knees to ground, their wills to mend.

Nineteen moons shall orbit bright, 'round the sun's commanding light.

Death will come within a day, the sacrifice will cause dismay.

In secret, treachery begins to rise, charting out her fate's surprise.

Along the path, she'll find one soul, its love, a weight, a heavy toll.

In every beat, their souls combined, a tapestry by stars designed.

Once contact graces trio's sight, inner strength unchains with might.

Called by powers, true and bold, she journeys forth to claim her hold.

Upon the sacred ground, she'll stand, with fate's dark price in trembling hand.

CONTENTS

PREFACE

The most profound prophecies often come to us as whispers in dreams—secrets so sharp they jolt us awake, heart pounding, breath caught. In those fragile moments between sleep and reality, the dreamer clings to this newfound knowledge, revelations so heavy they threaten to shift the axis of countless lives. They cradle the question of its significance with a reverence both cautious and profound, as if weighing the worth of a jewel capable of illuminating the darkest night—or igniting an unquenchable fire.

What am I meant to do with this?

The question hums like a haunting refrain, resonating through the fibres of existence. It echoes, ricocheting off the unseen walls of time and space, until it confronts the dual nature of all truths:

What stands to be lost? What could be gained?

Prophets are no strangers to such questions. They speak of ruin and rebirth in the same breath, their words capable of both splintering hope and sewing it anew. Haunted by foresight, one understands liberation's rarity.

Will my warning be enough?

Ultimately, those touched by prophecy must choose to embrace the truth in all its weight—the pain it brings, yes, but also the hope it unveils. For while the revelation of truth may cast long shadows of suffering, it can also light the way to redemption. Some battles and destinies are beyond our mortal grasp, shaping us whether we wish it or not. In their wake, there is both affliction and the promise of something greater—a chance for rebirth, a path to salvation.

This has always been, and it will always be, a condition of life... and I would know.

For I have lived two...

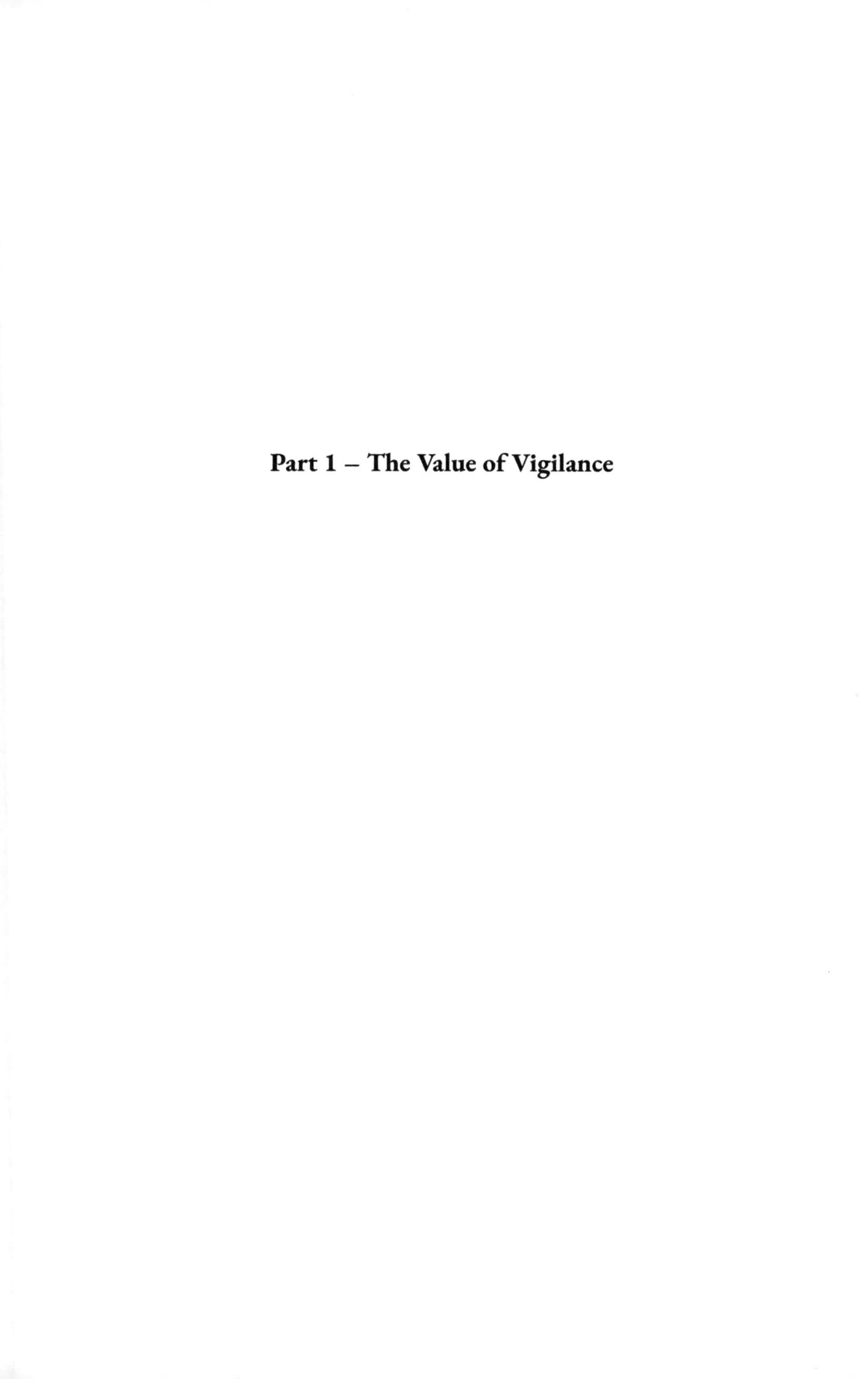

Part 1 – The Value of Vigilance

1

AT ALL COSTS

The Sinclair Family Home, Castle Connemara
1810 Keiss, Scotland

Ellen Sinclair was a woman of indomitable resolve, her unyielding nature a testament to her strength. Yet her youngest daughter, only six years old, seemed determined to match and surpass her tenacity. Triona's boundless energy and relentless stubbornness tested Ellen's patience like nothing else.

Her voice rang out, sharp with exasperation, from the doorway of her daughter's chamber. "Caitríona Sinclair, it's high time the stars bore witness to yer slumber!" Exhaustion weighed heavily on Ellen, her efforts to coax Triona to bed feeling as futile as waiting for the grass to grow.

The use of her full name, a tried-and-true tactic, finally did the trick. Triona froze mid-stride, her wide eyes snapping to her mother's piercing gaze. She stood motionless in the centre of the room; the whirlwind of her energy suddenly stilled by Ellen's commanding tone.

With a cautious gait, she approached the bed and carefully climbed on top. "Am I in trouble, Ma?" The crafty sparkle in her gaze was unmistakable; the art of persuasion was second nature to her, with her radiant green eyes and dainty nose. Hell come to any man that might consider giving his heart to her one day. She will surely have him bending to her every will.

Ellen, try as she might, bore no grudge against such gambits. She knew well the subtle power of a fluttered lash, of a gaze held just a moment too long—the silent wiles she had once wielded with effortless grace. In her tempestuous youth, those very charms had brought the mighty James Sinclair to his knees. He had fallen hard, utterly captivated from the moment their eyes first met, as if fate itself had conspired in her favour.

The mere thought of how deeply and completely he loved her, of the unwavering devotion woven into his every word and action, sent warmth rushing to her cheeks. He had made her feel like a queen then, cherished and adored beyond measure. Somehow, even after all these years, he still did.

Ellen lingered almost a moment too long, watching with a particular maternal fondness at the playful defiance Triona displayed.

Moments like these reminded her of how fleeting time was. Even at six, Triona's fierce spirit and vivid imagination left Ellen marvelling at her potential.

A tempest brewed beneath Triona's fiery spirit, one destined to shake the foundations of the world. Ellen had seen it in the way Triona fearlessly challenged her brothers, her sharp tongue unyielding even when outmatched. She had a gift for rallying those around her. This raw, untamed force could one day command the reverence due to a queen.

Ellen's demeanour lightened, and she playfully sighed as she walked up to the edge of her daughter's bed. "My little butterfly", Ellen spoke with playful exaggeration as she tucked a stray hair behind her ear, "Ye're not in trouble, but it is time for the house to settle, lest we wake yer brothers. Those trows would groan for hours should their rest be disturbed." Ellen smiled at her youngest, as a giggle escaped between Triona's lips.

She sat next to Triona to wrap her in a hug. Her little head smelled like her favourite flower: Scottish Primrose. "Ah, someone found their way into my scents again." A muffled laugh would be the only answer she would receive. Ellen did not mind. The scent brought nothing but fond memories, and a sense of calm filled the room.

As Ellen began to rise, a small hand tugged at her dress. "Ma, tell me that story. The one about goddesses." Triona said, her toothless lisp adding an endearing charm to her words. Her shimmering green doe eyes could sway even the most stoic of hearts. Mixed with her blossoming smile, Ellen's resolve melted in an instant.

"Aye, Ma," a mockingly high-pitched voice came from the doorway, "give my bonnie lass a goodnight tale."

Ellen turned her head to look at the tall man leaning against the doorframe. James Sinclair was indeed a welcome sight. After over ten years of marriage, he could still kindle an ember within her.

Ellen rolled her eyes playfully as she spoke. "Oh? If ye're that eager to please, why no' try yer hand at storytellin', *mo chridhe?*"

Laughing, he said, "Only ye tell the story with such justice. My poor grammar isnae match for such a fabulist like ye, dear."

Ellen threw her hands up. "What am I to do with ye?" The statement had his lip curling up into an all-familiar smile.

She appeared amused at first, but James noticed the faint shadow behind her smile—a sadness she tried to mask from the world, though never from him. The memories tied to the tale lingered, heavy and unspoken, brushing against her resolve.

Noticing the faint yet subtle change, James gave Ellen a nod of encouragement. Only he understood how difficult it was for Ellen to feel as if she were losing time with Triona, and the reminder sat laced within the lines of the story. Sharing brought Triona joy, and that was ultimately what mattered most to Ellen, so she was determined to push through, her feelings be damned.

"Ye spoil her, James," she said in jest as she forced every fatalistic thought away.

His gaze became wolfish, and she could not resist beaming a smile his way. He had a way of smiling that was equal parts loving and playful. His smile was one that would make others join in gleefully.

"I wonder," he mused, his eyes locked on hers, "where I might have first learned to be so dotin', not to mince yer words."

He was right, of course. Finding such an attentive man was rare. James had always been ever present in his ladies' lives, his playful involvement at bedtime a prime example. There was not a single thing he would not do for Ellen or Triona, equating them to a mighty queen and princess.

Triona gently tugged on Ellen's dress again, drawing her attention away from James. Looking down with a laugh, Ellen said, "Aye, keep yer *heid*, little butterfly."

She scooped Triona into her arms, the girl's laughter bubbling up as she squirmed playfully. Crossing the room, Ellen settled gracefully by the window, holding Triona close.

As she gazed out into the dark night, with Triona comfortably snuggled in her arms, Ellen felt the warmth of James' presence behind her. The gentle weight of his hand upon her shoulder urged her gaze toward him; his hazel eyes, reflecting starlight, conveyed silent promises as he softly said, "Ye are truly a wonder, Lady Sinclair." His words warmed her skin, but his gaze left her breathless, her mind yearning to move story time along—to feel his hands tracing her, igniting every inch of her.

In a whisper of a moment, James' lips brushed against hers, igniting a silent cascade of understanding. He whispered into her ear, "*at all costs.*" That tender, unspoken phrase had evolved into an oath more poignant than a thousand declarations of love. Together, they had an unwavering bond of devotion, steadfast in their resolve to protect their families, prepared to make even the most profound sacrifices should the occasion arise. They had built a beautiful life together, and they would valiantly defend the bonds of this family to their last breath.

In the hush of twilight, Ellen began.

"Long ago, before the rise of great kings and queens, when Ireland's emerald hills were young and unspoiled, beings of unmatched power roamed the land. The Tuatha Dé Danann, 'People of the Goddess Danu,' were a spiritual tribe of gods and goddesses cloaked in mystery.

Among them, Ériu and her kin held dominion over the realm. Born of the land itself, Ériu's essence was tied to the rivers and hills, representing unity and strength. Their presence wove magic into the land itself, breathing vitality into barren soil, calming stormy seas, and moving in rhythm with the tides of the moon and sun. Beneath their watchful gaze, mythical creatures pledged their loyalty, and nature itself obeyed their will. They stood as towering guardians of existence, timeless and revered.

Yet, shadows whispered of a destiny even they could not foresee—a truth that would shape the fate of the world.

Triona leaned in closer and whispered urgently, "Tell us about their powers already,

Mam! Did they shoot fire from their hands? Turn people into goats? Did they have swords that talked?"

Ellen gave her a sharp look. "If ye want me to continue, ye'll keep yer heid. Ye're rushin' me like a bard who's had too much mead an' forgotten his own tale!"

Triona huffed, crossing her arms. "But tell the good bits! The fightin'! The magic! The explodin' stuff!"

James, who had been lounging nearby, smirked. "Aye, Ellen, spare us the poetry. Were they hurlin' lightning bolts, shapeshiftin' into fearsome beasts, or at least turnin' some poor bastard into a toad? Because if there's no dramatic smitin' involved, I'll be terribly disappointed."

Ellen sighed dramatically, giving James an exasperated look before turning to Triona. "Ye ken, lass, ye're far too much like yer father. Impatient, an' full o' mischief. If the pair of ye dinnae let me finish, I'll start bletherin' on about the grand politics of auld Ireland instead."

James raised his hands in surrender. "All right, nae need for such cruelty. Continue, wise storyteller."

Ellen smirked before pressing on.

"Sacred within the beliefs of the Tuatha Dé Danann was the divine feminine—the conviction that goddesses alone would weave the threads of existence. These deities lent their essence to the very fabric of the land, blessing all forms of life with vigour.

Amongst them rose a triad: the Goddesses of Sovereignty, and foremost was Ériu—her might unrivalled, her power immeasurable. Such was her force she did not deign to grace the battlefield with her presence.

It wasn't just power she wielded. Ériu could change form and command the loyalty of any woodland creature, but above all, she chose the raven—a creature as enigmatic as the shifting tides of fate itself. Her raven was no ordinary creature. Black as the deepest night under the moon's watch, yet when the sun reigned, its feathers shimmered with an eerie violet sheen—an omen, a harbinger of fate, and a whisper of the unseen world.

Even the bravest warriors faltered at the sight. A bridge between the living and the dead, Ériu's raven carried the weight of fate itself. To see it was to know that destiny had begun to unravel—and none could escape its shadow. Warriors on the battlefield would freeze in terror at its cry, for they knew its presence heralded judgment.

Combined with the strength of her other parts, she wove destruction upon those who dared invade their sacred realm, ensuring that the spirit of the land remained unbroken."

Ellen cleared her throat and began singing a simple melody.

'In her stead, she sent a raven, cloaked in violet's hue. Then came the banshees, bold and fierce, vengeance swift, and justice true.

The villains' steeds on windswept heath would buck and bolt, unbound, untethered, their masters left to face their fate, their cries soon lost to winds that weathered.

With victory near, the triad stood, beneath the sky so vast and wide. Their blades like fire, their hearts burned bright, no foe could break their fearless stride.

Through shattered night and echoing wail, the foes did fall, their strength undone, and so the dawn in golden light arose to hail what they had won.'

With an abruptness only a child could muster, Triona blurted out, "What does that mean?"

Ellen blinked. "What does what mean, mo chridhe?"

Bundled in a shawl far too big for her, Triona wriggled around on her lap. "The raven. The banshees. The horses runnin' off."

Ellen nodded, settling deeper into her chair. "Well, they called Ériu the Raven Queen because, before battle, she would send her raven as a warning—a sign to put fear in the hearts of men. And once that fear took hold, she used it. While they fled for the safety of the woods, she lured them toward their victims—the very people they had wronged."

"Banshees?" Triona asked, eyes wide.

Ellen's lips curled in a knowing smile. "Aye."

James muttered under his breath, "Serves 'em right for layin' hands on a woman."

Ellen spoke, her voice low and steady. "Then, whatever men remained were left abandoned, because Ériu would call their horses away, leavin' them stranded... easy prey for her warriors."

Triona let out a long breath, her eyes shining. "So they were already afraid before the fight even started?"

Ellen smiled, smoothing back a stray curl. "Aye, mo chridhe. For the strongest warrior is no' always the one who wields the sharpest blade—but the one who makes their enemies drop theirs first."

Triona's brows furrowed. "And why did she not come herself?"

Her mother chuckled softly. "Because Ériu was so powerful, she didnae need to stand on the battlefield herself. She could bend the world to her will from afar, shaping fate with but a whisper in the wind. She was mighty, aye, and could hold her own—but she kenned there was more power in fear."

Triona's mouth fell open in awe. Then, before she could stop herself, she blurted, "That's hellish grand!"

"Triona!" Ellen spoke in a chiding tone.

The wee girl clamped a hand over her mouth, eyes wide.

James, who had been quietly listening mostly, let out a bark of laughter. "Well, she's no' wrong, Ellen. And she even used it correctly."

Ellen shot him a glare. "Dinnae encourage her, James."

Still chuckling, James ruffled Triona's hair. "Jus mind yer tongue next time, lass. But aye—it is hellish grand."

Ellen sighed, shaking her head before a reluctant chuckle slipped out. She glanced at James with a mixture of exasperation and fondness, and then muttered, "Ye're impossible."

James smirked. "Aye, so I've been told."

Ellen continued.

"Those words spread across the land to Hispania, where a race of men called the Milesians resided. They sought to challenge the pantheon of gods and claim the land they believed was owed to humankind.

Prophecy of their arrival came to Ériu in sleep. She saw visions of the Milesians descending upon Ireland; the gods fading from mortal memory. Torn between her duty to protect her people and the inevitability of fate, she foresaw a great challenge ahead. The Tuatha Dé Danann would be tested, and their era upon the Earth would wane. And she knew they were not beyond the reach of destiny.

When the Milesians arrived, they stormed the Sidhe with swift and relentless force, overwhelming the Tuatha Dé Danann at once. Despite their strength and wisdom, the gods found themselves divided. Lugh of the Long Arm urged a last stand, while the Dagda counselled retreat, fearing that fighting would bring ruin to the land they loved.

Caught between their pleas, Ériu knew she must act to preserve the spirit of Ireland. Though powerful, their divine sovereignty waned under the sheer determination and numbers of the mortal invaders. The Tuatha, who had once stood as unyielding guardians, now found themselves at the mercy of fate.

Mind made up, Ériu resolved to meet the Milesians upon the Hill of Uisneach, the sacred heart of Ireland. This ancient hill, known as the navel of the land, was the meeting point of the heavens, the earth, and the Otherworld—a place where all things converged.

The first to approach Ériu atop Uisneach was a handsome man named Amergin, a bard and judge respected among his people. She recognised the spark of potential within him. Her decision was set, and when she spoke, she said,

'Warriors, welcome to you. Your coming was prophesied. Yours will be the island forever. There is no better island in the world. No race will be more perfect than your race. The Tuatha Dé Danann will take the land below, and you shall have the one above. You shall seek assembly with the Three Kings to test the value and ability to sustain life within the bounds of this land.'

As she spoke, her voice was light and melodic, captivating Amergin. Yet her enchantment was soon shattered by a man named Éber Donn, whose heart was filled with disdain for the gods.

'We owe her no gratitude; our tribute is to the gods alone, to the might of our own hands and hearts.'

If provoked in such a manner, a dark power would rise from within Ériu. Such a direct affront would not go unanswered. With wrath surging through her veins, she invoked a fierce curse upon him, her ire uncontained and swift. Forcing the Milesians to kneel before her, she spoke.

'Naught to thee, thou shalt have gain of this island, nor will thy children. This wretched man shall drown in the deepest depths of the ocean. A resting place fit for a monster. A gift granted to me as retribution for his insolence, from the children of the Milesians, is that my name may be upon this island forevermore, as a reminder that I will always be here. Shall we fall, my people will find a haven in an eternal dominion, one of my creation, and I shall give myself over to the

land. Mankind that dare to gain ungranted entry shall face consequences of my making. It shall be swift, harsh, and unforgiving.'

With a wave of her hand, Ériu released them, her knowing smile lingering as Éber Donn departed, his pride stung. Paying heed to the gravity of the moment, Amergin agreed to both conditions on behalf of the Milesians. He expressed great regret for Éber Donn's slight.

Undeterred by Ériu's warning, Éber Donn advanced to challenge the three kings ahead of him—Mac Cuill, Mac Cecht, and Mac Greine. Sensing a similarity that matched Ériu's, they set terms. The Milesians were to endure nine days out at sea on two separate vessels, pitted against the ferocity of surging waves and sorcerous wings conjured by the druids. By virtue of pure heart, Amergin was granted the power to soothe the thrashing seas and make safe passage to shore. Éber Donn, by fault of his own, succumbed to the fate Ériu had spoken upon him and was swallowed by the ruthless waters.

Accepting fate's hand, Ériu prepared to make the greatest sacrifice of all. Many of her people wanted to continue fighting, but she had seen that outcome, and she would not let it fall upon them. With Ériu's arcane influence, the Tuatha Dé Danann withdrew into the Otherworld. This ethereal dominion shimmered with light and magic, where rivers of silver wound through forests alive with ancient songs. Ériu shaped it to mirror the beauty of Ireland, ensuring her people would forever remember the land they had left behind.

Her parting words hung heavily in the air, an ominous omen cloaked in mystery.

'Mankind shall do many great things, but should an era arrive for my resurgence, I will heed the summons. Through hubris or folly, mankind may summon its own undoing. Should that time come, when the balance is broken and the echoes of their own deeds summon forces long at rest, I shall rise once more'

In the breath that followed, none dared stir, and silence seemed to blanket them. Ériu laid herself in eternal slumber atop the high ground of Uisneach. She became one with the land, ensuring her essence would endure as a protector of Ireland for all time. The hill became a place of reverence, where violets bloomed year-round as a reminder of her sacrifice and enduring protection.

Amergin sat upon that hill in silence. Alone. The weight of Ériu's departure settled heavily in his chest. With Éber Donn out of the way, he was named Chief Ollam of Ériu.

He split the land in two, granting his brothers rule over their halves, while dedicating himself to documenting Ireland's wonders so that Ériu's legacy would endure for all time.

But Amergin knew that words alone were not enough. In his heart, he understood that the land would not always be left in peace, and so he made another vow—one spoken only to the winds and hills that had once carried Ériu's voice.

Should Ériu's lands ever need defending, his bloodline would rise—bound by honour, waiting for the call.

Ériu's solemn rest could be felt across the land, sending silent warnings that the Age of the Gods was over. The hour to seek refuge had dawned on them.

As the world above changed, the Tuatha Dé Danann did not vanish, nor did they fade from existence. Instead, they dwell in the radiance of their undying essence—

In the Otherworld."

Triona's brow furrowed in confusion. "Why are there still bad folk? Where is her magic?"

James placed a steadying hand on Ellen's shoulder, ready to take the lead. Crouching down to meet Triona's gaze, he said, "Ériu's magic still lingers, but it cannae always shield against human choice. It's woven into the land and lives in the hearts o' good folk, but even the strongest magic can fade if mankind allows hatred to take root."

Triona's posture shifted, almost in defeat. James took her small hand in his. "But there are far more good folk than bad, and as long as they're here, evil won't prevail. It's hope that fuels them, keeps 'em fightin'—for themselves and for those they'd sacrifice everything for. Hope gives 'em the strength to believe that a lass as fierce as mine might save 'em all. Ériu's magic still breathes in them, waitin' to prove themselves worthy of her return."

"How? You said she died." Triona questioned, her eyes wide with innocence.

"Not died—" James considered his words carefully, "just slumberin', in a sense." Despite Triona's puzzled expression, James pressed on.

"Do ye wanna ken what Ériu means now?" She nodded enthusiastically.

"It means Éireann." James paused for a moment to give Triona a moment to ponder the importance of what he was saying. Though her middle name was not a typical one, Ellen and James loved it.

He continued. "Ériu's spirit still lingers, not just in the land, but in those who refuse to let darkness take hold. Folk like ye, my fierce one, is why the world hasnae fallen to ruin. Ye're filled with the love of others, ye're bountiful, and life in ye is abundant and everlastin'."

She smiled at him. "Casey said it was a daft name." He chortled and looked up at Ellen.

"Remind me to have words with that boy come mornin'."

Beneath the warm glow of the flickering fire, the room brimmed with a tenderness that wrapped around them like a soft, encompassing embrace. Ellen, her heart brimming with love, brushed a tender hand over Triona's cheek and spoke softly.

"It isnae a silly name, my bonnie lass. Yer cheeky brother's just fond o' teasin'. The name ye bear is a promise of grand adventures yet to come—jus like the one ye got it from."

With a mother's grace, Ellen cradled Triona's cheek lightly, as if to leave a whisper of her affection. Ellen's eyes were deep pools of emotion, and danced with the light of a thousand memories, glistening with the sheen of tears unshed.

"Yer father speaks true. Ye carry more than jus a name, my love. Ye carry a spark of something greater—something the world cannae afford to lose. The fire in yer heart's set to turn the world on its heid. The name ye bear is the breath of Ireland herself. It's a strong name, like the emerald lands of old." Triona stared into Ellen's eyes, and frowned, noticing the silver glisten there.

"Mama, why're cryin'?" Ellen let out the faintest chuckle, and blinked forcibly, containing what was sure to be an onslaught of tears.

"Oh, I am jus so proud to be yer mother. Da and I-" Ellen paused, unsure how to even explain such emotions to a child. She continued, "We're so grateful the heavens saw fit to give us an angel on earth."

That single statement was as close to the truth as Ellen would ever willingly get.

With eyes wide and full of youthful curiosity, seeming to mull over some statement Ellen had made, Triona turned to James.

"Will I be stronger than ye, Da?" James let out a full belly laugh.

"Oh, my sweet girl, ye're gonna be strong enough to defeat many a foe. The strength ye wield will rival the legends! Grown men, in their pride and glory, will quiver at the mere mention of yer name!" James spoke with melodramatic flourish, making hand gestures as if he were a stage actor. The sight of it had Triona and Ellen rolling with laughter.

"I have no powers, I'm just a wee lass!"

James impulsively reached out and teasingly pinched the tip of Triona's nose. Like that of a little lion cub, she burst from Ellen's lap to unleash her playful wrath, pinning James beneath her. The surprise of the attack knocked the wind out of him, causing Ellen and Triona to laugh harder at his expense.

"Seems ye're already well equipped with that strength." With a resonant laughter that echoed through the hearth-warmed room, James stood, pulling her close as he twirled her in his arms. Holding her tight, he pressed a kiss to her temple, a seal of eternal fatherly love.

"In due time," he whispered with an air of mystery, as though speaking of an old secret, "all will be revealed. But until then, it's my solemn duty—nae, my sacred promise—to keep ye locked away from all the terrible groonies that lurk beneath veiled shadows."

James sat, Triona safely cradled in the crook of his arm, wriggling delightfully with every peal of laughter. He stroked Triona's head as she settled down, energy slowly starting to wane. He sat there with her for a long while, just relishing in the rarest of moments. Ellen hummed the sweetest of lullabies, and together they watched as Triona's eyelids began to sag.

When her lashes fluttered close for the final time, James gently stood, and walked to lay the cherished bundle down on her bed, Ellen at his heels.

Turning, they exchanged a look brimming with silent understanding—an unspoken pact to nurture and protect the wonder that was their Triona. In James's mind, the image of her smile mingled with fears of what lay ahead, a flicker of resolve hardening in his chest. Ellen's gaze, shimmering with unshed tears, spoke of her own quiet promise: no matter the cost, they would stand united against whatever challenges might threaten their daughter's light. This extraordinary girl they had been blessed with.

Gone was the playful smile that had just been plastered across his face, and an all too familiar gleam returned to Ellen's eyes. James grabbed Ellen's hand and pulled her in tight for an embrace, grounding himself in the warmth of her presence, though a chill ran through him. He pressed a quick kiss to the top of her head, the simple gesture unravelling her last fragile restraint as silent tears slipped free.

When he spoke, his tone had an unsettlingly eerie chill to it. Much unlike the typical light-hearted tone familiar to their household.

"Called by powers, true and bold, she journeys forth to claim her hold. Upon the sacred ground, she'll stand, with fate's dark price in trembling hand."

James's voice lingered on the last word, his gaze fixed on the firelight as though seeking answers in its flicker. The prophecy was as familiar to him as his own heartbeat, yet speaking it aloud made the weight of its truth settle heavily in the room. He clenched his jaw, his thoughts a tempest of pride and foreboding. "Ellen," he murmured, "this lass of ours... she's got a destiny grander than we'll ever ken. We savour every moment, every blessed second."

Ellen nodded solemnly, her tears falling in silence. She brushed a tender hand over Triona's brow, her voice hushed, almost reverent. "Each moment she's safe is a gift borrowed—one I'd trade anythin' to keep."

They stood there for a long while, watching over their daughter as she slept peacefully, her small form a flicker of light in a world so vast and shadowed by unseen dangers.

Though any road set before them remained uncertain, fraught with peril, they stood ready—knowing that even against the mightiest of foes, the love they bore for their daughter was a strength beyond reckoning. They knew that love alone could not shield her from the storms to come, but they would give everything, even the very marrow of their bones, to stand between her and the gathering darkness. Whatever the cost, their love would burn as a beacon, defying the shadows threatening to consume her light.

At All Costs.

2

WHERE ALL GREAT JOURNEYS BEGIN

Triona
Present Day
Friday, 18 April 1823
Edinburgh, Scotland

A sharp, rapid pounding jerks me from sleep, each knock a demand rather than a request. The sound doesn't linger—just a few decisive raps before heels strike the wooden floor in retreat, their clipped rhythm echoing down the corridor. Deidre Wallis never lingers. She announces, disrupts, and then vanishes before protest can form.

I groan, dragging the pillow over my head. The dim light slipping through the curtains tells me it's not urgency that's roused me—it's fussiness. Deidre has been restless these past few days, no doubt because we're preparing to part ways.

She is the reason I've been able to attend school so far from my family. My parents, trusting her beyond measure, have relied on her since I was twelve to oversee my education and well-being. Over the past six years, she's been more than a governess. She's a mentor, a maternal figure, and a maddening force of nature. Despite the friction between us, I can't deny her dedication. She's given me more than knowledge—she's helped develop some of the best parts of myself.

Deidre embodies contrasts. Middle-aged grace shapes her, with fine lines that hint at wisdom earned. Her deep brown eyes hold untold secrets, her rich, dark skin mirroring her steadfast strength. Just as the roots of an ancient tree, she's unyielding in her convictions. Everything she does, no matter how exasperating, is for others' benefit.

She doesn't need words to fill a room—her presence alone commands it. She carries herself with the certainty of a queen and the impatience of a soldier, her gaze a silent reprimand before she's even spoken. She's moulded me with that stare alone.

When she first broached the idea of my attending Mrs Lotraine's School for Girls, I remember the weight of her words settling over the room. She argued that time away from our secluded home would teach me to navigate the world, to forge connections and alliances I might one day need. '*Scotland has known its share of hardship,*' she'd said, her voice steady. '*And there will be many more to come.*'

Practicality was her shield—proximity to resources, access to books—but I suspect she saw the hunger in me, the restless yearning for something beyond our borders. Perhaps, in her wisdom, she knew I needed this more than I realised. After a heated debate, my parents agreed to her plan, albeit with strict conditions: relentless studying and almost daily sparring with my brothers, Callan and Casey, assigned as my reluctant guardians. Bound to the role out of duty rather than desire, fulfilling our parents' expectations rather than their own wishes.

I accepted the terms without hesitation, diving headfirst into a gruelling routine of academic studies and rigorous training alongside my brothers. There was no room for excuses, no leniency for failure—this had been my father's way since I was a child. It had shaped me, tempered me, just as steel in a forge. Not just tradition, but a way of survival. A foundation built stone by stone for a life filled with unknowns.

I learned the weight of a blade before the weight of expectation. I endured the sharp sting of bruises, and the sharper sting of failure, long before I understood how rare it was for a girl to fight for her own life, let alone receive the training to do so.

I may not be the strongest among my siblings, but I am certainly the fastest. My agility, both physical and mental, gives me an edge in contests of strategy and wit, much to my brothers' frustration.

Callan, my eldest brother, takes his role as guardian with a deep sense of duty. He sees himself as an extension of our parents, embodying their authority and values at every turn. His domineering nature leaves little room for sibling camaraderie, so weeks spent by his side drag on as if time itself has slowed to torment me. To him, being my brother is secondary to being my overseer, and I suspect he wouldn't have it any other way.

To top it off, he has a maddening habit of scaring off anyone I might show the slightest interest in. His hypocrisy only adds to my frustration. He scrutinises my every move, judging my virtue as if *he* is some moral authority, all while indulging himself in ways he thinks I take no notice of. How dare he preach restraint on me while ignoring his own? It is enough to make me want to lob the nearest heavy object at his impossibly thick skull.

Casey, the middle child, is a gust of wind in a stagnant room—chaotic, refreshing, impossible to ignore. Where Callan constrains, Casey liberates, turning arguments into laughter and competition into camaraderie. Our closeness is effortless, woven from playful jabs and whispered conspiracies. He admits, in rare moments of honesty, that Edinburgh has awakened something in him too—a yearning for more, for the stories we've read to become places we see with our own eyes. Only a year apart in age, we share a competitive streak that often turns playful. We bicker constantly, but Casey has a way of turning every argument into a joke, leaving me laughing and forgetting what I was mad about to begin with.

A sharp knock on my door snaps me back to the present. Deidre's unrelenting spirit will be the death of me.

Another sharp rap rattles the door, insistent. I groan, making sure she hears my suffering. "Triona isn't here! Try again later!"

The floorboards creak—my only warning before the door swings open with force. Deidre storms in, her presence as commanding as ever. "Caitríona Sinclair, get out of that bed this instant, or I'll fetch a pail of cold water!"

I bolt upright, rolling off the opposite side of the bed to escape her wrath. Deidre's warnings aren't idle threats. She gives one, and only one, before following through. It didn't take many incidents for me to learn that the hard way.

Raising my hands in surrender, I let out a resigned huff. "All right, you win this one." A playful smirk creeps onto my lips, but Deidre just rolls her eyes, muttering, "*gods help me.*"

She crosses her arms and surveys the room with a critical eye, her gaze narrowing as it settles on me. "Were you up late reading again? This chamber looks a bloody disaster!" she declares, gesturing dramatically, as if the room were in shambles.

The scene is far from the chaos she describes. A few scattered papers lay on my desk, a shawl hangs casually over the chair—but the rest of my belongings, meticulously gathered over nine months, sit neatly packed away.

"Triona, the necessity for departure is—"

"It's hardly chaos!" I protest. "Callan's training and your relentless studies have left me utterly spent. You loom over me like the *Abhartach*, draining the life from your victims!"

A sharp scoff escapes her, disbelief etching itself into her features. Amusement bubbles within me, threatening to spill over, but I bite the side of my mouth to stifle a laugh. I've overplayed my hand, and I know it. Her expression shifts, the faint trace of humour evaporating into something far darker.

"The bloodsucker, is it?" she muses, lips pursed as if seriously considering my accusation.

Then she moves—one step, then another—rounding the bed with purpose. My eyes widen, the humour draining from me as quickly as it had come. "Deidre..." I warn, my voice trailing off. Whatever her intention, I'm certain it won't bode well for me.

Shite.

To escape her advance, I roll over the bed to the other side—a nearly impossible feat in a shift—as she narrowly misses whipping me with a towel she's holding. As soon as my feet hit the ground, I run for the door, unsure where I'm going.

I make it only a handful of steps before I crash into a solid, immovable surface.

Casey.

His hands land on my shoulders to steady me, his gaze already full of suspicion as he gauges the source of my giddiness. His eyes shift over my shoulder, and I can only imagine the sight awaiting him. A grin spreads across his face, warm and infectious—the very image of our father's smile. Behind me, Deidre sighs, her tension dissolving into exasperation.

"Good morning, *piuthar*. Trouble so early in the mornin'?" he asks, his attention still fixed on Deidre, as if awaiting her account of the unfolding chaos.

"She's going to kill me," I whisper under my breath.

"She likened Callan and me to the Abhartach," Deidre replies, her tone dripping with theatrical flair. "You know—the bloodsucking *fiend* that drains the life from its victims. It seems this poor maiden—" she emphasises the word with a flourish—"has been so *cruelly* worn to the bone. Perhaps I'll inform Callan he's finally bested her."

My jaw drops as I turn to face her. "You wouldn't dare—"

Casey cuts me off with a booming laugh, turning me around before I can hurl an ill-advised retort. I caught a fleeting, mischievous glint in Deidre's eye before my back was to her once more. She looked as if she has a secret she wasn't sharing.

"That's not a fair match, Triona," Casey teases. "Ye're far too kind to our dear brother."

We laugh, Deidre included, and as if summoned, Callan enters the hallway from behind Casey. He appears just as tense as Deidre, no doubt eager to seize the day ahead.

Callan's sleeves are rolled to his elbows, revealing muscular forearms, while his usual partial topknot secures part of his dark-brown hair, as the rest cascades over his shoulders in effortless waves.

It looks as though it simply fell into place that way, without a thought. Here I am, battling the elements so my hair doesn't resemble a bramble bush after a stiff breeze. I have to bite back a sigh of irritation. How is it fair for him to look like that?

Casey steps aside, giving Callan a clear view of me. "What's all this banter about? We're leavin' in the next—" Callan stops mid-sentence, his expression freezing as he curses under his breath and turns abruptly toward the wall.

From my vantage point, I see Casey's brows knit in confusion as he glances between Callan and me. A strange stillness settles over Casey's face, his eyes widening before he groans and shields his own vision.

"Gods, Triona!" he bellows, voice half-laugh, half-horror. "You might as well be in the scud, like the day ye were born!"

A sickening chill slithers down my spine as realisation strikes. In my rush to escape Deidre, I completely forgot about my attire—or the lack thereof.

I'm not just in a shift. I'm in a *sheer* shift. Practically an invitation for the entire household to critique my sins.

My arms snap over my chest as heat rushes to my face in a near-searing manner. All I can think about is never facing either of my brothers again. I'd rather live as a wandering gypsy, selling trinkets on the road.

My movements are frantic as I dash from the hallway. I swear I catch Deidre laughing as I pass. I'll *certainly* be repaying her for this.

The last thing I hear before slamming my door is Callan's familiar, condemnatory tone. "Ye'd reckon a clan of cursed wolves raised her, the way she carries on some days."

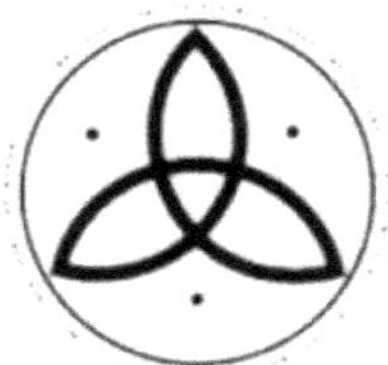

Goodbyes have always been hard for me. I'd rather slip away unnoticed than confront the festering ache of leaving. It's easier to avoid the pang of loss entirely, to push it aside until time blurs the edges. That's what works for me. At least, that's what I tell myself.

I linger, taking a few more minutes to walk through the house, my steps slow and deliberate. The weight of the moment presses down on me, heavier with each passing second. I draw in a deep breath, trying to etch every detail into my memory: the way sunlight filters through the curtains, casting soft patterns onto the wooden floor. The lingering scent of my mother's favourite flowers, the ones Deidre insisted must come with us to Edinburgh.

Beyond the window, the town murmurs its usual tune—wagon wheels crunching over loose gravel, the distant call of children at play, the fluttering of birdsong drifting from the rooftops and trees. I close my eyes, committing the melody to memory. After today, it will play only in the quiet chambers of my mind.

It's surreal, knowing this is the last time I'll see these sights, hear these sounds. A heaviness settles in my chest at the thought of leaving Deidre behind—of having this chapter of my life close for good.

My thoughts spiral, consumed by the reality waiting for me. The seconds ticking away feel like the last moments of peace before plunging into a world of womanly expectations and responsibilities—a world I'm not sure I'm ready for.

Soft footsteps behind me break the quiet. I turn to see Deidre approaching, her slight smile a balm to my fraying nerves. She takes my hands; her thumbs rubbing gentle circles into the backs of them. It's not her usual way—comfort isn't her strongest suit—but when it matters, she bends.

"Give me one memory." She murmurs.

I chuckle despite myself, and she squeezes my hands in response. "I jest not. Your final lesson with me will be practising *gratitude*."

There's no use fighting her, so I nod. She once told me her father used to do the same for her, and it always worked to distract her from her worries. Gods know, I could use a distraction now.

I close my eyes, searching for a memory worth sharing. A smile tugs at my lips as one comes to mind. "Do you remember when Casey left the window open in the sitting room, and that bird flew in?"

Deidre's face lights up with laughter, the sound ringing through the room like a song I'll miss. "I can still see your face as you came rushing in after hearing all the commotion from the kitchen. Casey and I must have looked like a pair of bampots trying to explain what had happened. Just when we thought the bird had flown the coop, it came rushing back in again! It took us nearly two hours to persuade it to leave!"

"That blasted bird caused such destruction for being no bigger than a paperweight!" She wipes at her eyes, still chuckling. "Irksome, yes, but a fine memory it makes."

As the laughter fades, she releases my hands and steps to a small wooden box on the mantle. Carefully, she opens it and retrieves a bundle wrapped in soft cloth. Turning back to me, her expression is serious yet tender as she holds it out.

"I have a gift for you, my dear. I might not see you for some time now that you have no real need for me, and I wanted to leave this."

The finality of her words hits me like a wave, bringing with it the goodbye I've dreaded all morning. The beginning of expectancy. The end of youth.

"I believe it has always been meant for you." Conflicting emotions of sadness and gratitude are washing over me. Too much, and not enough, all at once.

"I will always need you," I manage, hoping she knows just how true those words are.

Deidre's eyes soften as she places the bundle in my hands.

My fingers tremble as I take the bundle from her. I drag back the fabric to reveal a bracelet unlike anything I've ever seen. The band is crafted from dark leather, soft and worn with age, but what draws my attention is the intricate design woven into it. Delicate raven feathers are pressed flat and encased seamlessly in a translucent hardened substance, their iridescent sheen catching the light. Intricate patterns are etched into the leather edges, giving it an otherworldly beauty.

"This belonged to someone of great importance to me," she whispers, her voice trembling slightly. "It was entrusted to me long ago, and now it's time it found its rightful place—with you."

The weight of it feels heavier than its size suggests, its significance sinking in as I cradle it in my hands. My breath catches, the room tilting slightly as emotions crash over me.

"How can I...?" I whisper, unable to finish the thought.

"You'll wear it with ease." Her hands close over mine, grounding me. "This is a gift worthy of its new bearer."

A storm brews in my chest—gratitude, grief, love, fear. It all crashes at once, stealing my breath. I clutch the bracelet, its cool surface grounding me as the walls of my world shift.

"Triona," Deidre says, her voice firm. "I want you to listen carefully."

I meet her gaze, and in it, I see everything—hope, sorrow, an unspoken promise that lingers between us.

"You are going to do wonders. I need you to remember that when you get home, and I need you to remember it five years from now. More importantly, I need you to hold on to it when life feels unbearable. When everything is so hard, you'll want to give up, when it feels as if you've got nothing left to give."

Her grip tightens, willing the truth of her words into me. "Promise me, Triona, that you'll hold on to what I'm saying. That you'll remember, even in those moments."

A lump swells in my throat. I nod, pressing the bracelet to my chest, as though it might tether me to her faith in me. Tears sting my eyes, my voice trembling as I go to speak. "I promise to lock this away when I need to give away one memory."

I lean in, letting myself rest in her presence one last time. "I promise to take care of this much in the same way you've always taken care of me."

I pull back, and the smile across her face doesn't quite touch her eyes. She raises a hand to my cheek, her thumb brushing away a tear with a tenderness that makes my heart ache. She nods, voice a breath on the wind. "Until I see you again."

3

THE BURDEN OF DEPARTURE

Triona

Deidre and I step out of The House on Howe Street, and I steel myself against the tide of emotions threatening to overwhelm me. For nine months, this house has been a haven—a place of whispered conversations, creaking floors, and memories that seep into every corner. Its warmth became a part of me, grounding me in a life that now feels so fleeting. Leaving it behind is like losing a fragment of who I am.

I glance at Deidre, her composure masking the same weight I feel. She has always been my anchor, her presence steady. Yet, even her cheer can't chase the shadow of farewell hanging over us.

After the bracelet, Deidre handed me a copy of Frankenstein, passionately declaring it a masterpiece destined to shape the literary world. She feigned exasperation when I showed more interest in the bracelet than the book, throwing up her hands in mock outrage. We laughed together, the sound still fresh in my mind. She cited it as something Casey would quite enjoy reading, too. His fascination with tales of creation and destruction perfectly suited to its themes.

I spot my brothers waiting on the cobbled path, and the weight of the farewell is quickly replaced by lingering embarrassment from earlier. Straightening my shoulders, I force a confidence I don't feel. Casey bites back laughter, his gaze darting everywhere but toward me. Callan stands tall and rigid, arms crossed. Judgment sharpens his expression, but a faint edge of humour lingers beneath it. He shakes his head slowly as I approach.

"Glad to see ye huv'nae forgotten how to dress yerself properly," Callan drawls, his voice dry and laden with that unmistakable, biting wit. "The shamelessness ye've picked up here is a real bother." He speaks as though my time here has turned me into some wildling in need of taming.

I roll my eyes. "Let it rest. We need not speak of this incident further."

Casey, as always, takes the opportunity to twist the knife. "Time away turned you into a harlot, Triona. We cannae have you embarrassin' our dear brother." He casts a sidelong glance at Callan. "Although ye'll have to help me with this one, Cal. Which is worse? The town thinkin' Triona's a harlot, or you actually bein' one?"

Callan's expression falters, and he casts his eyes my way before his mouth presses into a thin line. He clears his throat to right himself. "I dinnae ken what ye're talkin' about," he mutters, his voice a touch too defensive.

Casey's laugh bursts free as he crosses his arms. "You speak of shamelessness, brother, but we all ken ye've got more hidden liaisons than ye'd care to admit. I'm simply helpin' to jog yer memory. Have you just forgotten about that time on the way—?"

"Keep yer geggie shut, Casey," Callan growls, his face flushing red as his glare sharpens. The tension between them crackles, but I arch a brow, glancing between them.

"You don't say? Seems every saint's got his sins," I remark, my tone dry as I watch the scene unfold.

Callan mutters something under his breath, refusing to meet my eyes, before lunging at Casey with an elbow. Casey dodges, letting out a triumphant "Ha!" before Callan recovers quickly and lands a slap to the back of Casey's head with a loud thwack. Casey retaliates in kind, wrapping an arm around Callan's neck, attempting to drag him off balance.

These two are unbelievable.

"Enough, boys!" Deidre's voice cuts through the scuffle, sharp and commanding.

I smirk, tilting my head. "Who's lost all sensibilities now? Reprimanded like bairns."

They pull apart reluctantly, each muttering under their breath, but before they can start again, Deidre steps forward, placing herself firmly between us. "Triona, you've caused enough trouble for one day. Stop while you're ahead. Unless you require a reminder of—"

"No!" My voice rises too sharply, heat rushing to my cheeks. "That won't be necessary," I add hastily, forcing a calm I don't feel. Payback brews in my mind. Her time will come.

With an easy change of manner, Casey approaches Deidre and leans in to kiss her cheek. "It's been wonderful to see ye, as always. We'll miss yer company—and how well ye've kept Triona in line."

As expected, his charm is undimmed by the chaos he leaves in his wake. Deidre grabs him by both shoulders, and smiles at him with great affection. She's always had a soft spot for Casey, as do many who find themselves in his company. He's someone hard not to love, with his sarcastic wit and warm features. His infectious zest for life just compels everyone around him.

Callan follows, enveloping Deidre in a hug, his tall frame dwarfing hers. She grabs both of their hands before they leave. "Take care of her, boys. She needs you more than she'll admit."

Callan nods, his tone steady. "Always."

Her words settle heavily in my chest. They love her as much as I do, even if my bond with her feels singular. As the pair head to the cart, Callan pauses, squeezing my shoulder. "A few minutes left. Make sure ye've got everything."

I roll my eyes, letting a smile tug at my lips. "Aye, father," I reply mockingly. "I'm as ready as one can be."

He huffs a laugh, shaking his head as he moves back to Casey.

As Deidre and I move to join them, Casey's grin widens as he takes a moment to read the cover of what I'm holding. "Something to keep us occupied on our journey home?"

"Were you spying on our conversation or something?" I shoot back, narrowing my eyes playfully.

Casey raises his hands in mock innocence. "Absolutely not," he replies with a smirk.

"Oh? How do you know what this is, then?" I ask.

"I just ken ye better than anyone else. The second that book touched yer palm, that's exactly where those thoughts of yers travelled. 'Sides, Deidre would have my heid if I'd interrupted the two've you cryin'."

I narrow my eyes and harshly shove his shoulder, throwing him off balance. He places a hand over the place where I'd just made contact, and scoffs.

"Now, now, Triona," he chides, "dinnae start something you couldnae possibly finish in a dress."

"Casey, the both of us know the dress wouldn't be the issue—it's your complete inability to keep pace with me," I shoot back, unable to resist. "Not even the dress could slow me down enough to give you the upper hand. In fact, I'm willing to—"

"Children!" Deidre's voice cut through the air, laced with exasperation and amusement. "Whatever will the three of you do in my absence? The Sinclair name must carry on, so you'll have to come to some sort of arrangement to keep from killing one another."

Casey moves to my side and throws an arm over my shoulder. "No promises about this ride back home, but we'll have plenty of space at home. Don't go losin' hope in us yet."

"Speak for yourself, you howling—" I snap, but Deidre cuts me off with a pointed look.

"A lady must watch her language,' Triona," she chides, her eyebrow arching.

I straighten, biting back a retort. Deidre spent years drilling speech lessons with me, insisting that the world beyond our home would expect refinement and poise. She believed softening my Highland brogue would grant me opportunities and spare me judgment.

On top of that, they scolded me just for considering using insulting language. The reprimand felt unfair, unnecessary—stifling, even. Now, as I walk between these two worlds, I see the practicality of her persistence.

Callan grins smugly. "Teach us that trick, Deidre. She listens to ye better than anyone."

Deidre arches a brow, her lips quirking into a playful smile. "Careful now, Callan. She'll remember that when she decides how much to trim from your ego."

"Indeed. At some point, the both of you will sleep, and I will be there when you do," I warn, narrowing my eyes. "You'll do well to remember that." The warning hangs in the air. They give each other a knowing look, remembering the last time they lost to exhaustion after one of their more vicious rows. Waking up with fewer tresses was an unpleasant surprise.

The thought alone should give both of them enough to dwell on for the next few days.

Deidre, ever the peacemaker, breaks the tension with a clap. "Enough now, lovelies. Time's ticking."

With that, Casey and Callan climb into the wagon. I linger on the cobbled path. My eyes trace the sand-coloured bricks, ivy clinging stubbornly to the walls, narrow windows catching the afternoon sun. Everything about the house feels alive, timeless, like a story I know by heart but have to leave behind.

"Come on, *piuthar*," Casey calls, his hand outstretched. "Time to go home."

I glance back at Deidre, her gaze steady and warm. Everything about this moment feels fixed in time, like a portrait in faded hues—steady, familiar, unchanging.

The air feels thick, heavy, as if it, too, recognises the weight of this farewell. Each breath pulls me further from the comfort of this life I'm leaving behind. I inhale deeply, holding that final memory close before letting it slip from my mind like sand through fingers.

With a deep breath, I turn forward. "Off we go, then," I say, a faint smile tugging at my lips. "No sense delaying the inevitable."

The cart jolts into motion. Each wheel's turn pulls me further from the life I've known. The townhouse shrinks, fading into a shadowed memory, until it's gone—like dust swept away by the wind.

Triona
Sunday, 20 April 1823
Somewhere in the Scottish Highlands

The temperature has taken a steady decline in the last hour. Unfortunate, considering the trip is already taking longer than expected. The rain has been relentless this time, and Callan refuses to let us stay in the cities—cities like Inverness, where we could have rested for the night. Could have had proper beds. Instead, he insists we avoid them dragging us through longer routes just to keep our heads low.

Tonight, that means sleeping in tanned leather tents, on the cold ground, near the small village of Golspie. A four-day journey has stretched into five, and patience is wearing thin.

My tent collapses in a heap at my feet as I fumble with the fastenings, my fingers stiff from the cold. One might think being near the woods would shield us from the wind, but luck has never been on our side.

"I wish we were already there," I mutter, not speaking to either of my brothers in particular. Casey and Callan glance at one another.

"Aye, we ken how you feel about bein' in the dark. It's just two more nights." Casey says.

"It's not the dark so much as the woods." I shift uncomfortably, glancing around. "That, and the air has an unusual chill. It feels... unsettling."

Casey moves closer, slinging an arm over my shoulders. I immediately wrinkle my nose. "Gods, Casey, you stink."

He snorts, unfazed. "What d'ye expect? We've been travellin' for days."

"I wouldn't know," I say primly. "Women keep themselves *clean.*"

Casey barks out a laugh, squeezing me against him. "Please... ye're no woman. A fearsome creature dwells within you."

"Oh," I say, eyebrows raised. "Please enlighten me. What matter of creature am I?"

"Ye're a hatchling we found in the forest one day. Probably why ye're so uncomfortable out here. Yer people are callin' to you," Casey teases, squeezing me tighter against him.

I roll my eyes, letting him have his fun. "Well, I'm sure the forest folk are keen to have me back. Shame, I'm stuck here with you instead of my kind."

Casey smirks, draping himself over me dramatically. "Honestly, I dunno how we ended up saddled with you. Imagine how much quieter things would be if we'd left ye in the woods where we found you."

I snort, shoving him off. "Aye, and imagine how much smarter we'd all be if you hadn't spent your entire childhood breathing up all the common sense in the room. I swear, we all had promise once—then you started talking."

Callan exhales, shaking his head. "She's not wrong. I *do* recall havin' a few good thoughts before ye learned how to string a sentence together."

Casey gasps, clutching his chest. "*Et tu*, Callan?"

I sigh, nodding solemnly. "Tragic, really. We had such potential. But no, Ma had to keep him."

Casey throws his hands up. "Ach, this is an ambush! I see how it is. A coordinated attack! I thought I was the heart and soul of this family."

Callan scoffs, shaking his head. "Ye just need to learn when to shut yer geggie. Then we wouldnae have to keep twistin' the knife to get a moment of peace."

I gasp dramatically, pressing a hand to my chest. "Oh, but we *need* Casey's voice, Callan! Without his endless prattling, how else would we know the important things? Like how much he hates running, or how many times he's *nearly died* from hunger, or—"

Casey groans. "Aye, all right, I get it! D'ye ever tire of bein' a misfit?"

I blink. "A *what?*"

He smirks, nudging me with his elbow. "An *outcast*, Tri. A wild thing. Always pickin' fights, always speakin' yer mind as if ye've no fear of consequence. Most lasses learn when to hold their tongue—but you? You just *never* stop."

Something in my chest tightens, my humour fading.

"Maybe I'm happy not being like most *lasses*." My voice is sharper than I mean it to be, but I don't soften it. "Maybe that's the point."

Casey snorts. "Aye, well, that's certainly one way to put it—"

"That's enough." Callan steps in before he can finish, his voice firm.

Casey blinks, his grin faltering. "Ach, Callan, I was only—"

Callan's expression darkens. "Aye, ye *always* are. Just a jest—a bit of fun. Until it's not."

The air shifts.

Casey glances at me, then back at Callan, finally noticing the way the mood has changed.

Callan's voice stays even, but there's steel in it. "If ye had half the sense ye claim to, ye'd ken she's had enough."

Casey exhales, rubbing the back of his neck. He nudges me lightly. "Sorry, Tri. Took it too far."

I shake my head and give him a small smile. "I know you're only teasing."

Callan lets out a huff. "Come on Casey. Let's get Tri's tent set up. We need rest," he says, his voice carrying that familiar tone that leaves no room for argument.

Casey doesn't argue. He gives my shoulder a light squeeze before joining Callan.

I look into the shadows cast by the fire, feeling an inexplicable unease creeping in, like the darkness itself is watching.

It was just a jest.

But the words still echo in my head.

"A misfit. An outcast."

Triona
Monday 21 April 1823
Somewhere in the Scottish Highlands

Perched atop a weathered, stony cliff, I take in the breathtaking expanse stretching endlessly before me. Rolling green hills, vibrant and alive, undulate far beyond what my eyes can trace, bathed in the soft golden light of the late afternoon sun. The Glen—our Glen—rests just below, cradled by the surrounding hills, its beauty untouched by time or toil. It's my family's hidden piece of paradise, sacred and unspoiled, a sanctuary we've always known.

As I gaze upon this great wonder, the land shifts. Ancient power stirs beneath the surface, awakening from its slumber to drain the land of its vitality.

Darkness falls.

I watch in horror as the once-green hills and valleys wither under a bleak sky. The river threading through our peaceful Glen—normally clear as glass—runs sickly black, poisoning all it touches.

The crops vanish, skeletal cattle lie where they fell, starved and forgotten. And the people... they are little more than shadows, hollowed by despair, their eyes empty, lost.

I try to reach them, try to call out to someone—anyone—but the wind swallows my voice. Silence presses in, heavy and suffocating, and with it, the creeping dread that everything we know is crumbling beneath us.

Paradise unravels before my eyes, and I am powerless to stop it.

Then, I feel it. A presence—vast, ancient, and cruel—watching.

A sudden clopping of hooves behind me sends ice down my spine. Unwelcome, unnatural. I turn slowly, dread coiling in my stomach.

A rider looms atop a shadowy beast, unmoving. The horse's eyes glimmer like dying embers, its breath curling into the cold air. Under the rider's arm rests a horrific sight—his own severed head, its decayed visage twisted into a baleful grin. Its eyes, glowing with malevolent light, pierce through the despair, locking onto me.

"Ériu," it speaks, the name rolling from its lips with a chilling resonance. The voice is an echo, a wail carried from the depths of a forgotten cave.

My heart races. Terror and fascination grip me, holding me fast in the web of his gaze.

The horse rears, neighing loud enough to shake the earth. I flinch, covering my ears.

"You have been chosen," the voice continues, ancient and inevitable. Though the words belong to no tongue I know, they settle into my mind as if they have always been there. "The darkness comes for you, and with it, the end of all you hold dear."

He draws nearer, and the chill seeps into my bones. The despair suffocating the land now coils around me. I want to run—to flee from the certainty of doom radiating from this wretched being—but my feet refuse to move. The weight of his presence roots me in place.

"Ready yourself, for I am the harbinger of what is yet to be—of a fate that cannot be stayed."

The Glen is lost.

The unravelling has only just begun.

It has waited centuries to resurface, and now, nothing and no one will stop it.

Not this time.

I wake with a gasping scream, my body jolting upright as if wrenched from drowning. Cold sweat slicks my skin, the air thick, suffocating. My chest heaves, my ribs straining against the frantic rhythm of my breath. The nightmare isn't gone—not fully. The phantom chill of it clings to me, curling like unseen chains tightening around my throat.

Before I can wrench myself free from its grip, heavy footfalls thunder outside my tent, followed by the frantic rustling of fabric. A heartbeat later, Casey and Callan burst inside, weapons drawn.

"Triona!" Casey barks, his voice sharp, cutting through the haze. His eyes—wild, frantic—sweep the dimly lit space, searching for a threat.

Callan, slightly more composed but no less tense, steps forward, his gaze locking onto mine with unnerving precision. "Nightmare?" His tone is calm, but his posture is rigid, his muscles coiled.

I try to speak, but the words lodge in my throat, trapped beneath the lingering weight of terror. My fingers clutch at the fabric over my chest as if I can physically hold myself together.

Tears blur my vision, hot and unwelcome. I hate this—hate the way my body betrays me, the way my breath shudders as I whisper, "It felt so real."

My voice is hoarse, raw, the tremor in it betraying the depths of my fear.

Casey exhales sharply, dragging a hand down his face before lowering his blade. "A nightmare?" he echoes, but there's no relief in his voice. "Sounded more like you were bein' flayed alive."

His words send another shiver racing down my spine. Because he isn't wrong.

Casey hesitates, his expression shifting, softening—not enough to dull the worry etched into his brow, but enough that his voice drops a notch. "I can stay. Just until you fall back asleep."

I want to refuse. The words are on the tip of my tongue, bitter and stubborn, but the silence waiting beyond them feels too vast, too dark, and too heavy.

I exhale slowly, hating the way my body craves the comfort I don't want to need. Hating how the thought of being alone makes my skin crawl. The remnants of the nightmare coil around me still, cold and merciless.

I clench my jaw, forcing myself to speak past the shame curling in my gut. "Fine," I mutter, reluctant, resigned. "Just until I fall asleep."

Callan, watching me carefully, crosses his arms. His gaze sharpens, pinning me in place. "This isn't the first time, is it?"

My stomach twists, and I hesitate. Then say, barely above a whisper, "No. But they've never been like this."

I swallow hard, avoiding Callan's piercing gaze. Because it isn't the first time.

And deep down, I know—it won't be the last.

4

THROUGH THE GATES OF CONNEMARA

Triona

Wednesday, 23 April 1823

Keiss, Scotland

When we reach the cliff's edge along the road to our home, the day greets us with a bright, welcoming sun. Dawn breaks, and the first rays spill over the horizon, casting a much-needed warmth that settles softly around us. Despite the lingering chill in the wind, the sunlight stretches across the rugged terrain in golden beams, illuminating every curve of the landscape.

My grandfather, Taskill Sinclair, named the castle after my grandmother—his 'Irish Gemstone'. Connemara is a well-known area in Ireland, celebrated for its beauty. According to my father, my grandfather often said no woman had ever been as strong or as beautiful as she had been. They loved each other fiercely. My parents have that same love. It is impossible to miss the way they look at each other across a crowded room, or how devoted my father is to my mother. One would hope that kind of gentlemanly comportment runs in the bloodline, though it has yet to manifest in either of my brothers.

From this point on the road, you can see every promise the Highlands offer. The sun kisses the water in a way that hints at endless hours of wonder. The cliffs, worn by centuries of waves, stand tall and unyielding. To the left, atop the hill, sits our home—a serene and steadfast presence.

I close my eyes, breathing in the rushing wind. The air carries a floral sweetness mingled with the briny musk of the sea, a potent bouquet that has become a profound comfort. Having lived here my whole life, it wraps around me like a familiar embrace.

The waves crash loudly against the cliffs, drowning out conversation. Not that we've spoken much. The past few hours have been quiet, a tense silence hanging in the air. Callan hasn't said a word, his eyes fixed on the horizon, his expression unreadable. He doesn't notice my gaze lingering on him, or how his face betrays emotions that ripple just beneath the surface.

Perhaps it's our arrival weighing on him. His usual gruff remarks and derisive comments while Casey and I bicker are conspicuously absent. I suspect there's more behind his silence, but I haven't worked up the courage to ask. A few days ago, I overheard him speaking in hushed tones with Deidre. Something about the last whiskey shipment going awry. Whatever happened sits heavily on his shoulders, and I suspect he's bracing himself for the potential fallout with our father.

A soft chuckle beside me pulls me from my thoughts. Casey, who I thought had been resting, grins as if he's caught on to something.

"What's got you gaggling?" I ask, half-curious, half-amused.

"D'ye think the reason he's so quiet," he whispers, gesturing toward Callan, "is because the sun's drainin' his dark magic powers?" His attempt to lighten the mood sends a ripple of laughter through me, his infectious humour impossible to resist.

"Oh, now *you're* on about him being the Abhartach?" I tsk playfully. "And laughing at your own jokes, like Da?"

"Ye're no fun."

"I'm plenty of fun," I retort, crossing my arms with mock offense. "*I'm* not the one brooding the day away." My voice carries just enough volume to ensure Callan hears, finally giving in to the incessant urge to pull him out of his dark, silent reverie.

"Naebuddy's broodin', Triona," Callan replies dryly, turning just enough for me to catch his narrowed eyes. "Some folk dinnae need every second of the day filled wi' noise. Or rather, dinnae feel the need to talk just to hear themselves."

I elbow Casey as he tries—and fails—to stifle his snickering. "Some of us require human interaction," I say, raising an eyebrow and daring Callan to challenge me.

For a moment, his lips twitch as though a smile threatens to break through, but it falters. He pulls away, retreating into himself, leaving me chewing my lip in mild disappointment. I thought I'd finally coaxed him out of the shadows that seem to cling to him.

The silence stretches between us again, and I'm about to give up when Callan mutters, "Speakin' of human interaction." There's a flicker of relief in his tone, as if grateful for the interruption. "Look who's ready to greet ye."

Curiosity flares, and I lean over the side of the wagon. In the distance, three figures wave enthusiastically. My face lights up and I wave back with equal enthusiasm. The knot of anxiety I've carried over this journey starts to fade.

I am home.

The first to move toward us upon arrival is my dearest friend, Dealla. Ignoring Callan's outstretched hand to help me down, I practically leap over the side of the wagon and go running toward her.

"Dealla!" I call out, lifting my dress to keep the hem clear of the lingering mud from the recent rain.

Dealla is more like a sister than a friend—she's a lifeline who found me in a time of need. Like a skilled storyteller, she opened me up like a book, coaxing out every hidden chapter. She took a chance on the quietest soul in the room, albeit forcibly, and her efforts changed us both for the better.

She's the sort of friend who mirrors the love and beauty you should see in yourself. Dealla has a way of silencing the noise within me. In my lowest moments, she doesn't wait to be called—she just appears. Her laughter isn't merely infectious; it revitalises me in ways I can't explain. She's a steadfast pillar of acceptance, reminding me to embrace every facet of myself in a world that often demands too much.

We collide just outside the gateway leading to the main courtyard, both of us on the verge of tears.

"Oh, how I've missed you!" Dealla practically squeals, her arms tightening around me.

I pull back slightly to get a better look at her, admiring the way her fair hair falls in soft waves around her face. The lilac dress she wears suits her perfectly, highlighting her graceful features. With a grin, I reach up to tug playfully at the ends of her hair.

"You look wonderful, Dealla. Are we wearing our hair down in defiance again?"

She laughs, her eyes gleaming with mischief. "Aye. I won't be told how to wear it simply to attract men." She sneers dramatically.

"And you," she says, stepping back to inspect me with mock seriousness, "look like you've just spent far too many days riding in a wagon."

I pinch her arm, earning a laugh. "You're such a little shite sometimes."

Dealla cackles and winks, her laughter spreading through me like warmth. She has a charm similar to Casey's, her voice a melody that lingers in the air, pulling everyone into her orbit. It's impossible not to laugh with her, and I find myself grinning wider.

"Ah, and are we nothing to ya now?" A high-pitched voice rings out behind me.

I turn to see Saoirse and Eamon standing a few strides back, Saoirse grinning wide, arms spread as if she means to gather the whole world into them.

"Come here to me, ya little rogue!" she calls.

Rolling my eyes but unable to keep the smile off my face, I oblige. Saoirse's slender arms wrap around me in a bone-crushing hug.

"What's wrong with you two? Squeezing me like that—are you trying to snap me in half?"

Saoirse and Dealla chuckle in unison.

"Eamon, get in here before she slithers away on us again!" Saoirse calls out with a mischievous twinkle in her eye.

Eamon steps forward, the faint blush creeping up his cheeks unmistakable. He wraps his arms around both of us with a sheepish grin.

Saoirse and Eamon share the same striking features—long waves of fiery red hair, piercing green eyes, soft Irish lilt's, tall statures—but their differences couldn't be clearer. Saoirse is bold, wild as a fox, the kind to dance barefoot in the rain just for the hell of it. Eamon, though, carries his past more quietly, careful where she is reckless, measured where she is free.

Their past still lingers like a shadow. They arrived at our home from Ireland four years ago, carrying nothing but the clothes on their backs and the weight of their history. My father caught Saoirse trying to steal from us in the dead of night. Instead of punishing her, he saw through the desperation in her eyes and offered them a place to stay. In a world where others would have condemned them, he gave them solace.

Saoirse wasted no time making herself at home, charming her way into all our hearts. Eamon, though—Eamon took time. He was a hard book to read, quiet and cautious. As Dealla had done for me, I earned his trust, piece by piece.

"Ye've been missed, Triona," Eamon says warmly, pulling back but leaving a hand on my forearm.

I smirk. "By you... or my parents?"

His eyes widen slightly, and his blush deepens. "Teasing Eamon," I say with a wink.

Behind me, Saoirse and Dealla are already focused on Casey and Callan, who are unloading our belongings.

"I missed you all so much," I mutter, half to myself, "but never tell a soul."

Eamon chuckles, his laughter soft and genuine. "It will remain our little secret."

"Where are my parents?" I ask.

Eamon glances over my shoulder toward Saoirse and Dealla, hesitating. They exchange looks before deliberately turning their backs on me.

"They're entertainin' someone," Eamon finally admits, his tone uncertain.

"Someone?" I raise an eyebrow, making it clear I expect more of an answer.

He shrugs playfully, his expression carefully neutral. "Ye'll have to see for yerself. I'd hate to spoil the surprise."

"Triona, your ma says to come in from the back," Saoirse calls, smirking over her shoulder.

I roll my eyes at her dramatic tone but laugh as she adds, "Lest ya drag all that muck through yer dear ma's entryway."

Pressing a quick kiss to Eamon's cheek, I dart toward the house.

But before I step inside, there's someone else I need to see. Someone who's been waiting far too long for me to come home.

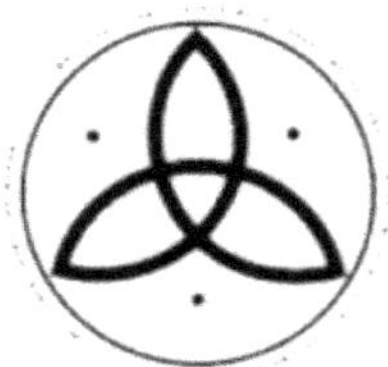

This late into spring, patches of wildflowers—some of sea pink, muted purple, and heather—dot the grassy slopes, offering subtle bursts of colour against the heavy greens and browns of the far-off landscape. The faint echo of waves crashing in the distance still reaches my ears, and the salty tang of the sea lingers in the air, ever-present.

Ancient stone walls, weathered by centuries of harsh winds and relentless rain, cross over the fields around our home. These walls mark old boundaries that once divided the land. These older stonewalls lead to the ruins of Old Keiss Castle, where our ancestors lived before it succumbed to the forces of time and weather. An attack many years ago destroyed the other half of the castle.

To the north, just beyond the sheep that graze lazily in the open meadows, the land flattens out gradually, leading to the village of Keiss. It's a small, quiet settlement with traditional stone cottages and winding roads. The people who reside in this village are more like family than neighbours; many work closely with my parents. Our whiskey business, along with my father's trading endeavours, help to sustain the village. Without the Sinclairs rebuilding our ancestral home after the fall of 1698, Keiss might not even exist today.

I approach the stables quietly, taking my time as I run my hand along the weathered wooden exterior. I know it's no use, though—my special companion is already awake and moving. From the sounds of it, he's been waiting for me for quite some time.

With a quick flick of my wrist, I unlatch the door. The familiar smell of hay and leather greets me, along with the soft nickering of the horses.

"Good day, my lovelies!" I call out softly, excitement building as I move further inside. In the far corner, a flash of pristine white hair glistens like moonlight against a sleek white coat.

"*Scáthfhóilt*." I mutter aloud.

As I step closer, my faithful stallion moves forward with a graceful step, his intelligent eyes meeting mine. I extend my hand, palm open, and his warm breath huffs against my skin as he nuzzles into my touch.

"Your mane is looking exceptional." I smile, running my fingers through the silky strands. Eamon has taken great care of him in my absence.

Scáthfhóilt is his Gaelic name, meaning "Shadow Mane", but I called him Shadow.

He'd been a tricky horse to tame—largely because I was the only human he seemed to tolerate. We had found each other one day in the village when I was eleven. I had gone into town with my father to gather supplies for my mother. While I waited outside the blacksmith's workshop, I saw four grown men struggling to control a wild colt. His soft eyes met mine, and within moments, he had broken free and charged in my direction.

I stood frozen in the middle of the road as he approached. For a moment, we simply stared at one another. Then, in a surprising show of trust, the colt lowered his head and rested his forehead against mine. There was a power in him, like a creature out of legend, and from that moment on, the bond between us was unbreakable. When my father came out to see what all the commotion was about, he found me ready to take my new companion home.

Shadow's huff against my arm brings me back to the present.

"I am sorry to have left you," I say, my hand sliding over his gleaming mane, the silken strands slipping between my fingers. "But, in truth, you are not one to keep company easily, are you? It is your own doing, not mine."

His ears flick, and he tilts his noble head, as if weighing my words with the wisdom of a creature far older than he appears. I laugh softly as I realise I'm addressing a stallion as though he might answer me in the tongue of men.

"Ah, but you remember, don't you?" I continue. "That day when poor Eamon, with all the kindness in his heart, sought only to offer you water, and you nearly sent him flying across the fields for his trouble. *Water*, Shadow! As though he were plotting some great treachery!"

The great horse snorts, his breath warm as it mists in the cool air, clearly unbothered by my accusations.

"Do not look at me with such disdain," I say, shaking my head in mock exasperation. "You know full well you carry the pride of kings in your blood. Were you gifted with the hands of men, I know you'd be seated upon a throne, demanding that I serve you grapes and finest fare, while I grovel at your hooves."

At this, Shadow tosses his head with an air so grand I can almost see the crown upon his brow. His gaze meets mine, and for a moment, I swear he understands every word.

"You see? That's precisely what I mean! " Shadow whickers, his eyes gleaming, as though he knows all too well the truth of my words.

He nuzzles my shoulder, his breath warm and steady against my cheek. I laugh softly. "Gods, how I've missed you."

For a few precious moments, it feels as if it is only the two of us—horse and rider, reunited after months apart.

Just as I'm about to reach for his bridle to pull him outside, the sound of hurried footsteps breaks the peaceful silence.

"Triona?" a voice calls from the doorway. It sounds unfamiliar, tight and anxious, which means it must be one of my mother's handmaidens.

"Ye're needed at the house," she calls from outside.

With a sigh, I give him one last affectionate pat and turn. "I'll be back soon," I promise quietly. He whinnies softly, as though sensing my rising unease.

As I approach the doorway, I recognise the girl standing there. "Oh. Hi, Colina," I say, surprised to see her. "I didn't realise you were working for my parents."

She gives a small, strained smile. "Aye, mistress," she replies, her voice dripping with a forced cheer that doesn't sit right with me. "Mistress Sinclair has been kind enough to offer me work after ma's injury."

"Aye, very kind and very like her," I say, noting the tension between us. "There's no need to call me mistress. Triona is fine." Colina and I grew up not too far from one another, but we hadn't been friends. Especially not after what her brother had done to Dealla. Thoughts I quickly push away.

Her round, plain-looking face gives her a youthful appearance despite us being close in age.

"Are you staying on the property?" I ask, hoping to ease the awkwardness.

"Aye, mis—Triona," she quickly corrects herself. "Durin' the week, yer ma's given me lodgin's."

"Ah, well, it's good to have you here." I offer a polite smile. "Never hurts to have an extra set of hands."

Colina nods again, her lips pressing into a tight semblance of a smile. Her eyes flicker toward mine momentarily before she shifts them away. The air between us feels thick, an unsettling aura creeping over me, though I can't quite place it. We continue toward the house in silence.

Hesitant steps carry me the rest of the way toward the house, and I wonder who—or what—I might find waiting inside for me.

Part 2 – One Promised, One Written in the Stars

5

THE WEIGHT OF THE UNWRITTEN

Finn

Saturday, 29 March 1823

Portugal

In my room, pale beams of light slip through a narrow chink in the heavy-drawn curtains. The parchment between my fingers feels heavier than it should, as though it bears the weight of these past three years. Each word tethers me to the promise of a future I've scarcely allowed myself to imagine. The inked curves seem to echo the ache in my chest—a longing so sharp it threatens to unmoor me entirely.

I rise, pacing restlessly, the letter trembling slightly in my grip. I read the last part of the letter again; the words sticking in my mind like an unshakable echo.

You have reasons for the silence you've kept, that I may not understand, but do come home. It has been an eternity since we last saw you, and we feel your absence keenly.

Safe travels,

Callan

A warmth spreads through me as I read those final words. Yearning is no longer a distant dream, but a reality. With each word, the tension in my shoulders loosens, replaced by something far more profound—a stirring hope that perhaps this distance kept has not been in vain.

I sink onto the edge of my bed, the letter still in hand, and fall back against the covers. The scent of wax and faint lavender lingers in the air. Closing my eyes, I let the weight of the moment settle over me.

"Why are you holding that like it might vanish?" Bran's voice cuts through the stillness, making me jolt slightly. My fingers instinctively tighten around the letter as I glance toward the door. He stands there, leaning casually against the frame, a smug grin plastered across his face, clearly pleased with himself for catching me off guard.

"I'll bet it's important," he continues, crossing his arms. "Judging by the death grip, maybe even life-changing?"

I roll my eyes and turn my gaze back to the ceiling. "Stop actin' as if you didnae fumble through my things to read it."

The grin in his voice is unashamed. "If it makes you feel better, I didn't read *all* of it—just most."

"Bloody insufferable American," I mutter, shaking my head. His nosiness and devil-may-care bravado burrow under my skin like a thorn. Yet for all his pestering, there's a strange comfort in his presence. He's maddening, yes, but grounding in a way I can't quite explain.

Bran barks a laugh. "What can I say? It's an American specialty—we take what we want and figure out the rest later."

"Aye, you said it," I reply dryly.

"Damn, Mac, you're not supposed to agree."

I cast him a sidelong glance. "I willnae lie to yer face, Mums. You deserve the truth."

Bran strides into the room and flops onto the bed beside me. His hazel eyes glint with mischief as he props himself up on one elbow. "So, what's got you in a twist? Excited to see someone in *par-ti-cu-lar*?" He wiggles his eyebrows suggestively.

"The day's new, Bran. Let's not feck it up with yer shite."

"Oh, come now." He flashes an exaggerated grin. "Let's not pretend your dashing good looks and charm didn't catch the eye of many back home. Give me a hint of something to work with. It's been near *impossible* to get through that stone wall of yours. You're practically crawling out of your own skin to haul it out of here. This is the most alive I've seen you since you ate leite creme for the first time."

Despite myself, I chuckle. "It's a damned delightful treat, you know that." I smirk, leaning back. "In truth, I'm just relieved to be rid of you."

I stand, hoping to end the conversation and busy myself with the few remaining tasks before we leave.

"Sure you are," he drawls, his tone teasing but softer now.

My movements are deliberate, but Bran, ever persistent, steps closer, matching my stance as if to challenge my attempt to disengage.

"*I'm* willing to bet there's someone back home you've been dreaming about."

I stiffen, keeping my voice even. "There's not a single soul I see that way."

"That's a load of bunk. Not even that *pretty little thing* you yammer on about?" His words strike a chord, and my chest tightens. Unease flickers to life, kindling into something harder to ignore. I glance away, unwilling to name her even in my mind. She's a presence I can't shake, a thought that lingers too long and leaves me restless.

"I've not called anyone *pretty* around you—hardly call it *yammerin'*—lest I be met with an onslaught of questions," I shoot back, unable to contain the grunt of annoyance that passes through my clenched teeth.

"Oh, but you have." He raises a single finger. "It's the way your eyes sparkle when you talk about home. As if you're a babe at Christmastime. Starry-eyed and giddy."

Before I can interject, he raises a second finger. "And the soft smile when you say her name."

My jaw clenches as a third finger joins the first two. "Or how many of the stories I pull from you circle back to her. You don't think I notice, but I do."

I open my mouth to retort, but he silences me with a fourth finger, grinning wider now. "Or maybe it's the fact that you've not let a woman so much as touch your—"

"All right!" I snap, swatting him in the stomach. "Shut yer trap."

"Ouch, you bastard." The movement momentarily stops his speech, but it's quickly followed by an obnoxious laugh. "Touchy subject? Just another sign, Mac."

I glare at him, but it only feeds his smugness.

"And anyway," he continues, utterly undeterred, "what else is there to talk about now that our grand, illustrious *assignment* is over? Aside from the fucking and drinking I do to keep myself occupied, I have to keep conversation creative to keep from going mad. And"—he claps a hand to his chest, his grin widening—"you're stuck with me until you dump me on my dearest popsies' doorstep, and I plan to squeeze as much information out of you as I can."

I groan. "Gods help me."

"Don't call to them. You brought this on yourself with all the mysteriousness," Bran quips, winking. "Now, tell me more—her hair, her smile, the way she—"

"Dinnae make me hit you again." I curse under my breath and turn back to the task at hand. Gathering what few belongings I have, stuffing them into my satchel. I pause as I note the last remaining object. The last letter she'd written me, with the pressed purple primrose still wrapped inside.

It had found its way in the back of the armoire, almost forgotten. I wish its delicate scent could still be found, but it'd been perfectly preserved to hold shape, not smell. The effort it had taken to send this sent a tinge of guilt to my stomach, but an action that I thought about often. It's brought me comfort in my darkest of days.

I fold the letter once more, tucking it into its designated box amidst the others.

"It's not so with her. Not in that way." The words leave my mouth too quickly, and I can't help but feel the lie curling around them. "When I stayed with the Sinclairs, she was just... kind, is all."

Bran doesn't interrupt, but I can feel his scrutiny. "She'll take a shine to some bonnie suitor capable of givin' her the moon and stars." My voice tightens as I wrestle with the ache in my chest, forcing it down like bile. "Not some workin'-class scut like me."

I force a smirk, though it feels like a knife is twisting in my gut as I openly spew falsities. "She's far too delicate to endure me. I'm far too rough and rugged."

Bran laughs. "In this fairytale version of her so-called future," he adds, "he'll be a fair-haired, soft-handed lad, who smells of lavender and fancies poetry? *Definitely* not the red-blooded stag you'll be in between the sheets?"

His cheek earns him a half-smile despite me. "Red-blooded stag? Is that how you see me?"

"Aye," he says, wagging his eyebrows. "You and me both. Dark hair, dark eyes, sun-kissed skin, toned bodies marked by our manual toil. Women dream of us while their soft-handed lads flop on top of them, carelessly."

I let out a small laugh, masking the way his words unearth something raw inside me. "Ye're hopeless."

"And you weave tall tales," he shoots back, smirking. "But I'll let you keep secrets—for now."

I'm mightily relieved he doesn't press further and hasn't delved too deeply into the unsaid truths that linger. I'm even more grateful he can't see the true turmoil etched on my face with my back to him once more.

The return of the pain churns in my gut every time I picture another man's hands resting upon the curves of her body, holding her in ways I can't allow myself to imagine. The thought of another man giving her his name, binding her to a life where his touch becomes her solace and his voice her comfort, is a weight I can scarcely endure. To think of him holding her in the quiet hours of the night, when she dreams and belongs most wholly to herself, cuts deeper than I dare admit.

The ache intensifies like a blade twisting in my chest when I imagine the sounds she'll make under his touch, her voice breaking with a softness meant for him as he draws out her pleasure. The image of her carrying his child instead of mine sears itself into my mind, a torment that leaves me gasping for control.

It's all a bitter draught to swallow, but a cruel torment I'd endure a thousand times over, just to bask in the light that surrounds me when she is near.

I can scarcely remember when the simple affection of our friendship shifted. When her laughter stopped being something I merely enjoyed and became something I longed for. When her absence felt like a hollow ache.

When I left Scotland, she was but sixteen—a vision of innocence and youth that should remain unchanged in my memory. But it hasn't. Not even close. It's as though she's grown in my mind, shaped by every letter, every word, every quiet moment I've spent imagining her. And that, I think, is the cruellest twist of all.

Perhaps it's the distance that's fuelled this deeper yearning—a longing for the familial closeness I'll feel at the Sinclair's home. It was the first place I ever truly felt loved, where I understood what it meant to be part of something bigger than myself. But that love is also what makes these feelings harder to bear. If I were to act on my urges, I'd have far more to lose than I ever thought possible.

Yet, I fear that the moment I lay eyes on her again, this fragile delusion will crumble. This burgeoning desire I've buried will rise, threatening to drag me under a tide of emotions I'm failing to navigate.

Before the thought can spiral further, Bran's voice cuts through the haze, snapping me back. "Mac, you've got that brooding look again. You're gonna wear a hole in the floor if you keep at it."

"I ought to tie you to a post and take sail without you," I say, with an even tone, as if I'm casually discussing mundane topics such as the weather.

Bran laughs and disregards the statement entirely, saying, "You know you'd find little joy in the world around without me. We're pariahs of society, after all. We band together for a damned good reason."

"Nae," I say, shaking my head in disagreement, "dinnae group me in with you. I'm not a rake—movin' around from bed to bed."

"Impossible not to *move around* here," he snaps. "There's fuck all to do while we've been sitting around with our cocks practically in hand, day in and day out for weeks. You'd know if you did anything other than mope around in the sleeping quarters."

"I've not been mopin' around. I just like my bits where they're at. No chance of having anything festerin' down there if I'm not in one bed and into the other while the sheets are still sweat-slicked."

He scoffs, showing a dismissive curl of his lips that hints at the bemusement he feels toward the observation. An over-exaggeration it might be, but only in the slightest.

Bran leans casually against the doorframe, his eyes glinting with mischief as he flashes that knowing grin. It's not just his words that carry weight—he wields his charm and easy confidence like a weapon, effortlessly turning the focus of every room toward himself. Whether by design or mere happenstance, he navigates his world with a confidence that suggests he is not only conscious of his allure, but also adept at wielding it to his advantage.

"You've no clue what you're missing. You know what they say... if you neglect it too long, it'll fall off or turn to stone." Bran's voice carries a teasing lilt, and he clutches his chest dramatically, staggering back as if struck by a divine epiphany. "Wait... is that the problem? Has it turned to stone? *Does it not work anymore?*"

"It works just fine, you bloody weasel!" I snap, irritation getting the better of me. "I have used it just recent—" I cut myself off abruptly, cursing inwardly, jaw ticking as I realise he's merely coaxing me.

"Oh, don't stop on my account," he drawls, that maddeningly smug grin spreading across his face.

His countenance, steeped in insolent arrogance that practically begs to be struck, infuriates me.

"Have you ever considered *properly* courtin' one of these women?" I challenge. "Maybe then ye'd spend less time up my arse, wonderin' what I'm up to behind closed doors."

His face scrunches as he shakes his head with exaggerated bewilderment. "Why should I? I've no plans to settle here," he finishes, gesturing dismissively toward the outside world with a flick of his wrist.

"Seems an awfully lonely life," I retort, watching as his playful facade falters for just a breath. A faint shadow passes over his face, softening the sharp edges of his usual grin. For a moment, the armour he wears so casually slips, revealing something raw beneath—something he'll never admit aloud.

Bran shifts his weight, and with a shrug that feels more practiced than genuine, he straightens. "Just having a bit of fun," he says, his voice lightening again, almost forcefully. "We're young, and we've the endurance of a pack of wolves. Besides, Portuguese women love an American accent. And the way they call out to me as I—"

"Stop bein' screwy," I interject quickly, rolling my eyes. "And shut yer mouth before I boak. Ye're far too comfortable around me. I've never met someone as absurdly divulgin' as you."

"Fine, fine!" He laughs, throwing his hands up in mock surrender. "But admit it, you'll miss me every second of every day. My absence is going to tear you apart, Mac."

I snort, shaking my head. "Aye, it'll be heartbreakin'... for no more than five minutes."

With a quick motion, I grab my satchel and head for the wagon waiting outside. The thought of returning to Castle Connemara stirs something restless in me, a mix of excitement and unease. The weight of Callan's letter lingers, its promises of home and reunion heavy in my mind.

"Not quite time to leave yet," Bran calls, catching up to me. He claps a hand on my shoulder. "Why don't we grab a quick drink?"

I nod in agreement. "A dram, then. But no nonsense, Mums. I leave today, with or without you." *Not a chance in hell I miss leaving.*

He squeezes my shoulder, his grin as persistent as ever. "You won't rid yourself of me that easily. Besides, I hold my liquor far better than you."

I arch an eyebrow disapprovingly. "I'm a *Scot*; we've boundless alcohol tolerance."

Bran snorts. "Do you forget my very *Scottish* roots?"

"Aye," I reply, smirking. "You act every bit an American. I've seen how well you hold a bevvy. Loose lips practically gobbin' off to anyone who will listen."

He scoffs, half-offended. "Loose-lipped in a fun way. Not in the *'pour-my-soul-out'* sort of way."

I chuckle, nudging his shoulder as we walk.

For all his bravado, Bran's presence eases the weight I carry. His teasing and constant chatter keep the darker corners of my mind at bay. Over the past three years, his lightness proved indispensable—a sharp contrast to my solitude and silence.

Three years of detachment, knowing full well—though unspoken—that I was chosen because I'm dispensable. Bran, with his relentless pestering, kept me anchored to the truth: being expendable doesn't strip away worth. He drives me mad, but I'd never truly wish him gone.

"In all seriousness, I can't wait to meet her," Bran says suddenly, as if the thought had been simmering since our earlier conversation and only now spilled over.

"Who?" I ask, though I know who he's referring to.

"The one from back home who probably keeps all of you in line."

He speaks with more truth than he knows.

I glance at him, shaking my head. "And here I thought you didnae read my letters?" The smile tugging at the corner of my mouth betraying my attempt at annoyance.

There is sincerity in his voice when he speaks. "I'm simply saying... she must be worth meeting for her to be cared for so well... and for her to keep a smile on your face from across the sea."

I don't respond, and Bran doesn't push the issue further. With each passing moment, anticipation settles in—home awaits, and I hope she'll forgive my prolonged silence.

Even though I don't speak this truth aloud, it lingers in every quiet moment—a presence I could never escape.

She's worth everything and more.

6

SHADOWS AT THE DOOR

Triona

Present Day

Wednesday, 23 April 1823

The Sinclair Family Home, Castle Connemara

I step into the house through the open library door, ignoring Saoirse's futile attempt to shield me from my mother's impending wrath.

I pause, letting the stillness of the room settle over me. It's the quietest place in the house—my father no doubt left the doors open to air it out, as he always does. His quiet thoughtfulness never fails to warm me.

I note the room remains untouched as I run my fingers along the familiar spines of the books. It feels like a sanctuary, a place that has served as my refuge since childhood. Lessons with Deidre turned it into my second bedroom, and many nights, I've fallen asleep here amid the pages.

I sigh and make my way toward the kitchen. Passing through the gallery room, I catch a fleeting glimpse of movement outside the windows. By the time I turn to look more closely, the figures—if there were any—have vanished. It seemed like two grown men walking together, which makes no sense. My brothers and Eamon are still out front.

Frustration stirs as I reach the foyer outside the kitchen. Deciding my mother deserves it, I shout, "Ellen Sinclair!" She abhors shouting indoors, and using her full name is the ultimate provocation.

The foyer is barren by design, maintained like a museum display rather than a lived-in space. From here, I hear hurried footsteps approaching. My father rounds the corner first, his face radiant with delight. He closes the distance between us in a few long strides.

"Mo nighean bheag!" he exclaims, pulling me into a crushing hug. Before I can return the embrace, he lifts me off the ground and spins me in a circle.

When he sets me down, he places his hands on either side of my face and plants a kiss on each cheek. "I missed you too, Da," I say, tears of joy springing to my eyes. He gently wipes them away. "But we've discussed this. I'm not so little anymore."

"Ye'll always be my little lassie, Tri," he insists. Then, leaning close, he whispers, "But even as yer Da, I cannae protect ye from what's comin'." Straightening, he glances over his shoulder as a hand clasps his arm. My eyes widen as he mouths a silent *'sorry'*.

My mother's radiant figure steps into view, her expression a blend of disapproval and elegance. Her gaze fixes on my father with practiced suspicion. "What did ye tell her, James?" she demands. Her uncanny ability to predict his every move is as sharp as ever.

Sensing trouble brewing, I intervene, slipping to her side and enveloping her in a hug. She immediately reciprocates, her hand rubbing my back in comfort before pulling away to inspect me.

"Hi, Ma," I breathe. Her composure falters, and a tear escapes down her cheek. She brushes it away quickly. "I missed ye so much," she confesses, her voice thick with emotion.

Grinning brightly, I reply, "I missed you, too." She gently pinches my chin, a familiar gesture from my childhood. "Ye're truly a sight, Caitríona," she says, her voice tender. "My little butterfly with emerald eyes and amber-brown hair... and a knack for gettin' under my skin like no other."

And there it is.

I glance at my father and catch him gazing adoringly at her, as if the rest of the world has disappeared. The two of them are always in sync, their bond palpable even in moments of conflict. I find it both endearing and frustrating—a united front against me.

Crossing her arms, my mother's expression sharpens. "Ye're lucky I love ye so much. Using my full name in front of company..."

Company? *I knew it.*

Before she can unleash a full-blown maternal lecture, salvation arrives in the form of loud bickering from the doorway. Callan and Casey stomp in mid-argument, voices growing louder by the second.

"Nae, I handled hoof care last time," Callan grumbles, throwing his hands in the air. "I willnae keep doin' it for ye, Casey. I'm not yer bloody stable hand."

Casey scoffs. "Aye, but ye're so much better at it—"

"That's not the point, ye lazy shite!"

Casey claps a hand over his chest, feigning deep offense. "Lazy? Lazy?! I'll have ye ken I work hard!"

Callan glares at him. "Oh, aye? Work hard at what? Sittin' on fences lookin' important?"

"I provide morale, you ungrateful bastard."

"Morale?! Is that what ye call sleepin' in the hayloft while I'm knee-deep in manure?"

"I was supervisin'!"

"Then tell me, Casey, did the horses mentally clean their hooves while ye were nappin'?"

"I—I was testin' the structural integrity of the hay!"

Callan throws his hands up. "Saints above, ye're insufferable."

Casey grins. "Aye, and ye're—"

"I swear on the saints, if ye dinnae stop yer yammerin'!" My mother's voice slices through their squabbling like a dagger.

The transformation is immediate.

Callan and Casey freeze mid-motion—one with arms raised in frustration, the other mid-step as if he's about to launch into a dramatic re-enactment of his supposed labour.

Just like that, Callan seizes the moment—striking first like a seasoned warrior—stepping forward to press a quick kiss to Ma's cheek. Casey follows suit, both of them suddenly transformed from bickering idiots into obedient sons, their earlier fight erased from existence.

Meanwhile, I stand back, watching the miraculous scene unfold, deeply impressed by their ability to switch sides at the first sign of danger.

I lean toward my father and murmur, "They're like rats fleeing a sinking ship."

He chuckles, shaking his head. "Aye, but clever rats."

My father pulls me into a tight embrace. As if I might vanish if he lets go. I look up to meet his gaze at him, offering a sweet smile.

"You owe me," I whisper playfully, to which he responds with a chuckle and a nod.

The commotion subsides as Dealla, Saoirse, and Eamon join us, their presence adding warmth to the gathering.

"It's good to have all three of ye back under one roof," my mother remarks. "Some of ye hardly wrote home." I fight the incessant urge to roll my eyes, knowing full well my brothers kept her updated on every detail of my life.

Turning her attention to me, she adds, "And Triona, we'll need to fit ye for new dresses. Ye're spilling out of that one." Her comment catches me off guard, and I instinctively cover myself up.

Flushing crimson, I stammer, "I can't help being blessed as I am!" Laughter erupts around me, breaking the lingering tension and filling the room with easy camaraderie.

Casey, always mischievous, chimes in. "Triona has a very interestin' story to tell ye'll about indecency. I'm sure she'd love to share with the ladies. Hows about us men leave you to it?" The collective sigh of relief from the menfolk is almost theatrical as they seize the opportunity to leave, practically tripping over themselves in their haste.

Dealla and Saoirse waste no time sidling closer to my mother, their curiosity as obvious as their grins.

"What's Casey going on about?" Saoirse asks, her bluntness slicing cleanly through the awkward tension.

"Ugh, I'm going to wring his neck, the bastard!" I mutter, my face burning with embarrassment.

"Language, Triona," my mother scolds.

I throw my hands up in exasperation. "I run out of my room in haste one time—*once*—and wouldn't you know that both my brothers were in the direct vicinity to witness it."

All three women exchange a glance, their faces unreadable except for the faintest hint of suspicion. Then, my mother fixes me with *that look*—the one that says she'll not let me off the hook without full disclosure.

I groan. "I ran out in my *sheer* sleepwear."

My mother gasps, one hand flying to her chest as if I'd just confessed to a heinous crime. "Triona! What were ye thinkin'?"

Meanwhile, Saoirse and Dealla double over in laughter, the pair of them nearly in tears as they lean on each other for support.

"I am *so* happy to know my misery brings such joy to the both of you," I say, crossing my arms and glaring at them.

Dealla waves a hand at me, trying and failing to catch her breath. "Oh, Triona, you've painted such a picture—I can just see Casey's face now. Mortified, wasn't he?"

"Mortified?!" I exclaim. "He's been bringing it up at every opportunity since, the little devil!"

"Sounds like Casey," Saoirse says, her grin wide and unapologetic. "But honestly, Triona? Ye're lucky yer da wasn't about, or he'd still be tryin' to recover."

I groan again, my face surely as red as Saoirse's hair. "That's it. I'm moving out and changing my name. You'll never hear from me again."

Dealla pats my shoulder, still chuckling. "Oh love, it's not half as bad as you think. Just be glad Casey didn't drag out your embarrassment in front of the men."

I sigh, shaking my head. "Give him time. He'll find a way."

"True," Saoirse agrees, smirking. "But 'til then, at least we've this moment to savour."

Just then, my father calls for my mother from the kitchen. She moves to squeeze my hand before calling back out to him. "Go get settled and freshened up, *dealan-dé*. I'll call for ye." Before she turns to leave, she lingers for a moment, her gaze locking onto mine.

In that fleeting moment, I detect a hint of sorrow in her eyes. Before I can say anything, she quickly masks it with a smile, releases my hand, and walks away.

As I watch her form disappear, an urge wells up inside me to throw my arms around my mother and offer her comfort. Sensing that beneath her composed exterior, she's grappling with something on her own—all alone with her thoughts.

Dealla clasps my shoulders, practically shoving me toward my room, wrenching me from the spiral of my own thoughts. "Gods, I thought we'd never get a moment alone! There are things no letter can capture, and we've so much to catch up on." Her words, warm and insistent, dispel the lingering weight of the day. With a gentle smile, I let her lead me away, and we step into the quiet refuge of our shared haven, leaving the chaos behind.

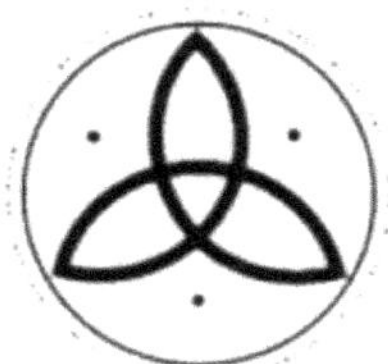

I change and situate myself just in time for my mother to walk in to us standing around one another, laughing.

"Ah, what a sight," she says as she beams at us. "Seeing ye three ladies back together makes me miss being yer age. My auld lassies and I used to find ourselves in all kinds o' trouble."

She smiles at us with such warmth, her face alight with joy, and for a moment, I wish I could freeze the scene—capture it and hold it forever.

The sounds of male laughter from somewhere in the house shatter the peaceful moment. My mother's gaze shifts, and she turns.

"Right, well, ye're needed, dear. Someone's here to see ye." She gestures for me to join her side and loops her arm through mine. I glance over my shoulder at Saoirse and Dealla. Their guilt is obvious and hard to miss. I mouth *'no warning?'* and Saoirse mouths back *'we were threatened'*.

Sensing my hesitation, my mother tugs me along. "There's nary a need for temporisation, Triona. He's been waitin' all day!" Her voice is light as she tries to comfort me, but the flutter in my stomach intensifies.

"He?" I repeat, my voice a blade of curiosity tempered by dread.

"Aye dear, ye heard correctly." With no further explanation, I'm dragged alongside her.

My father, Eamon, and Casey, crowd around the backdoor, speaking to someone just outside. I can't see or hear who the person might be, but Ma will undoubtedly make quick work of that. Callan props himself against the wall, looking displeased.

"Don't crowd him!" My mother scolds. Callan huffs from his position against the wall, and when I look at him, his jaw ticks.

As the doorway clears, my vantage point becomes obvious. When our eyes lock, as he walks through the doorway, my breath hitches.

I am all too familiar with the person before me, but everything about him has changed. No longer the boy I once knew—every bit a powerful man. His fair coloured hair, shorter than it used to be, brushes just below his ears, but those eyes—those same piercing blue eyes—haven't changed.

He steps through the doorway, his bright eyes fixed on me, and I feel my pulse quicken further.

"There you are, beauty... I have missed you." There's a new weight to his voice—richer, lower—curling around me as he closes the distance, his hand lifting toward me. I follow the silent pull of his gesture, watching, mesmerised, as he brings my hand to his lips—a token far more intimate than anything from our youth.

The boy that took my first kiss.

Marcus Murray is breathtaking—and the hunger in his eyes, raw and unrelenting, leaves no doubt about what he wants. He's not here to reminisce or rekindle an old friendship. He's here for something far more significant.

My mind reels as realisation sets in. This meeting, this moment, hasn't been left to chance. My mother, in her quiet, persistent way, has been planning this, setting the pieces in motion well before today.

As Marcus holds my gaze, a strange, unbidden thought weaves its way into my mind. For just a moment, I allow myself to imagine it—to wonder what it might be like to be his. There's something electric about the way he watches my every move, and it makes my heart race in a way I can't quite control.

I should not want this.

Within minutes of standing near him, I feel my resolve and the need for self-preservation slipping.

But somewhere, deep in the back of my mind, a voice calls to me. Faint but unmistakable. A quiet reminder that this—whatever *this* is—cannot be my fate. Somewhere in the world's vastness, another exists.

Someone who is meant for me, and I for him.

7

A WOMAN WHO WONDERS

Triona

The soft sound of Marcus clearing his throat breaks the heavy silence that encompasses the room. I feel all eyes on us, yet I remain fixated on how his bright blue eyes search mine.

The tumultuous storm of emotions churning within me is a complex web, too complex to articulate. Desire and doubt war for domain, twisting into a knot that refuses to unravel.

"I was hoping to steal you away for a moment," Marcus begins, his words hesitant, almost unsure. "I know you only just arrived, and need time with your family, so I am more than happy to return tom—"

My mother's voice cuts across his, a bright forced note ringing out. "S'no trouble at all! Take all the time ye need."

Marcus turns his attention to me, gaze searching mine for permission, for reassurance that I approve.

I offer him a reassuring smile, my lips pressed together in a thin line. His smirk falters for a moment, his eyebrows twitching in a silent apology he does not owe me. The gentle pressure of his thumb tracing lazy circles on my knuckles registers belatedly, and with it, the realisation he never released my hand after pressing those warm lips to my skin.

"Come now," my mother calls out, her voice a cheerful facade. "Best to give these two a bit of breathin' room. There's plenty else that can be done around here." She ushers everyone from the room with the efficiency of a sheepdog corralling a flock. Dealla and Saoirse are the first to comply, but not before they shoot me a furtive thumbs up from just out of Marcus' line of sight.

Casey saunters out behind them, his hands buried deep in his pockets, a wicked glint dancing in his eye. He's assuredly enjoying the spectacle of me being ambushed by this unexpected visit.

Marcus releases my hand to offer his own to my father, who meets it with a firm, clenched-jawed shake. Marcus, of course, misses the subtle tension entirely. More unsettling is the sudden shift in my mother's demeanour. Her smile, though aimed at Marcus, is thin and brittle—like glass stretched too far, ready to crack. I don't know why, but it makes my skin prickle.

My parents trail after Callan, whose face is a mask of barely contained displeasure. Callan never approved of Marcus' involvement in my life, especially not after the incident. The mortification I'd felt that day still feels fresh every time I sit and think about it.

My parents exchange a weighted glance, followed by a lingering look cast back at me, and the anxiety churning in my belly only intensifies.

A shaky breath escapes my lips as I pivot to face Marcus, a chuckle rumbling from his chest, likely to ease some of the awkwardness at the tense exodus of our audience. I catch myself smiling, my gaze locked on his, and a flush of embarrassment heats my cheeks. Such apprehension is unfamiliar territory for me; Marcus was never one to fluster me so.

Undeterred by the flush in my cheeks—or perhaps emboldened by it—Marcus steps closer, closing the distance between us with one long, deliberate stride. His confidence is palpable, unshaken, as if he knows exactly the effect he has on me. Before I can think to retreat, his hand finds mine, intertwining our fingers with ease.

The moment his skin meets mine, a jolt courses through me, sharp and undeniable, like the static spark of a storm. It's both startling and electrifying, leaving me caught between instinct and intrigue.

"Are you nervous, Triona?" he challenges, his voice dipping into a gentle murmur that carries more weight than his casual tone suggests. His piercing blue eyes search mine, and though his words are tender, they hold a challenge, as if daring me to deny it.

I can't. He's not wrong about my nerves, but they aren't born of awe. Not entirely. He may look like something divine, but my unease goes deeper—twisted with apprehension, resistance, and the quiet thrum of something I can't name.

While drawn to his outward appearance—the sharp line of his jaw, the effortless grace in the way he holds himself—those surface attractions do little to quiet the unease stirring inside me. I didn't return home just to fall in line with society's expectations, to be parceled off like a prize, handed to the man with the firmest grip or the most practiced smile.

Yet, his gaze pins me in place, fills with quiet certainty—as if he's already decided I'm something worth having, worth pursuing. A shiver runs through me as the truth sinks deep into my bones. They set expectations for me. They made decisions in my absence. And the weight of it crushes against my chest, heavy and unrelenting.

I manage a shake of my head, my words tumbling out in a rush. "I haven't stopped moving from the moment I arrived home. I'm overwhelmed, but if I'm being honest," I confess, my voice barely above a whisper, "after our last encounter, I'm surprised to see you so comfortable... so much in your element."

My words trail off, the path forward uncertain. But Marcus, ever the trailblazer, has no qualms about pressing on, undaunted. "You mean when Callan caught us lip-locked behind the stable house?" he asks, a hint of mischief dancing in his eyes.

Heat blooms across my skin, spreading to my ears, my cheeks, and down to my chest, as the memory crashes over me in vivid, unrelenting detail.

The feel of his hard body enveloped me, pinning me to the stable's immoveable frame. His chest melded to mine, rising and falling with a hunger that matched my own. One hand tangled in the hair at my nape, his fingers threading through the strands as though they belonged there, while the other splayed possessively on my hip. The weight of his grip grounded me, even as it hinted at his struggle to contain his own baser impulses.

I'd never felt so uninhibited before; my hands roaming his body, tracing the rugged lines of his neck, the defined ridges of his waist, delighting in the sharp hitch of his breath my touch was eliciting. When mere lips no longer seemed to suffice, he'd taken control—his hand at my hip, pulling me until his front was flush against my own, leaving no space between our bodies. The unmistakable press of his arousal had been a heady thing; burning into me with a hunger that left me wanton.

His forehead dropped to mine, his breaths ragged, his voice a low rasp that ignited every nerve in my body. "You taste like heaven above. I am burning for you."

Reason had fled in the face of such words, and I pressed closer into his thick length, seeking to rejoin our lips. The guttural groan that escaped from deep within him had driven my hunger forward. But before I could form a response, I was torn from his arms–or rather; he was torn from mine.

Callan.

I'd never seen such a rage in his eyes before that day. Without a word, he dragged Marcus back and landed a blow to his face, knocking him to the ground. Callan moved to strike again, but I'd stopped him with a firm grip on his arm. The pure hatred swimming in his eyes was still burning when his head whipped toward me.

"Callan, what is wrong with you?"

"Wrong with me?" his voice so sharp I flinched. "What were ye thinkin'?"

I started, "Callan, it's not —" but my words were interrupted. Marcus tried to speak over me, only to be silenced by Callan's snarl. His body language conveyed he was seconds from pouncing on him once more. The grip I had on his arm tightened, nails digging into his flesh to keep him tethered, if only for a moment.

"Feckin' save it, ye gods-damned wee shite!" Callan spat, yanking free from my hold. He glared at Marcus, his gaze venomous. "I ken what Sassenach scum like ye are capable of." Then he turned on me. "I willnae tell Ma and Da 'cause they may force yer hand in marriage, and I willnae have you locked to this one for the rest of yer life."

"Ye'll not say a word either," he said, staring holes into Marcus, voice, low and menacing.

"Callan, you're wrong!" I shouted, but even as the words left my mouth, a doubt stirred.

"Are ye prepared to wed?" he demanded, words cutting into me like a sharp blade. I went to speak, but the statement had caught me off guard, and I was unsure what to say.

"Are ye prepared for him to take what he wants and leave ye with a bairn?"

Marcus scoffed. "I would never do that to her."

The tension in the air crackled, heavy with unspoken fears and unresolved emotions. I felt trapped between two worlds: Callan's protective fury and the connection I'd just had with Marcus. My heart raced, torn between the loyalty to my brother and the fierce desire I was feeling in that moment.

"Ye think this is a game, Triona?" Callan's voice was strained, his anger barely contained. "Ye cannae be so naïve! This isnae just about ye and him; it's about everything that comes after!"

I had no argument after that, so I listened to what Callan had said. In the weeks leading up to me leaving for Edinburgh, I hadn't spoken to Marcus, nor had he attempted to make contact.

It was the biggest fight we'd ever had, but had Callan been wrong? Had things progressed with Marcus, would I be where I am today?

Marcus' voice tugs me from the haze of memory and intrusive questions. "It seems Callan has not yet seen fit to forgive my impudent act."

To mask the sensual thoughts roaming freely in my mind, I respond with a dismissive roll of my eyes. "It takes two to partake in such an act, *Mr Murray*." His name rolls playfully off my tongue, and a flash of pure desire ignites in his gaze before being swiftly smothered by his customary lightheartedness. The smile he offers now is practiced—a mask he hides behind.

"I would never alter a single moment of that day," he declares, his body inclining ever closer to mine. "I would gladly endure another of Callan's rebukes," his tone softened, suffused with earnestness, "because I meant every word I said."

The way his eyes are set upon me has me practically panting as I speak, my question barely audible. "And what was that?"

Marcus dips his head, his lips grazing the sensitive shell of my ear. "I burn for you... I have not tasted nearly enough of you, and I have thought of that kiss every single moment since I last beheld your beautiful face." A tingling sensation dances along my skin, electrifying every nerve.

He pulls back, shifting with effortless control as he guides my hands to his shoulders, his touch deliberate. I don't hesitate. Accepting his silent invitation, I splay my fingers wide, pressing into the firm muscle beneath my palms.

A subtle shudder rips through him, so fleeting I might have missed it—if not for the way his grip tightens. His hands settle, heavy on my hips, fingers flexing before he tugs me closer. Closer, until I'm caught in his gravity, until the space between us disappears into something charged, something inevitable.

"Marcus, someone could walk in at any moment," I say rather pointedly, though I make no move to pull away. His gaze holds me captive.

"I shall not kiss you—not yet, and not here," he counters, his voice low and sure. Relief washes over me. His restraint feels necessary; I'm all too aware that my inability to push him away is driven by the pull of my body to his. Sure, many women are likely to swoon over his words, but something about this doesn't feel right.

"But I will return within the week," he continues, his tone tinged with certainty. "This will afford you ample time to rest, and I would like more of your company—if, of course, you will indulge me." His words carry a confidence that suggests he has not entertained the possibility of refusal.

He draws back, his eyes still burning with unrestrained longing. "Marcus," I say, trying to diffuse the tension with humour, "If you stare at me any longer, your eyes are sure to dry out."

His smile softens, but instead of retreating, he lifts his hands, cradling either side of my neck. His thumbs trace slow, deliberate paths along my jawline, sending another tremor through me.

"I cannot fathom what I have done to deserve the attention of someone as breathtaking as you, Triona," he states, his voice quiet but brimming with conviction. "But I will not squander another moment pretending you are not what I want. I wish to resume what once was before you left."

His words land heavily, each one clawing its way past my carefully constructed defenses. This was not the homecoming I'd envisioned—not by a long shot.

I can't find the words to respond, so I lean into his touch instead, hoping the gesture doesn't betray the whirlwind of trepidation coursing through me. My heart pounds in my chest, and I manage only the faintest of nods.

He sighs, a sound that carries the weight of some invisible burden being lifted. His arms stay a moment longer, his hands firm yet gentle, before he brushes his lips lightly against my forehead. The touch is brief but tender, leaving a warmth in its wake. His arms fall away, the reluctance in his movements almost palpable.

"I will do whatever it takes to prove that I am worthy of you—and that you are meant to be mine," he murmurs, his voice laced with a newfound determination. Before I can gather my thoughts, he turns and strides from the room.

As the door closes behind him, the silence presses in. I'm left standing there—heart racing, breath uneven.

The realisation settles over me, cold and inescapable—nothing will ever be as simple as it once was.

8

Night Calls My Name

Triona

Thursday 24 April 1823

Keiss, Scotland

I stand at the cliff's edge; the wind whispering against my skin, carrying the scent of earth and rain. Below me, the Glen sprawls in quiet majesty, green hills rolling into the horizon, kissed by the golden light of a sun that feels distant, unreal. I know this place. I have walked this land, breathed its air, and traced its rivers with my fingertips. And yet, it is never mine to keep.

I brace myself, but it never softens the blow.

The air shifts. The golden light dulls to a muted grey, then deepens to a suffocating blackness. The warmth on my skin is ripped away, replaced by an unnatural chill that seeps into my bones. The hills tremble, but not from any storm or quake—something beneath them is stirring, something ancient, something insatiable.

Darkness falls.

I don't need to look to know what happens next. I've seen it before—the land choking, its very lifeblood siphoned from the soil, the once-glimmering river turning into a black, writhing thing. But this time, it's worse. The decay spreads faster, more violently. The trees don't just wither; they crack, splitting open as if something inside them is desperate to escape. The ground beneath me shifts, no longer solid, no longer safe. It wants to swallow me whole.

A howl rises—not wind, not nature, but something more guttural, something hungry. And then the screams. They are louder this time, more piercing. Not distant echoes, but near, surrounding me. Familiar voices twisted in terror, voices I should know but cannot place. I clamp my hands over my ears, but the sound burrows into my skull like nails dragging through my mind.

This is wrong. This is worse. This is new.

A crushing force clamps around my throat. Invisible hands tighten, suffocating, unyielding. My breath snags, my body fighting against a grip that doesn't exist. I cannot run. I never can. My limbs are locked in place, my voice stolen before it can even reach my lips. The wind carries my silent screams away, mocking me.

Then comes the sound of hooves.

The deliberate, measured clopping against the ruined earth. A sound I know all too well. A sound that never ceases to send ice through my veins.

I don't want to turn. I don't want to see him. But I always do.

The rider is there, perched atop his monstrous steed, his decayed form draped in shifting shadows. The beast's eyes burn like dying embers, its breath curling in thick, black smoke. And as always, the rider holds his own head beneath one arm. The distorted face grins at me, a grotesque mockery, its hollow eyes burning with something too ancient, too knowing.

This time, he moves faster.

"Ériu," he breathes, his voice not one, but many—layered whispers of the dead, wailing in unison, gnawing at my sanity.

"Ready yourself," it breathes, the voice no longer distant but right against my skin, a cold whisper that slithers down my spine. The rider hasn't moved—yet somehow, he is here, beside me, above me, around me. The scent of rot clogs my throat, choking, rancid. A decayed hand—cold, damp, wrong—trails along my jaw, nails scraping as if testing the fragility of my flesh. I can feel the grin in the darkness, wider than before, stretching impossibly,

grotesquely. "You cannot run. You cannot hide. The end is written, and I will be there when it comes."

I don't understand why it's different, why the nightmare is unravelling beyond its familiar bounds. But I know one thing.

This time, I won't wake up before the end.

The shadows surge forward, slamming into my chest. Air tears from my lungs, vision narrowing to pinpricks of darkness.

The pressure around my throat tightens one final time. My lungs seize, burning, screaming for air that will never come. My limbs go slack, the last of my strength slipping away as the darkness consumes me whole.

I am drowning. I am dying. I am gone.

I jolt awake, heart hammering wildly. The remnants of the nightmare still cling to me, leaving me disoriented and panicked.

In my frantic attempt to rise from the bed, I neglect to pay attention to the fact that I have tangled my legs in the blankets. The momentum sends me tipping sideways, and before I can steady myself, I crash to the floor with a resounding thunk.

A loud groan escapes my lips as I stare up at the ceiling, trying to reorient myself. The cold of the floor against my back aids in counteracting the heat of adrenaline still coursing through my body, the remnants of the dream lingering nearby. Just as I gather myself, the door swings open to reveal Saoirse, her expression wide-eyed and startled.

"Triona, in the name of the saints, what're you doin' sprawled out on the floor like a sack of spuds?" she asks, her voice barely masking her amusement.

I wave a limp hand in the air. "Can't you see? I've abandoned the burdens of vertical living. The floor is my home now."

I heave out a sigh of frustration. "I fell out of bed. You walked in at just the right time to witness my downfall—both literal and metaphorical. If you'll excuse me, I'd like to lie here a few moments longer, gathering up the shattered remains of my pride."

Saoirse bursts into laughter, the sound ringing through the room like a bell. "Well, I'd say ye've gone and shattered more than just yer pride. But there's no more time to wallow. Yer da's callin' for ya. Says there's no time for rest—time to train."

I groan louder, throwing an arm over my eyes. "Of course he is. Nothing like a bruised arse to really enhance my fighting stance."

There's a pause before she speaks again, a devilish lilt in her tone. "Triona?"

"What is it, Saoirse?"

"D'ye need something for yer arse? I reckon ye're mightily relieved ye've got such a plump one."

"Ugh, get out, you wee gobshite!" A pillow whizzes through the air, but she ducks, cackling as she darts out the door before I can aim another.

Left alone, I sigh dramatically and roll onto my stomach, smothering my face into the rug before muttering, "I hate her."

The begrudging smile tugging at my lips, however, says otherwise.

In truth, her cheery disposition is exactly what I'd needed after that dream, but the interaction only serves as a distraction for minutes. The moment she's gone, the dark shadows from the dream return.

A great famine. Blight. Death. Destruction. Chaos.

The visions swirl through my mind, and no matter how I try to shake them, they cling to me as I sluggishly get ready for the day.

As I'm leaving my chambers, I'm startled to find my father sitting just outside my door. The sight of my startled expression draws a deep chuckle from him.

"Da, what have I said about doing that?" I ask, shaking my head, grateful for the warmth of his familiar smile.

"Jus wantin' to walk with my wee one over to the farmhouse for our trainin'."

Eyeing him skeptically, I say, "What are you really out here for?"

He grunts, his eyes narrowing with a hint of a smile. "Aye, well. Got something for ye." He nods toward the back of our home. "Come on, follow along."

I hurry after him, struggling to match his long, purposeful strides. James Sinclair moves with a determination that makes everyone else appear sluggish. His legs eat up the ground with ease, each step covering what takes me two. I nearly jog to keep pace beside him.

"Slow down, Da. What's the hurry?" I call breathless, though I know better than to expect him to. When he sets his mind to something, nothing—least of all his daughter's slow strides—will stand in his way.

"We have much to do today," he asserts, glancing back with a grin. "I'm excited for ye to see what I have for ye."

The inside of the small stone room always smells heavily of worn leather and oil, not dis-pleasant, but not distinctly enjoyable. My father moves toward a bench where a large bundle, wrapped in cloth, rests. My heart gives a strange flutter as he picks it up and holds it out to me.

"Go on, lass," he says, his voice softer than usual. "Open it."

I hesitate before reaching for the parcel. I peel back the carefully wrapped layers, and the moment I see what's inside, something warm and wild unfurls in my chest.

It's a set of deep red fighting leathers, so dark they might as well be black in the right light. They're reinforced at the shoulders and waist.

Intricate stitching traces subtle patterns across the surface, not ostentatious, but deliberate. No unnecessary flourishes, just clean, careful craftsmanship. Made to protect. Built to move.

Every detail speaks of care and intention. Made with great purpose.

Made *for* me.

"Da…" The word barely makes it past my lips, thick with the emotion tightening my throat.

Tears prick at the corners of my eyes. "I appreciate this," I say, my voice hardly above a whisper. "These are—"

I clear my throat, trying to think of something to say, but my mind comes up empty. Instead, I look up at him, lips parted, utterly lost for words.

"Well," I finally manage, "you've gone and rendered me speechless. Mark the day."

He lets out a gruff chuckle, the pride in his eyes unmistakable. "Nary a need for words, mo nighean bheag. Jus keep trainin', keep gettin' stronger. That's all I'll ever need. I need to ken ye'll care for yerself when I'm no longer around to do it."

His smile doesn't quite reach his eyes, and something in the way he says it shifts the mood slightly.

"You're not going anywhere, Da." I lift my chin stubbornly. "I'll have you forever."

Before he can respond, Casey shows up, effectively ending the conversation.

"I'd like to get on with it, if that's all right by you, piuthar."

My father nods toward the door. "Well then," he says, stepping back with a spark of mischief in his eyes, "get on. Let's see if ye can defeat those trows and put yer auld man on his arse, aye?"

The training yard is awash in golden light from the early morning sun, casting long shadows over the worn ground beneath our feet. The space, bordered by weathered wooden posts, holds the marks of countless skirmishes, each one etched into the earth.

I step toward Callan, who stands tall in his familiar leathers, practice sword resting easily in his grip. A smirk tugs at the corner of his mouth, his gaze sweeping over me with appraising amusement.

"Think the new gear will give ye an edge in trainin', eh?" he taunts, his eyes gleaming with challenge.

"You're unusually chipper today," I counter, rolling my shoulders as I shake out my limbs.

Today carries a different weight. A thread of unease has wound itself through me since dawn. The remnants of my restless night still cling to my skin, and echoes of that dream I can't quite shake whisper at the edges of my mind, but I refuse to let it weaken me.

Instead, I seize that unease, forging it into something sharp, something I can wield. If my body hums with restless energy, I'll make it my strength. If my thoughts refuse to quiet, I'll carve them into every strike, every movement.

Whatever haunts me will not own me.

My father and Casey take position at the edge of the training yard, eyes brimming with amusement.

Callan shifts ahead, flexing his fingers around the hilt of his practice sword, the smirk tugging at his lips as infuriating as ever. "Ready, Triona?" His voice carries that familiar edge—low, taunting, meant to unnerve me.

"Aye," I reply, gripping my practice sword tighter.

Our father raises his hand, signaling us to take our stances. The moment his hand falls, the air between us tightens—but neither of us moves.

Callan's eyes gleam with confidence, the way they always do when he knows he has the upper hand. He doesn't just expect to win—he expects to remind me how easily he can overpower me. He delays the opening strike, savouring my restlessness, just to show me how quickly he can end it all.

This is the calm before a storm on open waters. But today, I won't brace for collision. *I will welcome it.*

Callan lunges, as relentless as a mountain stream carving its path through stone. His weapon crashes against mine, the force rattling through my bones, but I refuse to falter. I meet him strike for strike, each movement fuelled by determination—parrying, ducking, and driving forward instead of giving ground.

My new leathers creak under the strain of movement; a constant reminder of my resolve to win. The air shifts as more onlookers gather, drawn by the clash of wood on wood, eager to see how long it takes before Callan bests me.

My heart pounds hard in my chest as I parry each blow, my movements growing sluggish under his relentless assault. But then, something shifts within me, a spark ignites and flares bright against the uncertainty within me. I draw a deep, steadying breath, as if drawing strength from the very ground beneath my boots.

Callan's grin falters, his narrowed eyes sharpening with something new—assessing, calculating. He expected this to be over by now, expected me to buckle under his force. But I haven't. And now, the tide shifts.

He moves in again, swift, ruthless—but this time, I let agility overcome strength.

I pivot, slipping just out of reach, using his own momentum against him. With a sudden burst of movement, I strike first. The flat of my sword connects solidly with his ribs, sending him stumbling. A sharp intake of breath ripples through the crowd, the silence breaking into murmurs of disbelief.

And then—*the perfect opening.*

Callan overextends his reach. His balance shifts, the slightest miscalculation. In a breath, I twist my body, instinct taking the reins. Defying every expectation—including my own—I channel all of my strength into a final decisive strike. My sword swings upward, connecting with Callan's flank.

He crashes to the ground, dust kicking up around him, the wind knocked clean from his chest. For a beat, no one moves. The silence stretches, thick with disbelief—before it shatters.

Cheers erupt around us, jeers and whoops filling the air.

My breath comes hard and fast as I look down at my brother, his stunned expression a perfect mirror of the gathered onlookers. He blinks up at me, his chest rising and falling in uneven bursts. His fingers press into the dirt, bracing himself as if trying to make sense of what just happened.

The impossible just happened.

Victory tastes as sweet as the fight itself.

Casey saunters to my side, shaking his head in exaggerated disbelief. "The sight of the formidable Callan Sinclair, vanquished by our dear sister," he quips, barely holding back a grin. "Our wee Triona outmatchin' you—a man twice her size!"

I roll my eyes, dusting off my leathers. "I wouldn't say he's *that* big."

Casey chuckles, nudging Callan with the toe of his boot as our father extends a hand to pull him up. Callan grips it, his movements slower than usual, as if still reeling from what just happened. He dusts himself off, but when his gaze lifts to meet our father's, something shifts in the space between them.

They don't speak—don't need to. A look passes between them, heavy with something unspoken. Callan's brows furrow just slightly, his breath still coming hard, but there's no frustration in his eyes—only a flicker of something close to awe. My father, for all his pride and bluster, meets him with an expression just as full, a silent acknowledgment of what this match means.

"My lassie jus proved ye needna be the strongest in the pack to defeat the biggest foe," He declares, his booming laughter rolling through the yard. Before I can react, his massive hands scoop me clean off the ground, and the world tilts as he spins me.

"Da!" I shriek, half-laughing, half-protesting as I cling to his shoulders, but he only grins wider before setting me down. My feet barely touch the earth before he's pulling me into a hug, his brawny arms wrapping around me with a warmth that makes my chest ache.

"I've never been prouder," he says, his voice thick with emotion. "Ye fought with yer heart today, and that's what truly makes a warrior." He presses a kiss to the top of my head, and for a moment, everything else fades—Callan's bruised pride, Casey's teasing, the murmurs of the crowd.

For this moment, I am just Triona. Not a Sinclair, not a woman proving herself in a world built for men. Just a daughter, wrapped in the pride of her father, and it means everything.

As the noise swells around us, I find my gaze drawn back to Callan. He meets my eyes and gives me a small nod—a subtle gesture, but one that carries more weight than words ever could. His eyes, still narrowed with disbelief, soften with something else. Shock. Pride. Respect. A silent acknowledgment that speaks louder than the cheers.

A familiar voice breaks through the chatter. "Well done, Triona."

I turn to find Eamon approaching. The morning sun catches in his red hair, setting it ablaze like embers in the wind. His lips quirk into a warm smile as he takes in the scene before him.

"Callan's not so easily toppled."

A laugh bubbles up. "I think I surprised even myself. Truth be told, I never thought I'd live to see the day I'd put my brother on his back."

"Eamon!" Casey's voice cuts in, dragging the moment away. He saunters toward us with a boyish grin, arms outstretched as if he's about to announce something grand. "Are ye two just gonna stand there or join in the revelry? Triona's bested our mighty brother, after all!"

Eamon chuckles, shaking his head. "I reckon Triona's earned her victory and a bit of peace, and Callan's earned himself a bit of quiet reflection. I've no desire to steal this moment." He winks, and I laugh.

Casey claps him on the back hard enough to make him stumble forward. "C'mon now, Triona's practically a legend! The Great Topple of the Brutish Sinclair! They'll be singin' ballads about this one."

"*Ballads?*" I raise a brow. "I'm not sure my victory was quite *that* grand."

Casey nods sagely. "Aye. We'll need a proper title for ye now. Something with flair."

Eamon hums, considering. "*Triona the Triumphant.*"

Casey shakes his head. "Nae, that misses the mark entirely. It's not nearly dramatic enough. How about '*The Fearsome Fury of the Sinclair Clan*'? That'll make 'em tremble."

I arch a brow. "That sounds like a poorly penned folk tale."

Casey slings an arm around my shoulders with a dramatic flourish. "All the best tales are, lass."

I can't help but laugh at the exchange. Casey's enthusiasm is infectious, while Eamon's calm humour balances it out perfectly.

Eamon chuckles. "Callan might never live this down."

I shake my head, trying not to laugh too much. "We can cut him a bit of a break."

"Fat chance," Casey replies, giving me a playful nudge. "But no matter what they call ye, Triona, ye've earned every bit."

Then Casey grins, mischief sparking in his eyes. "Now come! There's no time for rest when Callan's pride is in ruins."

"Leave her be and let her rest, Casey." Eamon says as he playfully nudges Casey away.

He waves a dismissive hand. "Pish posh! There's no time for peace when there's opportunity to poke fun at our dear older brother."

Eamon raises an eyebrow, his voice dipping into a playful warning. "Careful now, unless ye fancy findin' yerself flat on yer arse next. Triona would be more than happy to oblige."

Casey nods, eyes twinkling with mirth. "Aye, cannae have her bestin' me next. I'm far too handsome to end up face down in the dirt."

He claps Eamon on the back and heads toward the others, leaving us in the easy silence I've come to cherish when I'm with Eamon.

"Your confidence is growin', Triona," Eamon murmurs, his voice steady. "And it suits ye. Never doubt that."

I glance down at my practice sword, still feeling the weight of the match in my hands. But also the truth in his words. The unease from earlier has entirely faded, replaced by something stronger.

Resilience.

"Many thanks, Eamon. It means a lot to hear that." I nod, hoping the sincerity in my voice carries the weight of my gratitude. He holds my gaze for a moment before offering a small, knowing smile, one that says he understands the true meaning to me.

"Now, go find your Mum. I'm sure this'll throw her for one."

With one last look at Callan, still at the mercy of our father and Casey, I can't help but feel a sense of peace settling over me.

Each step back toward home feels different, as if the earth beneath my feet recognises the shift within me. The weight of doubt lingers, but it no longer defines me. The girl who once questioned her place drifts further away with every stride, replaced by something steadying.

Beneath my skin, something hums—low and unfamiliar, a pulse just beneath the surface of my awareness. It's something reaching, and it pulls at me in ways I cannot name. Whispering of something just beyond my grasp.

As I walk beneath the sun's golden light, I know this truth—there is no turning back.

As I bound into the kitchen, my mother stands at the worn wooden counter, crooning softly to herself. Her hands move rhythmically as she kneads dough with practiced ease.

The kitchen hums with the warmth of home—fire crackling in the hearth, the mingling scents of fresh bread and wildflowers, no doubt my father's contribution, creating a gentle, familiar symphony of comfort.

"I come bearing great news!" I exclaim, my voice tumbling over itself in excitement. "I bested Callan! Finally knocked that smug look clean off his face."

My mother lets out a low chuckle, the kind that starts deep in her chest and rolls out slowly as she keeps kneading the dough. "Aye, aye. Ye're always full of grand stories."

I cross my arms. "No, Ma. I'm serious."

She hums, still smiling faintly, not looking up.

I lean in, voice firmer now. "Ask Da when he comes in."

That gets her attention. She freezes, the rhythm of her work faltering. Slowly, she meets my gaze and studies me. After a long pause, she tilts her head. "How?"

I beam, rocking on my heels. "Wild, right?"

She wipes her hands on her apron, still staring at me like I've just told her the sky turned green. "How did ye manage *that*?"

I cross my arms, near fit to burst with satisfaction. "I used my *brains*. And speed. He got cocky, and I found the perfect opening to catch him in the flank. Sent him toppling." I spread my hands dramatically. "The great Callan Sinclair, flat on his—."

"Language, Triona."

I huff.

Her mouth parts, then closes without a word. For a long moment, she simply looks at me, a quiet storm flickering behind her eyes—pride, astonishment, and the faintest shadow of concern.

Then, with an exhale, she shakes her head, a slow, wry smile creeping onto her lips. "Yer brother willnae let that lie," she says, her voice laced with amusement. "He'll go until he's clawed back every bit of that lost pride."

"He can try, but I'm the strongest Sinclair now," I declare, throwing my arms out dramatically. "Da's not what he once was, Callan's too soft, and Casey...well, we both know he's better with a bow than he'll ever be with a sword."

Her gaze softens as she rakes over my form, tracing the lines of my new leathers.

"Yer Da wouldnae let me look at those," she claims, her voice catching in her throat.

I fidget under her gaze, my fingers brushing absentmindedly over the reinforced seams. "It made me cry, seeing them," I admit, my voice quieter. "It just felt like..." My words trail off as I search for the right ones. "It felt like he might have been more excited to give them than even I was to receive them. And I *adore* them."

A small silence settles between us, warm and weighted. Then I clear my throat, trying to shake the emotion from my voice.

"Still," I say, forcing a smile, "Part of me still can't believe I outmanoeuvred Callan. Especially after the sleep I lost last night. Woke up in a panic—ended up flat on the floor."

"Ah, found her on her arse, I did," Saoirse chimes in, her voice ringing out from the doorway like a welcomed breeze. She leans casually against the frame, her lips curling into a mischievous grin. "Not her finest moment!" Her laughter bubbles up, light and infectious, effortlessly brightening the room.

"Mind yer tongue, Saoirse." Though her tone is sharp, there's a a lively glint in my mother's eye.

"Sorry, Mum." Saoirse steps forward, pressing a quick kiss to her cheek, the gesture so full of affection that it softens even the faintest trace of irritation. My mother's lips twitch into a reluctant smile as she turns back to her work.

Saoirse and Eamon had taken to calling her *'Mum'* not long after my father brought them into our lives. Though we never speak of the hardships they endured before, I can see the shadows of their past in fleeting moments—in the way Eamon's shoulders tense at loud noises, or how Saoirse sometimes glances at the door, as if expecting it to slam shut without warning.

Hearing them call her *'Mum'* stirs something deep in me. It's just another symbol of the love that binds our patchwork family together.

Saoirse's playful demeanour shifts. Her brow furrows as she steps closer, her gaze searching my face. "What's wrong then? Ya look like ye've seen a ghost."

I swallow, the vivid images of the dream flashing behind my eyes. "Ma used to tell us a story about a glen untouched by turmoil, but last night, my dream twisted it. At first, the glen was a paradise. The air was sweet, and the river glistened with purity. But then something dark crept in, like an ink stain spreading across a page. Everything that had been vibrant and alive became poisoned, consumed by darkness. Then this headless... *being* appeared. It stopped right in front of me and called me *Ériu*, as if speaking to someone else *through* me."

The steady rhythm of my mother's hands kneading the dough falters. The warmth of the kitchen seems to drain away, replaced by a cold, creeping tension.

"What d'ye say?" She turns toward me, worry etched into every line of her face.

"What is it?" I ask, confusion knotting my stomach.

Her expression hardens, shifting from uncertainty to an almost fierce intensity. "What else did it say?"

"It said..." I falter, the memory of the words chilling me all over again. "Well, the last thing it said was *'You cannot run. You cannot hide. The end is written, and I will be there when it comes.'*"

My mother's knuckles whiten as she grips the counter, her lips pressing into a thin line. For a long moment, she doesn't speak, her thoughts clearly racing.

"Another oddity," I add quietly, "was that it spoke in the old tongue. But I understood it, as if it spoke directly into my mind."

Saoirse throws her arm around my shoulders. "Och, what's got ya dreaming of The Dullahan, then? Who'd ye piss off to earn a visit like that?" She grins, her lighthearted tone coaxing a small, reluctant laugh out of me.

I glance at my mother, ready to jest along, but her expression remains unchanged. Her eyes brim with an anguish so raw that it steals the air from my lungs. I see something there I can't unsee: fear, tangled with a pain she's trying to hide.

"Ma, are you all right?"

She shakes her head, as if trying to dispel whatever thoughts have taken hold. "Ye ken how I feel about dreams, Triona," she says, her voice measured and careful. Her eyes flick up, meeting mine for just a heartbeat before she looks away again. She wipes her hands on her apron and sighs. "Dreams can be tricky things. But ye've always had a vivid mind, aye?"

Saoirse pulls me into a tight, reassuring embrace. Her warmth and the scent of wild-flowers wraps around me. "Ach, don't fret too much, Triona. Headless horsemen, magic dreams—whatever comes'll have to get through me to ya."

My mother clears her throat, smoothing her hands over her apron as if brushing away more than just flour. When she speaks, her voice is just a touch too light, too casual. "Change out of that before dinner," she says, nodding toward my dust-riddled leathers. "Ye're much too pretty to be trouncin' about smellin' like a boggin laddie."

Just then, heavy boots thud against the ground outside, followed by the creak of the back door swinging open. Laughter and deep voices spill in, my father and brother stepping inside with easy familiarity. My mother, still tense from our conversation, straightens at the sound of my father's voice.

"Ellen! Where are ye?" My father calls out, his voice warm and rich with affection.

My mother's entire demeanour shifts. Without even washing the flour from her hands, she hurries toward him. The moment their eyes meet, his face brightens, but as he catches the worry etched into her features, his smile falters. He steps closer, slipping an arm around her waist.

He quickly tries to mask it, his voice dropping as he leans in. "Come here, mo luaidh," he murmurs, guiding her gently toward the door. "Let's have a word before ye cover me head to toe in flour, aye?"

My mother chuckles softly, not resisting as he leads her away.

Saoirse and I exchange a glance, both of us feigning indifference as they slip into the next room.

Meanwhile, Callan and Casey exchange their own curious glances before turning toward me. Callan's ever-present scowl deepens.

"Triona," he says, folding his arms across his chest, "What've ye done this time, then?" he asks, his tone gruff, laced with mild accusation.

I scoff, mirroring his stance. "Why do you assume it's my fault?" I hurl back, raising an eyebrow, daring him to push the issue.

From the corner of my eye, I catch Saoirse suppressing her laugh. Casey's lips twitch, but he hides it well, rubbing the back of his neck as if the ceiling has suddenly become the most fascinating thing in the room. They both know exactly why Callan assumes it's me—my mother and I have been bickering with the energy of warring clans in legendary fashion since I learned how to talk back.

Callan tilts his head slightly, his gaze sweeping over me as if he is trying to read something just beneath the surface. I roll my eyes, unwilling to let him dig any deeper.

"Fine," I say, shrugging. "She's upset because she heard how her oldest son got his arse handed to him by his wee sister. In front of *witnesses*."

Saoirse snorts, trying to stifle her laughter. "Ah, stop it—ye're takin' the absolute piss."

Casey laughs outright, shaking his head. "Oh, she is *not*," he says, clearly delighted. "I saw his downfall with my own eyes, and I'm makin' it my personal mission to herald the news."

"Wait—*what*?" Saoirse's eyes dart between us. "Ya ain't pullin' my leg?"

She stares at me, jaw slack. Then slowly, her expression shifts. Her brows raise. Her mouth curves into a wide, gleeful grin.

"Holy shite, Triona. Ye flattened *Callan*?" she says, voice thick with disbelief and awe. "You glorious bitch."

"Many thanks," I reply with a mock curtsy. "I take coin, compliments, and I expect a toast in my honour tonight at the dinner table."

Saoirse laughs, slapping my arm. "I'd've paid good coin to see that. You must've hit him like a feckin' cart horse."

Callan mutters something dark and Gaelic under his breath, scowl locked in place like it's carved from stone.

Still grinning, Saoirse saunters over and rubs Callan's arm—a touch he doesn't pull away from. "Ya all right there, sweetheart? Should we fetch a mirror so ya can come to terms with yer defeat?"

With a glint in her eye, she glances down at his backside and back up at him with a smirk. "Ye've a fine plump arse, Cal. Not *quite* as plump as yer sister's, but almost. Bet it caught most of your fall!"

Saoirse looks over at Casey. "Shame about yers. This gift," Saoirse says as she taps Callan on his bottom—a gesture he jumps at—,"must have skipped right over ya and into yer sister. She has twice as much in the rear."

Casey scoffs, looking genuinely offended. "I am *perfectly* proportioned."

Callan and I both chuckle—heartfelt laughter this time, the kind that catches in your chest and pulls the sting out of the day. The teasing, the warmth in their voices—it untangles the knot in my chest just enough to let me breathe.

As I feel that settling in my chest, the sound of low voices murmuring from the next room catches my ear.

I glance toward the door.

My father and mother's tones are hushed, too hushed, the warmth of their earlier embrace replaced by something taut and weighted.

The knot in my chest returns.

Whatever had unsettled my mother—whatever flickered in her eyes—it was so much more than the contents of a lingering dream.

It was the look of someone hearing pieces of a story they already knew.

And she seemed haunted by the familiarity.

9

MEMORIES WORN BY TIME

Triona
Friday, 25 April 1823

I find myself standing alone amidst the dark, veiled embrace of the forest. Tendrils of fear coil in my stomach. I am that frightened little girl again. A memory that has my consciousness trapped, and terrors of the past envelop my soul. A memory with odd familiarity.

Out of my direct line of sight, a butterfly with ethereal hues of a perfectly combined violet and black adorned in its wings seems to beckon me. The light casts an ephemeral dance along its coloured scales, and I find myself captivated. An otherworldly allure emanates from its delicate form, and against all wiser instinct, I listen to its siren call that compels me to follow it deeper into the forest.

I walk through dense foliage for some time, treading a path unknown. Shadows deepen and surround me in uncertainty. When the butterfly lands abruptly, on top of a large and rounded mound, the world falls into a chilling silence that portends danger.

It's the jarring sort of silence that causes prey to heed warning that a predator lurks near. The silence of the forest is shattered abruptly, and before I have any chance to react, a stone is propelled, and collides with the back of my head. I crumble to the ground, screaming from the pain, mixed with the fear that's taken over all senses. My cries are the only sounds that can be heard until the faintest sounds of malevolent laughter rings out.

Death, a concept unknown until this very moment, asserts its presence. It's an intangible spectator that I can feel looming there, right on the precipice, ready to make its move on me.

Prey.

Just as darkness inches closer, a thunderous bellow rends the silence, and the fear and the darkness fade instantly, swallowed by a luminous surge of light. I feel protected by a force unseen. When I find the courage to look up, an enormous white stag peers at me from across the clearing; standing guardian like a majestic sentinel.

As it approaches with deliberate grace, it gazes down upon me, and much like the butterfly, I find myself ensnared in two sets of golden eyes that reflect wisdom transcending mortal understanding. A sense of tranquillity and peace descends over me, bringing with it a sudden drowsiness. Whether from fear, pain, or the exhaustion of the past few minutes, I cannot say.

I extend my hand tentatively, and the stag responds in kind, as it nuzzles into my outstretched palm. In that sacred moment, I am touched not only by the velvet softness of its muzzle but by an unspoken assurance—an ethereal connection and understanding between frightened mortals and benevolent guardians of the otherworldly realm.

My eyes shutter closed, and I begin to drift into the realm of dreams. The last thing my consciousness renders is the faintest whisper that sounds much like my name being called from afar.

Remnants of the dream cling to me like a fog that refuses to lift. My body is tense, gripped by a strange unease as fragments of it float in and out of my mind. The dark forest, the butterfly, the sharp pain from the stone striking me, and that white stag with its golden eyes—watching me, shielding me.

My fingers find the scar on the back of my head, in the exact spot it had been in my mind. The memory of the injury taunts me with its elusiveness. The thought unsettles me, leaving a restless energy crawling under my skin.

Once I'm ready, I find Dealla downstairs, seated in her usual spot by the kitchen table, a book resting open in her hands. She glances up when I enter, her expression brightening as she sets the book aside.

"Morning, Triona. You look... unsettled," she says, her brow furrowing. "What's wrong?"

I hesitate in the doorway, unsure how to begin. The images that woke me still swirl in my mind, and I don't know if I can articulate the strange mix of fear and familiarity gripping me. But the urgency bubbling inside me forces the words out.

"I had the strangest... memory? Nightmare? I don't even know what to call it. It's been clawing at me."

She gestures for me to sit, her curiosity immediate. "Go on," she urges, her tone gentle but concerned.

As I recount the things I remember, the images feel more vivid, but more unsettling. "It felt like something I should remember, but I can't. It's slipping away, and it's... it's driving me mad."

Dealla leans forward, her brows knitting together. "You said it felt like a memory. Why?"

I hesitate, my hand drifting to the back of my head. "There's a scar here," I say softly. "Right where the stone hit in the... whatever it was. I've had it for as long as I can remember, but I don't know how I got it."

"You never asked about it?"

"No," I admit, my voice dropping. "I just... I've never truly taken the time to think about it. But now? It feels as if it might mean something, as if there's this piece of my life I've forgotten."

"Well, you *do* have a shite memory."

The tease lands, pulling a small laugh from me. It breaks the tension—just for a breath.

Dealla's gaze sharpens, and her voice takes on a serious tone. "Why is this bothering you so?"

Before I can respond, Casey saunters into the room, an impish grin lighting up his face. He's carrying a bundle of firewood, clearly mid-task, but the moment he spots us, his attention veers off course. Whatever intention he had is immediately forgotten—his curiosity now far more interested in whatever conversation he's just walked in on.

"Well, look who's up bright and early," he quips, flashing a quick smile at Dealla. "Good morning, Dealla. Ye're practically glowin' today."

Then, with a smirk in my direction, he adds, "And Triona, still lookin' half-asleep, even when ye're upright. Truly impressive."

I roll my eyes, but a small smile tugs at my lips. "Nice to see your sense of humour is still as questionable as ever."

Dealla shakes her head with a playful smirk of her own. "Casey," she scolds lightly, "if you spent half as much time being useful as you do trying to be clever, you might actually have found a bride by now. Someone else to taunt for eternity."

"Ouch, Dealla! Right in the pride."

I stifle a laugh, and he grins, completely unfazed. "Lucky for me, I've already got a bride to be under this roof," he says, throwing Dealla a wicked grin. "Fair hair, bright blue eyes, *alarming* wit—ring any bells?"

Dealla arches a brow, lips twitching. "Oh *please*. You better hope your bride has poor taste and a high tolerance for nonsense."

Casey beams. "Aye, and a thing for hopeless charm. I'm her dream, really."

I snort. "If Dealla ever so much as *glances* in your direction with interest, I'll assume she's been cursed. Or concussed. I'd never let her succumb to whatever bizarre spell you'd have her under, you absolute bogle in trousers."

Casey turns, feigning fresh betrayal. "A *bogle*, Triona? That's low, even for you."

Dealla laughs under her breath. "I mean... if the boot fits."

"You wound me, Triona. And here I was, planning to name our firstborn after you."

"Ach, the poor bairn will be hexed from birth," I mutter, fighting a grin.

For a few minutes more, it's just the three of us caught in that easy warmth—the kind that comes from years of knowing one another too well. But as the giggles settle, something quieter creeps in. The kind of hush that follows laughter when someone remembers why we were gathered here to start.

Casey is the first to notice. He tilts his head, brows knitting slightly as his voice softens. "Alright then... what had the two've you whisperin' like old hens?"

Dealla gives him a measured look. "You're one to talk. You've done naught but squawk since you walked through the door."

"Aye, but my squawkin's charming. Yours is suspicious." He leans forward, gaze flicking between us. "C'mon now. I ken that look on yer face, Triona. Out with it."

Dealla scolds him lightly. "Casey, don't you have work to do?"

"Not before I find out what's so interestin'," he says, grinning as he leans against the table.

I hesitate, chewing the inside of my cheek, then I sigh and begin recounting the fragments of the dream—each image disjointed but vivid. I mention the scar, and how I've never known where it came from.

The teasing drops from Casey's face in an instant, replaced by concern. "You truly dinnae remember?" he asks, frowning now.

"Aye," I murmur. "I can't make myself any plainer, Casey."

He shifts, his arms crossing as something in him goes distant—like he's stepping into another time. "It was no a dream, Triona. We were playing—just runnin' around like we always did. One minute, you were beside me, and the next... you were gone."

"How did you find me?"

"It wasna me. It was Finn," he says softly. "Shortly after he arrived here for the first time."

The words land heavily, making me question how I could forget something so important.

Dealla's brow furrows as she looks between us. "I've *never* heard this story."

Casey glances at her, the teasing edge fading from his voice. "Finn's father died. He didnae have anywhere else to go. Ma's a distant relative of his, and they took him in without question."

He pauses, shifting his weight, the memory clearly lingering. "He was only about fourteen. Thin as a reed. Quiet. There was a look in his eyes even then—like he'd seen more than a boy ever should. Seemed he was just... holdin' it all in, tryin' not to break."

Dealla nods slowly, her expression softening as she absorbs the weight of this revelation. "I can't say that I've ever thought to question the how or why of his presence. Him being here has always just felt so right."

Casey nods his agreement. "Finn had only just arrived—barely said two words—but the second he heard you were missin', he took off after you. No one asked him to. He just *went*. Like he *knew* where to find you."

His voice grows quieter. "And the moment he came back with you in his arms, the sky just... flipped. Darkened so fast we thought we'd lose our way. It was the strangest thing I've ever seen. Ma and Da said it was the worst storm they'd ever witnessed—rain hammerin' down in sheets, lightning crackin' across the sky like it was splittin' the world in two."

A cold unease coils in my chest.

Then Casey's lips twitch slightly, easing the weight. "Finn watched over you the rest of the night. Callan and I thought it odd at the time, but once we learned how rough his life had been..."

Dealla leans in again, brow furrowed. "How do you mean?"

I glance at Casey, then speak up before he can. "Finn's father used to beat him black and blue. And often." I pause, swallowing hard. "For someone who's been through so much, he's one of the kindest souls I've ever known."

Casey nods, his expression softening. "Protectin' you just felt right to him. Hell, you were the only person he spoke to for days after that. He was such a timid thing back then. It's a shame you dinnae remember that day. I'm certain it's the only time I've ever seen Callan cry."

"Callan cried? And I *missed* it?" I exclaim, feigning disappointment.

"Aye... we were terrified. All of us."

I can feel the impact of that statement—of a memory I don't have, but one that clearly shaped them all. I watch him lean back slightly, as if the memory presses too close and he needs to breathe again.

"Well," he finally says, exhaling, "I've talked enough for now. Ye ken where to find me if you want more stories."

He glances at Dealla. "You keep Triona out of trouble, all right? It's a full-time job."

Dealla smirks. "I'm not sure anyone can manage that."

Casey strides over to me in a few easy steps.

"C'mere, you daft thing," he mutters fondly, and leans down to press a quick, warm kiss to my forehead.

I roll my eyes, but I don't pull away.

"Oh, and before I forget," he adds, straightening again, "Ma's looking for you. Said to meet her in her bedchamber."

He tosses a wink toward Dealla, whose cheeks flush instantly pink, and then strolls off with that smug Sinclair swagger—as if he isn't the embodiment of mayhem.

The second he's out of earshot, I turn to her, eyebrows raised. "Did Casey just make *you* blush?"

"Oh, shut it! He did not!" she protests, even as she presses her fingers to her flaming cheeks. "My cheeks are naturally rosy."

I smile, letting the silence stretch long enough to make her squirm. She groans and hides her face in her hands.

"Stop staring at me like that!" she mumbles.

"What? I'm just admiring that sudden complex change of colour you've got." I bite back a laugh.

Dealla peeks out from between her fingers, her expression a mix of exasperation and amusement. "I swear, Caitríona, one more word, and I'll throttle you."

Looping my arm with hers, I grin. "Come on, before you start daydreaming about my brother."

Dealla's jaw drops, and she pulls away, pointing an accusatory finger at me. "Caitríona Éireann Sinclair, stop while you're ahead!"

I double over, laughing, clutching my side. "I'll take it back when you stop blushing like a lovesick bairn!"

"I'll have you know I could *never* indulge in such thoughts about your brother," she huffs, crossing her arms but failing to hide her smirk.

"Good. Keep it that way. I couldn't look you in the eye ever again if you fell for Casey," I say, still laughing.

"You and me both," she mutters, rolling her eyes as we walk off, the sound of our laughter echoing behind us.

I pause at the door, one hand braced on the frame, and for a moment, I think about not going in. About turning around, walking back out into the fresh air and pretending Casey hadn't told me to come and see her.

But I relent. Because I know there's no avoiding the inevitable.

The door to my mother's bedchamber creaks open, revealing her silhouette by the hearth. Her face is half-shrouded by the dim light of the fire, and her eyes seem unfocused, as though she's somewhere else in her mind. For a moment, I linger in the doorway, watching her fingers tugging at the loose threads of her shawl. She's carrying a quiet, unshakable worry that colours her every move.

As I step closer, she glances up, her eyes sharpening slightly—but not enough to conceal the lingering shadows that shroud her.

This is so unlike my mother—a woman whose steady hands seem to hold the world together. Always so sure, always composed, with practical answers at the ready, even when they aren't the ones I want to hear.

Now, there's a fragility in her I don't recognise. As if something inside her has quietly come undone. Her eyes are shadowed with a sorrow I can't name, as if she's burdened by memories too heavy to speak aloud.

She has avoided my every attempt to speak with her—each time I'm met with a smile too thin to be real and a well-orchestrated deflection

'Dinnae fash, mo nighean bheag' she says, brushing off my concern as if it's a leaf on her shoulder.

Her expression changes, hardening into the calm and commanding presence I often relied on as a child. I can see right through it now, though, and it's disorienting. It feels like trying to hold water. Every lingering glance, every evasive answer deepens the chasm between us.

Finally, she speaks, her voice breaking the silence. "Triona," she says, almost cautiously. "I've been meanin' to speak with ye about Marcus."

Of course it's about Marcus. The irritation flares, but it's not just him. It's her evasion, her dismissal of the things I'm desperate to understand. I feel my body tense, an instinctive prick of annoyance rising. "What about him?" I ask, keeping my voice measured.

"He's quite taken with ye."

"You've only seen us together *once*, Ma," I reply, resisting the urge to roll my eyes.

Her gaze is steady, her eyes intent as she crosses the room to stand closer to me. "He's a good man, Triona. Strong, respectable. Ye'd have stability with him, someone to depend on."

"I hear what you're saying, Ma, but what I cannot see is the point?"

"I think ye need him," she says, her voice steady but firm. "It's high time to consider that."

"That's what you think I need? A man to *'depend on'*?" The words come out harsher than I intend, but I can't bring myself to soften them.

Her sigh carries more weight than usual, a flicker of weariness crossing her face. "It's no' jus about stability, Triona. It's about safety. Protection. Marcus could be that for ye." Her insistence only fans the flames of my growing frustration.

"Why are you really pushing this on me? I'm not some helpless damsel, Ma. I don't need Marcus—or any man—to protect me," I snap, crossing my arms. The space between us feels insurmountable now. "And don't I deserve the choice?"

"Of course, but that stubbornness wellin' inside might keep ye from makin' the right one." Her brow furrows as she studies me, her mouth opening and closing as though she's struggling to find the right words. "It's not about control, Triona. Things are changin' for this family. Ye'll want someone like Marcus by yer side."

"I want freedom!" The words tear from my throat like an escape. "That's what I want, Ma. Not Marcus, not your notion of stability, not your safety—just my freedom! To go where I please, without eyes following me. To make my own choices without whispers in the hallway. To see the world, to chase something bigger than duty or tradition. To live a life that's *mine*, far beyond the walls of this house."

Her face tightens, shock flickering across her features. I press on, unwilling to stop now that the words are pouring out.

"You say you're trying to protect me, but it feels as if you're locking me away. And if that makes me petulant, so be it. I'll not apologise for wanting more."

"Triona, that's enough," my mother snaps, her voice trembling—equal parts anger and something far more fragile. "Ye speak as if this is all some foolish game—as if I *enjoy* seein' ye this way, as if I take pleasure in bein' cast the villain in yer tale."

She shakes her head, her eyes shining with unshed tears.

"Everything I do—every choice I make—is to shield ye. To keep this family from failin' into ruin. Ye think ye understand, but you're still so young. Ye dinnae see the weight of the world beyond these walls—cannae understand the cost of choice."

"I'm old enough to make decisions about my life," I snap, "even if they're the wrong ones. I've earned the right to choose my path, even if I stumble down it."

"Ye dinnae see the bigger picture," she retorts, her hands balling into fists. "There are forces—people—who would take everything from us if they could. Marryin' Marcus could bring the kind o' strength ye need. It could be the only way to keep our kin safe. To keep *ye* safe."

"Safe?" I scoff, the word bitter on my tongue. "By selling me off like chattel? That's not protection, Ma. That's control. That's a blood prison wrapped in lace."

"Caitríona Sinclair."

My father's voice booms from the doorway, sharp enough to cut through the air and steal the breath from my lungs. I whirl toward him, startled.

His face is hard as granite, his eyes boring into mine with the weight of his authority. "Ye will not speak to yer mother that way."

My frustration is too hot to hold.

"So now you're defending her?" I demand. "Just the perfect wife, doing what needs to be done, aye? And I'm just the ungrateful daughter who understands nothing!"

"Enough!" he roars, stepping deeper into the room like a storm in human form. "Ye dinnae ken what ye're sayin', lass. She's sacrificed more for this family than is fair. Show her the respect owed under this roof."

My chest heaves, each breath feeling sharper than the last. The room feels smaller by the second; the walls pressing in. I can barely get the words out.

"Respect?" I choke. "Is that what you call it? Obedience, masked as respect?"

There's a beat of silence—sharp, aching—before my mother steps forward. Her voice is quieter now, but no less firm.

"Triona… please. Ye dinnae understand. Not yet. But someday, you will."

I stare at her. At both of them.

And then I break a little.

"Da… you've always made me believe I could live differently—*be* different. From the moment I was old enough to understand the world, you were the one who told me I didn't have to follow the path laid out for me. You never put limits on me, never tried to clip my wings. You let me run wild through the woods, taught me to track and fight when others said I shouldn't even lift a blade. You gave me a weapon and told me that my strength was something to *wield*, not fear."

"And now?" My voice breaks. "Now it feels as if you're trying to unmake all of that. As if everything you helped me become is suddenly… inconvenient. As if you're asking me to shrink back into something I *can't* be anymore."

Neither of them says a word.

I turn and storm out of the room, my boots striking the floor with each step. My vision blurs as I make my way down the corridor, but I don't stop. I need air, space—anything but the stifling confines of this house and the weight of their expectations.

Out in the corridor, I nearly collide with Casey. He stands there, frozen, his face etched with something between sympathy and dread. He heard everything.

"Triona—" he starts.

But I shake my head. The lump in my throat won't let me speak.

I push past him and keep walking, the sting in my eyes burning hotter with every step.

Just wishing I was anywhere but here.

10

THE SOUND OF HOME

Triona

I watch from my perch in the library as the sun begins its slow descent, casting delicate golden hues over the estate. The sight should bring comfort, but the world outside feels distant, muted by the weight of that argument.

When I hear footsteps approaching, I don't look up right away

"Mo chaitinn bheag... fancy a walk through the garden with yer auld Da?" My father's voice breaks through my thoughts, soft yet steady, carrying a tone that promises understanding.

I glance up, meeting his familiar warm smile. There's something in his eyes—a quiet knowing that tells me he senses my turmoil. With a nod, I rise, wrapping my shawl around my shoulders. The fabric is a slight comfort against the cool evening air.

The garden greets us with the earthy scent of damp soil and blooming flowers. It's vibrant and alive, but the beauty feels overshadowed by the storm in my heart. We walk in silence at first, the familiar crunch of gravel beneath our feet filling the space between us.

Finally, my father breaks the silence. "I ken things aren't always easy for you, lass. This world, this life... it's heavy."

"It's not just that, Da. Sometimes, it feels like there's this... ugh, as if Ma is so focused on the most mundane things. It all seems so small compared to everything happening around us."

He nods slowly, thoughtful. "Aye, lass, I hear what ye're sayin'. I truly do. But consider this for a moment—companionship disnae hold ye back. It pushes ye ahead. Ye've got a heart as big as they come, but even the strongest heart can tire. Yer mother disnae want to rid this house of ye. She wants to surround ye with support. An abundance of it."

His words cut through the fog in my mind, but frustration lingers. "I know I sound like a petulant child, Da, but I feel as if I'm not meant to waste away under the thumb of a husband."

He guffaws, loud and sudden, and it startles a laugh from me. "As if ye'd ever let a man keep ye under his thumb. Ye're Ellen Sinclair's daughter."

"There's a strength inside ye that'll never be silenced," he continues, his voice softer now. "It'll only grow. But strength disnae mean ye have to bear everything alone. There's a difference between resilience and isolation."

He pauses, thinking. "I'd like to tell ye about a friend o' mine... someone who meant a great deal to me, not jus for the man he was, but for the friend he was as well."

"He was a passionate revolutionary, full of fire and ideas. He believed he could change the world on his own without askin' for help. And in the end, that pride cost him dearly. He didnae just lose his cause, lass. He lost his life, and it broke those who loved him."

His voice softens as he continues. "He had a fire that burned so bright, it drew everyone to him. He was a man who inspired, who challenged the world to be better. But couldnae always see that leanin' on those who cared for him would have strengthened him. That's what I've tried to teach ye, Triona. It's not a weakness to let others in; it's strength."

I reach out, placing my hand over his. His eyes meet mine, and for a moment, the weight of his grief lingers in the air between us. "I'm sorry for yer loss, Da," I whisper. Something in my words makes his eyes glisten..

He clears his throat, his voice quieter now. "I appreciate that, lass. Ye ken, I've always had little reminders of him around me. Small things that keep his spirit close." His eyes linger on me, the hint of a smile softening his features. "And sometimes, those reminders grow up to be fiery and stubborn... jus like him."

He peers at me, his expression a mix of pride and something deeper, almost sorrowful. "Ye have that same passion, that belief in something greater. But ye've got a chance he never took—the chance to share that fire with those who love ye. To let it grow without burnin' out. That's why I've always pushed ye to lean on others, to build those strong connections."

"Ye've got a strength that's all yer own, and it disnae have to come at the cost of everything else. Trust in those around ye, and trust in yerself."

"I'll talk to yer mother, but promise me ye'll think about what I've said."

His eyes soften with memory. "Ye ken, yer mother didn't want me right away. And look at us now."

I roll my eyes, a faint smile tugging at my lips despite myself. He always brings my mother into these conversations, as though their story alone answers every question. And I guess, in some strange way, it does.

"I ken ye want the freedom to find what yer mother and I have on yer own," he continues, his tone thoughtful. "And I understand that, lass. I want that for ye, too. Real love, the kind ye're wishin' for, disnae demand ye give up freedom. It's something that feels so natural. Ye'll hardly notice its pull until ye're already there. When ye truly find it, freedom willnae be the first thing on yer mind—it'll be the last. Ye'll want to be wholly theirs. Not trapped, but enveloped. Loved so deeply, ye feel it deep in yer very bones. Love's no easy thing, lass. It's a battlefield of its own, but if ye've found someone worth the fight, ye fight like hell and hold tight."

Before I can respond, he pulls me into a warm embrace. The tension in my chest eases slightly as the steady beat of his heart presses against me. His arms are a haven, and for a moment, the strain of my fears feels just a little lighter.

"Ye dinnae have to ken what tomorrow brings," he murmurs, his voice soft in my ear. "None of us do. What matters is that ye face it head-on, surrounded by those who love ye. Ye're never alone, even when it feels like you are."

I pull back, wiping at my eyes. "Okay... you might be right. I might push back unnecessarily."

"Without a doubt." His words come without hesitation, but it's the quiet pride in his gaze that hits the deepest. "Ye've worked hard to prove yerself, and ye've grown stronger with every challenge. Trust in that strength. Trust in yerself. And trust that, even when ye feel different or out of place, ye're more equipped to handle this life than most. Maybe even more than yer brothers."

That earns a laugh from me, light and genuine.

We resume our walk; the sun dipping lower in the sky, casting long shadows that dance along the path.

"Thanks, Da," I whisper, my heart swelling with gratitude. "For always being here, even when it's hard to be."

He smiles, joy shining in his eyes. "Ye're no hard thing to love. Nae matter how dark the night is, the dawn will always come. And when it does, I'll be right by yer side."

As we walk, his words linger, settling deep within me, a steady reminder that no matter the trials ahead, I have those in my corner that wish me well.

The wind sweeps across my face, fierce and relentless, as I stand at the cliff's edge, staring into the vast, unbroken expanse of the sea stretching out before me. The waves below crash in a timeless rhythm, each one carrying with it the echo of my father's words—words that have seeped deep into my soul, shifting something unnameable within.

His tales of resilience, of love that binds tighter than iron, of strength forged in the quiet moments of trust and truth, have cracked me open, baring raw places I didn't know existed. The weight of his wisdom settles like a stone in my heart, a reminder, a promise, a question—a call I can feel in my bones but can't yet answer.

Lost in the currents of thought, my mind drifts with each rise and fall of the waves, and the quiet footsteps behind me slip past my notice. Then, large hands—warm, grounding—slip over my eyes. My breath catches, followed by a soft, startled laugh, the tension unravelling. There is something achingly familiar in the touch, something that reaches down to ease the ache in my chest.

"Cal," I murmur, lifting my fingers to trace one of the roughened hands, "or Casey? Three seconds and I'll know, so enjoy the mystery while you can." I try for levity, teasing, but my voice is softer, the edges fraying with anticipation.

But the voice that answers isn't theirs—it's softer, each word threaded with affection.

My heart stills, caught between breaths as his words wrap around me, a gentle steadiness grounding me against the wild cliffs and endless sea. His voice holds the warmth of something known, yet something that feels like a new beginning. The first hint of dawn breaking through the longest night. Sunshine in human form.

"Miss me, Little Doe?"

11

A THOUSAND NIGHTS WITHOUT HER

Finn

Friday, 25 April 1823

Sleep has become an elusive companion since receiving that letter all those weeks ago. Visions of Triona now dominate my thoughts.

In daylight, I envision her at my side as I complete arduous tasks. Chores I once resented seem bearable when I picture her there—laughing softly, fingers brushing mine as she passes. I imagine us sprawled on the library floor, the day's weight pressing into our limbs as her voice dances through the quiet, reading aloud while I let her words lull me into peace.

But the nights are worse.

They stretch long and hollow, filled with a hunger I cannot sate. I lie awake as my mind conjures the shape of her—the arch of her spine, the softness of her thighs, the warmth of her breath at my neck. I feel her, though she's not there. Her hair, like silk, spills over my skin in dreams that blur the line between what was and what I long for.

The desire burns so intensely within me it often becomes a physical ache—a constant reminder of the power she holds over me.

Though I fight it, there are nights when I surrender—to the darkness, to the silence, to the echo of her name. My hands move with a desperate rhythm, chasing a fantasy I know I shouldn't crave. But in that fevered moment, it's her. Always her. Her touch imagined, slow and knowing, teasing me toward the edge of bliss.

It's her name that whispers through my mind in that last moment before I tip over, the forbidden fantasy bringing me to completion, only to leave me hollow afterward. Shame and longing intertwine, but no matter how I fight it, the pull of her is relentless, consuming me in ways I'm powerless to escape.

Our horses slow to a halt before Castle Connemara, dust settling in a golden haze around us as I dismount. Before my boots fully touch the ground, I'm met by Casey's wide grin and Callan's steady, grounding presence.

Casey barrels toward me at full speed, wrapping me in a fierce hug, his usual boisterous laughter filling the air as though no time has passed since we last stood together.

"Look who's finally come home!" he shouts, his voice rich with warmth. "We thought ye might've forgotten where we were—or decided ye preferred the company of strangers to yer own kin."

He pulls me in tighter for another hug, his strength catching me off guard. When he speaks again, his voice is softer, more sincere. "It's good to see ye, brother."

I chuckle, clapping his back, before turning to Callan, whose smile is quieter but no less genuine.

"Glad ye made it back," Callan murmurs, his eyes steady with a depth of gratitude that doesn't need explaining.

I nod, a small smile tugging at my lips. "Yer letter was convincing enough."

Callan huffs a quiet breath, something like a smirk flickering across his face, but the look in his eyes holds steady—relieved, and maybe even a little surprised.

A throat clears behind me, drawing our attention.

"Who's that?" Callan asks, voice low and guarded, as he nods toward the figure looming just behind.

"Right," I say, steadying my voice, though a flicker of tension tightens my chest.

Casey's eyes spark with interest, and Callan raises a questioning brow as the tall, broad-shouldered man steps forward, his confident stride as unmistakable as his American drawl.

"This is Bran," I introduce, clapping a hand on Bran's shoulder. "He's been a tolerable friend to me these past few years. Couldnae leave him behind—not that he gave me much choice."

Bran, wearing his usual roguish grin, nods in greeting, his eyes glinting with curiosity as he sizes up Casey and Callan.

Recognition dawns on both of their faces, but Callan speaks the question aloud. "Alex's son?"

"Aye, that's my old man."

"Our father speaks highly of him. It's a pleasure to meet half of the illustrious Mumford father and son duo," Casey says with a playful edge.

"Pleasure's mine," Bran retorts, voice warm but edged with a playfulness of his own as he extends his hand to Casey first. "Finn's told me plenty about you both."

Casey laughs, shaking Bran's hand enthusiastically. "Aye, well, I hope he spared some of the more scandalous tales. Not sure I could live down some things you might've heard."

Bran chuckles, shooting me a playful glance. "Don't worry. Finn was mostly diplomatic."

Then he turns to Callan, offering a respectful nod while clearly sizing up the man's quiet intensity. "He's spoken highly of you... Callan, I presume? Said you were one to beat in a fight."

Callan's mouth quirks, a faint smile tugging at the corner of his lips. There's a glint of appreciation in his eyes—but also scrutiny.

"Aye, well," he says, stepping forward and clapping Bran on the arm, the force deliberate. "Clever of ye—to lead with flattery while scoping out the competition." His gaze sharpens just enough to make the point. "Suppose that means you're not entirely daft."

Bran's grin only deepens. "Flattery's just honesty with a smile, isn't it?" he quips, then leans in slightly, lowering his voice just enough to let the mischief settle in. "Figured I'd win more ground by working out which of you bites back the hardest."

Casey barks a laugh, clapping Bran on the back. "My coin's on you. Might not be so hard to put Callan down these days. Our sister—"

"Casey," Callan cuts in sharply, his tone low and warning. "Shut yer mouth and drop it."

Casey tries to suppress his amusement but fails miserably, laughter spilling out despite Callan's glare. "Aye, aye, fine," Casey says, holding up his hands in mock surrender, though his grin remains firmly in place. "Consider it dropped."

My gaze slides to Callan, curiosity flickering to life as I silently ask the question.

Callan meets my eyes with a look that says *don't even think about it.* Whatever Casey was about to say, Callan's not sharing—and if I so much as breathe a question, he'll make himself scarce faster than a shadow at sunrise.

The corner of my mouth twitches, amusement threatening to rise. I know better than to press, but I also know it'll come out—most likely when Casey decides the time is ripe to stir the pot, as he always does.

The four of us fall into laughter—the easy kind, worn in like an old coat. Camaraderie blooms in the way only old ties allow—jabs and jests tossed like stones across a quiet loch.

But when the mirth fades, I catch the edge of something in Callan's sidelong glance. Subtle—but heavy. A flicker of what still lingers beneath the surface. A reminder of why I've come back.

As Casey leads Bran off toward the stables, his voice animated as he regales Bran with some undoubtedly exaggerated tale, Callan steps closer to me. His hand lightly grips my arm, his voice dropping low enough that only I can hear.

"I'm glad ye're home."

He hesitates, and I see the vulnerability in his eyes, a crack in the armour he wears so well. "I'd wondered if my letter had gone unanswered," he continues, his words slower now, deliberate. "If maybe—" He pauses, the unspoken possibility hanging heavy between us.

He doesn't need to finish. I know what he's thinking, what he doesn't say aloud.

We were both raised to carry what others couldn't. To be unflinching, unshaken. There's little room for softness in the shape we were forced to take. It hollows you out over time. And he's been carrying too much, alone.

I place a hand on his shoulder, grounding him in the way only he and I understand.

"Ye never needed to doubt," I say, my voice quiet but certain. "I'd have come, Callan. Always."

His lips press into a faint line, his gaze dropping for a moment before meeting mine again. The tension in his shoulders eases, though the gratitude in his expression is something I doubt he'll ever put into words.

"Aye," he finally says, giving a small nod. "Good."

It's a simple word, but it carries more than it seems, and as he steps back, I feel the unspoken bond between us as strong as ever. A tether that runs deeper than blood. It's a connection forged in silence—in the heavy spaces where burdens are borne without complaint.

Beneath Callan's steady gaze, I sense the stirring of unrest—a shadow that has yet to take shape. There are questions in him, tangled and unsaid, and though he hides them well, I know their weight.

He needs someone beside him—not to lift the burden entirely, but to remind him he is not alone beneath it.

And when he's ready—when the silence breaks and the words finally come—I'll be here. He's never been one to speak before the time is right. And I?

I've always known how to wait.

"Right then," Callan says, nodding toward the familiar stretch of land behind the farmhouse. His tone softens, the edges of his usual gruffness smoothing into something almost wistful. "She'll be glad to see ye," he murmurs, as though speaking more to himself than to me.

As he steps back to give me space, memories of Triona flood my senses, as vivid as if she stood beside me. I can almost *feel* her there, our shoulders brushing as she catches me up on the last three years of life—three years spent without me—her voice weaving stories that linger long after the words fade.

"Ye ken how she is. She'll get bent outta shape if she finds out ye didnae see her the moment yer foot stepped onto solid ground." I nod in acknowledgment, though words fail me.

Callan claps a hand on my shoulder, his voice low. "She's out at the cliffs. Casey said her and Ma got in quite the row. Said it looked like she'd been holdin' back tears, but she's not the type to let 'em fall where folk can see."

I nod again, and my chest constricts as my gaze follows his—toward the worn path I know by heart, the one that winds through grass and wind and salt air until it reaches the sea.

Every nerve thrums. The steady beat of my heart begins to rise, louder now, pulsing with something I wish I could ignore.

Because beneath the anticipation, beneath the ache to see her again, there's something else—something darker.

Guilt flickers through me, sharp and unwelcome. I shouldn't feel this way. Not about her. Not when she's always been Callan's little sister... and one of my greatest friends, in every way that's meant to matter.

But no amount of reason or restraint has loosened her hold on me. Not time. Not distance. Not blood that was never truly shared.

I take a breath, long and steady, trying to brace myself, not just for the moment I'll see her again, but for whatever stirs inside of me when I do.

I realise, as I watch her from a distance, that the moment I dreaded isn't dreadful at all. There's a strange sort of peace in seeing her again.

No other woman could ever hope to compare to the allure that she possesses. She's become the measure I never meant to make, the standard by which all others fall short. It's not fair to them—and it's not her fault—but it's the truth.

Her absence carved something into me, a hollow space that no one else has filled. But even in that emptiness, I grew. The ache of missing her shaped me, forced me to become a man worthy of more.

She'll likely never know that. Never see the way her memory has steadied me, how the thought of her lit a path when everything else went dark.

But *I* know. And somehow, that's enough.

As I draw closer, I can see a great tension in her shoulders, the heaviness that weighs her down. I want to say something, but the moment feels too delicate to break with words. Instead, I step up behind her and gently place my hands over her eyes.

She gasps, which slowly turns into a chuckle that I can feel hum through my body. "Cal... or Casey?" She quiets as she runs a hand over my calloused knuckles. "Three seconds and I'll know, so enjoy the mystery while you can." She laughs, light and teasing, and a smile tugs at my lips.

I let my voice slip into the quiet between us. "Miss me, Little Doe?"

She stills, her whole body freezing as though the world has paused around her. I watch eagerly as she turns, her movements laced with disbelief and awe. Her gaze lifts, and for a heartbeat I can see so much there—surprise, relief, and a light that banishes the shadows that are haunting her.

We stand here, eyes locked, her expression vulnerable and beautiful. In this instant, I want to tell her everything—that she'd been in my thoughts, in my heart, that every moment leading me to this cliff had felt like a race against time just to be here, just to be with her.

Then, in a rush, she launches herself at me with reckless abandon, crashing into me with such force that I stumble backward, nearly toppling to the ground. In my arms, she feels like pure fire, igniting every nerve ending in my body. I hug her tightly, the instinct to hold her anchors me in place. Selfishly, I choose to take this moment for myself—if only for a moment, I can be hers, and she can be mine.

The intoxicating scent of her skin—primrose and something wild, like the moors in springtime—saturates every breath I take, the fragrance stirs something deep within me, awaking desires I want to keep buried. Three years without this fragrance, three years of wondering if I'd ever breathe it in again, sharpen every second she's in my arms, heightening everything until it's almost unbearable.

Our bodies intertwine tightly as she presses herself against me in such an intimate manner that I can sense every flawless contour of her figure melding harmoniously with mine, creating a fiery passion that simultaneously thrills and terrifies me.

I can't help but to imagine what the softness of her velvety skin would feel like beneath my fingertips, the delicate heat pressed directly against me. I can picture her skin yielding to my touch, smooth and supple, as if made to fit perfectly with mine.

My mind runs wild as I accept the fact that this far exceeds any touch experienced before. I find myself grateful for the layers separating us, shielding my aching arousal provoked by how flush she is against me.

Her arms wind around my neck in a tender, unrelenting embrace—each gentle squeeze is a tether that binds me to this fleeting moment. And though I hold her now, I know well the sorrow that will come when the embrace is but a memory, a whisper of warmth lost to the cold.

"Your heart is hammering," she says.

I huff out a laugh, shaking my head. "Aye, well, you nearly knocked me flat—gave me a wee start, you did."

She leans back enough to look up at me, so close that her warm breath is dancing languidly against my skin. She's searching my face as her teeth graze her lower lip—just a whisper of pressure at first, then a slow, thoughtful bite. She holds it there long enough that the soft swell of her lip deepens into a flush. The sight sends a fresh bolt of heat through me. My fingers itch to tangle in her hair, to tilt her head back, and claim that perfect mouth.

Her emerald eyes are wide, shimmering with emotion she isn't attempting to mask. A single tear falls from her eye, and without thinking, I move my hand to her cheek, brushing it away gently with the pad of my thumb. The touch is so natural—so instinctive for me.

Triona lets out a soft, nervous chuckle, wiping the corner of her eye. "Gods, I'm sorry," she whispers, her voice catching in her throat as she tries to pull away. "I didn't mean for you to—"

"Stop." My hands find her waist, gentle but unyielding—an anchor against the pull of her retreat. "Never apologise for that. Not with me."

She swallows hard, and I track the movement. Without a word, she steps closer. Her arms slip around my waist, slow but sure, and she rests her head against my chest. I feel the soft hitch of her breath, the faint tremble in her shoulders as she lets herself cry—she lets me see the most vulnerable version of herself.

My hands stay firm on her hips, holding her as if she might vanish with the wind. This simple closeness, the weight of her against me, her warmth seeping through every layer—it undoes me.

It's not enough. And yet somehow, it's everything.

"I was just... so surprised. So happy to see you. It... caught me off guard."

"It's all right," I murmur, rough-voiced and aching.

"It was hard," she says, quieter now. "Not hearing from you. I didn't realise how much I'd come to depend on you being around... until you weren't."

The words hit like a blow I saw coming and still didn't brace for. I should've written more—something, anything—but every time I began to write, it felt impossible. How could I endure longing for the place, the people that were home without unravelling completely?

"I'm sorry, Triona," I say, voice low, with nothing but compassion clear.

She looks up at me, her brow furrowed, and she pulls away from my embrace in order to wrap her arms around herself.

"Why didn't you? You got my letters, right?"

There isn't anger in her voice, just a quiet hurt. The kind that twists the knife even deeper. Her anger is something I knew I deserved, but the hurt is a harder burden to bear.

I run a hand through my hair, exhaling slowly as I try to find the right words. "It was... hard to write home when I missed it so much. I thought if I tried to put it all into words, I'd never stop thinkin' about how much I wanted to be back. I never intended to hurt anyone. But I missed this... I missed *you*."

Her lips part slightly, as if she doesn't know what to say. After a beat, she nods slowly and reaches for my hand. Her thumb brushes over my knuckles in a soft, reassuring gesture.

"Say no more. I should have considered that," she breathes, her eyes softening. "I was here with family, and you were there alone. I missed you too, Finn. You have the kindest heart... and I'm so grateful to know it."

She pauses, her gaze steady. "To call you a friend is an honour," she finishes quietly.

Friend. The reminder I need at the moment. The reminder I needn't ignore.

I let out a quiet chuckle, rolling my eyes in mock exasperation as I try to shake off the ache sitting too close to my ribs. "Oh, I wasna alone. Not by a long shot."

"How do you mean?"

I give her a sly grin, leaning in slightly. "They stuck me with a particularly obnoxious bugger. Bran Mumford."

"Mumford?" Triona echoes, eyes narrowing as recognition ignites. "Is his father's name Alexander? The American?"

"Alex. Aye... it is. I've not had the pleasure of meeting his father yet."

I chuckle and nod as I cross my arms. "If Bran's anything to go by, let's just say subtlety isn't exactly in their blood. Bran can be... crass, to put it lightly. I used to wonder if all Americans were alike in that way, but I truly believe he's one of a kind."

Triona laughs, eyes dancing with amusement. "Poor, long-suffering you. Enduring all that confidence and charm—how *did* you manage?"

"Ye've no idea," I say, smirking. "He'll stride into rooms as if he were born to command them. Every time he opens his mouth, I stare and wonder how a man can be so bold and not even blink."

She snorts, clearly enjoying herself, and I can't help but grin.

But then the humour softens, giving way to something quieter. "He nearly drove me mad," I admit, the smirk fading. "But... I'll never say it to his face, not unless he's dyin' or something... but havin' him around helped. A lot. There were moments I might've lost my head if it weren't for him."

"Well, if he's anything like his da, I can only imagine the whirlwind," she says with a soft laugh, shaking her head. "Da says Alex can turn a tumble through a rainstorm into an adventure—talks nonsense half the time, but somehow makes you feel you're part of something bigger just by being there."

My grin widens. "Aye, that sounds right. Bran's cut from the same cloth. Half the time it felt as if he was leadin' us into some kind of chaos just for the thrill."

"*Americans,*" she sighs, clearly leaning into the jest.

I tilt my head, watching her for a moment. "So, Callan mentioned you'd been away at school."

Her smile softens at that, touched with something quieter. "Aye," she says, but doesn't linger on it. Instead, she shifts the conversation with practiced ease. "That's part of why I've not had the chance to meet Alex. He moved here permanently a few months ago. Works with my da, mostly, but he just bought the Sutherlands' tavern—since they couldn't pass it on to their son..." That flicker in her eyes says more than her words ever could.

She still carries the blame. As if the sins of another are hers scars to bear.

"Triona, it wasna yer fault," I say, more firmly than I mean to. "The things that boy did... what he was up to..."

"I know, it's just... my mother *hired* Colina while I was away. Her father's passed, and her mother has taken ill. So of course my mother's trying to help where she can."

She pauses as if she's warring with the truth of her words. "But you should see the way she looks at me, Finn. Like I've taken something from her and she's just waiting for the right moment to say it."

Her words make every protective instinct in my body come alive.

She plays with the loose ends of her hair as she continues. "It's unsettling. I try not to let it get to me, but it does."

"Triona, d'ye feel unsafe or—"

"No!" She shakes her head.

"No," she says, much more evenly toned. "I didn't mean to sound as if I felt that way. I know it likely saved Dealla."

Why does she feel the need to reassure me she feels safe? Why does it feel as if she's apologising for voicing her concerns?

"Tri," I start, running my hand through my hair again, "if something's off with her, you need to trust yer gut. I've seen what people can do when they're pushed into corners." My voice is soft but firm.

She attempts to maintain calm by brushing it off, but she can't fool me. Her down-played tone, the casual dismissal—it all feels too familiar, as if she's trying to convince both of us that there's nothing to worry about.

But I know that look in her eyes. I've worn it myself.

Her unease plants a seed of suspicion deep in my gut—one that takes root fast. And now, the knot in my stomach refuses to loosen.

Before I can speak again, the moment shifts.

A familiar voice cuts through the air, full of swagger and poorly concealed amusement.

"Talking about me, are you?"

Bran saunters up, all effortless confidence and too-perfect charm, flashing the kind of grin I've seen disarm more than a few hearts—and test the patience of even more.

Triona glances at him, immediately clocking his energy. She appears unimpressed as she waits for introductions.

"You are *quite* divine." Bran announces, voice dripping with charm.

Before I can tell him to behave like a functioning adult, Triona crosses her arms and cuts in with a dry tone. "I'm not buying whatever it is you're selling."

Bran chortles, feigning surprise. "These are *premium* goods, beautiful," he says as he gestures to his frame.

She rolls her eyes dramatically. "Don't flatter yourself."

Something about her response pleases me more than I care to admit. A warm satisfaction settles deep in my chest at seeing her brush off his usual swagger with such ease. I bite back the smirk threatening to break free, but it's a losing battle.

Bran, ever unbothered, chuckles and throws me a look. "Oh, she's immune, Finn. I see. A tough crowd."

Triona is clearly holding her own—living up to the strong-willed woman he expected her to be.

"This *bugger* right here is Bran." I say, even if the statement is pointless.

She extends her hand hesitantly, unsure of his intentions. When Bran leans in to kiss it, I swat him away before he can land it.

"Oi!" he yelps, rubbing his knuckles. "Can't blame a man for trying."

Triona crosses her arms, though her grin remains in place. "Finn was right to warn me about you. You *are* trouble."

"You'll give in, eventually. They all do."

She raises an eyebrow, still grinning. "You sound *awfully* confident for someone who just faced rejection."

Bran smirks. "Confidence is key, love. And you haven't rejected me yet—you're just playing hard to get."

Triona scoffs, crossing her arms tighter. "Oh, is *that* what this is?"

Still watching the back-and-forth with mounting amusement, I step a little closer to Triona, feeling that familiar protective tug. "Bran, ye're gonna run out of charm if you keep chuckin' it around like that."

He chuckles, unabashed. "Not a chance. I've an endless supply."

Triona shakes her head, rolling her eyes but still smiling. "Well, don't waste it here. You're chasing shadows, *Brannie*."

Bran's eyes sparkle. "See? You've already given me a nickname. Progress." He leans in a fraction too close. "I'll wait for you to come around to me properly—I pride myself on being a patient man."

With one last wink and a devilish smile tossed my way, he backs off, hands raised like a saint. "I'll leave you two to your fun. But remember, Triona—I'll be around."

"He really thinks he's irresistible, doesn't he?"

I grin, my heart lighter than it's been in days. "He does. But you handled him admirably."

She shoots a sideways glance my way, a spark of something playful in her eyes. "I'm willing to wager you enjoyed watching that."

I shrug, though my smile gives me away. "More than I should have."

She laughs again, soft and real, the last traces of tension between us completely diminished. "Him and Casey are going to get along famously."

I light up with amusement. "I thought the same thing."

As we stand here, the conversation flowing easily; I feel a sense of balance return, the easy camaraderie between us masking the deeper feelings I still can't voice.

But for now, this—this ease, this warmth—is enough.

Part 3 – Nineteen Moons Shall Orbit Bright

12

A THORN AMONG THE FLOWERS

Triona

Sunday, 27 April 1823

The first light of dawn spills through the curtains, soft as breath, casting a warm glow across my room.

Lately, sleep has offered no rest. My dreams—sharp, vivid things—are filled with lengthening shadows, with whispers I can't quite hear, with the feeling of running and never reaching safety. I wake with the weight of them, always a moment too late to grasp meaning.

But today, something anchors me. A familiar scent.

Turning my head, I find a small bundle of primrose resting on my bedside table, tied with twine, delicate as memory. Their soft purple petals catch the morning light, and for a moment, I forget the dreams. I trace the edge of one bloom with my finger, and it feels like being touched by a version of myself I'd long put away.

It's been years since I've last seen them placed here. Their absence has nearly faded from my memory.

As I lift the flowers gently, the scent of earth and morning dew rises, carrying me back to childhood mornings when I would wake to find them waiting for me. Primrose has always been resilient, growing wild in the Highlands despite the rough soil and harsh winds. Seeing them in bloom serves as a reminder that I, too, can endure much.

My mother used to leave them when she thought I needed quiet reassurance—a way to let me know I was loved and protected. We've never spoken about it, and maybe that's why it means so much. A silent language, written in petals and placed gently in the dark.

I haven't spoken to her since our fight, and maybe this is her way of reaching across the silence—offering a hand I'm not quite ready to take.

I ready myself and make my way down toward the stables. I've seen very little of Finn since he arrived two days ago, and there is a strange urgency in me to find him, to see him away from the hustle and bustle of everyone else.

As I near the stables, muffled voices and bursts of barely stifled giggles filter through. Curious, I pick up my pace, stopping just at the edge of the fenced perimeter where I can see Dealla and Saoirse standing with their backs to me, shoulders pressed together as they stare out at where we let the troop roam freely.

"Will you look at him?" Dealla whispers. The awe in her tone is unmistakable. "I swear, the man looks like he stepped out of a dream."

Saoirse nods, cheeks flushing as she mutters, "A dream I wouldn't mind stayin' in longer."

Curious, I creep closer, my amusement bubbling just beneath the surface. I stop when I see what has them both in a trance.

Finn.

He's shirtless, the early light gilding over his skin in gold. His dark hair falls into his eyes as he brushes down his mare Aisling, every movement slow, deliberate. His back is a sculpture in motion, muscles flexing under skin slick with the sheen of morning effort. But it's not just the strength that draws the eye—it's the ease. The quiet rhythm of the moment. The way Aisling leans into his touch, trusting, content.

But what catches my attention more than anything are the markings between his shoulders. Black ink swirls into an image, bold and striking, something almost primal in its beauty.

My eyes trace the curve of ink, following the shape of his spine, and the way his muscles shift and stretch under the design. I catch myself staring, caught not just by the ink, but by the man beneath it. For a moment too long, I forget myself entirely. It takes effort to pull out of my daze to speak.

"Shameless, ladies." Dealla and Saoirse startle, then dissolve into giggles.

Dealla barely spares me a glance before sighing again, utterly unrepentant. "You can't blame us, Triona... I mean, by the gods, *look* at him." She practically purrs the words.

I hadn't even realised I was staring again until Finn looks up, his gaze locking onto mine. A flicker of amusement dances in his eyes. He raises his voice to bridge the distance between us. "Didnae expect to see you up so early, Little Doe!"

"Aye, well, I came out to stretch my legs," I reply smoothly. "And Shadow's."

Finn raises an eyebrow, that warming smile still tugging at his lips. "Ah, so ye've bullied poor Eamon into saddlin' up Shadow for you, have you?"

I scoff. "Of course not. I *kindly persuaded* him. There's a difference."

He chuckles and returns to his task. Behind me, Dealla sighs audibly. "He's going to ruin us all. Just look at him."

"Settle yourselves," I mutter under my breath. "You two look as if you're about to faint dead away."

They exchange amused glances, not the least bit abashed, and Saoirse smirks. "Ye'd be doin' it too if ye weren't tryin' so hard to hide it."

"Don't you ladies have *anywhere* else you could be right now?" I ask, arching a brow.

They groan dramatically but slink off, casting one last look over their shoulders.

Finn chuckles at their antics, shaking his head. As I near him, he turns toward me, wiping his hands on a cloth tucked into his waistband. There's a brightness in his eyes as they meet mine.

I offer a smile—small, a little uncertain. He returns it with that familiar smirk, the one that always feels like an invitation.

"When did you get that?" I ask, gesturing toward his back.

"Not too long ago."

"Did it hurt?" I ask, though I can imagine the answer.

His laugh rumbles low in his chest, and something about it loosens a knot inside me. "Aye, more than I thought it would. But some things are worth the pain."

I take a small step closer. "Turn a bit?" I request, my voice softer than I mean for it to be.

He shifts, angling his body to give me a better view. My gaze traces the lines across his skin, following each curve and edge. It suits him—fierce, grounded, quietly defiant. Just like him.

"Why a stag?" I ask.

He turns to face me, his expression endearing to look at. "It's a bit of home, something permanent I can take with me no matter where I go."

I tilt my head, playful. "This home?"

He gives a tiny eye-roll, but the smile that follows betrays him. "Of course. This is the only true home I've ever known."

The accuracy of those words settles into me as easily as a breath: he belongs here. With the Sinclairs. With me.

Having him home again feels right in a way I can't quite explain. As if something that had been missing slipped quietly back into place.

"It's quite lovely, Finn," I murmur, and as he holds my gaze, I see the tiniest flicker of vulnerability in his eyes. A glimpse of the man beneath all that steady, unshakable strength. The one who carries so much, so silently.

His face gentles further, the movement overtaking his usual reserved mask. "I'm glad you came out, Triona. I actually have something for you."

Surprise flickers through me, but before I can speak, he gestures toward the stables. We walk side by side, silence stretching between us, filled only with birdsong and the rustle of wind through the grass. My mind spins, but I hold on to the quiet, letting the anticipation bloom.

At the stables, he moves to a leather bag hanging from a post and pulls out a small cloth pouch—worn, but sturdy.

"Go on," he encourages, a hint of a smile playing at the corner of his mouth. "Open it."

I loosen the ties and peer inside. Nestled in the soft fabric is a necklace unlike any I've ever seen. As I remove it from the pouch, the pendant catches the light and gleams, its surface etched with intricate spirals and wavelike patterns. The craftsmanship is delicate, unmistakably ancient. It feels as if it carries history within it—belonging to another time entirely.

"It's beautiful," I whisper as I hold it further up to the light. I tilt the pendant to watch the iridescence dance along its edges. Hues of blue shimmer across its surface—deep sapphire, pale glacier, the flicker of moonlit water. "Finn, I... I don't know what to say."

He shrugs, but I can see the quiet pride in his eyes. "It's a birthday gift."

"You didn't have to get me anything."

"I know," he says, his voice low. "But I wanted to."

"Here," he murmurs as he takes the necklace from my hand. "Turn around, and I'll help you put it on."

I lift my hair, and his hands move carefully, the chain brushing my collarbone. His fingers graze my skin—light, precise. The pendant settles against my chest, and for a moment, I feel... anchored. As if it's always been meant to rest here.

I turn back to face him, feeling oddly exposed. "Thanks," is all I can get out.

His expression softens into something shy. "Ye're welcome, Triona. It... suits you."

Caught up in the moment, I feel a sudden urge to close the distance between us. Before I can talk myself out of it, I lean in and wrap my arms around him.

He stiffens, surprised—but only for a second. Then he exhales and pulls me in, his arms folding around me with quiet sincerity. The burden of everything—of fear, of tension, of uncertainty—eases as I rest against him. For longer than is necessary, I let myself stay there in his arms.

Then he gently pulls back and nods toward the pasture.

"Come on," he says. "Follow me to go grab Aisling before she eats her weight in clover."

The mare lifts her head as we approach, ears flicking forward. She's halfway through munching a patch of wildflowers, unbothered by our presence.

But just as I step forward to greet her, my boot catches on a rut in the ground—small, invisible, and perfectly placed to sabotage me.

I overcorrect when I try to catch myself, and I go down hard, landing flat on my back with a surprised yelp. The fall knocks the wind out of me for a second—but then the absurdity hits. I burst into laughter, clutching my stomach, helpless to stop.

Finn leans down, laughter dancing in his eyes. "Are you all right?" he asks, though the grin on his face tells me he is more entertained than concerned. "Ye'd think someone as *attentive* as you would be more mindful of yer surroundin's."

The corners of his mouth twitch before they fully surrender to amusement, and when he laughs, it's not loud or mocking—but soft, warm, and impossible not to feel. The mirth in his smile lights up his entire face, a glow that chases away any trace of embarrassment I might have felt with anyone else.

I roll my eyes at him, but there's no hiding my smile. It tugs at my lips before I can stop it, betraying the way his laughter always gets to me.

Then I gasp, bolting upright, hands flying to my pocket.. "The flowers!" I exclaim, frantically checking the small bundle of primrose I'd brought out with me. To my relief, they're intact—not a petal out of place. I hold them up, grinning in triumph.

I catch a flicker in Finn's eyes—a softness, maybe even curiosity.

"What've you got there?" he asks, his tone genuine.

"If you must know," I say, holding up the bundle, "it's primrose. I woke up to them on my bedside table."

A breath passes before I add, "It's something my mother used to do. I hadn't seen them in so long, I almost forgot she ever did this. You know I've such a shite memory, so that's hardly a surprise."

We both laugh at that.

I bring the purple flowers with their heart-shaped petals down on my lap, a fond smile tugging at my lips.

Finn lowers himself to the ground beside me, crossing his arms over his knees, watching me with that steady gaze of his.

"So?" he finally says, a bit of teasing in his voice. "What's got you leapin' to save a handful of flowers?"

I shrug. "It just... it feels important. To keep them all. Or it used to."

Finn tilts his head, his voice softer now. "You keep all of 'em?"

I nod, brushing my thumb over the edge of a petal. "Most of the time. Except in instances where I trip and fall and crush them into oblivion."

I smile, but there's a hint of shyness tugging at the edges of it now. "I used to press them into books," I admit. "Slide them between the pages so I'd come across them again when I was reading." I glance over at him, my voice softer still. "And when you were away, I sent them to you. Tucked in with the letters. Like you said before—I wanted you to have a piece of home."

The grin slips from his face, replaced by something softer, more thoughtful. He says nothing at first, but I can feel the shift—the quiet settling between us like the scent of the flowers, warm and subdued.

There's a beat before I speak again. "You know, this flower is what my father used to win my mother over," I tell him, gently turning the bundle in my hands. "He always said, '*In the language of flowers, it represents the joy of youth and a celebration of adolescent love.*'" I mimic my father's dramatic tone, and Finn lets out a muted chuckle.

"In full bloom, the primrose is hard to ignore. He said the love he had for my mother was like that—not always out loud and proud, but hard to miss."

I can almost see my father, bent over, carefully picking the flowers, waiting for the right time, the right season, to give her that special gift. "They bloom their brightest from May to July, so he waited, patient as anything, collecting them to make that one bottle of scent for her." I shake my head, laughing softly.

Finn is quiet for a long moment. When he finally speaks, his voice is low, thoughtful even. "You should wake up to flowers on yer bedside table every day, Triona."

I look his way, drawn in by the tenderness in his tone. There's something in his eyes—a genuine acknowledgement. A depth of sincerity that roots me in place. "*Never* settle for less. Yer da wouldnae want that."

For a heartbeat, I'm lost—studying the lines of his face, the way the light brushes against his skin. The way his golden-brown eyes find mine. I've met his gaze more times than I can count, but now they hold something new—more grounded, more certain.

An ache rises slowly, blooming like something long buried, and I feel myself poised at the edge of a truth too heavy to name.

I avert my eyes. There's so much I could say—so much I *want* to say. About my mother. About Marcus. About the fear clawing at the edges of everything lately. The words burn at the back of my throat, desperate to escape.

But something about this moment feels too delicate. A hush I'm too afraid to disturb. And I *do* trust him. More than anyone.

More than anything, I'm clinging to the quiet comfort of him beside me—unwilling to break it by acknowledging what waits beyond this stillness. I want it—want him—a little longer before the world presses in again.

"I know he wouldn't," I say finally, voice quieter than before.

I pause, eyes fixed ahead. "My mother feels differently."

Out of the corner of my eye, I see Finn exhale—sharp, as though he's been holding it in. His jaw tenses, and I know that's all the answer I need. That broaching this topic is risky.

I stretch my legs out, keeping my gaze forward, my voice dropping to a quiet murmur. "I think—I *know* she wants me to marry Marcus Murray. We got into a particularly awful row about it. It's the reason I went out to the cliffs the day you returned—why we haven't been talking. I can't stand this sort box she's trying to fit me in. I won't fit. I never have."

There's a tense pause before Finn speaks. His tone is softer, but there is an unmistakable edge. "And you? What is it *you* want?"

I swallow, not daring to meet his gaze. "I don't know." The words fall out in a hesitant whisper.

The quiet stretches, taut as a pulled thread. Then Finn shifts, his hand reaching out—slow, deliberate—and he gently tilts my chin toward him.

"Look at me," he says, voice barely above a breath.

And I do.

His eyes search mine, as if he's trying to see through the fog. My heart stammers beneath the power of his gaze—and if I hold it for too long, I'll say everything I've tried so hard not to feel.

A sharp, chaotic clamour erupting from behind us abruptly interrupts our conversation.

The piercing, desperate whinny of a horse in full panic cuts through the air, reverberating across the yard and setting every nerve in my body alight.

Shadow.

He's thrashing violently in his stall, hooves pounding against the wooden walls like a battering ram. The entire building shudders with the force of his panic. Splinters fly. Dust rains from the rafters. The sound is unbearable—desperate and wild, the cry of a creature gripped by a fear beyond reason.

Without hesitation, I run toward him, skirts clutched in my fists, boots thudding over the packed earth. Logic flees. Instinct takes over.

"*Triona, stay back!*" Finn's voice is sharp, panicked—but I'm already halfway there.

The air is electric, crackling with something unnatural. Shadow seems more beast than being, his eyes wild, his body trembling with restless energy. His hooves slam dangerously close to the stall door just as I reach for him.

For a moment, he seems to settle, nostrils flaring, the whites of his eyes beginning to fade as I edge closer—calm, steady.

Then—movement behind me. A sudden rush of air.

Finn barrels into me, arms locking tight around my waist.

The world lurches, tilting off its axis. In the next breath, I'm pulled against him—his grip fierce as he hauls me back. Shadow's hooves crash down exactly where I'd been standing only heartbeats before.

My back presses to his skin, bare and burning. I can feel the rapid thunder of his heartbeat, wild beneath the surface. The heat of him pours into me, chasing away the cold bite of fear. His breath grazes my ear, ragged and warm, stirring loose strands of my hair.

And clinging to him is the scent of sweat, leather, and earth. I can't tell if it's the danger still pulsing through me or the nearness of him that makes my knees threaten to give.

My fingers curl around his forearm, still braced tightly across my waist. For a moment, neither of us moves, the world narrows to breath and heartbeat.

"He's not right," he breathes into my ear.

I nod, breathless, trembling.

"Let me handle it."

Finn's presence changes—solid, commanding. He steps into the stall as if he's done it a thousand times.

Shadow rears, hooves flashing. Finn doesn't so much as flinch.

"Settle," Finn says low, stepping closer with terrifying calm. "Ye ken me, Scáthfhóilt. Stand down."

The Gaelic name hits the air heavy—old, familiar, binding.

Shadow bares his teeth, kicking hard against the ground—but Finn doesn't waver. His hands move until they are iron clamps around the reins. His voice isn't loud when he speaks, but it feels omnipresent all the same.

"I said *settle*."

And somehow—he does.

The transformation isn't instant, but it's unmistakable. Shadow shudders. His ears twitch, nostrils flare. But slowly, the tension bleeds out of his body.

I stare, heart caught in my throat.

Finn doesn't tame him with strength. He doesn't wrestle him into calm. He *calls* it into being.

It humbles me, watching it. Watching *him*.

Finn murmurs something under his breath and gently coaxes Shadow forward, out of the stall and into the clearing. The big stallion follows, quivering but no longer fighting. There's trust in the movement. Hard-earned. Absolute.

And I can't tear my eyes away.

Finn moves alongside him, keeping one hand on the reins while the other glides slowly over Shadow's flank, feeling for heat, for swelling—anything out of place. His palm presses lightly over the stallion's sides, down his legs, across his chest. A quiet, thorough search.

Then he shifts to the saddle.

His attention sharpens, and then he freezes.

"Finn?" I whisper, barely able to speak.

He doesn't answer. Just reaches beneath the saddle straps and pulls something free. The moment it clears the leather, a sudden biting cold hits my face, sharp enough to sting. It's a branch—twisted, gnarled, black as coal. Thorns that are like jagged fangs.

"*Blackthorn...*" Finn mutters, holding it up for me to see its twisted branches and sharp thorns catching the light.

Revulsion twists in my gut. My skin crawls. Blackthorn isn't just wood—it's weaponised *malice*.

"Why would this be here?" I whisper, fingers curling around the necklace he gave me earlier, seeking anything to ground me.

Heavy footsteps thunder across the gravel. Callan barrels into the clearing, shirt half-buttoned, eyes wide. "What the hell happened?! I heard screamin'—"

Casey and Eamon's entry cut Callan off. Both of them barge in with hair wild, blades drawn.

"What happened?!" Casey practically screeches out.

Finn holds up the branch.

Callan recoils instinctively. "*Is that—?*"

"Aye, blackthorn," Finn growls. "Wedged up under his saddle. Just waitin'."

Eamon blinks hard, shaking his head. "I saddled him not half an hour ago..."

Casey takes a step closer, inspecting the branch with narrowed eyes. "That's *placed*. You dinnae just pick that up in a brush."

Shadow snorts, still rattled, still watching the thing like it might leap from Finn's hand.

Eamon's voice is quiet, almost too small. "That kind of wood... it's used in binding spells. Dark ones. And curses. Sometimes... sacrifices."

"It could mean nothin'," Finn says, his tone soothing but his eyes shadowed with worry. "Could be it *was* tangled in the saddle?"

A shudder rolls through me.

"Not a chance. *Someone* did that," Eamon urges. "I swear to the gods it wasn't there, Finn. I'm certain."

"Burn it," Callan demands. "Now."

Dealla and Saoirse approach with apparent hesitation.

"What's this then?" Dealla asks, voice tight.

Saoirse takes one look at the Finn's hand and her face drains of colour. "That's cursed wood."

Without ceremony, she takes it from Finn's hand. Her fingers barely brush the bark before she grimaces.

"I'm burnin' it. Right now."

She moves to the firepit with a strange urgency—swift but silent, her skirts barely whispering over the ground. As she lowers herself to her knees, she does so with a practiced steadiness, like someone performing a rite.

Beside me, Finn pulls his shirt back on, fingers moving quickly, jaw tight. Then, without a word, he wraps an arm around me—grounding me.

But the cold lingers. My skin prickles. My pulse won't settle.

Shadow isn't thrashing anymore. But he isn't calm, either. He watches the fire, ears pinned back, a deep unease radiating from his enormous frame.

"Dinnae fash, Little Doe," Finn murmurs, voice low enough for only me to hear.

We *all* feel it—that heaviness, the shift in the air. As if something's been disturbed. Awoken.

A gust of wind rushes in, stirring ash and loose straw across the ground. Somewhere nearby, a raven caws once—sharp and out of place.

A chill skitters down my spine. My gaze shifts to the far end of the stables, drawn by movement in the gloom.

A figure looms, half-shrouded in shadow.

Colina.

She's staring, arms at her sides, the sunlight barely brushing her face. Her eyes aren't on the fire Saoirse is trying to coax into life, or the blackthorn still smouldering in the pit. They're not even on Shadow, still tense as he seems to pace around us.

Her gaze rests on Finn's arm across my body, on the way I'm leaning into him. Her brow tightens, almost imperceptibly. A small flicker of something passes over her face. There, then gone.

Focused in such a way that she doesn't notice that I'm looking at her.

But then, as if some current between us jolts to life, our eyes meet.

Colina straightens.

And without a word, she turns and walks away, disappearing behind the stable with quick, purposeful steps.

I blink, uncertain.

The silence thickens again.

I shift in Finn's hold. My pulse is still uneven, my body trying to catch up with the chaos that's only just settled.

His arm tightens around me—not forcefully, but firm. Protective. Reassuring. A response born of instinct, not thought.

My body responds before my mind does. The tension in my shoulders eases, my breath finds rhythm again. The cold crawling up my spine—the one that has nothing to do with the wind—retreats.

And I settle.

Not because the fear is gone.

But because *he* hasn't moved.

Finn
Wednesday, 30 April 1823

Triona steps outside, her gaze sweeping over the group as though she has stumbled upon a council of kin in deep discussion. At the centre stands Alexander—Bran's father—his presence commanding, his authority unmistakable. The resemblance between father and son is striking, their shared lineage evident in their bearing and expression. Easy smiles convey an effortless sense of belonging, as though they have long been a part of the family's affairs.

Alex carries himself with quiet confidence, a steady demeanour, and tranquil strength laced with wry humour—traits his son has unmistakably inherited. Bran's smirks mirror his father's, though his edges are softer, his charm more playful.

Even Callan, typically ensconced in an armour of guarded reservation, has abandoned his customary frown. A rare flicker of approval crosses his face—so brief it could be missed. Yet, it is enough to suggest that even he cannot deny the quiet steadiness the man exudes. Alex's bond with James is one of deep camaraderie, and it appears forged through years of shared history.

Casey takes it upon himself to play host, waving Triona over with a look that practically sparkles with mischief. "Triona, come meet Alex."

There's no denying what the light in her smile means—it's the warmth that only comes from a sense of belonging. Blood relation or no, we're family to her, and that now extends to Bran and Alex, just as naturally.

"So wonderful to meet you, *officially*, Mr Mumford."

Alex playfully winces at the formality, pressing a hand to his chest as if she'd struck a blow. "Ach, *'Mr Mumford'*—you make me sound ancient," he laments, though his eyes gleam with amusement. "Just Alex, please, unless you fancy putting a few more grey hairs on my head."

He casts a knowing look toward her, a grin tugging at his lips. "Much like you and your brothers have done to your poor father, aye?" He chuckles, shaking his head. "I imagine the man's due for sainthood, putting up with the lot of you."

Triona snorts, tossing her hair back with exaggerated flair. "Aye, well, I've two clarty bampots for brothers to wrangle, so if sainthood's on offer, I'll take mine with a crown, a castle, and a lifetime supply of whisky. Seems only fair."

"From what I've heard," Alex says with a chuckle, "you've got this bunch of hooligans well in hand."

His glance sweeps over us as if he's known us his whole life, and a ripple of laughter stirs through the group.

"They *do* know better than to cross me—don't you, *lads*?" She glances at each of us with a raised brow, daring us to disagree.

Casey is the first to break, his laugh echoing as he nudges Callan. "Oh, Callan most assuredly. She kicked his arse the other day. Laid him out—flat on his back, legs in the air, lookin' like a tavern girl who'd just been tossed onto a mattress too quick." The laugher spreads quickly, causing a scowl to form on Callan's face. A hint of red creeps into his cheeks.

I glance over at him, raising an eyebrow with feigned seriousness. "You failed to mention this to me."

Casey's grin stretches wide, pure delight shining in his eyes as he steps forward, arms crossed as if he's been waiting a lifetime for this moment. He rocks back on his heels, savouring the scene, the way Callan's pride is about to take a hit.

"I *tried* to tell you the other day when you arrived," he says, his voice carrying that familiar, too-pleased lilt. "But now? Now seems an even *better* time to mention it. Bigger audience. Better impact."

Callan's glare deepens. "Aye, well, it wasna really worth mentionin'," he mutters, but his eyes betray a mix of pride and begrudging respect for Triona.

Triona's grin widens, satisfied, and she leans in, eyes twinkling with amusement. "Och, I'd say it's worth mentioning, Callan," she drawls. "How often does one get to witness the great Callan Sinclair—Highland warrior, legend of the glen—sprawled on his back, looking as if he had no idea what hit him?"

Casey's already mid-performance, lifting his hands dramatically. "Imagine it, aye? Triona—cool as a breeze—sidesteps him so fleetly he stumbles forward like a lost bairn, all arms and no balance. Then—before he even knows what's happenin'—*bam!*—she's got him flat on his arse, his own weight havin' worked against him, and all he can do is blink up at her like he's beggin' for mercy."

The entire group howls. Someone chokes. Even Eamon's grinning now, shaking his head.

Callan's jaw flexes tight, eyes narrowing, but even he can't fight the twitch at the corner of his mouth.

I can't help myself; a grin spreads across my face as I watch Triona, pride and admiration swelling in my chest. I give her a playful wink when she looks my way. "Now that's impressive, Triona. Layin' Callan out? That's a thing of legend. The stuff ballads are written about."

Casey gasps, clutching his chest. "That's what *I* said!"

Triona groans, dragging a hand down her face. "What is it with the lot of you suddenly wanting to go into bloody songwriting?"

"I'm just sayin'," Casey says, eyes gleaming, "it's a crime if we dinnae immortalise that moment in a tune. We'll call it *'The Lass Who Felled the Highland Ox.'*"

Eamon nods solemnly. "It's got a pleasant ring to it."

Callan mutters something under his breath that definitely includes the word *"eejits,"* but he's already fighting back a smirk.

The laughter is still echoing when Triona turns to me. Her eyes find mine, and for a moment, the world around us fades.

"You didn't even question the truth of what happened," she whispers, her voice low, meant only for me.

I furrow my brow, not out of doubt, but something closer to disbelief—that she doesn't already know.

"I dinnae need to," I murmur. "I'm not surprised to hear what ye're capable of."

Because I'm not. Not in the slightest.

I've seen it even when she can't—her fire, her fight, the way she walks through the world like it hasn't earned the right to break her. And it hasn't. It never will.

If she wanted to raise hell, I'd strike the match.

If she wanted to rule, I'd kneel without hesitation.

If she wanted to run, I'd be right behind her—every step.

The one truth I can't outrun, no matter how hard I try—is that she can't be mine. And gods, that thought stings like open flame, but it wouldn't stop me from being here.

She pauses for a moment, and in that fleeting instant, I catch the faint blush blooming on her cheeks—one that contrasts beautifully with her smooth, fair skin. I want to memorise that sight, to tuck it away for days when she holds herself so guardedly.

Bran coughs—pointed and far too dramatic to be anything but intentional.

I glance and find one eyebrow raised at me, catching the way I'm admiring her, and I roll my eyes, trying to play it off. But it's pointless. I look at her like she's hung the moon and the bloody stars.

Seeing her like this—confident, laughing, surrounded by people who admire her—it's impossible to look away.

She fits here, shines here.

And me? If she wants me beside her, even just in the quiet spaces, even just as a shadow in her corner—I'll go willingly. Always.

As her attention shifts to Alex, her focus entirely on him, I trace every line, every curve, appreciating how stunning she looks just... *existing*.

It's maddening, the way she can pull the air from my lungs without even trying, without even knowing. I'm supposed to be the calm, steady one, but here I am, heart hammering like a lovesick fool, praying the others don't notice how my focus has shifted entirely to her.

I shoot Bran a sharp look—the kind I usually reserve for when he's one word away from getting smacked upside the head. But as always, he's undeterred. His smirk only grows wider as his gaze flicks between Triona and me.

He casually saunters over to where I'm standing, all smug ease and far too much awareness for my liking. He leans in, voice pitched just low enough to keep the others from hearing—but loud enough to set my nerves alight.

"Careful, Finn," he murmurs, amusement thick in his tone. "You're looking at her like she's the last pint in the pub."

I don't flinch, but it takes effort. A *lot* of effort.

"Knock it off," I mutter through clenched teeth, keeping my eyes forward.

He hums, clearly enjoying himself. "Might want to ease up before you start drooling. Or worse—*confessing*."

I shoot him a glare sharp enough to slice bark off a tree, but he just grins wider, completely unbothered.

The bastard *lives* to test me.

"Can't say I blame you," he murmurs, his gaze drifting back to Triona. "She's absolutely stunning. But pick your jaw up before she notices, aye? Wouldn't want her thinking you're about to pounce on her right here in front of the family."

I clench my jaw, praying he'll shut up before anyone else catches on. But the quiet chuckle that slips from him says otherwise—he's enjoying this far too much.

"Finn? Bran?" Triona's voice cuts through the moment, sharp enough to jolt me.

"Sorry, Bran willnae stop buzzin' in my ear. What'd you say?"

She grins, full of fire. "Feel up for a game of hurling?"

I scoff, grateful for the shift in attention—but not enough to stop the corner of my mouth from lifting. "Triona, you might've bested yer brother, but—"

She holds up a hand, cutting me off. "I will *not* be joining in. First of all... I don't trust *that* one to keep his wandering hands to himself." She jabs a finger at Bran.

Immediately, Alex and Callan tense like hounds scenting blood.

Ah. Karma. A fickle, glorious mistress.

Bran's smirk falters. A flush creeps up his neck as he throws out a nervous scoff. "Whoa, whoa, whoa—don't get me wrong, you're beautiful, but you're not *'I'm ready to meet my maker today'* beautiful."

He glances over at me as if I might step in and save him. I just raise a brow and let him burn.

"...It was a jest," Triona adds smoothly, winking. Her tone is light, but the glint in her eyes says she knows exactly how deep inside his head she's crawled.

Bran lets out a nervous laugh. "All right, I see how you keep these menfolk in line now. Felt as if I was about to have my insides rearranged for a second."

"Oh, I dinnae ken. Could still happen." James's voice rumbles from the side as he strides up beside Bran, cutting through the laughter.

The group goes silent, all eyes on James, who's staring at Bran with that unflinching look of his, making Bran visibly tense. He's trying to keep his cool, but I can practically see the sweat rolling down his temple. Finally, James breaks the silence with a booming laugh, slapping Bran on the shoulder.

Bran lets out a dramatic sigh before turning to Triona with a look of mock solemnity. "By all the gods, I solemnly swear to be the picture of restraint in your presence. Pure, untainted innocence."

Triona steps forward and reaches up, patting him on the head like a tamed pup. *"Good boy."*

Bran chuckles, but her voice—soft, teasing—lingers in my mind. Those words echo as if they were whispered just for me, warm breath against my ear. It sends a shiver down my spine so sharply I have to swallow hard and drag my gaze away from her.

Focus.

I turn from the group and head toward the hurleys—the whole reason we'd gathered out here in the first place. I take my time, letting the rhythm of movement steady me while the banter continues behind me.

"Aye, it will be much more enjoyable overseeing this informal match as Brehon," Triona finishes.

Casey lets out a low whistle, shaking his head. "Aye, brilliant idea—give Triona unchecked power. What could possibly go wrong?"

"Go on and amuse yourself now, but mark my words—when calamity inevitably befalls you, and the lot of you are stumbling about in utter disarray, you'll be pleading for my guidance. And, being the benevolent soul that I am, I shall deign to save your sorry hides."

A chuckle ripples through the small group, a mixture of amusement and reluctant acknowledgment, as if they half-suspect she might actually be right.

I rejoin them just in time to catch Bran elbowing Casey. "She says that like she hasn't already planned the downfall herself."

Triona smirks, unbothered. "I prefer the term *'strategic foresight.'*"

I hand off the hurleys, slipping easily back into the circle as the surrounding energy sharpens. The sun is climbing; the field is wide, and the tension—friendly or otherwise—is about to explode in motion.

Her gaze flicks to mine, eyes glinting with mischief. "Now then," she calls, "how shall we divide the teams?"

"I believe," I say, clearing my throat as I step back into the circle, "since ye've claimed the lofty title of overseer, Little Doe, the selection falls to *us.*"

She gives me a mock-curtsy. "How generous of you."

"I think two captains should do the picking." She turns, eyes already twinkling with a playfulness I admire. "Da, Alex—would you do us all a favour and take up the noble mantle as the elders of the group?"

Both men let out low chuckles and move to stand opposite one another like it's some kind of ceremonial duel. There's a dramatic hush for all of three seconds before Bran loudly whispers, "Place your bets, everyone. It's the beard versus the biceps."

James strokes his chin. "The beard *and* the biceps, if ye please."

Alex cracks his knuckles and grins. "Aye, but mine are younger. Less likely to lock up halfway through."

The group laughs, the energy warm and buzzing with anticipation.

Triona raises her hand with mock authority. "Right then. Captains, prepare to choose your warriors."

"Wait," Casey says, "we only have seven here."

"Actually, Marcus is inside. He was stuck in a conversation with Saoirse, but should be out momentarily."

Callan huffs, his mood shifting instantly.

"Marcus?" I say, body tensing. *Why would he be here?*

"Aye," Casey says. "He's courtin' our dear sister."

"Casey, shut it!" Triona snaps, her tone sharp, but there's colour rising in her cheeks.

I feel Casey's words viscerally, as if someone just reached into my chest and took my heart into their hands.

It's just another reminder—another brutal, silent blow—of how completely and hopelessly gone I am for her.

Only yesterday, we talked about Marcus. She opened the door to that truth, and I sat there in silence. Didn't say what I wanted to say.

Didn't shout that he wouldn't be good enough.

That I could *see it*, even now, in the way her jaw tenses, in the way she won't quite meet anyone's eyes—that maybe, just maybe, she knows it too.

And gods, I should've said something. But I didn't.

Now I can barely contain the storm that's risen in me. The jealousy. The ache. The helpless fury. I wear a mask of indifference, but my breath is uneven, my hands clenched too tight.

Beside me, Bran shoots a look—quiet sympathy written across his face.

It's a kindness I don't want. Not right now. Not when the woman I care for more than anyone might end up with the wrong person, purely out of duty.

"Moving on," Triona says as I stand beside her with a bleeding heart, "since this is just a puck-around, you'll each need a goalkeeper, midfielder, centre-forward, and forward. Agreed?"

She glances at each of us, her eyes lingering on me just a second longer. I meet her gaze, and she gives me the warmest smile. I can only manage a quick one in return before she carries on.

"I think it's only fair for our captains to play goalkeeper, given their progressed age. Any issues with that?" Triona says.

The two older gentlemen scoff at her statement before grumbling in agreement.

"Da, please choose your midfielder."

"Well, that's easy—Finn, join me over here." I nod absentmindedly and move without making eye-contact with anyone.

"Alex, please select your *midfielder*."

"Callan, you look like a beast of a man."

"Thanks for the vote of confidence, Dad." Bran says.

We're down to the last two people when Marcus saunters out, his eyes set wholly on Triona.

She doesn't seem to notice—too busy brushing a loose strand of hair from her face—but I see it. I *feel* it. The way his eyes linger on her like a man assessing property. Intense. Possessive. Calculated. There's no admiration in it—no softness. Only appetite.

"And what is all of this?" Marcus asks, his tone carrying more curiosity than warmth.

"Hurling," Triona replies, a faint blush rising to her cheeks. "And I might've volunteered you to join."

I clench my fists, the sight of him staring her down making my stomach churn.

"And you, love?" His words drip with something that feels more like judgment than affection. "Are you playing as well?"

Triona gestures down at her attire with a coy grin. "Do I look ready to play a contact sport?"

He chuckles. "No, you look far too pretty and delicate to take these mongrels down. Best keep this sport to the men."

I see it—the slight clench of her fists, the tightening of her jaw. Triona doesn't back down easily, but she reins herself in, offering him a tight, toothless smile. By the gods' teeth, this man's got the gall of the devil.

"Ye've got the gall—" Callan starts, stealing the very words from my mind, but Triona slices through his outrage before it can catch fire.

"All right then," she snaps, pivoting sharply and redirecting her frustration. Her glare swings to Callan. "Da, pick your forward."

James doesn't miss a beat, his eyes flicking over Marcus as if he's inspecting a broken wheel. "Eamon," he says, the choice deliberate.

With that, the sides are set. James's team includes me as midfielder, Bran as centre-forward, and Eamon as forward. Across from us, Alex's team is equally matched: Callan as midfielder, Casey as centre-forward, and, of course, Marcus as forward.

As we gather into position, Bran sidles up to me, leaning in with a mischievous grin. "You know, the midfielder has the best chance to take the forward down. If you needed that reminder. I personally wouldn't mind assisting."

He shoots me a playful wink, his expression smug as ever.

I crack a smile. "Noted."

"All right, you lot!" Triona calls, playfulness glinting in her eyes. "Play fair, or I'll call a foul faster than you can blink."

James and Alex stand ready in front of their respective goals, each nodding in quiet acknowledgment. Callan and I move to midfield, the spark of competition clear between us. Bran and Casey, grinning as centre-forwards, look ready to stir up trouble, while Eamon and Marcus, stationed as forwards, tightened their grips on their hurleys.

"Let's go, lads!" James roars.

The game is on.

Bran is quick off the mark, sending the sliotar flying toward Alex's goal, but Alex deflects it cleanly back toward midfield. Callan intercepts, leaps, and flicks the sliotar toward Marcus, who surges forward with a smug glance in Triona's direction.

He swings.

James dives, blocking it with a grunt. The sliotar rebounds, and Callan is already moving, barreling past me with purpose. He passes to Casey, who breaks toward the goal with wild speed.

Sweat beads down my back, muscles tight with exertion—and frustration. Even as I chase the sliotar, I can *feel* Marcus nearby. He's cocky, all swagger and easy arrogance, and it grates on every nerve.

But I'm faster. And far more motivated.

Callan, usually stride for stride with me, lags—just a fraction. He glances my way, gives me a subtle nod.

"All yers," he mutters.

All mine.

Closing the gap, I lock onto Marcus, waiting for the right moment. He turns, oblivious, likely expecting an easy run. That's when I barrel into him with a solid shoulder check. The impact is more satisfying than I could've hoped. He stumbles, his balance shattering, and hits the ground hard, dirt spraying everywhere.

For a moment, I want to smirk—maybe even laugh—but I keep my face impassive, jogging forward as if I hadn't noticed.

Behind me, I can feel Callan's amusement radiating, and I know he's enjoying the spectacle.

"Really into the game, eh, Finn?" Callan calls, laughter laced in every word.

I shrug casually, keeping my voice steady. "Just playin' the game, Callan."

From the ground, Marcus shoots me a glare, resentment blazing in his eyes as he dusts himself off. Triona raises the whistle, her lips twitching as though she knows *exactly* what just happened.

She blows it, voice calm but firm. "No fouls here, but keep it clean, lads."

I refocus, a quiet satisfaction buzzing in my chest. Callan jogs up beside me, gives a small nod—his silent seal of approval.

Winning or losing doesn't matter. Not today.

Not after Callan handed me the perfect opportunity to knock the smugness off Marcus's face.

And gods, I'd do it again in a heartbeat.

When the game ends, our team celebrates a 5-2 victory. James is reveling, clapping Callan and Casey on the back as he grins from ear to ear. Their laughter echoes around me, but my focus is elsewhere entirely.

Just a few paces away, Marcus leans in close to Triona. Too close.

He's saying his goodbyes, one hand lingering on her arm. She smiles up at him, laughing lightly.

And something in my chest tightens. Not at her laughter—it's the way *he* looks at her. As if she already belongs to him.

Then he leans in, presses a kiss to her cheek, and lingers too long. His gaze drags over her face as he pulls back. She doesn't move, her attention fixed on him even as he walks away.

I can't look away.

She must feel my stare because she turns, her eyes meeting mine. The silence between us feels heavy, her expression softening for a moment before she looks away and rushes inside.

And I'm left standing here with her smile and *his* kiss seared into my mind.

Triona

I sit on the ground, knees tucked to my chest, gazing up at the sky as the last of twilight melts into night. The cool evening air wraps around me, and everything feels still. I don't hear Finn approach until he drops beside me, settling onto the grass with a quiet ease that's so completely... him. His presence is grounding, familiar, a comfort I didn't realise I needed.

He reclines, legs stretched out. "Thought you could use some company."

I glance over, meeting his eyes, and can't help but smile. "You always seem to know."

He shrugs. "Call it a skill."

Silence settles between us until a question rises, unbidden but insistent. "Finn," I begin cautiously, "where did you go for the past three years? Why were you gone so long?"

His expression shifts, the lightness dimming, replaced by a quiet gravity. "There are people in this world far less fortunate than us," he says finally, voice heavy with sorrow. "People who have no one, nowhere to turn. Bran and I spent two years fighting the illegal slave trade throughout the west coast. Travelling to places where hunger and despair were as common as breath. We saw terrible things—things that change you, that force you to grow in ways you never expected."

I hesitate before asking, "And that last year? The year you didn't spend fighting slavers?"

He takes a breath. I can tell he's hesitant to share, but he's resigned to do so anyway. "I was helpin' James and Alex with things they needed taken care of. Quiet matters, things that required a certain discretion. It wasna easy work, but it was important."

He pauses, his gaze distant, fixed on a memory only he can see. "I learned what it means to truly fight for something—for someone—who has nothin' left. It's humblin', and it's not something I can ever forget."

He shifts slightly, his focus returning to me. "When I received Callan's letter, though, I didn't hesitate. I came back immediately."

I watch him closely, seeing the shadow of those years etched into the lines of his face, the depth in his eyes. "You came back different," I say softly.

A wry smile tugs at the corner of his mouth. "Aye. But for the better, I think."

I reach out and lay my hand on his shoulder—firm, steady, a promise without flourish. "If you ever find the weight of it to be too much and need someone to listen—or simply to sit in silence beside you—I'll be here."

His eyes hold mine, calm and steady. "Aren't we doin' just that?"

I study him for a breath longer, then let my lips curve into a small smile. "I suppose you're right."

My hand lingers for a heartbeat longer before I ease back, a playful smile tugging at my lips. "You are welcomed company, Finnis MacGregor," I say lightly.

The comfortable quiet stretches until Finn speaks again, his tone thoughtful. "You huv'nae told me about boardin' school," he says, tilting his head as he looks at me. "How was it?"

I'm unsure how truthful to be. "It was... different, I suppose," I begin, casting a glance in his direction. "Not like home."

He waits for me to continue. His silence isn't empty; it's attentive, as though he's giving me all the space I need to find my words.

"It was strange being there at first," I admit, glancing out into the open space before us. "Everything felt so big, so polished. And I didn't know anyone. It was just me, in this place, that felt far away from everything familiar."

I look at him, and he frowns a little, his brow furrowing in that way it does when he's deeply invested in what someone is saying. "Were you lonely?"

I nod, a small, bittersweet smile tugging at my lips. "Far more than I expected. Eventually I found companionship, routine. I even grew to enjoy aspects of it. But I always felt like an interloper. As though belonging was a performance I couldn't quite master."

He listens, truly listens, then replies simply, "Their loss was our gain."

"Thanks, Finn," I murmur, barely registering I've said it aloud.

He tilts his head, a soft smile lifting the corners of his mouth. "For what?"

"For this," I reply, gesturing to the space between us—to the quiet and the way he seems to know exactly what to say, even when I don't quite know myself.

He gives me a small nod, his eyes holding mine a moment longer before he glances back up at the sky. "Anytime, Triona. I mean it."

A deep chuckle rumbles in his chest, his lips twitching with a familiar smirk and a glint of mischief in his eyes.

"What's so funny?" I ask, arching a brow, though I'm already smiling.

He turns his gaze back to me, still grinning. "You know, ye're a little too good at overseein'."

"Oh?" I tease. "Flawless officiating, I'm sure."

He reaches out, brushing a stray lock of hair from my face. His touch is brief, but it lingers—an echo across my skin. A thrill shoots down my spine, and though my cheeks warm, I hold his gaze, doing my best to mask the grin tugging at my lips.

"Flawlessly terrifying, more so."

"Terrifying?" I scoff. "You're just sore because I called you out. Maybe I ought to go easier on you next time—if you can't handle the *heat*."

He chuckles, shaking his head. "Nae, wouldnae dream of it." His gaze lingers on mine, and his grin fades, leaving an expression that's far too sincere, far too real.

"But ye're tougher than any of the men that played today. I'll give you that," he adds, his voice dropping to an indistinct murmur.

I huff a laugh, swatting at his shoulder. "I beat my brother once, and now you're all acting as if I'm some fearsome supernatural being."

A low, rasping chuckle escapes him as he catches my wrist before I can pull away. His thumb grazes the rapid beat at its centre. When his eyes lift to meet mine—shadowed, unreadable—my breath falters.

"I think it suits you," he says, his tone soft, almost reverent as his eyes move over me in a slow caress. "Keepin' us all in line."

I wet my lips, and Finn clocks the movement instantly.

"Don't think you'll sweet-talk your way out of this," I state, tugging at my wrist. But he doesn't let go.

Instead, he grins—slow and wicked.

When I go to swing at him with my free hand, he catches it midair, fast and firm.

"Ah, ah," he warns softly, and in one fluid motion, he shifts.

I don't have time to react before I'm on my back, his weight pinning me to the ground.

He's everywhere. His body flush against mine. My wrists pinned above my head. His breath hot on my face.

And just like that, the moment turns.

Neither of us moves.

Time folds in on itself. My pulse roars. My breath stutters. The space between us vanishes, and the silence sings with tension so taut it trembles.

One move could change everything.

And it feels like something I want. Something I shouldn't want.

I find my voice, but it's weaker than I want it to be. "Finnis MacGregor—"

His name is a tremble on my lips. And then he's there—closer. His breath ghosting over my mouth, his lips barely brushing mine.

"If you don't get off me, I swear—"

But the words dissolve because there's no true meaning behind them.

"Ye'll what?" he breathes, and the sound of it unravels something deep in me.

A noise escapes me—soft, fragile, shamefully wanting. A whimper. Barely there. But it betrays everything.

His grip tightens. His body stays locked against mine. His breath fans across my cheek, uneven now, as if he's holding himself back.

"You might handle Callan and Casey with ease..." his voice dips lower still, his breath dragging slow and hot across my skin, "but *they're... not... me.*"

A shiver rolls down my spine.

The silence between us stretches—thick, molten. It hums, strung tight like a bow pulled to breaking.

And he's right.

There is no one in this realm quite like him.

No one whose words soothe the storm inside me, yet set my skin aflame. No one else that can hold me down like this and make me feel as if I belong here. No one who makes me feel as safe and seen as he does.

His strength should unnerve me. Should make me fight back harder, make me remind him—remind myself—that I bow to no man.

Instead, it makes me want to yield.

I want him pressing me down, keeping me here, making me feel every bit of his dominance until I forget how to fight it.

And his breath alone is enough to make my thighs press together with aching, helpless need.

I shouldn't feel this way. Not about Finn. Not about the man who's always been my steady ground.

But I do. *Desperately.*

I buck my hips in a last-ditch effort to dislodge him—to escape the direction my mind is going—but it only pulls us closer.

He groans, low and strained. His grip tightens, his body tenses, and his expression darkens.

His eyes drink me in as if I'm something sacred and dangerous all at once. Like he's been starving for me—holding this craving back for far too long.

And for a single, suspended heartbeat, I can *feel* he's going to kiss me.

Then he blinks, and the spell breaks.

He releases me like I've burned him. He rolls off of me, and the loss is sudden and cold.

He sits beside me, his back half-turned, jaw clenched, breath uneven.

A beat passes. Then another.

He clears his throat. His voice is rough, scraping low. "Despite what society says," he murmurs, "and despite my jest... ye're a natural leader. You always have been."

I sit up slowly, heart still thundering against my ribs. Despite the lingering tension, his words settle warmly in my chest.

Finn turns to me, unflinching.

"Listen to me, Triona. *You* dinnae wait for permission. You *never* bend for comfort or tradition. Do what's right for you, and you hold it. And the ones who matter? They'll follow."

It feels like the kindest, fiercest thing anyone's ever said to me. Not flattery. Not comfort. But truth. A truth he's handed me like a weapon I forgot I already held.

"Thanks," I manage, unsure what I'm thanking him for—the reassurance, his steadiness, his presence when I need it most, or for stopping when I wasn't sure I wanted him to.

"When things matter—well, you've always been good at this," I say. "This sort of thing."

He offers me a reassuring smile. "It's always been easy with you."

The quiet confession lands between us, heavy with meaning.

Silence lingers, taut with words neither of us can say. It feels as if we're teetering on the edge of something fragile—one step forward could change everything.

But neither of us moves.

Eventually, the silence softens, unravelling into quiet conversation. We speak of the day, of old memories and new ones waiting to be made, and of nothing in particular. His quiet presence grounds me in a way so few others can. And when I pause, he doesn't rush to fill the silence. He simply waits—constant, unwavering, like the stars above.

13

NIGHT OF MANY CHANGES

Triona

Thursday, 1 May 1823

Day of the Ceilidh: Triona's Nineteenth Year

Peering out from the overlook above the courtyard, I watch as my father directs preparations for tonight's festivities. I've been ordered to rest for the day—a task easier said than done. I take pride in helping when I can.

Anticipation stirs as I imagine the lively music and rhythmic dancing that will fill the air at the first ceilidh my parents have hosted in years. The details of the evening have been kept a mystery, no small feat in a house brimming with chatterers.

Sensing my presence, and in true James Sinclair fashion, he blows me a kiss, and I pretend to catch it and place it upon my cheek. We both chuckle, and he waves, returning to the work at hand.

My gaze drifts out to the ocean. I watch as the waves crash, sending whitewater curls onward. Sunlight catches the foam, transforming it into an ethereal visage. The scene is both chaotic and graceful. There's something so hypnotic about watching this endless ebb and flow of the ocean; where great power meets grace in the most enchanting way possible.

Behind me, the sound of approaching footsteps breaks the spell. Turning, I see my mother standing in the doorway, cradling a thick bundle wrapped in linen and tied with twine. She looks tired, as though sleep has evaded her for days.

"I wanted to give ye something before the day gets away from us," she breathes, her tone uncharacteristically hesitant.

As I examine her face, I notice the lines of worry and the weariness that seem to consume her; something I noticed days ago. Today, a vulnerability clings to her movements, deeper than is even recognisable to many.

"I dinnae ken if ye'll like it," she says, hands toying with the edges of linen.

"Ma, you didn't have to get me—"

"Hush," she interrupts. "I'll admit I've been hard on ye, and maybe I huv'nae always been fair. I'm no' too proud to admit it now. I want there to be peace between us." She inhales slowly, as if her words cut into her.

"I fear for ye—for the world I'll leave ye in when I'm gone from it. But not for what ye're lackin', or things unknown to ye. I fear what the world will demand o' ye, and I ken it's unfair to place such a burden upon yer shoulders. I pushed things on ye thinkin' I kent what was best. I've pushed *people* on ye because I've thought the connection might be of great benefit..."

Tension unwinds thread by thread beneath the weight of her honesty.

"You speak as if you plan to leave tomorrow," I say, trying to keep my tone light.

She shakes her head resolutely, determined to keep herself composed. "Nae, love, jus the ramblin' thoughts of a mother who longs for a brighter dawn for her daughter. I wish for a world where the path ye'll traverse be less replete wi' uncertainty, where each step is easier to navigate than the century that came before."

She motions for me to follow her inside. I move without question, leaving the sounds of the courtyard, the feel of the May breeze against my skin, and the calming smell of the ocean behind.

We settle into a quiet corner, and I place my hand atop hers, a silent reassurance.

"Time has flown," she murmurs. "One day yer da and I are rocking ye to sleep, and now yer nineteenth year has come. Time isnae kind to us—we dinnae get nearly enough of it."

When she looks at me, her green and brown hued irises are clouded with emotion. "I've told ye stories since you were little. Do ye remember yer favourite?"

"As if I could ever forget an Ellen Sinclair retelling." I tease, earning a small smile.

"There were parts I left out. The parts about aimless sacrifice—decidin' without consulting others. I know we speak of Ériu's strength... but she acted in isolation, and it cost her."

"Well, it's a good thing that it's just a story."

"Even the tallest tales are rooted in truth. The meaning and morals stick around. We may grow in age, but thousands of years later, the fact remains that everyone needs someone to lean on."

She meets my eyes, voice shaking with emotion. "There will come a day when ye'll have to make choices that will feel impossible. Not out of fear or fate bidden obligation, but because of those impacted if ye refuse. I never thought I'd be an overbearing mess, not until I had ye, but I've myself had to make some of those choices. Motherhood turned me into a bit of a madwoman." We chuckle in unison at that.

She places her hand on my cheek, and a tear rolls from her eyes as she stares into mine. "I want ye to trust yerself. I've spent every second since the moment I first saw ye draw breath, believin' in ye. Truly. I regret not showin' ye more."

I squeeze her hand in mine. "Ma... you've shown me plenty."

She smiles, though it trembles at the corners.

Then she presses the bundle into my hands, and I unwrap it to reveal the Sinclair Clan tartan—made of deep blue, green, and yellow—beautifully woven and edged with fine embroidery.

"I made this for ye," she whispers. "To keep ye bundled in the cold, and when ye're away from home, to remind ye, no matter where ye are or who ye're with, that ye'll always have a home. Ye'll always be loved, and despite the distance between us, ye'll always have me."

My hands tremble as I run my fingers over the fabric. The weight of her love is palpable in every stitch.

"I dinnae ken what I did in this life to deserve ye as a daughter." She admits.

"I love you, Ma. Even when I push back out of pure stubbornness. I'm blessed to have such love."

She pulls me into an embrace. "Ye've done enough in every life to be loved a thousand times over."

She stands, pulling me with her. She carefully drapes the tonnag around my shoulders. Its comforting weight feels like a hug that will stay with me wherever I go.

"Happy day o' birth, mo nighean bheag."

The early night air outside the gallery doors carries a lingering chill, just enough to make my new tonnag feel welcome on my shoulders. Its significance deepens as I take in how my family and friends have transformed the courtyard for this night.

My father has worked tirelessly since dawn, and his efforts are undeniable. The once simple space now shines with life and warmth. Each table boasts a floral arrangement that brings an absentminded smile to my face.

"They bloomed early for ye this year, lass," my father says, appearing at my side. He traces the delicate heather blooms with his finger. "Must've kent we needed 'em to show face to celebrate my wee lass."

Heather—the first to bloom in early summer, symbolising good luck and protection. Flowers symbolise many things; beauty, renewal, patience, protection, life, death... All things that resonate with someone who values all things granted in this life.

In these particular arrangements, he used many wildflowers, but each of our favourites is present; bell heather, thistle, lavender, and of course... "Primrose," I whisper.

"Aye, wouldnae be a proper bouquet without it," he says with a proud grin.

"They're sunning, Da." My smile is one of the most radiant of warmths I can muster. He stares down at me, as if memorising every detail of my face—each line, freckle, and flicker of emotion.

"Nae, my thanks are to ye for bein' the best daughter a man could ask for."

"Your opinion is highly biased, Da. After all, I'm your only daughter—no great competition there."

His serious demeanour cracks, and a low chuckle churns from deep in his chest. "Ach, lass, always givin' me strife. Still, if there were a hundred more, ye'd still be the best."

I nudge him playfully. "Flattery will get you nowhere, auld man."

He raises an inquisitive eyebrow at me. "Auld man? We'll see who's got the energy to outlast this ceilidh, eh?"

"Usual stakes, then?" I say, shooting him a mischievous grin.

His eyes shine with amusement as he crosses his arms over his chest, his expression mock-serious. "All yer mornin' rolls," he declares. "Hope ye're prepared to go starvin'!"

I laugh and give him one last playful shove. "We'll see!"

"Better go see that yer ma needs no aid, lest I get put in the bad books. Keep out of trouble, lass." He kisses my head and strides off, leaving me to admire the courtyard.

Lanterns, wrought iron with elegant scrollwork from my grandparents, flank each floral display. The Sinclair Clan Tartan is draped over every table, chair, and archway, completing the scene. Nearby, guests are gathering around a table laden with fresh bread, bannocks, roasted meat, and Scotch broth. The aroma is heavenly.

I turn at a burst of laughter and spot Callan near the bonfire. Before I can join him, an imposing figure steps through the archway of the portcullis.

Marcus's broad shoulders and confident smirk command attention. He bears a sinful smirk as he leans against the heavy stone wall and crooks his finger at me, which might work to curry favour from more obsequious females, but is vexing to me given the well-known fact that I don't enjoy being summoned by men.

However, I decide it best to smile coyly and oblige to his request, and vow to mention it later. His usual gentlemanly and urbane manner still lingers underneath the man attempting to gain my attentions.

A chill sweeps through the air as I suddenly find myself rooted in place, held against an unforgiving frame as an arm holds me tightly at my waist. The very earth holds its breath at his arrival.

Finn's touch is protective, but as I stare up at him, I see he isn't looking at me, but at Marcus. There's a visible challenging possessiveness in his eyes.

"Finn," I whisper, drawing his attention.

He leans in to murmur, in a tone meant for my ears alone. "Ye've no reason to obey when summoned like a sheepdog." His eyes burn into mine, and the frustration in his tone only serves to further my aggravation.

"I don't believe he intended it that way, Finn." I turn away from his searing gaze momentarily to glance at Marcus, and see his focus remains on where Finn's hand clings to my waist.

Unspoken challenge hangs heavy in the air, thick with unyielding pride between the two of them. I can feel the tension between them—Finn's open defiance, and Marcus' silent demand.

"My statement stands," Finn says, words as finite as the tight set of his jaw.

"You'll have to let me be the judge of that." My tone is resolute, matching the hard-pressed steel of his words.

I feel his fingers flex slightly, as if realising his overstep. A flicker of something—regret, perhaps—passes through his golden eyes before they retreat from mine. Slowly, he lets me go, a grin dancing at the corners of his mouth.

It's then that Callan makes his presence known. "Triona, come sit by the fire." Eager to dissuade overlookers, I stride toward where Callan stands at Marcus's side.

When I near Callan, he crosses his arms, so I decide against further conversation. "I'll leave the three of you to sort out whatever is necessary to get through this night," I mutter, slipping past Callan and Marcus's towering forms.

The hum of guests' arrival sweeps through the air, creating a contagious excitement that permeates the grounds of our home.

Laughter and chatter ripple through the crowd like wildfire, hinting at an unforgettable evening yet to unfold. Any lingering unease fades as I catch sight of the joy lighting up every face.

Each new arrival brightens the festive ambiance, filling me with pride in my family. Fragments of conversation float my way—promises of first dances, whispered desires for stolen moments beneath the stars. It stirs something deep within me, a growing yearning.

I long for stolen glances, a secret rendezvous, hushed words carrying the weight of longing. The idea of stepping away from the crowd, of finding warmth in another's presence, calls to me despite my best efforts to ignore it.

These exchanges paint a vivid picture of the life my parents have built—a world full of allies, joy, and celebration. As I take it all in, a sense of belonging washes over me. Amid the discord of life, there are always moments of magic waiting to be embraced.

Finn

I watch Triona's retreating figure, filled with a mix of satisfaction and unease. I hadn't initially intended to interfere in her interactions with Marcus, the blethering clot. Not outwardly anyway.

I resigned myself to a life of misery, knowing the day she'd find a husband was inevitable. I long to see her happy, so I wear a mask of calm around her. But the shadow that looms around my heart twisted my actions in ways I know will bear no favour, but I couldn't stop myself from interfering. I was drawn to conflict at that moment.

She wore apprehension like a cloak, and I felt her hesitation as I watched her. Seeing Marcus attempt to summon Triona—*my* Triona, whose presence has become the anchor to my happiness, made me react in a way that felt as mindless as taking a breath. The powerful pull to guard her, despite knowing she's more than capable of handling herself, is a grievous burden I'd bear for a lifetime.

Callan's shifting form breaks my line of vision, and I move to join his side.

The two of them differ notably in size and strength. Marcus carries a much leaner tone, lacking the brute force present in Callan. He may stand in even height, but Callan is a mountain of muscle that speaks of both natural strength and hard-earned skill.

His physicality matches mine, so the glance Marcus casts between Callan and me establishes he understands how an altercation between the three of us would end for him; bloody, bruised, and broken.

"I dinnae trust ye," Callan says, voice low and full of the surety I never question. "Not with her. Yer intentions aren't pure". He may appear sullen more times than not, which can be mistaken for casting judgement when it isn't due, but something Callan is notably efficient at is reading people. None of us can explain it, but it's as if he possesses a sixth sense of sorts that is unique to him and him alone.

"Regardless of this mistrust, Triona's choices are her own to make," Marcus says.

"Aye, that they are," Callan confirms, "But they're also clouded from yer lies and schemin'. Catchin' ye with yer tongue down my sister's throat, practically ruttin' into her like a beast in heat, more than affirmed that to me."

The inferno of protectiveness blazing through me shows plainly on my face, and in the way my body tenses without thought.

My fists clench, knuckles popping audibly. Marcus notices, and he gives me a contemplative once over. I see as recognition takes hold of him just before he glances back to Callan.

"I'll not stop until ye're out of her life."

Marcus smirks as Callan's statement rolls off. He grins pompously as he reiterates his earlier point. "As I stated before, that decision is not one that you can make. You are mistaken if you think I would ever do anything to harm Triona, *mate,*" he asserts, clipping out the last word.

"For all your posturing, you failed to see that she was more than pleased to give herself over to me. The way she was writhing against me as I ran my tongue down her neck—"

That sentence alone seals his fate.

Callan's fist flies—swift and merciless—cutting him off mid-sentence. It connects with a sickening thud, the sound of bone meeting bone sharp in the stillness. Marcus staggers back into the stone wall, curses spilling from his lips as the crowd gasps in collective shock.

Silence falls over the courtyard, the tension thick enough to cut.

Triona bursts through the crowd, her eyes wide with shock. Her hands crash against Callan's chest, halting him before he can throw another punch.

"Callan!" she whisper shouts. "What have you done?" It's not really a question—more an accusatory reeling.

Callan opens his mouth to justify himself, anger etched in each harsh word he utters. "His actions make him more than deservin' of—"

"No!" Triona cuts him off sharply. "You've just turned this into a spectacle. On a night meant for celebration, you've made it about violence." Her voice trembles with disappointment. Callan's defiance falters, and his shoulders slump.

The weight of her glare shifts at me. The implied *why did you allow this to happen* lands like a blow. Guilt twists in my gut, not because I feel bad for Marcus, or regret stepping in, but for handling it publicly.

The crowd parts as James and Ellen approach. Ellen's expression is a mix of disapproval and concern, and reflects Triona's mortification. It appears she's unsure whether to console Marcus or chastise Callan.

James remains composed. His eyes scan over Marcus, still being doted on by Triona, then to his oldest son. A flicker of emotion dances in his eyes. It almost appears to be pride, though he says nothing outright.

"What happened here?" Ellen demands, voice sharp.

"Looks like a bit of a scuffle, aye?" James says evenly, his gaze settling on Callan.

That sets Ellen off. "A scuffle? James, Marcus is bleedin' from the side of his mouth! At the ceilidh of all places. The first time we have a large celebration in years, and my boys are out here throwin' fists before a drop of scotch has even been consumed!"

"He's a feckin' outsider," Callan mutters. "Ye think they *care*?"

Ellen's jaw tightens, but James intercedes as he places both of his hands over her shoulders. "Ye'll both be joinin' us in the study." Not posed as a question, Callan and I nod in unison.

He kisses the side of Ellen's face and whispers, "I'll handle it. Go inside, and I'll meet ye there." Ellen leaves without uttering another word.

James' expression seems to soften as he meets Triona's eyes. "Go get him cleaned up inside," he orders, gesturing to Marcus' bloodied lip. She shoots him a tentative look as she reaches up gently to cup his chin between her forefinger and thumb.

"Do not bother, Triona. I am more than capable of handling this," he says, gesturing to his bloodied lip. "Go take up place beside your friends."

"Are you certain?" Triona asks. Marcus smiles down at her and draws his hand outward to encircle her wrist.

"Of course, love. I want you to enjoy your night." And like something out of a bad dream, I watch as he brings her palm to his lips and places a saccharine kiss in the centre. He uses his other hand to draw her body in closer against his.

James clears his throat, clearly as taken aback as the rest of us. Callan stands beside me, eyes focused anywhere but at the bastard with his hands on his sister. The one who just publicly laid claim to her.

Triona steps out of his embrace, seeming uncertain and torn.

James lingers, assessing what to do next. His gaze shifts back to Callan, and he gives a dismissive nod, then turns to usher Triona back out into the beginnings of the party.

"We need to talk," Callan mutters under his breath.

No shite.

What have you been keeping from me, Callan?

Callan paces in James's study, his boots heavy against the floorboards. His jaw is set, his voice low but vibrating with tension. "Before she left for Edinburgh, I saw them. Out in the open—as if they didnae care who might walk by. His hands were all over her, Finn, and his mouth..." He stops short, exhaling sharply. "Anyone could've seen it. Anyone."

Frustration with everything simmers in my chest. "And you said nothin'? Ellen's practically planned their nuptials, Callan. You sat on yer hands while this went on?"

He stops pacing and turns to glare at me, his eyes dark with something more than anger—guilt, maybe. "What was I supposed to do? Be the cause of 'em forcin' her hand on the spot? Have her married to that feckless scunner just to save face? Ye ken me better than that." His voice drops, sharp with emotion.

"When I looked at him, Finn... I swear his eyes were like the Earl of Hell himself. I kent from the first moment he walked up to her in town that he was trouble."

"If you thought all that, why hold yer tongue?"

Callan shakes his head, running a hand through his hair. "Because I thought I had time. Time to stop this before it went too far. Thought to take care of it without her bein' involved. I didnae want to be the one to pile another unknown burden on her."

That stops me cold. "What unknown burdens do you mean?"

Callan's lips press into a thin line, his shoulders tense. He doesn't answer, his gaze darting toward the door as if willing someone—or something—to interrupt. The silence stretches, thick and charged, until it's broken by the soft creak of the study door.

James and Ellen step inside, their faces tight with urgency. Ellen clutches her shawl as if it's the only thing anchoring her. James's expression is harder, his usual calm replaced by a fierce intensity.

"Da—" Callan starts, irritation clear in his tone, but James cuts him off with an incisive look.

"Enough," James says, his voice like a crack of thunder. "We've a lot to discuss, and little time to do so," he asserts. "So for now, we need ye both to keep yer eyes open and yer mouths shut. No more bloody feckin' fights. No room for mistakes. We'll explain more... but no' tonight."

"What are ye on about, Da?" Callan asks.

James doesn't answer immediately. Instead, he turns an unusually icy glare at Callan. When he finally speaks, his words come in a long forgotten language: *"Tagann aimsir ar cách, toilteanach nó ainneonach."*

Callan's shoulders slump, and his defiance drains away. For a moment, he looks more like a lad caught misbehaving than the strong, stubborn man I know him to be. His hands fall to his sides, limp and defeated.

I make a note to question the meaning of those words later.

James steps forward, his towering frame casting long shadows in the dim light of the study. "Someone tried to poison the whiskey Callan brought to Edinburgh on this last trip. They added the feints back into the barrels."

I stiffen, my gut twisting as pieces fall into place. "How d'ye know it was tampered with?" My voice is calm, but the tension ripples beneath it.

Callan glances at me, his jaw set. "I tested it. I always have the right mind to test before I sell. The feints were added back—someone knew exactly what they were doin'. I tested it for impurities myself," he says again, more assured this time, as if repeating it might drive the truth in deeper. "It wasna sloppy work on my part; it was deliberate."

"How come you didnae tell me sooner?" I ask, my voice steady but probing.

James fixes me with a look that brooks no argument. "Because we needed time to be sure of what we're dealin' with. We're tellin' ye now because yer crony here has a temper that could blow everything if he loses his head."

Callan exhales sharply, bristling but holding his tongue.

Ellen steps forward, her voice trembling but firm. "Ye've got to understand, Finn. There's more to this than ye know—than any of us fully ken. But for now, ye must promise us something."

"What?" I ask, though I can already sense the answer.

"Be cautious," James says, his voice like iron. "Watch yerself, watch the property, and by all the gods, keep a watchful eye on my ladies. Don't go stirrin' trouble, no matter what ye see or hear. We'll tell ye the full truth soon enough, but for now..." His gaze hardens. "Jus do as we ask."

A chill runs down my spine, though I don't let it show. Instead, I nod, my voice calm and deliberate. "Aye. Ye've got my word."

The room falls into a heavy silence. Callan stands rigid, the tension rolling off him in waves, but he doesn't speak. James's jaw tightens, and Ellen's hands twist the edge of her shawl until her knuckles whiten.

"We've made enemies," I breathe, my voice steady as I meet James's gaze. "That's what this is? Someone who wants to hurt us. Or worse."

James doesn't confirm it outright, but the flicker in his eyes is enough. "Aye," he says after a long pause. "But we'll deal with it. Together. As a family. No rash actions, no mistakes. Understood?"

Callan mutters something under his breath, but he nods. I nod as well, the unease in my chest hardening into resolve. I'll be damned if I let my guard down.

For now, I'll play the part. I'll wait. But my mind is already working, piecing together what little I've been told. And Triona...

She needs protection, so I'll be the one to give it.

"What did James say in there?" My voice cuts through the stillness.

The door to the courtyard groans in protest as we step beyond the threshold. The night air offers no respite from the tempest churning within. Callan follows in my wake, his presence a tangible force, his boots grinding against the earth as he halts beside me.

He exhales, the sound deliberate, measured. "He said, '*Time comes for everyone, willing or not.*'" His voice bears no inflection, but his gaze betrays him—a flicker of unease flashing through his eyes, his fingers twitching ever so slightly at his side before curling into a loose fist. His throat bobs as he swallows, as though forcing something back, but he remains otherwise still, an unreadable mask barely concealing what lingers beneath.

I huff, shaking my head. "How appropriately forebodin'."

Callan merely shrugs, his arms folding across his broad chest. "It's something I've heard since I was a lad, when my gran was still alive. She never wavered in the belief that, regardless of our readiness or resistance, change is inevitable. The only way forward is to prepare and brace yerself. She bore no fear for the end, whether from wisdom hard-earned, faith unshaken, or sheer defiance in the face of the inevitable."

His voice turns distant, as though recalling a time long buried beneath the weight of years. "I didnae think much of it then—just old words, old wisdom, wisdom that seemed more akin to folly than foresight. Toward the end of her life, I thought my gran a bit batty, murmurin' of winds that carried whispers, of unseen forces at play. But now..." He trails off, exhaling sharply. "Now they toll like bells in the dark—no mere sayin', but a true warnin'."

I draw in a slow breath, steadying myself before speaking. "You know you have to apologise, right?" My words are firm but not unkind, an anchor to pull him from the thoughts threatening to drag him under.

Callan's near cracking a tooth as frustration courses through him. He hates apologising. Almost as much as he hates being wrong. I can see it written all over him, the stubborn set of his shoulders, the way his lips press into a thin line. For a moment, he looks as if he wants to argue, to push back against the truth. Instead, he exhales sharply through his nose. "Aye, I ken," he grumbles, voice tight with reluctance. "And I hate that ye're right."

Without another word, he pivots on his heel, striding away, tension coiled within him like a beast held at bay. The air remains thick with all that remains unsaid, lingering even as his footfalls fade.

I hardly have time to collect my thoughts when I hear footsteps approaching. The sound of purposeful strides disrupts my quiet, and Bran emerges, his usual roguish grin playing at his lips.

"Just the man I was looking for—and, might I add, the most devastatingly handsome man to grace this fine gathering." Bran smirks, waggling his brows. "By the gods, Finn, you could make a nobleman look akin to a stable hand, and I hate you for it."

I let out a long, slow breath, dragging a hand down my face. "It's a true wonder how I've put up wi' you for as long as I have."

His laughter rings out, entirely unbothered, as he extends a hand, offering a flask. "That's the last time I try to sweeten you up. I'll just have to pour all of this honeyed talk into Triona's ear instead. Can't let it go to waste, after all."

"We both know that ye've made a muck of yerself more than once in her presence. Ye're sayin' this to get a rise out of me, and it isnae gonna happen."

His smirk widens, a knowing glint in his eyes. "Aye, but one of these days, you're going to trip over your own stubborn pride and say what you mean. And I'll be there when it happens—probably with a drink in hand to celebrate the occasion."

Bran watches me for a beat longer, his smirk lingering but his gaze sharper, more perceptive than ever. He exhales, shaking his head before shifting topics. "Word is there was a bit of a stir earlier." His tone wavers between mirth and concern, though amusement lingers at the edges of his lips. "Are you well?"

I snort, shaking my head. "Remember that fair-haired, soft-handed perfumed fop I laid flat the other day?"

The corner of his mouth lifts in amusement as he shakes his head knowingly. "Aye, I remember the—what did Callan call him? A *lily-livered dandy*?" He chuckles, the words rolling off his tongue with exaggerated mockery before he tilts his head at me, eyes gleaming with curiosity. "Why? What happened?"

"Callan planted a fist into his face earlier."

Bran lets out a low chuckle, the sound echoing into the quiet night. I attempt a smile, but it falters, never reaching my eyes. The levity is fleeting. Bran notes this, his laughter dimming as he studies me more closely, unearthing what I strive to conceal.

"Are you going to tell me if you're all right?" Bran challenges.

I stand unmoving, the burden of the evening pressing against me. I exhale, long and measured. For a moment, I consider my usual deflection—a jest, a dismissive shrug. But tonight, it rings hollow. My jaw tightens, and I release another breath through my nose.

"No," I admit, the confession rough-edged, unvarnished. "But I must be, aye?"

Bran's brow furrows, the humour draining entirely from the moment. He steps closer, resting a hand on my shoulder. "There's no dishonour in acknowledging when things are amiss, Mac."

"Perhaps not. But at present, I lack the luxury of breakin'." I shake my head, voice quieter now. "I cannae falter, Bran. For her sake."

Bran doesn't push, but the weight of my words hang between us, unspoken truths too heavy to unload in the fleeting moment.

Triona

I stand with my parents, the air heavy with anticipation. Around us, people form a loose circle near the unlit bonfire, their murmurs hushed in the growing darkness. The transition from day's warmth to night's mystery feels almost sacred.

A presence shifts at my side. I glance to find Callan lingering nearby, his usually unshakable confidence subdued.

"Triona," he murmurs, his voice low enough that no one else can hear. He rubs the back of his neck awkwardly, his fingers moving in a slow, nervous rhythm as if searching for the right words. "About earlier... I was out of line. Shouldna let things get to that point. I'm sorry."

His words catch me off guard. I hesitate before giving him a small nod. "As you should be."

"He said things about ye that made my blood boil."

"If that's so, I'll let *him* tell me. I can handle myself, Callan."

"Triona—"

"Callan... listen to me. I *know* you think you mean well, but that anger inside you isn't doing anyone any favours." He seems to mull that over and nods.

"I can handle *myself*, Callan."

He meets my eyes. "I think ye showed me a bit of that the other day when ye knocked me on my arse."

I laugh, the tension easing between us. A reluctant smirk tugs at his lips. The moment lingers, a rare instance of unspoken understanding between us.

The sound of footsteps echo through the quiet, measured and deliberate. I know who it is before I turn.

Finn steps closer, his expression resolute, though hesitation shadows his eyes.

"I—" he begins, but I stop him with a gentle shake of my head.

"You don't have to, Finn." My voice is sweet when I speak. "I know you were just doing what you thought was best. You don't owe me an apology."

Finn's shoulders relax, though his eyes linger on mine. With a wry tilt of his head, he asks, "How'd you know what I was about to say?"

I press a finger to the centre of his chest, a small smile playing on my lips. "Because I know *you*... and what thrives in here."

His chest rises with a slow, measured breath. Something raw and unguarded passes through his eyes before he tamps it down. His jaw feathers, then softens, as if caught between the instinct to retreat and an undeniable pull that keeps him rooted.

The moment between Finn and me shatters as a stillness falls over the gathering.

My father steps forward, his broad shoulders silhouetted against the evening sky. His posture exudes both pride and solemnity, as though the weight of tradition rests squarely on him. His deep voice commands attention as he gestures for my mother to join him. She steps to his side, and he places a tender kiss on her temple before addressing the crowd.

"Lá Bealtaine," he begins, "a day when the veil between worlds thins, and the power of renewal reaches its peak. It's a time to honour life, love, and the blessin' of the earth." He pauses, his eyes settling on me with a smile full of joy. "And tonight, we celebrate not just the season's turnin', but the birth of a soul destined for greatness."

I roll my eyes with a smirk, defusing the gravity of his words. "You act as if I possess magic powers." The crowd chuckles along with my father.

My mother's gentle voice follows. "Since the day ye were born, Triona, ye've been a light in this family. Not as the sun, but alike the brightest moon—steady, constant, casting its glow even in the darkest nights. And that, my dear, is the kind o' light that never blinds, never burns, but guides. Ye've brought strength and joy to all of us. Great things await ye, and what an honour it has been to watch ye come into yer own."

I lower my gaze, my chest tightening with an unexpected swell of emotion. The sincerity in their voices, the weight of their belief in me, near undoes my composure. Before tears betray me, my father gestures toward the unlit bonfire. "And now, lass, it's ye turn to light the flame. Set Bealtaine in motion."

Nerves get the better of me as I step forward, the small ceremonial torch in hand. Its faintly glowing tip feels heavier than it should. Tonight, this flame represents more than tradition; it marks a moment of transformation. My breath mingles with the crisp air as I approach the kindling. Everything around me falls silent—the murmurs, the crackling of smaller fires—as though the world holds its breath.

I glance up, seeking reassurance, if only for a moment, and find Finn. I wholly welcome his presence. His smile meets mine with a warmth that steadies me. With newfound confidence, I kneel, lowering the torch. As the flame touches wood, it ignites with an almost supernatural vigour. Its light chases away the evening's chill as the crowd erupts in cheers.

The celebration quiets once more as my father nears me. The flickering flames paint his face with a warm glow as he raises his cup to speak. "Now, I ken ye lot are a buncha proud Scots!"

The crowd responds with exuberant cheers and raised mugs, causing him to whoop heartily.

"Aye, aye, we're proud, but dinnae forget our family has strong ties to Ireland too—thanks to my dear Ma, gods rest her soul. Ye all ken my da renamed their home, *our* home, wi' her in mind, and I have to agree with the beauty my da always said it housed because... well, my lovely daughter here," he says, pulling me into a hug, grinning ear to ear. "She's the most beautiful thing I've ever laid eyes on."

My mother chuckles. "I'd have to agree. She is a vision."

My father pulls my mother to his other side, pinning both of his ladies against him. "I'm a lucky man."

From the back, Casey's voice breaks the sentiment. "Da, just admit who yer favourite is already!" Laughter ripples through the crowd.

Without missing a beat, my father strides toward Casey with a mischievous gleam. Before my brother can react, my father pulls him into a dramatic, exaggerated embrace, planting a sloppy kiss on his cheek. "Ye want to ken who my favourite is, lad?" Casey squirms but can't break free, much to everyone's amusement.

"It was said in jest, Da!" Casey splutters.

"We all know it's Saighdear, anyway," Callan adds dryly.

Casey, red-faced, sputters, "Yer bloody horse?"

"Watch yer mouth, Casey," My mother chides.

My father raises a hand dismissively. "Aye, the horse disnae talk back like the rest of ye. Now, focus. This is important!"

The laughter ebbs, and the firelight bathes the gathering in a warm glow. Da's voice softens. "In all earnestness, this night is special. It's about growth, renewal, and new beginnings. And our Triona—" he gestures to me, his voice thick with emotion—"she will bring more light to this world than any fire we could ever kindle."

Finn takes that moment to step forward as he raises his cup, capturing everyone's attention. I see vulnerability in his eyes—a depth of feeling that tugs at something within me.

A small, heartfelt smile creeps onto his face, one that always has a way of making my heart falter. "To Triona, the heart of this family and the light of our lives."

Our eyes catch and linger. "May you find the courage to chase each dream, and the strength to weather each storm, may joy and laughter let yer spirit beam, and enduring love keep you warm."

As the crowd recites his sentiment, his eyes stay on mine, steady and unwavering. Such simple words have my heart swelling with emotion. Spoken aloud to the crowd, but his words—they were for me.

I raise my glass, and when I smile, it's all for him, a silent thanks for always seeing me in a way no one else does.

"Here's tae us—wha's like us?" Finn shouts, raising his glass high.

"Gey few, and they're aw deid!" the crowd answers in roaring unison.

"Slàinte mhòr!" he calls out over the laughter, and the crowd echoes him once more, glasses clinking all around.

His eyes never leave mine.

The surrounding noise fades in that shared moment, the cheers of the crowd becoming a distant hum as the weight of what he said—what he meant—takes root in my heart.

My life is infinitely better for having him in it.

As Finn steps back, his presence lingers like a calming force.

The musicians strike up a lively tune, and the air fills with the high skirl of pipes and the quick bow of fiddles. Around me, the ceilidh begins. Saoirse tugs at Callan's arm, teasing him into dancing. Casey and Eamon exchange jests, their laughter infectious. Nearby, Dealla sneaks glances at Bran, whose nonchalant demeanour is betrayed by the way his gaze lingers on her when she isn't looking.

In the centre of it all, my parents stand close, their love a steady anchor. They share a look, one of those quiet, intimate exchanges that speak of decades spent together. Through every trial and triumph, their love as strong as ever. The sight of them, so deeply content in each other's presence, makes my heart swell with adoration.

The night feels like something out of a dream—alive with laughter, music, and the glow of the fire that flickers against the darkening sky. But more than anything, it's the people, my people, that make this moment perfect.

My family. My heart. My home.

Casey claps a hand on my shoulder, pulling me from my reverie. His grin stretches ear to ear. "Come now, birthday lass, no hidin' in the shadows tonight. Let's show 'em how it's done."

Before we can step forward, a tall figure blocks our path, arms outstretched as if commanding the attention of everyone gathered.

"That's a grand idea. Come now!" My father's voice booms, louder than necessary, echoing over the laughter and music.

"I believe the guest of honour must sing the laird of this land one song."

"What song?" I ask, feigning ignorance, though I know exactly where this is heading.

"Tartan Troubles, my wee lass," he announces, a playful glint in his eyes.

"Da, please don't make me," I protest half-heartedly.

"Ach now, who else but me brought ye into this world?" He puffs out his chest, mock pride writ large across his face, like a cockerel strutting through the yard.

"I believe Ma did most of the work. Wouldn't you agree?" I shoot back, trying to suppress a grin.

My mother, standing behind him, lets out a gentle laugh. She gives me a conspiratorial wink, but still sides with my father. "Casey, fetch the bodhran for us, aye?"

"Me? Why do I have to do it?" Casey protests, but the laughter in his tone is unmistakable.

"Ach, jus do what yer mother says!" My father replies, hands on his hips, a playful challenge in his eyes.

"Ye're only backin' her because—oh, nevermind." With a loud huff, he complies, drawing chuckles from those nearest to us.

Callan snickers from his position, clearly enjoying the spectacle.

"Ye as well, Callan!" My father husks, pointing at him with mock authority.

"Not really a two-person task..." he trails off when he catches Ma's pointed look. Callan sighs dramatically, heading off together with Casey.

"You're going to make me the laughingstock of the evening, Da."

He roars, his eyes twinkling. "Nae such thing, lass! Ye're the star of the show tonight, and it's time ye show them what ye're made of."

Bran cuts in then, his grin devilish. "I would love to perform alongside you, if that's all right, Triona."

"You know it?" I ask, surprised.

Bran's grin widens. "My father owns the pub in the village, and he owned one back home. Doesn't take but a handful of times hearing it to pick it up."

Bran's grin widens further, all effortless charm and wicked intent. His eyes spark with mischief, the kind that makes trouble look inviting.

By the gods, he's unfairly handsome. Not that I'd ever admit it to him—his ego's already unbearable—but I can see why people are drawn to him. The charm, the wit, the devil-may-care grin—it's a dangerous combination.

"Fine," I sigh dramatically, a teasing smile on my lips. "But none of that funny business you're always on about."

Bran raises his pinkie finger to me, eyes gleaming. "I swear, only serious business tonight."

I stare blankly at his hand

He wiggles his finger expectantly. "Go on."

I arch a brow. "Bran, what am I to do with that?"

With a grin, he grabs my pinky with his. "It's called a pinky promise. You wrap your pinky around mine, then you lean and seal it with a kiss."

I chuckle. "Is this an American thing?"

"Are you really going to leave me hanging?"

I laugh, but oblige to his playful demands.

"There you go! I knew you were my favourite for a reason!"

There's a twinkle in Bran's eye when he meets my gaze again. "In honesty, I can sense your affections are otherwise engaged elsewhere. So, I promise to be on my *best* behaviour with you." He winks.

I blink, momentarily thrown. I can't form the right words to respond.

Casey stomps up, fiddle in hand, his excitement bubbling over. Callan follows behind, holding our grandfather's bodhran.

"Are you joinin' in?" Casey asks, brows raised with a mix of curiosity and concern. "You sound worse than a wounded hound, if I recall correctly."

Callan's eyes narrow, and he responds curtly, "Even if I *could* sing, ye should ken by now that I'm not a trained dog like my two younger siblings."

Casey scoffs, crossing his arms. "Aye, because ye're far too dignified for a bit of fun, aren't ye, Cal?" He smirks, eyes glinting with mischief. "These folks would throw silver to see ye try a reel without lookin' like a bear that just woke up from hibernation—angry, clumsy, and in desperate need of a bath."

Callan levels him with a pointed look, unimpressed. "Eejit."

Casey grins, completely unfazed, before looking down at me with a spark of challenge in his eyes. "All right, Triona, let's give 'em a performance they'll never forget!"

Bran hums thoughtfully beside me, and I glance toward Casey. "Bran is joining in alongside us," I say, watching as flared excitement flashes in Casey's eyes before he coolly masks it.

He tilts his head, feigning nonchalance. "Aye? And can he play anything worth hearin'?"

Bran smirks, stepping forward with an easy swagger. Without a word, he suavely plucks the fiddle from Casey's hands, giving it a quick, effortless tune before tossing a wink my way. "Why don't we find out?"

My father claps his hands together. "All right, ye lot! In close now. Ye're in for a treat!"

As the first notes rise into the air, a spark of energy surges through me, lifting my heart with the rhythm. The world fades, leaving only the music and the fire it stirs within me.

Oh, Lachlan MacDougal, a bonnie Scots lad,

Strolled into the tavern, finest kilt he was clad.

He danced on the tables, not givin' a care,

When he woke the next morning, his kilt was not there!

"Oh, where's my kilt? Oh, where could it be?

I had it last night after pint number three!

I searched high and low, but to my dismay,

My kilt up and vanished at the break o' day!"

Lach wandered the village, his arse in the breeze,

Hands hidin' his pride as he shook at the knees.

He shouted, "My kilt! It's gone far an' wide,

If ye see it flappin', please tell it to bide!"

"Oh, where's my kilt? Oh, where could it be?

I had it last night after pint number three!

I searched high and low, but to my dismay,

My kilt up and vanished at the break o' day!"

He checked wi' the barkeep as he came into sight,
"Was I wearin' my kilt when I left ye last night?"
He laughed till he cried, and he started to say,
"As ye slept in the bushes, the wind took it away!"

"Oh, where's my kilt? Oh, where could it be?
I had it last night after pint number three!
I searched high and low, but to my dismay,
My kilt up and vanished at the break o' day!"

He ran to the pub where the ceilidh was loud,
But all that he found was a mocking wee crowd,
"If ye want yer kilt back, there's no' need to cry,
Ye'll just need to jump up and reach for the sky!"

"Oh, where's my kilt? Oh, where could it be?
I had it last night after pint number three!
I searched high and low, but to my dismay,
My kilt up and vanished at the break o' day!"

They hung it up high on the tavern's tall beam,
And Lach had to jump, wi' a wobble and scream.
But each time he'd leap wi' a huff and a shout,
His kilt fluttered higher and the crowd would cheer out!

"Oh, where's my kilt? Oh, where could it be?
I had it last night after pint number three!
I searched high and low, but to my dismay,
My kilt up and vanished at the break o' day!"

At last, dear Lach, with a desperate heave

Caught hold of his kilt, then he started to leave.
He threw it back on with a grunt and a spin,
And vowed he'd no' drink so much ever again!

"Oh, where's my kilt? Oh, where could it be?
I had it last night after pint number three!
I searched high and low, but to my dismay,
My kilt up and vanished at the break o' day!"

Now Lach wears his kilt wi' a belt o' strong leather,
And ties it on tight in all kinds o' weather.
So shed not a tear for the skin he was showin',
For the lasses come flocking, bright smiles a glowin'.

"Oh, there's my kilt, right where it should be
I lost it last night after pint number three!
I searched high and low and found it at last,
And thanks to misfortune, I'm no longer chaste!"

As the last verse rings out, I can't help but laugh as the crowd's cheers ring in my ears. Performing with Casey and Bran feels as if I'm reclaiming a piece of my childhood—a moment of unbridled joy. This is a memory I'll hold on to forever.

Others take the position around the fire to play their own music once more, allowing us a moment of reprieve.

Couples spin and twirl, creating a whirlwind of flashing kilts and skirts, stomping boots, and the rhythmic claps of dancers mingling with the lively tunes that fill the space.

The firelight flickers off the stone walls, casting golden hues on faces flushed from joy and whiskey.

Casey gives Bran a playful shove, both of them laughing, getting along as if they've known one another for years. It warms my heart to see how easily Bran has fit in.

I am still soaking in all the sights and sounds when I feel a presence approach me from the side. He steps into my line of sight, exuding a confidence that borders on intoxicating.

"Triona," he begins, his voice a velvety timbre that wraps around my name like a caress. The way it's said sends a flutter through me. "I wanted to talk to you about what happened earlier."

His gaze holds mine with a smouldering intensity that sends a flush creeping up my neck. I nod for him to continue.

He sighs, a slow, deliberate sound, his fingers brushing the back of his neck in a gesture so casual yet irresistibly magnetic. When his eyes meet mine again, they smoulder with a heat that feels both dangerous and enthralling. "I said things to your brother... out of frustration. I did it knowing it would upset him."

I arch a brow, intrigued despite myself. "Is that so?"

He nods, a roguish glint sparking in his eyes. "Quite so. Show me a man who would not bristle at the intrusion upon a moment shared with the woman who commands his heart."

I feel my breath catch at his words, the weight of them settling over me like a warm cloak. I can't deny the pull between us—inescapable and undeniable—and moments like this threaten to undo my resolve.

He takes a step closer, his voice dropping to a husky murmur. "Triona, you have long held my heart—since the moment I first laid eyes on you. Everything I do is for you, because you have become the centre of my world, the only thing that truly matters."

I cross my arms over my chest, hoping to convey with body language that I'm in no mood for his coyness. "Tell me what you said."

"They did not tell you?"

"I told them I'd hear it from your lips, or not at all. I wanted you to tell me."

"Your brother told Finn about that kiss in the woods, and I just got so protective of you... over that special moment. Then he—"

I hold up my hand, hearing enough. "I can't believe you're both still going on about that."

His words are careful, as if he is weighing each one before speaking. "I meant no disrespect. I only intended to rile him up, and things got out of hand, and that is my fault. But believe me, Triona, I should have handled things better, especially for your benefit. I truly care about you."

I'm unsure what to say, still feeling uneasy about it. His words, so effortlessly polished, leave me torn. They're like honey—sweet and golden—but laced with something sharper, something that both captivates and unsettles me. There's a charm to him—one I've never denied—but tonight, something feels rehearsed. "I appreciate your words, but—"

"Wait," he interrupts, flashing that devastating smile that seems capable of disarming even the fiercest resolve. "Allow me to prove my devotion, not with empty words, but through actions that reflect just how profoundly you have touched my life."

He steps into me, his hand gentle as it cups my cheek, his thumb brushing against my skin with such tenderness.

"May I have this dance?"

I hesitate for just a moment, feeling a mix of emotions swirling inside me. But the inviting spark in his eyes, the way he looks at me, makes my steadfastness waiver. With a deep breath, I nod, allowing him to pull me toward the circle of dancers.

The music picks up, lively and full of cheer, and as we move together, I try to focus on the rhythm, the hum of the strings, and the energy of the surrounding crowd.

Marcus's hand is warm and steady on my waist, his touch igniting a thrilling current that seems to spark through every fibre of my being as he guides me effortlessly into the dance.

He leans in, his voice a rough murmur meant only for me. "When I am near you, the rest of the world fades into insignificance. In your presence, there is only us, and I would traverse seas and scale mountains to preserve that."

Fuelled by the sweet caress of scotch, I find it easier to push aside my lingering doubts. I allow myself to be swept up in the music, his words, and the intoxicating warmth of his presence.

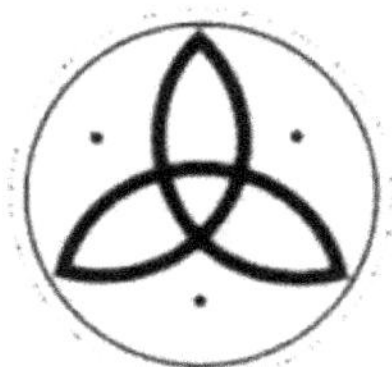

Finn

I stand in the shadows, arms folded across my chest, watching the scene unfold. My usual, affable grin is nowhere to be found. Instead, my jaw is clenched as my gaze darts to Marcus, who is pulling Triona close in a slow, intimate sway.

His hand lingers at the small of her back, and my blood boils. Triona tips her head back, a soft smile teasing her lips as Marcus leans in—too close, too familiar—murmuring something in her ear. There's a looseness in her movements, the kind that says she's had a drink or three. She laughs, light and unguarded, unaware or unwilling to care who's watching. He pulls her in, nuzzling her hair as they sway to the lively beat.

James's words from earlier replay over and over in my head every time I want to grab hold of her.

'We've a lot to discuss, and little time to do so. So for now, we need ye both to keep yer eyes open and yer mouths shut.'"

I need something to occupy my mind—anything—or I'll go mad. Deciding on more drink, I turn to refill my cup, but before I can take another step, Colina steps into my path, blocking the way.

"Finn, dance with me?" she pleads, her eyes bright with determination.

I give her my best smile. "Aye, let me just put my cup down."

She grasps my hand, leading me out to the centre of dancers. The lively music wraps around us, the rhythm infectious and lighthearted. I move easily with the steps, though the pull of Triona and Marcus lingers in my mind like an invisible tether.

"Why do ye look so sombre, then?" Colina inquires, her voice soft against the backdrop of the laughter and chatter. "Ye should be enjoyin' yerself! Gods know ye've overworked yerself wi' all that ye've been doin'."

"Aye, well, I'm glad I took a page from yer book to join in the revelry," I reply. "Maybe this is exactly what I needed."

"Ye deserve some happiness, Finn," Colina replies, leaning closer, her voice dropping to a conspiratorial whisper. "What if I told ye that I could be that happiness?"

Colina's gaze softens as she twirls in front of me, her laughter light and melodic.

"Have ye ever considered," she begins, attempting to steer the conversation, "that ye'd be a good fit for someone like me? Ye've got a way about ye, Finn. I'm sure there are many women who'd be lucky to have ye, but none to service ye like I could."

I hesitate, every instinct screaming at me to keep my distance. "Colina, ye're a fine lass, but I—"

"—Have been *too* focused on Triona," she finishes, her tone teasing yet insistent. "But she's with Marcus now. What about ye? Ye want someone who appreciates ye, no?" She presses as tightly as she can, feigning seduction.

The warning bells in my mind grow. "I appreciate yer kindness, but I'm not lookin' for that, at present," I say, trying to sidestep her advances. "I've my own—"

"—issues to deal with, I ken." She interrupts, stepping closer, her eyes sparkling with mischief. "But I could help ye with that, Finn. Just think of what we could accomplish together."

I feel the heat rising in my chest from the tension. "Colina, really, I think you should—"

Before I finish, she leans up, attempting to kiss me, but I shift at the last moment. Her lips brush my cheek instead, and I can see the flush creeping up her face, mingling with satisfaction.

"Colina, I—" I begin, but the urgency in her gaze makes me wary. She isn't giving up easily, and the realisation settles heavily in my stomach.

"Just tell me what ye want," she presses, her voice low and sultry. "I can be what ye need. I can be better for ye than she ever could. I'd satisfy *all* yer needs."

I take a step back, creating a space between us. "I can see ye've been drinking, which explains a lot of this." I say, gesturing between the two of us with a finger. "I'm not interested in marriage with anyone, includin' Triona."

That lie feels like ash on my tongue.

"She's like family, and ye're mistaken." The words, a shield, but the way Colina's eyes narrow, suggests she won't relent.

"Look, come to me tomorrow, and we'll talk then. Not around pryin' eyes and listenin' ears. Let's discuss this alone, just you and I."

Her face lights up, her eyes alight with triumph. "Ye feel it too, then?" she whispers, voice dripping with a relieved sort of victory, as short-lived as it may be.

Refraining from an outright lie or deception, I keep firm. "Tomorrow, Colina."

"Tomorrow, then. Just the two of us."

Keeping the ruse, I commit to another dance or two.

The music shifts, laughter rises, and just as I start to drift toward the edge of the crowd, James, already a few drinks deep, claps a hand on Triona's shoulder.

"Sing for us, lass!" he shouts, eyes bright with excitement.

Triona moves from Marcus's hold, catching her breath, and glances at Casey and Bran, who nod enthusiastically. "Ériu's Promise," she calls out, earning cheers from the crowd.

Colina reluctantly steps away to listen, her fingers trailing down my arm in a lingering caress. I suppress a shudder at the unwelcomed touch.

Triona closes her bewitching eyes, letting the lilting melody of the old song wrap around her voice, delicate and haunting, her words carrying the weight of promises made in love and sorrow. My gaze softens as I watch her, chest tightening with emotions I don't want to acknowledge. Her voice is that of a siren's call, goading gooseflesh along the surface.

The last note of the song fades, and James breaks into a raucous cheer.

The music surges, the temporising, and within seconds, Marcus finds Triona's waist—his hands returning to their favoured place of the night. The ceilidh reaches a fever pitch.

A circle forms once more, the musicians driving the rhythm faster; the cadence climbing with each passing second. Feet pound against the cold ground, matching the heartbeat of the tune. Couples spin, faster and faster, skirts flaring, hands clasping and releasing as bodies weave through the dance in a dizzying, breathless blur.

I catch sight of Triona as Marcus spins her, the two of them moving as one. The music fades into a distant hum as I watch Marcus pull Triona from the crowded circle of dancers, his grip firm on her wrist.

I feel a dull ache settling deep in my chest, twisting with something I can't push away. I finally lose the will to stand idle in the madness. Looking away, I catch Bran's eyes, a single question swimming in their depths, as if he, too, can feel the weight of this burden I carry.

I stare down at Colina with obvious distress on my face. She frowns as she attempts to lift a hand to my cheek. "What-"

"I... I need a moment."

I turn abruptly, pushing through the dancers, the laughter and joy a cruel mockery of my inner turmoil.

It was supposed to be a good night. It was supposed to be easy.

Colina calls after me, her voice laced with concern, but I barely hear her over the pounding in my ears.

I hesitate in the dark, the instinct to follow battling against the voice that tells me to just let it go. But the way he leads her—so possessive, so sure—churns my stomach.

Every instinct screams at me to stop, to turn back, but my feet move of their own accord, quickening with every step.

Then—I see them.

And the ground rips from beneath me.

Marcus has her pinned against the sidewall of the farmhouse, his hands firm on her waist, fingers pressing in a claiming way. His stance is possessive, assured, as if he knows she belongs beneath his touch. He leans in slightly, his head tilting, his gaze sweeping over her face—not searching, not questioning, but savouring.

His thumb strokes the fabric at her hip, a deliberate motion, his confidence unwavering as he lifts a hand to brush a stray lock of hair from her cheek. His touch lingers, his fingers trailing down her jaw, grazing her skin as if testing her silence, as if waiting for even the slightest resistance.

It never comes.

When his lips meet hers, she doesn't push him away. She doesn't struggle. She lets him claim her.

The jealousy that has simmered all evening erupts, white-hot and all-consuming. The sight of her in Marcus' arms feels like a betrayal I have no right to claim.

Last night, it had been me above her. Me pressing her into the earth, her laughter breathless as I pinned her wrists playfully. It had been nothing, just a teasing match between us—until it wasn't. Until she stilled beneath me, her chest rising and falling against mine, and I swore I saw something in her gaze that mirrored my own hunger.

I had almost convinced myself she wanted me, too. Almost lost control and claimed her mouth, desperate to know how she'd taste, how she'd feel bared beneath me.

And now, knowing exactly how good she felt pressed against me, how her breath had trailed over my neck like a brand, has the inferno inside me raging to unimaginable heights. Wanting her and not having her is a living nightmare—one I fear I will never wake from.

With a muttered curse, I storm out of sight, each step echoing the pulse of anger and hurt surging through me. The cool night air does nothing to temper the fire burning in my chest. I rake a hand through my hair, fingers trembling with grievance. I'll never erase the image from my mind.

It feels like a punch to the gut, one that leaves me staggering toward something to help ease this heartache.

What did I expect?

She is with Marcus. She *chose* Marcus. And here I am, like a fool, burning with jealousy over someone that was never mine to begin with.

Triona

As Marcus kisses me, I pull my head back as his lips find my neck. My voice is gentle but steady. "Marcus, wait. Someone might see." It isn't angry or forceful, but there is a clear hesitance in my tone.

He lets out a low, seductive chuckle, leaning closer, brushing the hair back from my face. "Sorry, my love. I got carried away. You just have this way of making everything else disappear," he murmurs, his breath warm on my skin, voice soft yet insistent, as if trying to will away my hesitation.

I feel a warmth rise in me at his words, but the thought of prying eyes lingers. "It's not that I don't…" I trail off, biting my lip. "It's just—this isn't the right time."

Marcus nods and steps back with a small, understanding smile. "You need not explain," he whispers, his eyes remaining on mine.

Before the moment can stretch further, a voice calls out, breaking the tension. "There ya are!"

Saoirse's voice rings out, her tone brisk but tinged with relief. Her sharp gaze moves between Marcus and me as she steps closer.

He hesitates for a moment, confusion and disappointment clouding his features. His gaze passes between us, searching for a sign that this isn't over. The warmth that had enveloped us dissipates, leaving an awkward chill in its wake.

He nods toward Saoirse before looking back at me, his grin softening into something almost tender. "I shall see you tomorrow, Triona."

Saoirse doesn't wait, slipping an arm through mine and pulling me away with a purpose. "Come on, ya promised me a drink, and I'm collectin' on it."

I manage a tight smile before Saoirse tugs me away, my pulse still racing.

Once we're out of earshot, Saoirse releases me and turns, arms crossed, her expression as pointed as a blade. "I saw him take ya back there," she says, her voice lowering. "And so did Finn."

My stomach twists at the mention of Finn, a sharp pang cutting through the haze of the evening. Tension is coiled tight beneath my skin—and now, the thought of his disappointment feels like a blow to my stomach. "I wasn't—nothing happened," I mutter, the words tasting hollow, defensive. Too fast. Too guilty.

Saoirse exhales through her nose, shaking her head. "Ah, love, I know ya. And ya know I love ya, but after tonight…"

"I know," I reply quickly, cutting her off. "You're right. I don't know what I was thinking."

She scoffs, her voice tight. "Ya weren't. Yer mind's muddled by drink, and *he* should've known better."

"He didn't—" I start, but she cuts me off with a look.

"Don't." Her voice is firm, but not unkind. "Don't make excuses for him."

Saoirse watches me for a beat longer, then exhales again—this time softer, letting the tension go with it. Her tone shifts, light but still laced with care.

"Come on now," she says, nudging my arm. "One more dance before we both fall into bed, aye? Let's not waste the music."

I huff a quiet laugh, more breath than joy.

There's something about Marcus—a pull I can't explain. It feels as if two forces are tearing at my soul. One whispers to lean in, the other screams at me to run. My thoughts churn, a storm I can't quiet, my body caught in its turbulent centre.

Finn wouldn't have noticed. Wouldn't have seen the tension in my shoulders or the way my breath caught at the thought of my family's disdain.

Wouldn't have felt the guilt coiled tight in my chest, or the way Marcus's nearness leaves me teetering on the edge of something I don't fully understand.

We step back into the glow of the bonfire. The lively music and cheerful clamour of the ceilidh wraps around me like a lifeline. I cling to Saoirse's arm—her presence grounding me, even as my thoughts drift back to the chaos still brewing inside me.

14

THE LAST DAWN OF INNOCENCE

Triona

Friday, 2 May 1823

The morning air bites against my skin as the sky above bruises with the first light of dawn. Still rubbing away the haze of sleep, I step outside, pulling my shawl closer. And there he is.

Standing with his back to me, silhouetted against the silver-washed fields, his stance as unmovable as the mountains beyond. Something in me exhales. Relief rises—unexpected, quiet, and sharp. In the hush of morning, with everything still unsettled, his presence feels like the only thing that hasn't shifted.

"Finn," I call out, my voice barely a breath in the lingering fog. He doesn't turn, but I follow the weight of my own words, unwilling to let them die in the mist between us. "I wanted to say something. About what you might have seen last night."

He tenses and looks over his shoulder, gaze sharp as broken glass. "Triona, you owe me nothin'." The tone of his voice holds none of his usual warmth.

"But—"

"But nothin', Triona. Leave it alone."

His words are rough and cutting. My cheeks flush with something akin to shame. The ache rises sharp in my chest, but I press on, even as his coldness sets me on edge.

"Finn, please," I murmur, my words catching like brambles. "I only want to explain—"

"Enough!" His words hit like a lash. "I'm not yer brother. I'm not gonna speak on who you should or shouldna talk to, even if I agree with Callan."

I square my shoulders and lift my chin. "It sounds as if you *do* have issue with my happenings that need discussing."

"Triona," He warns with a voice as biting as a winter's breeze. "I said to leave it alone. *Stop* tryin' to provoke an argument."

But—stubborn as ever—I don't listen. "Marcus provoked Callan, but if he'd stop looking for a fight every time Marcus so much as breathes, it wouldn't have got so out of hand!"

"Out of hand?" His voice is a low growl, simmering with an anger that seems to shake the ground beneath us. "You think yer brother was just lookin' for a reason to pick a fight in front of all of those people?"

"Well, no—"

"Open yer eyes. Callan's not just pickin' fights for the sake of it, and he damn sure isnae doin' it for selfish reasons!"

I cross my arms, feeling a chill settle in my expression. "Callan's never approved of Marcus; he's always jumping to the worst conclusions. Marcus is respectful. Kind."

Finn's fists clench, every muscle in his body pulled taut. He draws a slow, deliberate breath, as if wrestling down something volatile.

"*Respectful?*" he echoes, voice dropping to a dangerous whisper. "That's what you think?"

The silence that follows crackles, brittle and bruised.

"You didnae seem so fond of him when we spoke the other day—and look how quickly that changed."

I open my mouth to speak—to tell him he's wrong, that he didn't see what he thought he did, that I'm not fond of Marcus, that *none* of it was what it seemed—

But I don't get the chance.

The moment the anger overtakes him, it swallows everything else.

"You think so highly of a man who takes liberties with you in public not once, but *twice*. Ye're so blind to him—it's as if you dinnae ken yerself anymore."

Finn's face is taut with frustration, and his voice is filled with unmistakable disappointment. "And the way you talk about yer brother? *Against* yer brother... All I hear is someone who's blind to how lucky she is. Yer family loves you, given you everything—protection, a home, love—and yet here you are, soundin' as if it's all some burden, because they want the world for you."

Shame and regret are all I know at this moment. He's relentless, his gaze hard. "Ye're actin' like a *wee bairn*, Triona. Throwin' their care back in their faces like it's something to be ashamed of. I'd have given anything to have parents half as decent as yers, and I'd have been grateful for it every *damned* day."

A fierce defensive anger fuelled by embarrassment spurs me into action before I can stop myself. "You're *just* like Callan. It's why you're both alone—because you can't *stand* the idea of anyone not needing you, so you smother people under the farce that it's for their own damn good!"

My voice cracks, but I don't stop. I *can't*.

"You both need to find other ways to occupy your time that doesn't involve being completely and unabashedly unnecessary."

His face drains of colour, the weight of my words pressing down like stones.

I open my mouth to take it back, to say *anything* and undo the damage, but the words won't come, tangled in the knot of my regret. As he looks away, his regard distant, it's as if he is already pulling himself out of my reach. I feel a sudden, hollow ache in my chest.

When he finally speaks, his voice is dangerously soft. "If that's how you feel... then all this talk is cheap, and I'm *done*. I'm done tryin' to make you see it. Maybe one day ye'll realise what ye've got before it's too late."

He turns on his heel, his steps firm and unhesitant, the lines of his shoulders tense as he walks away, every step widening the space between us. There's no hesitation, no glance back—just a finality that settles in the silence, heavy and unforgiving.

I stand frozen, the space between us filled with everything I wish I hadn't said, and every word I wish I could take back. It feels as if I've just rebuilt the walls between us, stone by painful stone. Walls I may never break through again.

A sinking horror grips me as I realise that I've wounded him in a way that echoes back to the time before he came here.

During a time when a frightened, lonely child spent years wondering if he'd ever feel the tender touch of a hand, instead of the biting strike of a drunkard.

Before he knew the love my parents pour into these halls.

Before he felt the bond of brotherhood with Callan and Casey.

Before us—our heartfelt friendship we spent so much time nurturing. One we've shared so freely. One I felt getting stronger.

He isn't unnecessary. He never could be.

Telling him otherwise—seeing that devastation in his eyes—might be a cruelty I'll never forgive myself for.

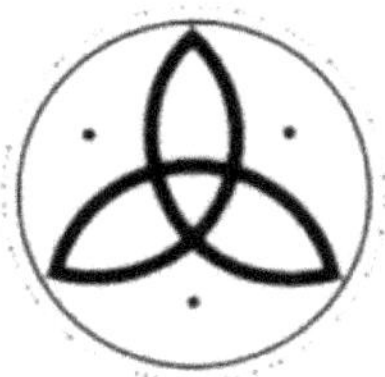

Finn

I find myself alone; the silence pressing heavily against me. Her words echo painfully in my mind: *'You both need to find other ways to occupy your time that doesn't involve being completely and unabashedly unnecessary.'*

The words strike in the worst way imaginable because of the truth that I desperately avoid at all costs.

I close my eyes, a bitter laugh escaping as I press a hand to my face. I'd lost control, let my frustration and protectiveness tear out of me without thinking. It didn't matter that she pressed me. I hadn't meant to hurt her, hadn't meant to imply she was naïve or incapable of understanding reason, but in my anger, that's exactly what I'd done. And like the fool I was, I backed her into a corner. Now I'm left wondering if I've shattered something between us I can't mend.

I exhale slowly. "*Eejit,*" I mutter to myself.

I want to protect her, but I'd been too forceful, too... possessive. She didn't need me trying to dictate her choices, even if I know—I *know*—Marcus isn't what he seems.

I enter the stables, thoughts in a haze, to find Eamon sporting a wearisome face as he stands just outside the largest stall reserved for the sick, injured, or foaling mare.

"What's going on?"

"It's Aisling," Eamon says, his voice low with concern. "She got out somehow—probably someone feckin' about. I found her before first light, grazin' in the patches of rich grass."

I move closer, my chest tightening at the sight of her. She looks worse for wear.

"I don't know what we're dealing with, Finn," Eamon continues. "She's in a bad way."

I nod grimly. "We're supposed to meet at the still today, aye?"

"Aye," Eamon mimics. "But Callan says he's stayin' behind—said something about needin' to be here for Triona?"

Thoughts of our recent spat come rushing back, and I get lost as I replay every glaring mistake.

"Finn." Eamon says, pulling me from my thought spiral. "Did ya hear me?"

"Sorry, Eamon. I have a lot on my mind. What did you say?"

"I said, ye'll have to take Shadow. Maybe ask Triona—"

"She's busy, and we're short on time. This needs to be handled before midday."

"Why the rush?"

"Last night, they told me the last of the product was... compromised."

Eamon's brow furrows. "How do ya mean?"

I relay what was said to me in the study.

Eamon ponders for a moment, his features darkening as realisation strikes. Fear flashes in his eyes. "So someone..."

I nod. "Properly distilled whiskey burns with a golden flame. But when Callan lit the top of the glass, it burned a deep, intense blue. We're lucky Callan had the sense to bring the 3-year-aged barrel. His quick thinkin' saved this family from a lot of trouble. The other batch would've poisoned anyone who drank it."

"What does this mean, then?" Eamon asks, brow furrowing.

I shake my head. "Someone tried very hard to ruin the Sinclair name—tried makin' it look as if they made a big mistake. It was a calculated attack."

"Why wait until now?" he presses, echoing the very question I'd first asked.

"I think they wanted to inspect things before causing panic," I explain.

"I'll have Saoirse watch over Aisling for the day. She needs monitorin'."

I glance at where the mare is sprawled out on the ground and kneel to stroke her head.

"A bit of fresh air might actually do Shadow some good. Every time Aisling has made the tiniest sound today, he's started neighing like his heart's broken. Real mournful sound, it is." Eamon says.

I glance up at him with a crooked smile. "D'ye speak the language of a horse now?"

Eamon rolls his eyes. "Take this serious for just a beat. Something's wrong."

He's right, something *is* wrong.

"All right," I say, standing and placing a hand on his shoulder. "If the stubborn auld man'll let me, we'll head out now. Let's get him ready to leave."

Triona

I watch with peaked interest as Eamon pulls Shadow from the stables. It's not unusual for him to do this.

What's odd is that he's donned in his endurance saddle.

"Oi," Saoirse says from the doorway of my open chamber.

"Gods, Saoirse!" I jolt, a hand flying to my chest. "You gave me a fright!"

She chuckles. "Yer door was *open.*"

"Aye, guess I'm a wee bit jumpy. But if you'll excuse me, I have to go see why Eamon is saddling Shadow."

"That's what I'm up here for. He told me to tell ya that Aisling is too sick to ride today."

"Oh, poor girl. I bet Shadow is beside himself..."

"It's funny ya mention that. It's the first thing Eamon said he'd been bothered by."

She continues, "Apparently, he's been up carin' for her since before the sun had even come up, which is *strange* 'cause he's not usually up that early. Anyway—" she pauses for a breath. "Finn has to take Shadow if they're gonna have all the help they need at the still today."

"Wait, *what*? What's going on at the still?" I ask.

Saoirse pauses as if trying to remember pieces of a conversation she had only half-heard. *Typical.*

"Eamon said something about a bad batch in Edinburgh."

"The ride home!" I shout. "I knew it! Something *was* wrong." Then the second part of her statement hits me. "You said Finn is taking him?"

"Aye—I mean, we all know he's the only other person Shadow allows to ride him."

I nod absentmindedly.

"What's wrong?" Saoirse asks, her gaze sharpening.

"How do you know something is wrong?"

Saoirse rolls her eyes. "Because I know ya, Triona. Now tell me."

"I really messed up. I said something incredibly cruel to Finn. I was embarrassed about last night, and I just lashed out at him. I pushed him until he broke. Even after he asked me to let it rest."

Saoirse grips my shoulders. "Gods, Triona, ye're ramblin'. Breathe." I take a shaky breath, but the knot in my chest barely loosens.

Her expression is one of understanding. "Triona, I know it might not feel like it, but they all just want the best for ya."

"I'm tired of everyone thinking they *know* what's best for me. I don't even know what's best for me, so how is them telling me supposed to make me feel?"

She nods. "So, ya feel confused. That's fair."

"I'm unsure if I can trust my feelings. Then there's the actual reality that Ma and Callan are asking me to choose two very different things."

Saoirse squeezes my arms gently, her expression warm. "It's not their expectations that have ya upset, though, is it?"

I shake my head. "I think I surmised that during my blowup at Finn... I'm afraid of disappointing them. I let shame in the decision I made overcome all reason."

Saoirse's eyes soften, and she pulls me into a quick, reassuring hug. "Listen... whatever happened with Finn, it's not as broken as it feels right now."

I pull back, biting my lip. "You didn't hear what I said to him. I practically told him he's a bother in my life. That he clings to people because he's too afraid of being alone. And he just... walked away, silent."

She winces, but quickly covers it with a small smile. "Och, Triona, ya know, for all the stubbornness and fire that Finn has...he's not one to hold grudges, especially not with his *Little Doe*. He'd never hurt ya—"

"—in the same way I just hurt him?"

She blanches. "My apologies, love. Should have thought that sentence through."

"No, you're right, he wouldn't say those things." I glance out the window, where Eamon is fastening Shadow's bridle, Finn standing nearby with an unusually stoic stance. The sight sends a pang through me. "I don't deserve his forgiveness, not for this."

"Then do something about it," Saoirse says, her tone brightening as she nudges my shoulder. "Go down there, apologise, make it right. Tell him what ya feel, not just what ya think he wants to hear."

"And if he doesn't forgive me?"

She arches a brow. "Then ye'll know, won't you? But... Triona, I'd put all my winnings on him forgiving ya."

"I almost hate when you're so incredibly *right*."

Saoirse's laugh carries like a tune. "You're lucky Dealla isn't here yet. There's no telling what she'd be spilling in your ear."

"Thanks, Saoirse. For being here, for...understanding."

She squeezes my hand and steps back. "Go on, then. Before he rides off and ye're left sittin' here all day, wonderin' how he's feelin'."

With one last look, I turn and make my way down to the stables, my heart racing as I step outside.

I call out for him, but he's already mounted on Shadow, his broad back stiff as he spurs the stallion forward, the sound of hooves muffling my voice.

"Finn!" I call again, louder this time, the urgency spilling out. But they're already moving faster, the gap between us widening. My voice dissolves into the cool morning air.

A pang of something sharp and hollow settles in my stomach. Did he really not hear me? Or...did he choose to ignore it?

I stand there, rooted in place, feeling the weight of what I'd said this morning pressing down on me. I turn toward my father's garden, intent on heading there to walk through it, but I'm met with a troublesome glare from Colina. The intensity in her eyes bothers me immensely. A prickling unease settles at the base of my neck, creeping down my arms like icy tendrils.

As I lift my hand in a tentative wave to ease some of the discomfort of the moment, her face darkens, and her eyes narrow with a look that borders on antipathy. Without a word, she pivots on her heel, leaving me standing there with my hand still raised.

The silence she leaves in her wake feels heavier than words she could have spoken. I let my hand fall, watching her retreat—each step echoing louder than it should against the stone path, as though the world itself refuses to soften her departure.

I swallow, unease settling over me like a shroud.

"I just need to wander through Da's garden." I say out loud, as if I weren't alone.

The fondness I feel as I lose myself in the natural beauty of the garden is unmatched. It feels like a sacred haven of the old world. Its tranquility is unmatched—a place where time seems to slow down.

But the moment I set foot among the familiar flowers, a wave of foreboding crashes over me, making the air feel weighted. The awaited hum of life muted, and the usual rustling leaves and swaying flowers are eerily still. This place, my sanctuary, now feels foreign, as though something unseen has crept into its heart.

I weave through the garden, my steps quickening as I near my favourite corner, where delicate flowers sway in the breeze. The air hums with the scent of earth and blossoms, each one thriving under my father's careful hand—except one.

My chest tightens as my gaze lands on a single primrose, its petals curled inward, edges tinged with decay. Its stem bows under its own weight, lifeless amid the riot of colour around it. A stark contrast.

A silent warning.

I reach out, running a finger along the fragile petals, but it crumbles before my eyes, causing me to pull my hand back and gasp. It dissolves as if my very touch were a virulent venom; spreading disease from my fingertip and snuffing out its life-force.

Somewhere beyond the barriers of this garden, something is shifting—something I can't yet see, but I feel its presence threading through the world.

I glance at my hand, still dusted with the remnants of the primrose. It seems I'm leaving a mess of everything I touch today.

I force myself to rise, a dizzying unease swirling in my chest, leaving the world slightly off-kilter. One last glance at the ruined flower—silent and accusing—and I turn away, my steps quickening toward the library. Whatever truth once lived here has withered. This place offers no answers now. The unease follows me like a shadow, clinging to my every thought.

The wind picks up behind me, whispering through the trees, carrying with it a message I cannot yet decipher.

But I feel it in my bones—the world is shifting, and I'm not sure I'm ready for what awaits.

Finn

As Eamon and I near the clearing, my eyes lock onto Callan's broad-shouldered figure among the group gathered near the still. A surge of confusion shoots through me.

He's supposed to be back home, keeping watch. Keeping watch over her.

I dismount in one swift motion and sprint toward the others, urgency tightening in my chest with every step.

A cold knot of anxiety coils in my gut. Images flare behind my eyes: Triona, trapped—endless halls swallowing the light, shadows slithering through the silence. The faint creak of empty rooms echoes like a warning, a hollow sound that underscores just how vulnerable she is—alone, with no promise that anyone would hear her scream. Not anyone with the ability to do anything.

Callan's eyes snap to mine, his face tightening as the same dreadful realisation dawns on him. His shoulders go rigid, his hands curling into fists. James, usually unshakable, shifts where he stands, his steady confidence replaced by a taut, unfamiliar tension.

It's Alex who finally breaks the silence, his voice low but charged with the weight of our shared fear. "Who's back at the house?"

Eamon, Casey, and Bran exchange uncertain glances, their brows knitting in confusion.

"Dad, what's going on?" Bran asks, his tone edged with unease.

But it's Callan who cuts in, his voice sharp, accusatory. "Finn, why are ye here?"

I glare back, the knot in my stomach tightening. "I should ask the same thing, Cal. Eamon told me you were stayin' behind."

Eamon nods, stepping forward. "Aye, that's what I was told." His gaze flicks between us, confusion written across his face.

Callan's jaw tightens, frustration rising as he snaps, "And who told ye that?"

"Colina," Eamon replies, hesitant but firm.

Callan bellows. "I'm only here because she insisted Finn wouldnae make it because his horse had takin' ill. Got me out of bed to tell me she'd ready my mare."

I hardly register the rest of the conversation, focus already pulled elsewhere.

It's faint at first, just a whisper tangled in the wind. But then it's unmistakable—*her* voice.

"Triona?" I murmur, almost afraid it's just my mind playing tricks. In the distance, Shadow's unmistakable neigh cuts through the night, only tightening the knot in my chest.

Then I hear it again, more urgent, drifting through the trees with a haunting clarity that makes my heart seem to stop beating.

"Finn... Help... Please."

"Triona!" The name rips from my throat, shattering the tense silence and echoing through the trees. Every head snaps toward me. I see Callan's face change as the colour fades and dread flickers to life in his hazel eyes. James's gaze locks with Callan's, and a thousand unspoken words pass between them in the briefest of moments.

Something is *wrong*. And they can feel it too.

The plea slices through me, raw and unfiltered. The world narrows. Nothing exists but her voice—reaching for me like a lifeline.

My legs propel me toward the waiting stallion before I even realise I've moved.

Shadow paws at the ground, restless. I vault into the saddle in one motion. Behind me, the others shout, but their voices drown beneath the thunder of my pulse.

"Where the hell are ye goin'?" Callan's voice cuts through the noise, sharp with alarm, but I don't stop, almost forgetting to answer entirely. I kick hard, urging Shadow forward. The reins bite into my grip as I finally twist in the saddle, shouting over my shoulder, my voice raw and fierce.

"She's in trouble!"

In a heartbeat, they all spring into action, mounting their horses with practiced ease.

The air grows colder as I race deeper into the woods. The trees seem to close in around me, their shadows stretching long and ominous. I clench my jaw, my grip on the reins so tight my knuckles burn. Every pounding hoofbeat is a second slipping away—another moment lost when I should already be there.

I lean forward, urging Shadow faster, every fibre of my being pulling toward hers. The whisper of her voice lingers in my mind—fragile, desperate, fueling the urgency clawing at my chest.

Hold on, Triona. I swear to the gods—I'm coming.

The wind picks up, sharp and stinging, shoving me forward as if mocking my urgency. In its gusts, I swear I hear her voice—faint, distant, threading through the trees like a phantom whisper.

Shadow's muscles bunch beneath me as they veer around a narrow bend, the forest looming taller, thicker. My mind races, every dreadful possibility assaulting me. Every instinct in me screams to reach her, protect her, to bridge the distance between us with sheer willpower if I have to.

Behind me, Callan's caught up, and shouts something—maybe a command, maybe a warning. I barely register it. The echo of her voice—whether real or imagined—drowns out everything else.

It grips me, relentless. And with it, the chilling thought that whatever awaits us at the end of this reckless race won't just change everything—it will tear our lives apart.

Another voice—James this time—cuts through the chaos. Desperate. Sharper than I've ever heard from him. It tugs at the edge of my focus, but I don't slow. I don't give them the chance to stop me.

I drive Shadow harder until their voices are only ghosts in the wind. The world becomes a blur—trees flashing past like streaks of shadow—and all I can hear is the call that started it all.

She called for *me*. And I know, with a conviction that pulses in my bones, I won't stop until I'm the one who finds her.

Triona

I've tried for over an hour to lose myself in *Rob Roy* by Sir Walter Scott, but it's of no use. Paragraphs blur together, the words slipping away before they can take hold. I take a sip of the tea beside me—stronger than I'm used to, its sharp taste lingering on my tongue. Rather than grounding me, it only heightens the restless energy already thrumming beneath my skin.

Outside, the day mirrors my inner unrest. A heavy canopy of ashen clouds dims the day, shrouding the world in quiet desolation. Wisps of fog curl around the rolling hills, transforming the landscape into something mythical yet haunting. The wind has deserted the day, leaving a stagnant silence that deepens my sense of unrest, and amplifies the stillness that echoes my thoughts.

Just as I rise to retreat to my bedchamber, a speck of brown adorned with cream-yellow spots catches my eye. It lands on the bay-window windowsill, and the very movement stirs a long-buried memory.

I'm surrounded by a sunlit glen, where a variety of wildflowers bloom in patches of colourful beauty. The air is crisp, filled with the distant sound of a babbling brook.

I'm kneeling in the grass making a flower crown when a butterfly lands on a flower just out of reach. "Look, Da!"

He walks over slowly; the butterfly remains unperturbed by his movements. "It's lovely, aye, but ye ken the stories, don't ye? They say speckled wood butterflies can carry messages from the other side."

"What kinds of messages?"

"They're seen as symbols of transformation, and can signify positive change to come, but sometimes... sometimes they come with warnin's. It's not always good news."

I look up at him. "What about this one? D'ye think it brings good news or bad news?"

He shrugs his shoulders. "It could bring either. When one flutters near, it might be a reminder to pay attention. To be cautious."

"But what if it's just a butterfly?"

"In our world, even the simplest things can hold weight. Everything has its own purpose. It's about knowing where to look and what to feel."

My father retreats, but I stay to watch the butterfly dance from flower to flower. I feel an irresistible pull to follow it. I stand, mesmerised, my worries fading away like the soft whispers of the wind. Each flutter of its delicate wings draws me deeper into the glen, and soon I'm laughing, chasing it through a riot of wildflowers that sway in the breeze.

With every step, the world around me fades into a blur of colour and light, the joy of the chase lifting my spirits. But then, a sudden stillness creeps in, and I paused, realising something is off.

"Da?" I call, but my voice echoes back at me, swallowed by the silence. The familiar sounds—the babbling brook, the rustle of grass—disappear. I turn in a slow circle, and the vibrant glen I was so enchanted by now feels like a maze of tall, shadowy trees.

Panic bubbles in my chest as I take a deep breath, trying to steady myself. The butterfly lands abruptly on top of a large, rounded mound. The sun has all but vanished, leaving me alone in a forest that suddenly feels vast and strange.

"Okay, just breathe," I whisper to myself, trying to remember the way we had come. I glance around, trying to find a familiar landmark, but everything looks the same—an endless sea of dark green and brown.

"Stay calm," I mutter, but my voice trembles slightly. I am lost, and the magical adventure has turned into something altogether different. Something that makes my heart pound with fear. A silence unlike anything I'd ever witnessed before surrounds me.

That's when the stone collides with the back of my head.

The memory hits me like a formidable wave. That familiar foreboding surges through me, echoing similarly to when I was yanked from that strange trance all those years ago. I had known better that day, much as I do now, to heed whispers of intuition when they warned of danger lurking in the shadows. But somehow, it was as if I was *made* to follow the butterfly that day. The compulsion to do so overwhelmed all reason.

Colina's voice, soft but urgent, snaps me from my thoughts. She stands in the library doorway. "Yer mother's askin' for ye in the stables. It's Aisling." Gone is her intensity from earlier, now replaced by what appears to be a surface level tolerance.

My heart lurches at the mention of Aisling.

The stable is quiet when I arrive. Aisling stands in her stall, looking far stronger than she had this morning. Her eyes are bright, her posture steady—nothing like the weak, motionless state I left her in.

The second door, usually left open, stands firmly shut. I call for my mother, but my voice echoes in the silence. A wave of dizziness hits me out of nowhere, my stomach twisting as sudden nausea rolls through me. I grip a stalls frame, swallowing hard, trying to steady myself. Unease creeps in when there's no answer, and I turn back to find Colina standing close behind me.

"Oh!" I start, the suddenness of her presence unnerving me. "Colina! You gave me a fright. Where's Ma?"

She just watches me, unblinking, something cold flickering in her gaze. "It's just the two of us."

I force a laugh, though it sounds hollow. "Well, if Ma's not here, I'll be heading back then—"

"Stay." Colina says, as she steps in front of the door, arms crossed behind her back. "Ye know, ye made this simple by walkin' down here alone. Didnae think it'd be so easy to get ye down from yer room without a fuss. I worried that mouth of yers would ruin my fun."

"Colina…" My voice wavers. "This isn't funny. I don't know what you're on about, but I'll not—"

"It's no jest, Triona." Her voice sharpens, eyes narrowing. "Ye should see the look on yer face, thinkin' yer mother needed help. Nae… Aisling was just a tool to get ye here." She lets out a dry laugh. "I had ye all believin' she just fell ill this morning. Got ye here all *alone.*"

A sickening realisation grips me, tightening a knot in my stomach. "Colina, what have you done?"

"Poisoned her, of course," she says with a cold, gleeful smile. "A small dose, mind ye. Wouldnae want my precious Finn to lose his mare. Just enough to weaken her, make them worry—force Finn to take yer *precious* stallion."

My mind spins, trying to make sense of the situation. "Why? What could possibly make you do this?"

"Tried twice before to be rid of ye," she says, the indifference chilling. "Never expected ye to last this long. Seven years I've waited, watchin' ye take everything that should've been mine." Her voice hisses as her gaze sharpens. "Thought maybe if that horse kicked ye hard enough, I'd be done with ye. But no, ye found the blackthorn. And then… *he* came along and saved ye that day, and ye took him from me with whatever sin ye promise him."

My heart races, anger bubbling beneath my fear. "What day? Are you saying this is about *Finn*?"

"Dinnae say his name!" she snaps, eyes blazing with rage. "My *hatred* for ye started burnin' when ye fibbed on my brother. Got him in trouble over a lie."

"I did not lie! He *forced* himself on Dealla. I saw it!" My words come fast and sharp.

Her face twists, her shriek so loud it makes me flinch. "He did not! Ye bewitched everyone just like ye're doin' with Finn. Yer witch ways have him actin' like a simple fool, hangin' on yer every word. And the others… the way they look at ye, like ye're something special. I ken better."

Each of her words drips with fury. "He was meant to meet me here in the morn', but ye—jealous, scheming witch—ye scared him away with that fight ye started!" Her eyes are wild as she takes a step closer, her rage palpable. "Finn. Is. Mine. And once ye're gone, once *he's* come to claim ye, Finn will have all that he needs… *me.*"

I ache to ask who she's talking about, but I think better of it and hold my tongue. She's not in a state to understand reality.

"Colina, I don't know what you think is happening, but I don't want—"

She laughs—a jagged, cruel sound. "Nae, Triona. All that ye say will be a filthy lie. Justice is comin' for ye; by my hand if necessary."

A memory hits me sharp and sudden, pulling me back to that day in the woods.

"Come on, Triona!" she says, her hand outstretched. Her smile is warm and inviting.

"Don't ye see it? The butterfly? It's so pretty—like a wee fairy. Let's catch it!"

I hesitate, glancing back toward the clearing where my family's voices fade into the distance. Something deep in my belly twists. A shadow of uncertainty brushes against my thoughts, but it disappears as quickly. Colina tugs at my hand, her excitement contagious. "We'll be quick. I promise."

Her words are a net, and I follow her into the thick of the woods, our laughter mingling with the rustling leaves. The butterfly flits just ahead, its wings catching slivers of sunlight that peek through the canopy.

Then it happens.

Colina stops suddenly. The butterfly darts away, but she doesn't seem to care. Her face shifts, like a cloud passing over the sun. The warmth drains from her eyes, replaced by something colder, darker. Her fingers, once soft around mine, tighten before she lets go. "Wait here," she says. Before I can ask why, she disappears behind the trees, leaving me alone.

"Colina?" I call, but the trees swallow my voice. My legs feel rooted in place, my chest tightens as the minutes stretch into an eternity.

When she reappears, relief floods through me—until I see she is holding a rock

Her lips press into a thin line. "Justice is makin' things right, no matter what it takes. And ye... ye're the reason it's all wrong. Ye ruin everything, Triona."

"Colina, what are you doin'?"

The last thing I remember is the weight of the blow—heavier than I expected, sharp, merciless. Pain shatters through my skull, a white-hot explosion behind my eyes. The world tilts sideways, and then—nothing. Darkness rushes in like a wave, swallowing me whole.

I wake to warmth against the cold. I expect to see Colina's face leering down at me, but she's gone. Instead, there is a boy, crouched beside me, his face blurring in and out of focus. For a moment, he is light against the dark, like something conjured from a dream.

His hands tremble, hovering as if he's afraid to touch me. When he finally brushes my hair away, his breath catches. His fingers come away red. His eyes—wide, stricken—lock onto mine, as if looking anywhere else might break something inside him.

"I've got you," he whispers, as if saying it makes it true. His voice is young, raw with conviction, and yet—fragile. "Ye're safe now." A pause. A hesitant breath. "I won't let anyone hurt ye... not if I can help it."

I feel every bit of the truth in his words.

Colina wasn't a friend that day. She *was* the storm.

Finn just another piece in her twisted game. No, this is about me. About her sick need to erase me—not for what I've done, but for what I am. A shadow she cannot shake. A reminder she cannot stand.

"Colina," I say, my voice measured, hiding the tremor beneath, "my brothers and Finn will be back soon. They'll find you here, cornering me."

She cackles. "They won't because *ye'll* be gone, and there's no one here that can stop that from happenin'."

"Colina, enough of this," I mutter, forcing my voice to remain steady. I edge around her, aiming for the door, but the dizziness that's been lingering crashes over me in full force.

My vision blurs, the edges darkening, my stomach twisting violently. A low, dull ringing settles in my ears, warping Colina's words into something distant and distorted. My knees buckle, the ground rushing toward me—too fast, too soon, and I can't stop it.

My palms slam against the stable floor as I collapse onto all fours, struggling to fight the dizziness that threatens to pull me under. My breath comes in short, sharp gasps, the scent of hay and damp earth overwhelming me. The world tilts again, nausea curling deep in my stomach. The ground feels unsteady beneath my hands. Then—a shift in the air, the snap of a riding crop slicing through the stillness. Before I can react, fire lashes across my back.

A scream rips from my throat as I pitch forward, barely catching myself before my face hits the ground. My arms shake as I press my palms harder against the stable floor, forcing myself up—trying to run, to escape—but the nausea surges, colliding with the fresh agony ripping through me. I gag, my stomach heaving violently. I hardly have time to brace before the next lash comes, searing across my back.

I cry out, my body jerking forward from the force, but I can't collapse—not yet. The rough hay scratches against my palms, my fingers digging into the dirt as I fight to stay on all fours. I fight against the nausea, swallowing hard, but the bile rises again.

Colina moves to my side, no longer lingering behind me, but close enough that I can see her on the edge of my vision. Her lips curl into a wicked smirk, her eyes gleaming with something dark and twisted. She tilts her head, slow and deliberate, her eyes drinking in my helplessness, her presence pressing in on me like a suffocating shadow.

"Ye ken, some women just cannae hold their laudanum very well," she murmurs, her voice lilting with cruel amusement. "Slippin' it into yer tea was as easy as they said it would be."

Colina's laughter is sharp, cruel. She moves closer. "I ken about what ye do in the dark!" ***Whip!***

The next strike sends me sprawling onto my side, my cheek pressed against the cold, unforgiving ground. My limbs are heavy, too slow to push myself back up.

"Sirr warned me. Said ye'd be beggin' Finn to fill ye with his cock the moment ye got a chance!" ***Whip!*** My vision swims, my breath ragged. "How easy it is to get ye on yer back!" ***Whip!*** "Ye—" ***Whip!*** "Are nothing—" ***Whip!*** "But a worthless—" ***Whip!*** "Filthy, vexin' whore!"

Colina lets out a breathless chuckle between strikes, drawing out each one as if she's reluctant to let the moment end. She steps forward, slow and unhurried, then crouches beside me, her grin widening as she tilts her head, watching me struggle. The scent of blood and damp earth thickens in the air between us.

"Aye," she murmurs, her voice almost tender, mockingly sweet. "Ye don't look so special now, do ye?"

Through the haze of pain, I try to roll, to curl inward, anything to shield myself, but my limbs betray me. My muscles won't obey, won't move fast enough. The world is tilting, slipping, breaking apart at the edges. Colina strikes harder, faster, forcing me down, attempting for harsh words to cut deeper than the blows.

I sob as blood seeps through my clothes, hot and slick. The air stings as it meets raw, open flesh. I shudder, bracing for the next strike. Fire rips across my back, stealing the breath from my lungs.

"Finn isnae yers to take!" she spits, her face twisted in hatred. "Ye tried to slither in like a serpent and take what's mine! Ye'd be naught but a sullied wench to him—no wife, no standing, no future! What man would keep a woman like ye?"

The words are nearly as relentless as the blows, each one landing with the weight of her twisted resentment. Each hit blurs into a storm of agony.

The pain is all-consuming, and it's all I can do to keep breathing, each ragged gasp an insignificant victory against the darkness closing in around me.

"Ye willnae get the chance—" Colina's howl ricochets off the stable walls, her words severed mid-breath. The pain stops, but my body doesn't believe it. I brace for the next strike, every nerve still flinching, waiting—expecting more. The silence is deafening, my body tense, too shocked to turn, too afraid to hope.

Then, through the pounding in my ears, a voice—low, commanding, and steady—cuts through the haze like a lifeline, slicing the silence clean in half.

"Drop it, *now!*"

The sound reverberates around me, but I barely register it. My body gives in at last, sinking into the darkness that waits to claim me.

15

SHATTERED

Finn

I arrive as the last glints of sunlight illuminate the horizon. Shadows stretch across the property, cloaking everything in darkness, but it's the stillness, the eerie quiet, that tightens a knot in my gut. Everything feels familiar yet foreign, a place I should feel safe. And yet, something is terribly amiss.

The stable door swings slightly, left ajar, and every instinct in me says to move. Nothing seems out of place at first, but as I get closer, a sound cuts through the silence.

A scream. *Her* scream.

The sound rips through me, a raw, guttural cry that lodges deep in my bones, freezing my blood before it sends it blazing hot through my veins. Then, the unmistakable snap of a whip cuts through the air, sharp and deadly.

"Triona," I breathe, the horror already clawing at my chest.

I bolt for the stables, legs pushing harder than they ever have, and every fibre of me trained on getting to her. I can hear the others behind, but I don't look back, don't wait for them to catch up. It's only me and the desperate need to reach her.

I see red. Red like blood, like rage, like the fire roaring through every inch of me as I take in what's happening before me. Colina's standing over Triona, whip in hand, poised to strike. Triona—*my* Triona—curled up on the ground, battered and broken.

I can hardly breathe through the rage twisting in my chest. My hands shake with unbridled wrath as I reach her, snatching Colina's arm mid-swing. I don't just grip her wrist—I twist it, relishing the sharp snap of bone beneath my fingers. She screams, a high, piercing sound, but I don't let go. She lets out a shriek, but I feel nothing—nothing but contempt.

"Drop it, now!" I growl, each word dripping with venom. My grip tightens, and she gasps, her eyes wide with terror. "Or I'll make sure you never lift anythin' again."

She complies, her fingers trembling as the whip slips from her grasp, but I see it—the disbelief in her eyes, as if she never thought I'd dare to lay hands on her. As if she still believed she held any power here. As if the very idea I'd disapprove was unfathomable to her.

"Ye'll regret every action you took tonight."

I keep her close, my grip unrelenting, my fingers digging into her arm as she squirms. Let her feel it, let her know she's at my mercy. When Callan, Casey, Bran, and Eamon come charging in, I don't hesitate. "Think I broke her wrist," I mutter, my voice flat, unbothered. The men falter, their eyes flicking between me and Colina, concern flashing across their faces.

Callan's brow furrows. "What in the hell is goin' on?"

I tighten my grip on Colina, feeling her tremble beneath my hold. "She whipped Triona. And she wasna done. She'd have kept going—might not have stopped 'til Triona couldnae breathe anymore."

Their concern shifts in an instant. Their confusion fades, replaced with something colder, sharper. Bran's mouth presses into a grim line, Casey's hand clenches at his side, and Callan's expression turns lethal. The air thickens with unspoken fury, and their attention now fixes squarely on Colina.

Only then do I throw her toward Callan, watching with grim satisfaction as she stumbles into his grip.

Colina's eyes dart between us, panic and desperation overtaking whatever madness drove her to this. "But Finn, ye dinnae understand. Ye wurnae supposed to be back yet." She stammers, her voice weak, pleading. "This was all for ye—"

"Enough!" The word erupts from me like thunder, a raw, primal snarl that reverberates through the stables. Colina flinches, shrinking back, her breath coming in sharp, uneven gasps. The word hangs heavy in the air, a final verdict, sealing her fate.

"Tie her up. I dinnae care where or how. We've little time to deal with this mess. Callan, Bran—we need answers, and we need 'em now."

"Aye," Callan replies, his voice as hard as his grip on her. Bran gives me a nod, a look that tells me he'll take care of it, no matter what it takes.

I turn back to Triona, shrugging out of my coat and draping it over her bare back, gentle as I can manage. My hands tremble as I lift her from the ground, careful to keep her close, feeling the wet warmth of blood soaking through my coat as I cradle her to me. Her whimpers cut through me, each one like a blade to my chest.

"I've got you now," I whisper, low and soft, just for her to hear. "Ye're safe, Doe. I swear it."

Her eyes flutter open, dazed, her voice faint. "It hurts…"

"Shhh, dinnae speak. I know it hurts, lass," I say, my heart twisting at the pain in her voice, her little whimpers that make me feel weak enough to buckle.

"Finn," she whispers, her breath hitching. "I'm sorry."

"Not now," I murmur, clutching her closer. *Not ever.* I bear no grudge against her. All I want is for her to be okay. I see her trying to hold on, trying to stay present, and I press my lips to her hair, reassuring her, letting her know she's safe.

"Colina said… '*he put her up to it*,'" she whispers, her voice thin, trembling as if the words themselves weigh her down. My jaw tightens, muscles feathering as rage flares hot and bright in my chest. Someone put her up to this—someone dared to orchestrate this hell, to think they could harm Triona and walk away from it.

As we reach the front door, I kick it open, not caring about the splintering crack as it slams against the wall. Saoirse rushes in first, her face draining of colour the moment she sees Triona's battered form in my arms.

Then Ellen appears at the top of the stairs. She takes one look at her daughter, and a sound escapes her lips—a broken, guttural cry she tries, but cannot stifle.

"Saoirse," I snap, sharp but not unkind. "We need medical supplies. Now. Go."

She doesn't hesitate. She spins on her heel and bolts, feet pounding down the corridor.

I cross the floor of the sitting room in a few swift strides, lowering Triona gently onto the divan. Ellen rushes forward, her hands trembling as they hover over Triona's face—afraid to touch, afraid of the pain she's endured. Behind me, Casey and Eamon approach, their expressions tight with anger and anguish.

Casey steps in beside Ellen, wrapping a steadying arm around her shoulders.

"Ma," he says, his voice rough and quiet, "we need to talk. But we'll wait for Da." He glances down, face taut with anger and worry. "Can you tell us if he beat us here?"

Ellen gives him a small, barely there shake of her head, still too overcome by shock to answer properly. Her gaze stays fixed on Triona, her fingertips brushing softly over her cheek as if to reassure herself that she's still breathing, still here.

I want to say something to Ellen, to comfort her, but decide better of it and focus on what I can fix instead.

Dealla comes rushing into the room, and stares for a heartbeat too long, frozen as she watches the blood spill from where Triona lies slumped across the divan. The dark stain spreads fast, blooming across the fabric like ink in water.

A strangled cry rips from her throat. "Triona!"

Casey is at her side in an instant, pulling her into his arms. She doesn't resist—just clutches his shirt, her body trembling against his.

It doesn't take long for Saoirse to return, breathless and wide-eyed, clutching the supplies in her arms.

I turn my attention to Triona's wounds, hands working with a practiced steadiness as I clean every mark Colina left on her. She doesn't wake, but every so often, a faint tremor runs through her, a shallow breath hitching as though she can feel the pain even in unconsciousness.

It cuts through me like a blade to the bone, but I keep my face like stone, my hands steady. The field taught me how to mend wounds, how to steel myself against the surrounding horrors, but nothing prepared me for this. For the sight of Triona, lying motionless, her presence reduced to shallow breaths and fragile stillness.

Ellen pauses for a moment, her eyes catching on the necklace Triona wears—the pendant resting on the back of her neck, glinting in the dim light.

"Where... where did she get this?" she chokes out.

My throat tightens, but I answer. "I gave it to her for her birthday. I came upon it durin' my travels."

A flicker of recognition sparks in her eyes, something heavy with meaning. Her expression shifts, softening into an ache I hadn't expected. Then, as if something inside her shatters, she reaches for me, her fingers trembling. Awe and remorse cloud her gaze.

"Gods, I've been such a fool," she murmurs, voice breaking. "It's been ye this whole time."

I look at her in great bewilderment. "Ellen, what—what d'ye mean?"

She shakes her head, unable to look at me, her focus fixed solely on the pendant. Her fingers trace its edges, as though afraid to let go. "Finn... do ye even ken what this is?" Her voice wavers, thick with urgency.

"No, it just... called to me."

"Ye might have jus saved her, Finn." She swallows, her gaze floating between the necklace and my face. "This is more than just some trinket. It's a necklace of Manannán mac Lir."

Confusion knots in my chest, but Ellen presses on.

"Manannán is a protector, a guardian of realms. His magic is ancient, Finn—powerful enough to create barriers between worlds, between life and death itself. This necklace... it's imbued with his essence. It was crafted to shield the wearer from unseen forces, from dark intentions. And *ye* gave it to her."

Her fingers clutch mine for a moment, a fierce intensity in her grip. "I thought *I* was protectin' her all this time, but I was blind. And ye—ye've been the one watchin' over her."

I swallow hard, glancing from her to Triona's peaceful face, my confusion and dread mounting. "Ellen... what's happenin' here?"

Ellen doesn't answer. Instead, she takes Triona's hand, her grip fierce and unyielding, as if she can somehow take the pain away, somehow bear it for her. Silent tears spill down her cheeks, her lips parting to speak—but no words come.

Across the room, Eamon leans close to Saoirse, murmuring softly, piecing together what he can. Saoirse covers her mouth, horror flashing across her face as her wide eyes snap to Triona. Her voice, usually bold and untamed, cracks when she finally speaks.

"Who...who would do all of this?" she whispers, her words barely more than a breath.

I can't bring myself to answer. Not when I know that once I speak, I'll only add fuel to the fire already blazing within me.

Instead, I look around at each of them—Ellen, Casey, Saoirse, Eamon, Dealla—a family torn open by violence yet clinging to each other in its wake.

And then I look at her.

Wounded, fragile, still fighting even in unconsciousness.

Something inside me snaps. The fury roars louder, drowning out everything else, consuming every trace of hesitation.

Whoever planned this—whoever pulled the strings, whispered in Colina's ear, made her their pawn—*I will hunt them down*. I will drag them into the depths of their own darkness and make them choke on the suffering they inflicted.

And they will pay for it in full.

For every bruise. Every wound. Every breath they tried to steal from her.

I swear it to her in this room, a promise as unbreakable as the steel at my side. They will know what it means to have crossed her—crossed *us*—and I will not rest until they suffer for the agony forced upon her.

And if I fall along the way, if I must sacrifice everything to see justice done, then so be it.

I will *die* before I let them escape the wrath I've summoned—the vengeance that now surges through my veins like poison.

16

FAREWELL AND FURY

Finn

Bran and Callan make a sudden, forceful entrance into the room, and a deep churn of apprehension rises in my stomach before Bran even speaks.

"Colina went and alerted the authorities about the still," he says, breathless. "Before... well, before everything."

For a moment, there's a heartbeat of silence—then the room erupts. Shock and fury spill from every corner, voices overlapping in disbelief. They all know what this means. The still isn't just a way to make scotch; it's survival, defiance, the only thing keeping some families living on Sinclair land fed. And now the gaugers will come. Fines, prison—worse, perhaps.

"That's not all," Callan adds grimly, his voice slicing through the chaos. "She's the reason the whisky was tampered with."

I let out a sharp, bitter laugh. "Colina? She's not clever enough to pull that off on her own." Contempt drips from my words, and though no one openly agrees, no one rebukes me either.

Callan's jaw feathers. "Well... she didnae do it on her own." His voice is full of loathing. He exhales sharply, shaking his head. "She wouldnae say a name, but she said it was a high-ranking military officer. Offered her coin on top of it."

My fists clench, tight enough to shake. "What'd she sell us for?" I ask, though I already know.

I know this circles back to me.

Callan hesitates. His gaze flicks to Triona, then back to me. "They asked her to make sure Triona would be weak enough to go without a fight. And in return, they'd leave *ye* unharmed... so she could have *ye*."

A heavy silence spreads dragging an icy rage with it.

Saoirse breaks the silence, voice sharp and incredulous. "That mad feckin' eejit thought the Reds'd leave survivors behind—so she could ride 'em like trophies?"

Across the room, Bran and Casey scoff. "She's delusional," they say in unison.

Saoirse snarls. "Aye, I swear to the gods, I've never wanted to strangle the life outta someone so badly in all my days. I'd have wrung her neck like a bloody chicken and smiled while doin' it—"

Before she can spit another word, Eamon steps up behind her, wrapping his arms around her middle, anchoring her to the moment.

"Easy now, beag gráinneog," he mutters near her ear, his tone dry but fond. "She's not worth burstin' a vein over."

Delusion or not, Colina set things in motion that can't be undone. And some-one—someone *powerful*—is behind her.

Casey leans forward, jaw set. "If they think we're still in the dark, we have the element of surprise. We use that against 'em."

Callan shakes his head, his voice flat. "Casey... ye ken that's not how it works in the Highlands."

Casey exhales sharply, rubbing a hand over his face. "So what, then? We sit here with our heads up our arses and wait for them to come take everything from us? Or worse, take *us?*"

Callan's gaze darkens as he looks around the room, his voice heavy with something colder than anger. "Ye need to understand—this was never meant to be a fair fight. They planned for us to be gone, to leave the women defenceless, so when they came, there'd be no one to stop 'em."

Casey lets out a slow, irritated breath. "And yet, here we are. Not gone. Not out of the fight." His eyes flick around the room, landing on each of us, his voice steady now. "We know they're comin'. That's more than we had an hour ago. But either way...we fail?"

A heavy hush settles among us, heavy with the truth of it.

Bran speaks, his voice measured but laced with something precarious. "If law is on their side—that is, if we believe all that Colina has said, all that she's done—why hurt Triona? Why was it so important to get her alone? What did they think would stop them from taking her, regardless of injury?"

Too many bloody questions. Not enough answers.

My blood surges, hot with indignation. I push up from the divan so fast that Ellen gasps. "If she willnae talk to you, I'll force it out of her." The words come low, dark, shaking with the need to do something. To make someone pay for this.

My boots thud heavily against the floor as I stride toward the door. The room is a blur at the edges, my vision tunnelling, my mind fixed on one thing—Colina. I will *drag* the truth out of her if I have to.

"Stop!"

The single syllable cuts through the fury coursing through my mind.

I freeze, fingers curled around the doorframe, but Ellen's voice, raw and desperate, pierces through the rage clawing at my ribs.

Slowly, I turn.

She stands rigid, eyes locked onto me, chest rising and falling too fast. But it's not anger on her face. It's *pain*.

"Finn..." Her voice wavers, but her resolve doesn't. "That isnae *ye*. Ye dinnae hurt people. Especially not women."

The anger is still burning, still demanding release. "Ellen—"

"Nae." She steps forward before I can argue, her eyes fierce, her voice steady. "What's done is done. What happens next is crucial to all of ye survivin' this night."

Her words press against my ribs, heavier than my fury, heavier than the betrayal choking the air in this room. The others are waiting, watching, to see if I'll push back, if I'll let this anger consume me.

The heat of my fury hasn't faded, but it's trapped beneath the sharp edge of her gaze, pinning me in place.

Before the tension can fully settle, a side door into the sitting room swings open.

James steps in first, moving with a quiet, deliberate stillness that makes the hairs on my arms prickle. Alex is close behind him, his presence a storm barely contained.

His gaze sweeps over the room, sharp and assessing, lingering on every face until it lands on Triona. The sight of her—broken, fragile, wounded—stops him cold.

His boots echo against the floorboards as he crosses to her in a rush. And then the unthinkable happens.

A sob so rare and powerful escapes him. It turns the air into glass.

A man I've never seen shed a tear crumples to his knees beside her, trembling as he gathers her hand in his own. His shoulders quake, but still he holds on, as if his touch alone might keep her tethered to this world.

"Ellen," he chokes out. She moves to his side, her own face a mask of grief. He meets her eyes, and the years of love, pain, and shared battles speak in silence. He presses a kiss to her forehead, their foreheads meeting in a shared moment of sorrow and strength.

The tears vanish as if scorched away. A darkness settles over him, not of grief, but of purpose, forged like iron in the fire. His jaw locks, and his eyes blaze with a fury that no one dares to challenge.

We watch as a husband, father, warrior, rises from the ground. More determined than ever.

"There's something we've kept from ye all. About Triona. About what's coming. But there's no more hidin' it now."

Ellen hesitates, glancing at James, who gives her a small nod. "Some years past, we received confidential information from one now departed—a secret concerning our sweet lass. She's long since been tied to a prophecy. One we've been guardin' against for years. And tonight..."

She swallows hard, then looks at each of us. "Tonight, evil comes, as it was foretold."

"What's the prophecy?" I ask, my voice rougher than I meant it to be.

"It's a warnin'. And a truth," James intones.

Ellen steps forward, closing her eyes for a moment before beginning her recitation. Each word falls slowly and deliberately from her lips, as though the phrase is indelibly inscribed into her memory.

In whispering woods where shadows play, a life unfolds with grief's first day.
Some souls in solemn vigil bend, their knees to ground, their wills to mend.
Nineteen moons shall orbit bright, 'round the sun's commanding light.
Death will come within a day, the sacrifice will cause dismay.
In secret, treachery begins to rise, charting out her fate's surprise.
Along the path, she'll find one soul, its love, a weight, a heavy toll.
In every beat, their souls combined, a tapestry of stars designed.
Once contact graces trio's sight, inner strength unchains with might.
Called by powers, true and bold, she journeys forth to claim her hold.
Upon the sacred ground, she'll stand, with fate's dark price in trembling hand.

My chest tightens. "What the hell is that supposed to mean?"

Ellen clasps her hands tighter in front of her, guilt flickering across her face. James exhales heavily, rubbing a hand over his jaw before he finally speaks.

"It means we should've seen this comin'." His voice is rough, edged with something bitter—something that sounds a lot like regret. "We kent, as Triona's nineteenth year came, that the clock was tickin' toward this moment. Toward whatever was meant to happen."

Ellen nods, her voice quieter, but just as heavy. "We dinnae have all the answers, which is why ye must go away. Alex will lead the way. But the prophecy speaks of a chosen soul who bears both a great gift and a terrible burden. A force that can either unite or destroy. She's always been special."

James meets my glare, his own expression carved from stone. "We thought we had more time." His gaze flickers to Triona, pale and unmoving, then back to me. "We were wrong."

James continues. "But dinnae think for a second we've done nothin'. There's reason she was trained as a warrior when others were raised as daughters of the hearth, learnin' to mend and weave. It wasna just for survival, but because we kent—one day—she'd have to fight. Not jus for herself, but for all of us. And her strength is growin'. Callan *felt* it himself."

I shake my head, disbelief surging through me. "But why not tell us? Why wait until now?"

James's face hardens. "Because no parent wants to burden their child with something like this. But the signs are here now, and we cannae shield her anymore. Evil moves, and it's searchin' for her."

Just then, there's a knock at the door. A sharp, deliberate sound. I move swiftly to pull it open, primed to pummel whoever stands on the other side.

Marcus appears in the doorway—disheveled, breathless, wild-eyed. He staggers forward, barely catching himself against the doorframe.

"I came as quickly as I could," Marcus says, his voice strained, though his gaze remains sharp. "I heard a few men speaking of clearances at the Prentiss Street Club... when I heard your family name, I headed straight here. They are not far now. Well, they will be here by nightfall. At the latest."

James straightens, his face hardening. "So, they plan to take our home under the guise of a '*clearance*'?"

Marcus steps forward. His gaze locks with James's, his resolve unshakable. "I shall remain here to reason with them. I can aid in your defense."

"Why do that?" James asks, his voice edged with incredulity. "This isnae yer fight, lad."

"Despite what some of you may suppose," Marcus counters, looking Callan's way, his voice steady and low. "I hold your daughter in the highest regard. I care deeply for her. They are not here to forge alliances or negotiate a truce—they come with nothing less than murderous intent. They are out for blood. I beg you, allow Triona the chance to escape, and permit me to offer aid."

Callan speaks up. "What? Ye think because ye're a filthy Englishman, they'll look the other way?" No one corrects him. No one speaks up to defend Marcus, because we're all feeling the same thing.

Distrust. Agony. Betrayal.

Marcus remains impassive in the wake of Callan's jab. In a measured tone, he replies, "I believe, given my... cultural background, that I can help. I can pull what strings I have and assist." He then turns his earnest gaze to James. "I will do whatever I can to keep her safe. To keep those she loves most safe. Let me try. Please."

James hesitates, his jaw working as he considers Marcus's words, and the intention. Finally, he exhales, his voice heavy with resignation, and he nods.

Marcus fixes his gaze on each of us. "You all have to leave... now."

"Aye", James says. "Ye'll take the wagon with what's left of the scotch, and ye'll be tradin' it for safe passage."

Across the room, Bran speaks up, brow furrowed. "Safe passage to where, exactly?"

Alex turns to him, his expression unreadable but resolute. "We're going to Portugal."

Casey's voice cuts through the quiet. "That's no fair trade, Da."

"Yer lives are worth more than what's in those barrels," James replies, his tone firm but thick with feeling.

A long silence stretches between us—grief, resistance, and reluctant understanding hanging in the air.

Then Ellen speaks, her voice soft but certain. "Triona would fight us if she could." Her hand trembles as it brushes over her cheek. "But this is the way it must be."

James nods slowly, his throat bobbing as he swallows hard. "This way... she willnae have the chance to argue."

I break my silence, my voice raw with desperation. "There's got to be another way. You shouldna bear this alone. Let me stay—"

James cuts me off with a firm shake of his head. "Yer job is to protect *her* now. Keep her safe, lad. That's what we're askin'. You owe us that much."

I glance to Callan, desperate. "Cal, tell them. We could help—"

"And what, Finn?" Callan snaps, his jaw tight. "We dinnae ken who or what's comin'. And as of now... every single one of us is a marked enemy. She spared no one in her attempt to harm Triona."

Alex steps forward, his expression grim. "I'd wager my tavern's already their first stop."

Ellen leans down, pressing a kiss to Triona's forehead. "Be strong, mo nighean bheag. Stronger than I ken ye can be."

James hesitates, his fingers briefly threading through Triona's hair—a fleeting touch, soft and reverent—before he straightens, his expression hardening like forged steel. His voice is firm, leaving no room for argument.

"Take her. Get her as far from here as possible. And dinnae look back."

He turns to Alex, eyes locking with unwavering trust. "Ye ken the route. Take them to Port Oban. Our allies there will see them safely to Lisbon. That's the path laid before ye—follow it, no matter what."

Alex steps forward, and without hesitation, the two men clasp forearms in the kind of steadfast grip that speaks of trust and respect. A warrior's promise. A brother's oath.

"I'll see them through," Alex says, his voice ironclad. "Every one of them. I swear it on my life."

James holds his grip for a beat longer, his jaw tightening as if committing the words to something deeper than memory. Then, with a sharp nod, he releases Alex's arm. "Good man."

Ellen pulls me aside, her hands clutching mine tightly, her eyes searching my face. "Finn, listen to me," she says, her voice low and urgent. "Triona has a long road ahead. A dangerous one. She cannae afford any chinks in her armour. What we're askin' of ye... it's no small thing. It's *everything*."

"I'll keep her safe," I say, though the weight of her words press hard on my chest. "Ye have my oath."

Ellen nods, her expression serious. "I ken ye will. That's why this falls to ye. Ye have to be her strength. Her shield. No weaknesses, Finn. None. It's more than protection, lad. It's about... it's about seein' her through this. Standin' by her when she needs ye most."

I swallow, the meaning settling like a stone in my gut. No *distractions*. Human or otherwise.

"What's comin', Ellen?"

She shakes her head. "This is as far as we get, Finn. This was always meant to be."

Her gaze holds mine, unyielding, and for a moment, something in her expression twists that I can't quite name. A pang of hope, chased swiftly by sorrow. Resignation. Or... something more.

Does she know? About what I feel? About what I've been trying so hard to bury?

Ellen exhales softly, the kind of breath that carries lifetimes. Her hand finds my arm, squeezing once.

"I trust ye'll do what's right," she says, voice thick with meaning. "What's best for her?"

My throat locks up. I should say something—anything—but the words won't come. I nod instead, hoping it's enough.

Ellen's words claw at my thoughts, but duty anchors me.

Protect Triona.

It's as natural to me as drawing breath, as ingrained in me as my own name. Whatever I feel, whatever I've longed for, it counts for naught.

I'll be her strength, her shield, her blade, her keeper in the dark. But never her weakness.

Ellen and I sit in vigil beside Triona while, throughout the entire house, the others are bustling to gather what little they can in order to leave. Her hand absently strokes Triona's dark hair.

Within the hour, they've loaded what we can carry. Our four horses—Aisling, Shadow, Casey's horse Iona, and Callan's horse Meara—sturdy creatures whose hearty spirits mirror our own, stand ready to bear us to our destination within the narrow window we have to secure safe passage. We exchange silent glances, each look heavy with trepidation and an unwavering determination.

Shadow's eyes dart anxiously, but the moment Triona comes into view, he settles, as if sensing the purpose behind the simple cart to which he's yoked. The intent is unmistakable—Triona won't be able to sit upright for days, perhaps even weeks. This journey promises to be a torment to her body.

"Finn, we'll need ye to keep her in the saddle until we reach safer ground," Casey declares in a firm tone. I nod without hesitation.

James carefully lifts her limp form into my arms, adjusting her gently as she moans softly in protest. His movements are deliberate, as though the weight of her is more than he can bear—not because of size, but of what she represents. His eyes burn with determination even as unshed tears shimmer against their edges.

Nearby, Casey and Callan stand with Ellen. Ellen, as resolute as ever, cups each of their faces in a touch that is both tender and commanding. Callan's expression remains impassive, his jaw set as though steeling himself against the inevitable storm. Meanwhile, Casey, who wears his heart on his sleeve, appears mournful, his lips drawn tight as he struggles to hold back words that threaten to spill forth.

Despite the differences in their outward reactions, the shared burden of fear—fear of the unknown, of what lies ahead, and the possibility that this may be the last moment they stand together as a family—is unmistakable.

"There will be things on this journey," James begins, each word deliberately spoken, "that defy all earthly explanation. Many things will not be as they seem."

He continues, "Ye'll face obstacles that test ye in ways we cannae explain. But never lose sight of one another—if ye allow fear to divide ye—then whatever lies ahead will win."

This moment, this goodbye, isn't one of parting but of transformation. We are not merely leaving behind a home or a family; we are abandoning everything familiar, stepping into a realm where the rules we have always known no longer hold sway.

Ahead of us lie endless stretches of rugged terrain. Mountains loom ominously in their grandeur, rivers running swift and icy cold, while forests abound with unknown dangers lurking behind every tree's shadow.

Our hearts grow heavy as we stand on the threshold of this journey—a passage we never sought and for which we feel woefully unprepared.

Dealla's trembling voice cuts through the tension. "What's to fall upon my family?" Her hands clutch the folds of her dress, as though she were gathering the very threads of her courage to hold herself together.

Alex's expression is hardened by the weight of leadership. "I can't guarantee their safety, my dear. For that, I am sorry, but we won't have time to go back. No time to warn anyone, no time to change what's already in motion." His words land like stones, and it's Casey and Bran who step forward to steady her.

They share a look, a silent conversation passing between them.

Casey wraps a steady arm around Dealla's shoulders, and she leans into him, her tension easing, if only slightly.

With her free hand, she reaches for Bran. Their fingers find each other without hesitation, locking in a quiet clasp.

His grip is firm, grounding. His gaze meets hers, and in it is an unspoken promise—strength, steadiness, and something that feels a little like hope.

"I'll take these three and the whisky ahead," Alex says, gesturing to Saorise, Eamon, and Dealla. "We need to remain separated so as not to draw attention."

"The two of ye will have to share a horse," Callan declares, addressing Casey and Bran. They exchange a look—a silent acknowledgment of the arrangement.

Bran speaks up, "I don't mind riding with Casey; this one time." His playful smirk, however, belies the turbulent feelings he hides beneath the facade.

Alex casts a steady glance at his son. "Bran, we meet in eight days' time at Port Oban."

Then he turns his gaze toward me. "I assume, given your training alongside Bran, you can tend to a wound?" I nod in acknowledgement.

"Good, that one will need constant care. Keep it clean. Keep it bound."

Nearby, Casey and Dealla exchange a long embrace. He whispers something I can't make out, then presses a quick kiss to her hair. Whatever words pass between them seem to bring her comfort, though her face is still sorrowful when they pull apart.

Then, each of them mounts atop a horse and disappears down a hidden back road. The rhythmic thud of hooves fade into the night. Silence follows, pressing down with the weight of all that has been lost—and all that is yet to come.

James and Ellen stand before us, their expressions grave. James's hand rests on Ellen's shoulder as she speaks. "Much will unfold on yer journey. Keep an open mind, all of ye. What lies ahead...face it together."

She doesn't need to ask for our promise. We already know. A shared look passes between us, unspoken yet absolute. There is no other way forward but together.

There's a faint glow in the distance, flickering unnaturally, and James's eyes narrow. Ellen's voice grows urgent. "Go. Ye need to leave."

Without another word, they turn and run back toward the house, their figures disappearing into the growing darkness. We linger, hidden in the shadows, unwilling to part. Not yet. Not when every instinct screams that this moment, this place—it's a fleeting breath before the tide of fate sweeps us forward.

Our breaths are shallow, our hearts pounding, but it's more than fear keeping us rooted—it's the gnawing knowledge that this is the last time we will stand here as we are. Once we leave, there is no coming back.

"They're here," Casey says.

A low murmur ripples through the approaching group before a commanding voice cuts through the night.

"Search the property," one barks, his tone slicing through the uneasy hush like a blade drawn from its sheath. "We bring in everyone the filthy bog rat mentioned."

Another man snorts. "Are you still planning to pay her the twenty shillings agreed upon?"

The first man laughs, a low, cruel sound that cuts through the tension. "Not in the slightest. Far as I'm concerned, she did exactly what's expected of a dirty Scot. She just didn't realise she'd sell out this family for nothing."

The second man laughs sinisterly. "What exactly does Sirr want us to do?"

"He said to have them all out here waiting when he arrives."

Minutes stretch into eternity as the men ransack the house. The crack of breaking furniture punctuates the night, followed by the distant clang of metal and the sharp sound of something heavy striking the floor. Shadows shift behind the broken glass of the windows. We hear shouts and the faint sounds of a scuffle.

It's torture watching from this position, unable to help, unable to do anything but listen as our world is torn apart piece by piece.

Then, they emerge—dragging James first. Blood drips from his face, his clothes torn and his gait unsteady. Yet his eyes are fierce, unbroken.

Behind him, Ellen stumbles, a fistful of her hair wrapped in the man's hand pulling her forward. Lip split, blood trailing down her chin, but she holds her head high.

Casey shifts beside me, a quiet gasp escaping his throat. Before he can make another sound, Bran hisses in his ear. "Don't, Casey. You'll give us away."

Callan's sharp gaze locks on the figures emerging from the darkness. His knuckles whiten around the hilt of his blade, but he doesn't move.

Two figures haul Marcus into view, his battered face streaked with blood and his body sagging lifelessly. They toss him to the ground in front of James and Ellen without a shred of care.

"So much for his damned help," Callan growls, his voice like gravel, thick with barely restrained fury. "He stayed behind, swore he'd buy us time, make a difference. And yet here he is—bloodied, beaten, and thrown at their feet like a useless scrap."

Hooves thunder in the distance, and a new group of riders arrives. At their head is a man whose presence seems to draw the warmth from the wind itself. He dismounts in one fluid motion. His boots, polished black leather, are sturdy but finely crafted. They're not the scuffed footwear of a common soldier—they speak of wealth and power, a reminder that he is not like the men he commands.

His long coat billows slightly in the wind, a dark woolen garment with reinforced shoulders. The fabric is well-fitted but functional, its deep black colour blending into the night. The high collar, turned up against the night, frames a face carved in sharp, angular lines.

His hat—a broad-brimmed, dark felt affair—sits low over his brow, casting his face in shadow. He lifts it, revealing sharp, calculating eyes that glint like steel in the torchlight. His presence radiates control and menace, a man who orchestrates violence not for the thrill, but for the cold efficiency of achieving his goals.

The man stops in front of James, his tone coiled in mock curiosity.

"Where is she?" he asks, his tone cold and sharp.

"Henry Charles Sirr," James says. "Fancy seein' ye after all these years." He meets Sirr's gaze without flinching. "I dinnae ken who ye mean."

A ripple of shock grips me, and my gaze snaps to Callan and Casey. Their eyes mirror my disbelief, their subtle shakes of the head confirming what I already suspect—they know nothing of this. Nothing of James's past with this man. And yet, here it is, unfolding before us like the turning of a hidden page in a story we were never meant to read.

Two men emerge from the house, shaking their heads. "The place is empty. Whoever was here didn't leave long ago. The house is in disarray, and it's still got a bit of warmth to it," one says.

Sirr's eyes narrow as he steps closer to James. "So, you were warned, I presume?"

James says nothing, his silence a wall Sirr cannot breach.

Sirr's gaze shifts to Marcus, lying in a crumpled heap. A cruel smirk plays on his lips. "The poor fool was so desperate to fuck the girl that he threw away his future without a second thought. How tragically predictable." He clicks his tongue, almost amused. "His father will be *thrilled* to hear about it—when he arrives to collect what's left of his disgrace of a son."

"How the hell did they know about Triona?" Bran questions rhetorically. We all exchange glances, unsure what the hell is happening.

James's head tilts slightly toward where we hide, his gaze sweeping the darkness—too precise, too knowing. It shouldn't be possible for him to see us, but the way his eyes pause, the way they seem to linger just a moment too long, sends a shiver down my spine.

Is it instinct? A final, desperate hope we aren't there?

My body feels paralyzed, my feet rooted to the ground, refusing to obey the silent command in his stare.

Sirr slowly unsheathes his blade. The metal catches the flickering torchlight, its edge glinting with deadly purpose. Time feels as though it slows, each breath drawn shallow and quiet.

"What a pretty pity," he murmurs, voice like silk drawn over steel. "All that fire, wasted on what's already mine to take."

Then, in a flash, the tension shatters. Sirr moves with brutal precision, his blade cutting through the air. James doesn't flinch, doesn't struggle—he meets his fate with a quiet, unwavering defiance, his eyes burning with the last embers of resistance—a last act of rebellion that sears itself into my memory like a brand.

A spray of crimson, stark and vivid, is followed by the sickening sound of air escaping from James' severed throat.

He falls forward, his hand instinctively reaching for his neck, but it's futile. Blood pours from the wound, pooling beneath him as he falls forward, his body crumpling in a lifeless heap.

Stop*!*

The word claws at the back of my throat, desperate to escape, but I bite it down, my fists clenched so tightly they tremble. Callan grips his blade, his whole body taut like a coiled spring, ready to explode.

Ellen's scream cuts through the night, raw and anguished, a sound that doesn't just echo—it scars. She lunges toward her husband's fallen form, but the man holding her yanks her back by her hair, forcing her to her knees.

"Ellen Sinclair," Sirr muses coldly, as if savouring the moment. He takes a step toward her, the blade dripping with James' blood. "You've always had a firm voice. Let's hear it now."

Her sobs turn into a feral growl as she struggles against her captor. "Ye bastard," she spits. "Ye'll *rot* for this."

Sirr smirks, tilting his head like a predator toying with its prey. "Perhaps. But not tonight."

With a single, ruthless motion, he drives the blade through the side of her neck. The sound is sickening—a wet, gasping slice that cuts through the hush like a shriek. Blood spills in a violent arc, catching the firelight as it splashes across the ground and Sirr's boots.

Ellen crumples beside James, her knees giving way as her outstretched hand just barely grazes his. Her lips part, as if to speak—to call out to him one last time—but no words come. Only a shallow, shuddering breath.

Her body trembles once... then goes still. Her lifeblood seeps out, mingling with his until it's indistinguishable.

Two lives. One final act of defiance. One cruel silence.

The world feels as if it's spinning. Casey makes a sound—a choked, animalistic cry—but Bran clamps a hand over his mouth, pulling him back into the shadows. "Steady," Bran hisses, his voice barely a whisper. Tears streak Casey's face, and for the first time, I see Bran's resolve start to tremble as he holds him.

Tears burn in my eyes, but I force myself to look away... and my eyes find Callan, who looks absolutely distraught with grief.

Sirr wipes the blade against a cloth, the motion casual, as though slitting the throats of James and Ellen Sinclair meant nothing to him. Torchlight flickers against the blood pooling at his boots, staining the ground beneath him.

"Burn the castle down. They resisted our attempt to clear them from the home, leaving us no choice but to engage. That's what started this, right, men?" They all laugh in unison, the sound sickening.

"Do what you will with their corpses... but no fucking the dead, gentlemen. I have to draw the line somewhere." Disgust churns violently as they speak about two of the kindest humans, as if their lives meant nothing.

"This is it," I whisper, my voice barely audible. "We have to leave, Cal." I steer Shadow quietly over to him, to shake him out of the daze he's in. He's trembling, grief barely contained. He looks over at me, sheer panic in his eyes.

Shadow shifts beneath me, sensing the urgency, but Callan remains rooted to the spot, his eyes shifting back to the lifeless forms of James and Ellen. The glow of the torches reflects in his eyes.

"Cal," I urge, my voice barely audible. "We have to go. Now." For a moment, I worry he won't move, that he'll charge out there and get himself killed, but then something shifts. He shuts his eyes tightly, his body trembling as he struggles to compose himself.

"We're leaving 'em like they mean nothin'," he whispers hoarsely, his voice cracking.

"We have no other choice," I say, my throat tight with grief as I gesture toward Triona. "For her—for all of us."

When he opens his eyes again, the fury and anguish is still there, but a flicker of willpower has returned. He nods, a single curt motion, and grips the reins of his horse.

"We ride," I whisper, meeting Bran's gaze, barely audible over the sound of my pounding heart.

Behind us, Sirr's voice rings out, sharp and commanding. "Leave nothing standing!" The faint echoes of Sirr's men shouting carry through the night as we slip into the darkness, silent shadows swallowed by the wilderness. The images of James and Ellen—broken, lifeless, and betrayed—are forever burned into my mind.

The reality of our situation sinks heavily into my chest, pressing against my heart with unrelenting force. We're on the run—venturing forth into the unknown, armed with only our fragile resolve.

Flames rise as we slip into the darkness, our bodies moving but our souls left behind, watching the only world we knew turn to ash.

And when Triona wakes... we will have to relive this all over again.

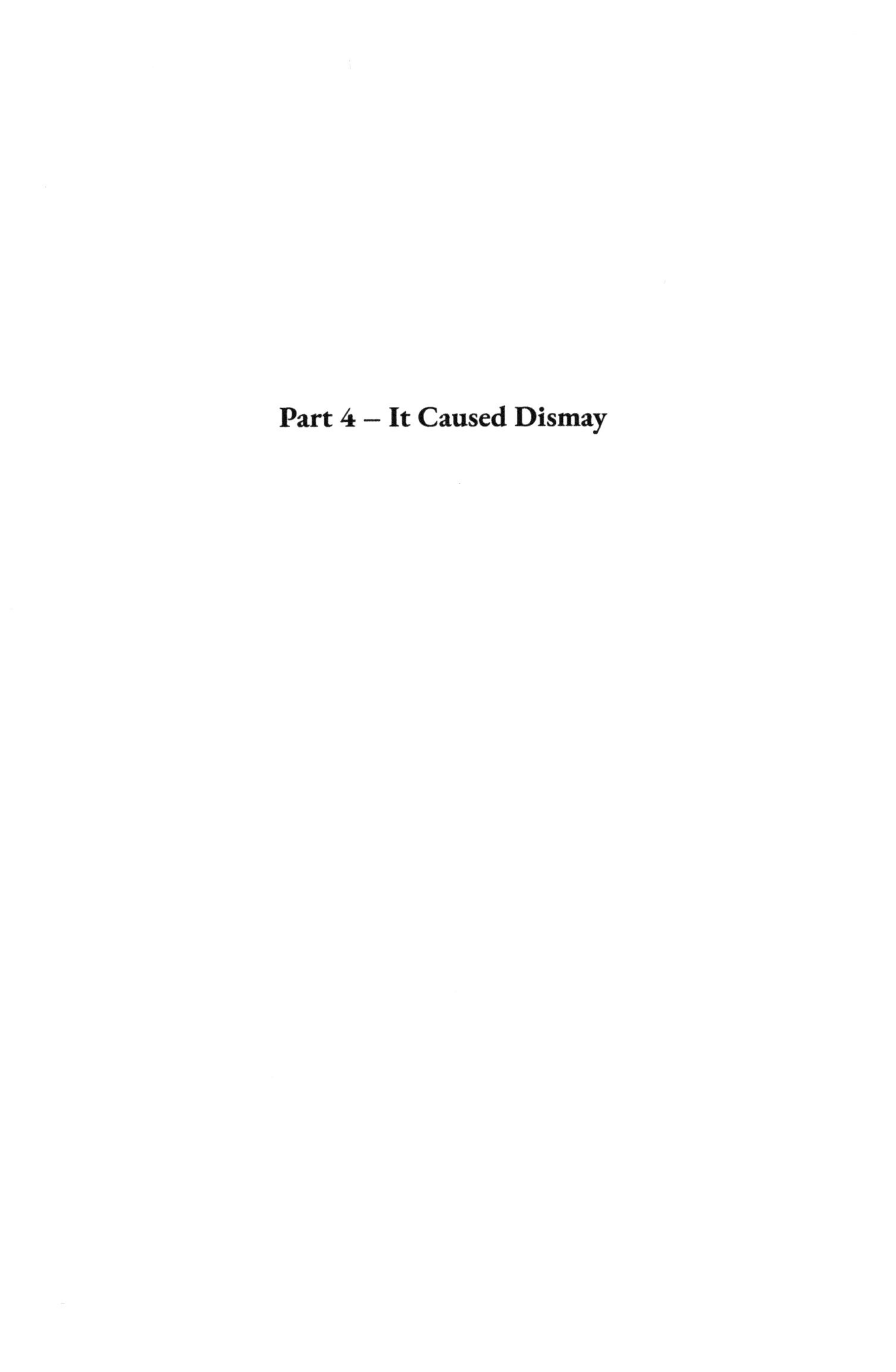

Part 4 – It Caused Dismay

17

THE ROAD OF SILENT FOOTFALLS

Finn

Hours after the Attack

We travel in silence with the cloud of death hanging over us. The steady clop of hooves on the dirt road and Casey's muffled cries are the only sound in the cold, empty night. The weight of grief hangs heavy in the air.

Callan rides ahead, his jaw tight and his hand gripping the reins as though they are the only thing keeping him anchored.

Bran is the first to break the silence, his voice unusually subdued. "This doesn't feel real," he mutters. "None of it does."

Casey, riding with him, keeps his gaze down. His voice trembles as he speaks. "I think…" He hesitates, then swallows hard. "I think they saw their end comin'."

I snap my head toward him, brows knitting together. "What are you talkin' about, Casey?"

"What Ma said," Casey states, his voice firmer now. "'*Nineteen moons shall orbit bright, 'round the sun's commanding light. Death will come within a day, the sacrifice will cause dismay.*' Triona turned nineteen yesterday... and now..."

A bitter taste rises in the back of my throat.

"Ma... the way she hugged me before we left. The things Da said. As if they were sayin' goodbye, and they'd made peace with it." Casey says.

"They knew, and they didnae say a bloody word. Why?" I ask.

Callan pulls his horse to a halt and turns to glare at us, his eyes cold and fierce, as if he can will us all into silence. "Enough." His voice is sharp, a blade slicing through the tension. "They kent, aye. So what? Does it change what's done?"

"It changes *everything*," Casey snaps back. His reins shake in his hands. "Why not warn us? Why not tell us what was comin'?"

"They have to have had good reason," Bran says quietly, his voice carrying a weight I'm not used to hearing from him. "They didn't want you going into this carrying their burden. They carried it alone."

Casey scoffs, wiping angrily at his face. "And now they're dead, and we're homeless, clueless, and just aimlessly followin' the vague directions given in the heat of the moment. On a road we can barely see with orders so rushed they might as well have been spoken by the wind. Fat lot of good that did in the end. How does not havin' a clue what to do help honour their memory? How can their deaths mean something?"

I tighten my grip on the reins, the leather biting into my palms. He isn't wrong. We are lost in every sense of the word, floundering in the dark with nothing but fragments of warnings and riddles to guide us.

"They trusted us," I say, my voice low, steady. I meet Casey's glare, refusing to look away. "Whatever reason they had, whatever they knew, they trusted us to figure it out. To protect her. To stop this madness."

"And we will," Brans says, his voice rough, the fire in his tone as sharp as steel. "But this,"—he gestures to the lot of us—"this blaming and doubt... it ends here. So much has been lost already. We have a purpose, and we see that through with the information we *do* have."

Casey sobers a bit, his shoulders sagging as he exhales slowly. He gives a small, wary nod, his gaze fixed on the ground.

Bran shifts in the saddle they share, leaning closer to Casey. He places a steady hand on Casey's shoulder, giving it a compassionate squeeze. "I know I've not known your family long like I have Finn, but I've got you. *We've* got each other," he says smoothly, his usual smirk replaced by a rare earnestness. "No one is alone in this."

The road stretches out ahead of us, dark and uncertain, but there is no turning back, and it's best we all face that.

"We keep ridin'," I say. "And maybe now, we can truly empathise and feel the despair James and Ellen did when they were told a child of theirs would one day have to face such hardship. We'll do what they did, and bear it... and choose to fight for her, anyway."

Triona
Saturday, 3 May 1823
Somewhere in the Scottish Highlands

The first thing I notice is the warmth. Soft sunlight filters through the canvas above me, casting golden streaks across the pale fabric. The air smells of fresh grass and earth, mingled with something faintly medicinal. My eyelids feel impossibly heavy, but I force them open, squinting against the dappled light.

A tent. I'm in a tent.

Confusion swirls in my chest as my eyes adjust. The sunlight glints off something metallic nearby—a basin, perhaps. Slowly, I turn my head, wincing as pain lances through my skull, spreading like ripples in water. My body feels heavy, pinned down by an invisible weight. I groan, the sound faint and unrecognisable in my own ears.

"Triona?"

A voice cuts through the haze. Familiar. Grounding. It tugs at me, pulling me back from the abyss. I blink against the light, my lashes damp with tears I don't remember crying. Slowly, the blurry edges of a face comes into focus.

"Casey?" My voice cracks, dry and raw. I blink again, harder this time, forcing the world to sharpen. His face hovers above mine, his usually mischievous features drawn tight with worry. His lips press into a thin line, and his eyes—hazel like our mother's—are red-rimmed and glistening.

"Thank the gods," he breathes, his hand gripping mine so tightly it almost hurts. "I thought—" He stops, shaking his head, his throat bobbing as he swallows whatever words he can't say.

My head throbs, memories swimming just out of reach. "What... happened?" My voice feels foreign, weak. "Where... where are we?"

I try to push myself up, but the sudden rush of dizziness and a searing pain in my back knocks me down. I let out a string of pained moans and curses.

Casey's hand flies to my shoulder, steadying me.

"Dinnae move yet," he says quickly, his tone gentle but firm. "Ye're hurt, Triona. You need to rest."

Rest?

The word feels wrong. Foreign. Like it doesn't belong. Shadows flit through my mind—screams, fire, chaos. My heart begins to race, pounding a frantic rhythm against my ribcage.

"Casey," I whisper, my voice trembling now. "What happened to me?"

"Colina... she whipped ye." He shifts uncomfortably, glancing around as if unsure how much to reveal. "Ye've been in and out of sleep for some time."

"Is it bad?"

"I dinnae ken. After Finn cleaned it—"

"Where is he?"

"Him, Callan, and Bran went to wash up in the creek."

"Why are we in the woods?"

Casey's discomfort grows. His fingers twitch against mine.

Before he can answer, a sound outside draws my attention. The tent's canvas rustles, and Bran's head appears. His eyes widen when he sees me.

He whistles, the noise sending a fresh wave of pain lancing through my head.

I flinch further at the sound of hurried footsteps approaching the tent. Casey's grip on my hand tightens as Bran steps aside to let them in. Finn's tall frame ducks through the opening first, his face set in a hard line. Callan follows, his eyes raking over me with a concern so intense I can hardly breathe.

"Triona," Callan says softly, his voice carrying the weight of concern. He crouches beside me, his broad shoulders blocking some of the light streaming through the canvas. "How are ye feelin'?"

I blink at him, my lips parting to respond, but I don't know what to say. How am I feeling? Pain ripples through me with every breath, but that's not what he's asking. There's something else in his gaze—something deeper. A growing sense of unease gnaws at the edges of my mind.

"I'm dizzy," I say, my voice barely above a whisper. "But I'm confused. You're all scaring me."

Finn and Callan exchange a glance, their silence only amplifying the tension. Casey shifts uncomfortably beside me.

Callan clears his throat—his usual gruff demeanour softens. His movements are slow, deliberate, as if he's approaching a wounded animal. "Ye've been through a lot, lass. Like Casey said, ye need to rest."

Rest.

That word again.

I shake my head, and pain pulses sharp behind my eyes. "I need to know what's going on. Why are we in the woods? Where is everyone else?"

The question hangs in the air, with a suffocating presence. No one answers.

Finn looks away, jaw clenched so tight I can see the muscle feather. Callan sits tight-lipped. Casey lowers his gaze, his fingers fidgeting with the edge of the blanket draped over me.

"Someone answer me," I demand, my voice cracking under the weight of my rising panic. "What happened? Why are we here?"

Bran, still lingering near the tent's entrance, shifts his weight, his usual humour absent. "It's... it's not something easy to explain, Triona," he says cautiously.

"Try," I snap, the sharpness of my tone surprising even myself. "Because I can't remember anything after—after Colina..."

My voice falters, my mind catching on the fractured memory. The whip. The blinding pain. Then... nothing.

Callan reaches for my hand, his touch gentle but firm. "Triona," he begins, his voice low and steady. "Ye need to stay calm."

"Calm?" I repeat incredulously. "How am I supposed to stay calm when none of you will tell me what's happening?"

"Right now, ye need to listen to us, and ye need to focus on healin'." Callan says bluntly, his deep voice cutting through the tension like a blade.

The finality in his tone sends a chill through me. My head aches as a thousand possibilities flood my mind, each more terrible than the last.

"Stop," I whisper, shaking my head. "I need to know. Please."

Casey leans in, his voice low and tight. "There was a fire," he says. "The house... it's gone, Triona."

"What caused the fire? Are we outside because—"

Casey places a hand on my shoulder, halting my racing thoughts.

He stiffens as I reach up to grab his hand, a move I regret immediately as it causes the muscles in my back to move in a way that has pain radiating in all directions.

I scream out in pain, and Casey jumps back.

In an instant, Finn and Bran are both at my side.

Finn cups my face. "Triona, I need to look at yer wounds. We have more laudanum for pain," he says, gesturing to Bran. "It won't taste good going down, but it'll help you sleep and ye'll heal better if ye're not movin'."

"Stop!" I shout.

"Finn," I say, panic rising. "Please. Tell me. You're *scaring* me." I stare into his golden-brown eyes long enough to see an unbearable pain in their depths.

Bran hands Finn a cup with liquid in it. "Drink this, and we'll tell you," he says with a finality unusual for Bran.

I do as I'm asked.

"They protected us, Triona." Casey's voice cracks when he speaks after I've consumed every drop of the foul liquid. "They protected *ye*. Da—he fought to keep us safe. Ma... she—" His voice breaks completely, and he closes his eyes, as if the memory alone is too much to bear. "They didnae make it."

Through my still clouded memory, I attempt to process what they're saying.

The realisation of what he's suggesting drops like a stone into a deep, dark well. I stare at Casey, his eyes misty, at Callan who's body is tense, and then at Finn and Bran, who both avoid my gaze as though my eyes might burn them. The silence presses against me, thick and suffocating, and my mind struggles to pull the pieces together.

"No," I murmur, my voice raw, barely more than a breath. "That's not—" The words crumble as my throat tightens, and I shake my head, vision blurring with tears.

"You're lying." The denial scrapes against my ribs, desperate, trembling. "They can't be gone. They can't."

"They saved us, Triona," Finn says softly, his brogue roughened by emotion.

My chest tightens painfully, as if the very act of breathing might break me. "No," I whisper again, my voice trembling. "No, no, no." My head shakes violently. A sob wrenches free from my throat, raw and ugly. I try to push them all away, to sit up, to do something—anything—but my body refuses to obey. Nothing compares to this storm raging inside me.

Casey takes me into his chest as gently as he can manage.

"Let me go!" I cry, though my arms cling to him in desperation. "This can't be real. Casey, it can't—"

"I'm sorry," he whispers, his voice thick with grief. "I'm so sorry, Triona."

The memories resurface, disjointed and painful. My father's tears, a rare and shattering sight, falling onto my cheeks. My mother's hands trembling as they cup mine, her voice steady despite the quiver in her breath. The sound of shuffling feet, of hurried whispers and suppressed sobs. The clatter of horses' hooves fading into the distance.

It's all too much. Too much to hold, too much to bear. My chest is near bursting, my sobs wracking through me until I feel as if I might splinter into pieces.

I cling to Casey as though he's the only thing tethering me to the earth, and he holds me like I'm something precious, something fragile that might shatter if he lets go. His tears drip steadily, soaking into my hair, and the quiet sound of his grief reverberates in his chest. I clutch at him, desperate for his strength, his presence, his reassurance that some part of this world—of my world—remains intact.

My breaths come slower, weaker, as if the effort to stay awake is more than I can bear. The laudanum's grip pulls at me, its weight like a tide dragging me under. My eyelids grow heavy, my body slackens, but I fight it for just a little longer.

"Ma used to hum to us," I say, my words thick and clumsy. "When we were sick... do you remember Casey?"

His body tenses, and I feel the hitch in his breath against me. For a moment, I think he won't answer, that the memories will be too much.

"Aye, I'd never forget. Not ever." His voice comes low and raw. The way he says it—soft but weighted—means much more than the words being said.

Then he starts.

The sound is shaky at first, but it steadies as he continues. It's a tune I remember from countless nights when fever or nightmares kept us awake—the melody of a mother's love, now carried by the brother holding me together.

As the sharp edges of pain fade, so do I, the darkness taking me gently this time.

All that remains is the thrum of Casey's heartbeat beneath my cheek, and the sound of sweet, familiar humming—leading me where I hope the pain can't follow.

Finn

While Triona is in a deep slumber, I kneel beside her, carefully pulling back the fabric dressings covering her wounds. I'm prepared to change them, prepared for the pain I might find beneath, but the sight before me stills my hands mid-motion.

The wound is healing—far too quickly, impossibly so—and for a moment, all I can do is stare, disbelief rooting me to the spot.

"Callan," I call out, my voice low, but urgent. "Ye need to see this."

He strides over, his scowl deepening as he takes in the sight. He crouches beside me, his sharp gaze assessing her back.

The gashes, raw and angry just hours ago, are now pink, shrunken, and scabbed, as if days—no, a week—has passed since the injury. The physical truth is undeniable and jarring.

"How is this possible?"

"I dinnae ken," I mutter, brow furrowed. My fingers hover over the wounds, careful not to touch. "This... this shouldna be happenin'. Not like this."

"Da warned us," he says, his tone clipped. "Said we'd encounter things movin' forward that might make little sense—things like the body healin' quicker than humanly possible."

"That, and that the answers to what's ahead lie in the mind of someone we're meant to meet in Portugal." He meets my eyes, and I can see the scepticism in their depths.

"Which begs the question. What's waitin' in Portugal, Finn?"

I stiffen, his implication stirring something akin to fury. "Why d'ye think I know?" I ask.

His expression hardens. "'Cause ye've just come back from there," he says, his voice growing cold. "So ye must ken something ye're not tellin' me."

The words hit like a slap, and I recoil, his doubt carving deeper than I care to admit. My voice lowers, tight with frustration. "Have I *ever* lied to you, Cal?"

His refusal to answer unsettles me. Frustration laced with something darker rises, pushing me to reveal just enough of the truth I've been burying for years. The truth about why I never wrote, why I let my poison stay locked away, kept from spilling onto pages I could never send back to them.

"The past three years were far worse than any torment my bastard of a father ever put me through," I say, my voice quiet, but steeped in emotion sharp enough to cut stone. "Some places Bran and I were in—there were no allies there, Callan. No kindness. No mercy. Every hardship found me, and not one spared me. So dinnae suggest I'd keep things from you now, when we need to be aligned, now more than ever. I'd never ask of you what was asked of me."

My voice cracks slightly, but I push through, my gaze steady, even as the weight of my memories threatens to pull me under. "If I knew what was waitin', I'd bloody tell you, you stubborn arse of a man."

He doesn't answer right away. Just watches me, as if he's still deciding whether to believe me or break something. His scowl is carved from stone, but it softens—barely.

No apology comes. Of course not. He's Callan. And apologies don't come easy to men who've spent their lives building walls out of pride and pain.

Instead, he shifts his attention back to Triona, but the tension between us still pulses like a wound left open.

"We need to keep movin'," Callan mutters, voice rough. "Because whatever's drawn to *this*"—his gaze lingers on Triona's unnaturally healed skin—"it might not be far behind. And it won't come gently."

18

NO HOME, NO HAVEN

Finn

Sunday, 4 May 1823

Just Outside of Inverness

The path to the tavern is barely visible, overgrown with brambles and heather, and the looming Highlands offers no comfort from the biting wind that howls around us. Bran leads the way, his hand instinctively resting on the hilt of his dagger, his sharp eyes scanning the dim surroundings.

Behind him, Casey is humming under his breath, his usual swagger muted but not absent, while Callan brings up the rear, his broad shoulders tense with unease.

Triona is nestled in the cart in the rear, bundled beneath layers of blankets as the pain medication continues to keep her in a deep slumber.

"This is madness," Callan mutters, his voice gruff. "We're wanderin' the Highlands with no plan, no home, and we're barely holdin' on."

"We have a plan," Bran snaps without turning. "Find shelter. Regroup. And make sure she's safe."

"Aye," Casey chimes in, his tone lighter, though there is an unmistakable tension beneath it. "Because nothin' screams '*safe*' like a mystery tavern in the arse-end of nowhere. What next? Gonna tell me it's run by kindly Highland monks with a flair for hospitality?"

"Stay out here then," I growl, shooting Casey and Callan both glares. "But if you keep blubberin', I'll throw you to the wolves myself."

"Easy now," Casey says with a grin. "Just tryin' to lighten the mood, aye?"

Callan huffs. "Wouldnae need to lighten it if we'd stayed put on a pathway."

I stop abruptly, turning to face Callan, my expression dark. "Stayed put on what pathway exactly, Cal? Tryin' to come upon people lookin' for us? Would you rather be back there lettin' Colina finish what she started?" My voice is low, sharp, and deadly quiet, careful not to wake Triona. The air between us thickens, the tension coiled like a watch spring.

Callan tenses, his jaw tightening. "How could ye even suggest—"

"Ye're sayin' nothin' that wasna already considered," I clip, my voice barely above a whisper but brimming with restrained anger. "And ye're lucky Triona's dead asleep right now. If I didn't have her to think of, I'd remind ye—"

"Dinnae test me, *Finnis*, lest ye've the spine to finish that thought and follow it wi' swift action." Callan interrupts, his tone low and lethal, matching the dangerous glint in his eyes.

Bran intervenes with his usual effortless charm.

"All right, break it up," he asserts with a cool and even tone, though his voice carries an edge. "We're on the same side, remember? We shouldn't be at odds with each other. Let's save the sparring for when we're not starving, dead on our feet, dragging horses that look ready to drop, and in need of a dram."

Callan glares at me, his eyes simmering with unvoiced accusations, but he says nothing. I force myself to unclench my fists, jaw tightening as I turn back toward the path.

We rarely fought—being so alike often kept us in step—but the past few days have been a nightmare, wearing on both our patience. And neither of us has said a word about our last row, the one where Callan had accused me of hiding things from him. It's something he's not got over yet—and he's being too much of a blethering gowk to apologise and move on.

The glow of the tavern's window flickers just ahead, its promise of warmth and shelter tugging at my focus.

Bran glances between the three of us, his usual grin fading as he takes in the tension still ripe in the air. Without a word, he adjusts his jacket, and takes a step forward, his usual cocky energy suddenly sharpened with purpose.

"I'll go ahead," he says, his tone lighter but lacking its usual teasing edge. "See if this fine establishment's got room for a few wanderers."

I narrow my eyes at Bran. "Dinnae cause a scene, Mums."

"Me?" Bran shoots back, feigning offense. "I'm charm itself, Finn. You worry too much."

Before anyone can argue, Bran sets off at a brisk pace toward the tavern. His silhouette grows smaller with every step until he's swallowed whole by the shadows.

Callan lets out a frustrated breath, adjusting his grip on his reins. "He's too eager to run headlong into trouble."

"Aye," I mutter, eyes still fixed on the path ahead, "but if trouble's waitin', better it finds Bran first."

Callan lets out a grudging huff of agreement, his lips twitching as if fighting a smirk. Then, to my surprise, a low, gravelly chuckle escapes him. It's quiet, almost like he didn't mean for anyone to hear, but it was there.

Casey glances sideways at him. "Did you just laugh, Callan? Thought ye'd forgotten how."

"Dinnae get used to it," he mutters, though there's a telltale twitch at the corner of his mouth. "Just a momentary lapse in sanity brought on by exhaustion, and too much of yer voice."

"Aye, the delirium's settin' in proper," Casey shoots back with a wicked grin. "Give it another hour and ye'll be singin' lullabies and askin' Finn for a cuddle."

"If I do," Callan says dryly, "assume I've been possessed, and do the merciful thing."

Casey smirks. "Gladly. I'll make it quick... right after the lullaby."

Levity lingers for only a breath before the quiet swallows it whole. Minutes stretch as heavy exhaustion creeps back in. The faint rustle of the wind and the distant hoot of an owl are the only sounds breaking the silence.

Finally, the loud creak of the tavern door echos down the path, faint but unmistakable in the stillness. Moments later, Bran emerges from the shadows, his hand raised in an exaggerated gesture of triumph as he jogs toward us, his grin wide enough to rival the moonlight.

"There's a room," he calls out, a grin spreading across his face. "A small one, mind you, but it's got a proper bed and a roof that won't leak."

My shoulders relax, though my face remains guarded. "Any trouble?"

"Quite the opposite. There's a barmaid in there, Lori, jugs the size of a—"

"Focus, Bran." I say flatly.

"Right, the point. She won't be asking questions. Told her we needed to take the room for the night, and she happily obliged."

I shoot him a look. "And did you pay her favour for that, or did yer charm take longer to turn on than normal? You had us waitin' out here for a bit."

Bran rolls his eyes. "Neither. I got stopped at the door by a rather interesting woman. She asked if *'her eyes met the light of this day, or any since the last.'"* He shrugs. "It seemed as if she might have thrown a few too many back. I even entertained her and asked if she would clarify, and she just shook her head in disappointment and said *I'll wait where time holds its breath—when the one meant to lead us stirs, I'll reveal the hand.'"*

I frown, unease pricking my skin. "What the hell does that mean?"

Bran shrugs, still grinning despite the oddity of his encounter. "No idea. She seemed harmless enough, touched in the head, but harmless. I figured it was best to humour her."

Callan shifts uneasily as he glances at Triona. "Drunk ramblings or no, I dinnae like the sound of it."

"Nor do I," I mutter, my gaze fixed on the dimly lit tavern ahead. I shake my head, pushing the unease to the back of my mind. "But we need to get her inside before we freeze to death out here. Just keep your guards up."

Bran nods, motioning toward the tavern. "Room's just off the main hall. Cosy, if you're into tight spaces."

Casey smirks. "Sounds like yer kind of setup. Ye've always been good in tight spots, eh, Bran?"

Bran halts mid-step, turning to throw an exaggerated hand over his chest in mock offence—dramatic, but with a glint of challenge in his eyes. "I know not of what you speak."

Casey just grins. "Ye're a heartbreaker, Bran. Ye're likely to leave a trail of broken vows and weepin' barmaids from here to bloody Port Oban."

"I leave them all better than I found them," Bran says with a shrug. "Confident. Glowing. Sometimes singing, depending on the time I'm spared."

"Singin'?" Casey scoffs. "More like sobbin'. Probably writin' poetry about their stolen virtue and mysteriously missin' underthings."

Bran lifts his chin, unbothered. "Well, art inspires art, mate. I consider it a cultural service."

Callan groans under his breath, but the corner of his mouth twitches.

"A cultural service?" Casey chokes on a laugh.

"I give them memories," Bran says, smug as sin. "And sometimes a mild limp. Depends on the evening."

I let out a sharp breath, somewhere between a laugh and a warning.

Casey clutches his chest. "Saints preserve us. Ye're not a man, but a walking cautionary tale."

Bran winks. "Only to the lonely and the curious."

"And the easily impressed," Casey mutters. "Come on then, ye wee magpie. Let's see if that silver tongue of yours can charm us two rooms for the night."

"Aye, just watch," Bran replies, his grin widening. "They'll be begging me to stay forever."

"I reckon this goes without sayin'," Callan cuts in, dry as smoke, "but Triona gets the room. Finn, ye'll stay with her."

"Why me?" I ask, confusion lacing my voice, though my tone feigns annoyance.

"Aye, why him?" Casey echoes, crossing his arms with a raised brow.

Callan doesn't blink. "Because he's not slept well in three days. Been tendin' to Triona nonstop. We both ken he needs it more than anyone else, and she cannae be alone."

I hesitate, guilt and weariness tangling in my chest. "Are you certain?"

Callan's eyes meet mine, steady and firm. "Aye. Get some sleep, Finn. Ye really need it. I'll stay in the common room with Bran. Someone will need to watch him before he gets us kicked out by flirtin' with the barmaid and her... *jugs*."

Bran snorts, clearly pleased. "Now, that's the spirit, Cal! I could use a minder. Lori's got a smile that could turn a saint unholy, and what's one drinking companion when you can have two?"

"Go tend to the horses, will ye, Casey?" Callan says, his voice losing its usual edge. There's a rare softness to it—something quieter, almost weary.

Casey nods, eyes flicking between us before trailing after Bran with a muttered, "Try not to bloody each other up too badly."

Their figures fade into the night, leaving me and Callan alone. The tension from earlier still simmers beneath the surface, but it's heavier now—shaped by grief, shaded with guilt, and filled with the silence of things neither of us knows how to say.

I glance at Triona; her face is still pale but peaceful. "She willnae need another tea," I murmur, more to myself than Callan. "She's practically healed. But when she wakes up again..." My words falter. The physical wounds might be fading, but the pain she'll carry when she's fully conscious again will be far deeper, far crueller.

"Aye." Callan's eyes drift toward the faint tavern glow, his shoulders stiff. After a beat, he adds, voice low and gruff, "I never really gave my thanks. For what ye did. For whatever sent ye racin' back home. And... for what it's worth, I believe ye dinnae ken how it is we're bound for Portugal. Ye're an honourable man, Finn. And I'm sorry... for what I said yesterday."

His words hit harder than I expect.

"Aye, prove it then, Cal," I say, nudging him lightly, trying to ease the tension.

He huffs a laugh. "Guess I'll prove it with a pint or two."

"That's the spirit."

Then his eyes meet mine—still tired, still shadowed.

"I wish things were different," I murmur.

"We all do," he says. "But I'm glad ye're at my side. Even when it seems like I want to wring yer neck—and ye want to wring mine."

A reluctant smile tugs at the corner of my mouth. "That's more often than you think."

"Aye, probably," he concedes, a faint chuckle escaping, though it's coloured with sorrow. His gaze drifts back to Triona as she stirs faintly, her brow twitching as if she feels the weight of our grief. "But what ye did... Finn, ye saved us."

The weight of his words settles heavily in my chest. "I didnae save them all."

"That's not on ye to bear," Callan says sharply.

"And it's not on *you* either," I shoot back.

We stare at each other for a long moment, until he nods—just once, but it's enough.

He claps my shoulder, solid and grounding. "I'll see if someone can gather what's needed to make her comfortable. Can ye carry her in?"

I nod my agreement.

Callan steps up to Shadow, eyeing the horse like he half expects trouble. With a sigh, he takes the reins.

"Right then, *beast*," he mutters, giving the reins a tug. "Do us all a favour and behave yerself. Finn's got his hands full, and I've no interest in bein' dragged through horse shite tonight."

Shadow snorts, but follows willingly.

Callan shakes his head. "Aye, that's what I thought. Pretend ye've manners for once."

And with that, he leads the horse off toward the stables.

I turn back to Triona and lift her gently from the cart, cradling her with as much care as I can manage. Her weight against me is familiar, grounding. It quiets something restless inside me.

"Almost there," I whisper—whether to her or to myself, I can't say.

As I near the door, her eyes flutter open. Glazed. Wandering. But then they find mine, and the world stills.

She blinks, her hand lifting weakly, and I don't move—not when her fingers reach for me, not when they brush softly across my cheek. Her touch is feather-light, reverent.

"You are a necessity in my life, Finn."

The sentence is nearly inaudible, yet it carries the weight to crush the last fragile remnants of pride and anger from our argument days ago—an argument so insignificant now it feels almost foolish to recall. Her words, her touch, and the way she looks at me as though I'm the only steady thing left in her world... it threatens to undo me entirely.

Her hand drops slowly, falling limp against her chest as her eyelids flutter closed once more. The peace on her face feels fragile, like glass that could shatter at the slightest disturbance.

I swallow hard, the lump in my throat nearly choking me as I whisper, *"And ye're mine."*

The others bid me a quick goodnight, but say nothing else as I head toward the room where Triona rests. My steps are heavy, the tension of the day dragging me down. I'm not sure how much rest I'll find, but something is better than what I've got over the past few days.

It's eerily quiet as I approach the door. Just as I reach for the handle, a figure emerges from the shadows—a young woman, her presence as sudden as it is unexpected. She stands before me, her dark eyes sharp, expression unreadable. She is beautiful—hair a pale yellow, skin like moonlit snow.

She's wearing a long cloak that brushes the floor, and the surrounding air is a stillness I've never felt before.

"Warrior, first of many," she says, her voice melodic, like the haunting tune of a distant lament. It sends a shiver down my spine, raising the hairs on my neck.

There's no masking how taken aback I am by the strange greeting. "Can I help ye, lass?"

Her gaze flicks to the door behind me, then back to my face. "You carry the burden," she says, her tone scolding. "But you do not yet see it for what it is."

I frown, unsure if I'm dealing with a drunk, or someone whose mind has wandered far from reason. "I'm not sure I know what you mean."

The maiden tilts her head, studying me with unnerving intensity. "Safety is what you offer, but the bond is what you fight. You stand at a threshold, blind to the weight of your own heart. Do you not see? She is the thread that binds you to the stars."

I stiffen, words cutting through the exhaustion clouding my mind. "You confuse me with someone else."

"No," she says firmly, stepping closer. "It is you who mistake yourself. You carry the blade, but she is the reason you wield it. You see the door, but not the path. And if you do not learn, warrior, the door will close. The path will vanish."

Her gaze burns into mine, and for a moment, I can't speak. Her words unsettle me, a strange mix of truth and nonsense that makes my chest tighten. I want to push her away, to tell her she doesn't know me, but something in her tone, in the way she speaks, makes me hesitate.

"Lass, I've no time for riddles," I say, voice quieter now, edged with uncertainty. "I'm no warrior, and I've no path to walk but the one I'm on."

Her eyes soften, but the intensity in her voice remains. "You are blind, warrior. But the time will come when the choice is clear. Do not wait too long to see. It is a path you once knew so well."

Without another word, she turns, leaving me standing in the hallway, heart pounding in my chest. I stare after her, mind racing, but the sound of a faint stir from behind the door pulls my focus back.

I push the door open swiftly, the faint creak cutting through the stillness. My eyes dart around the room, instinctively searching for movement. Triona lay undisturbed, her chest rising and falling in a steady rhythm. Her lips move faintly, a soft murmur slipping past them, but the words are too quiet to catch.

The dim glow of the lantern on the bedside table casts a warm, flickering light over her face, highlighting the delicate curve of her cheek and the shadows beneath her eyes. She's turned toward the light in her sleep, as if seeking its comfort.

I exhale slowly, the tension in my shoulders easing just enough to remind me how tightly wound I am. Lowering myself to the floor, I settle onto the bedroll I'd laid out just beside her. The floorboards creak under my weight, but Triona doesn't stir.

Though I try to shake off the maiden's word, I fail. *The thread that binds you to the stars.*

I don't understand them. But I *feel* them—because I have something that pulls me back when the world threatens to tear me apart.

My gaze drifts to her—pale, still, her chest rising in quiet, measured breaths. The ache in my chest tightens, a pressure with no name.

And then her lips part, barely moving, and in the faintest whisper that feels like a prayer, she breathes my name.

19

A Promise Between the Living and Dead

Triona
Monday, 5 May 1823
The Kelpie's Tavern

I wake to a world that feels distant and hazy, as if I'm surfacing from a dream I can't quite grasp. The room is dim, unfamiliar in a way that unsettles me. A dull ache lingers throughout my body, but it's nothing compared to the gnawing emptiness in my stomach. Hunger claws at me, fierce and insistent, and the pressing urge to use the chamber pot forces me to move.

My limbs feel as though they're weighed down with stones, sluggish and reluctant to obey, but the pull of hunger still outweighs my fatigue. It's only as I shift I realise something odd—my back, the source of so much pain before, feels... fine. No burning, no sharp stabs of agony. Just a faint stiffness, as if the injury had never been as dire as I remembered.

Confusion thickens in my mind like fog. Had I imagined it? The memories of the past few days blur at the edges, dulled by pain draughts and fevered exhaustion, but I know I didn't imagine that. Right?

With hesitant fingers, I pull my arm from the sleeve of the humorously large linen shirt draped over me. My breath stutters as I reach back, heart hammering. My fingers find smooth skin. No open wounds. Only the faint ridges of scars remain. The sharp, searing pain that had consumed me?

Gone.

The rustle of blankets behind me startles me, pulling me from my thoughts. Finn stirs, his head snapping up from where he's slouched beside the bed. The sight of him immediately eases some of the unease coiling in my chest.

If I had the mind to notice him before, I might have scrambled for some shred of modesty. Right now, however, my dignity is a distant concern, buried beneath the weight of exhaustion and the lingering fog of pain. There are greater burdens pressing down on me.

His eyes, wide with alarm, meet mine, and he bolts upright, his face drawn tight with panic.

"Triona?" His voice is rough from sleep. "Ye're awake."

The words are a statement, seeped in relief, like a prayer fulfilled. He eyes me as if he's confirming the validity of my existence. "Do you... how do you feel?"

I blink at him, still shaking off the grogginess. "Hungry," I rasp, the dryness in my throat making my voice sound rough. I shift slightly, testing my body, and the absence of the sharp, searing pain in my back hits me like a shock once again.

"And... I don't hurt."

Finn steps around the tiny bed, his massive form filling the space. "How d'ye mean?" His tone carries something subtle—a suggestion that he's not as oblivious as he'd like me to think. But fine, I'll humour him.

"I don't hurt." My hand instinctively reaches behind me, brushing over the places where I'd felt the wounds the most. I can feel the faint ridges of scars beneath my fingertips, but no pain—nothing even close. "They're gone," I say, my words trembling with disbelief.

Finn keeps his eyes locked on mine as he steps closer, his movements measured. "I dinnae ken how else to explain it, except to say the scars remain, but the injury itself..." He exhales sharply, his throat bobbing as he swallows. "Triona, when I found you after—" He stops, jaw tightening, as if the memory alone is too much. "It was bad. Worse than bad. You should've been bedbound for weeks—maybe longer—before you could even think about moving without pain. But now..."

"Months?" I whisper, trying to wrap my mind around what he's saying. I can see the truth of it in his expression—the way he's looking at me, as if I'm a riddle with no solution.

"Aye," he murmurs. "It's as if time sped up. As if ye've been recoverin' faster than... faster than is possible for anyone."

He hesitates, his gaze flickering downward before returning to my face. "The necklace," he says, his voice quieter now. "The one I gave you." His fingers twitch, as if he almost wants to reach for it, but stops himself. "Ellen said there was something about it. Something meant to heal." He exhales, shaking his head slightly. "I didnae think much of it at first, but after seein' the impossible with my own eyes..." His voice trails off, the unspoken thought hanging between us.

I glance down, my fingers brushing against the cool metal resting against my collarbone. My mind reels, struggling to grasp what he's suggesting—what any of this means.

Finn exhales sharply, dragging a hand through his hair. "We're all tryin' to make sense of it, Triona. Everything—this, you, the world itself—none of it feels..." His voice falters. His gaze turns searching, almost haunted. "Things are changin'. Faster than any of us can understand."

This explanation should be a relief. It should make me feel stronger, grateful even. But a cold unease creeps into my chest. My hands go still, my gaze shifting away as my shoulders slump beneath the weight of it all.

I struggle to hold on to his words, to piece them together into something that makes sense. But another pain surges forward—one sharper, deeper, more unbearable than any wound I've suffered.

My parents.

For a moment, silence stretches between us. I stare at the far wall, my thoughts tangled in something I can't quite name. Finally, I exhale. "It's strange, isn't it?" My voice is soft, but there's no mistaking the anguish beneath it. "My body heals faster than I can make sense of, yet the things that matter most—the things inside me—feel as if they'll never heal."

Finn's brows pull together, concern etched across his face. He doesn't speak. He just waits.

Because he knows.

Because he understands.

I swallow, my chest tightening, and then—"Finn," I whisper, hesitant, fragile. "I remember that day. The day you found me in the woods."

He nods slowly, his expression unreadable. "Aye, the first day I met you..."

I pause as a tiny weight presses against my chest. "It's unthinkable that I ever forgot," I murmur, my gaze drifting. "But the memories started coming back—first in dreams, and then, during my talk with Colina, the truth hit me. The horrible truth of it."

My throat tightens. The truth sticks, but I force it out. "Finn... Colina hurt me that day. She's the reason I was in the woods. The reason you had to come find me."

His face darkens, tension rippling through his body. "What?"

I exhale shakily. "I followed her into the woods. I thought—" My voice cracks, but I push through, even as my hands tremble. "I thought she wanted to play. But she didn't. She was leading me away, Finn. She was going to leave me there."

The admission sours on my tongue, bitter and raw, and my breath stutters beneath its weight. "And if you hadn't found me..." My voice drops to barely more than a whisper. "I might have never come back."

Finn's jaw clenches, his hands curling into fists. "I'm sure someone would have—"

"No, Finn." I cut him off, my voice firm despite the tears brimming in my eyes. "You saved me then, just as you saved me the other day."

The first tear slips free, trailing down my cheek, and then another. I don't wipe them away. I let them fall, let the grief and gratitude settle between us. Let Finn see the depth of what he's done for me—what he's *always* done for me.

He swallows hard, looking as if he wants to say something, but nothing comes. Instead, he just nods, his expression raw, his eyes dark with something unreadable.

"Finn, what I said the other day—"

"Don't," he interrupts quickly, shaking his head. "You dinnae have to—"

"No!" I shout, cutting him off just as fast. My breath is ragged, my chest rising and falling too quickly. I force myself to even out, to steady my voice. "Finn, you deserve an apology." My voice softens, but the conviction remains. "I didn't mean a word of what I said to you. Not a single word. I owe you my life, twice over. And what I said... it wasn't fair. It was selfish."

My hands tighten at my sides, my heart pounding. "I was lashing out. I was trying to protect myself from something I didn't even understand. Some idiotic form of self-preservation. But I see the light of it now. And I'm sorry, Finn. I'm so sorry."

I take a breath, the next words tumbling out in a rush before I can lose my nerve. "And Marcus... I *never* really wanted him. Not before I left for Edinburgh. Not when he showed up again after I came home. Not even the night of my party. It would never be him."

His lips part as if to argue, but I don't let him. Instead, I push aside every morsel of hesitation, the heat of embarrassment flickering in the back of my mind. It's nothing compared to the need to reach him. To feel something solid, something real. My dignity can wait—this moment cannot. Before he can react, I wrap my arms around his neck, holding on tightly.

For a heartbeat, he doesn't move—just stands there, as if frozen by the weight of my touch. Then, slowly, he exhales, the breath shuddering from his chest. His arms come around me—not just to hold me, but to keep me. The warmth of him cascades through me, steady and unyielding, mooring me in a way I hadn't known I needed. As if he alone can still the chaos that trembles beneath my skin, in a way I never knew I craved.

His voice is quiet when he speaks, but there's no mistaking the weight of it, the promise woven into every syllable.

"You should know, there was never a world where I wouldnae have found you, Triona."

He presses his cheek to my hair, his breath warm, his heartbeat strong against mine.

"And there'll never be a world where I couldnae."

Something inside me stirs, something I can't name, can't face—not now. But I feel it, thrumming beneath my skin, winding around my heart like an unseen thread, pulling taut in a way I never noticed before.

I close my eyes tight, gripping onto him as if he's the only thing keeping me tethered to this world. And the truth of it? At this moment, *he is*.

"I wanted to become more than what others expected of me. But not like this." My voice is a whisper, raw, scraped thin by grief. "Not when the price is in lives that can never be reclaimed. Not when all of you sacrificed everything—bound to this sick and twisted reality of mine."

Finn's grip on me tightens slightly, his voice low and steady. "Triona, none of us choose how the world changed, and that includes you. It happened to all of us. This isn't something you *did* to anyone."

I shake my head, but the motion feels weak. "It hurts," I admit, my voice trembling. "It hurts that I didn't get to say goodbye. That I'll never get to say goodbye." The thoughts crack open something deep inside me, raw and bleeding. My fingers tighten around the back of his neck, holding on as if he's the only thing keeping me from breaking apart. "And if I keep thinking about it—if I let it sink too deep—I feel like... like it'll devour me whole."

Finn exhales, a sound both heavy and certain, before wrapping me closer. His lips press briefly to my hair, his voice a quiet vow against the storm raging inside me, as if his words alone could hold back the tide threatening to pull me under. "It won't," he murmurs. "Because I won't let it."

His words don't mend the cracks or dull the ache, but they steady me. He steadies me. My breath shudders against his shoulder, and his fingers press firmer against my back, as if he's trying to hold me together.

My eyes fill with tears, but I blink them away quickly, nodding even as my lips press tightly together. "You have the heart of a saint, Finn," I whisper, my voice barely audible.

The silence stretches between us, an unspoken reality wrapping around us. This path that pulls us forward is heavy, but the weight of everything doesn't feel like mine alone to bear.

Finn reaches for my hands, hesitating for just a moment before gently prying them from around his neck, his touch uncharacteristically careful. "I've some things to see to," he says quietly, almost shyly. "If you need me, just call for me. I'll not be far." He lingers for a moment, his gaze searching mine, as though there's more he wants to say but chooses not to. Instead, he steps back, his expression soft but resolute.

"Go on, then," I say, my voice steadier than I feel. He slips out, the door closing softly behind him.

The quiet settles around me like a heavy cloak. A tremulous breath escapes me, as I decide it's all right to let the tears come—just for a moment. No prying eyes, no comforting words. Just a few silent sobs to help me face the rest of this day, and the rest of this chaos I've yet to untangle.

I stand naked in the small tavern room, the basin of lukewarm water on the table beside me, its surface rippling faintly as I dip the cloth into it again. The simple act of washing up, of moving without wincing, feels almost foreign. Days ago, I couldn't even imagine lifting my arm without agony, let alone scrubbing my skin clean. Now, my movements are slow but steady, but I feel human again.

I reach for the small, cracked mirror propped against the wall, angling it carefully to help glimpse my back. I can see them clearly—silver lines trace the skin across my back like threads woven into my flesh.

My breath quickens as I stare, a mix of disbelief and wonder washing over me. Finn hadn't been exaggerating. The scars, faint and almost delicate, are all that remain of the wounds I had felt tearing through me only days ago. I brush over the ridges and shiver at the odd sensation—neither pain nor numbness radiates where it was once overbearing.

The image in the mirror doesn't feel real. I turn slightly, watching the way the scars catch the light, tiny and intricate, almost beautiful in a strange, unnatural way. But they are also a reminder. Of pain. Of loss. Of survival.

A knock at the door startles me, and I nearly drop the mirror. I sigh, setting it down gently before turning toward the sound. "A moment," I call, my voice steady despite the sudden rush of emotion.

I move to pull on the fresh clothes Finn left for me, my fingers lingering on the fabric. As I slide them over my head and smooth it down, a thought strikes me: I'm not the same as I'd been before. Not entirely. Something has changed—something more than just my body.

And no matter how hard I try to push it away, the weight of that realisation presses into my chest, heavier than ever.

I move to open the door, and there they are—all four of them. Finn, Casey, Bran, and Callan stand shoulder to shoulder, their faces etched with a mix of worry and anticipation. Their eyes scan me as I might collapse at any moment, and I sigh, leaning my head against the edge of the doorframe.

"I can sense what you're waiting for," I say dryly, though the emotion in my voice betrays me. "And if you keep staring at me like that, it might actually happen."

The weight of their worries press on me. It's not that I don't appreciate it—I do. But if they ask if I'm all right, or worse, try to comfort me, I know it'll break the fragile dam holding back my tears. And once I start, I'm not sure I'll be able to stop. That's the cruel thing about kindness; sometimes it hurts more than the ache you're already carrying. It's easier to let the silence hang in the air than to hear the words that might push me over the edge.

Before I can protest further, Casey steps forward, wrapping me in a hug so tight it nearly knocks the breath out of me. "I'm glad ye're okay," he murmurs, his voice low but thick with relief. He presses a kiss to the top of my head, a gesture so tender it sends a sting straight into my eyes.

Do not cry. Do not cry.

"As am I," I manage, my voice wavering but sincere. The words hang between us, and for the first time in days, I mean them completely. I *am* glad. Despite everything, despite the ache and the scars and the weight of what's happened, I'm alive.

And I can't waste that.

I step back, meeting Casey's gaze, and his eyes are full of something unspoken yet steadying. I glance toward the others, taking a shaky breath. "Will you tell me where we're going?" I ask, my voice soft and measured as I continue to fight back a wave of unshed tears.

Casey squeezes my shoulders, his hands grounding me. "We'll tell ye," he says, his tone firm but kind, "as we go. I promise."

The warmth in his words eases me.

Callan's voice cuts through the lingering quiet. "It's time we left," he says firmly, his arms crossed as he glances toward the door. No one argues.

We move outside, the chill of the early morning air biting against our skin. Casey walks ahead, his hand resting lightly on the hilt of his dagger, while Bran and Finn exchange a quiet word as they fall into step. Callan, as always, saunters suspiciously. His shoulders squared and his eyes scan the horizon for threats.

I trail at the rear, my steps slow and deliberate as I adjust to moving on my own again, and look at the surrounding scenery. The tavern is well hidden, surrounded by woods on all fronts. The breeze stirs my hair, and the sound of the others' boots crunching against the ground feels oddly distant. My thoughts are elsewhere—on the past, the promises I've made to myself, and the weight of everything ahead.

Then, I feel it—a light tapping on my back. I jump, my breath catching as I twist. Standing behind me is a beautiful young woman, her features delicate and otherworldly, her gaze piercing but calm.

She smiles faintly, tilting her head as if studying me. There is something unsettlingly familiar about her—an air of mystery that makes my chest tighten.

"Can I help you?" I ask, my tone cautious. She does not respond, her eyes continuing to examine me.

"Who are you?" I press, my voice quiet but firm, hand instinctively moving toward the knife at my belt.

"I am but of no threat to you," she replies, her tone calm, almost dismissive, as if my question is absurd.

"But who are you?" I press again, unwilling to let it go.

"It's of no importance," she says with a soft shrug, her enigmatic smile remaining in place.

"Why are you here?" I press, the grip on the hilt of my knife tightening. "What do you want?"

The maiden doesn't answer. Instead, she reaches out and places a gentle hand on my shoulder. "It is not what I want, but what you must see," she says cryptically, her tone almost gentle. "The thread binds tighter now," she mumbles, her voice lilting and melodic. "Do not look away when the path reveals itself. Not again."

My frown deepens as confusion floods my mind. "What are you talking about?"

"You are the thread that binds him to the stars. You walk beside a child of the sun, his light drawn to your shadow. You are the moon, ever turning, your cycle complete. Together, you balance the sky, for one cannot rise if the other should fall."

The maiden stares ahead, as her eyes seem to cloud faintly. Then, in a tone that carries both melody and gravity, she speaks.

You journey now with sun-born kin,
To find the spear, the battle's twin.
The warrior bold from Gorias' might
Seeks the blade of eternal light.
Two hearts entwined, a cauldron they crave,
A vessel of plenty their fate will pave.
And you, my child, seek what's been torn—
The shard of your soul, to be reborn.

I blink, the cryptic words weaving into my mind, unsettling and strange. "I don't... I don't understand," I say, shaking my head.

The maiden smiles faintly, her eyes holding a knowing sadness as she steps back. "The answers you seek are not mine to give," she whispers, her melodic voice carrying a mystical weight. "This is the end of the road for the knowledge I possess."

Her words settle like stones in my chest, but before I can question her further, Finn's voice pierces the stillness. "Triona!" he shouts, his tone tight with concern. His hurried footfalls grow louder behind me.

The maiden's gaze lingers on me for a moment longer, her expression unreadable. Then, as though the mist itself swallows her, she hurries off into the haze; her form disappearing into the woods just as Finn reaches my side.

"Triona," he says, spinning me around by the shoulders, his eyes searching mine. "What did she say? Are you all right?"

I hesitate, the weight of the encounter still pressing down on me. "She sounded like a loon... but, I can't help but feel..." My words trail off, my eyes drifting to where the maiden stood just moments before.

"Feel what?" Finn asks, his voice soft but insistent.

I shake my head, an uneasy smile tugging at my lips. "I believe she might have been trying to get coin out of me." The lie rolls off my tongue far too easily.

Finn's brow furrows, concern flashing in his eyes. But I can't bring myself to say more. Her words didn't just unsettle me—they felt like they'd slipped past some invisible barrier and rooted themselves deep within me. And no matter how much I wanted to dismiss them, part of me knew they weren't nonsense.

Finn does not press the matter further, seeming to be lost in thoughts of his own.

We mount our horses, the cool air biting at my cheeks as Finn swings up behind me on Shadow. His arms come around me, steadying me, and I feel the solid warmth of his chest against my back. It's a closeness I've never experienced with him before. It steadies all of me. Being alone is harder than I want to admit, and I'm reliant on his touch now. It grounds me.

As we move into an easy stride, the maiden's words play over and over in my mind, unrelenting. Her voice whispers through me.

"You are the thread that binds him to the stars."

The weight of it fixes itself deep in my chest, heavier with every repetition. Something about those words feels undeniable—*unavoidable.*

I glance up at the horizon ahead; the path stretching endlessly before us, and realise with a chill that some truths don't wait to be sought. They find you—whether you're ready or not.

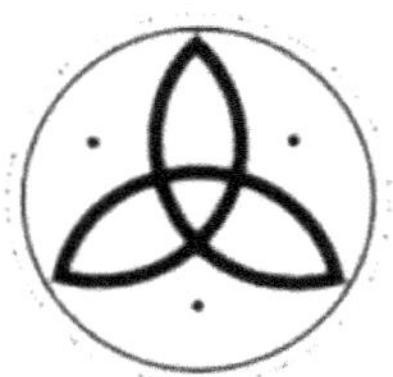

Triona
Tuesday, 6 May 1823
Somewhere in the Scottish Highlands

On tired legs, we trudge forward, giving the horses a much-needed reprieve from carrying us. The crunch of boots against the dirt road mingles with the distant rustle of leaves. It isn't quite night yet, but the day is rapidly slipping away, the last remnants of sunlight bleeding through the trees like liquid fire, casting the woods in a hazy, golden glow that seems to stretch the shadows longer and deeper.

"We're three days' ride from Port Oban." Callan says, his voice weary. "Accordin' to Alex, it's the safest one to port from. Ships there make the fewest stops, and the sailors ask the least amount of questions. Makes sense, considerin' we're tradin' whiskey for safe passage."

"That's assuming they don't drink half of it before we board, and start getting mouthy," Bran mutters. His usual cocky grin is absent as he adjusts the straps on his pack, his steps lagging slightly.

I stay quiet, my thoughts elsewhere, but my focus snaps back as Shadow suddenly snorts, his ears flicking back and forth as he shifts uneasily.

"Shadow?" My voice trembles, swallowed almost immediately by the looming quiet surrounding me.

"What's wrong?" Finn asks, his hand instinctively going to the blade at his belt.

"I don't know," I say, trying to calm the horse, but his unease is contagious. "He's nervous... spooked by something."

Before I can react, Shadow rears slightly, then bolts to the left, disappearing into the dense line of trees at the edge of the road.

"Shadow!" I shout, my pulse spiking as his form vanishes into the shadows. My feet move before my mind catches up, and I sprint after him, ignoring the frantic shouts from behind me.

"Triona! Wait!" Finn yells, but his voice barely registers.

Fear claws at my chest as I plunge into the woods, the thick darkness swallowing me whole. My heart pounds in rhythm with my steps, the cool air biting at my skin. Shadow's hoofbeats thunder ahead, crashing through the underbrush. I have no plan, no thought beyond the instinctive need to reach him.

The trees close in, their branches clawing at my arms like skeletal hands. I stumble over an unseen root, catching myself just before falling, and keep running. Dusk's dim sunlight barely pierces the canopy, turning everything into a chaotic blur of shadows.

"Shadow!" I call again, my voice hoarse and desperate. But the only answer is the haunting echo of my own words.

And then, silence. The hoofbeats stop.

I freeze, my breath ragged, my chest heaving as I strain to listen. The world around me seems to hold its breath, the oppressive quiet pressing down like a weight.

"Shadow?" I whisper, taking a cautious step forward into the thick blackness ahead.

A sudden crack of a branch to my right makes me spin, every muscle in my body tensing. The hairs on the back of my neck stand on end, and I reach instinctively for the dagger at my side. Something—or someone—is out here with me. And whatever it is, it isn't Shadow.

The world around me morphs into a verdant blur, damp leaves and rough bark creating a symphony under my touch as I steady myself against a towering trunk. My breaths come sharp and shallow, each one an echo in the eerie stillness.

The air feels heavier here, clinging to my skin, and my heart pounds with the growing certainty that I've ventured into something far beyond my understanding. The shadows ahead deepen, forming into shapes that send a shiver down my spine. My path forward has been cut off, a sinister trap laid just for me. I played right into their hands.

They've awaited this moment, biding their time as I stumbled, blind and witless, into their web. Foolishness, sheer foolishness. I have done many a reckless thing in my day, but this... this surpasses them all. Never have I been so unwise.

I tighten my grip on my dagger. The instinct to defend myself rises faster than I thought possible, flooding my veins with purpose. My heart thunders, not with fear but with a raw, defiant energy.

I count eight threatening figures in the shadows, their lecherous grins glinting menacingly in the bracken. I freeze for a moment, but the danger they present sparks a rage in my heart that quickly melts away my fear. I unsheathe the dagger from its baldric at my side, its polished metal gleaming.

Eight against one—those are grim odds, even for someone as stubborn as me. Let them come. If they think I'd go quietly, they are sorely mistaken. My back straightens, the dagger steady in my hand, the instinct to defend outweighing the fear present throughout my body. I'll be damned if I don't carve my mark into every one of them before the end.

"Look at the *scary* little doe we've trapped, fellas." The voice is smooth, taunting, and unmistakably British. "And we didn't even have to work for it, as she left her guard willingly."

It could be a coincidence, but it likely isn't.

Their presence means one thing—they've found us. The men that had a hand in the murder of my parents. And if they are here, it means others are nearby, watching, waiting. The rage that fuelled me moments ago wavers, replaced by an icy dread that twists in my stomach like a serpent. My absence isn't just reckless—it's endangered the group. If they are out here searching for me, they'll be walking straight into this trap.

I can't help it as my mind wanders back to the stables—remembering how it felt as Colina came down against my flesh, whip after whip, relentlessly.

That momentary slip of focus is all they need. A sharp yank at the nape of my neck sends pain flaring across my scalp as one of them grabs me forcefully.

I hiss and twist instinctively, bringing my dagger up in a blur. I flip the hilt in my hand, ready to drive it backward into my attacker.

But he is faster.

His iron grip clamps around my wrist like a vice, twisting sharply until my fingers betray me and the dagger clatters to the ground. I barely have time to react before he yanks my arm behind my back, the sharp pressure in my shoulder sending a jolt of pain rippling through me.

"Feisty, aren't we?" His breath is hot against my ear, and the smugness in his tone makes my stomach churn.

I grit my teeth, swallowing the cry that threatens to escape. Panic claws at the edges of my mind, a wild beast desperate to break free, but I force it back, summoning the same defiance that burned within me before.

I thrash against his grip, twisting and straining with all the strength I can summon. His hold is unyielding, his fingers like iron chains gripping the hair at my nape. My father's warnings ring in my mind, each word sharper than the dagger I dropped.

'Don't let them grab your hair, lass. It could be the end of you. Always tie it up.'

But I hadn't listened. Vanity or carelessness—it didn't matter now. I'd ignored his guidance, and I had no one to blame for this predicament but myself.

"She fights back. We like when they fight back, don't we, fellas?" The voice behind me drips with cruel amusement, his breath hot and sickening against my ear.

He yanks my head back sharply, forcing my neck to arch, and before I can summon another burst of defiance, his wet tongue drags up the side of my throat. I recoil instinctively, bile rising in my throat, but the brute only laughs, the sound low and guttural.

"So bloody sweet," he mutters, drawing out the words, reveling in his own twisted triumph

The fear begins to course through my veins, thunderous and all-consuming. My limbs tremble as I claw at his fingers, trying desperately to pry them away from my scalp, but his grip tightens further.

"No, no, no," he tuts mockingly, his amusement dark and vile. "Ye ain't slippin' away this time." Then, like the filthy pig he is, he leans closer and sucks the tender skin just below my ear, his audacity a searing brand against my spirit.

A wave of disgust and fury surge through me. My hands ball into fists, nails digging into my palms. I can't let this monster win. I can't let them break me further.

Not now. Not ever.

"Ya know," he continues, his voice low and mocking, "We was told ye've got a tight little virgin cunny—warned to leave ya nice an' untouched." He chuckles darkly; the sound rumbling like gravel and reverberating against my skin—a filthy, calculated taunt meant to unsettle. "But 'ow could I resist, eh? A prize like *you*? They can sod off wi' them orders." He presses in behind me, and I can feel the unmistakable press of his arousal. A fresh wave of revulsion crashes over me, twisting my stomach and sending an involuntary tremor through my body.

His hand snakes forward, grazing the side of my neck, his touch light yet deliberate, as if savouring the moment. "Ya shiver so pretty," he sneers, his voice low, almost playful. "Makes me wonder 'ow much more I can make ya squirm."

His chuckle grows deeper, more sinister, as if my silence only fuels his twisted delight. "He'll get ya, aye." His hand tightens slightly against my throat, his breath brushing my hair like a ghost of what's coming. "But he won't be findin' ya all nice and tidy like a pretty doll. Oh, no."

"Y'see," he sneers, his voice dripping with malice. "We'll each be takin' a turn with ya. Gotta bring ya in alive, but he never said we couldn't bring you in bloody. So while each of us takes every filthy hole of yers, ye'll bleed and break, just like he wants ya to."

The words send a fresh wave of horror crashing over me, mingling with the disgust that boils in my gut.

How can someone I don't even know hate me so?

I shift my stance, feeling the damp forest floor beneath my boots and searching for any advantage. "Now then, ye're gonna be a right filthy little tart and take me cock like the wicked slag ya are," he grits out, his panting breaths on my neck threatening to overwhelm my senses in the most vile way.

He clumsily snakes his hand toward my waistline, his movements uncoordinated but full of vile intent. A surge of anger and revulsion rises within me, stronger than the fear that's been paralysing me. I thrash violently, my body reacting before my mind catches up. The motion surprises me—surprises *him*—but not long enough to gain the upper hand.

"Get your filthy hands off me!" I snarl, my voice a guttural growl even I didn't know I possessed.

His grip falters, if only for a moment, and I wrench against him with everything I have. My body twists like a trapped animal, desperate to escape the vice of his hands.

"Ah, ye've got some fire, eh?" he sneers, tightening his grip again, but there is a flicker of something else now—a crack in his smug confidence. He sneers, his voice dripping with mockery. "Makes it even more fun."

I bare my teeth in a snarl, my breathing sharp and fast. "Try again," I hiss, venom dripping from every word, "and I swear you'll regret it."

His grip tightens to unbearable levels. I blink hard, refusing to let tears form, refusing to give him the satisfaction of seeing my fear. Fear won't help me now.

I need to think. I need to act. I need to escape.

With a savage tug on my hair, he pushes me to my knees, the sharp pain ripping through my scalp like fire. I grit my teeth, swallowing the cry that threatens to escape. My hands claw at his fist, nails digging into his skin, but his grip remains ironclad.

"Come an' hold 'er down while I take 'er in the dirt—right where she belongs," he barks, his voice a sickening blend of cruelty and triumph.

My stomach drops as two shadowy figures move closer, their dark shapes looming over me.

"No!" The word rips from my throat, raw and desperate, echoing into the stillness of the forest. If anyone—*anyone*—is nearby, they'll hear. They *must* hear.

I feel his movements behind me and hear the distinct sound of fumbling as he attempts to undo his pants. Panic surges, and I thrash harder, my whole body bucking against the two surly men now forcing me toward the ground.

The first grabs my arm, his hands rough and cruel. The second closes in on the other side, pressing me downward with unrelenting force. I twist, bucking against them, but their combined strength pushes me closer to the forest floor. My heart thunders, the world around me narrowing into a chaotic blur of survival instinct and blind panic.

One of them reaches for me, his rough hand snaking downward with vile intent. His touch grazes my thigh, and bile rises in my throat as his fingers creep closer, aiming for what he has no right to take. "*Oi!*" the brute behind me barks, voice cutting through the chaos. "None of that. She's *mine*. Ye'll not be touchin' 'er before me."

The vile hand recoils instantly. A slap cracks through the air, sharp and jarring, as the brute strikes the man hard across the side of his head. The impact reverberates through the suffocating silence, shattering—for just a moment—the grotesque tension hanging over us.

A surge of anger wells up within me, burning away the edges of my fear. Determination floods my veins, sharpening my thoughts. I make a split-second decision, forcing my body to go still.

Let them think you're defeated—just for a moment.

The instant I feel their grips ease, I strike.

With every ounce of strength, I throw my head back, aiming true. A sickening thud meets my effort, and the brute howls in agony. He stumbles, his hands releasing me as he cups himself between the legs, writhing in pain.

I don't wait to savour the moment. Seizing the opportunity, I rip my arms free from the men's grasp, grab my downed dagger, and twist, rolling away with all the speed I can muster. The forest floor scrapes against my hands and knees, but I don't care. Distance is all that matters.

"Ya daft bitch!" the man roars, his voice raw with fury and humiliation.

Every nerve in my body screams at me to run, to flee this nightmare as fast as my legs can carry me. But before I can take even a single step, the air itself seems to split open, and a blood-curdling scream tears through the stillness of the night, cutting into the quiet like a jagged knife. It isn't just loud—it's piercing, primal, and haunting, a sound that claws its way beneath my skin and roots me to the spot.

I whip around, my breath catching in my throat as the scream hangs in the air, stretching out like an endless wail of torment.

It's high-pitched, laced with sorrow so raw it feels tangible, as if the forest itself mourns with it. My chest tightens, and the hairs on the back of my neck stand on end. The sound reverberates through the trees; the echoes overlapping in a way that makes it feel as though the source is all around, nowhere and everywhere at once.

It came from no man—or creature I'd ever encountered. For a fleeting moment, confusion eclipses my fear, my mind scrambling to identify the source of the sound. But nothing I can think of matches the sheer, bone-chilling horror of it.

The men's bravado vanishes in an instant. They freeze, heads snapping around, searching for the source of the unholy sound. Even the one who violated me stills. His pained groans cut off beneath the crushing weight of the scream.

Their attention snaps toward the comrade standing furthest from the group. My heart hammers as my eyes struggle to adjust to the dim light filtering through the trees. And when I finally make out the scene before me, my stomach knots with terror.

His head is gone.

Not just gone—removed cleanly, severed in a single stroke. His lifeless body stands motionless for a brief, heart-stopping moment before crumpling to the ground like a felled tree, the sound of his collapse reverberating through the oppressive silence.

The men's confidence shatters, giving way to chaos. They scramble to unsheathe their weapons, their shouts frantic and disorganised, clashing with the eerie stillness of the forest. The one who violated me remains hunched over, clutching himself in pain, oblivious to the severity of the danger bearing down upon them.

I can't waste the chance. The opening is clear. I inch backward, preparing to sprint into the shadows, but just as I turn, something appears and pauses my retreat.

It materialises from the darkness as if born of the shadows themselves.

A phantom figure—tall, unnaturally pale, its ghostly pallor shimmering faintly against the blackened backdrop of the forest. It has the distinct form of a woman, clad in a ragged silver dress that ripples as if caught in an unfelt wind. Wild, wispy silver hair frames a face I can barely discern, its features obscured but radiating a haunting intensity.

The figure moves with a speed and grace that is impossible to track. One moment it stands motionless, the next it seems to glide through the darkness, its ethereal form shifting in and out of the shadows like smoke caught in moonlight.

The men barely have time to react before it descends upon them with terrifying precision.

One assailant, bolder—or more foolish—than the others, lunges at the phantom with his sword, a guttural shout escaping his lips. But the figure moves as if expecting his every action. With an effortless sidestep, it avoids the blade, its movements a fluid blur.

Before the man can adjust, the phantom's hand shoots out, seizing him by the throat. He struggles, his hands clawing uselessly at the pale, unearthly grip that holds him aloft. For a moment, his legs kick violently in the air, and then comes the sound.

A sickening crack.

The man's body goes limp, his head lolling unnaturally to the side as the figure drops him to the ground like a discarded doll.

The others shout in horror, their panic now spiralling out of control. One of them stumbles backward, his weapon slipping from his trembling hands. The ghostly woman turns toward them, her glowing form seeming to grow brighter as the surrounding darkness deepens.

My breath stutters, my limbs locking as the scene unfolds before me. Every instinct begs me to run, to turn away—but I can't.

I take a slow step back, a tangled rush of relief and fear surging through me. But the movement is clumsy, my foot pressing down on a brittle twig. The sharp snap shatters the fragile silence.

The creature's head jerks up with unnatural speed, her eyes locking onto mine—bright, furious, unyielding. They blaze with an intensity that roots me to the spot.

She lets out another bone-chilling scream, more powerful and fear inducing than the first. The sound vibrates through the air like a physical force, rattling my teeth and sending a piercing ache through my skull. I drop to my knees, clutching my ears, desperate to block it out.

But the scream isn't meant for me. I don't know what it is—whether ally or enemy—but for now; it stands in my favour.

The slim figure darts through the underbrush like an arrow loosed from a master's bow, swift and precise, each movement a seamless blend of grace and urgency as the shadows of the forest swallow her whole.

I truly can't believe what I'm seeing. It's as if the creature has risen from the depths of forgotten legends and childhood night terrors. Its eyes flaring with fury as it launches itself at the remaining six men. Their screams echoing through the woods. My hands press harder against my ears as I bend at the waist, my gaze fixed on the forest floor. Each crunch of bone and wet thud is a grisly punctuation to their cries.

One of the men that pinned me down falls into my line of sight with a heavy thud, his body crumpling like a discarded puppet. His lifeless eyes stare back at me, frozen wide in a terror that even death can't erase.

I can't look away, the image searing itself into my mind. My chest heaves, each breath catching on the edge of a sob as I try to ground myself.

Then, from the shadows, a hand snakes around my waist, firm but gentle. Before I can cry out, another hand covers my mouth, silencing the gasp that tears from my throat.

"Shh, Little Doe. Calm down. It's me." The voice is low and familiar, pulling me back from the precipice of panic. "Ye're safe now. I've got you."

He wraps himself around me, his body a shield, his arms steady and sure as they anchor me against him. For a moment, I sag into his hold, too drained and overwhelmed to resist. The tension in my limbs gives way to a trembling exhaustion as I let his words sink in.

Safe.

The last man remaining is the pathetic man who tried to defile me. He crawls backward through the underbrush, his face a mask of desperation. His pants, still bunched around his knees, keep him from fleeing outright. He stumbles and falls, his breaths coming in ragged gasps as he tries to put distance between himself and the phantom still lurking in the shadows.

I sense the moment Finn considers the scene in front of him. Finn's arms tighten around me, and his grip on me is incorruptible. He's trying to regulate his breaths, but the tremor in his hands is betraying the storm of emotions he's failing to suppress.

"Did he—" Finn's voice cracks, his question cutting off as he tries to steady himself. I shake my head, needing to reassure him and myself that I'm still in one piece. That the proclamations this morally repugnant man made weren't a permanent reality for me.

Finn's hand slips from my mouth, his touch trailing down to the base of my neck, where it lingers. His fingers are warm and steady, a quiet reassurance in the chaos still swirling around us.

"We need to get out of here," he says, his voice tight, but the weight of the moment keeps us both frozen.

I know better.

We aren't leaving. Not yet. Something holds us here, rooted to this place, to the man cowering before us. I can feel it in the stillness of Finn's body, in the way his breathing slows but remains heavy with rage. The air itself feels heavier, charged with an energy I don't fully understand.

The man's eyes bulge with terror, his pitiful attempts to scramble away thwarted by his trembling limbs and tangled trousers.

"Please, no!" he begs, his voice a high-pitched whimper. "We was only playin' around. It wasn't serious. We would never—"

He doesn't finish.

There is no mercy in her movements. The spectre descends upon him with the precision of a predator and the fury of vengeance long overdue. Her long nails sink deep into his abdomen, and with a sickening sound, she drags them upward. Blood gushes freely, his screams turning to weak, gurgling gasps as his body convulses.

She rears back; her face splattered with crimson, and lets out a piercing scream directed solely at Finn. The sound tears through the air, vibrating like the toll of some unholy bell.

On instinct, I rip myself from Finn's grasp, stumbling forward as I brace for an impact that never comes.

The creature freezes, her head tilting slightly as her glowing, rage-filled eyes shift from Finn to me. Slowly, the fury seems to dull, her ethereal form trembling as though caught in some internal struggle.

Up close, she is more human than I'd imagined. Beneath the blood and wildness, traces of what she had once been linger. She'd been young, vibrant, even beautiful. But those qualities are distant echoes now, buried beneath the weight of her hatred and sorrow.

Her lips move as if trying to form words, the effort strained and unfamiliar. A fragmented, guttural sound emerged, soft and hesitant.

"*An gortóidh sé thú?*" she asks at last, her voice carrying the lilting tones of a question.

I don't understand, but Finn's breath hitches behind me. His voice comes low and steady, laced with a conviction that makes my heart twist.

"I would *never* hurt her," he says, his grip tightening on the hilt of his blade as he rises and steps closer. "She is *mine*. I would die before letting harm come to her."

The creature's glowing eyes flick back to Finn, narrowing as if weighing the truth of his words. Her bloodied hand rises slowly, pointing toward the man still gasping weakly on the ground. The gesture is deliberate, her meaning clear.

"*Cosain í, onóraigh í.*"

I glance at Finn, my heart pounding. I don't know what she is saying, but somehow Finn does. The creature's eyes return to mine, and for a fleeting moment, something softer flickers within them—an emotion I can't name, but one that makes the tension in my chest ease.

She moves back; her form fading slightly as the shadows of the forest creep in to swallow her whole. But before she disappears completely, she pauses, her head tilting once more toward Finn.

Her voice, faint and distant, carries a last whisper.

"Cosain í."

The forest seems to hold its breath as the creature's presence fully dissolves, leaving us alone with the task she'd silently entrusted to Finn—and the man still writhing on the ground, his pleas now nothing more than feeble whimpers.

Finn's focus shifts entirely to the man.

Something changes in his stance—his usual steady presence now radiates an unrelenting, burning fury. His shoulders square, his jaw clenches, and his breaths come harder, faster, as though his rage is the only thing keeping him upright.

"Finn," I whisper, reaching for him, unsure of how to anchor him at this moment.

But he doesn't look at me. His eyes, stormy and dark, locked on the figure writhing in the dirt.

With deliberate steps, Finn closes the distance between them, the weight of his footsteps like distant thunder. There is no hesitation, no faltering in his movements.

The man's eyes widen further, his whimpers turning to desperate pleas as Finn looms over him. "Please—help me."

"You think you can beg yer way out of this?" Finn spits, his voice trembling with rage.

I stand frozen. This isn't the Finn who always holds his emotions in check, who thinks before he acts. This is raw, unbridled rage—passion so intense it borders on terrifying. Driven by a fire I've never witnessed in him before.

"Tell me who hired you, and I'll consider sparin' you." The man coughs, choking on his own breath.

"Speak," Finn commands, his voice low and lethal, sending a shiver down my spine. "Who sent you?"

"A... man," he rasps, barely audible. "Tall... gold hair..."

Finn edges closer. "Give me more, or I'll make sure it's slower."

The man's body shudders from the pain. "Said... some pudgy lass reckoned... reckoned she knew where ya was headed. We split up in three... to find ya quicker."

Finn's head snaps toward me, his stormy eyes lock onto me, and they promise destruction.

"*Colina?*" I say so low I'm not sure the wind will carry the sound to him.

He turns back to the man. "I need names."

The man groans, his head lolling to the side. "Didn't... say. Just said... she told 'em where ye'd be... she was sure of it."

Finn's expression darkens further, a shadow falling over his face. He grips the man's tunic tighter, dragging him closer with terrifying ease. "No names, no faces? Just a girl's word and gold in yer pocket? And her blood," he spews, pointing at me, "her blood on yer disgustin' hands."

The assassin whimpers, his body convulsing in pain, but Finn doesn't waver. His voice drops to a low, dangerous murmur. "So here's what's gonna happen now." He kneels, his presence towering even as he crouches. "I'm leavin' you to fate. Ye'll feel every bit of pain you tried to put on her. Ye're gonna die alone in the dirt. And I hope you find just as much misery in yer eternal life."

Finn rises with a deliberate finality, the man letting out a faint, sputtering sound as his hand weakly reaches toward Finn. But Finn doesn't look back. He grabs my arm, his touch firm but steady, and leads me away without another word.

I glance back only once, just long enough to see the man writhing in the dirt, gasping for air as his life ebbs away. A hollow pit forms in my stomach, but it isn't sympathy that fills it—only relief that he'll hurt no one again.

"Finn," I whisper, my voice barely audible over the pounding of my heart as we put distance between ourselves and the scene.

He turns to me abruptly, his eyes gleaming with the same fire that had driven his fury. But as his gaze meets mine, something shifts. The flames dim, replaced by something softer—wounded, familiar.

"It's more than he deserves," he murmurs, his voice hoarse.

I step forward, placing a trembling hand on his arm. His skin is hot to the touch, his muscles still tense beneath my fingers.

"I thought I'd been too late to you," he murmurs, his voice cracking under the weight of his emotions. "When I heard you scream, I—" He breaks off, eyes dropping to the ground as though he can't bear the thought.

"You weren't," I breathe, my voice steady despite the tremor in my hands. "I'm right here. I'm safe. Right here with you."

Tentatively, I step closer, sliding my hands upward until they rest lightly around his neck. His breath hitches, his eyes lifting to meet mine again. Slowly, as though testing the reality of my presence, his hands settle at my waist. His grip is gentle, but there's a desperation in the way his fingers curl slightly, grounding himself in this moment.

He exhales sharply, his body sagging as the weight of my words settle him. "I'll let no one hurt you, Triona," he says, his voice thick with emotion. "Not while I'm still breathing."

His lips part to say more, but no words come. Instead, he leans forward, forehead resting against mine. The proximity is electric, our breaths mingling in the forest's stillness.

"I'd die for you," he says, his voice barely above a whisper. "And I'd kill for you, too."

"You'll never have to make that choice," I reply, my voice just as quiet, my heart thundering in my chest.

When we break apart, his eyes search mine, his hands lingering on my waist, the touch mooring me as much as I hoped mine did for him.

"Let's get back," he murmurs after a moment, his voice steadier now.

Without a word, he offers me his hand. His fingers curl around mine with a gentle strength, the kind that says more than words ever could. There's no hesitation, no uncertainty in his grip.

Together, we step further into the darkness, leaving the blood and horror behind us. But as Finn's grip tightens on my hand, I know we carry something else with us—something unbreakable.

20

THE LANGUAGE OF TOUCH

Triona

The moment we step out of the dense forest, the cool night air hits my skin like a balm. I hear him before I see him.

"Triona!" Callan comes barreling toward us, his face a mixture of fury and relief. His arms wrap around me in a crushing embrace, so tight I can barely breathe.

"Never run off like that again!" He exclaims, voice raw and trembling with an emotion that isn't entirely anger. "How could ye ever think that was a good idea?"

"I—I'm sorry," I stammer, my voice cracking. "I didn't mean for—"

"*Sorry*?" he growls, pulling back just enough to grip my shoulders and scrutinise me. "Ye're filthy! What in the name of all that's divine happened in there? And where—" His voice breaks off as his eyes dart to the edge of the clearing.

Shadow.

Callan exhales sharply, dragging a hand down his face.

"Of course he returns now." I say, my voice soft and laced with frustration.

His eyes narrow at me, dark and piercing, as if searching for something deeper in my words. "What do ye mean? Ye went in there for him."

My stomach churns as the memory of the forest comes rushing back. "I ran for as long as I could, but I lost him. I tried to stop long enough to sense what direction he'd went, but that was a mistake because... because I was attacked."

Casey, who had been pacing nearby, stops dead in his tracks. Bran, leaning against a tree, straightens instantly, his easygoing demeanour melting away.

"What?" Casey says, his voice sharp.

"Attacked?" Bran asks, his usual smirk replaced with a furrowed brow.

I take a deep breath, forcing myself to meet their incredulous stares. "There were men in the woods. They—" I swallow hard, the words sticking in my throat. "They tried to..."

Finn steps forward, his presence solid and reassuring. He places his powerful hands on my shoulders. "She fought them," he says firmly, his voice cutting through the tension like a blade. "And when she couldnae fight anymore, someone else... *something* else stepped in."

Their gazes snap to Finn, disbelief etched across their faces.

"*Something* else?" Casey asks, his voice tinged with confusion and skepticism.

"It looked like a... woman. But it wasn't human. It... it might have been long ago, but not anymore," I breathe. "She killed them. *All* of them."

The weight of my words settles heavily over the group. Casey and Bran stare at me, their disbelief palpable. Bran opens his mouth to say something but closes it again, his usual quick wit failing him.

But Callan, he doesn't look surprised.

His jaw tightens, his expression unreadable as his gaze flicks to Finn and back to me.

"Callan," I say, narrowing my eyes at him. "You're not surprised. Why aren't you surprised?"

He clenches his fists, the muscles in his jaw twitching. "Not tonight, Triona," he says tersely. "We'll discuss it tomorrow."

"No," I press, stepping closer to him. "You know something. You *knew* something. Why won't you—"

"Not tonight," he snaps, his voice low and final.

"We leave now," he says, his tone brooking no argument. "We cannae stay in this area for the night."

"It sounds like everything was handled, Cal. Why move?" Casey argues.

"Casey," I interject, my voice trembling slightly as I look at him and then back at Callan. "Those men... they knew me. They've been following us."

The weight of my words crashes over the group. Casey's face pales as Finn stiffens beside me, his hand resting instinctively on the hilt of his dagger.

"They knew exactly where I'd be," I continue, my words rushing out in a mix of fear and anger. "One of them even said they split into groups to find us faster."

Finn steps forward, his voice tight with barely restrained fury. "They wernae after just anyone," he growls, his gaze flicking to Callan. "They knew her. And they knew her movements."

Callan's jaw works as though he's waging a silent battle with himself. Finally, he exhales sharply. "It's not safe to talk about here," he says, his tone clipped. "Jus trust me when I say we cannae risk stayin' another night."

Finn's glare sharpens. "Ye're holding something back, Callan. Spit it out now, for *her* sake."

Callan rounds on him, his temper flaring. "Dinnae start with me, Finn. I've been tryin' to keep this from turnin' into something worse!"

"Aye, well, felicitations," Finn bites out. "It's damn near worse."

"Stop it!" I shout, stepping between them. My heart is pounding, the reality of everything crashing down on me. "Arguing will not help."

Finn's nostrils flare, his jaw clenched tight, but before he can speak, I turn to him. "Finn. We can wait to discuss when things have... settled."

His chest rises and falls with slow, measured breaths. Anger still lingers in his eyes, but when he looks at me—really looks at me—something shifts. He exhales sharply through his nose, nodding once.

Callan's mouth presses into a thin line as he nods. "We go now. I willnae risk givin' whoever another chance to find us."

No one argues this time. Our group moves quickly, gathering their things in tense silence. But as we step into the night, Finn stays close beside me, his hand at my back.

Tomorrow.

Tomorrow, I'll have more answers.

Finn's fingers curl lightly around my arm, his warmth a quiet reassurance against the chill seeping into my bones. The weight of him at my side is the only thing keeping the gnawing uncertainty at bay.

Behind us, Callan, Bran, and Casey murmur in hushed voices, their words low and urgent, yet not so discreet as to escape my notice. Though I cannot make out the whole of their exchange, the clipped tones and sharp glances they throw over their shoulders betray their unease. It does little to quiet the disquiet thrumming in my chest.

Ask I continue walking at Finn's side, another thought takes root deep within me, heavier than the rest, curling into the hollow spaces fear has left behind.

I hesitate, glancing toward Finn. The moon casts its pale glow over his features, turning the sharp lines of his face into something unreadable, almost unearthly. His grip on my arm tightens ever so slightly, the smallest gesture, yet enough to make my breath catch.

I swallow, my voice barely more than a whisper. "Finn... the others..."

His gaze snaps to mine, and I see it—the same fear twisting inside me reflected in his eyes. His voice is quiet, steady, but laced with something raw.

His fingers flex slightly around my arm, his voice just as quiet as mine. "I know, Little Doe. The same thought crossed my mind."

A cold weight settles in my stomach.

If they faced the same danger... if they were hunted as we had been...

The mere thought of losing anyone else is enough to bring me to my knees.

I pray fate's hand had not been crueler to them than it had been to us.

Well into the middle of the night, exhaustion finally forced us to stop. We found a place hidden well enough, concealed beneath the thick canopy of trees—no firelight to give us away.

After doing my best to clean my body, I stand at the edge of my tent, wringing my hands as Finn tends to Aisling. His movements are slow and methodical as he runs a hand down her neck, murmuring something too quiet for me to hear. The dim moonlight catches on the curve of his jaw, his focus so absolute it makes my request feel even more absurd.

I hesitate, the words caught somewhere between my heart and my throat.

"Finn," I finally say, my voice barely louder than a whisper.

He glances up, his eyes immediately softening at the sight of me. "Aye, lass?"

I shift on my feet, my cheeks burn. "Would you sleep with me? In the tent, I mean." The words tumbled out in a rush, and I can't bring myself to meet his gaze. "Just for tonight."

For a moment, he doesn't answer, and I risk a glance at him. His brow furrows in a way that makes my chest tighten.

"You're scared," he says. Not a question, just a simple truth.

I nod, embarrassed, my arms folding around myself as though I can shield the vulnerability bleeding through me. "I just... I'd feel better if you were close."

He crosses the space between us in a few quick strides, his presence grounding me before his hands even touch me. When they do, they are gentle, steady as they grip my shoulders. "If that's what you want, it's what ye'll have," he says, his voice quiet but resolute. "Ye've no reason to be embarrassed, Tri."

I look up at him then, unsure if I've ever seen someone look at me in the same way he does—as if I am something *worth* protecting. The knot of tension in my chest eases, though my heart still pounds as his strong arms wrap around me, and the icy fear that grips me thaws.

"I'll be right here," he murmurs against the top of my head. "Always."

And I believe him. It's not a belief born of mere words. It's in the way he holds me, as if the world could shatter around us and he'd still shield me with everything he is. The weight of his promise presses into my chest, a vow that thrums with quiet power. In that moment, I realise he's not just offering comfort; he's offering a piece of himself, raw and unwavering. And I take it greedily.

"Go on inside," Finn says gently, pulling back just enough to meet my eyes. "Lie down and try to rest. I'll not be far behind."

Nodding, I turn and slip into the tent, the cool air inside wrapping around me as I settle onto the blankets.

I try to make myself comfortable, but I feel restless. Finn ducks inside, his presence filling the small space as he settles down beside me. I keep my back turned to him at first, unsure how to navigate this unfamiliar intimacy. The rustle of the blankets as he adjusts and the steady rhythm of his breathing become my focus.

After a moment, I turn to him, the question pressing against my lips. "Finn," I say softly, "How did you know what that... creature was saying?"

His brow furrows in thought. "I dinnae ken... truly," he admits, his voice low and thoughtful. "It worried me, but if it somehow saved you, I'll not question whatever gift was granted in that moment."

"What did it mean?"

Finn shifts, his fingers curling slightly into the blanket. "She asked if I'd hurt you."

A pause lingers between us, thick and heavy.

His voice is quieter when he speaks again. "Then she told me to defend you."

The response slips easily from my lips. "I know... given the chance, I'd not hesitate to do the same for you. To defend you with my life."

I swallow hard and turn my gaze away, focusing on the slow rise and fall of his breath.

Moments pass, and though I try to keep to myself, the tension in my body refuses to dissipate. Suddenly, Finn shifts, his arm tentatively wrapping around my waist, drawing me closer until I'm turned, and my back presses against his chest.

My heart races, but it's not fear that fuels it now. There's something settling about the weight of his arm around me, the way his body moulds protectively against mine. His touch is firm yet careful, as though he's afraid I might shatter if he eases his grip. I let out a shaky breath, and the sound of it draws a soft murmur from him.

"Easy now, Tri," he whispers, his voice low, soothing, and far too close to my ear. "I've got you."

And I truly believe that. I feel safe—not just from the dangers outside the tent, but from the doubts and fears that tangle in my heart.

As my breath evens out, he moves his hand to my hip. It lingers, not moving, not pressing, just there. It should feel out of place, but it doesn't. It feels right. Warmth spreads through me, seeping into places I hadn't realised were cold.

My fingers brush against his, tentative, testing the reality of this moment. Beneath my touch, his muscles shift, and I feel his breath hitch. Emboldened by his reaction, I grasp his hand, guiding it to rest just above my breasts, lacing my fingers through his.

It is as brazen a move as I have ever made, my heart pounding at the intimacy. The heat of his palm sears against me, and for a moment, I am caught between hesitation and desire.

What am I doing?

The thought flickers, but his steady breathing drowns it out, his presence anchoring me. Is this what it means to trust—offering a piece of myself without fear? I can't explain why I need him this close, only that it feels inevitable, as if every unspoken word and stolen glance led to this shared moment.

It's not just the safety that lulls me, but the quiet strength of him, the way his presence seems to fill every corner of the tent, and every part of me.

"Thanks," I whisper, barely audible over the rhythm of his breathing.

He doesn't respond with words, just presses me further into his body. It's a slight gesture, but it feels like everything.

As sleep slowly pulls me under, I realise I have never felt more protected—nor more vulnerable. In Finn's presence, I don't feel the need to run from anything.

Triona
Wednesday, 7 May 1823
Somewhere Near Inverness

The morning sun filters through the trees, casting shifting patterns of light across the forest floor as I make my way toward the creek. Callan crouches low at the water's edge, sharpening his blade with slow, deliberate strokes, his focus unyielding.

A few paces away, Casey and Bran sit in hushed conversation, their words occasionally broken by bursts of laughter that feel oddly out of place in a world that's tipped off its axis.

"Callan," I call softly.

He glances over his shoulder, his sharp gaze softening when it lands on me. "What is it?"

"I'm holding you to your promise," I say, folding my arms to hide the tremor in my hands. "No more secrets. I want the full truth."

He exhales heavily, setting his blade and whetstone aside.

For a moment, I think he might brush me off, but then he looks at me, really looks at me. Something in his expression shifts—an older brother's love mingled with reluctant acceptance.

"There's no sane way to say it—in fact, that it's a truth is something I'm still sortin' through," he begins, running a hand through his hair, his eyes darting to the trees as if searching for the right words.

"It's not uncommon for families like ours—families tied to the old ways—to attract... protectors. Guardians of a sort."

"Protectors?"

"Banshees," he says bluntly, watching my reaction. "Spirits drawn to families—especially bloodlines with daughters. They're not just harbingers of death, like the stories say. They watch over us, protect us—especially the women—from horrors they themselves endured when they were alive..."

A chill races down my spine. "And you think... one of them is protecting me?"

"I dinnae *think*, lass. I *ken*." His gaze locks onto mine, unwavering. "I was told long ago that Sinclairs never walk alone in the darkness. Even if we dinnae see them, guardians linger. They're there, in the shadows, tied to us in ways we cannae hope to understand."

"Who told you that?" I ask, though I'm not sure I want the answer.

Callan hesitates. "Triona—" he starts.

A bark of laughter snaps the tension like a whip.

"Ach, you're havin' a laugh," Casey says, shaking his head as he strides closer. "So we've got a family banshee now? Hauntin' us, but bein' downright civil about it?"

Bran flicks a pebble into the stream. "Sounds like the start of a bedtime story gone wrong. 'Once upon a time, your ancestors were so tragically tortured that the spirits belonging to the great beyond stuck around.'"

Callan rounds on them. "It's no jest, ye daft bastards. I'm tellin' ye what's real."

Bran raises his hands in mock surrender. "I'm just saying it sounds like something out of a fairytale. Banshees lurking around like some sort of spiritual escorts?"

"It might not make sense to you two eejits," Callan snaps, "Seein' as ye've been too far up each other's arses to see what's happenin' around you. But Triona's healin' ability doesnae make much sense either, now does it?"

That shuts them up. Casey's smirk fades. Bran's humour dims to curiosity.

Casey crosses his arms. "All right. So how would *you* know all of this?"

"Because I was told," Callan growls. "Years ago. By someone who knew more about this sort of thing than ye ever will."

Bran tilts his head. "By *who*? A wise old mystic? A local seer? Someone drunk off his tits at the pub?"

"By someone who *cared* if we lived," Callan snaps.

Casey steps forward. "Say it's all true. How—"

"Enough!" I snap, my voice cracking as I cut him off.

They all freeze, playful banter fading as I glare at Bran and Casey.

"I saw her." The words tremble out of me. "I *saw* her. So whether you believe in banshees or ghost stories or bloodline curses... I'm telling you. She's real." I pause, swallowing hard.

"They almost... if I'd been held down a minute longer..." I trail off. My throat tightens, the memory searing.

As if summoned, Finn steps into the clearing. His presence steadies me, and when words fail, he speaks for me.

"They were gonna force themselves on her," Finn says, his voice low and cold. "And I watched as they were torn limb from limb. So I dinnae care what it was, but I'm damn grateful for its arrival. I'll be thankin' it every night I draw breath."

Silence chokes the clearing.

Even Bran doesn't have a quip. Casey's expression twists with shame and something deeper—fear, maybe.

Casey lowers his voice. "Triona... I'm sorry."

"No, I'm... *we're* all just as confused as you," I say, gesturing toward Finn and Callan. "This hasn't been easy to process."

They nod in unison, their earlier skepticism replaced by a quiet understanding.

Bran exhales, running a hand through his hair, the humour that usually dances in his eyes tempered by a flicker of something softer. "Banshees... it's... bloody wild, and eerie as the grave. A spirit woman smiting deceptive cunts in the woods."

A small smile tugs at the corner of my lips, but before I can respond, Bran speaks again.

"So... just to be clear, she's on our side, right? No sudden appearances to scare us while we're taking a leak in the woods?"

Casey snorts. "Bran, I swear—"

"Are you afraid she'll try to steal yer cock?" Finn deadpans.

"What? No!" Bran balks. "I've a strong bladder, but I'm not made of steel. One jump scare and I'll be down a pair of trousers. I don't know about the rest of you, but I don't fancy pissing myself."

The tension breaks, a ripple of quiet laughter passing between us. Even Callan smirks, though he quickly hides it behind a scowl.

Bran's grin widens as he leans back against a tree. "That's all I needed to hear. Banshees, welcome. Just... give a bit of warning so I don't greet you with my arse out."

The laughter that follows is sharp and strange—but welcome.

Callan rolls his eyes but mutters, "Bloody eejit," under his breath.

Casey shakes his head, his voice a touch more serious as the moment settles. "Truth be told, we should've believed him straight off. I've been this lad's brother for twenty years, and I can tell ye—Callan doesnae know how to tell a joke, let alone make one up."

That draws a few more quiet chuckles, even from Callan himself. For a fleeting moment, it feels like we might be okay.

Callan exhales, rolling his shoulders, blade back in hand. His voice, when it comes, is softer.

"Deidre told me. Long ago. When I was just a lad." He stares down at the blade like it holds the memory.

I swallow, something uneasy curling into my stomach. "How would Deidre even know that?"

"Deidre has been a presence in our parents' lives since before we were born. I can only assume... she must've kent the truth of it all'."

The truth of everything.

Had she known what was coming?

Had she known my parents' fate long before it unfolded—watched it, carried it in silence, never speaking a word?

"I'm startin' to truly believe what Da meant... what he said before we left. That the world we're steppin' into—it's not the one we knew. Not anymore."

No one speaks, but I feel the quiet acceptance of the truth—that the world *has* changed.

And somehow, I know—we are only just beginning to grasp its depths.

21

FAITH AND FOLLY

Triona

Saturday, 10 May 1823

Port Oban: The Day of Departure

The harbour is a hive of activity, bustling with sailors unloading cargo, shouting dockworkers, and the sharp tang of brine in the air.

Beneath the noise, beneath the movement, a suffocating unease lingers as the same thought loops in all our minds.

Did the others survive the journey?

We move through the throng, our urgency at odds with the ordinary bustle of the port. Each glance over a shoulder, each pause of hesitation, carries the weight of unasked questions. We make our way to the inn where we were told to meet Alex. The common room is noisy, filled with the hum of conversations and the clink of mugs. Bran wastes no time approaching the innkeeper, a stout man with a sharp eye for newcomers.

"We're looking for Alex Mumford," Bran says, his voice steady despite the tension in his jaw. "He left word for us to meet him here."

The innkeeper doesn't answer right away. The world seems to slow, the din of the common room fading into a dull hum as we wait—each second stretching unbearably long. My breath catches in my throat, and though no one speaks, the weight of our shared fear presses down like a stone.

The innkeeper studies Bran, his expression unreadable, dragging the moment out further.

And then he exhales, leaning in slightly. "Mumford? Hmm, no' sure," he mutters. Then, quieter still, he recites: *"Born in the West, yet I wander with ease..."*

Bran hesitates, the faintest flicker of something—relief, maybe—crossing his face before he responds. *"My laughter echoes on the salt-kissed seas."* His voice is sure, but there's an edge to it. A warning not to play games with us.

The man grunts in approval. "Yer da's gone. Left word wi' the harbourmaster, he did."

Bran exhales, nodding. "Thanks."

We step out of the inn, the noise behind us doing nothing to drown out the frustration boiling in the group.

"Sweet shite on a biscuit." Bran paces, as his mind seems to race ahead.

"He's just *gone*?" Callan mutters, throwing his hands in the air.

Bran grunts. "Let's go get answers before panicking."

For the first time since we set foot in this harbour, something settles inside me—not entirely at peace, but steadier.

They made it.

That is all that matters right now.

We stride toward the harbourmaster's office, but the man himself is barking orders at a group of dockworkers when Bran approaches. He stands tall, unaffected by the man's sharp gaze. Their conversation is barely audible from where we wait.

"If ye're here for a berth, ye'll need to wait," the man says to Bran, barely sparing him a glance.

"I'm not here for a berth," Bran replies, his voice firm. "I'm looking for Alex Mumford. He left word for his son, Bran."

The harbourmaster pauses, then looks him over. "He did, did he?" Then the man clears his throat and gets close to Bran's ear. Bran produces a compass from his pocket, which seems to satisfy whatever question he'd asked.

"He left instructions," the harbourmaster says, gesturing toward his office. "Covered transport for you lot, and anything ye'd have wi' ye. Also, left coin to see you through. Gave little else, but he seemed to know what he was about."

"Where did he go?" Bran presses.

"Ireland," the harbourmaster replies, narrowing his eyes. "Said yer paths would cross soon enough."

Bran's jaw tightens, but he nods. The harbourmaster hands him a small pouch of coin and a folded note. "Here. He left this, too."

Bran returns with the note. One with his name scrawled on the front.

His fingers tremble slightly as he unfolds the letter, but the moment his eyes scan the words, his entire body sags with relief. His chest rises and falls in a heavy exhale, the tension that had coiled in his shoulders finally breaking.

For a second, he just stares at the letter, his knuckles tightening around the edges as if anchoring himself to the words before him.

"They're all alive. All and well." His voice, though thick with emotion, carries the weight of absolute certainty.

A breath I hadn't realized I was holding escapes me, my limbs suddenly weak with the sheer force of relief. Finn lets out a quiet exhale beside me, and Callan rolls his shoulders, the tightness in his expression easing—but only slightly.

Bran lifts the letter slightly, his grip firm. "My father did indeed leave for Ireland. It doesn't say why, but I know he wouldn't make an unnecessary decision." His expression hardens, his voice steady, decisive. "But this changes nothing for us. We still need to forge forward. Our destination remains the same—we continue to Portugal."

Callan's eyes narrow. "That's it? He just *left*?"

"Do we even know it's really from Alex?" I ask, stepping closer. "This could be a trap for all we know—anyone leaving us a message."

Bran doesn't flinch under the barrage of questions. Instead, he lifts the note, scanning it carefully. "He'll have left something. Something only I can find."

"And if that's not the case?" Callan presses.

Bran doesn't answer. He walks to the edge of the dock where the sunlight is strongest and holds the note up to the light. For a moment, it looks like an ordinary scrap of paper, but as I step closer, I make out a faint wolf's head, its features sharp. Beneath it, four words glow faintly in the sunlight:

We endure, we prevail.

Bran exhales softly, folding the note with care. "That's his mark. It's him."

Silence settles over the group, thick and uncertain. Callan crosses his arms, his expression hard. "And we're just supposed to trust this?"

Bran turns to Finn suddenly, his gaze steady and direct. "Do you trust my judgment on this?"

Without hesitation, Finn meets his eyes and nods. "Aye, I do."

Bran's shoulders relax slightly, and he looks at us. "Then we trust the plan. My father has *never* let me down before, and he's not about to start now."

Callan mutters something under his breath, but doesn't argue further.

Casey sighs, rubbing the back of his neck. "All right. We trust the plan. We'll stay the course. I trust you too, Bran." Casey gives him the faintest smile, which Bran returns in kind.

We settle into the corner of the dock, waiting for the next steps. Bran stands a few paces away, his gaze fixed on the horizon, his hand absentmindedly brushing the note in his coat. The tension lingers, thick and heavy, despite the despite the assurances laid before us.

I sit on a crate nearby, elbows on my knees, head lowered. Finally, I break the silence, voice low and trembling with frustration. "I'm trying so hard to push forward, but I don't know how much blind faith I have left in me."

To my surprise, it's Bran that crouches in front of me.

"I feel it too," he says, his voice low but fierce. "The uncertainty and doubt clawing at the back of my mind. Wanting something solid when all we've got are whispers and shadows. I've never been so torn in my life."

He continues. "What matters now is that we keep stepping, even though it feels as if the ground could fall away at any moment."

All that I find when I look at him is steadfast sincerity.

"You've been through fire before, and you came out stronger," he continues. "We all see it. And I know we'll see it again."

His words hit something deep, cracking the wall I'd built around my frustration. A reluctant smile pulls at my lips, and I let out a shaky laugh. "Who could resist feeling better after that?"

Bran grins, standing and offering me a hand. "Now get up. We've got a long road ahead, and I'd rather not face it without your sharp tongue keeping us all in line."

I take his hand, and he holds mine as he says, "*We endure, we prevail.*"

I loop my arm through his and repeat his words with quiet conviction. "*We endure, we prevail.*"

With that, we turn toward the brigantine moored at the dock. The ship is smaller than I expected but sleek and sturdy, its masts stretching skyward like black spires. The name *Bán Sídhe* is painted in bold letters along its bow. One by one, we load up, horses included, the creak of wood and the rhythmic thud of hooves filling the air.

Curiosity gets the better of me as I approach a deckhand near the gangway. "Excuse me, sir. What does the name of the boat mean?"

He raises an eyebrow, a smirk playing at the corner of his mouth. "*Sir,* is it? Ah, that's rich. Ye hopin' a bit o' sweet talk'll get ye far? We're crammed on this floatin' tub for a good stretch—plenty o' time to learn how to handle a man proper, if ye've the nerve for it."

I blink at him, my lips parting in disbelief before settling into a firm, unimpressed line. My brows lift just enough to convey silent exasperation—the same look a mother gives a child when they find themselves toeing the line of trouble.

Before I can retort, Finn sidles up beside me, one hand resting on the hilt of his weapon, the other pulling me in against his side. His voice is smooth but edged with quiet authority. "Answer her question, and mind yer tongue—before I decide ye're better off without it."

I don't have to look at Finn to know how he's staring at the man—it's written in the tension coursing through his body, in the way his presence feels heavier, more certain, as if he's just waiting for an excuse to make good on the threat.

The deckhand straightens sharply, the teasing edge vanishing as he swallows hard. "Aye, well," he clears his throat, glancing between us, "Bán Sídhe," he replies, his thick Irish accent making the words roll like a song. "Means '*white fairy*'."

Another deckhand passing by snickers and calls out, "Naw, cap'n calls 'em banshees! Says they're death bringers, he does. Thinks name alone'll warn off wrong-doers. Superstitious feck, full o' notions, that one." His mirth lingers as he continues past us.

The first deckhand seizes the moment to scurry away, casting a nervous glance at us before disappearing below deck.

When I glance at Finn, his glare is sharp enough to slice through the rigging, his golden-brown eyes dark with warning. Every muscle in him is taut, like a man barely holding himself in check.

Without thinking, I reach for his hand and squeeze, just enough to steady him.

At first, he stays rigid, but after a moment, his fingers shift—slow, deliberate—curling around mine with certainty.

I glance back at everyone, expecting a quip or a sharp remark, but they're all quiet. Casey's fingers tap anxiously against the hilt of his dagger. Bran avoids my gaze entirely. Even Callan stands silent, his brow furrowed.

My voice cuts through the silence, steady but soft. "It's just a name."

"Hell's own britches," Bran grumbles under his breath, just as Casey groans. "Of course it is. Of course, it's called a damn banshee."

I raise an eyebrow at both of them, lips curving into a ghost of a smirk. "Well," I say dryly, "guess it's a fitting vessel for us, then."

Bran groans again, dragging a hand down his face. "Couldn't it have been something a little less... I don't know—ominous? Nothing screams *'we might not make it to our next destination'* quite like our ship being named after a screeching death spirit."

"What would be more to your liking, pray tell?" I counter, tilting my head with exaggerated thoughtfulness. "The Buoyant Bosom? The Twin Treasures? The Corset Conqueror?"

Casey snorts so loudly I think he might choke. "HMS Plump Peaks? Oh, no—wait. The Glistening Gudgeon." His grin is wide enough to split his face.

Finn interjects in his usual calm drawl, "The Lusty Lancer."

That earns a laugh from me, but before I can respond, Callan clears his throat. He doesn't look up, just mutters under his breath, *"The Veined Voyager."*

The laughter dies instantly, and every head turns toward him.

Bran looks at Callan, then at the rest of us, and finally throws up his hands with a wide grin. "Well, hell. Callan wins out, but I have to give it to Triona for second place with *The Corset Conqueror.*"

Callan shrugs, completely unfazed. "Takes a keen mind to name a ship," he says, the ghost of a smirk tugging at the corner of his mouth.

Bran claps him on the shoulder as they walk ahead. "Aye, mate. And you have a far filthier one than I'd expected."

The rest of us follow, the tension from earlier easing slightly as we settle into the rhythm of the task. Whatever lies ahead, we have a ship, a direction, and each other—our path set, even if the destination feels uncertain.

22

COLLIDING TIDES

Finn

Tuesday, 13 May 1823

Third Day Out at Sea

The late afternoon sun glints off the rolling waves, stretching golden across the ship's deck. The scent of salt and tar lingers in the air, carried by the breeze that rattles the rigging and sends ropes slapping against the mast. The steady creak of wood beneath our feet is a quiet reminder of forward motion, of distance growing between us and everything we left behind.

Once we settled on the boat, we told Triona everything she had missed while unconscious—Marcus stepping in, and his failed attempt at helping. Colina's betrayal that set everything in motion. Then, finally, about the men who came for us.

Each word felt like peeling back a scab, exposing wounds that had barely closed. It wasn't easy. The telling made it real. But it was necessary.

By the time silence settled over us, it wasn't the heavy, suffocating kind we'd known since that day. It was a quiet that allowed us to breathe again. For the first time since the chaos, the weight in our chests felt shared, no longer something we each carried alone.

I linger in that fragile quiet, lost in thought, often reciting the events in my mind. It's only when movement catches my eye that I'm snapped back to the present. Bran leans against a coil of rope near the mainmast, his grin as cocky as ever, but his eyes are fixed on Triona, studying her with a sharp intensity that sets my teeth on edge. My jaw tightens before I catch myself, forcing a deep breath as I refocus. "I want to spar with Triona," he announces.

He's loud enough to make a few deckhands pause mid-step. Triona's face is calm, but there's a flicker of amusement in the curve of her lips as she eyes him.

"You jest," I say flatly, though Bran's expression says otherwise.

He fires back without missing a beat. "C'mon, Finn, she's got spirit. Let's see if she's got skill."

"Ye're built like a bloody draft horse," I growl. "This isnae a fair match."

"First, my thanks. A strong form isn't a gift; it's earned. I have to keep myself in top physical form for the ladies. And second..."—Bran spreads his arms wide, grinning like the devil—"To hell with fair! Let skill speak for itself!"

Casey barks a laugh, shaking his head. "Ye seriously underestimate what ye've just done, mate. She's gonna knock you flat."

I glance at Triona again, expecting her to wave this off, maybe laugh and let it go. But she stands, head high and eyes shining with something that sets my teeth on edge.

"I accept," she says, her voice calm but firm.

Bran's grin grows devilishly.

I open my mouth to argue, to tell her she doesn't need to entertain this, but I know it's useless. She's as stubborn as a mule on a wet day.

Bran chuckles, rolling his shoulders as he steps into the centre of the clearing. "All right, *lass*. Let's see what you've got."

The makeshift sparring match begins with a slow circle. Bran moves, loose and confident, his cocky grin intact. My fists clench as I watch him tower over her, like a wolf squaring off with a raven. But Triona doesn't flinch. She moves light on her feet, her eyes fixed on him, sharp and calculating.

Bran lunges first, feigning left. She doesn't take the bait. Instead, she sidesteps, darting in with a quick jab to his side that forces him to stumble back. The grin slips from his face for just a second before he resets, this time more cautiously.

It doesn't matter. She's too fast, too precise. Every time he tries to land a blow, she's already one step ahead, her movements fluid and relentless. When Bran overextends, she ducks low, driving her shoulder into his ribs and forcing him off balance. With a sharp twist, she sweeps his legs out from under him, and he crashes to the ground with a heavy thud.

The ship falls silent, save for the lapping of waves against the hull. Bran groans, sprawled on his back as he stares up at the rigging.

Propping himself up on his elbows, he rubs his ribs with a wince. "It's unnatural," he mutters, "for a woman to hit a man so hard he sees stars."

Triona steps closer, crouching beside him until their faces are level. She tangles her fingers in the hair at the top of his head—not enough to hurt, but enough to command his undivided attention. His dazed eyes snap to hers, wide with surprise.

Her voice is low, laced with steel. "I am not just some woman. I am *the* woman who will bring comeuppance in full force, so it's best for all to keep out of my bloody way."

She rises, brushing her hands off as if the fight were only a casual chore. She's radiant, her expression one of quiet satisfaction. Not gloating, not boastful—just steady, unshaken.

"Maybe next time," she says with a smirk, "you'll think twice before underestimating me."

Casey's laugh is contagious. "Tried tellin' ye—never stood a chance." For a moment, his laughter fades, replaced by something more reflective. "She's come a long way. Always had the fire, but now... she's a true force to be reckoned with."

Bran lets out a weak chuckle. "Aye, a goddess to flatten all men like sacks of flour," he says, still fighting for breath. "Never thought I'd lose my pride, my spine, and my bollocks all at once, but here we are."

He shifts slightly, wincing. "Next time, full body armour. From head to cock. A man's got to keep all of his parts where they belong."

Casey barks out a laugh, shaking his head. "Aye, well, let this be a lesson: never bet against a Sinclair."

Bran groans dramatically as he shifts. "Didn't even get a kiss for the trouble."

Laughter ripples through the group once more, loud and easy.

Triona stands tall, the fading sunlight painting her in gold, her breath steady, her fire undimmed. She's light personified, standing there like a queen, and I can't take my eyes off her.

As the others drift apart, laughter giving way to murmurs and motion, I step toward her. My voice is low, meant for her alone. "Ye've nothing to prove, Little Doe."

Triona glances at me, her gaze softening, but the edge of her smirk remains. "Maybe not, but it wasn't for him. It was for me. After everything, I needed to feel strong again."

As I look at her, I know two things: she'll never stop surprising me, and gods help me—I'll never stop wanting what I can't have.

Triona
Sunday, 18 May 1823
Eighth Day Out at Sea

As I finish the last word of *Frankenstein*, I close the book with a soft thud and release a contemplative sigh. The story lingers in my mind, its weight settling in my chest. "That was brilliant," I murmur, the fondness in my voice unmissable.

Beside me, Casey lounges against the side of the boat, hands tucked behind his head, long legs stretched out as if he owns the space. His easy sprawl clashes with the stiffness in my legs and the numbness creeping into my backside—a reminder of how long I've been perched on this wooden bench, lost in Shelley's words while the boat rocks beneath us.

A few paces away, Bran, Callan, and Finn sit in contemplative silence, their gazes shifting between the open water and the worn pages in my hands. They're listening, but their minds drift—half here, half caught in the world the story has spun around us.

Casey's gaze drifts toward the sky. "It's eerie. The creature wasna born a monster. He just wanted to belong, to be loved. But he became something dark because no one could see him as anythin' else."

Bran, who has been uncharacteristically quiet, speaks. "It's tragic—and familiar," he muses, his voice thoughtful. "A soul rejected, forced into the shadows because the world wouldn't make room for him."

Casey shifts, his face taking on that rare thoughtful look. One I used to tease him about as a child. "Do ye remember Ma's story about Lugh Lámhfhada?" he asks suddenly, turning to meet my gaze.

"Aye, the master of many skills," I say, recalling the tale with a smile. "He had to prove himself to the Tuatha Dé Danann—show that he was worthy of their favour. They tested him, but when he succeeded, he earned his place among the greatest beings of his world."

Casey nods, his expression thoughtful. "Ma always said if they'd turned him away, he might've become like the creature. Bitter, desperate, tryin' to prove himself for the wrong reasons. But Lugh was lucky. He found his place. The creature... he never had that chance."

"There's a truth in there," Finn says, his tone thoughtful. "We should treat those we dinnae understand with decency. "

I glance at him, a small smile forming. "Exactly. That's the real test of humankind. Who knows what one might become if we give them a chance?"

Casey's nod is slow and deliberate. "That's what makes Triona different, lads," he says, his voice quiet but steady. "Most folk wouldn't pity the creature—they'd fear him. They see the surface and stop there, never thinkin' what's beneath. But she's always had a way of lookin' deeper. Seein' what could be, not just what is."

His words hit me like a warm light in the cold. Casey's rare compliments always settle in places I didn't know needed filling.

I blink at him, a grin tugging at the corner of my mouth. "By my troth. Was that a compliment? From you?"

He huffs a laugh, rolling his eyes. "Dinnae let it go to yer head."

I deflect. "Maybe it's just because Ma raised us with those stories. She made sure we knew there's more to a person than what the world sees."

He nudges me with his elbow, a wry smile softening his words. "Dinnae go givin' Ma all the credit. That kindness? That's all *you*. I see it in the way ye treat folk, even when they dinnae deserve it... even when your brother's huv'nae earned it."

I snort, shaking my head. "Gods know what you've *ever* done to earn it. Miraculous, really."

"Miraculous? I'm a proper saint for puttin' up with you."

I laugh softly, shaking my head. "You're my family.... that's reason enough, I guess."

He falls quiet for a moment, his grin fading into something softer, more genuine. Callan exhales, glancing toward me before speaking, his voice steady. "Aye, we're family. But it's more than that, Triona. Ye've got this way of makin' folk feel like they matter—like they belong. Casey and I... we'd be lost without ye, truly. Ye keep us steady—keep us whole. It's no small thing what ye give us."

Bran nods, his voice quieter but firm. "He's right. You've got a way of holding people together, even when they don't know they need it. You're something to come back to—you feel like home, in a way."

Casey chimes in next, nudging me lightly with his elbow. "Aye, even when we're bein' right impossible, you never give up on us. No matter how much we bicker, ye'd stay by us if the entire world turned its back."

Finn, who has been listening silently, finally speaks, his tone filled with certainty. "It's why we stand with ye, Triona. At all costs."

Their words settle around me, warm and solid, and for a moment, I don't know what to say. I just let myself hold on to the feeling, letting it root itself deep within me.

A lump forms in my throat as warmth spreads through my chest. I blink rapidly, feeling the sting of unshed tears. "Thank you... all of you," I say softly, my voice trembling just enough for them to notice. A half-laugh escapes me as I swipe a hand across my eyes. "Now stop before I start crying like a bairn."

Casey takes my hand in his and squeezes, his own rare softness showing. "Whatever happens, wherever life takes us, ye'll always have a place with us. Never doubt that."

Before I can respond, Callan's voice cuts through the moment. "Careful, Triona. If Casey gets any softer, we'll need to pack him in straw so he doesn't fall apart."

Casey groans, his sincerity breaking. "Ach, Callan, can you not let a man have a moment?"

"Oh, aye, have yer moment. Jus dinnae ask us to call ye Saint Casey anytime soon." Callan quips.

I laugh, shaking my head. "Don't worry, I'd never let it go that far."

Casey rolls his eyes. "And now the two of you have me thinkin' I should've been an only child."

The sound of our combined laughter fills the space, but then we sit in comfortable silence. Bran clears his throat, breaking the quiet. "All right, now that we've all had our sentimental moment, back to the book. We can all agree that Mary Shelley's got a mighty unusual way with words, aye?"

I chuckle, tilting my head in curiosity. "How do you figure?"

Bran leans forward, his voice thoughtful. "Doc thinks he can play God, so he builds himself a monster and then *blames* it for everything wrong. The real villain isn't the creature—it's him. He's less human than the monster itself."

I nod, considering his perspective. "But it's more than that, isn't it? It's about what it means to be human. To long for connection, for belonging. The creature's desolation—that's the real tragedy."

Finn tilts his head, letting my words sink in. "Aye, desolation. It's not just loneliness—it's something deeper. A hollow that makes a person take what they want without carin' for others."

"Unmonitored power's a dangerous beast. We've seen the destruction it brings," I say, then glance around at them, my voice softening. "We know it all too well."

Casey looks at me with an expression that conveys understanding—to pain lived and felt. "'*Beware; for I am fearless, and therefore powerful.*'" He adds, with a deep mocking tone, quoting the book word for word.

I set my eyes upward, watching the stars flicker faintly against a velvet black. "They say power corrupts," I murmur, "but I don't believe that—not entirely. Power doesn't change someone. It unveils them. Shows who they've been all along, buried beneath the quiet."

Casey lets out a bitter laugh. "We've faced the worst of unchecked power—our land, our kin, our culture taken from us by those who saw us as nothin'."

As the impact of Casey's words settle, Callan cuts in, low and resolute.

"And that's why we fight," he mutters. Then he turns, his eyes locking onto mine, and there's a fire in them, something fierce and unyielding. "One day, they'll reap what they've sown."

Words hang heavy in the air surrounding us, as promises etch themselves into the silence.

Callan glances ahead, then shifts his posture. I can tell that his body is just as tense as my own. "We should probably rest for the night," he says.

Casey stretches with a sigh. With a laugh, he starts, "I cannae believe a woman—" he cuts himself off, all too aware of the blunder he was about to make.

"Casey Sinclair, why do I feel as if you were about to say something senseless?"

The look on his face is one of a guilty man. "I might've been about to say something senseless."

"Possibly about, oh I don't know, the gender of the novelist?" I cross my arms, awaiting his confession.

"Oh, what was that Callan? Did you need something?" Casey gestures towards Callan's position near the deck's railing and darts off.

Bran snorts, shaking his head as he watches Casey flee. "Aye, run while you can, Sinclair. That tongue of yours will be the death of you one day."

With a chuckle, he pushes himself up. "Ah, might as well see what trouble they're getting into. Don't do anything I wouldn't do. Or do," he adds with a smirk.

Finn shoots him a look, unimpressed.

Bran just grins and winks before striding off to join Callan and Casey.

The boat rocks gently, the sounds of the night settling around me. My thoughts drift, tangled in the conversation's weight, in the meaning of the stories we tell.

I don't hear Finn move until he's beside me. He lowers himself onto the bench, his presence steady and quiet. After a beat, he speaks. "Not headin' to bed?"

I shake my head, exhaling softly. "Too restless."

He hums in understanding. "Aye... me too."

There's nothing more to say. He just stays sitting with me as the boat sways beneath us. The silence between us isn't heavy—it's comfortable, as it often is with him. I feel my body slowly relax, exhaustion settling in despite my earlier words. My head tilts, finding its way to rest against his shoulder. In my sleepy haze, I feel Finn shift slightly before his arm comes around me, steady and warm. Instinctively, I nuzzle into him, seeking the quiet comfort he offers. A breath later, his head rests atop mine.

The night stretches on, and in the gentle lull of the waves, my eyes drift closed.

Finn
Saturday, 24 May 1823
Fourteenth Day Out at Sea

Moonlight cuts across the deck, silvering the ropes and casting long shadows against the masts. The distant sound of waves slapping against the hull is the only rhythm, save for the occasional creak of wood as the ship shifts. I lean against the railing, staring out at the black expanse of water, but my thoughts are far from the sea.

"Why do you call her that?" Bran's voice cuts through the quiet, pulling me from my thoughts.

"Call who what?"

He smirks, one brow cocked, and leans back on his elbows. "You call Triona '*Little Doe.*' Why?"

The memory sits heavy in my chest, not something I share lightly. It's always been a story I held close—one I never spoke aloud because the weight of it belonged to me alone. But now, after Triona's revelation, the truth twists through the edges of that moment, poisoning it.

I exhale sharply, gripping the railing a little tighter. "I've been calling her that from the first day I came to the Sinclairs' home."

Bran's eyebrows lift, but he stays quiet.

"I'd barely arrived when the family was in uproar," I begin, my voice low. "Triona was missin'. They said she'd gone off to play but never came back."

Bran's smirk fades, his gaze sharpening. "What happened?"

I rub a hand over my face, the weight of that day pressing against me. "I didnae ken the land, or anyone, but something in me screamed at me—demanded I find her. So, I entered the forest, and the moment I did..." I pause, my throat tightening. "I saw a flash of movement."

"A flash of movement?" Bran echoes, leaning in closer now.

I nod. "It was a massive white stag. Bigger than any I'd ever seen. It stood there, starin' at me, steady and knowing. Then it turned and started movin' deeper into the trees."

"You followed it." Bran's voice a statement, rather than a question.

"I didnae ken why, but I felt as if I had to." My tone softens, reverence creeping in as I recall the memory. "Something in me said to follow it. Every twist, every turn, I stayed on its trail. And sure enough... it led me straight to her."

Bran's breath catches. "Where was she?"

"She was in a clearin'. Badly injured—scrapes, bruises, a nasty gash on her head. She looked so small lyin' there." My voice wavers, but I push through it. "But when I knelt beside her, she opened her eyes. And in that moment... the most beautiful set of green, doe-like eyes stared back at me."

Bran exhales slowly, his voice soft with understanding. "*Little Doe.*"

I nod, a faint, bittersweet smile pulling at my lips. "Aye. She's been that to me ever since."

For a moment, I hesitate. The memory sits heavy in my chest, not something I share lightly. Finally, I sigh and lean heavier into the rail. "She told me something at the inn about that day that she'd forgotten. And then a truth that wretched bitch Colina confessed."

Bran lifts a brow, but he stays quiet.

"She told me she was the reason she was in the woods that day." I run a hand over my face, the weight of the revelation pressing into me all over again. "Colina led her out there, hit her over the head with a rock. She meant to leave her lyin' there."

Bran's smirk vanishes. He stands straighter, his gaze sharpening. "What?"

I nod, swallowing hard. "Triona said she only remembered it recently, but she gives me the credit for saving her life." My voice drops, tightening with something I don't want to name. "She told me that if I hadnae found her, she might never have made it back."

Bran exhales sharply, shaking his head. "Bloody hell."

For a moment, neither of us speaks. The sea stretches endlessly before us, dark and unknown, much like the past I can't seem to let go of.

I can feel Bran studying me, and when I turn to look at him, a slow, knowing grin spreads across his face. "Sounds like she thought that was quite the romantic notion, Finn."

I shoot him a flat look. "It's not like that."

Bran raises his hands in mock surrender. "Aye, sure. Just a young lad following a mystical stag to rescue a lass, giving her a secret name and keeping it close to his heart for years. Definitely not romantic."

I shake my head, but Bran just grins wider.

"Doesn't that make you want to tell her the truth of your feelings?" he presses.

I tense, my gaze snapping to his.

Bran stares at me for a long moment, his sharp gaze studying me. Then his grin breaks through. "You're ferociously hopeless, you know that, right?"

I roll my eyes, but I don't bother arguing.

He goes quiet again, his grin fading into something more thoughtful. "She doesn't know about the tattoo you've got on your body? Doesn't know why you've got that, I presume."

My shoulders tense, but I don't look up. "No," I admit quietly.

There's something closer to concern in his tone when he speaks again. "You've been carrying this for years, and when the moment to tell her everything surfaces, you don't?"

I glance at him; the moonlight casting shadows across his face. "It's not something I can just tell her. What am I supposed to say?"

Bran raises an eyebrow, and I see the sly grin creeping in. "You could start with," he says, clearing his throat. Then, in the worst attempt at a Scottish accent I've ever heard, he mimics, "Oi, Triona, did ye ken ye've been hauntin' me since the day I met ye? Oh, and by the way, I've got yer spirit guide tattooed on me body."

I stare at him, completely unimpressed. "That was atrocious—a crime against accents. Ye've been around me for how long, and *that* was the best you came up with?"

Bran grins, completely undeterred. "Well, it could use a wee bit of refinement. Maybe if you spent more time baring your soul to me, I'd get it just right. So go on, Finn, pour out your heart. Tell me all your deepest, most tragic thoughts. Hell, cry if you want to add flair. You'd be doing me a great service in the name of accuracy."

I groan, dragging a hand down my face. "You're insufferable."

"And you're a tragic mess. It's a miracle you've kept it bottled up this long without expelling it out into a soppy confession."

I shake my head, trying to ignore the way his words hit too close to home. "It's not like that."

Bran raises a brow. "Aye, sure. That's why you look like you might vomit every time she so much as breathes in your direction."

I shoot him a glare. "Go to hell."

He throws his hands up. "Fine, I'll pack my bags and call a ferry to come whisk me away."

Despite myself, I huff a small laugh. But Bran's expression sobers slightly as he leans back against the railing.

There's something deeper in his gaze, like he knows everything in my heart. "You're just too stubborn to admit the truth to yourself." He grows serious. "I think you're scared, and it's okay to be, but fear is a lousy compass."

His voice is quieter now, all teasing gone. "You can't just carry this forever. One day, you'll have to tell her."

My only response is a quiet, almost broken, "To what end, Bran?"

Bran watches me carefully. "You tell me."

"She deserves more than what I can give."

He shakes his head, a quiet scoff escaping him. "And yet, you're the only one she looks for when the world starts falling apart."

He lingers just long enough for his words to take root, settling in the quiet between us. Then, with a heavy exhale, he steps back. The boards creak beneath his retreat, each step fading into the hush of the night, until only the rhythm of the waves remains.

My fingers curl tighter around the railing, my gaze fixed on the dark expanse ahead, where unspoken words sink beneath the endless tide.

Part 5 – The Path from Treachery

23

THE UNEXPECTED

Finn

Saturday, 31 May 1823

Port of Lisbon

The ship sways beneath us as the harbour comes into view, the scent of salt and citrus filling the air. Portugal is a feast for the senses even before we set foot on its soil. The city sprawls out before us, whitewashed buildings with terracotta roofs gleaming under the afternoon sun. The gentle hum of life reaches us on the breeze—distant voices, the cries of seagulls, and the faint strum of a lute carried from somewhere unseen.

I grip the railing tighter, the warmth of the metal surprising after the chill of the voyage. The waves lap at the sides of the ship, their rhythm almost hypnotic. Triona stands a few feet away, the wind catching strands of her hair and tossing them around her face. She's dressed simply—travel-worn but radiant in a way that seems unfair to the rest of us. I can't look at her without feeling a pull in my chest, like the tides bending to the moon.

Her smile breaks through the haze of my thoughts when she glances back at me. "Are you just going to stand there all day, or are you going to help unload?" she teases, her accent thick with home, yet her voice feels at odds with the foreign shores.

Casey appears beside her, slinging an arm over her shoulder and ruffling her hair like a pup. She swats him off with a mock scowl, but her laughter bubbles up anyway, light and carefree.

"Ready to face what lies ahead, *piuthar*?"

The gangplank is lowered, and a cacophony of sounds greets us as the dockworkers shout instructions in rapid Portuguese. The language is a melody I don't know the words to yet, but its rhythm is intoxicating. I follow the others off the ship, my boots landing on solid ground with a thud that reverberates up my legs. The sun feels different here, warmer, softer—like it kisses rather than scorches.

I look back, watching Triona as she takes it all in. Her lips part slightly, her expression one of awe. She's always like this—open to every new experience, drinking in the world as if it might vanish tomorrow. She catches me staring, and I don't look away this time.

"What?" she asks, tilting her head, curiosity sparking in her eyes.

"Nothing," I say, though my chest feels full, like I've swallowed too much air. "Just... it suits you."

She blinks, confused, then laughs softly. "Portugal?"

"No," I reply, my voice lower, barely audible over the surrounding bustle. "The sun."

Her smile falters for a moment, something flickering in her gaze, but she doesn't press me. Instead, she reaches up and squeezes my arms before calling for Casey to help her with their bags. I watch her go, the space she leaves behind heavier than it should be.

The city waits for us, alive with possibilities. I pull my pack higher on my shoulder and follow.

As we wait for our herd to unload from the ship, I glance toward the others. Callan is busy haggling with a merchant, but Bran? He lingers at the edge of the group, arms crossed, staring at the water.

He's been slipping away since last night. Distant. Tense.

Normally, he'd be right at Casey's side, trading jokes or making some sarcastic remark, but now? He's barely acknowledging anyone.

Before I can second-guess myself, I grab Bran by the arm and pull him to the side. He yelps in protest, nearly dropping the pack slung over his shoulder.

"Mac, what's your problem?" His voice is sharp, but the moment he sees my face, his expression shifts—something uneasy flickers behind his eyes.

"I need a word," I say low enough that the others won't hear. I glance over my shoulder, just to be sure. The last thing I want is for this conversation to turn into a spectacle.

Bran frowns, his usual smirk absent. "A word about what?"

I cross my arms, leaning closer. "Are we goin' to talk about what happened last night?"

"We are not having this conversation," he says, his voice clipped, "and we will never speak about it again."

I exhale slowly, forcing my voice to remain level. "Bran, I'm not here to judge," I say, keeping my stance firm while my tone softens. "I just need to know ye're all right."

His jaw tightens, and he glares at me, but it's not the sharp, cutting Bran I know. There's fear there, buried beneath the irritation, and it makes my chest ache. "Finn, I am not discussing this with you."

The heat of his anger catches me off guard, but I refuse to back down. "So you can talk about my life, but the moment I bring up yers, I'm supposed to shut my mouth?"

Bran's jaw clenches, and his eyes narrow. "Your choices won't get you killed," he snaps, his voice biting. "So fucking drop it, Finn."

The breath punches out of me. My fists curl at my sides, but I force myself to stay calm. "Ye think I'd ever do anything to risk yer safety?"

His hands curl into fists at his sides. "You don't get it, Finn. You can't just... waltz in like some storybook hero and set everything right. I don't need you to protect me, and I don't need your pity."

"It's not *pity*," I say firmly. "It's me lookin' out for someone I'd do a whole hell of a lot for. That's what this is."

For a moment, the bravado slips. His gaze flickers away, his jaw working like he's chewing over words he doesn't want to say. Then he shoves past me, his shoulder brushing mine. "Drop it, Mac. Whatever you think you saw—whatever you think you know—you're wrong."

Finally, I let out a sharp breath, shaking my head. "Fine. Keep your secrets, if that's how you want it."

Bran doesn't respond immediately. He stares at me, his expression unreadable, before stepping back and adjusting his pack. "You've got enough to deal with, mate. Focus on that."

Then he turns and walks away, leaving me standing there with too many gods damned questions and a knot of frustration tightening in my chest.

Triona

The weight of my pack presses down on me, each step toward the harbour's end burdened by the growing anxiety inside. Callan leads the way. A slip of paper with an address is clutched firmly in his hand, his brows drawn in an unwavering, determined focus.

The rest of us follow in silence, and despite Casey attempting to lighten the mood, it seems to fall short. Something about that feels odd.

Bran's quiet isn't the comfortable kind; it's the heavy, brooding kind. He's been off since Finn pulled him aside this morning. The usual spark in his eyes is missing, replaced by a tightness in his jaw and a brooding air that clings to him like a storm cloud. He lingers a step behind us, his gaze flicking toward Finn now and then, only to snap back to the street ahead.

Casey keeps looking at Bran like he's holding back from saying something. A look that promises an argument if Bran so much as breathes the wrong way. It's strange. They usually get along like a house on fire—teasing, joking, backing each other up. Now, the air between them feels thick, like a storm about to break.

And then there's Finn. He's striding ahead of us, his shoulders tense and his mouth set in a hard line. He hasn't said a word in what feels like hours, and the scowl etched into his face makes him look older, harsher somehow. He glares at Bran every so often, though he says nothing, which is almost worse than the alternative. Finn isn't one to simmer in silence unless something's really eating at him.

Bran glances my way, and for a moment, I catch something raw in his expression—something almost vulnerable—but it vanishes as quickly as it appeared, replaced by a familiar smirk that doesn't quite reach his eyes.

"You're quiet," I say, keeping my tone light, hoping he'll take the bait.

He shrugs, his usual swagger muted. "Long trip, Sinclair. Even I get tired."

"Since when?" Callan asks, his tone sharp enough to make Bran's smirk falter.

Bran's shoulders stiffen, his smirk vanishing. "Don't start, Callan," he mutters, his voice dangerously flat.

"Start? I huv'nae said anythin'," Callan replies, his tone dripping with mock innocence. "Jus seems odd, is all. Usually, ye can't stop running that mouth o' yours."

Bran stops walking abruptly, turning to face Callan. "Maybe I just don't have the energy to be chatty today."

"Or maybe," Callan says, taking a step closer, his voice dropping lower, "there's something else eating at you."

Finn glances back at the exchange, his jaw tightening as he mutters something under his breath. He doesn't intervene, though, his focus staying fixed on the road ahead, his shoulders tense and his steps heavy.

"Leave it, Callan," I say sharply, stepping between them before it can escalate further. "We've all been through enough the past few days without adding to it."

If the four of them don't work it out soon, I might be the one losing my patience—and none of them will want to see that.

The harbourmaster's office comes into view, its sun-bleached walls standing out against the blue sky. But before we reach it, everything stops. Every sound, every step, every thought halts as if the world itself has drawn a sharp breath.

I freeze mid-step, my heart skipping as my eyes lock on the figure ahead. A woman stands there, arms crossed, her dark hair catching the sunlight. Her familiar grin is wide, filled with mischief and warmth, the expression that could light even the gloomiest of days.

"Deidre?" I whisper, my voice barely audible above the din of the street.

She lifts a hand in a casual wave, as if she hasn't been missing from my life for what feels like an eternity.

"Deidre!" The cry rips from my throat before I can think. My pack slips from my shoulders, clattering to the ground as I take off at a sprint. My legs move faster than they have all day, carrying me toward her, toward home.

When I reach her, I throw my arms around her, holding on as tightly as I can, like letting go might make her vanish. She hugs me back just as fiercely, her presence solid and warm, grounding me in a way I didn't realise I needed.

"I thought—," I murmur, my voice trembling as tears sting my eyes. "I—I didn't know if—"

Deidre pulls back just enough to look at me, her hands still resting on my shoulders. Her gaze softens, and I can see the sorrow etched into her features, mingling with the joy of our reunion.

"I know, love," she says, her voice low and tender. "I know about your parents. I'm so sorry, my girl."

Her words hit like a stone dropped into still water, ripples of confusion spreading through me. "How…?" My voice falters. "How could you know?"

She hesitates as she considers how much to say. "There's much we must discuss, Triona," she finally declares, her tone steady yet laden with gravity. "But not here. Let us return to my home first—we shall have all the time we need."

I glance back over my shoulder at the others, who stand rooted to the spot, staring at us with expressions ranging from shock to tentative relief. Callan nods once, as if to say we'll follow Deidre's lead.

"Finnis MacGregor," she says teasingly admonishing him, gesturing for him to come over. "Still tall, still brooding, but a little more handsome than the last time I saw you."

His head lifts at the sound of her voice, and the faintest hint of a smile crosses his face as he steps toward her. There's something unguarded about the way he moves, a quiet eagerness in his stride that I rarely see from him.

Finn chuckles as he returns the hug. "I could say the same about you," he replies, a rare lightness in his voice.

"You always were a charmer." Deidre steps back, studying him with a fond smile. "You look well, boy. I was worried about you."

"Dinnae fash yerself over me," Finn says, shaking his head. "I'm not the one with a secret residence in Portugal."

Deidre's laughter rings out like a bell, clear and unapologetic. "Touché, lad. But I think you'll find I had my reasons." Her expression softens, her gaze searching his. "It's good to see you. Truly."

Finn nods, his grin dimming slightly, though the warmth in his eyes lingers. "Good to see you too, Deidre."

Deidre's grin widens as Callan approaches, his stride purposeful as always. She steps forward to meet him, arms open, and pulls him into a brief but fierce hug.

"Still a grumpy bear, I see," she teases as she pulls back, her hands lingering on his shoulders. "Though maybe with a few more grey hairs this time."

Callan snorts, a rare flicker of amusement crossing his face.

Casey's next, striding up with an easy smile that matches Deidre's energy. "Aye, and here's my favourite troublemaker," Deidre says, wrapping him in a warm hug.

"Always yer favourite, aren't I?" Casey quips, his grin widening as he hugs her back.

"You know good and well that you're tied with the others," Deidre replies, winking at me over his shoulder.

When they part, her gaze lands on Bran, who's hanging back slightly, his expression unreadable.

"This is Bran Mumford," I say, stepping slightly to the side to let him come forward. "He's... well, he's one of us."

She steps closer, studying him for a moment before speaking.

"You look so much like your mother," she says, her voice tinged with something akin to nostalgia. "And you're tall, just like your father."

Bran's usual guardedness falters, replaced by a look of sad fondness that makes my chest tighten. He blinks, his mouth opening slightly as if to respond, but no words come out.

Deidre smiles gently, her gaze unwavering. "They're a rare people, your parents. The kind that are loyal to the very end."

Her words hang in the air, heavy with meaning, and for a moment, none of us speak. Casey and Callan exchange confused glances, while Finn straightens slightly, his brow furrowed. I can feel the questions rising to the surface, clamouring for answers. How does she know his parents? How does she know Bran at all? And why did Bran look so affected by it?

But before anyone can voice the obvious, Deidre claps her hands lightly, breaking the spell. "Come now," she says briskly, her tone shifting to one of warm authority. "We've lingered here long enough. There's a meal waiting at my house, and I'll not let it go cold because of your dawdling."

We're left with little choice but to follow as she turns and leads the way, her steps sure and steady. Bran lingers for a moment, his gaze lingering on her retreating form before he pulls himself together and falls into step beside me.

He doesn't say a word, his expression carefully neutral now, though the sadness in his eyes lingers. I want to press him, to ask what's going through his mind, but the look on his face tells me now isn't the time.

One by one, we mount our horses, the soft creak of leather and jingle of bridles filling the air. I swing into the saddle just as Finn steps up beside me. Without a word, he grips the back of my saddle and swings up behind me, his presence solid and unshakable. His arms settle around me as he takes hold of the reins, the warmth of him impossible to ignore.

Whatever Deidre knows, it's clear we're not getting the answers here on the dock. I glance toward her; her figure moving confidently ahead of us, and I resolve to understand it once we're settled. For now, the questions will have to wait.

As we approach the villa, the rhythmic clatter of hooves on the gravel path fills the air. The house rises before us, its terracotta roof glowing in the soft light of evening. Ivy curls along weathered stone walls, and the scent of wildflowers drifts toward us from the sprawling gardens. A fountain, chipped but elegant, sits at the centre of the courtyard, its gentle trickle the only sound besides the horses.

Casey shifts in his saddle, his eyes scanning the house with measured curiosity, while Bran lets out a low whistle. "Fancy," he mutters, though there's a tightness to his tone, as if he's trying to distract himself from the uncertainty. Callan rides ahead, as if ready to face whatever—or whoever—might greet us first.

I shift to glance over my shoulder at Finn. His jaw is tight, his eyes fixed on the house. The pressure of his hand on my waist steadies me, though my own nerves flutter. We trust Deidre, but stepping into the unknown always carries its weight. The estate looms larger with every step, alive with possibility, and I can't tell if it's comforting or unnerving.

Deidre swings down from her horse with practiced ease, her boots crunching softly against the gravel. She turns to face us, her expression unusually serious as she gestures for us to dismount.

One by one, we slide from our saddles, the air thick with an unspoken question. I'm the last to move. Finn's hands are firm at my waist as he helps me down from atop Shadow. The moment my boots touch the ground, his grip lingers—warm, steady, as if reluctant to let go.

For a heartbeat, neither of us moves. Then, as if remembering himself, he exhales and releases me, stepping back just enough to put space between us.

Deidre sweeps her gaze over the group, her voice steady yet heavy with meaning. "No matter what happens from here on out, know this—it was done to protect, not to deceive."

We exchange glances, uncertainty flickering between us. I can feel the tension ripple through the group. Finn shifts slightly behind me, and I know he's watching Deidre closely, waiting for any sign of what's coming.

Then Deidre's eyes settle on me. Her expression softens, but the intensity of her gaze doesn't waver. "Triona," she says, stepping forward and holding out her hand. "There's someone inside who's been waiting to see you for a very long time."

Around me, the world feels still, despite the horses shifting and the breeze whispering through the leaves. My heart pounds, my mind a storm of questions, but I remain still. Then, with a glance back at Finn—his warmth now gone, yet his presence an anchor in the space between us—I reach forward and take her hand.

The villa's interior is just as breathtaking as its exterior—warm, inviting, alive with quiet charm. The soft scent of lavender and citrus drifts through the halls, mingling with the distant crackle of a hearth.

Deidre leads us into a spacious sitting room, where a large table awaits, set with an array of fresh breads, cheeses, and ripe fruit. The spread is simple yet abundant, a quiet luxury that suits her perfectly.

She turns to face us, her hands on her hips and a knowing smile playing on her lips. "Before anything else," she begins, her tone firm but warm, "I want you all to settle and clean up in your rooms. You'll find clean clothes and basins at the ready. Then you're all to come back down here. Understood?"

Casey raises a hand lazily, grinning. "And how will we know—?"

He's cut off—as if on cue—when several staff members glide into the room, their movements swift and precise. Without a word, they incline their heads toward Deidre in silent acknowledgment before gesturing for us to follow.

I glance around at the others, momentarily stunned by the sudden appearance of help, the quiet efficiency of it all rattling in a way I can't quite place.

"Seems she's thought of everything," Callan mutters, his tone half-amused, half-impressed.

"Go on, then," Deidre urges, clapping her hands lightly. "Get settled. You'll want to be fresh for what's coming."

A woman with kind eyes and a soft smile steps forward, her posture poised yet welcoming. She motions for me to follow. I glance back at the others, each now paired with their own attendant, before falling into step behind her.

The walk through the villa feels like a journey in itself. The halls are long and winding, adorned with paintings of sprawling landscapes and sea vistas. The light filtering through the windows casts golden hues on the tiled floors, and the air feels calm, almost sacred.

When we reach my room, the woman opens the door with a gentle push, revealing a space that takes my breath away. The room is spacious but cosy, with soft linens draped over a wide bed, a small writing desk by the window, and a basin of water already set on a stand. Sunlight pours in through the open shutters, illuminating the delicate patterns etched into the walls. A fresh set of clothes lie folded neatly on the bed, simple yet elegant.

"Many thanks," I whisper, and the woman inclines her head before retreating silently down the hall. I close the door behind me and take a deep breath, letting the tranquility of the space wash over me.

It's then I realise how quiet it is—too quiet. My room feels removed, distant from the others, as though it's on the farthest side of the house entirely.

I feel the faintest twinge of unease. But as I look around the room again—the inviting bed, the basin with clear water, the view of the sea stretching endlessly outside the window—I let the feeling go. This place is a sanctuary, a reprieve from everything we've endured. I may be alone on this side of the villa, but maybe that's exactly what I need.

With that thought, I step toward the basin, preparing to wash away the grim clinging to my skin. My gaze flickers to the mirror, catching sight of the gown hanging there, and I nearly gasp. It is unlike anything I've ever seen—delicate, luxurious, as if made for someone who is not me. But right now, that doesn't matter.

My fingers trail over the buttons at my back, each one loosening the grip of my dress against my body. The fabric sighs as it slips from my shoulders, pooling at my feet. A shiver prickles down my spine as the cool air kisses the newly bared skin, leaving nothing between me and my reflection but the thin shift clinging to my form.

I watch myself, drawn to the way sunlight dances over my skin, the way the sheer fabric moulds to my body, revealing more than it conceals. The curve of my waist, the soft swell of my breasts, the long lines of my legs—all things I rarely stop to notice. A strange warmth coils low in my stomach, not quite embarrassment, not quite pride. Something new. Something unnameable.

I move to wash away the remnants of travel from my skin. I take my time at the basin, letting the cool water chase away the dust and weariness, trailing damp fingers over every part of me—my arms, my legs, my neck, the curves of my body—until I feel clean, refreshed, renewed.

With a steadying breath, I reach for the hanging gown and begin to slip it on.

A knock at the door startles me. "Come in," I call, turning slightly.

The door opens, and a young handmaiden steps inside, her presence quiet but efficient. She dips her head in acknowledgment. "I'll help you tie it properly, my lady," she says, her voice soft but assured.

I nod, exhaling as I step forward, letting her guide me into the dress. The emerald fabric slides over my skin like water, cool and weightless at first, before tightening as she laces the bodice. I grip the bedpost for balance as she pulls the stays snug, pressing the gown to my curves.

The fabric feels decadent against my fingertips, like liquid moonlight shimmering in the golden glow of the room. It clings in places I'm not used to, the bodice dipping low, baring the delicate slope of my shoulders, revealing more of my breasts than I've ever dared to before.

I fidget, smoothing the skirt with trembling hands. The woman in the mirror stares back, mesmerising yet foreign, like a version of myself I don't quite know.

Deidre steps inside, her expression brightening when she sees me. "Well, look at you," she says, a glint in her eye as she takes me in.

"It's so beautiful," I admit, gesturing to the gown. "But... isn't it a bit, well, revealing?" I glance at the mirror again, my cheeks heating. "Won't my bro—"

Deidre cuts me off with a tut and a wave of her hand. "They'll have to get over it," she says firmly, but her tone is light. "That's how most of us dress here. They're not so... modest in this country."

Her playful smirk makes me smile despite my nerves. "Come on, the others are waiting."

Before I can argue further, she grips my arm and guides me out of the room, leading me down the hall and into a sitting room that feels like a scene from a dream. A grand table overflows with trays of fruit, pastries, cheeses, and delicate cakes, while the mouthwatering aroma of fresh bread and herbs fills the air.

My band of merry men are already there, lounging comfortably in their chairs, their earlier tension washed away by the food and the ambiance. Callan and Casey are deep in conversation while Bran is inspecting a glass of wine, as if it holds the secrets of the divine. Finn stands at the edge of the group, his arms crossed as he leans back against the frame of a door, his gaze distant.

"My, don't you lot look absolutely dashing," I announce as we step into the room.

They all turn to look at us, their laughter fading as their gazes settle on me.

Callan and Casey's reactions are immediate. Casey chokes on his drink, sputtering, while Callan nearly drops the pastry in his hand, his eyes narrowing on me. Bran's jaw simply falls open, his usual bravado completely wiped away.

Finn's reaction, however, is different. His eyes flicker over me for only a moment before his expression tightens.

"Well, then," Deidre says, clearly delighted by the chaos she's caused. She pats my arm and nudges me forward. "Go on, love. Join them. Don't let their stares frighten you off."

I hesitate, suddenly feeling exposed under their scrutiny, but Deidre's encouraging smile steadies me. I step forward, my movements careful, and take a seat near the end of the table.

Callan recovers first, though I see in his eyes he's about to lie into me before a rather well-timed cough on the other side of the room halts him. "Ye, uh... clean up well, Triona." he says, though his tone is sharper than it needs to be.

Casey lets out a nervous laugh, still coughing a little. "Aye, well, she's... um..."

"Stunning," Bran finishes, his voice quieter than usual. He walks over. "Since no one else has the courage to say it properly..." He leans down, placing a quick, friendly kiss on my cheek. "You look absolutely radiant."

"Many thanks," I say, trying to sound casual, though my cheeks are on fire.

Finn doesn't say a word, doesn't even look over toward the exchange, and I can't help but wonder what's going through his mind. I force myself to focus on the food and conversation, but his silence lingers like a shadow.

Casey waves me over from across the room, his excitement palpable. "Triona, come look at this," he calls, gesturing toward a large portrait hanging prominently on the wall.

I make my way over, the sheer size of the painting commanding my attention. The woman depicted in the portrait is striking—dark, thoughtful eyes, her features soft yet determined. There's something almost haunting in the way she gazes out from the canvas.

Casey points to the plaque beneath the frame, his brow furrowed as he reads aloud. "*'Beware; for I am fearless, and therefore powerful.'*" He glances at me, his confusion mirrored in my expression. "Why d'ye think this quote is under this portrait?"

Before I can reply, Deidre's voice drifts from behind us, calm and certain. "That, my darlings, is Mary Wollstonecraft Shelley."

Casey and I turn to look at her, my curiosity piqued. "Why is she hangin' on the wall?" Casey asks, tilting his head.

Before Deidre can answer, the sound of footsteps echoes through the room, and a woman appears from the shadows of the doorway. She's stunning, her beauty so arresting that it's almost disarming. Her long red hair falls in waves over her shoulders, and her face—her features—strike a chord so deep and chilling that my breath catches in my throat. She's familiar, I can't explain how, and a shiver runs down my spine.

"She's on the wall because I painted it in her honour when she published her first book," the woman says, her voice smooth and confident.

I blink, trying to process what she just said. "You know her... personally?"

The woman steps closer, a smile curving her lips. "Aye, she's a dear friend of mine."

I'm too stunned to speak for a moment. My eyes flicker between the portrait and the woman in front of me, the sensation of familiarity growing stronger by the second.

Deidre steps forward, her expression softening as she glances between us. "Allow me to introduce Amelia Curran," she says with warmth, though her voice carries a hint of caution.

"Curran?" The name feels heavy on my tongue, as though it carries a significance.

Amelia's gaze remains fixed on me, her smile fading slightly. "There's no easy way to say this," she begins, her voice steady but careful. "So it's best I just come out and say it."

The room feels impossibly still, the air thick with an unspoken weight.

"Caitríona Sinclair," she continues, "I am your aunt. My sister, Sarah Curran—she was your mother. Your *true* mother."

24

A Name She'll Never Know

Finn

"**C**aitríona Sinclair, I am your aunt. My sister, Sarah Curran—she was your mother. Your *true* mother."

The words land like a hammer. I stand up straighter, my eyes darting to Triona. She's frozen, her face pale, her arms moving to cross her middle, as if it's the only thing that will keep her grounded.

"That's not... no, that's not possible," she whispers, her voice trembling.

Amelia takes another step closer, her eyes never leaving Triona. "It is," she says gently. "This is going to be a lot to take in."

Triona looks at Casey, her wide-eyed shock mirrored in his expression. I feel the weight of it, too, the magnitude of what's just been said pressing down on all of us.

Deidre moves to Triona's side, her hand resting lightly on her arm. "Let's sit," she says softly. "We'll take this as slow as you need, okay?" Triona nods weakly.

She sinks into the chair, her fingers trembling against the armrests. The room feels heavier now, the air thick with unrelenting tension. Her gaze locks onto Amelia, emotions warring just beneath the surface—betrayal, disbelief, hurt.

But outwardly, she is a portrait of control, her warmth stripped away, leaving only the sharp edges of restraint.

Her voice is flat as she breaks the silence. "Please, just—just start from the beginning, and tell me the whole damn truth."

Amelia flinches at the sharpness of her words but nods, her gaze softening as if she had steeled herself for this reaction. "All right," Amelia says finally, her voice trembling. "It might be hard to hear…"

Triona doesn't flinch, doesn't move. "I don't think I'll like it any less than being lied to my *whole* life."

Amelia takes a deep breath and starts. "Your mother, Sarah, was my younger sister. Your father, Robert Emmet—he was a man of conviction. A revolutionary. He dreamed of a better world—for Ireland, for all of us. But the Crown didn't see ideals. They saw defiance. They saw a threat too great to ignore."

She pauses, her gaze distant. "Men like him have always been cut down for standing up to the wrong people. And women are left behind—bearing the weight of grief and survival. The names change, but the ending doesn't."

Amelia turns back to Triona, her voice steady now. "But Robert wasn't *just* a revolutionary. He was a teacher, a thinker. He wanted more for the people who'd been crushed under the Crown for centuries. He believed in freedom, equality, justice. And for a while, he thought words might be enough. But words changed nothing, not for the starving families or the children who'd never know a life without chains." She exhales, as if releasing something heavy.

"He started planning secret meetings and forming quiet alliances. He thought if they could unite, if they could find collective courage, that they could reclaim the country."

Her voice takes on a darker edge. "But dreams weren't enough. Careful planning wasn't enough. In the summer of 1803, Robert led an uprising in Dublin—a fight for freedom against the Crown. Every detail planned, every move calculated, but the night spiraled into chaos." She swallows hard.

"The streets erupted in violence. Civilians became unintended casualties. A government official, Lord Kilwarden, fell dead amid the fray. Some claimed it was friendly fire, but the justice would hear none of it. The rebellion collapsed before it truly began, and all blame landed on Robert's shoulders."

Amelia presses on. "He tried to stay hidden, but the distance from your mother became unbearable. He risked everything to see her again, writing letters—confessions of his plans, his failures, his dreams."

She draws a slow breath, as if the next words pain her to say aloud. "That was his undoing. Those letters never reached her. They were intercepted. Someone betrayed him—and threatened my sister's life if he didn't surrender."

Her throat bobs as she swallows, shaking her head like she still can't believe it. "That's how they caught him. He didn't even hesitate. He gave himself up willingly to keep her safe. They used the only weapon that could ever bring him to his knees."

Then, softly, as if delivering a final blow, she utters, "Mere weeks after learning of your existence... he was sentenced to death."

Amelia's eyes begins to fill with tears that she tries to quell. "We had to leave to keep safe. Sarah was devastated, leaving the only place she'd ever known. The place her love story had blossomed, but knowing a part of Robert would live on comforted her. She told me, *'This child will be everything we dreamed of, Amelia. Everything Robert and I fought for.'*"

Amelia pauses, her gaze distant, as if the memory pulls her back. "Sarah grew sick after your birth, so we had to make a very hard decision. She knew her time was running out, and she was desperate to protect you. She begged me, Triona. Begged me to take you somewhere you'd be safe. Somewhere far from the danger that had already stolen Robert."

"We agreed on the Sinclairs," Amelia continues. "Not just because they were good people, but because they loved you before they even knew you. James and Ellen—bless them—they didn't hesitate. Not for a moment. When I told them about you, they agreed with a gleam in their eyes."

Amelia's voice catches, her throat tightening as she looks down at her hands. "That was the last time I saw you. You were swaddled in my arms, so small, so perfect. And I had to let you go."

Triona's face crumples, her hands curling into fists on her lap. "You just... left me?"

"I had no choice," Amelia says softly. "It was the only way to keep you safe. If I stayed, they'd have found me. And then they'd have found you. The same people that intended to harm Robert never knew of your existence. If they had, they might have done everything in their power to harm you like they had your father." She looks up, her eyes glistening with unshed tears. "It was the hardest thing I've ever done, but I knew, with James and Ellen, you'd have a life. You'd have love."

Triona exhales sharply, her voice barely above a whisper. "But they still found us. So now I learn I lost a father before I knew what life was, a mother before I could walk, and now..."

Her gaze flickers between Amelia and Callan, searching—grasping—for something. Denial. Reassurance. Anything but the truth unravelling before her.

Then a spark. That familiar flicker in her eyes—the one she gets when realisation strikes like a blade through fog.

She swallows hard, her head shaking, as if sheer defiance could turn back time, could unmake what's already been spoken. "Cal... did you—did you know I wasn't your sister?"

The second the words leave her lips, my stomach turns to stone.

Callan doesn't answer right away. The silence drags and the weight of it presses down on all of us.

She's searching his face, her expression caught somewhere between disbelief and betrayal.

I want to move. To reach for her. To offer something—anything. But I don't, because this isn't a wound my hands can mend, nor a battle my presence alone can shield her from.

He finally shifts, his broad shoulders stiffening, but his eyes stay steady on hers. "Aye, but Triona... ye're no less my sister now than ye have been most of my life," he says, his voice low, heavy with conviction. "I respected our parents' wishes, their secrets—their burdens. It wasna my truth to spill."

Her lip quivers, but she doesn't say a word, letting his explanation unfold.

"They wanted ye to learn this now," he continues, his words careful, deliberate, "with the answers ye'd demand close at hand. I waited so ye wouldnae face this unarmed... so ye'd know the why as much as the what."

The flicker of guilt in his eyes is unmistakable, but there's something else too: tenderness, unwavering and fierce. "Would ye rather fate ripped it from my lips," he says quietly, "without caring for yer heart, yer choice?" His words strike like a blow, sharp but with no malice. Triona opens her mouth, then closes it.

Her breath quivers, and for a moment, she just stares at him, unblinking, as if she's trying to see past his words to something deeper.

And that's when I see it—the moment she realises a thought that had been echoing in my mind. This wasn't just Callan's secret.

She turns to Amelia, her chest rising and falling too fast, her voice sharp with something close to desperation.

"Who else knew?"

From the corner of my eye, I see Deidre straighten, her usual calm demeanour unshaken—but her hands, pressed together in her lap, are too still.

Amelia inhales deeply, then exhales, slowly. "Deidre has always known," she says, her voice quiet but steady. "And so has Alex Mumford."

She doesn't falter. "He may be a recent ally to you, but he's known your parents for a long time. His presence now was no happenstance."

"How do you even know all this?" Triona demands. "You weren't there."

Amelia doesn't flinch. "It's... a long story. Too much to unravel all at once," she says gently. "And best saved for another day."

Then she turns on Bran. "Did you know? Did you know any of this?"

His eyes widen as he lifts both hands, palms out. "Are you kidding? I'm just as shocked as you are. I didn't exactly expect my family to be tangled up in some secret rebellion legacy."

He lets out a half-laugh, more nerves than humour. "Though... I can't say I'm all that shocked to learn my father was involved. Prickly bastards got a slew of secrets up his sleeve."

"Wait..." he murmurs. "Does that mean my mother—?"

Amelia nods slowly. "Your parents met through the Sinclairs."

Bran swallows hard, the realisation settling deep. His gaze drops, voice quieter now. "Right. Of course they did."

A heavy silence falls over the room—thick with everything that can't be undone.

Triona sinks back into her chair, hands trembling in her lap. "I don't know how I'd have preferred hearing this," she whispers, her voice cracking. "I just... I wish it didn't have to be like this. Any of it."

Callan's gaze softens, and he steps closer, lowering himself onto one knee. He is a man of presence, always standing tall, unshakable, yet here he kneels, not out of submission, but out of the weight of what he needs her to understand. "Triona," he says gently, "it's not the blood between us that makes us family. It's the life we've lived, the way we stand by each other. Ye're my sister, and that's a truth I'll carry to my grave. No matter what changes now, that'll never change for me."

Amelia's voice follows. "He's right. Family's not in the blood—it's in the love. And there's been no shortage of that."

Triona lets out a shuddering breath, her eyes glistening as she glances at Callan. "I don't even know who I am anymore."

I watch helplessly. Rooted to the spot. Feeling the moment she breaks.

I step closer, my boots heavy against the floor. "Ye're still you, Triona." Her eyes flick to mine, searching, lost, but I hold her gaze, refusing to let her slip away into doubt.

"One of the fiercest souls I've ever known. You stand against those who seek to break you. You never let the world decide yer worth—or the worth of those you love. You love with every beat of yer heart, fight with every shred of yer spirit. Blood doesnae change that. Nothin' ever will."

She exhales a sharp laugh, empty of humour, shaking her head. "That's not accurate," she mutters, bitterness lacing her words. "And not to be wallowing, but if I had the sense the gods gave me, we wouldn't be here. I dragged us into this mess with my foolishness."

Casey's voice cuts in, soft but firm. "That's not true, Triona. Ye—"

"Stop," she interrupts sharply, turning to him with a hard glare. "Don't coddle me, Casey. I can't... I can't bear that right now. You don't want to admit it to yourselves? Fine. But stop pretending as if this all makes sense." Her voice falters, but her expression stays resolute.

Her hands tremble as she presses them to her lap. "I'm just... swarming with guilt right now," she whispers, the words spilling out as if they'd been locked inside too long. "And I don't want to make this all about me. I don't want to bring everyone down." She swallows hard, rising from her chair with deliberate movements. "I need to leave the room," she says, her voice trembling but clear.

Her breath hitches, and for a moment, the weight in her eyes lessens. She looks away, her fingers curling into fists. "I need time." Her voice is a whisper, but it's steady enough. "I need to... think."

Callan nods, stepping back. "Take all the time ye need."

Amelia's hands wring together, but she doesn't press. Deidre moves closer to Triona, her presence steady and silent, as if to guard her without words, but Triona stops her with an outstretched hand, and she turns to leave.

I linger near the door, torn between giving her space and the unbearable thought of letting her walk away alone. If I follow, will I be offering comfort or pressing too hard? If I stay, will she think I don't care enough to go after her? The weight of indecision presses down on me, heavy and suffocating. Triona's movements are deliberate as she walks toward the door. As she passes me, her shoulder brushes mine, and I catch the faint tremble in her step.

The door closes softly behind her. I lean against the doorframe, my arms crossed tightly over my chest. Callan's eyes meet mine, heavy with unspoken questions.

"She'll be all right," He says, though I'm not entirely sure if he's trying to convince me or himself.

A muscle tics in my jaw as I push off the doorframe. "Aye," I murmur. "But let me make sure she gets to her room."

Before Callan can reply, I'm already moving.

I step out into the dimly lit corridor just in time to see Triona turn the corner. Without thinking, I chase after her, my pulse a steady thrum in my ears. She's hardly made it a few strides before I reach out, my fingers wrapping gently but firmly around her wrist.

She stills, and slowly she turns, her gaze lifting to mine. And sweet mercy from the gods above. There's something in her eyes that nearly undoes me.

It's not the irritation I half expected.

It's something softer.

She doesn't pull away.

And for the first time in a long time, I don't second-guess what I'm about to say.

My grip stays firm, but my thumb moves—slow, steady circles against the delicate skin of her wrist.

"You saved *me*," I murmur, my voice low but certain. "Directly, indirectly... Naught but a broken lad arrived in Connemara, Little Doe. And you—" I shake my head, the words thick in my throat, "—you breathed life back into me in ways I can never repay."

I swallow hard. "That's who you are—a healer."

A breath shudders through her. Then, before I can react, she launches herself at me, arms wrapping around my neck in a fierce, unrestrained hug.

I barely catch her, my hands seizing her waist as she collides into me, clutching me as if she never intends to let go. Her grip is desperate, and without hesitation, my own arms tighten around her, holding her just as fiercely.

She leans in, her breath ghosting against my ear.

"I've always loved who I am with you," she whispers.

I close my eyes, fighting the ache in my chest, the longing that coils deep inside me.

She leans back slowly, just enough to meet my gaze. Her fingers skim my jaw—tentative, searching. And before I can even process what's happening, she presses the softest, slowest kiss to my cheek.

It lingers.

Steady. Certain.

And then, just as quickly, she pulls away and turns, walking toward her room without another word.

I stand there, frozen, watching her go.

And all I can do is *feel*—the ghost of her touch, the whisper of her breath, the truth of everything I've ever wanted wrapped up in a single moment.

Damn it all.

I *am* nothing without her.

Triona
Sunday, 1 June 1823
Casa da Prímula

The door to my room is closed, but faint light spills from beneath it. I hear footsteps pause outside, then soft voices. My body tenses as I clutch the embroidered pillow tighter against my chest.

"Are you sure about this?" Deidre's voice is low, trembling with worry.

Amelia's answer is quieter but firm. "She needs to know we're here. Even if she doesn't want to see us right now."

Deidre hesitates. "I'll go in first to see if she's upset."

"Bless you, love," Amelia murmurs.

A light tap on the door makes me flinch. "Triona? It's me and Amelia," Deidre calls gently. "Can we come in?"

For a moment, I don't answer. I don't know if I want to see anyone, but the silence feels heavier than my thoughts. Finally, I manage, "Fine." My voice sounds distant, like it belongs to someone else.

The door creaks open, and their footsteps are soft on the wooden floor. I don't look up. My legs are curled beneath me, and I'm sitting on the edge of my bed, gripping the pillow like it's the only thing keeping me tethered. My hair falls around my face in a messy curtain, hiding my swollen eyes.

Deidre moves first, crossing the room and sitting beside me. She doesn't speak right away, just slips an arm around my shoulder. I stiffen but don't pull away. I'm too tired to pull away.

Amelia lingers by the door, her hands clasped tightly in front of her. "I'm sorry to intrude," she says quietly. "I just... I needed to see you. To make sure you're okay."

A bitter laugh slips from my lips before I can stop it. It's hollow, jagged. "Okay? Sure, I'm fine. Why wouldn't I be?" My voice wavers, but the sarcasm cuts through clearly enough.

Deidre's arm squeezes gently around me.

I tighten my grip on the pillow, my knuckles white. The words I want to say feel tangled in my throat, but eventually, I whisper, "I don't even know how to feel right now. Angry? Hurt? Betrayed?" I shake my head, and my voice breaks. "All of it, maybe."

Amelia takes a step closer but stops, as though afraid of crossing an invisible line. "You have every right to feel all of those things," she says, her voice trembling slightly. "I won't try to take that away from you."

"Why wasn't I told sooner? Why didn't anyone tell me?"

Amelia exhales slowly, her shoulders slumping. "Because we were protecting you, as hard as that is to believe," she admits.

I stare at her for a long moment, my jaw tight. "Do you have any idea how much this hurts?"

Amelia's eyes glisten with tears, and she nods. "I do. And I'll carry that guilt for the rest of my life." Her voice wavers as she continues. "But I love you, Triona. I loved you from the moment Sarah told me she was carrying you. And I've never stopped."

My lip trembles, but I bite down on it and turn away. Deidre leans in closer, her voice soft but firm. "Triona," she begins softly, her voice steady but heavy with emotion, "you have every right to be angry. To feel betrayed. But there are things you must understand about why this secret was kept from you."

I keep my gaze fixed on the floor, my jaw tight. "I'm listening," I say, with far too much bite than is deserved.

Amelia clasps her hands together, her knuckles white. "Your father wasn't just a man who dreamed of a free Ireland. He was a symbol. A martyr. Even now, decades later, his name carries weight. To some, it's hope. To others, it's rebellion. And there are those—powerful, dangerous people—who would see anyone connected to him as a threat. Someone to be silenced. Someone to make an example of."

I lift my eyes, narrowing them. My voice cracks as I spit the words out. "So, you all hid who I am because you thought I couldn't handle *that*?"

Amelia's face tightens, but she nods. "Aye. Knowing the truth too soon would have sent you searching for answers. Answers that would have led you straight into the crosshairs of those who still fear what your father stood for. You would have been drawn to his legacy, to the fight he left behind. And you wouldn't have been ready."

My fists clench in my lap, and I feel the heat rising in my chest. "You don't know that. You don't know what I could have handled!"

Her voice hardens, but her eyes soften, filled with sorrow. "No, I didn't know. But I couldn't take that risk. Sarah—your mother—made me promise to protect you. To give you a life where you could grow strong before the weight of all this was laid upon your shoulders. And I kept that promise, even when it broke my heart to stay away."

I shoot to my feet, pacing the room as the anger boils over. "So everyone decided what I could and couldn't know? Everyone decided what I could handle? I'm the one whose life is a lie, and you all thought that was fine as long as it suited you?"

"Triona," Deidre's voice cuts through the room. I stop mid-step, turning to face her. The anger flickers in my chest, but her steady gaze stops me in my tracks.

"Enough," she says, her eyes searing into mine. "You think this was easy for any of us? For Amelia? For your parents? Do you think we don't wish things could have been different? But wishing doesn't change what the stars have written." She pauses, her gaze softening slightly. "We were all so close once, Triona. James, Ellen, Alex, his wife, Amelia, Robert, Sarah, and even me. We were family—a chosen family. But Robert's death... it shattered everything."

I blink, the weight of her words making my chest feel even heavier.

She continues, her voice steady but tinged with sorrow. "After Robert died, Sarah began having disturbing visions. They grew stronger every day, consuming her. She saw things none of us could understand, things we barely believed at first. And then... when she died, James and Ellen had no choice but to leave Ireland. The danger was too great. They took you and returned to Scotland, while Alex went to America to keep his family safe. We all scattered, trying to pick up the pieces."

My heart pounds in my chest, my anger momentarily forgotten. "She had... visions as in...."

Deidre exchanges a glance with Amelia, her lips pressing into a thin line. "Your mother believed she saw things before they happened... and sometimes, the things she saw came true."

I blink, stunned into silence as she steps closer, her tone softening but still firm. "Your path was set long before any of us could even dream of changing it. The only choice any of us had was how to prepare you for it. And that's what they tried to do. To protect you until the time was right."

"What we had hoped for, to protect you... they still found you."

I look between Amelia and Deidre, searching their faces for answers. "Who found me?"

Amelia takes a hesitant step closer, her hands wringing together as if trying to crush the weight of her own guilt. "The ones who never stopped watching. The ones who see you not as who you are but as what you represent."

My breath quickens. "What do I represent?"

Deidre kneels in front of me, her hands resting gently on mine. Her voice is calm but unwavering. "You represent hope, lass. They believe you're the one to finish what your father started. And that terrifies the people who thrive on control, on silence, on oppression."

I shake my head, my throat burning with unshed tears. "I don't even know who my father was! How am I supposed to carry a legacy I never even knew existed? How am I supposed to fight for something I don't understand?"

The fire in my chest dims, replaced by a sinking weight. My shoulders slump as I sink back onto the bed, gripping the edge to keep myself steady. Guilt creeps in, sharp and unwelcome.

"I'm being selfish," I whisper, my voice barely audible. "Acting as if I'm a child, throwing my anger around and... proving your point. I'm sorry."

Deidre's hand rests gently on my shoulder, her voice firm but kind. "Triona, you're not selfish for feeling the way you do. You've been handed so much all at once, and no one expects you to handle it perfectly. But let me tell you this... I think you're handling it as well as anyone could. Better than most, even."

Her words settle over me like a fragile shield, not quite enough to banish the guilt entirely, but enough to stop it from crushing me. I glance up at her, and she gives me a small, encouraging smile. "You're showing great strength, Triona. Even if you don't feel it right now, it's there. I see it."

Amelia steps closer, her voice gentle again. "You love fiercely and stand tall in the face of adversity. Knowing where you come from doesn't change who you are. It adds to it. When you're ready, I'll help you find the answers you seek. But only when you're ready."

I close my eyes, taking a deep, shaky breath. When I open them, the hardness in my chest has lessened, replaced by exhaustion. "I'll need time," I breathe.

Amelia nods. "Take all the time you need."

The sound of footsteps echoes softly down the hall, and I hear murmured voices before the door creaks open. Casey is the first to appear, leaning against the doorframe with his signature smirk firmly in place, arms crossed as if he's already prepared to break the tension. Callan follows, his broad frame filling the doorway before he steps inside. Bran trails behind, settling on the edge of the chair near the window, his usual humour subdued but still present in the twitch of his lips, as if waiting for the perfect moment to strike. Finn doesn't appear, his absence lingering like a shadow in the room.

"So, ye're *full* Irish then?" Casey asks, pausing just long enough for dramatic effect. "You make much more sense as a person now."

His grin widens as he expertly dodges the small pillow I hurl at him.

"What?" he says, feigning innocence. "It's not an insult. It's practically a compliment! The fiery temper, the stubborn streak, the whole... *'hell hath no fury like a woman on a mission'* attitude—aye, it all checks out now."

I roll my eyes, but a faint smile tugs at my lips. He always has a way of cutting through the weight of a moment, leaving something lighter behind. "And here I thought finding out I wasn't your sister might make you less insufferable," I quip, tilting my chin up. "Maybe even earn me a little sympathy."

"Less insufferable? Me?" Casey gasps dramatically, clutching his chest. "Never. You wouldnae know what to do with a dull brother."

He steps closer, kneeling in front of me, taking my hand in his. His grin is still in place, but his eyes are earnest. "Besides," he says, flashing a grin, "I think no less of ye. Ye're still my favourite sister... Even if you're more Irish rebel than Scottish lass, blood or not, it doesn't change a thing. We've got your back."

Callan's voice rumbles from the corner, quiet but steady. "Aye. Ye've always been a Sinclair to me. Most days I forget ye dinnae have the same stubborn blood flowin' through yer body."

The lump that rises in my throat catches me off guard, but the love in his tone steadies me, the way only Callan can.

Still, my thoughts linger elsewhere. My gaze flickers to the window, the dim light casting long shadows across the room. "My Da... James," I murmur, almost to myself. "He told me about Robert once. He never used his name, but said he always had little reminders of him around. Said that reminder grew up to be fiery and stubborn."

My fingers tighten slightly, memories resurfacing—small trinkets on the mantel, a worn leather journal he never let me read, the way his eyes would cloud over whenever he spoke of loss.

I swallow, exhaling shakily. "And now... I know why."

My father carried Robert with him, always. In the way he spoke, in the way he grieved. And now I carry him too.

The realisation lands deep in my chest, settling alongside everything else. For so long, I thought I was searching for myself. But maybe... maybe I've always known. Maybe I was just waiting to understand.

The weight in my chest shifts—not disappearing, but changing. What once felt like loss now feels like something else.

Purpose.

My voice steadies as I straighten my shoulders. "So, I refuse to let evil win. For all of them. I'll make a stand and fight back with all that I am."

I brace myself, waiting for someone to challenge me—to tell me I'm being reckless, that I don't understand what I'm saying.

But no one speaks.

Casey's gaze flickers downward, his usual smirk absent. Callan exhales slowly, rubbing the back of his neck as if turning something over in his mind. Even Bran, who never lets a moment sit for too long, watches me in quiet contemplation.

Then—finally—he lets out a slow, impressed whistle. "Well, damn—already plotting vengeance? I'm in."

Callan exhales, shaking his head. "Aye... and here I thought I was the stubborn one."

He runs a hand over his jaw, thoughtful, before meeting my gaze. Something in his expression softens, just barely, before he gives a slow nod—approval, understanding, something between just the two of us.

Whatever comes next, I'll face it. For my parents. For those I care about. For myself. For anyone who has ever suffered at the hands of cruelty. For anyone who thought they didn't have the strength to fight back.

Even if it means becoming something I don't yet understand.

The late afternoon sunlight cascades over the garden, illuminating the patch of primroses nestled beside the doorway. Their soft, purple petals seem to radiate warmth in the golden light, delicate yet striking. A smile tugs at my lips, a gentle warmth spreading through my chest at the sight of them.

I know exactly what they signify, and I treasure their presence here. Primroses aren't merely flowers—they are silent sentinels standing guard against the unseen. Shielding homes from the most mischievous, their placement marking the threshold between the human world and the Otherworld. There's an intrinsic magic in them, a connection to something greater that has always captivated me. Somehow, the revelations of the past few weeks have brought clarity. Now I understand why my family surrounds themselves with these flowers, as if weaving protection and meaning into every petal.

"It's lovely to see you out of bed, my dear," Deidre's voice calls out warmly from the side. She stands a few paces away, wiping her hands on her apron, her cheek streaked with a bit of soil. "You're admiring my handiwork, are you?" she adds with a teasing smile, though her tone softens as she moves closer.

I give her a small, self-conscious smile. "I know it does nothing to wallow away in my room," I reply, though my voice betrays the lingering heaviness in my heart.

Deidre pauses, her gaze steady. "It's strange, isn't it? How loss reshapes us. Sometimes it feels like the grief will consume us entirely, but the heart has a remarkable way of creating space for both the sorrow and the joy. Don't rush yourself, love. Healing takes time, as so does learning to carry the love left behind." She gestures toward the flowers with a faint smile. "And speaking of love, those primroses there—they're brimming with it, aren't they?"

Her words linger in the air as I glance back at the blooms, my smile returning, but tinged with a hint of sadness. "They're perfect," I breathe. "Ma loved them..." The words catch in my throat as a wave of emotion swells within me. I quickly avert my gaze, ashamed of the tears that threaten to fall. "I'm not even sure how to stop calling her my mother," I add quietly.

"Don't stop," she says. "She will always be your mother. Blood doesn't determine that kind of love."

"It just hurts twice over," I admit, "mourning the loss of a second mother I never even had the chance to meet."

"I'll never smell a primrose and not think of Ellen."

The sentiment catches me off guard, my breath hitching slightly, but before I can respond, Deidre adds, almost absently, "Sarah loved them, too."

"Truly?" I ask. Hearing her name is foreign and carries the ache of a connection I'll never fully know.

Deidre's gaze lingers on me, unreadable for a moment before she steps closer. "Very much so. She'd have adored seeing you so drawn to them."

I brush my fingers lightly against a bloom, careful not to damage its fragile beauty. "They're beautiful, and they feel right here."

"There you are," Amelia calls, stepping lightly into the garden. She's dressed impeccably, her smile warm but carrying that glint of determination I associate with her. "I've been looking for you, dear. May I steal you for a moment?"

I straighten, brushing off my skirt. "Of course. What is it?"

Amelia's gaze flits to the primroses, her smile softening. "I was wondering if you might accept an invitation to a ball being thrown tomorrow night."

The question catches me off guard, and I blink at her, unsure how to respond. "A ball? I... I'm not sure." My voice falters as doubt creeps in.

Amelia doesn't miss a beat. "It's going to be held here, at my villa," she says lightly, as though that might ease my hesitation. "And before you protest, all the gentlemen seem onboard with the idea."

I raise an eyebrow, skeptical. "Oh, really? All of them?"

She laughs softly, shaking her head. "It's true, I promise. But there's a reason for their enthusiasm." Her expression softens as she steps closer, her voice lowering. "We're throwing it for you, Triona. To celebrate you."

"For me?" I repeat, unable to mask the disbelief in my voice. "Why?"

Amelia's eyes glisten, her smile tinged with something bittersweet. "Because you deserve to be celebrated. I've spent the last nineteen years honouring your birthday from afar, and now that I finally have the chance, I want to make up for all the time I've missed. Please, let me do this."

The earnestness in her gaze leaves no room for refusal. Slowly, I nod. "All right," I breathe, a tentative smile forming. "If it means that much to you, I'll accept. But it seems a polite decline might not have been an option, either way."

The smile that crosses her face is mischievous. "You would be correct, but I *promise* you won't regret it." She takes my hands, giving them a reassuring squeeze before releasing me. "Now, come inside. There's much to plan."

With a deep breath, I follow her, the quiet resolve within me shifting to something lighter, brighter.

25

A DANCE OF DESIRE

Triona

Monday, 2 June 1823

Casa da Prímula

The door to the hall swings open, drawing my attention to Aunt Amelia stepping in with a man at her side. There's something about his presence—so effortlessly commanding—that causes the room to fall silent. I barely register Amelia's sly smile as she prepares to address the room. "Everyone, this is Mannie, a dear friend who has planned to stay for a short time."

My breath hitches when his piercing blue-grey gaze locks onto mine.

His hair, a silver hue flowing freely down his back, catches the light like moonlight on water. His presence is an enigmatic force that fills every corner of the hall, demanding attention without a word. I can't help but notice the fluid grace in his movements as he steps forward, dressed in a tunic of deep blue that shifts shades like ocean waves. The silver clasp of his cloak catches the light, and his boots gleam with a polished finish that reflects his meticulous appearance.

A faint smile plays at the edges of his lips, and when he finally speaks, his voice is smooth, and has an unmistakable Irish lilt. "Ah," he murmurs, his eyes never wavering from mine. "You must be she, the one for whom this night is adorned. Tell me, do you always command such attention?"

My cheeks burn, and before I can respond, he strides toward me with singular focus, his every step confident and deliberate. The sound of my heartbeat pounds in my ears.

He stops just short of me, bowing slightly in a gesture that feels both respectful and intimate. His hand extends toward me, and before I fully understand what is happening, his cool fingers close around mine.

"Forgive my boldness," he says, lifting my hand to his lips. "But beauty such as yours deserves to be honoured properly."

His lips linger against my knuckles—a touch that feels both foreign and unnervingly familiar.

I'm acutely aware of every pair of eyes now trained on us. I swallow hard, unable to find words as confusion mixes with an unshakable sense of recognition.

A throat clearing from behind me snaps me from my trance. Callan stands rigid, his jaw locked so tightly I half expect him to snap. Every line of his face is carved with warning. His hand flexes at his side, as though ready to act should Mannie overstep in the slightest.

Near the hearth, Finn remains still, his expression unreadable, but apprehension coils in his frame.

"Who are ye?" Callan's gruff voice cuts through the silence.

Mannie's chuckle is soft, almost melodic, a sound that holds both amusement and subtle intrigue. Straightening, he meets Callan's gaze with a calm, self-assured demeanour. "I have walked many paths with Amelia over decades past. It seems my steps have aligned to bring me here at this very moment. Amelia spoke of your arrival mere days past—a timely coincidence, it seems."

Only then does he release me, his thumb brushing my knuckles one last time before his hand falls away.

"A lot of things seem to happen at *just* the right time these days," Bran quips from the corner, his grin cutting through the tension like a flicker of sunlight on stormy waters. His tone is playful, but there's an edge to it, as though he's testing those waters.

Aunt Amelia chuckles softly, her grin widening as her eyes dart between me and Mannie. There is a knowing look in her expression that makes my stomach flutter with curiosity.

"Well," Amelia says, her tone light and teasing, though a subtle edge cuts through her words. "I trust you'll all behave yourselves, properly, as *gentlemen* ought. Mannie is my guest, after all." Her eyes meet all in the room, but linger on Finn.

Mannie inclines his head toward Amelia, his smile widening slightly. "It is an honour to be in such esteemed company—a privilege I am so rarely granted. We will all make such quick companions," he says smoothly, but his attention returns to me, his voice softening as he adds, "And to gaze upon the exquisite beauty that is Amelia's niece—a radiance not bound by mortal years, is a gift I had not expected."

My flush deepens as I try to make sense of his words—of him. I've not met anyone quite like Mannie. There is a flamboyance to him, a deliberate, theatrical quality in the way he speaks and moves, as if he is well aware of the attention he commands, and revels in it. And something about him that feels... untouchable. Not threatening, but hypnotic, and utterly beyond comprehension.

"You flatter me. If I didn't know better, I'd think you were trying to charm me." My voice is soft and teasing.

Mannie's smile deepens, and he takes a deliberate step closer. "How could I not? A woman as radiant as you should hear what effects she has over men. Truly transcendent beauty." His gaze flickers behind me for the briefest moment before returning to me, his expression laced with amusement. He glances down at my hand, and reaches out to brush over my bare finger, before he lifts his gaze to mine again.

"Yet no ring adorns your hand. No oath set in stone. A strange thing, for one such as you. Perhaps fate is merely waiting for the right hands to lay claim?"

Bran, ever the opportunist, lets out a low whistle. "Saints above, and here I thought I had all the allure in the room."

I shoot Bran a pointed look, my eyes warning him to hold his tongue. He just grins, holding his hands up in mock surrender, though the dashing smile he flashes me makes it clear he's enjoying every bit of my discomfort. I roll my eyes, exhaling sharply as I try to shake off the heat creeping up my neck.

Before the tension can stretch further, the door creaks open again, and Deidre steps inside, her gaze sweeping the room before landing on Callan. "Callan, could you assist me with something?" she asks, her voice cutting through the heavy silence.

Her timing isn't just convenient—it's deliberate. A well-placed hand on the reins before the horses bolt.

Callan's eyes flick to her, his jaw still taut, but after a beat, he nods. With one last wary glance at Mannie, he strides toward Deidre, who turns and leads him out of the room.

Bran, sensing the shift, claps his hands together. "Well, then!" he exclaims, rocking back on his heels. "I think I'll go see if there's anything left of that apple tart from earlier."

Casey, who had been standing stiffly, eyes darting between Finn and Mannie, exhales and nods quickly. "Aye... I think I'll just go busy myself with something incredibly important and entirely made up. Seems like the safer option right now."

I glance toward Mannie, and he winks before offering a slight bow. "Enjoy the rest of your evening. And perhaps, if fate allows, you might save me a dance?" His voice is smooth and teasing. With that, he turns and strides toward Aunt Amelia, slipping effortlessly into conversation as if he hadn't just set the room ablaze with tension.

From the corner of my eye, I catch a flicker of movement. Finn steps toward the door with quiet purpose. He does not slam it, does not storm out. He simply slips away, his broad shoulders carrying a weight he does not speak aloud.

My heart clenches as I hesitate, but ultimately I let the pull in my gut push me forward. The echo of my footsteps down the corridor seems to amplify the pounding in my chest.

"Finn!" I call out, quickening my pace to catch up. "Finn, wait!"

He doesn't stop. His strides are long and unsteady, as if he's trying to put as much distance between us as possible. I hear his breath, ragged and uneven, betraying the storm inside him.

"Finn, talk to me!" My voice cracks slightly, desperation seeping through. The sound makes him falter for just a moment before he turns on me abruptly, his expression raw, stripped of the usual control he holds so tightly.

"What is it, Triona?" he demands, his voice tight, thick with something unspoken.

I stop in my tracks, startled by the rare intensity of his tone. "What is it? Finn, this isn't like you. You're—" I swallow hard. "You're not yourself. This... anger radiating from you."

His chest rises and falls, his golden eyes burning into mine. The tension in his jaw trembles, his hands clenching and unclenching at his sides as if warring with himself. "I cannae stand it, Tri."

"Can't stand what?" I whisper as my heart hammers against my chest.

"To see his hands on you," he grits out, his voice hoarse. "Just as I couldnae bear watchin' Marcus touch you. Standin' there, pretendin'... As if it were naught to me, when it burned through me like a brand."

I blink, his words sinking in like a stone thrown into deep water, rippling outward. My breath stutters as I take a step closer. "Finn..." My voice is barely above a whisper, hesitant but searching. "What are you saying?"

"You cannae just trust anyone, Tri."

I take another step closer, the space between us charged. "I trust my aunt, Finn. And besides," I press, my voice quieter but unyielding, "That's not what I asked."

My voice is quiet but firm, my heart hammering against my ribs. "You can't stand to see them touch me, but *why*?"

His throat bobs as he swallows hard. I search his face, desperate for an answer, for confirmation of what I hope is true.

"Say it, Finn," I whisper.

Finn's mouth opens slightly, but no words come out. His hands flex at his sides, his breathing uneven, as if he's on the verge of saying something he can't take back.

"Finn... please," I press, willing him to say it, to admit it out loud.

Just when I think he might, when his lips part with something more than silence, the air shifts. Mannie steps forward, his movements as fluid and graceful as ever, an ambiguous smile curving his lips as he approaches.

"It is so rare," Mannie says, his voice smooth and resonant, "to see a bond so deep it eclipses its original form."

Finn's glare at Mannie is blistering, but Mannie doesn't flinch. Instead, his gaze lingers on me, and I feel as though he's seeing straight into my soul, peeling back layers I didn't even know existed.

"A bond like this is not something to take lightly. Not something to run from, either."

Finn's voice is tame as he responds. "This *bond* was forged over years of friendship. Deep and unbreakable, aye, but grounded in trust and shared experience."

The words sting, as though he's just rejected me in front of an audience, dismissing the possibility of anything more. I swallow hard, keeping my expression neutral.

Mannie tilts his head. *"Friendship?* Yet you would bristle at the thought of her in another's arms? Strange, would you not agree?" A moment of silence stretches between them, heavy and charged, as though Mannie's words are testing the very air around us.

Finn steps forward, his movements sharp and deliberate, his voice steady but laced with fury. "We dinnae trust so easily these days. Not with people unknown to us."

He stays rooted in place, his glare fixed on Mannie until the man finally inclines his head and steps away, his smile lingering as he retreats. Just before he turns fully, Mannie glances back at Finn and says, "There are bonds in existence that have much power... ignore them and they may consume you. Deny them, and they may *break* you."

Finn exhales sharply, his jaw tightening as he finally speaks. "You dinnae ken what ye're sayin'." His voice is low, controlled, but there's a tremor beneath it—something raw, something unguarded. Mannie only smirks before he turns on his heel and strides away, leaving the room with effortless ease.

Finn remains where he is, his shoulders still rigid, his breathing slow but heavy. He doesn't move until Mannie is gone. Only then does Finn's gaze shift back to me, his eyes softening for a fleeting moment. I feel every muscle in my body urging me to stop him, to force him into a conversation he clearly doesn't want to have. The words are there, trapped behind my teeth, but with impossible strength, I hold them back. I know if I push now, it won't go well.

Without a word, he turns and walks away, his retreating figure taut with emotion he doesn't dare show. The silence he leaves behind is deafening.

I stand there, frozen, as my thoughts spiral.

This is no mere friendship for me now. It has transformed into something deeper, something that sets my heart alight. The sound of his laughter has become not just pleasant, but necessary. I catch myself memorising the way he looks at me, searching for something more in his gaze. His absence doesn't just leave a space beside me, but an ache in my very soul.

And the thought that he might not feel the same? That terrifies me. Caring for someone this deeply is a danger. Handing over your heart means giving someone the power to destroy you. If something happens to them—if they leave, if fate is cruel—it doesn't just hurt. It rips a part of you away, a piece you never get back. Perhaps that is why I should turn back now, before it is too late.

But such thoughts are a folly. I fear I am already lost to him.

The sight of the bundle of fabric my aunt left for me is both thrilling and unnerving—unlike anything I've ever worn.

Deidre sidles up beside me, her sharp eyes catching my wide-eyed expression. She lets out a soft chuckle, her amusement warm but tinged with mischief.

"Let's get you all gussied up, my sweet," she teases, her tone light and coaxing, as if I were a skittish horse she's determined to saddle.

I hesitate, glancing at her as my cheeks heat. "Shouldn't there be..."

"No room for undergarments in this one, love," she says, cutting me off with a wave of her hand. "The dress will do all the work."

A fresh wave of nerves ripples through me. My mind fixates on the absence of that missing layer, the stark susceptibility it creates.

The soft brush of fabric against naked skin magnifies the sensation, turning the dress from something merely daring to something scandalously intimate. It's not just revealing—it's a shedding of armour, a deliberate unwrapping of restraint. I should be mortified. I should demand something more modest, more... *safe.*

And yet.

The vibrant red hue, the daring cut, the way the fabric slides over me like whispered temptation—it all sends a thrill racing through me. The fabric clings like a lover's embrace, and celebrates every curve as if it were made for me alone.

The bodice is made of a sheer, nude fabric that gives the illusion of bare skin, embroidered with intricate red and gold detailing that curves across me like living art. The delicate embellishments bloom like flower petals, trailing into a plunging V at the front and skim dangerously close to the edges of my nipples—leaving me achingly aware of just how exposed I am.

The skirt is unapologetically bold. The daring slit at my hip leaves my leg fully exposed with every step—a deliberate choice, a provocation I'm unaccustomed to.

The dress commands confidence.

As I catch my reflection, I'm transfixed by the woman staring back at me. I see a version of myself I scarcely recognise—a woman fierce and unafraid. I behold a strength that effortlessly silences lingering doubts, a willpower capable of shattering even the most obstinate barriers.

Unshed tears glisten in my eyes as I realise I have, in many ways, been remade. It's as if the woman before me has emerged from a long-forgotten dream, ready to seize life with unbridled passion and grace.

Deidre stands behind me, her hands on her hips, a satisfied grin spreading across her face. "There she is," she sighs softly.

"Who?" I ask, still in awe.

"This version of yourself they won't be able to stop talking about."

Deidre works quickly but skilfully, weaving my hair into a loose, cascading style—long waves tumbling down my back and over my shoulders. Small red flowers are nestled into the strands, their delicate petals standing out against the rich brown hue. A few soft tendrils frame my face, grazing the curve of my neck, adding to the romantic, almost ethereal effect. She adds a touch of colour to my cheeks and lips before leaning close to dab a familiar fragrance behind my ear.

"Is that primrose?" I ask, excitement slipping into my voice.

Deidre's smile widens knowingly. "Your aunt's favourite," she says. "She loves how it gives off a profound fragrance—"

"And just the right balance of the florals and woods that surround it?" I interrupt, laughing as the words leave my mouth. My mother's voice echoes in those words, and Deidre's expression softens with recognition.

My laughter fades as the bittersweet memory settles, tugging at my heart. Smiling feels wrong when I think of how she'd gasp at the sight of me, dressed the way I am now, her wide eyes filled with both shock and admiration. My body tenses, but Deidre's hands settle firmly on my shoulders, grounding me. Her eyes meet mine in the mirror, steady and full of warmth.

"She'd faint, wouldn't she?" I murmur, a small, wistful smile tugging at my lips. "Seeing me so… scandalously dressed."

Deidre chuckles softly, her grin widening. "Perhaps for a moment there'd be an immediate shock—a panic, given how far things here stray from the expected order," she says gently. "But then she'd be awestruck. Your mother would marvel at the sight of you, just as I am now." Her gaze drops briefly to the dress.

It takes great resolve to keep the tears back. Tonight, of all nights, I want to hold on to the illusion that everything is fine. My hand moves to hers, giving it a gentle squeeze. "You have my gratitude, Deidre. For everything you were to my family."

Her eyes glisten, but she keeps her composure, reaching out to brush a tear from my cheek before it can fall. I turn to face her fully, grabbing her hand again. "You were a mother to me, even when I fought you at every turn. I will never forget that."

She gives a soft laugh, squeezing my hands. "I'm most proud of that stubborn determination of yours," she teases, her voice thick with emotion. After a moment, she clears her throat and steps back, her tone shifting to its usual no-nonsense practicality. "Now, are you ready to step out there and knock the breath from the lungs of every poor soul waiting to meet you?"

I laugh. "As ready as I'll ever be."

When I step out of my room, Aunt Amelia is waiting in the hallway. Her face lights up, her eyes widening as she takes me in. "Oh, spin for me, my darling girl!"

I laugh and oblige, twirling dramatically before dipping into a playful bow. Her laughter is contagious, filling the space as she claps her hands in delight.

"This dress is magnificent," I say, though nerves edge into my voice. "My only concern is—"

"Tut, tut," she interrupts, waving her hand as if batting away my worry. "I've already dealt with your brothers. I practically threatened them, so don't even *try* to use them as an excuse to get out of wearing something so *marvelous*."

I blink at her, a smile tugging at the corners of my lips. "You threatened them?"

"Aye," she replies, a wicked gleam in her eyes. "And if they so much as *breathe* too loudly around you tonight, they'll find themselves escorted to the stables and tied up. They'll behave. I promise." She finishes with a wink, and I can't stop the laughter that spills out of me, the sound bubbling up unexpectedly.

I can picture Callan's ever-present scowl, his brooding silence meeting its match in Amelia's razor-sharp tongue. And then there's Casey—his effortless charm usually lets him slide through life untouched, but somehow, Amelia remains uniquely immune to it. The image tugs a smile from me, warmth blooming in my chest, admiration swelling like a tide I don't fight.

"You are mighty, Auntie," I say, shaking my head. "I'd have paid to see their faces when you said that."

She smirks, clearly enjoying my amusement. "The big one—Callan—looked like he'd swallowed a stone. Hasn't made eye contact with me all day."

I shake my head, marveling at her unmatched boldness.. "I wish to be as brazen as you when I'm older."

She pats my hand as we stop just outside the grand doors leading to the party. "Stepping into that room wearing *that* dress is your first step to finding that part of you. You are a fearless warrior, my girl, and I have every confidence that tonight, you'll shine brighter than any star in the sky."

I nod, straightening my shoulders as I meet her gaze.

Her smile is steady, her eyes shining with a fierce pride that settles something deep within me. "You carry great strength within you, my darling girl. Tonight, the world will see it too."

Nothing in my wildest dreams could have prepared me for this.

I haven't visited this room in my aunt's villa before, but I've seen ballrooms—none like this. The very air seems alive, humming with divinity, the grandeur both overwhelming and enchanting.

The ceilings stretch impossibly high, frescoes unfolding above me like a celestial tapestry. I recognise the story from the carvings alone—Ériu's story, the same tale my mother told me night after night as a child. Seeing it here, immortalised in paint and stone, leaves me breathless.

"I can't believe it," I murmur, my voice barely audible. "To see this here... it's incredible."

Amelia steps closer, her smile soft, yet tinged with pride. "I may not live in my home country, but I bring it with me wherever I go," she says, the weight of nostalgia woven into her words.

Towering marble columns line the walls and are adorned with gold leaves that catch the light. The chandeliers are massive, each flame encased in a glowing orb of ethereal light that seems to pulse as I stare.

The floor is a mosaic of polished stone, its green and white hues familiar. Amelia catches my expression and laughs.

"Connemara marble," she says, tapping it lightly with her foot. "One of the strongest marbles you can find, and you can only find it in—"

"Ireland," I finish, grinning as our eyes meet.

She nods, pleased, and places a hand on my shoulder.

The air is thick with a fragrance too beautiful to belong to this world. It clings to the room, softening every breath. Music drifts through the space, a supernatural symphony that hums with divine energy, threading itself into the laughter and movement around me.

Hundreds of flowers spill across the tables, their vibrant blooms bursting from perfectly placed arrangements. The sheer beauty of it steals my breath, striking me as both overwhelming and deeply moving. Amelia did all of this—for me. To celebrate my *homecoming*, as she'd called it.

Patrons dance with carefree abandon, their movements more expression than coordination. Their attire is a spectacle in itself—flowing gowns adorned with shimmering embellishments, richly coloured tunics, capes that glisten under the chandeliers. Their confidence is effortless, fused into every laugh, every step. The sheer joy in the room is palpable, swirling through the air like a tangible force.

Eyes fix on me—some curious, others admiring. The attention doesn't unsettle me. Instead, it fuels something stronger, a boldness I've never fully embraced. I stand taller, the nerves that once gnawed at me dissolving into something heady and exhilarating.

Confidence drapes over me like my gown—deliberate, daring. I feel worthy of the celebration.

"Auntie, this is—" Words slip from my grasp as I stand there, mouth partially open, trying to take it all in.

"This is all for you, dear," she says, her voice warm but laced with something bittersweet. "For nineteen years of missed birthdays and holidays. For moments I should have been there, but wasn't. Time I can't get back, no matter how much I wish I could. But tonight—tonight is ours. Tonight, I wouldn't have it any other way."

She takes my hand and pulls me along, her energy urging me forward. Whether it's keeping me from crumbling under the weight of her sentiment—or to shield herself from lingering in the same thoughts—I can't be sure. But I let her guide me, my heart full and my throat tight as I silently promise to make this night one to remember.

Casey spots me first, standing in the far corner with a drink in his hand. His jaw drops, his expression frozen in disbelief, before he hurriedly claps Callan on the back with enough force to make him flinch. Callan turns, irritation clear on his face as his conversation—with a small group of partygoers, mostly women—comes to an abrupt halt.

His narrowed eyes lock on me, and I can practically see the wheels turning in his head as he weighs his options. Is he really willing to test Aunt Amelia's warning? Judging by the tension in his stance, every muscle in his body aches to storm over and drag me away. The nerve of him—standing there, chatting with women dressed just as boldly as I am, yet looking at me like I'm the one committing some unforgivable sin.

With a mischievous grin, I stick my tongue out at them both. Childish? Maybe. Satisfying? Absolutely.

It's a minor act of rebellion, one they can't retaliate against tonight. Not here, not with Amelia's warning hanging over their heads like a storm cloud.

Taunting them without consequence fills me with a small, delicious sense of victory. They'll just have to sit with their opinions, because tonight is mine—and I don't intend to waste it.

Amelia must sense the hesitation in my step because she glances back, her brow lifting ever so slightly in silent question. I don't answer with words, my gaze fixed on the boys. The moment they catch her eye, their reactions are nothing short of comical—Callan stiffens like he's been caught stealing, and Casey dramatically averts his gaze.

Amelia's lips twitch with a barely concealed smirk, and I swear I hear her whisper, "*Cowardly bastards*," under her breath as we continue walking.

"You must have said more than you mentioned, Auntie," I say, side-eyeing her as her expression remains maddeningly composed.

She merely shrugs, a picture of innocence, though her silence tells me everything.

Despite myself, a laugh escapes me, soft but genuine.

Amelia slows, resting a hand lightly on my arm. When she looks at me, her voice is gentle but resolute.

"You have a soul so beautiful, Triona, it radiates outward. You're gleaming—and I want you to stand tall tonight."

Her sharp, kind eyes meet mine. There's no room for deflection in her gaze—only quiet insistence. "And I want you to stop denying yourself the things you've been pushing away."

My voice catches, and it's thinner than I mean it to be. "What do you think I'm denying myself?"

She lifts her brows slightly, her expression unreadable but knowing. "Only you can answer that." A pause, then with a glint that borders on amused:

"But I've my suspicions. And I trust you'll come to your senses—sooner rather than later."

The words land with more force than I expect. I'm left wondering if I've been more transparent than I thought—or if Amelia simply sees right through me.

With her, the latter never feels entirely impossible.

I realise something unusual as I'm led further into the room: no other woman in the crowd wears red. While the other patrons embrace boldness in their shimmering fabrics and intricate designs, the crimson of my gown stands alone, commanding a unique kind of attention.

"Auntie," I begin, glancing around the room again, "why am I the only one in red?"

She chuckles softly as she places a reassuring hand on my back. "Triona, you are not the *only* one in red."

I turn to her, my brow furrowing in confusion, but her gaze drifts past me, settling at the far end of the room. A soft smile graces her lips as she gestures with a subtle nod. I follow her line of sight to a figure standing with his back turned, deep in conversation with Bran. His outfit catches the light—a deep red fabric that clings to him, adorned with floral embellishments that mirror the design of my gown.

He's the finest man on the floor.

I'd know it was him whether he was dressed up or in tatters, but to see him like this is thrilling—his presence commanding the space effortlessly, exuding a gentleness and unshakable calm that steadies me in the crowd's chaos. *My* everlasting centre-point of serenity.

Bran glances my way, his eyes widening in shock, mirroring the slack-jawed disbelief my brothers wore.

Before my footsteps can even whisper my approach, Finn turns, as if sensing me before I arrive.

The air vanishes from my lungs as I take him in—bathed in the fading light. He looks like a god carved from myth.

Up close, he's even more devastating.

His hair, normally a touch wild, is pulled back, though a few strands fall rebelliously against his forehead and down the nape of his neck. It softens his look in a way that's charming. He's a picture of refinement and ruggedness, all at once.

His eyes travel over me, and the fire in them could set the room ablaze.

He lingers on every detail—from the exposing neckline to the daring skirt. My skin tingles under his focused gaze. It's overwhelming, as if his fixated look alone can unravel me. Each movement of his throat as he swallows reveals the depth of his restraint.

"Finn," Amelia says, cutting through the charged silence.

After what feels like an eternity, he blinks and glances over at Amelia, as if searching for an anchor.

"Evenin', Amelia," he rasps.

She nods slowly as her eyes flit between us with a playful smile. With a gentle pat on my arm, she declares, "Bran, my dear, follow me to the refreshment table." Her tone brooks no argument.

Without another word, he follows Amelia, his movements comically stiff as they vanish into the crowd.

Then our eyes meet—and everything around us seems to pause, not in some grand, sweeping way, but in the still, breathless quiet of something about to begin.

He blinks once, slowly, as if he's trying to make sense of what he's seeing. His gaze moves over—reverently, longingly—as if he's seeing something he hadn't let himself believe could be real.

Finn clears his throat, his voice rougher than usual.

"Little Doe," he murmurs—softer now. "You look... exceptional."

His words hold meaning far heavier than their simplicity. The name—once playful, once a tease—now inspires an entirely unfamiliar emotion.

The air between us shimmers with unspoken words, a fragile thread pulling tighter with each breath we share. I ache for him to let me in, to shatter the barrier he holds so firmly in place, to offer me just one fragment of what hides behind those guarded, golden eyes.

One word. One touch. One *moment* that assures me this means as much to him as it does to me. That I am not just a fleeting thought, a brief spark in his endless storm, but something more. I'd give anything for proof, even the smallest hint, that this connection is not just borrowed time. That I could have more of him if I dared to reach for it.

"Our outfits match almost perfectly," I murmur, my voice softer than I intend, as my fingers reach out to brush along the lapels of his jacket. Divine doesn't do him justice. The deep crimson fabric, the intricate embellishments—it all seems crafted to make him look otherworldly, untouchable, yet here he stands, so close I can feel the heat radiating from him.

His expression doesn't shift, but his hand moves, catching mine before it falls away.

His grip on me is firm and unyielding, its heat coursing through my body and igniting an ache deep within my core. My thighs clench instinctively, desperate for relief. If he notices, he gives no sign, his attention steadfast.

"It's almost as if it were meant to be. Or a—not at all heavily orchestrated—coincidence," he teases, affirming what we know to be true.

"I do wonder if Amelia was born with that meddlesome streak, or if it's a skill she's had to fine-tune over the years."

He steps in closer, the space between us charged. His gaze flicks to my mouth, then slowly rises to meet mine again. He catches his lower lip between his teeth and releases it with a subtle exhale, as if he's burying wicked intent.

"Must run in the family," he murmurs, his voice huskier now.

Before I can fire back, his fingers slide along my wrist, slow and deliberate, as though he's memorising the feel of my pulse.

I draw in a sharp breath, trying to hold his gaze, but it's like looking directly into a flame.

"Let's not pretend you don't love it," I whisper, breath hitching, the words a challenge.

He hums in response, as his gaze makes a final pass over the entirety of me. His jaw flexes once before he leans in, his mouth brushing the shell of my ear, not touching, just letting the heat of his breath skate across my skin.

A shiver rolls through me, sharp and immediate.

"Have I ever pretended," he murmurs, voice like a touch meant to linger, "not to love how headstrong you can be?"

Then—slowly—he pulls back.

Not far. Just enough to watch the change in my expression. To see how his words land.

As if guided by instinct, he releases my wrist and steps in closer. Slowly, deliberately, he takes my hand and places it against his chest—right over his heart.

The steady thrum beneath my palm is impossible to ignore.

Then his other hand slides to the small of my back, his touch warm through the thin fabric of my gown. The contact robs the air from my lungs, leaving me weightless and wanting.

His lips curl into a slow, appreciative smirk, his mouth lowering just enough to hover near the curve of my neck.

"Dance with me, Doe," his voice a velvet command.

When Finn takes charge, I want to surrender—completely. It's a dangerous contrast to the fierce woman I know myself to be, and yet it feels like coming home.

My lips part, and the words spill out—unbidden, but true. "I'd love nothing more than to dance in your arms, Finn."

His hand tightens at the small of my back. Without a word, he leads me onto the floor. His movements are sure, effortless—as though he's always known how to move me this way.

"You're quiet," I murmur, my voice low, my eyes searching his. "What's going through your mind?"

"Just enjoyin' the moment," he replies, though his tone is too careful, too controlled.

His grip on my back tightens, drawing me imperceptibly nearer, as though closing even the smallest distance between us is a necessity. "I'm tryin' to form coherent thoughts, and they all just keep leavin' me."

The tension between us hums like a drawn wire, ready to snap with the slightest movement. An eagerness I've never known coils tight in my chest—hope and frustration warring in equal measure. I'm wrestling with the unbearable thought that he might let this moment pass untouched.

"Why do they seem to leave you?"

Every beat of my heart is a lull, challenging him to cross the chasm between us. This all feels too meaningful to just be a fleeting dance. It feels... destined.

The last note of the song lingers in the air. He slows to a near stop, his thumb tracing slow, aching circles against my back. His lips part—but the words never come.

"May I have a dance?"

The voice cuts through the moment like cold water on an open flame.

Mannie.

His fair hair gleams under the chandeliers, and his tailored suit speaks volumes. He smiles at me, but his eyes flick to Finn, assessing the situation.

Finn's hand stiffens on my back. For one breathless second, I think he might speak—might *do* something. His lips part, the shadow of resistance flickering in his eyes as he looks at Mannie, then back at me. The pause lingers, just long enough for hope to stir in my chest... only to tremble.

"Ah," Mannie says, his smile shifting into something sly as he catches Finn's hesitation. "Is she now spoken for? It seemed she was not when you arrived. Forgive me if I've trod where I should not."

My heart pounds in the silence that follows. I look at Finn expectantly, my breath stills in my throat as I wait for him to say the words I've been longing to hear. *Say the words—say I'm yours.*

But he doesn't.

Finn shakes his head, his expression unreadable as he steps back, releasing me. "No," he whispers, the single word a jagged knife in my chest.

The sting of his refusal radiates through me. My face falls before I can stop it, the hope I'd carried extinguished in an instant. If he won't fight for me, then I won't stand here waiting for him to decide I'm worth it.

With a sharp smile that doesn't reach my eyes, I turn to Mannie, sliding my hand into his outstretched one. My heart protests, each beat a silent plea for the man beside me to stop me, to fight for me. But I bury the yearning deep, layering my actions with feigned confidence. If Finn won't step forward, then I'll do what I must do to protect myself—even if it means hiding the truth of how deeply his rejection cuts.

A small spiteful voice inside urges me to push forward, to show him what he's letting slip through his fingers. "I'd love to dance," I say, my voice laced with a forced sweetness.

Mannie glances at Finn, a faint smirk tugging at his lips before leading me back to the floor. My steps are deliberately lighter, my laughter too bright as I throw myself into the dance. Bitterness threatens to ruin this night if I don't tamper down this hurt.

Fighting to hold a smile, I let Mannie lead me deeper into the crowd. With each step, Finn fades from view, swallowed by the sea of dancers and gilded light.

26

SURRENDER

Finn

I watch Triona from a distance, the only one in the room who gleams with a light all her own. The gown wraps her in defiance, absorbing the shadows around her and amplifying the fire in her every movement. She is a flickering flame amidst a sea of polished elegance, untouchable, hypnotic. Her steps are graceful yet deliberate, but it isn't her poise or the elegance of her dance alone that keeps my gaze locked—it's the way she moves with Mannie.

With his smooth charm and effortless grace, he guides her through the steps as if they've done this a hundred times before. His hand rests high on her back, fingers splayed possessively against the intricate fabric of her dress. I see his thumb move, brushing lightly against her, and my pulse quickens, heat rising to the surface.

To those watching, they must seem the perfect pair—their bodies aligned, their movements effortless, their smiles exchanged as if they exist in a world of their own. But to me, the sight tears at something raw and primal. It's like watching another man lay claim to what is mine—no, what *should* be mine. What *would* be mine if I only dared to give life to my dreams.

For a split second, I nearly lost control—almost pressed my lips to hers, and dragged her out of the room. Let the world watch as I made it known she was mine, consequences be damned.

But I didn't.

I'm a cursed man with a heart too full and hands too empty—and now I'm watching someone else touch the fire I've been burning for.

Each touch, each laugh she throws Mannie's way sharpens the edges of my frustration, carving my restraint down to brittle remnants. when she tilts her head, catching the chandelier's light, her smile glimmers as if meant for no one but him. Tension coils its way through my muscles, winding tighter, tighter. I struggle to keep from acting on every primal instinct, screaming at me to rip her away.

"You're staring."

A voice cuts through the haze.

Bran steps beside me, casual as ever, his usual humour tempered by something more knowing. He watches me, watches them, and the weight of his gaze is unbearable.

I drag my eyes away from Triona. I can feel the frustration and pain bleeding through, despite my best efforts to mask it. My voice is tight, coiled with something I can't quite mask. "How can I not?" I gesture toward the dance floor. "Look at them."

With an exaggerated nod, he mutters under his breath, "I know. That dress is something else."

I turn to him with a murderous look, my jaw clenching so tightly it aches.

He raises his hands in mock innocence, eyes glinting with amusement. "What? I'm honestly shocked at your restraint. I think I just saw a priest in the corner crossing himself. That dress is a religious experience."

He has no idea how close I am to snapping. "Say one more thing, Mums. Just one. And I swear, they'll be peelin' you off the ballroom floor."

That first glimpse of her in that dress didn't just steal my thoughts—it obliterated them. The rush of blood to my cock was so sudden, so overwhelming, I thought I might pass out.

It wasn't just lust. It was *need*. Raw, instinctive, all-consuming. The kind of need that makes a man forget where he is, who's watching, or what damnation he might earn if he touched what he shouldn't. I nearly stumbled under the weight of it—of *her*

But I won't admit that.

What I admit—gritted out through clenched teeth—is, "I just want to cover her up so no one gets the wrong idea."

He snorts, clearly not buying it.

I drag a hand down my face, exhaling sharply before I add, "So no one else sees it and takes it as an invitation."

A beat.

Then, more pointedly, "Especially not Mannie."

He follows my gaze to the duo, his expression shifting from sharpness to something more cautious, even concerned, as if he's measuring my breaking point. "They're just dancing, Finn."

"*Dancing,*" I echo bitterly. "It's more than that to him. I can see the way Mannie looks at her, like he's claimin' what isnae his to take."

His eyebrows lift, expression turning pointed as he considers me with the patience of a man about to deliver a killing blow. "Whose is she to take?" he asks, the challenge clear in his tone.

I glare at him, but his narrowed eyes cut through me, tenacious as he studies my face. His words hang heavy in the air, unspoken but implied: *She isn't yours, either.*

"I'd say you're not mad at him," he says, his voice deceptively light, "so much as you are at yourself. Because he's doing what you won't."

The truth in those words stings sharper than I want to admit.

Bran shifts closer, his voice quieter but no less cutting. "If you can't give her what she deserves, someone else will. That's the choice you're making—every time you swallow the truth."

His words slice through the chaos in my mind, cutting straight to the marrow of the fear I've buried for far too long. "You're just standing here, letting her slip away because you're too afraid to take what you want. And for what? Fear? Rejection? Judgment? Losing her?" He scoffs, shaking his head. "You're already losing her, Finn. Right now. Toying with fate as you continue to push her into the arms of someone—anyone—who *will* tell her everything you're too afraid to say."

The weight of it lands like a punch to the ribs. My jaw tightens, frustration burning hot beneath my skin. "It's not that simple," I mutter, but even I hear the weakness in it—an excuse, flimsy and worn. A deflection to justify the weight of my hesitation.

Bran lets out a sharp laugh, not unkind, but scathing enough to snap me out of my haze. "Not that simple? Gods Finn, the woman you want is dancing with someone else right in front of you, and you're standing like a spectre in your own life. She's waiting for you... for you to show her she matters more to you than the fear in your head. You have the chance to love her openly. Not all of us can afford that risk."

His last words stick, and in another time, I'd heed them—turn them over, dig for the meaning buried beneath.

But right now? He's baiting me, dragging me out of the fog—and it's working. I round on him.

"The last thing her mother said to me was to let no one impede her path."

Bran steps into my space, eyes blazing. "And you already have. We both know you've already proven how wrong that was."

I open my mouth, but he barrels on, not giving me the chance to deflect.

"In fact, we're *all* so far off the so-called *path* that we'll likely never find it again." He huffs out a bitter laugh, something haunted behind it. "And you know what? That's all right. Maybe the old path was never meant for us. Maybe what matters now is what we choose in the mess we're in—*who* we choose."

My pulse pounds in my ears. "You think I dinnae want to? You think it doesnae gut me to see her in his arms?"

"Then fucking do something about it," Bran fires back, his voice rising enough to draw a few passing glances.

He doesn't blink. Doesn't back down.

He places a hand on my shoulder, his tone razor-sharp. "Stop hiding behind excuses. Stop letting fear control you. Grow a damn spine and show her she matters before it's too late."

Then, softer, he adds, "And if you don't, I swear on every cursed step we've walked together, I'll remind you of your stupidity every day for the rest of your miserable life. With *graphic detail.*"

He flashes me a wicked grin, but it doesn't reach his eyes. "Don't make me do that. Neither of us would enjoy it. Well, I might, but you'll go mad before I let up."

I snort, the sound low and bitter. "You're a bastard."

My eyes drift back to Triona just in time to see Mannie's hand shift again, this time settling brazenly on her hip as the music slows. My heart stutters as I see the slight tension in her shoulders, the way her body stiffens at the move.

That's all it takes for my resolve to shatter like glass underfoot.

"Mac, calm down—" Bran begins, but the words are distant, lost beneath the roaring in my ears. I shrug off his grip, the world narrowing to a single point.

The sight of Mannie as he leans in, murmuring in Triona's ear.

Unrelenting frustration mounts with each passing second. Bran's attempts to rein me in is laughable.

"Finn! I wasn't suggesting you handle it so abruptly," Bran whisper shouts, realising the fire he's stoked has grown beyond his control.

I cross the floor in a few quick, deliberate strides as a lifetime of restraint unravels in an instant. The moment I reach them, Mannie's smug expression only fuels the fury burning within me.

"Ah, Finnis," Mannie drawls, voice oozing mockery. "What seems to be the matter?"

"I believe you asked for *one* dance."

"Is there a problem with taking more? Your face suggests I have somehow touched a nerve," he says, amusement twinkling in his eyes. "But I suppose it must be challenging, standing back while someone else gives her the attention she deserves."

I grab Mannie's shoulder roughly, yanking him away from Triona without hesitation. One moment he's standing tall, the next he's sprawled across the polished floor.

Gasps ripple through the nearby crowd. A few heads turn—enough to draw attention, but not enough to raise alarm. Triona's hand flies to her mouth, her wide eyes darting between me and Mannie, who lies sprawled on the floor, rubbing his jaw.

"Whatever was that for?" he sneers, each word dripping with a patience so practiced it borders on contempt, even as he struggles to push himself upright.

I step closer, my chest heaving as I fight to control the storm inside me. "You had yer hands all over her like she was yers to take." My glare narrows, unyielding. "And that'll *never* be an option for you."

Mannie's smirk widens as he wipes a trickle of blood from the corner of his mouth. "Who does she belong to, then, *Finnis*?" His words are slow, deliberate, and heavy with an unsettling confidence, each syllable a calculated taunt that stirs something primal within me.

"That's none of yer concern," I snap, restrained only by the look in Triona's eyes.

He chuckles darkly. "It seems very much my concern. The fire in your eyes, the recklessness in your fists—those are not born of trivialities. Such passion drives you to strike me for dancing with a lady unclaimed by vow."

Triona cuts in, her eyes wide with disbelief and simmering anger. "Finn, what are you doing?" she demands, her voice trembling slightly. "This isn't necessary!"

I glance at her, my resolve faltering under the weight of her disappointment. "He was oversteppin'," I say, struggling to keep my voice steady. "Touching you as if—"

"As if *what*?" she interrupts, her gaze piercing. "As one might when asking someone to dance? A dance I gladly accepted?" Her tone is sharp, each word a deliberate challenge. "You're needlessly causing a scene, Finn."

Mannie stands tall and adjusts his jacket, the smug expression never leaving his face. "You are undermining her agency, casting doubt on her discernment."

"Stay out of this," I growl, levelling a glare at him.

"How can I when your actions have simply drawn me into this spectacle?" Mannie gestures around us. Guests are whispering, eyes fixed on our confrontation. "The weight of your temper can break more than objects."

Bran appears at my side, his hand gripping my shoulder firmly. "That's enough," he says under his breath. "This isn't the time or place."

I shrug off his hand, but the weight of the stares—Triona's wounded expression—it all sinks in. The anger that had driven me dissipates, replaced by a hollow ache of regret.

Bran steps forward, gaze locked onto Mannie with a pointed intensity. "Mannie," he says flatly, voice low but carrying a quiet authority, "I think it's time you left this to them."

Mannie nods his agreement. "Gladly. Triona, should you tire of misguided protectors, and find yourself in need of proper accompaniment, I would ready myself at the drop of a hat." Before I can react, Bran takes a deliberate step closer, his presence cutting off Mannie's lingering theatrics.

Bran watches him go, ensuring he's well out of earshot, before turning back to me.

Out of Triona's sight, he shakes his head and mouths, *"Fix it. Now,"* his sharp gaze hardening before he exhales.

"I'll... check to see if Callan and Casey saw any of this," he mutters. Then, with a dramatic sigh, he adds, "And get myself a drink. Maybe six."

My gaze softens as I look at Triona, regret pooling in my chest. "I'm sorry, Little Doe—"

"Don't you dare," she snaps, her voice trembling with a mix of anger and pain. "Don't '*Little Doe*' me right now."

"Triona, I just didnae want him to—" I begin, reaching out to her.

She steps back, avoiding my touch. "To what? Enjoy an evening with me? To be treated with kindness? Why do you care now, Finn? You made your choice, no go live with it."

She pushes past me as if I'm nothing but mistake she refuses to make. She doesn't hesitate, doesn't glance back.

The world carries on; the music rising once more, as whispers fade into laughter. But I stand frozen, drowning in the truth I can no longer escape—I have no one to blame but myself.

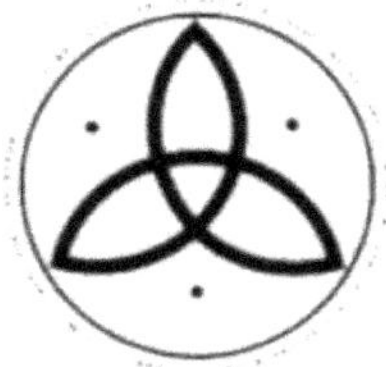

Triona

I flee the ballroom, my heart pounding and my cheeks burning with humiliation. The cloying mix of wine, perfume, and candle smoke still lingers in the air, but I can't focus on anything except the heat of my anger. I quicken my pace, desperate for distance from my embarrassment.

"Triona, please," Finn calls, his voice tight with desperation, cutting through the heavy silence of the corridor.

I whirl around as I reach the archway just before the staircase, my eyes blazing. "Return to the revelry," I snap, my voice sharp with contempt. "You'll surely enjoy your night more now that you've ensured I can't enjoy mine."

He halts a few steps away, his expression crumpling at my words. "Triona, I—"

"No, Finn," I cut him off, my voice trembling with the force of my emotions. "You were a brute in there!"

He steps closer, his face etched with regret. "I wasna tryin' to ruin yer night."

"It matters not!" I snap, my voice rising with frustration.

His breaths come in harsh, heated waves as he strides toward me, his movements deliberate. I press my back against the icy wall, willing myself to stay strong, to not flinch beneath the storm in his gaze.

There's an incessant desire burning inside me, a need to push him to his breaking point, to force out the emotions he keeps buried so deep.

"You're acting as if I did something wrong, when I have not. I was politely putting an end to his advances. I am more than capable of defending myself—far better than you give me credit for—"

"I never suggested *you* acted inappropriately," he says, tone elevated.

"Then why was all of that necessary when you seemed so fine with it mere minutes before?"

"Because I was a jealous feckin' git!" He snaps. "I couldnae stand to watch his hands on you!" he shouts, his voice raw, cutting through my tirade like a blade.

"This again? *Really*, Finn?" I spit.

He's so close now that I can feel the heat of his breath against my chest, his proximity making my heart thunder in my ears.

He takes a shuddering breath, and his voice softens, though the intensity remains. "I lied when I said you looked exceptional in there," he begins, his gaze locking with mine as though the words are being drawn from the deepest part of him. "You aren't just exceptional—you are *indescribable*. A vision so arresting I could barely breathe. That dress—gods help me. You walked in, and I forgot everything but you. How that gown clings to every inch of you, and the way the light dances on your skin... it's bloody unfair."

He pauses, jaw tightening, as if the truth burns on the way out.

"You are temptation itself," he says, his voice low, rough. "And I've never—*not once*—had to hold myself back the way I am right now. Because all I can think about is touchin' you... feelin' if you're as soft as you look. Tastin' the heat of your skin. And showin' every bastard in that room that they never stood a bloody chance."

His throat bobs as he swallows hard, his restraint fraying at the edges. "Is that what you want?" he continues, his voice trembling with the weight of emotion he can no longer hide. "D'ye want to hear how bloody crazed with jealousy I was? How it felt like fire ripping through me? How it took everything in me not to pull you away from him and—" He cuts himself off, his fists clenching at his sides as he fights to rein himself in.

"And what, Finn?" I demand.

My mouth opens again, but the words catch in my throat. Understanding dawns like a lightning strike—he isn't angry with me, and he isn't truly angry with Mannie. He's angry with himself.

Finn's palm presses flat against the wall beside my face. He doesn't lean in fully, but his sheer presence, the weight of him so close, keeps me rooted.

"You test my patience every single day, without even realisin' it, and it's drivin' me mad." The restraint in him is palpable—I can feel it, almost taste it, as though he's holding himself together by the thinnest thread.

"Finn, I don't want half-truths and hesitation." My voice is steadier than I feel, but my heart pounds like a war drum. I dare him to answer. I dare him to prove he's not just saying what I want to hear.

"You dinnae believe me?" His other hand comes up, pressing into the wall on the opposite side of my head. His scent—earth and leather, something wholly *him*—fills my lungs, making it impossible to focus on anything but *him*.

"I've tried," he says, his voice low and jagged, "tried to stay away, tried to tell myself you deserve better, but—"

I shake my head, the tears I've been holding back threatening to spill. "Stop, Finn. Have I not made it clear? I don't want better. I don't want anyone else. *I want you.*"

He closes his eyes, as if trying to block out the truth in my words. When he opens them again, they're brighter, fiercer, filled with something that steals the air from me. "I cannae be something you wake up regrettin'," he asserts, his voice rough with emotion.

My fingers curl into his shirt, fisting the fabric, pulling him closer. "I could never feel that way," I whisper fiercely. "I know *exactly* what I'm asking."

"I'm afraid to risk ruinin' what we have," he admits, the words shaky.

"What do we have, Finn?" The question slips from my lips before I can stop it, before I can shield myself from the answer.

His gaze doesn't waver. It darkens, deepens—stripped bare and trembling. "Somethin' I cannae fathom livin' without."

"I—"

The word has hardly passed my lips before a loud crash reverberates through the air, echoing from the archway just behind us. The sound is sharp, jarring, cutting through the tense bubble of energy between us.

I step toward the source of the sound, peering cautiously around the corner. Finn follows, his presence an unshakable shadow, standing far too close behind me.

My breathing quickens as my eyes lock on the scene before us. I should feel shame from witnessing such intrusion. I should shut my eyes and turn on my heel, but I don't. I can't.

Past the archway, a man has a woman pinned against the stone wall, his hands possessive, his body flush with hers in a tangle of urgency. A fallen case of wine lies at their feet, shattered bottles bleeding red into the stone like an afterthought—unnoticed, unimportant. His shirt is gone, discarded in a careless heap nearby, baring a back carved with muscle and slick with sweat.

Their bodies writhe against one another as the man's hands work with swift efficiency, pulling the woman's dress up past her thighs, exposing her olive complexion to the dim light. Her back arches against the rough surface of the wall as his fingers dig into her with a possessive grip.

In one fluid motion, he releases himself from his trousers, the urgency in his movements leaving no room for subtlety or decorum. Their breaths, heavy and uneven, echo faintly in the surrounding space.

He grips her firmly, hoisting her up against the wall with an eager desperation. She responds by wrapping her legs tightly around his waist, anchoring herself to him as their bodies meld together in an unrestrained display of passion.

There's no hesitation, no thought of their surroundings—only raw, unbridled need. I hear the moment he enters her, both of them releasing breathless, broken moans that spill into the quiet corridor like a confession.

The man groans low, praise spilling from his lips in a broken whisper. "Por todos os santos... you take me like you were made for me." His voice is thick with hunger, extolling in a way that feels all-consuming.

"Tão apertada... tão boa, meu amor." He presses deeper, his breath rough against her skin. "You were carved from sin—meant for nothing but this."

His movements are brutal in their rhythm, driven by a desperation that feels almost feral. With each thrust, he lets out a guttural sound—low, hungry, ragged. The wet slap of skin against skin echoes in a rhythm too primal to ignore, their bodies colliding with wild abandon.

As he moves against her, the woman's hands slide to the bodice of her dress, pulling it down in one swift motion to free her breasts.

He moves from sucking her bottom lip, tongue, and neck to flick his tongue against her nipple. She hisses as he takes her into his mouth, only letting go to suckle roughly over that silky soft flesh.

"Harder," she pants. "Take me like you mean to ruin me, meu amor. Fill me full. Leave your name written beneath my skin." Her words come out in broken gasps, her toes curling, eyes rolling back as he angles her neck to the side to bite the flesh just above her collarbone.

He says nothing, his only response a growl that vibrates through the air as her nails drag down his back, leaving angry red streaks in their wake.

She brings two fingers to his mouth, and he eagerly sucks on them. Without hesitation, she trails that hand downward, her fingers sliding between them to meet him at her core. Her movements are deliberate, teasing, and he lets out a ragged breath, his control unravelling further with every touch.

"You love being wicked to me, don't you?" His voice is low, dripping with dark amusement as his grip on her hair tightens. From where I stand, it looks almost painful, as her head is pulled back at a sharp angle.

So why is it arousing to me?

The question burns in my mind, unsettling and impossible to ignore. Heat rushes through my body, a mixture of shame and fascination pooling low in my belly. I hadn't known it could be like this—so raw, so unrestrained. The intensity of it holds me captive, even as my cheeks flush and my breath comes quicker.

When the man speaks next, his voice is commanding, dripping with raw seduction. The intensity coils in my chest, so overwhelming that my hand drifts to my throat, as if to steady myself.

"Quero ver tudo—cada tremor, cada suspiro. Watch the way you unravel for me... the way your soul reaches for mine when you break." His voice is dark, molten, a command wrapped in silk. "And when I do, I'll spill so deep inside you, you'll still feel me long after I'm gone."

Her screams tear through the air, the sound so intense it gives me chills.

"When you're still trembling, still catching your breath, I'll press you over this barrel—claim you all over, slow and relentless, until the memory of me lingers in every part of you. Até não haver dúvida nenhuma de quem é que você pertence."

A few final thrusts, and their cries of release tear through the air, echoing in the stillness like something sacred and profane all at once. I finally turn away, shame crawling hot beneath my skin. My cheeks burn, my heart pounds, and an aching discomfort twists in my chest—because I lingered. I watched for far too long, held captive by something so visceral, so private. And now I can't unsee it. Can't undo the way it stirred something in me.

I don't make it far. A strong hand catches my elbow, halting my escape before I can slip away.

My body betrays what my mind refuses to admit. My nipples tighten against the fabric of my dress, and between my thighs, a slow, aching thrum pulses in time with my racing heart. With Finn so close, his hand lingering at my elbow, every thought and sensation courses through me in a flood I can't control.

"Tri..."

His voice is low—velvety, sultry—a dangerous melody that undoes me with a single note. The way he says my name makes my knees weak. I hold my breath, frozen, unwilling—or perhaps unable—to pull away.

He steps in closer, the heat of his body licking at the space between us. His breath skims along the curve of my neck, and a tremor steals through me, unbidden.

Then, with deliberate slowness, his fingers drift to the nape of my neck. The pad of each fingertip skates across my skin, delicate as a whisper—but it feels like lightning.

Each brush of his fingers feels like a vow, whispered not in words but in touch. My skin hums beneath him, every nerve alight with awareness. There's a gravity in his nearness, a pull I can't—and won't—resist. The thrum deep in my belly isn't just desire; it's recognition. Of him. Of this. Of something that feels inevitable.

Despite the hardened warrior Finn has become, there is nothing harsh in him now. His calloused hands move with aching gentleness, as though he's trying to memorise the way I fit against him. He maps my body with reverent precision—like a man discovering sacred ground.

"You feel it too, aye?" Finn's lips graze my ear, his voice a low, intimate growl. "That ache, that hunger—I feel it too, Triona, gods help me. I've never felt anythin' stronger."

Then his hand moves—steady, sure—rising to wrap around my neck. Not to control. To anchor. To claim. A silent vow spoken in flesh and heat.

A soft, unbidden whimper escapes my lips as I finally exhale the breath I hadn't realised I'd been holding. The sound is my answer, raw and unguarded, leaving no room for denial.

His hand at my neck tightens, the roughness of his calloused palm a stark contrast to the tenderness of his hold, anchoring me to the moment, to him, in a way that feels both dreamlike and achingly real.

"Aye," he murmurs, his voice deeper now, rough with his own need. "I thought so."

"This is no game to me, Little Doe," Finn murmurs, his voice thick with emotion. "You know that."

My breath tangles in my throat, his words cutting through the defenses I've so carefully built.

"You see me, Triona. Ye've always seen me. And you know almost every part of me. And I knew from the moment you looked at me like I was worth seein' that I'd never tire of you."

My skin tingles under his palm, and despite my better judgment, I lean back slightly, letting my body move closer to his. The moment I do, he groans, the sound deep and guttural, his breath hot against my neck.

His other hand finds my hip, firm but not forceful, anchoring me in place. "I would not move again," he warns, his tone devoid of playfulness as he groans into my neck. It feels hungry, almost desperate. A command wrapped in a plea.

"Finn..." I whisper, my voice trembling, caught between surrender and self-preservation.

"I dream about you. Whether I'm awake or asleep, ye're there, hauntin' every corner of my mind. You consume me, Triona, until there's nothing left—only this *yearning* that refuses to fade. The weight of it is unbearable."

"Thinkin' I couldnae have you the way I wanted—it's been torment. Pure and cruel." His voice breaks slightly, each word a confession dragged from his very soul, before he exhales sharply.

"If we were sleepin' outside under the stars," he begins, his voice dropping to a husky whisper, "even with everyone around us, I watched yer chest rise and fall, lingerin' on every breath you took, wonderin' if you ever dream of me the way I dream of you. Wishing to the gods above that it was me."

His voice grows steadier with each word. "I pictured how it'd feel holding you in my arms, feelin' yer bare skin against mine. I thought about how ye'd look after I worshipped every inch of you... kissin', touchin', tastin'... until you could take no more. Pleasurin' you for hours, until the stars themselves envied what we shared."

"From the moment I saw you standin' on that cliff's edge, the wind tanglin' yer hair, as if it wanted to claim you for itself, I knew you had ruined me. No one else could ever compare."

His words hit me like a wave, the weight of them sinking deep into my chest. My breath catches as I turn to search his face, looking for some sign of hesitation, of doubt—but there's none. His golden eyes are steady, filled with an honesty that leaves me bare.

"I've tried to fight it," he continues, pressing closer, his presence overwhelming. "Tried to convince myself that I could ignore what I felt. That I could go back to bein' the man I was before. But I—." He lifts a hand, his fingers trembling as they trace the curve of my cheek.

"Ye've claimed me, Little Doe, in a way no one else ever could."

Without thinking, I move, brazenly placing my hands against his chest. His body tenses beneath my touch, his breath hitching sharply.

"I thought... I convinced myself that what I felt was one-sided. That I was foolish to think you'd ever look at me the way I look at you," I manage, my voice trembling with the weight of my admission.

He lets out the slightest laugh, a soft, muffled sound that somehow makes my heart flutter and ache all at once.

With Finn... there's no hesitation, no fear, only an ache that consumes me, a longing so deep it feels like it's always been there, waiting for him. This moment feels inevitable, as if the world itself conspired to bring us here. I won't stop it—not this time, not with him. Not when his touch feels like salvation.

His lips graze my neck, each kiss sending chills over me, stealing my breath. "I wouldnae wish this torment on anyone... Ye'd drive a man mad and straight off a cliff, Triona. Ye're drivin' me mad, challengin' me every chance you get."

His words make my head spin, but I move closer, needing the contact, the heat of him. His hands shift, one sliding to the back of my neck, his thumb brushing against my skin, the other pressing firmly at the small of my back, holding me to him.

I press closer, feeling the friction, the undeniable proof of his desire. He hisses, the sound rough and ragged, and I revel in the power I seem to have over him.

I tilt my head up, my eyes locked on his, refusing to tear my gaze away as the tension between us swells. "Tell me, Finn," I whisper, tilting my head, letting my lips hover just out of reach. "Would you really stand by while another man claims me?"

I press into him again, daring him, testing the limits of his restraint. "Could you handle it, Finn?" I ask, my voice dropping to a sultry murmur. "Could you handle another man laying claim to me?"

I can't hide my taunting look. I want to rile him up. Some, albeit childish, part of me delights in seeing the side of him that only I bear witness to.

In truth, I *want* to give in. I want Finn to dominate me completely. I'm ready for him to take what he wants.

"I want no other man to have you," Finn growls, his voice low but fierce, each word vibrating with raw intensity. "I want all of you. I want my scent so profoundly embedded in you that, even in my absence, they'd scent my claim on every part of you I've touched."

His words send a shiver racing down my spine, the possessiveness igniting a fire in me I can't ignore. His hand releases my hair, the tension easing only for him to slide his hands down to my waist. His fingers trace slow, deliberate circles on my stomach, a tenderness that contrasts with the rough edge of his voice and the hunger in his touch. The contradiction only heightens the need building inside me, making every nerve feel alive under his fingertips.

For a moment, he doesn't move, the tension between us sharp enough to cut. Then, slowly, he presses his forehead to mine. "If I give in now—" he rasps, his breath ragged. "I'll take you apart, piece by piece, and I won't stop until ye're ruined for me."

I press until I'm a whisper away from his lips. "Then ruin me, Finn."

His hands move with sure and steady intent, gripping my rear possessively as he grinds into me. The contact sends a jolt through me, igniting the ache already pooling deep inside.

And then, at last, he claims me.

Finn crashes his mouth to mine, a groan tearing from his chest like it's been caged for years. It reverberates through me—through skin, through bone—until I feel it in the deepest parts of me, where longing has lived in silence. His kiss is not careful. It's consuming. Devouring. A beautiful ruin. He kisses like he's starving and terrified this might be the only taste he'll ever get.

The first touch of his lips is indescribable. I press closer, needing more, needing him. His tongue brushes the seam of my mouth, seeking entrance not with aggression, but with an aching urgency that makes me dizzy.

My hands tangle in his hair, desperate to anchor myself. With a low, broken sound, he lifts me like I weigh nothing at all. Instinct takes over—I wrap my legs around his waist, our bodies aligning in a way that leaves no air, no reason between us. I chase the contact I've craved for so long, desperate for the connection, overwhelming all rational thinking.

With ruthless determination, he presses my back against the wall, the cool stone biting through the fabric of my dress—a stark contrast to the searing heat of his body against mine

He shifts against me, his hips rolling in a slow, deliberate grind, eliciting a loud moan from deep within me. The pressure is unbearable, exquisite—his need meeting mine in a rhythm that makes the world fall away. A moan builds in my throat, raw and desperate, but before the sound escapes, his hand gently covers my mouth.

His eyes find mine, burning with something feral and protective, as if to remind me we're not alone. But the danger, the sheer risk of it, only fuels the fire.

Nothing matters but this—him and I, tangled in the heat of our desire.

He lowers his hand from my mouth, fingers trailing down my jaw. One arm braces beside my head, the other wraps tight around my waist, anchoring me to him, to this.

I can feel him—hard, ready—pressing against my centre with a pressure that sends shockwaves through my core. My breath stutters, caught between desire and disbelief.

His gaze drops between us, and something shifts—a quiet, dangerous certainty. When his eyes meet mine again, they burn with a promise.

"Triona," he mutters, brogue thick with desire, "are you bare under yer dress?"

"Aye." I breathe, the word a sultry whisper.

"By all the gods, you're drenched for me," he rasps, his statement a sinful praise.

His hand glides lower, following the dip of my waist, his fingers barely ghosting over my skin. Each slow inch is deliberate, a silent plea for permission. His eyes burn into mine, waiting—demanding.

The instant his thumb grazes that aching bundle of nerves, pleasure sears through me. My body jolts, arching against him, chasing the friction I crave.

I am absolutely crazed for this man.

His touch is consuming every inch of my being. There is only his mouth, his tongue, his eager hands, and the strength of his well-sculpted and taut body pressing against me.

I run my tongue along the seam of his lips, and he eagerly grants me access. It feels as if I know every part of his body without ever having touched him before; every movement feels instinctual.

"Triona," Finn groans, in a voice unlike his own, but one I know I'd beg to hear again. He thrusts his hips between mine with unparalleled fervour as I continue to writhe and lose all sense of control. His arms flex with each powerful movement as he continues massaging my centre.

I'm a mix of urgency and lust; I don't want the moment to end, but feel a throbbing forming under the pressure of our combined movements.

Finn pulls away, tugging a moan from me to look me in the eye.

"Have you done this to yerself before?" He demands between his heavy moans. His movements slowing as he awaits my answer.

I nod, and the relief on his face is immediate as his pace quickens.

His tongue traces delicately along the column of my neck, drawing out soft whimpers as he moves, finally settling just below my ear—the spot that makes me clench against him. I can feel his grin in the way his breath tickles my skin.

"Like that, aye?" he murmurs, right before mimicking the motion once more.

"Finn..." is all I manage to gasp as my back arches off the wall.

"That's it. Let go, Triona. Let go and give your pleasure over to me."

Beads of sweat trickle down my skin, their cool trail contrasting with the scorching heat that radiates through my entire body.

Then it happens—the build of the unmistakable release his body promises, a sensation so overwhelming it feels as though the world vanishes. My body shudders, the intensity consuming me entirely.

It's the most intensely pleasurable sensation I've ever experienced, and I feel it everywhere—coursing through my veins, leaving me weightless. I grip him tightly, my nails pressing into him as I ride the crest of this overwhelming feeling, every thought, every word dissolving into the sheer bliss of this moment.

Finn never moves his eyes from mine as he watches my undoing, only taking my mouth again to stifle the moan I'm helpless to suppress, and growls in satisfaction as an undeniable wetness coats him.

My body aches with need, still so desperate to feel him—flesh against flesh, every bit of him claiming me. I want to feel him pushing deeper, his body overwhelming mine as he licks, sucks, and possesses me completely.

I eagerly wedge my hand between us, seizing the narrow space he's allowed. The moment I cup him through his damp trousers, he emits a long, low groan that sends a shiver down my spine—and makes my mouth water with anticipation.

I grapple with the laces coated in my arousal, but he jerks away, halting my desperate movements.

"Not here. Yer first willnae be against a wall," he says adamantly. "We need to—"

I cut him off with a searing kiss. I won't be swayed from claiming him the way he just irrevocably claimed me. *I need his release.*

I lock eyes with him as I trace the heel of my palm along the full length of his thick shaft, following its smooth contour until I reach his tip, resting just beneath his navel. His breath quickens, and he tilts his head back, exposing his throat in silent invitation. Leaning forward, I let my tongue explore his sweat-slicked flesh, every caress a promise of unspoken desire.

"Triona, I'm about to—" he begins, his voice hoarse with desire, but I silence him as I suck the skin at the base of his neck.

He groans and thrusts into my hand with a strength that has me aching and imagining him buried deep inside of me. "Oh, feckin' hellfire," he breathes, voice wrecked. With one final stroke, he shudders against me, his body going taut before he unravels completely. I feel his cock pulsing under my touch, and the guttural sound emanating as he finds release sends another wave of heat crashing through me, reigniting the ache between my thighs.

As the intensity of our embrace fades, Finn buries his face into my neck, his breaths slowing as he savours the aftershock of ecstasy. His grip on me remains tight, as if he never wants to let go.

A breathless laugh rumbles from his chest. "I cannae believe I came in my trousers like a lad fresh off his first kiss." His voice is low, rough with embarrassment, but there's a spark of wicked amusement in his eyes as his gaze locks with mine. He smiles, his thumb brushing tenderly along my cheekbone before pressing the lightest of kisses to the corner of my mouth.

"You can't possibly fathom how intoxicating you are," I murmur, voice hushed with reverence, my fingers still trembling from the aftershocks. "Hearing the sounds you made for me..." The confession slips from my lips unbidden, the vulnerability of the moment wrapping around us.

The moonlight pouring in through the window casts a soft glow over Finn's face, illuminating the sharp planes of his features. A sheen of sweat clings to his forehead, and his lips are swollen and red from our kisses. He is utterly mesmerising.

Reluctantly, he lowers me back to the ground, his body, lingering close, pressed against mine. Neither of us speaks, unwilling to let the fragile magic of this moment slip away.

My fingers weave into his dark hair as I tug him closer, desperate to capture his lips again. But the blissful haze shatters as the unmistakable sound of footsteps and cheerful whistling bounds toward us.

We tear away from each other like sinners caught in the act; the intimacy shattering as reality slams back into place. My heart races in my chest, hammering so loudly I'm certain Finn can hear it. I smooth my dress with trembling hands, the lingering heat between us making it almost impossible to compose myself.

The footsteps grow louder, closer, and panic blooms in my chest. Finn leans casually against the wall on one side of the hall, his posture deceptively relaxed. I move to the opposite side, creating a distance between us that already feels unbearable.

Casey rounds the corner, his steps uneven but sure enough. He pauses, his sharp gaze flicking between us. My breath stalls, bracing for the inevitable spark of realisation—the knowing look, the teasing remark. But it doesn't come.

His usual perceptiveness dulls beneath the flush on his cheeks, the slight sway of his stance. He's had more than his fair share of drink tonight. A small mercy. One I silently thank the heavens for.

"There you are, dear sister," he says, his voice light and sing-song. He bounds toward me with the carefree energy of a boy, tapping my nose as if I were still a child.

Casey slings an arm around my shoulders, his warmth a sharp contrast to the cold guilt settling over me. "Ye've been missin' all the fun," he says with a grin, oblivious to the tension hanging thick in the air. "Come on, we'll find something to drink."

I nod, forcing a weak smile, but my gaze flicks back to Finn. He leans against the wall, golden eyes locking onto mine for a single aching heartbeat. Something flickers there—regret, longing, something I can't name—but before I can breathe it in, he looks away.

27

A HOUSE OF GLASS

Triona

Tuesday, 3 June 1823

Casa da Prímula

My body feels leaden as I wake. I lie still, listening to the silence that followed the iron wall clock's chime, signalling morning meal. It rang at least half an hour past, but I know the state of the house—heads aching, stomachs turning, nursing other consequences of last night's excess.

After Casey collected me from the hallway, I became his reluctant shadow as he continued drinking. By night's end, he'd been a prickly bastard, starting a fight with Bran after catching him, stealing a kiss from a rather curvaceous party guest. The dispute reeked of drink and wounded pride. After that, Casey left me alone, so I'd carted myself to bed.

I didn't see Finn for the rest of the night. As much as I longed to find him, I thought it wiser to give him space.

An intrusive thought has been playing over in my mind since I left him standing there in that hallway. The thought gnaws at me. *Was that look I saw in him as I made a last pass at him regret?*

But that kiss.

The memory floods me, searing my cheeks with a heat that defies the morning's chill. It consumes my every thought. The press of his lips—firm yet tender—lingers as though he had restrained himself for an eternity, only to surrender after that constraint was broken. His gaze laid me bare and reached the core of me. Even now—I can feel him hot between my thighs—his deft fingers playing my body as if I were a tune he'd spent years perfecting. He moved as if he knew me better than I even knew myself.

I force myself upright, though the weight in my limbs makes it feel as if my emotions have taken root there. My gaze drifts to the bedside table—and a small, startled sound slips from my lips, a quiet mix of excitement and disbelief.

There, nestled in the soft morning light, is a bundle of primrose.

For a moment, I don't move. The purple petals are tied with a thin piece of twine. Slowly, I reach out, brushing my fingers over the stems.

They are still cool, the dew on them fresh, as if plucked only minutes ago.

The flowers are a stark reminder of my mother, as they will always be. Her quiet grace, unshakable love, and the way she knew what I needed before I did. I reach out to grab the bundle, tears pricking my eyes, and an overwhelming wave of guilt rises.

I clutch the flowers to my chest as though they might vanish, much like the bloom in Da's garden that day—when life as I knew it turned to ash. A day I'd wasted away, not knowing it'd be the last in our home. I'd never again hear my mother's chiding, which I'd needed more often than I cared to admit.

I'd never feel the warmth of my father's embrace, arms wrapped around my frame as if he alone could shield me from all. My steely composure completely shatters.

And suddenly, I'm falling.

A sob escapes from between my lips, unbidden and raw. My shoulders shake violently, and I clutch the bundle as if it can anchor me to something no longer present in this realm.

"Triona?" Aunt Amelia's voice cuts through the haze, sharp with concern.

I glance toward her, barely able to meet her pitying gaze before she crosses the room and gathers me into her arms.

"Oh, my love. What is it?" she murmurs as she strokes my hair. "What's hurting you so?"

I can't answer. My throat burns, my chest heaves, and the only sounds that escape are broken, guttural cries, echoing all around us.

Aunt Amelia rubs comforting circles on my back, though I can feel her own trembling. "It's all right, love," she whispers. "Let it out. Let it all out."

All I can think of is how much I miss them. How much I miss *her*. My mother. My father. My home. The life I'll never have again. How ungrateful, selfish, and foolish I had been.

I'm afraid—afraid that one day I won't remember the sound of my mother's voice or the way my father laughed. Afraid they will fade from me entirely, leaving only this aching void in their place.

At last, the torrent of tears subsides, leaving me hollow and spent. Amelia leans back, brushing away the remnants of my grief with a gentleness that cuts through the ache. Her eyes are soft, yet shadowed by her own sorrows.

"You needed this," she breathes, her voice steady. "You've not allowed yourself to grieve, have you?"

I shake my head, the motion weak. My gaze falls to the crushed primrose in my hand, its petals crumpled and bruised—a fitting reflection of the ache that refuses to heal.

"I'm sorry," I croak, my voice hoarse.

"There's nothing to be sorry for," Amelia replies, pressing a kiss to my brow. She takes the flowers from my trembling hands and places them carefully on the bedside table. "Grief is no fault of yours. An absolute burden, but one you need not carry alone. You hear me?"

"But I am sorry," I whisper, my voice trembling. "I'm sorry for not appreciating them more. For not saying the things I ought to have said. For not being... better."

Amelia's sigh is soft. "You were loved as you are, Triona," her Irish lilt curling around my name. "Not for things said or unsaid. You need not be anything but yourself. And I'd wager now they'd be telling me to knock sense into you for thinking otherwise."

A weak laugh escapes me, and I know she's right. Even in the darkest moments, our family always found humour—sometimes sharp, sometimes absurd, but always there. It was how we endured, how we remained whole.

She brushes a strand of hair from my face and stands. "Think you're ready to face the day?" She asks as she moves about the room.

I go to answer, but my focus goes to the crushed primrose. For a moment, I consider tossing it away, but I pick it up, smoothing the petals as best I can. They're so very broken, yes, but still so beautiful.

Who left these here?

Through muddled thought, I had not considered before.

"Auntie," I ask softly.

She turns, pausing in her tidying to look at me. "Did Deidre leave these, or was it you?"

She tilts her head, a sly smile playing on her lips. "Not I, my dear girl, though it seems the type of gesture Deidre would offer. She said not a word to me about it."

Deidre spent hours learning proper primrose care from my father. I can still see her crouched in the garden beside him, her sharp focus softened by the gentleness of her hands. She'd listen with rapt attention as he explained how to cut the stems just right, how to keep the flowers vibrant for as long as possible.

"I'll say," Amelia continues, smiling fondly. "Sometimes, folks can't always say what they mean with words. Sometimes they use gestures, minor acts of kindness, to say what they feel. It's an awfully lovely gesture, if you ask me."

Her words hang between us, and I study her carefully, noticing the way her expression softens. There's something in the way she speaks, the way her voice dips slightly when she mentions Deidre, that feels significant.

She eyes me as if she's deciding how much to say.

"You talk about her," I begin slowly, "in a way that suggests..." My words trail off, the weight of the unfinished thought sitting heavily in the room.

Amelia's breath hitches, just barely, but it's enough. She looks at me, her gaze steady but filled with vulnerability, and without a single word, I know.

My chest tightens, and a soft, breathless laugh escapes me. The realisation crashes over me, bright and undeniable, filling me with a warmth so intense it feels like sunlight breaking through a storm.

"You and Deidre," I whisper, my voice trembling. "You're..."

"She's my heart, Triona."

The pieces fall into place—the seamless way they move together, the reverence in Amelia's voice whenever she speaks her name.

The confirmation sends a wave of emotion through me—shock, curiosity, and something deeper, something softer. "How long?" I ask, my voice trembling slightly.

A bittersweet smile tugs at her lips. "Long enough to know what it means to love someone with your whole heart and still be afraid of what the world might do to you for it."

My throat tightens as her words settle into me, heavy and raw. "And you have given her up—for months, every year, for six years—just for me?"

Amelia moves to cup my face. Her eyes meet mine, filled with a fierce, unshakable love. "And I'd do it again a thousand times over."

Tears blur my vision, spilling over faster than I can wipe them away. "None of you asked for this. You should have lived your lives freely. None of this is worth the cost."

"Hush now," she whispers, her thumbs sweeping tears from my cheeks. "You may not understand it yet, but you will. I would walk through fire for you. And Deidre—she would too. You are worth all of it, every sacrifice. Never think otherwise."

Her hands tighten, holding my face as if she can force her conviction into me through touch alone. Her eyes burn with a fierce, unyielding love. "*You* did not ask for this life. The life you live now—it was never a choice you made, but one of destiny's making. Whatever guilt you carry, what blame you place on yourself, let it go. Not a single word is accurate. The world may take much from you—it may strip away comfort, joy, and even the ones you hold dearest—but it can never take this."

"I don't deserve that," I choke out, shaking my head. "I don't deserve you. Or her. Or them..."

Her grip never wavers. She leans closer, her voice dropping to a low, determined murmur. "Deserving has nothing to do with it. Love can never be won like some prize. Love—genuine love—is given freely. Fierce and unrelenting, not caring a whit for what you think you deserve. It simply *is*."

She holds me close, her arms a fortress. "Not love like this. Love that burns eternal, brighter than the darkest night, hotter than the fiercest fire. It will not fade, it refuses to falter, no matter what storm rages against it."

Her words settle deep into my chest, wrapping around the ache like a balm. They're not just words—they're a lifeline, pulling me back from the edge of despair.

Her voice dips lower, almost reverent. "This love, Triona—it's unyielding. It's the kind that anchors souls, that defies even death itself. It's in the blood, the bone, the very air you breathe. And it is ours to give, so promise not to push it away."

Her embrace never falters. I cling to her, letting the truth of her words seep into every broken part of me.

I nod again, my fingers brushing absently over the quilt beside me. "I'll try," I whisper.

Amelia smiles, the corners of her lips trembling slightly as she presses another kiss to my forehead. "That's all anyone can ask of you."

For the first time in what feels like ages, the crushing weight on my chest eases—just slightly, but enough to breathe.

"Now come, love," she says, her tone lightening just enough to lift the heaviness in the room. "Let us work to get you cleaned up and fed. A beauty such as yerself ought not waste a day crying, aye?"

I give her a weak smile, slowly rising to my feet. My body feels shaky, legs unsteady, but I let Amelia guide me toward the basin. As she splashes cool water on my face, I catch my reflection in the mirror. My eyes are red, cheeks blotchy, but there's something else there—an echo of resilience, faint but growing.

I follow Aunt Amelia out of my room, her steady presence grounding me. The weight of my earlier emotions still clings to me. We tread quietly through the hall, our steps soft against the worn wooden floor. The house feels heavy, almost suffocating in its stillness.

We halt as a door swings open ahead. My breath catches. From Bran's room, the woman I saw with him last night emerges. Her gown hangs loose, hair in wild disarray. My cheeks burn as my gaze drifts past her to the open door, revealing Bran sprawled on the bed like some half-drunk Irish god.

Completely naked, cock rising with the dawn.

A sharp shriek escapes me, and I clap my hands over my eyes. "Bran!" I yelp, my voice a mix of outrage and embarrassment.

The commotion draws a low groan from the bed. "Please," Bran groans, voice thick with sleep. "Heard enough of my name last night between cries of pleasure."

Amelia mutters something under her breath—likely a prayer for patience—and steps in front of me, blocking my view. "Cover yourself, you daft lad," she scolds, her tone low and firm.

Bran groans again. Sheets rustle, but I refuse to look to confirm.

Before the moment settles, another door creaks open. I peek between my fingers as Casey emerges, leaning against the frame. One hand rakes through his disheveled hair while the other shields his eyes. He carries the unmistakable air of someone deeply regretting last night's choices.

"Who in the name of the blasted gods just screamed like that?" he demands, his voice rough with sleep and laced with irritation.

"It was me!" I snap, still flustered from the sight of Bran laid bare. "If you saw what I just did, you would have screamed, too."

Casey raises an eyebrow, his gaze drifting toward Bran's open door. A knowing look crosses his face, mingled with something sharper—annoyance, perhaps? Or a hint of disappointment?

"Ah," he mutters, voice tight. "Try not to wake the dead next time, Triona."

Casey looks away, and, without a word, slams the door behind him with enough force to make me flinch.

Amelia exhales sharply beside me, crossing her arms. "What's got him in a tizzy?" she mutters. Then, turning to me, she asks, "What's all this about?"

I hesitate, stealing a glance at Bran's door before leaning closer. "He started a fight with Bran last night," I whisper. "Over *her*." I tilt my head toward the stairs, where the woman had disappeared moments earlier.

Amelia's eyes widen briefly before narrowing in thought. "A fight? Those two? The fun bunch of the group."

I nod, still keeping my voice low. "It was completely out of character. Casey caught Bran stealing a kiss with her at the party. Things got... heated."

Amelia exhales again, her expression unreadable. "Men and their pride. Nothing like a pretty lass to set it ablaze." She shakes her head, casting a sideways glance toward Bran's door. "And that one, lying about as if butter wouldn't melt in his mouth."

"A bit early for dramatics, isn't it?" Bran's voice cuts through the tension, his grin entirely too self-assured as he props himself up on one elbow.

"Early?" Amelia snaps, rounding on him. "I've no quarrel with what you do behind closed doors, but for the love of decency, could you at least pretend to be discreet? The lass was sneaking out like a thief in the night, and you're lying here like you've just conquered the world. Have some shame, love."

"Shame?" he repeats, feigning shock. "Why? Not my fault you lot took a morning stroll past my room."

She says nothing, just gives him *the look*. "You're right," he says, scrambling to sit straighter and brushes a hand through his unruly hair. "I didn't mean any disrespect, Amelia. This is your house, and I should've been more careful. Will not happen again."

The sincerity in his tone takes me by surprise, and judging by the slight softening of Amelia's expression, it catches her off guard, too. She tilts her head, studying him for a moment, before letting out a small chuckle.

"You're lucky to be so handsome, Bran Mumford." She waves a hand at him. "But mark my words—next time, there will be hell to pay."

I glance at Bran one last time, his grin as infuriating as ever, and let out a huff. "You're insufferable. Not even going to take the threat with the seriousness it deserves?"

He winks. "And yet you both adore me."

"I wouldn't go that far," I mutter, linking my arm with Amelia's as she nudges me gently down the hall.

As we move away, she exhales under her breath, so softly I almost don't catch it. "Not my thing, mind you," she murmurs, "but I can see the appeal."

My steps falter, and I glance at her, frowning in confusion. "How do you mean?" I ask hesitantly.

She tilts her head toward Bran's room with a small, mischievous smirk. "The lad's well-built, is he not? A hard sight to miss."

I take a moment to process her meaning, and when I do, my face flames. "Auntie!" I hiss, horrified, my hands flying up as if to block out the thought. "Stop. Just—stop."

She bursts into laughter, the sound rich and unrestrained as it echoes down the hall. "Oh, come now, love," she teases, wiping a tear from the corner of her eye. "I'm only saying what anyone with eyes could see."

"Well, I don't want to hear it," I snap, mortified, quickening my pace to escape the conversation.

She chuckles behind me. "You're too easy to rile, Triona," she says fondly, catching up to me. "But I'll spare you. For now."

"How kind of you," I grumble, though her laughter lingers, and despite myself, I feel a smile tugging at my lips. Leave it to her to find humour in the most mortifying situations.

Just like Deidre. Which reminds me...

Amelia leads me into the dining room, her arm still linked with mine as my mind churns with thoughts of payback. The room is warm and inviting, sunlight streaming through the tall windows, casting a golden glow over the table set with an impressive spread of pastries and breakfast treats. My stomach rumbles faintly at the sight.

"There you are, love," Amelia says, gesturing toward the table. "Help yourself. And don't miss the leite creme—it's Deidre's absolute favorite."

I'm busy preparing a plate when Deidre walks into the room. "Good morning," Deidre says brightly, her tone light and warm as she approaches. Her gaze sweeps over us, lingering briefly on Amelia before settling into her usual poised demeanour.

"Morning, love," Amelia replies, her tone easy, though there's a glimmer of something playful in her eyes. Deidre's gaze flicks to mine.

"Deidre," she begins, her tone casual. "She knows."

With quiet grace, Deidre leans over and presses a gentle kiss on Amelia's cheek, her hand resting lightly on her shoulder. Amelia's expression softens, and she tilts her head slightly toward Deidre, her fingers brushing against her wrist in a gesture so natural it feels like second nature.

The sight tugs at something deep in my chest. There's no hesitation in the way Deidre's eyes linger on Amelia's, no awkwardness in the tender exchange. Just love—quiet, steady, and unshakable.

A warmth spreads through me, and I find myself smiling softly. The chaos of the morning fades away in the face of this moment, simple and profound.

I seat myself while the two of them share a private moment.

They sit down, and we chat about nothing in particular.

Deidre goes to take a bite of her leite creme. The second it hits her tongue, she freezes, her eyes widening. She moves swiftly to grab for the nearest cloth, and spits everything into it. Slowly, her gaze lifts to meet mine, her lips pursing in suspicion.

"How's that taste? Auntie said it was your *favourite.*"

"What did you do?"

I shrug, feigning innocence. "Whatever do you mean? Does something not agree with you?"

Amelia glances between us, her eyes narrowing. "Triona..." she begins, but there's no mistaking the flicker of amusement behind her words.

"She looked like she needed something savoury *and* sweet to start the day."

Amelia sips her tea, oblivious to my quiet amusement. "What am I missing?"

"Your lovely niece salted the leite creme."

Deidre dabs at her lips with a napkin, her composure quickly returning. "You'll regret this," she mutters, though the faintest hint of a smile tugs at the corner of her mouth.

"Will I?" I ask, unable to hide my grin.

"Oh, you will," she says, pointing her spoon at me like a weapon.

Amelia shakes her head, her lips twitching with suppressed laughter. "You're as bad as each other," she mutters, sipping her tea.

As Deidre's gaze lingers on me with playful menace, I feel a minor victory warm my chest. Harmless payback.

The soft clinking of plates and cups fills the air, our conversation light and unhurried. Then, the door to the dining room creaks open, and everything changes.

Finn steps inside, and it feels as if all the air has been sucked from the room. My breath catches, and a quiet tension ripples through me.

Amelia glances up first, her greeting poised and warm. "Good morning, Finn," she says, breaking the spell just enough to remind me to breathe.

Deidre follows, her smile just as warm and inviting as Amelia's.

I hear his steps, slow and deliberate, as he moves toward them. My pulse thrums loudly in my ears when he leans down to kiss Amelia's cheek. Her soft laugh follows, a sound as natural as breathing.

Deidre greets him with her usual composed charm, tilting her face slightly as he places a kiss on her cheek as well. They exchange a few pleasantries, their voices low, but I can't make out the words. I don't need to. Every movement, every sound coils tighter in my chest as he finishes with them.

The air shifts again, the weight of his presence circling around the table as his footsteps grow louder. I feel him approach before I see him, his shadow casting long across the table as he comes to a stop beside me.

For a moment, nothing happens. My gaze remains fixed on my plate, my knuckles white as I clutch my fork. Then, slowly, I lift my eyes, drawn to him as though by some invisible tether.

His face is calm, unreadable, but his eyes—they burn with something unspoken, something raw and overwhelming. It's too much and not enough all at once.

"Good mornin'," he says, his voice low and rich, each word laced with quiet intensity.

Before I can muster a response, he leans in, his movements deliberate and unhurried. His lips brush against my cheek, soft and warm, a fleeting touch that chills me.

My heart is near to bursting, and my eyes sting with the threat of tears. The emotion in his gaze, the tenderness in his touch—it's overwhelming. He lingers, his warmth so close it's almost unbearable, before pulling away.

He straightens, turning to the table where the pastries and fruit are laid out, and begins assembling a plate with the same calm precision he always carries.

Amelia clears her throat, her voice cutting through the lingering tension like a lifeline. "We were just saying how lovely a trip to town would be," she says, her tone light and casual.

Deidre hums in agreement, pouring herself another cup of tea. "It's high time we visited the market. I'm sure we'll find something delightful."

"Is this leite creme?" Finn asks, with so much excitement that the guilt momentarily distracts me from the mix of emotions in me.

"Don't bother," Deidre says as she eyes me. "Triona went and salted it all to get back at me."

Finn chuckles. When I dare to glance up, his eyes meet mine for the briefest second, and it's enough to undo me all over again.

"I'm sure she had good reason. Triona does nothin' without purpose."

Amelia arches a brow, setting her cup down with a soft clink. "And what, pray tell, *did* Deidre do to deserve such culinary vengeance?"

Deidre doesn't hesitate. "I encouraged a brisk trot through the house."

I groan, burying my face in my hands.

"She *chased* me," I mutter through my fingers, "out of the room in nothing but a sheer slip. Practically see-through, Amelia. I flashed my *brothers*."

Amelia sputters and chokes on her tea.

Deidre lifts her chin, completely unapologetic. "Wouldn't have chased you if you hadn't called me the *Abhartach*."

Amelia gapes. "You called her the Irish vampire?"

"She was practically hissing at me!" I argue, flailing a hand. "Bloodthirsty eyes, waking me out of a dead sleep, just to yell."

Deidre lifts her cup with an amused smile. "You've a flare for the dramatics, just like your dear Auntie."

Finn picks up the tray of leite creme, inspecting it with a small, amused smile. "Still," he adds, setting the cream down with a mock sigh, "it's a shame. It's my second favourite sweet treat."

His gaze flicks briefly—pointedly—to where I sit before returning to his cup, the curve of his mouth deepening into something dangerously close to a smirk.

Deidre laughs lightly, a sound as warm as the morning sun. "Next time, I'll make sure it's unsalted. You have my word."

Their conversation flows easily, laughter and light banter filling the room, but I can't focus. The air feels thick, every glance and word a weight pressing down on me.

Finn is still at the table, handpicking pastries and fruit, but I can feel his presence like a beacon, drawing my attention no matter how hard I try to look elsewhere. It is all too much.

I push my chair back, the sound loud enough to draw a glance from Amelia and Deidre. "Excuse me," I say quickly, my voice tight, though I try to force a polite smile. "I need some air."

Amelia's brow furrows slightly, her concern clear, but she nods. "Take your time, love," she whispers, her tone as gentle as always.

Deidre's gaze lingers on me a moment longer, her expression unreadable, but she says nothing.

I don't dare look at Finn as I rise. My heart hammers in my chest as I make my way to the door, my steps quick but measured, trying to appear composed.

The moment I step into the hallway, the cool air hits me, and I let out a shaky breath, my hands trembling as I press them to my sides. My mind races, torn between the pull of what just happened and the need to steady myself.

I lean against the wall, closing my eyes and letting the quiet of the house envelop me. It doesn't dull the memory of his eyes or the warmth of his kiss, but it gives me space to breathe, to gather the pieces of myself that feel scattered in his presence.

Behind me, the faint hum of conversation continues in the dining room, but I push forward to my room, determined to stay in it for the rest of the day while I sit with these confusing feelings.

28

Mystery Unraveled

Triona

Wednesday, 4 June 1823

Casa da Prímula

As I hoped, no one came to my bedchamber yesterday. It was cowardly of me to hide, but I couldn't bring myself to face anyone—not with these feelings swirling inside me. Too afraid to act as if what happened in that hallway *didn't* happen. Too afraid to pretend I'm fine when I'm not.

Looking out the window, I catch sight of Casey sitting alone near the garden's edge. His shoulders are hunched, and there's a heaviness in the way he sits, like the weight of the world is pressing down on him. I'd wanted to seek him out anyway, to ask about what happened in the hall yesterday. His behaviour was just so... unlike him.

I move through the villa quietly, my steps careful as I weave through the hallways. No one sees me, and I step outside into the cool air. The distinct sounds of sparring drift from the training yard. Bran's laugh echoes, followed by Callan's gruff retort. I don't linger long enough to see if Finn is there. Instead, I head toward Casey, who remains motionless by the garden's edge, his head bowed.

"You've got a look about you," I say, breaking the silence.

Casey doesn't glance up. He just lets out a long, tired sigh. "What look, Triona?"

"As if you're waiting for that blade of grass to sprout legs and take off."

A slight smirk tugs at the corner of his mouth, but leaves in a flash. "I dinnae have a look."

"Aye, you do." I nudge his arm with mine. "It means something is eating at you—and refrain from saying my delusions are getting the better of me. I know you better than anyone."

"Ye're relentless," he says, his voice heavy.

The teasing drops from my tone. "Did you and Callan get into it? Or is it Bran? I saw how upset you were that night, and again yesterday morning. You seemed... off."

His jaw tightens, and he keeps his eyes fixed forward. "Bran's fine. Everything's fine with him."

I study him, my chest tightening at the obvious lie. "You don't believe that any more than I do. So what is it? Just tell me."

"I cannae explain it, Tri." His voice is quiet now, almost too quiet, like he's afraid of the words getting away from him. "It's just... hard to talk about. Like no one would understand."

"Then don't explain it. Tell me how it feels." I lean forward, trying to meet his gaze. "Maybe no one else would, but I'm not everyone else. You've always been there for me, and now it's my turn. You never have to hide from me, Casey." I reach out tentatively to take his hand in mine. "You don't have to hide who you are, or what you feel. There's nothing you could say or do that I would not love you through."

He speaks so softly I have to strain to hear him. "I'm afraid to be myself," he murmurs, his voice fragile, as if saying it aloud might break him. "I hide behind laughter, jesting as if it's all I'm made of, but... I dinnae ken how long I can wear this mask. It's as though I'm lost in a place I don't belong—trying to be someone I'm not."

His words hit me like a stone in the chest, and my teasing falls away completely. "Casey..." I pause, unsure what to say. "You're not out of place."

"How do you say that so easily?"

"Because I'm sure of how you make me feel. You are the strongest thread between us. You keep me steady. When everything feels too heavy, when the rest of us lose ourselves, you remind us to laugh, to breathe."

"Anyone can do that."

"No, Casey, they can't," I say firmly. "You are not a compilation of jests. You see us. You see when Cal's about to boil over, so you cut in before he explodes. You see heated arguments rising, and you change the topic to settle everyone. And me?" I pause, throat tightening, remembering waking up in that tent to see Casey hovering above me. "You see me in one of my darkest hours, and you hold me. You are the peace amongst us."

"It's not an effortless task."

"Then let someone else carry the weight when it feels too heavy a burden. You'll still be our safe place. I'll still find peace in your presence, even if you can't find it in yourself."

I move to wrap my arms around his shoulders. "You don't have to carry this alone anymore," I whisper. "When you're ready to talk, I'm right here. You've got me, Casey. And I'll remind you every day how much you matter until you believe it yourself."

"Thanks, Triona," he whispers hoarsely. "I dinnae ken what I'd do without ye."

I smile softly, holding him close. "Lucky for you, you'll never have to find out."

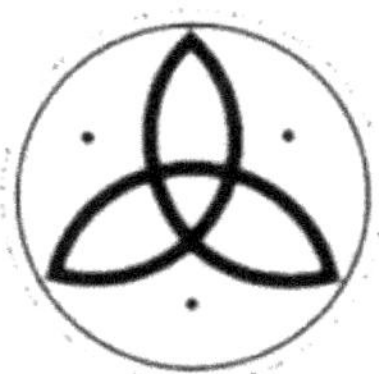

After the weight of the morning with Casey, I finally feel steady enough to find Deidre. The primrose left for me... it's been sitting where I left it yesterday morning. A delicate reminder that even in chaos, someone sees me, cares enough to bring light into my day. I need her to know how much it meant.

I find her near the kitchens, rolling dough at the large wooden table. The faint scent of fresh bread fills the air, and she hums softly to herself as she works. When she notices me lingering in the doorway, she pauses, wiping her hands on her apron.

"Triona," she says with a kind smile, her eyes warm. "What brings you here, my dear?"

I grin, stepping closer. "Honestly? I just wanted to see you. You're different here, Deidre—so relaxed, so in your element. It's nice to see you in your own space, truly happy."

Deidre smirks, wiping her hands on her apron. "It's easy to be this way when I'm not being driven *mad* by a maddening girl and the bickering that often follows the three incredibly *vexing* but loveable Sinclair children."

I laugh, crossing my arms. "Admit it, Deidre, you miss the chaos."

Deidre's expression softens, and she gives me a fond smile. "Maybe I do, Triona. Life is never dull when you're around. Chaos or not, I wouldn't trade you or the Sinclairs for all the peace and quiet in the world."

I smile, feeling a warmth settle in my chest. "Good to know I'm appreciated," I tease lightly before my expression grows more serious. I step forward, clasping my hands nervously. "but... I also wanted to give my gratitude, Deidre. For the primrose. It... it meant a great deal to me. After everything, finding something so thoughtful waiting for me..." My voice falters, but I press on. "It reminded me I'm not as alone as I sometimes feel."

Her brow lifts slightly, a flicker of surprise in her expression. "Oh, as sweet a gesture as it was," she says gently, "I cannot claim credit for it."

The words hang in the air, and for a moment, I feel utterly untethered. "You... didn't leave it?"

Deidre shakes her head, a soft chuckle escaping her lips. "No, I am not the one to thank, but I'm glad it brought you comfort, whoever it came from."

"My mother, though? She used to leave it?"

Deidre's gaze sharpens, her expression unreadable. She studies me for a moment, then leans back, her voice careful. "I can't say for certain she didn't, but she never once mentioned it to me."

She gives my arm a light pat. "Now, if you'll excuse me, I've bread to finish before the day's half gone." She turns back to her work, humming again, as though she hasn't just turned my world on its head.

Part 6 – Find One Soul

29

THE STARS ALIGN

Triona

I stand frozen, my thoughts a jumble. *If not Deidre, then who—?*

The answer is glaring at me, clear as day. Before my mind can catch up, my body moves with a will of its own. My skirts whisper against the stone floor as I hurry from the kitchen, while my heart beats a relentless cadence in my ears. Each step feels laden with a mix of trepidation and anticipation, and with each twist of the corridor, my pulse surges.

Past the dining room, up the staircase, through the narrow halls, I press on until I stand before his door. My breath comes in rapid, shallow bursts, and the certainty of what I know—what I hope—presses down on me.

I don't bother to knock. I wretch the door open, the air in my lungs held as I step into the room—and freeze in place.

Finn stands near the hearth, damp hair curling at the edges, droplets tracing slow, glistening paths down his bare back. A bath linen hangs low about his hips, and his skin is flushed with the lingering heat of the bath, lending him an almost ethereal glow in the flickering firelight.

He turns, startled by the sudden intrusion, his brows furrowing. "Triona? What in—?"

I prepare for a tongue-lashing, but words die on his lips when our eyes meet.

My gaze betrays me, trailing over the curve of his neck, the broad sweep of his shoulders, the taut muscles of his chest, the trail of hair that disappears beneath the fabric of linen—each detail illuminated in a way that renders him otherworldly. He is raw masculinity.

My heart pounds fiercely, and a blush of heat paints my cheeks. I know I should look away, yet I remain transfixed, unable to manage it.

"Triona," he says again, his voice lower now, almost cautious. "You all right?"

The sound of his voice snaps me out of it. I blink, tearing my eyes from him as I spin around, pressing the door shut behind me. I turn and press my back into the cool wood, and I try to steady my breathing.

"I—" voice faltering, sound coming out a mere breath.

"Just... just let me get dressed," he says.

The barrier he goes behind hides him from view, but I can picture him pulling on his trousers, raking a hand through that unruly hair. And the thought—gods help me, the thought—sets my skin ablaze.

He steps back into view, trousers on, barefoot, damp shirt clinging to his frame in ways that make it difficult to look away. I force myself to meet his eyes.

His tone is softer now, but his brows are still drawn, his concern clear. "What's wrong, lass?"

Wrong? The question hangs in the air, and I almost laugh at the absurdity of it. Everything feels wrong—the way my pulse races, the way the air between us seems to crackle, the way my traitorous eyes keep flicking to the hollow of his throat, where there's still an obvious glisten. And yet, it somehow feels exactly right.

"How long, Finn?" I demand, my voice barely above a whisper.

His brows knit. "What do you mean?"

"... the Primrose?" I state, each syllable saddled with hope.

He hesitates, his gaze dropping as if weighing the cost of his own truth. Then, without a word, he turns and walks toward the small table near his bed. I watch his movements, slow and deliberate, as he pulls something from among his belongings.

When he turns back to me, his eyes locked on mine, he slowly runs his thumb along the edge of the envelope. With deliberate care, he peels it open and removes the worn parchment inside. My throat tightens—I'd recognise that letter anywhere. It's the last one I sent him.

"You kept them?" I ask. He meets my gaze, and in the silence that follows, he offers a slow, smouldering look that silently declares, '*Of course I did.*'

"Part of me wondered if ye'd known," he breathes, his voice carrying a weight that makes my heart twist. His fingers trace the edges of the folded paper as if the words still hold power over him.

"Known what?"

He shakes his head, not answering. "I think this is the letter that truly did me in." He opens it and produces the pressed primrose. I remember the day I'd done that. The first day they'd bloomed.

"A single damned flower, and I was undone."

"Finn..." I whisper, my voice trembling. "How long?"

He still doesn't answer, but he steps closer. "Undone by a flower... that I'd been leavin' on yer bedside table since the morning after you'd told me about their significance." He moves closer still. "That their presence can protect someone from evil."

I take a shaky step toward him. I can feel the tension radiating off him, but I can't stop now. My words tumble out, unguarded, as I summon the courage to hold nothing back.

"I woke up yesterday thinking Deidre must have left them for me. So I went to thank her for the gesture, only for her to tell me it wasn't her." My voice cracks, and I can feel the heat of tears stinging my eyes. "And she said she couldn't confirm whether Ma had done it."

I step closer, my chest heaving. "I went years without waking up with them on my bedside table." My voice falters. "Just after you arrived back was when I received the first bundle after *years*. The realisation hit me in a rush. I never once stopped to question why. And I feel like a fool."

"Every time you'd stir in yer sleep, I could feel it," Finn says, voice laced with something raw. He takes a careful step closer, his curls framing his face as his proximity causes him to look down at me. I'm utterly transfixed—chiseled cheekbones, and eyes that are more golden than brown in the moment—unable to tear my gaze away.

"So I'd go out," he continues, his gaze fixed on me, "and I'd search for the brightest flower in the bunch. I'd clip it, place it in the centre of the bundle, and place it right there—right on your bedside table. And then, as if by magic, you'd settle."

He pauses, and I see a pass of hesitation in his eyes, the way his jaw feathers before he forces the words out. "I convinced myself it was my presence—that I calmed you as ye've always calmed me." His voice wavers as he exhales shakily.

"So I kept bringin' 'em. Watching from the shadows like a coward. I'd watch you roam the house, holdin' the damned bundle as if it were gold. And every time, I'd see it. That smile. That pure, unguarded smile, I'd wish—gods, I'd *wish*—I could tell you it was me who'd made you smile like that."

He looks down at the letter in his hand, his fingers tightening around it. "But I knew I never would. And it broke my heart, Triona. Every single time, it broke me. But I could never stop, because seeing that smile? Knowin' I could give you that, even if you'd never know it was me? That had to be enough."

At last he meets my eyes. There's something devastating in the way his gaze bores into mine, a weight I'm scarcely prepared to bear. The room feels impossibly still. His words hang heavy in the air, and the sheer depth of his pain leaves me stunned, rooted to the spot.

"What do you feel for me, Finn?" I mutter, my voice trembling but resolute, carrying the full force of my pounding heart.

His eyes soften even as they glisten with unshed tears. He takes a deliberate step forward, then another, closing the gap until no space remains between us. The raw sincerity in his eyes threatens to undo me.

"To most folks, I had but a single purpose. To fight. To protect. To be the weapon they needed. To be *used* for their advantage. To my own father, I was no more than a burden—a broken lad. But then you came into my life, and through your eyes, I discovered a reflection of who I truly am. You saw the best in me, kindlin' a belief in myself I'd long forgotten."

He pauses, his gaze falling for a moment, his shoulders sagging under the burden of words he's never spoken. "To the one person I was doing it for... the one person I'd give everything for... I've always been more." The heat of his body, so close to mine, coils around me.

"I've never been what they expected me to be—not with you," he declares fiercely, his eyes searing into mine. "Ye've always cared for me—just me—not for what I can do, or the benefits I can yield. Only me."

His voice gathers strength with each word, even as it trembles with barely contained emotion.

"I've told the stars about you more times than I can count. On nights when the world felt impossibly heavy, I'd look up at the sky and speak your name into the silence, as if the constellations could carry my words to you. I'd whisper all the things I refused to say aloud—the way your laugh feels like sunlight breakin' through a storm, the way your eyes hold more kindness than I deserve, the way the thought of you has kept me tethered when I was on the verge of fallin' apart. The stars know every piece of you I've ever cherished, every hope I've dared to dream, and every fear I've fought to silence. They hold, within their glow, the version of you I hold closest to my heart—the one I'll never stop yearnin' to truly know—despite my best efforts to subdue these overwhelming feelings."

"So, in short...," he says as he lowers to his knees in front of me. Gently, he brings one hand to my hip, then takes my hand and presses it tenderly against his beating heart, as if urging me to feel the truth of his devotion.

"I am who I am because of you." His voice trembles through his confession. "My fiercest ally. My unwaverin' refuge." He pauses, his throat working against the emotion threatening to break him. Then, softer, but no less certain, "And the love of my life—all of it, all of you—wrapped in one maddeningly beautiful, impossible package."

Tears glisten in his eyes, but he doesn't blink them away. Instead, he holds my gaze unflinchingly, as if daring me to see the truth in every shattered piece of his heart.

I stare at him. All I can do is feel. Feel the weight of his words. Feel the undeniable, inescapable truth of them.

"I have always been in love with you," he breathes, his eyes searching mine as though he's afraid of what he might find. "In one way or another, from the very first moment I saw you. When I found you in that field, I felt I had known you all my life—and then some. Helpless against a lassie with big, doe-shaped emerald eyes who saw the world with wonder, who carried storms in her soul and starlight in her laughter. I never stood a chance, Triona. Not then. Not now."

My chest tightens as the memory floods back. The woods. His arms lifting me, rain soaking through every layer until I could feel the cold in my bones. But with him carrying me, steady and unyielding, it's as if I can't be touched—I'm calm, safe, indestructible.

"I told myself not to love you. That I couldnae. That protectin' you meant I could never truly have you. If I let myself feel... if I gave in, I'd fail you. But my heart..." He falters, his hand trembling in mine. "Caitríona Sinclair, my soul has always known you are my home. Even before I knew what it meant to love. My beginning and my end."

Tears spill down my cheeks as his words root me where I stand, binding themselves to the marrow of my bones, to the very breath that sustains me.

"There is no one else in existence that my heart will ever belong to. You are everything for me, Triona."

He looks at me as though the world itself hinges on my response, his golden eyes raw with devotion. The world beyond us dissolves into shadow and silence, leaving only him, only us, caught in a moment suspended beyond time itself.

"As long as I draw breath," he whispers, his voice a vow, trembling but obstinate, "there will only ever be you. Even if you cannae love me back, even if this is unrequited... it's you, Triona. You are the last woman I will ever love."

I pull my hands away from his only long enough to weave them through his hair, my fingers trembling as they sink into the silken strands. A shudder ripples through him, a breath caught between restraint and longing. His eyes are wide, unguarded, brimming with the desperate hope I will not break him in this moment.

Finn, a man brought to his knees, not by defeat, but by devotion. Offering himself to me without pride. And the strangest thing is that he is all I thought I'd never find in a partner. A man who surrenders to no one, surrendering only to me. Powerless in this moment, and yet, somehow, stronger than anyone I have ever known.

My life was torn asunder, shredded at the seams. Yet through every shattering moment, I never felt that unbearable pain alone. Finn has been my constant, my unyielding foundation, carrying me through the wreckage—sometimes in the most literal sense.

And now, as he kneels before me, stripped of armour, of pretense, of anything but truth, I do not see the man who believes himself unworthy. I see the force that has held me together when I should have broken. My shield, my anchor, *my* unwavering strength.

"Finn, you are wrong," I say softly, reaching out with steady hands to cup his face. In that fleeting moment before our skin touches, a brief flash of panic sparks in his eyes.

"How could you ever think yourself undeserving of love?" I whisper, my thumbs softly following the rugged lines of his face—etched by time and trials, yet still strong and beautiful. "If I could go back, if I could change it all, I would. I would seek you in every moment of your life, and with a fervour unbound, I would tell you what you should have always known—that you are worthy. That you have always been worthy." My throat tightens with emotion. "Of love. Of joy. Of *me*."

I sink to the ground before him, our knees brushing. "You're the reason I've made it through, Finn. And I..." My breath hitches, the weight of my heart pressing into my words. "I regret every moment I spent being too blind to see your love for what it was. Because every second I wasted not loving you back was time—precious time—ill spent."

He's watching me, drinking in every word as if they might slip through his fingers if he is not careful.

"You are my haven, Finn. My safe place. And I love you... with everything I have to give, and everything I never knew I offered."

Finn's eyes bore into mine with a ferocity that makes me tremble. The fire reflected in them is nothing compared to the one building between us.

A broken sound escapes him, something between a whispered prayer and a lingering sigh. And then—

The world tilts as I reach for him, as his arms wrap around me, pulling me against him in a fierce, desperate embrace. My fingers thread through his hair, and when his lips find mine, it is not a kiss of possession, nor of conquest. It is a kiss of surrender.

Even as destiny itself may strive to tear us apart, I know in my heart this truth: no power in this world or beyond can change what I feel for him. We will always find our way back to each other.

Always.

All barriers between us disintegrate in a blaze of heat and need as the kiss deepens, leaving nothing but raw, unfiltered desire. The weight of our pasts, the fears that kept us apart, dissolve as though they never existed.

"I am forever yers, Triona," he murmurs, the words threading through the air like an oath before the gods. My heart answers in a thunderous rhythm, a beat that belongs to him entirely.

He travels a feverish path along my jaw, down the curve of my neck, lingering in a way that makes me weak. Our shared truths hang suspended in the air, as eternal and untouchable as the stars overhead.

His lips are a perfect contradiction of velvety softness and rugged fever, moving against mine with unrelenting need.

When he lifts us off the ground, there's no resistance, no hesitation. My body, my soul, surrender entirely, pliant and eager for him. I wrap my legs around his waist, drawing us closer, and feel the unmistakable press of his desire.

My fingers tangle in his hair as he carries me, his grip firm, his breath ragged with restraint. His hands roam with a confidence that speaks of a man wholly captivated, as though every inch of me is his to discover, to worship. Every touch sends a wave of heat surging through me, building and building until I'm drowning in the inferno he's awakened.

His lips burn against my collarbone, my pulse hammering beneath his touch. The sensation is maddening, every stroke of his hands a declaration, every kiss a promise.

"Finn," I sigh, my voice quivering as his hands grip the small of my back, pulling me closer until our bodies align. The desperate moan that escapes his lips sends a rush of heat coursing through me, pooling low in my core.

"*I need you.*" I whisper.

He stops, his eyes fixed on mine, and a shudder ripples through me—my nipples pebble under the intensity of his look.

"I've dreamt of you sayin' those words for longer than I care to admit," he rasps, his voice thick with longing.

A mischievous smile tugs at my lips as I lean in, letting my lips brush the sensitive skin just beneath his ear. "So," I murmur, my breath teasing against his skin, "what do you plan to do about it?" I trail a series of deliberate kisses down to the base of his neck, my lips lingering before I slowly drag my tongue along his skin. The taste of him—rich and heady, like warm scotch and wild heather—floods my senses, leaving me utterly intoxicated.

The reaction is immediate. His body tightens against mine, and he presses into me, his hard length meeting the very centre of my need. The ache inside me deepens, a demand rising in every nerve, pleading for his touch, his attention—his everything.

Finn

The words spark like flint against steel, igniting something deep, raw, and primal inside me.

Her lips graze the sensitive skin just below my ear, featherlight, teasing, and every part of me tenses, sharpens, and locks onto her—attuned to nothing but the heat of her body against mine.

My grip tightens at her waist, fingers pressing into the soft, heated curve of her body, holding her steady—but it's me who's coming undone.

Then, her mouth moves lower, tracing slow, deliberate kisses along my throat, her lips parting just enough for me to feel the warm slide of her breath, the wet tease of her tongue.

My willpower frays at the edges, thread by thread.

Her tongue drags over my skin, unhurried, taunting, her breath hot, her touch devastating.

I swallow hard, my pulse hammering, the ache of my need coiling tighter, thicker, more unbearable with every passing second.

The taste of her lingers on my tongue, sweet and sinful, a blend of wildness and warmth, of temptation and ruin.

The scent of her—utterly intoxicating, utterly hers—fills every corner of my senses, drowning me in her, pulling me under, leaving me lost.

She's so close, so completely overwhelming—so perfect.

I have to close my eyes, just for a moment, just to keep from falling apart entirely. If I lose myself now, there will be no turning back.

"Triona."

Her name leaves me in a rasp, weighted with everything I feel, everything I want, everything I'll never be able to give to another soul.

Her body moulds to mine, her legs holding steady around my waist as if by muscle memory. My hands grip her tightly, settling her against me as I carry us further into the moment. Her thighs, full and enticingly soft, form a sumptuous barrier of warmth and power that draws me in with irresistible allure.

As my lips trail along her collarbone, tracing the delicate line of her skin, I can feel the rhythmic pounding of her pulse beneath my touch. Every kiss is a vow, a promise I can't put into words. She's everything I've ever wanted, and everything I'll ever need.

"I love how your thighs feel," I whisper, my hand sliding seductively along her exposed flesh. "They're so deliciously thick. And yer breasts... so full, so soft—they drive me wild."

When she sighs, "*Finn*," the sound is a plea and a command all at once.

I let my arousal, firm and insistent, pulse steadily against her centre. I hold her close enough to feel every beat of my desire, yet deliberately leave a trace of space to test the strength of her will.

"What I love most about yer body..." My voice is a slow, deliberate drawl, thick with intent, each word dripping with sinful promise, "is that ye're strong—woman enough—made to take everything I'm about to give you... every stroke, every shuddering breath. And I know, deep in my bones, I needna worry whether you can handle it."

I tilt her chin up, fingers firm, claiming her gaze, refusing to let her look anywhere but at me.

"You can handle it, right, Triona?" My lips brush hers, close enough to taste, never enough to satisfy. "You *want* to."

She shudders, her breath catching, her fingers digging into my arms, grasping, pleading. "Undress me, Finn."

Her emerald eyes burn with a heat that steals my breath, her body already arching, offering—mine for the taking.

"I want you to see all of me."

I stare, searching for even a hint of hesitation, but all I find is an unspoken plea—a trust so profound it shakes something loose inside me.

My hands tremble as I set her down, slow, deliberate, reverent, as if setting something sacred into place.

A wicked smile tugs at my lips, teasing despite the urgent fire licking beneath my skin. "I was just waitin' to hear you beg," I murmur before I dip lower, aiming to place another lingering, taunting kiss to the base of her neck.

She scoffs, the sound vibrating softly against my lips—a quiet protest, laced with amusement, edged with want.

But the moment my mouth grazes her skin, I feel her shiver, the teasing edge in her breath giving way to something deeper, something consuming.

I trail my mouth lower, my hands mapping the delicate curve of her spine, fingers tracing slow, deliberate lines as if committing her to memory—every reaction, every shiver, every soft intake of breath.

Slowly, she turns for me, and I reach for the ties of her dress. I slide my fingers beneath the fabric, teasing over her shoulders, my knuckles ghosting down the length of her spine. A shiver wracks through her, and I feel it everywhere—in the way her breath stutters, in the way she leans into me, trusting me to unwrap her like something sacred.

I breathe her in, dizzy from the sheer presence of her—of this moment, of everything we've fought to have. I continue to explore, revealing every delicate curve of the body that I only ever dreamed of laying bare for my eyes alone.

When the last barrier falls away, I step back, memorising her in this moment of raw, unguarded beauty. She's luminous, like something carved out of light and shadow, and it's so much more than I ever imagined.

"You are... stunning," I finally manage, the words a whisper, thick with everything I feel. My hands ache to touch her, to learn her from memory and keep her safe in this moment forever.

She reaches for me then, pulling me back into her world, into her warmth, and I surrender to her completely. My hands find her again, and I vow, in the here and now, to show her exactly how much I adore every part of her—inside and out.

My mouth is on her an instant later, drawing a nipple deep. She cries out as her fingers find their way into my hair, pulling me further into her as I lap at her sweet flesh. My teeth and tongue playing her body like a finely tuned instrument.

I cup each breast, thumbs grazing the sensitive peaks until she arches into my touch, a wanton moan escaping her lips. She gasps as I roll the other nipple between my fingers, suckling and teasing until pleasure borders on exquisite pain.

I pause only long enough to lay her down on the bed with deliberate care; the mattress dipping beneath her as her body settles into the softness. The sight of her there, framed by the flickering light and utterly captivating, washes away any hesitation that idles. My hand lingers on her cheek, thumb brushing the flush of her skin, and I can't help but marvel at her—at us—at the fact that this moment is real and ours.

Every touch, every kiss, feels like a promise I can finally keep. Her skin is soft beneath my lips, her breath hitching with every press of my mouth as I make my way lower.

I am insatiable.

Triona deserves to be worshipped, and I'm helpless to do anything but oblige. As I settle between her thighs, the heat of her need calls to me. She is so damned addicting.

I tremble in anticipation, wanting to make this as perfect for her as it will be for me. My fingers brush against her centre, finding her wet and wanting. "Ye're dripping for me." She moans as I stroke her slick heat, thumb circling the sensitive bundle of nerves at her centre. She rocks against my hand, chasing the pleasure I draw out.

I look. Linger. Let the hunger rise until it's unbearable. Until the aching, throbbing need to have my mouth on her is too much to deny.

"I *need* to taste you." The words slip out, rough, ragged, dragged from the very depths of my hunger.

I let my fingers drift, featherlight, trailing up the inside of her thigh, her warm, flushed skin searing into my palms as she spreads wider, parting for me with a reverence that borders on desperation.

I grip the back of one thigh, fingers kneading, pressing, until I can lift one leg up, guiding it over my shoulder.

She lets me, pliant, eager, offering herself up so sweetly.

I graze my lips over her ankle first—soft, slow, worshipful—a teasing contradiction to the hunger burning in my veins.

I trace my way down, mouth dragging, teasing, along the delicate line of her calf, over the soft dip behind her knee. My lips part, tongue skimming just enough to make her squirm, to make her tremble in my hands.

"D'ye want it as badly as I do?" I murmur.

Her answer is in her body, in the way her thighs quiver, in the way her fingers fist the sheets, in the way a tiny, helpless moan slips out the second my lips move higher.

I drag my tongue slowly, tasting her, teasing her, letting her feel what's coming before I ever give it to her.

"Want the warmth of my mouth?" I whisper the words against her skin, my lips barely brushing where I know she's burning. I press a single, wet kiss, then another, trailing lower, pausing when I reach the smouldering centre between her thighs, savouring the way her body quivers in anticipation. The way her breath hitches as I hover there, so close to where she needs me most.

"Spreading you open... tastin' you... pullin' you apart with my tongue until you cannae do anythin' but sob for me?"

She whimpers, her back arching. I press my mouth closer, close enough that she can feel every word I say, every breath that fans over her soaked skin.

"Say it, mo ghrá," I breathe, dragging my lips up her inner thigh, pressing wet, open-mouthed kisses until I can feel the heat of her core against my mouth.

Her answer doesn't come out as a moan.

It comes in a wrecked, desperate plea. Voice shaking, her body already breaking for me.

"Finn—" she gasps, her fingers tangling in my hair.

"Ruin me. Make me scream, make me beg, make me *yours*."

A low, guttural growl rumbles from my chest as I drag my hands down her thighs, spreading her wider, forcing her to open for me completely.

I lean in, my breath hot, thick, spilling over her sensitive skin, letting her feel the anticipation, the certainty of what's coming.

Then, finally—I let my tongue drag through her slick heat. I give in, my mouth claiming her with an intensity that is as much about love as it is about need.

A gasp—sharp, breathless, uncontrollable—rips from her throat, her hips jerking up, chasing my mouth instinctively.

It's the most tantalising thing I've ever heard, her voice wrapping around me like silk, stoking the fire already raging in my veins.

"You taste like wild honey," I murmur against her. Her gasp is my reward. She arches into me, her hands tangling in my hair, urging me deeper, and I obey.

There is no part of her I won't worship, no sound or sensation I won't commit to memory. She is mine to taste, to love, to bring to the edge and beyond, and I intend to take her there again and again.

My lips find their purpose there, savouring the taste of her. Her body responds to my every move in a way that fills me with a heady mix of pride and devotion. My tongue dances against her clit, coaxing out melodic cries that only deepen my longing to give her more. Every noise she makes is music, a song only I can play, and I give myself over to the rhythm of her pleasure.

"Please, Finn," she begs. "I want to feel you inside me. Filling me..."

My tongue falters for half a second, the weight of her words like a lightning strike to my spine. Her words are almost enough to have me giving into my need to claim her, but the desire to coax every moment of pleasure out of her before the night is over is stronger.

I drag my lips up her thigh, savouring the way she trembles, and press a final, open-mouthed kiss over her pulsing heat before pulling back.

My eyes meet hers, and the flush dancing across her bare skin further fans the flames of my resolve. "Aye. I'll give you everything. Every part of me. But I want you ready to take me in, and ye're not there yet."

She whines, frustrated.

I smirk. Filthy. Taunting.

I press two fingers deep inside her, and the way she clenches around me is enough to send a shudder down my spine.

She is silken heat, wrapped tight, soaked for me, her body welcoming me with a need that borders on desperation.

I let her feel it, the slow stretch, the deliberate curl of my fingers as I find that spot within her that will undo her completely. The second I stroke it, she gasps, writhes, her thighs quivering at the sheer pleasure of it.

"That's it, Tri," I murmur, voice low, nearly lost against the delicate skin of her inner thigh.

Then I seal my lips over her clit, sucking her deep, dragging my tongue over that aching bundle of nerves, rolling it in slow, deliberate strokes.

She is helpless beneath me, her hands fisting the sheets, her legs shaking, her body nothing more than pleasure and need—

And *mine.*

"Let me hear you fall apart."

Her head lurches against the pillow as the sound of her pleasure, that exquisite cry right before the final peak, fills the room. The intensity of the moment surges through me—my arousal thunders painfully, and I can feel that all-too-familiar wet heat gathering at the tip.

"*Finn!*"

My name erupts in a raw, primal cry as she shatters beneath me. It's the most beautiful sound I've ever heard. Her surrender is my undoing, a perfect blend of vulnerability and strength that leaves me in awe. As the aftershocks ripple through her, I rise, sliding into position above her, just as I've dreamed of for countless nights.

"Make me yours. I need to feel you stretching me, filling me," she entreats, her voice trembling with desperate fervour, the sound weaving through me like a siren's call.

In response, a moan erupts from me, a sound that speaks of unbridled desire and instinct, echoing her plea without a single word.

"By the gods, Triona," I rasp. "Ye've got a sinful tongue."

She meets my gaze with a sultry smile, her eyes twinkling with mischief. "Aye, Finn," she purrs as she reaches for me, her hand finding the bulge straining against my trousers. I groan as she strokes me through the fabric. "You pull it right out of me."

Then, with a soft, commanding urgency, she adds, "I need to see you, Finn. All of you."

I rise and begin shedding the rest of my clothes, each piece falling away at a measured pace as I hold her gaze. I slowly remove each piece with purpose, giving her time to admire my body, just as she asked, revelling in the hungry way she drinks me in. With measured care, I undo the string at my waist and free my aching cock, savouring the profound pleasure of watching her take in all of me for the very first time.

"Oh, Finn," she says in awe. "You're magnificent."

She rises gracefully, her perfect breasts bouncing with each movement. With a deliberate slowness, she loops her fingers around my cock.

"Is this what you want? What you like?" Kneeling before me, she looks dangerously sinful—her eyes blazing with a wild, untamed allure that both seduces and challenges.

All I manage is a low "hmmm," a murmur of surrender that betrays my helpless passion.

"You feel like the softest velvet in my hand." She exhales a sultry, heated breath that causes me to jerk in her grasp. My eyes flutter closed as she strokes me, root to tip, marveling at my size and the way I twitch at her touch.

The head of my cock is weeping with arousal.

Hesitantly, as if testing whether I might retreat, she leans in and swipes the tip of her tongue over my slit, collecting the glistening evidence of my need, and I become a man possessed.

I lose the fight to keep my hands to myself, and I move one hand to the back of her head while gently tangling my fingers in her hair, drawing her closer as our shared hunger ignites into a fierce, consuming passion.

I tilt her head up, silently ensuring this is okay.

"Your taste… it's an an enchanting elixir. I want more. Show me how to move. How to make you come undone at my touch."

Holy feckin' inferno and all that is divine.

I take a slow, steading breathe to quell the need for release. Wanting to draw this out longer. "Wrap your hand around my base," I bite out, and wait for her to position herself there, "and take the tip of me into your mouth." She smiles before biting her lip.

I leave enough space for her to set the pace, holding my breath in awe as I watch her wet her lips, and draw me into her mouth without ever breaking our locked gaze.

A feral groan escapes my throat—a sound echoing the frenzy of our passion.

Then, as the heat of desire surges through me, a rugged exclamation bursts out—"Ach, you feckin' braw thing!"—followed swiftly by a raw plea, "Gods… please dinnae stop," the unfiltered desperation mirroring the savage intensity consuming us both.

She chuckles around my length, and the throbbing vibration sends shudders cascading through me. I'd laugh too if I wasn't so focused on the exquisite interplay of her mouth and hand, while I struggle to maintain my composure long enough to give her exactly what she's been begging for.

"That's it, *mo chroí*," I rasp.

The sentiment fuels something wild inside her, spurring her on, and she picks up speed. Every nerve in me ignites, as I can no longer handle the overwhelming sensation, my body trembling beneath the fierce intensity of her movements.

"Triona," I groan, as my hand covered hers. She pops off of my cock with a look of disappointment in her eyes. I sense her oncoming protest, so lean forward, capturing her lips in a kiss that's fierce, desperate, and utterly consuming.

"I cannae wait any longer," I murmur against her mouth. "I need to be yours, fully and completely."

Her fingers tighten around me as she whispers, "Then take me, Finn. Take all of me."

I push her back and make quick work as I lower myself onto her with a care that belies the storm raging within me.

I settle between her thighs, the warmth of her drawing me closer. My hands slide down her sides, her skin soft and trembling under my palms, until I reach her hips. I steady myself, my body poised at her entrance.

"It might hurt at first, and you might bleed."

"I know, Finn. I want it. I want you, and nothing is going to change that."

I pause, breathing her in, feeling the weight of the moment—the gravity of what we're about to share.

"Look at me while I enter you," she nods, gaze locked on mine, and what I see there steals the breath from my lungs. Love, longing, and something so achingly raw it makes my chest tighten.

I grip her hip tight, fingers digging into heated skin, holding her still, steady, open for me as I drag myself through her slick heat—letting the thick, swollen head of my cock tease her entrance—but not giving in yet.

"*I'm yours.*"

The words spill from me, a vow, a promise, a surrender, spoken just as I push the tip of me into her.

Her body yields to mine, welcoming me, and the sensation is indescribable—a blend of heat and connection so deep it feels as if our souls are colliding.

A throaty moan rips from her as she lifts her hips, taking me all the way in, all at once—we both cry out, the sensation too much, too perfect, too right.

Her body welcomes mine as if she were crafted for me, opening instinctively, perfectly. The first thrust steals my breath, the connection instant and electric, as though the universe itself has aligned just for us.

Her nails bite into my skin as I drive deeper, setting a rhythm that leaves us both trembling.

"*Triona.*"

Her name is a prayer, a plea, a worshipful groan as I press a line of kisses down her throat, my teeth grazing her skin just enough to make her shiver beneath me.

"I want to hear you." My voice is thick, dripping with need as I drive deeper, hips rolling in slow, deliberate, relentless circles. "Every gasp, every moan. Let me know how good I make you feel."

Her body trembles, her breath hitches, her nails raking down my arms as she clutches me tighter, pulling me impossibly closer.

"Finn," she moans, voice dripping with both need and impatience. "Please. Harder."

My hand drifts lower, claiming her, finding a firm grip on her plump arse, using it to pull her into every thrust, guiding her to take more, to take everything.

She arches beneath me, her back bowing, her thighs spreading wider, cradling me as though I belong inside her.

She whimpers, pleads, voice breaking as I slip a hand between us, my fingers finding that swollen, aching place, stroking it with measured precision, matching every movement to the rhythm of my thrusts.

"More," she pleads in a breathless whisper, every word heavy with longing. "Don't hold back. I want all of it. All of you."

Each thrust elicits a chorus of soft, trembling gasps and husky moans—sounds that signal her nearing the edge, that whisper of a pleasure about to burst forth.

Every exhalation, every subtle, yearning cry from her lips, drives me onward, compelling me to worship her body as though it were my salvation.

"Come for me," I command, the movement of my hand against her swollen bundle a perfect tempo. "Come for me. Let me feel you fall apart."

Her head tips back, and a broken moan escapes her lips as her body tenses beneath me, trembling on the very edge of release. With one final, perfectly timed stroke—synchronised with the rhythm of my hips—she shatters, her body convulsing around me as every nerve ignites in a wild pulse of surrender.

Her cries of pleasure push me over the edge.

My rhythm falters, and a deep groan tears from my throat as I bury myself fully.

"Triona—"

Her name erupts from me, a raw, guttural groan, my hips locking to hers as my climax rips through me, pleasure so intense, so overwhelming I can do nothing but give her everything I have left.

I spill deep inside her, my body shaking with the aftershocks of it, my arms trembling as I brace myself above her, refusing to let us part just yet.

I press my forehead to hers, our ragged breaths mingling, my hands still caressing, still claiming, still worshipping.

"Ye're mine," I whisper, my voice hoarse with emotion.

"Now and always."

Finn

In the aftermath, we lay together, bodies entwined. The fire crackles softly in the corner, its warmth a pale reflection of the heat still lingering between us. My chest rises and falls beneath her cheek, her breath brushing against my skin in a way that feels familiar. As her fingers brush against me, a flicker of worry surfaces. I shift slightly, tilting my head to look down at her. "Are you hurting?" I ask softly, concern thick in my tone.

A faint, wry smile tugs at her lips. "It's a pain unlike any other," she says, her voice soft and angelic. "It's bittersweet, because I'll miss it when it's gone. It reminds me of something so beautiful it's worth hurting for."

A laugh breaks from my chest, warm and unrestrained. "Leave it to you to make that sound poetic," I say, my grin widening as I brush a stray strand of hair from her face. "Ye're impossible, you know that?"

Her soft laugh joins mine, the sound weaving its way into the quiet intimacy of the moment, and I can't help but marvel at how perfectly she fits into my arms.

She continues to trace delicate, aimless patterns across my chest, each touch igniting something deeper than desire. It's as if she's trying to memorise me, to claim every inch of me, and I let her, gladly giving her all of me without hesitation.

"Ye're the most stunnin' woman in existence," I murmur, as if speaking too loudly might shatter the delicate intimacy of the moment.

She looks at me then, her eyes—those captivating eyes—glistening with unspoken emotion.

"Your woman... And you, Finnis MacGregor, are *mine* now," she mumbles, her voice tinged with a quiet, unshakable possessiveness. A declaration... a truth that settles over me like a warm, merciless embrace. My chest tightens, overwhelmed by the sheer power of her words and the depth of what they mean.

"Aye," I whisper, my hand finding hers, threading our fingers together. "For every breath I take and long after I'm gone."

Her lips curve into the faintest smile, and I press a kiss to her knuckles, lingering as if to seal the vow we just exchanged.

Her body curls into mine, soft and warm, her breathing even and peaceful. My arms wrap around her, protective and steadfast, and I press my lips to her hair, breathing in the faint scent of primrose that clings to her. The quiet rise and fall of her chest becomes my anchor, a rhythm that soothes every restless part of me I hadn't realised was still there.

She isn't a dream anymore. She is mine now. Every answered prayer, every whispered wish cast into the wind, every quiet hope I clung to in the darkest hours of my life. She is real—warm, soft, breathing steadily in my arms—and for the first time, the weight of what she means to me isn't an ache, but a balm, soothing every broken piece of my soul.

I know with unshakable certainty that I'll give her my last name. That she will be mine in every way the world will allow. The thought isn't fleeting; it's a truth that settles deep in my chest. Not a question of if, but when—when I'll hear her say my name as hers, when I'll see the joy in her eyes as she realises she is my future, my forever.

But tonight, this moment, holds something even more precious. For the first time in my life, I get to do the one thing I spent countless days only dreaming of doing.

I get to hold Triona while she sleeps.

30

Bold and Unyielding

Finn

Thursday, 5 June 1823

Casa da Prímula

If I knew nothing else, I knew this with unshakable certainty: no power, no force—neither of this world nor beyond it—would ever take her from me.

In this moment, with her in my arms, that vow feels less like a promise and more like the undeniable truth of my existence.

The first rays of dawn filter through the curtains, painting the room in a warm, golden hue. I stir slightly, her body pressed against mine, grounding me in a way I've never experienced before. For a fleeting moment, I stay motionless, reluctant to disrupt the serene intimacy of the morning, unwilling to let it slip away.

Her hair, sprawled across my chest in wild tangles, catches the sunlight like a golden halo. Her breathing is steady, her lips slightly parted in sleep. I trace a light touch along her shoulder, marveling at the softness of her skin beneath my fingers—so warm, so impossibly perfect.

Triona stirs, murmuring something unintelligible as she stretches lazily against me. Her eyes flutter open, those stormy depths meeting mine with a vulnerability that steals my breath. For a moment, neither of us speaks. We simply look at each other, the weight of what we shared lingering in the space between us.

"Morning," she whispers, her voice husky with sleep, sending warmth coursing through me.

"Mornin', mo ghrá," I reply softly, brushing a strand of hair from her face. "How do you feel?"

Her lips curve into a slow, tender smile that seems to light her entire being before twisting into a devilish grin. "Deliciously sore... but safe."

Her words strike something deep within me in the best way. I lean down, pressing a soft kiss to her forehead, lingering as I murmur, "Ye'll always be safe with me."

"I have to admit, I didn't know a man could go three times in one night."

Her cheeky comment catches me off guard, and I burst into laughter, the sound loud and full, shaking away the quiet reverence of the moment. But the laughter fades quickly as I look at her, something serious settling in my chest. "I've never slept with anyone else," I admit, my voice steady, my gaze locked on hers. "But I know it never would have felt as right as this does... with you."

Her eyes soften, a flicker of emotion passing through them that makes my chest tighten. "Last night..." she begins, her voice trailing off as if she couldn't quite find the words.

"Was everything." I finish for her, my thumb brushing over her cheek. "All I've ever wanted. Everything I'll ever want."

"You *really* mean that, don't you?" she asks, though the question feels more like a declaration, as if she believes the answer already.

I catch her hand, pressing a kiss to her palm. "Aye, Triona. I mean it with every part of me. As I said last night—ye're mine now."

Her lips part, as if to respond, but she leans up and kisses me. It's slow, deliberate—a kiss that seals the words between us. When she pulls back, her smile returns, soft and radiant, leaving me feeling as if I'm the luckiest man alive.

But then her expression shifts, a flicker of hesitation crossing her face. "Finn," she begins cautiously, her voice quieter now. "I don't... I don't think we should tell my brothers just yet."

Her words hit me like a stone. I keep my expression neutral, though disappointment bites sharply. "And why's that?" I ask, keeping my voice steady even as my grip on her hand tightens slightly.

She sighs, sitting up slightly, the sheet slipping down to pool around her waist. The sight of her naked form before me, so vulnerable and beautiful, tempers some of my frustration. "It's not that I don't want them to know," she says quickly, as if she can feel my tension. "It's just... you know how they are. They'll overreact. Casey will have something to say about it, and Callan—well, Callan will probably throw a punch before we can even explain."

Her attempt at humour falls thin, her smile apologetic. I nod slowly, shifting to lean back against the headboard. "So, what then?" I ask, my tone even. "We pretend none of this happened? Act like I didnae hold you all night? As if I dinnae love you with everything I am?"

Her eyes widen, and she reaches for me, her hand curling around my forearm. "No, Finn, not at all. This—us—it's real. It's everything. I just... I want to keep it ours for a little while longer. Before the chaos starts."

I study her, my jaw tightening despite myself. Her logic makes sense, but it doesn't make it easier to swallow. I want the world to know she's mine. I want her brothers to see it, to respect it. Hell, I'd even welcome a fight if it meant claiming her openly. Because I'd fight for her—every damn time.

Her gaze softens further, her fingers stroking over my arm as she whispers, "Please, Finn. Just a little while longer. For us."

I exhale slowly, forcing my shoulders to relax even as my heart feels heavy. "Aye, Triona," I say finally, my voice quieter. "If that's what you want, then I'll respect it."

Her face lights with relief, and she presses a quick kiss to my lips. "I thank you, love. I know what an ask it must be," she murmurs.

I give her a faint smile, though frustration simmers beneath the surface. I've given her my word, and I have the intention to keep it. But that doesn't mean it sits well with me. Keeping quiet feels wrong. She deserves to be claimed, to be celebrated. And the thought of waiting—of hiding what we share—feels like denying the best thing that's ever happened to me.

Still, I say nothing more, pulling her back into my arms and holding her close. My mind churns with the weight of her request, a quiet storm I can't seem to calm. Her warmth against me is both a comfort and a torment—a reminder of what I have and what I can't yet claim.

She rests her head on my chest, her fingers tracing idle patterns against skin. "You're my rock, Finn," she whispers, so soft I almost miss it.

I press my lips to the top of her head, closing my eyes against the ache in my chest. "And ye're my world," I murmur back, though the words feel too small for what I mean.

For now, I'll wait. For her, I'd do anything. But as the silence stretches between us, I can't help but wonder how long I can keep this part of myself locked away—how long before the truth demands to be spoken, no matter the cost?

I move with sharp, controlled precision, striking at an invisible opponent, every movement fueled by the restless energy surging beneath my skin. Sweat drips down my back, proof of how long I'd been at it—how long I'd been trying to fight off the thoughts chasing me. Training alone wasn't unusual, but today, every strike felt more desperate. Stopping meant thinking—about promises made, about the weight of waiting. And I wasn't ready for that.

But my muscles stay tense, my thoughts refuse to quiet. Every time I close my eyes, I see her—feel her—*hear* her. It's maddening, and I'm once again trapped with a truth I've long kept hidden.

A familiar voice cuts into a thought spiral. "You keep fighting like that, and you'll end up knocking your own head off."

I glance over my shoulder to find Bran leaning against a post, arms folded, watching me like he already knows something's off. I grit my teeth, refusing to slow.

He waits a beat before stepping closer. "All right, out with it. What's got you so pent up?"

I hesitate for all of two seconds before the words rush out like a dam breaking.

"The night of the ball—when Triona stormed out—and I chased her... we got in a heated argument, tempers flarin', both of us talkin' over each other. Then, out of nowhere, this couple started goin' at it in an alcove close to us. And we just... stopped and watched the show."

Bran blinks. "Wait. *What?*"

I let out a short laugh, shaking my head. "Aye. It was impossible not to look the way they were goin' at it. And then, before I knew it, we were both worked up, and—" I drag a hand through my hair, exhaling. "Then we kissed, Mums—bloody hell. Fire meetin' silk. Her lips were soft and warm, but her kiss—pure hunger. She was desperate for me, and gods help me, I was just as lost. And her body—her curves—absolute sin, and the way she pressed against me felt like she was made for it. Her scent was divine—I was drownin' in her before I could even think to come up for air." I pause for a necessary breath.

"And I swear to the gods above, nothing has ever felt as good as when I picked her up and she wrapped her legs around my waist, and I brought her to climax against the wall."

Bran looks as if he's barely breathing, eyes wide, completely enraptured.

I continue, "And then she made me come in my bloody trousers."

He blinks, utterly stunned, his mouth opening and closing like he's searching for words that refuse to come. Then, after a beat, he snorts—once, twice—before the dam breaks entirely. He throws his head back and lets out a bark of laughter. "Gods above. I think that's the most I've ever heard you talk in one go. If I could trap this moment in a scrying glass for all to see, I would." He shakes his head, still beaming. "I guess that pep talk of mine really paid off in the end, eh?"

I groan, rubbing my face. "She woulda let me take her right there against the wall if I hadnae stopped her."

Bran looks at me like I've grown two heads. "*You* stopped her?"

I drop my hands and glare. "It was a *public* hallway. I may be a fool for her, but I've still some propriety left."

He smirks. "Could've fooled me. You rutted against her until the two of you—"

"I get it!" I groan, shaking my head. "I dinnae have it in me to jab back at you fully, because I still cannae get over what happened next."

Bran's grin widens, practically vibrating with anticipation. "Well, don't just leave me hanging, man. Spit it out!"

I shake my head. "We didnae speak for a whole day, and it was drivin' me mad. Then—" I let out a breath, a slow smile creeping in. "Then she *stormed* into my room, fire in her eyes, after findin' out I'd been leavin' primroses on her bedside table. She stood there, all flushed and expectant, and I just... I had to tell her. A more perfect moment would never exist."

Bran's grin falters for a second, and he holds up a hand. "Hold on—back up. You've been doing what?"

I blink. "I've been leavin' primroses for her since—well, since not long after I met her. She never knew it was me until yesterday."

Bran just stares at me, his expression shifting into something utterly spellbound. Then, with a slow shake of his head, he bursts into a grin. "Finn, my dear lovesick fool, this is spectacular." Bran's grin only grows. "So you confessed?"

I nod, the memory washing over me, warming my chest. "Told her everything. Told her I loved her, that I'd always loved her. And she told me she loved me too. And—" I huff a laugh, shaking my head. "Then, when we finally slept together, I told her again. And again. And again."

Bran lets out a low whistle, shaking his head. "Mac, my friend, you're living in a damned romance novel. This is absolute gold."

"Aye."

"Her virginity?"

"...Aye. And mine."

Bran goes utterly still. No laughter, no teasing quip—just silence as he stares at me like I've grown another head. His mouth opens, then shuts. He blinks once, twice. Then, slowly, he exhales as if he's trying to process something truly monumental.

Abruptly, he grips my shoulders, shaking me once as if to make sure I'm real. "You mean to tell me, Finn—"

I frown. "Bran—"

"No, no, no, let me have this moment. This—" He gestures wildly between us. "This is historic. Finnis MacGregor was an innocent man until last night. Gods above, this is better than I could've ever imagined. I almost feel privileged to be the one hearing it first."

He finally releases me, stepping back, hands on his hips as he shakes his head, utterly dumbfounded. "I mean, hell, Finn. I just assumed you were picky."

"I've loved one woman for the better part of my life. Of course I'm picky. There was never even a choice—just her. The thought of lyin' with another felt wrong on a level I cannae even name."

He drops his hands from my shoulders, brows drawing together. "So... what's the trouble, then?"

My smile falters slightly. "She doesnae want me tellin' anyone."

Bran blinks. "But you're telling me."

I shrug, rolling my shoulders to ease the weight of it. "She means anyone of importance. Like her brothers. Mainly Callan."

His mock hurt melts into a lopsided grin in an instant. "Harsh, but I'll let it slide for a lovesick fool." He exhales, rubbing the back of his neck. "I would not want to be on the receiving end of that blowup. The man's got a temper like scotch on an empty stomach."

After a beat, he lets out a quiet chuckle, shaking his head once more. "Well, you have the girl..."

I huff a laugh, rubbing a hand down my face. "Ye're not thinkin' anythin' I huv'nae already thought of myself."

Bran chuckles, shaking his head. "I enjoy a harebrained plan, and there's only one way you're getting out of this, so you might as well go full throttle."

He pauses, then squints at me. "How long did she ask you to wait?"

I sigh. "She said a *little while longer*."

He raises a brow. "And how long ago was that?"

I glare at him. "Bran. I'm a man of my word."

He smirks. "You've kept your word, as far as I'm concerned. Be honest, Finn. How long are you willing to fight the inevitable before you do something reckless?"

I stand there for a long moment, Bran's words sinking in. My jaw tightens, my grip flexing around the hilt of my sword. I've spent so long holding back, waiting for feelings to fade, for the pain of wanting her and not having her to come, only to be met with an undeniable truth. A truth Triona herself made reality when she came to me. When she told me she wanted me. To hell with waiting. The right moment isn't some far-off thing we wait for—it's what we claim for ourselves. I made a vow when I confessed my truth. I have to make damn sure we have what we both want.

I exhale sharply, something fierce settling on my chest. "I hate when ye're right. Hate it. Worse still, I cannae argue. But if I'm already halfway to damnation, I might as well sprint."

I'm through holding back.

Triona

The room is alive with chatter and laughter, everyone immersed in their own conversations, but a sudden commotion in the hallway makes the noise falter. The sound of heavy, deliberate footsteps echo, growing louder with each second. I turn toward the doorway just as Finn storms in, his presence demanding.

Golden eyes ablaze, jaw clenched with intensity. I can't help the way my heart races. His presence fills the space, and though a knot of anxiety twists in my stomach, butterflies erupt in its wake. Every step feels like a declaration, and it's unmistakable—he is here for me.

"Finn—" I start, my voice barely above a whisper, but he doesn't slow. He doesn't stop.

Within moments, he's in front of me, his gaze locking onto mine with a force that robs me of breath. Without a word, his hands cup my face, calloused thumbs brushing tenderly over my cheeks. His touch is possessive, yet heartbreakingly gentle. I can't suppress the way my breath hitches.

"What are you doing?" I stammer, my voice trembling under the weight of his intensity.

"What I should have done long ago," he growls, his voice low but loud enough to still the room. Every pair of eyes shifts to us, but Finn's gaze doesn't waver. "What I should have done that day at the cliff's edge."

"Finn—" I try again, but he cuts me off, his words unravelling any coherent thought.

"You are no secret, Triona," he declares, his voice fierce. "You are mine, and I am yers. Not in silence or shadow, but boldly, for all the world to see. I'm through denyin' it."

His words overwhelm me, and before I can respond, he narrows the gap between us. His lips crash into mine, fierce and consuming. It's not just a kiss; it's a claim, a confession, a release of a weight he's carried for far too long. My knees falter beneath the weight of his ardour, yet his hands at my waist hold me firm. The room seems to dissolve, leaving only Finn—the heat of his lips, the strength of his touch, the raw, desperate emotion that has us both trembling.

The murmurs of shock ripple through the room, and seem a distant echo. I kiss him back without hesitation, my hands curling into his shirt as though I can secure myself to him, to the raw power of what we'd just claimed. Every thought and worry drowns in the torrent of emotion we've unleashed.

"Finally!" Aunt Amelia's voice breaks through the haze, her exclamation followed immediately by Deidre's identical one.

The laughter and applause swells, but just as quickly, the room quiets as Callan steps forward.

His nostrils flare, shoulders rising and falling with uneven breaths. His eyes flick from me to Finn, disbelief warring with fury. His hands curl into fists at his sides, knuckles white. The room feels too small, too suffocating. My stomach knots as I feel Finn's grip on me tighten, his body bracing instinctively.

Then—without warning—his fury erupts.

"Callan, don't—" I start, panic lacing my tone, but it's too late.

His fist shoots out, connecting squarely to Finn's jaw. The sound of the impact reverberates in the suddenly silent room. Finn staggers a step but doesn't fall, his hand brushing his jaw as he straightens, his golden gaze settling on Callan with a calm, simmering defiance.

The entire room holds its breath, waiting for Finn's reaction. Casey steps forward as if to intervene, but Finn holds up a hand, stopping him. His eyes meet Callan's, calm yet burning with resolve.

"Solid blow, Callan." Finn works his jaw once, then wipes the corner of his mouth where a small line of blood appears. "You get one punch on me. I'll give you that."

Callan's chest heaves as he glares at Finn, his fists still clenched, his anger barely contained. Finn takes a deliberate step forward, still calm, almost unnervingly so.

"But I'll not let you have two." Finn's voice is sharp, eyes narrow, and tone firm. "You can be angry. You can hate me if you so wish. But ye'll respect what Triona and I have. Ye'll respect her."

"That's my sister, ye feckless bastard! Who are *you* to tell *me* what to do?" Callan bellows.

"How long, Finn? How long have ye been hidin' this from me?"

Callan's nostrils flare, his gaze burning as he glances between Finn and me. For a moment, I think he might swing again.

"How long?" Callan repeats, his tone dripping with venom.

"I haven't lied," Finn says firmly, his gaze unwavering. "But this is... a recent development."

Callan snorts, his tone biting with disbelief. "Did ye take her to bed?"

Underneath Finn's calm exterior, a simmering anger boils. "You have no right to ask that. What happens between Triona and me is our business, and no one else's."

Callan's face contorts with rage, his voice rising with a venomous edge. "So ye did... dinnae stand there and pretend to be an honourable man! D'ye ken how humiliatin' it is to find out like this? My best mate lyin' to me, treating me like some damned eejit?"

"That is not what is happening!" I snap, pushing myself between them, my voice quivering with a mix of anger and disbelief. "You don't get to twist this into something it isn't."

I step closer still, laying a steady hand on Callan's arm, my tone resolute. "I love you, Callan, but I'm not asking for permission. This is my choice."

Callan wrenches himself away from me. "Aye, yer choice," The spits, then he's tearing away from the room, leaving a trail of stunned silence behind him.

Casey steps in, his attempt at levity strained beneath tension. "Ye'd best sleep lightly," he quips, clapping Finn on the back. "Ye're fortunate he held his second strike," Casey says with a grin.

Finn smirks. "Aye, but I was ready if he had come at me again."

As the room buzzes back to life, my chest tightens with a mix of relief and lingering unease. Callan's reaction, though predictable, was fierce—too fierce. Even Casey's laughter echoing through the room does nothing to ease the ache in my chest.

Finn sees it, the worry etched across my face, because he cups my cheek. "I'll make it right," he murmurs.

I blink up at him, my brow furrowing. "Finn, he's furious. You saw him. He—he feels betrayed."

Finn nods, his expression serious now. "Aye, he does. And maybe he's right to. I should have gone to him first. Callan's been like a brother to me, and I've no excuse for not tellin' him sooner."

He pauses, his thumb still tracing gentle circles on my cheek. "I'll talk to him. I'll fix it. There'll be no bad blood between us, okay?"

"You promised we wouldn't—" I start, my voice trembling as frustration seeps into my tone, but he cuts me off with a devilish smirk, his hands sliding to frame my face, grounding me despite the fire in my chest.

"I gave you half a day's mercy, Triona," he says, his voice playful. "And that was plenty. Any longer and I might've gone mad."

"And in that half day, did you consider what chaos this would cause? Or did you simply think of all the ways to make a grand gesture?" My words cut sharper than intended, but my heart betrays me, twisting as his unwavering gaze meets mine.

His smirk deepens, and his thumb brushes against my cheek, soothing. "I made a promise to be yers first. If waitin' longer meant pretendin' not to love you, then no, I couldnae do it. Ye're mine, Triona. The world needs to know that."

Without waiting for my response, he lifts me off the ground as though I weigh nothing. A startled gasp escapes me as my legs instinctively wrap around his waist. My cheeks burn, heat flooding through me as I feel the strength of him holding me so effortlessly. His golden eyes lock onto mine, searing with an intensity that makes my heart stutter and my breath catch.

"Finn—this is hardly—" I start, my tone somewhere between protest and surrender. But with a look, he silences me, voice dropping to a husky whisper meant only for me. "I'll be takin' you back to bed to apologise for my brash behaviour. I intend to lay you out and worship yer body with my tongue until ye've forgotten every reason to be angry."

My heart thunders as his words settle over me, stealing whatever resistance I might have had. A small whimper escapes me as I feel his sultry heat against my core. I tighten my hold on him, burying my face in his neck as the world fades, leaving only Finn, the wicked promise of his words, and the heady pull of everything he is.

"You're impossible," I mutter, though my tone holds no real heat.

"Aye," he admits, as he races us from the room. "And ye're an impossibility, come true." My heart swells at the sentiment. I forget the eyes that might be watching, the murmurs trailing behind us, and decide it's best to beat fire with fire.

Heat coils in me as I press my lips to his neck, tasting the salt of his skin. His response is immediate—a beast-like groan reverberates through his chest, sending a shiver down my spine. The sound fuels the reckless energy between us.

Without a moment's hesitation, he puts me down just long enough for him to hoist me over his shoulder. In that instant, his strength makes me forget the formidable woman I am, replaced by a yearning to be carried and tossed about by the only man I'd ever let take control of me.

His hand lands on my arse with a sharp, possessive slap, the sting eliciting a gasp I can't hold back. He strides forward, his voice dripping with dark amusement.

"That was just a wee taste."

I meet his challenge with a swift, playful smack of my own, surprising him. "I thought you said I was woman enough to take more of you—someone you didn't need to be gentle with, if I'm remembering correctly? I don't want a *wee taste*, Finn."

My taunt hangs in the air, charged with mischief and defiance. Finn bursts into raw, joyous laughter and dashes off, the sound of our shared mirth filling the room.

"Let's put that sinful mouth of yours to work them, hmm?"

With. Pleasure.

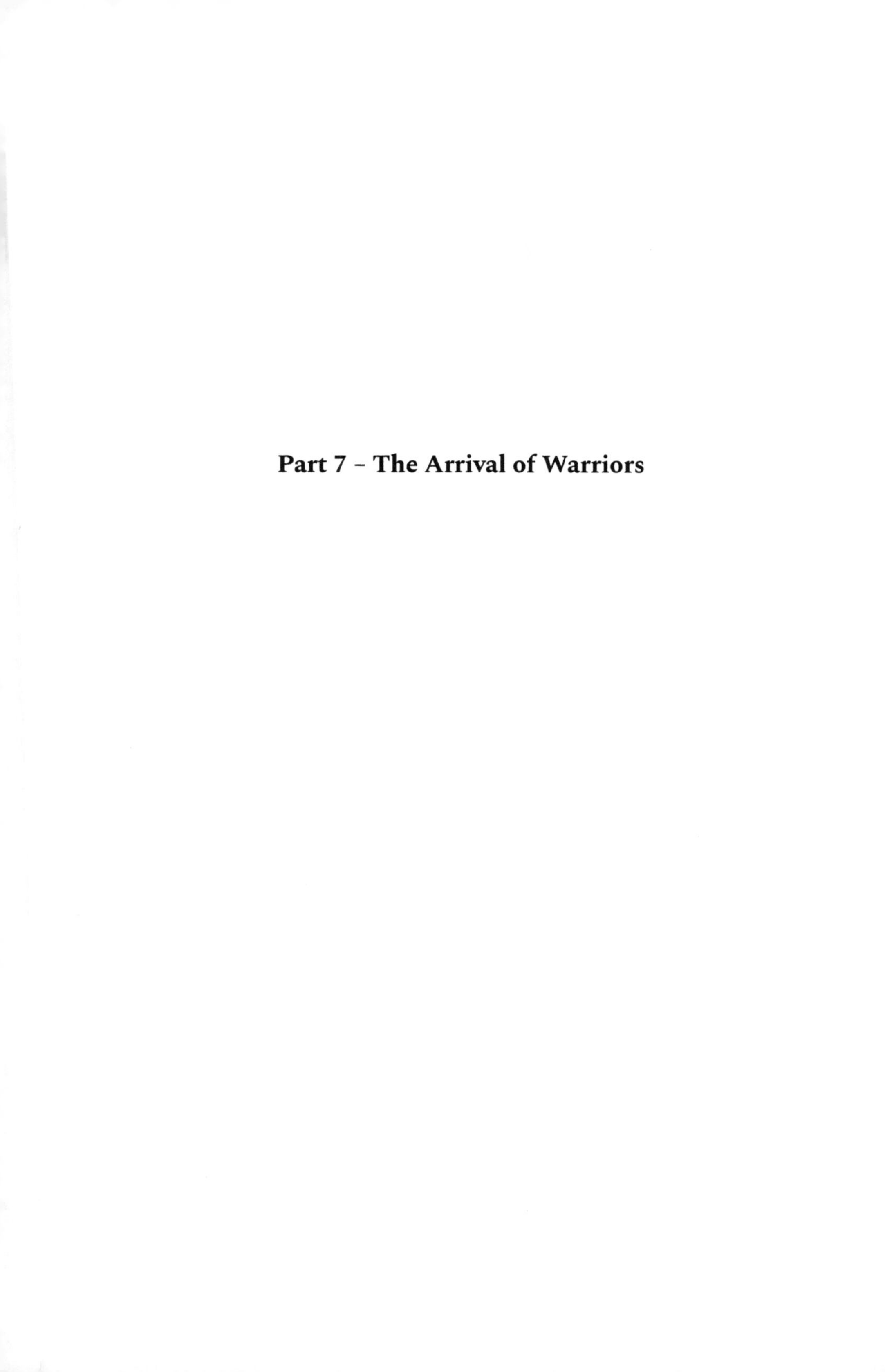

Part 7 – The Arrival of Warriors

31

THE FALLEN

Triona

Friday, 6 June 1823

Casa da Prímula

The room is quiet, save for the crackle of the fire. Amelia sits near the hearth, her expression far off. There's something about the way she carries herself tonight—sombre yet purposeful—that tells me her thoughts are far away, heavy with something that must be a great burden to bear.

Deidre gathered us here, emphasising the significance of listening to what Amelia has to say.

"Auntie, you requested an audience with us?" I ask, my voice breaking the stillness.

Her gaze meets mine, uncertain and vulnerable, a fleeting expression that looks misplaced on her face. "There's something I must discuss with you—with *all* of you," she says, her voice barely above a whisper. "The other half of the reason you've come all this way to see me... to prepare you for what lies ahead."

She studies me for a long moment before speaking again, her tone carefully measured. "Do you feel as if you might be ready to hear everything?"

I nod, the weight of inevitability settling over me. Our last conversation feels like it happened a lifetime ago, though only days have passed. So much has shifted, so much uncovered. Finn, as if sensing my unease, places a steadying hand on the small of my back. The simple gesture quiets my own mind.

Amelia's hands are tightly clasped in her lap, her shoulders stiff as though holding herself together by sheer will. She gestures to the chair closest to her, and I lower myself into it. Finn stays close, standing protectively by my side.

A small, wistful smile tugs at her lips. "Some could spend a lifetime searching for what your parents had," she says fondly. "Their efforts would be most unsuccessful. I have never seen a man so devoted to another as your father was to my sister."

My chest tightens at her words.

"Sarah learned she was with child just before your father was apprehended, as I have recounted, but what I refrained from mentioning was that she blamed herself for his capture. For his death. For the loss of love and freedom of her country. Your father fought to be here for you and for Sarah, even as the rope rung 'round his neck. This beautiful face was undoubtedly the last thing he thought of," she says, reaching out and pinching my chin between two fingers.

"Amelia, I dinnae think—" Callan starts, but she hushes him quickly.

"Your sister is tougher than you give her credit for. She *needs* to hear this." She speaks in a tone that suggests she doesn't intend to take Callan's opinion into account.

I'm truly tired of fearing the truth. Of running from the pain of loss. Of facing sacrifices made for me. It's not fair to do so in honour of those who have lost their lives.

"She's right, Cal. What's sacrifice if not spoken of? What good is it if we don't learn from it?"

A life I hadn't even known about has been ripped away, and nothing I could do—nothing anyone could do—would ever give it back.

"I tried so hard to care for her, your mother," Aunt Amelia recalls, her voice trembling now. "To protect her, but my father sent her away after Robert's death, to live with good folk. The bastard felt his image was compromised. I went too, refusing to leave my dear sister alone. But Cooper Penrose…" She pauses, her face softening. "He was a kind and noble man. His whole family helped care for her through the pregnancy."

I try to imagine my mother—her world shattered, finding solace among strangers. It feels impossible, a story that belongs to someone else.

"But after your birth, *a leanbh*…" Her tone shifts, her words chilling to the core. "Your mother saw something, as I told you the other day."

"She felt your significance the moment you took your first breath." Amelia's voice grows quieter, as if afraid to speak the words too loudly. "That night, she had the first dream about *what* you were to become. She dreamt of you. In a different time, with a face that had aged." Her lips quirk into a sad smile. "She said you looked so much like your father. It was almost as if it were him she was looking at."

She turns her face away, but not quickly enough to hide the single tear that escapes. A knot forms in my throat, as if the weight of her words has wrapped around it.

Amelia's voice trembles as she adds, "Losing Robert was hard enough, but when Sarah realised she would lose you too… she couldn't handle it."

The words sink into my chest like stones.

She pauses, her hands trembling faintly as they clutch her skirts. "Sarah stopped eating, stopped tending to herself," she whispers. "She succumbed to her sorrow one day, unable to hold on any longer. She let it take her, just as she said you both had been taken from her."

Her words hit me like a physical blow, but Amelia's gaze remains steady, anchoring me. "Your mother saw so much of the world's pain, Triona. She carried it like a weight on her shoulders, and she didn't know how to let it go."

Tears blur my vision, but I keep my focus on her as best I can.

"I'm so sorry for your loss, Auntie," I say, my voice thick with emotion. "For losing your sister. For carrying this pain all these years."

Amelia stares at me, her lips parting in awe. "Oh, Triona," she utters softly, her voice breaking. "How is it you… after all I've told you, you still have this strength in you to comfort me?"

"Because I see the love you've carried for her. You didn't fail her. You gave her hope when she had none, and now you're here for me. If that isn't strength, I don't know what is."

A deep sadness is present in her features, but something else lingers too—pride, perhaps. "Sarah saw a strength in you, a grand purpose," Amelia notes. "One she knew was destined, though she could not see it fulfilled. And that is why you must not falter, a leanbh. You are her legacy, and through you, she lives on. I think you've felt it. That pull to resist what is normal. The strength you once did not possess. You might have even had dreams of your own..."

I nod, many things coming to mind—being able to spar with Callan and Bran, besting both of them. The wounds on my back, healing in record time. Dreams of my fragmented past. Nightmares of chaos and ruin.

"You must try to listen," she pleads, her voice trembling. "With your heart wide open." She pauses, gathering herself as though bracing for a storm. "What I have to tell you won't be easy to hear. You won't understand at first, but I'm asking you to believe the impossible right now. I'm asking all of you to believe that. Can you do that?"

My heart thuds painfully in my chest, but I nod, knowing I would do anything she asked of me.

"What is it?" I whisper. My voice feels small, like a child's, desperate for answers but terrified of the truth.

Then, as if drawn by an unspoken oath, the men gather tightly around us. "You were never meant for normalcy in life," she says, her voice barely above a whisper. "You are something far greater than you realise."

The room seems to draw closer around us, the flickering fire casting long shadows on the walls.

"Ireland wasn't always the way it's known now. There was a time when the land and its people were one, inseparable, intertwined in ways you can't imagine."

Deidre steps into the room, as if sensing Amelia's unease. The faint clink of porcelain chattering breaks the silence. "Here, love," she murmurs, pressing a teacup into Amelia's hands. Their eyes meet for the briefest moment—steady, knowing—before Deidre steps back, fading into the background.

Amelia exhales slowly, her grip tightening around the cup as she gathers herself. "Then came the Milesians," she continues, her tone sharp, tinged with bitterness. "They arrived with their ships and their swords, but they did not claim Ireland through conquest—not truly. They made a pact with the Tuatha Dé Danann. The kings of old, as they were known," she says, her voice steady, "were bound to Ériu herself—the very spirit of Ireland. You know this story, aye?"

I nod, and she presses on. "It wasn't a crown or bloodline alone that made a ruler legitimate. It was Ériu's blessing—her sacrifice. She gave herself to the land so that her kings could rule justly. And when they did, the land thrived. Crops grew plentiful, rivers ran clear, and the people knew peace. But when a king was unjust..." She stops, her gaze meeting mine, her lips thinning. "The land withered. Famine and sorrow followed."

A chill runs down my spine despite the fire's warmth. Amelia's storytelling has a way of making myth feel like history.

"That's the version you've been told?" she asks, her brow arching.

I nod again, unsure where this is leading.

"Well," she sighs, leaning forward, her voice dropping as if revealing a long-buried secret, "here's the part lost to the destruction of time itself—ancient scrolls and tomes stolen or destroyed by those who seek to claim what is not theirs."

Her gaze holds mine. "The *Fomóire*—or Fomorians, as they're called in modern tongue—are hostile and monstrous beings that come from under the sea and deep within the earth. They are personifications of chaos, darkness, death, blight, and drought. And they have a singular purpose: to steal the very magic that works to keep their primal destruction at bay."

I swallow hard, the weight of her words settling over me.

"They learned long ago that they could never harness their own magic. But they discovered they could steal it—drain it from the land, from people, from anything tied to the earth's essence."

Her voice grows quieter, as though the very air might betray her words. "For centuries, the Fomorians have sown chaos across the Celtic regions. Their presence isn't random—it's deliberate. The havoc they wreak fuels a poison, an insidious corruption that seeps into the land itself. This poison feeds them, strengthening them while the land grows weaker."

"Our once-mighty Tuatha held them at bay, their light and power countered the darkness of the Fomorians, maintaining a fragile balance. But when the Tuatha retreated into the fairy mounds, the chaos of the Fomorians grew unchecked, their poison spreading through the veins of the earth, choking the life from Ériu and her people."

"They are not mere myths, Triona," she states, her voice firm now. "The Fomorians are still here, lurking in the shadows of this world, feeding on the discord and suffering that plagues the land. Manipulating events to weaken the land further. Every war, every famine, every moment of despair—they *thrive* on it. And the longer they endure, the closer we come to losing our connection to the land entirely."

"The time is coming when their poison will threaten more than just the land. It will threaten everything, and it's more urgent than you know," Amelia cautions, her expression darkening further. "They're setting the stage for something catastrophic. If we do nothing, in twenty years' time, the land will wither beyond recovery. Crops will fail. The rivers will run dry. And famine... what we'll call '*The Great Famine*' will sweep through Ireland like fire through dry brush. More than half of the country's population will starve or be forced out."

My dreams of the poisoned glen resurface in vivid detail—the disease creeping through the land, unstoppable. The kind of devastation that leaves scars not just on a person but on the soul of a place.

My stomach churns as the enormity of her words sinks in. "I've dreamt of this..." I reveal, my voice barely above a whisper.

Amelia leans closer, her gaze piercing. "I had wondered when you might share that bit of information."

Casey titters from behind me. "All this time, all those dreams ye've talked to me about. They've had true meanin'," he states.

Amelia nods her agreement. "See... you have a purpose in this. You can stop it. That is why you must be prepared. Why you must understand what is at stake."

"Where would I even start?"

Amelia's hands grip mine tighter. "You start right now by believing. Believing in yourself, in the connection that still lingers, faint though it may be. By remembering who *we* are. By rekindling the bond with Ériu herself. The land has not forgotten, Triona. And neither must you."

"Why me?" The words tumble out before I can stop them, laden with fear and doubt. "Why am I the one tasked with this? I'm just... me. I don't have the strength of the *Tuatha* or the wisdom of someone such as you. How can I possibly do this?"

Her face softens, a flicker of understanding breaking through the sombre lines of her expression. She leans closer, her voice low but firm. "Do you think the events leading up to this very moment were happenstance? You, Triona, were born with a connection to Ériu. Your existence is no accident. The blood of kings and guardians flows in your veins; it's what makes you different—what makes you capable."

"You were right to believe I would doubt your words," I whisper, the weight of her expectations pressing heavily on my chest. "It sounds unreal."

"Let me do my best to convince you," she says, her grip on my hand grounding me. "You carry a legacy older than you can imagine. You were chosen, not because you are perfect, but because you will fight for it. Despite all hurdles, all pain, you *care*."

The fire pops, startling me into the quiet room. How can I believe this? It feels as if I'm going mad. I should have long since stopped questioning the impossible. I've seen the impossible, and somewhere deep inside, I can feel what she's talking about. The stirrings inside me.

The faintest ember of resolve stirs within me.

"It's not just you who has been tasked with this," Amelia says, pulling me from my thoughts. "There are others... others who carry their own pieces of this fight. Together, you are meant to stand against what is coming."

I furrow my brow, the words barely sinking in before she continues. Her voice drops, becoming almost melodic, her eyes distant as if she is recalling something from deep within her memory.

"You journey now with sun-born kin,
To find the spear, the battle's twin.
The warrior bold from Gorias' might,
Seeks the blade of eternal light.
Two hearts entwined, a cauldron they crave,
A vessel of plenty their fate will pave..."

As the words linger in the air, the door creaks open, and Mannie walks in, his voice carrying the last line as if summoned by fate.

"And you, my child, seek what's been torn—
The shard of your soul, to be reborn."

His tone is grave, and Amelia's eyes cut to him as mine widen in recognition. "That…" I stammer, feeling as though the floor just dropped from beneath me. "That's what the maiden in the tavern recited to me. Weeks ago. Word for word."

Finn stands straight, looking me in the eye. "Triona, why are we just hearin' about this?" His voice is low, raw, but not angry. "When I asked, you said she'd approached askin' for coin."

I open my mouth to respond, but Callan's sharp voice cuts through the space before I can form words.

"Ye didnae think this was worth mentionin'?" His hands rake through his dark hair, frustration radiating off him like heat. "What else are ye hidin'?"

"I wasn't hiding it!" I snap, my voice breaking. "I—I didn't even know what it meant! I didn't think—"

"You didnae think," Callan interrupts bitterly, his voice dripping with anger. "That's just it. Ye've got strangers in taverns and gods know who else comin' to ye with riddles, and ye think it's nothin' worth sharin'? Should've told me the moment it happened!"

My face flushes with frustration. "I was still reeling from our parents' deaths, Callan! It made no sense, and I didn't want to worry anyone. Least of all you! At the time we hadn't met a bloody feckin' banshee, and you'll have to excuse me if I've been a little muddle-brained since then!"

"That's enough, Callan. You willnae speak to her in anger," Finn says. Callan's glare cuts toward Finn, and it looks as if he's contemplating laying Finn out where he stands.

Amelia stands to walk to Callan. When she places a gentle hand on his arm, his posture seems to loosen.

"Settle, dear," she says softly. "I know a rage grows inside your heart, but there is no enemy among you."

Callan exhales sharply, clearly still brimming with restraint, but he gives her a tight nod.

Amelia turns her gaze to Finn. "Finn, please. Share what you heard."

All eyes settle on him.

Finn hesitates, furrowing his brow. "How did you…"

"Amelia is a Pastseer," Mannie supplies smoothly, his voice even and deliberate.

Finn's jaw ticks, and suspicion flashes across his face as he shifts his gaze to Mannie. "Aye, and what about you? How would *you* know any of this? Why are you even here?"

But before Mannie can answer, I interject, eyebrows raised in alarm. "Wait—she *talked* to you too?"

Finn glances at me, still rattled. "Aye... though it was *after* Bran said she'd approached him at the door like a ramblin' fool."

Bran, sprawled like sin itself in a chair, lifts a lazy hand. "I said no such thing," he retorts, tone lofty. "I said she was touched in the head. Big difference." He pauses, then squints. "Though, in fairness, she *was* muttering about eyes meeting light, and time and... revelations, I think?"

He turns to the room at large, expression caught somewhere between bemused and deeply unnerved. "Are you actually suggesting that the batty maiden—appearing out of nowhere at a crumbling tavern in the middle of nowhere—has something to do with *all* this?"

Silence follows.

A charged, prickling silence.

Then Amelia, perfectly calm, sips her tea. "Not suggesting, love. Confirming."

Finn's brow furrows, and he tears his gaze from Bran to pin Mannie with a glare sharp enough to draw blood.

"I'll ask again," he snaps, voice low and dangerous. "How do *you* know any of this? And why in the seven hells are *you* here?"

Mannie's eyes settle on Finn, steady and measuring. There's no jest in his expression now, no trace of the playful irreverence he so often cloaks himself in. "I am what they call *Sí uaisle*—Noble Fae, in your modern tongue. My... ancestors have walked this earth longer than you can fathom. They have seen empires rise and crumble, their ashes scattering to winds that carry whispers of truths long forgotten. The threads of fate have woven a path that leads here—to you. This moment is no accident; it is the culmination of a purpose forged before your ancestors drew breath."

Amelia steps forward, her voice soft but steady. "I owe you an apology," she says, looking at each of us. "I should have told you more, but I thought easing you into this world might make it less overwhelming. I see now that withholding has only deepened your confusion and mistrust. Mannie and I have been aligned for longer than you can imagine. Trust that his presence here is no coincidence—it is necessary."

Casey's brow furrows, his frustration spilling into his voice. "What does that have to do with any of this? How does this help?"

He exhales sharply, running a hand through his hair. "The past weeks have been naught but chaos. We are struck repeatedly, without reason or sense, to guide us. Our world—it's turned upside down, and now we are expected to simply abide this madness as if it were the natural order? Tell me, how."

Mannie speaks, not truly acknowledging Casey's questions directly. "A Pastseer peers deeply into what has come before. It is a gift of immeasurable potency, but one fraught with pain, for she carries the weight of choices made and unmade. Her insight arrives only after time is set in stone. Yet, despite this burden, Amelia carries it with a grace few could muster. To dismiss her insight is to dismiss the weapon history provides. Trust in what is spoken to you now," Mannie says, his gaze briefly hardening as it falls upon Casey. "She has endured far worse than this inconvenience you so readily question."

Casey, his jaw tightening, fires back quickly. "You expect us to shoulder it without question?"

Finn's voice cuts through the tension. "It's not her word we dinnae trust," he asserts, his tone sharp. I place my hand in his, giving a reassuring squeeze. His gaze softens, steadied by my touch.

"Finn, please... share with us what you were told," Amelia says.

Running a hand down his face, Finn meets Amelia's gaze as he continues. "The same woman approached me."

Finn looks down at me, his expression troubled. "In the same tavern the night before. She came up to me out of nowhere, as if she'd been waitin' for me. She spoke of things that defied explanation—words that felt like riddles spoken by a troubled woman. But now..." He looks directly down at me. "She was speakin' about you."

I ask, my voice rising with urgency, "What did she say?"

Finn hesitates, as though the words weighed heavily on his tongue. Finally, he exhales, his voice low and steady. "As you said, it seemed the speech of a madwoman. She said, *'She is the thread that binds you to the stars.'*"

My breath catches, and I stand abruptly. "She told me *'You are the thread that binds him to the stars,'*" I add softly, the weight of the revelation sinking into the space between us.

Finn's eyes search mine. Slowly, he reaches out, his hand trembling slightly as he cups my cheek. His thumb brushes against my skin, sending a shiver down my spine. "It's as if... we were always meant to find each other," he murmurs, his voice raw.

Emotion wells up inside me, threatening to spill over. I cover his hand with mine, leaning into his touch. "What does being bound like this mean?"

His forehead rests lightly against mine, his breath warm against my skin. "It means we're stronger together than we are apart."

"*Quite* the opposite of what you've believed of yourself, right Finn?" Bran says.

I place my hand on the back of his neck. "I could have told you how wrong that was years ago if only you'd told me how you felt then," I say as I kiss his cheek.

Finn's hand slips to the back of my neck, grounding me with his touch. "If the stars bind us, then they've already seen what we can be."

Tears sting my eyes as his words settle over me. There is a strange comfort in the way he speaks. As if he possesses the knowledge of our future.

Before either of us can delve further, Mannie claps, breaking the moment. "Ooo, I do so love the joining of two souls, don't you, Amelia?"

"Indeed, but such bonds are not without trial. Threads must sometimes fray to find their true strength." Amelia turns her gaze to Deidre, their eyes meeting briefly. Something unspoken passes between them—pain, perseverance, love earned.

Mannie's grin widens as he leans closer. "Trial, indeed. Though I suspect these two are not ones to let their thread snap so easily."

Finn shifts beside me, his jaw tight. "Tell me something, Mannie," he says, voice cool and clipped. "Have you been screwin' with us this whole time? Flirtin' with Triona, buttin' in to compliment her, touch her, dance with her—was that all just some game to you?"

Mannie doesn't retreat. If anything, he tilts his head with maddening calm, that ever-present smile twitching like he's tempted to laugh—but doesn't.

"Hardly a game, Finn. I only ever meant to push you two together—seemed the only way to get you to move."

He lets that linger, then adds, "Though I will admit, watching you stew was a delightful bonus."

Finn steps forward, but I place my hand firmly against his chest. His breath hitches under the weight of my palm, and his jaw loosens just enough.

"Who exactly is this maiden?" Finn asks sharply.

Mannie sobers. "She is a Keeper," he says with more weight than flair this time. "An oracle's guide. The Mirror of Whispers she carries would have pointed her directly at you."

Finn's brows draw together. "To Triona?"

"To you both," Mannie corrects. "The mirror does not see faces. It sees ties—what is bound, what is meant. That is how she found you."

My hand remains on Finn's chest. "So she was sent?"

Mannie nods. "In a way. Called, rather. By fate."

His expression softens. "Your mother," he says, his voice quiet, "was a Timewhisperer. She could hear the echoes of what has yet to come, the whispers of fate weaving through the air."

I blink, the words barely registering. "A Timewhisperer? My mother?" My voice trembles as I speak.

Mannie continues as if his words aren't an absolute shock. "And you, Little One..." His voice takes on a reverence that makes my stomach twist. "You have the power to do both."

"What?" The word falls from my lips like a stone, disbelief wrapping tightly around me. "That's impossible. I can't do that. I've never—"

"You may not yet feel such power," Mannie interrupts, his voice as gentle as a breeze. "But the power is there, waiting. Hidden."

"How would I not remember?" My frustration boils over. "If I could do this, why—why wouldn't I know?"

"Because you do not remember yourself," Mannie says simply. "But that is why I have come. It is my duty to untangle the mess in your head. I can see you are overwhelmed, so let me make this simple." He stands and shakes out his limbs.

"The Tuatha Dé Danann came to this realm with four treasures that symbolised sovereignty, strength, sustenance, and victory—foundational elements for the Tuatha's survival and dominance."

He points to where Finn stands. "*You journey now with sun-born kin, to find the spear, the battle's twin.*"

Then to Callan. "*The warrior bold from Gorias' might, seeks the blade of eternal light.*"

Bran and Casey come next. "*Two hearts entwined, a cauldron they crave, a vessel of plenty their fate will pave.*"

Finally, Mannie stands before me, his expression grave. *"And you, my child, seek what's been torn—the shard of your soul, to be reborn."*

"These are four great items," Mannie continues, "that have never met battle at the same time. If they were united, the force threatening their wielders would face an impossible challenge."

He raises his hand as if summoning the weight of history itself. "The first, from the great city of Falias, imbued with a force far greater than any man could ever comprehend: The Stone of Fál." Then he turns to me. "Little One, it is *your* task to go to The Hill of Tara, for *your* item sets all others in motion."

"Why me?" My voice wavers.

"*Lia Fáil* roars when touched by true nobility, a voice great like thunder. It has *not* roared for millennia. It must be taken to Uisneach Hill, where it took its last breath."

"It has to be moved to work?" Callan challenges, a furrow forming on his brow.

"How useful is a key to you without a lock to open?" Mannie counters with a quiet gravity.

"It holds no use at all," Callan answers with confidence.

"Indeed. A lock is impassable without a key, and the key is meaningless without a lock. Think of the stone as the key, and what lies inside Uisneach the lock, and Triona the one given right to unlock a truly spellbinding power. The object will only respond to those made worthy, as told by her mother. The threads of fate are tightly bound to her, and only through her presence will the ancient forces respond, allowing the journey to truly begin."

"And then?" I inquire.

"Then... your path will reveal itself to you. And as the maiden made it so, you will know your next task."

"You mentioned four items?" Casey presses.

"Ah yes, the other three. A sword, a spear, and a cauldron."

"Ye want us to follow you into the unknown, trust ye with our lives," Callan grunts, his tone heavy with skepticism. "And why should we? What makes ye so certain we willnae be led to our deaths?"

Amelia steps forward, her expression calm but firm, and places a hand on Mannie's arm. "You need to show them, dear." She addresses the room. "Be warned, visions are your truths to unravel, but they are not the end. Only a guide."

Mannie nods and holds his palms out to us. "Each of you, my dear chosen ones, shall see why fate—or perhaps sheer lunacy—has deemed you worthy of these sacred relics. If the price of your trust is proof, then so be it." He winks, and with a flourish, the room seems to still, the air thick with anticipation. Then everything descends into darkness.

32

SEPARATION OF PATHS

Triona

A path lay before me, stretching out in two distinct directions. To my left, a shadowy road, twisted and gnarled, leading through a dense forest where the trees loom like dark figures. The air is thick with an oppressive fog, and I can hear distant cries—a sense of danger, of death in every rustling leaf. The path feels cold and unwelcoming, but necessary to save what calls me from within.

To my right, the path is bathed in a soft, golden light. Clear and wide, bordered by flowers in full bloom, with birds soaring overhead. This path is warm and filled with potential—yet it is obscured by a mist that warns something is hidden.

Both paths are shrouded in mystery, but one whispers of hope, while the other of destruction, and I'm not entirely certain the answer is obvious.

More images flash before my eyes, overwhelming all of my senses, until a voice calls out to me.

"Decide, Raven Queen," the voice calls from the shadows, echoing softly in my mind. "But be warned that the path that seems impossible may be for the right of the whole. Living for all is the only choice, for living for one will end in destruction."

It continues, "The items you seek are a power unyielding, a convergence of forces far beyond the understanding of mortal minds. To unite them is to awaken long slumbering foes who would see your purpose undone. You must choose to sunder your paths, for only apart can the whole be preserved."

My heart pounds as the image fades, leaving me standing in front of Amelia and Mannie, shaking.

"Sweet mercy and a six-day hangover," Bran mutters, his voice shaky as his eyes focus, pulling me from my thoughts.

I glance around, noticing unease on every face, mirroring my own. But it's Finn's face I can't ignore. His brow furrows, lips tight. His eyes are darker, distant, as if he's seen something unspeakable.

I'm about to ask when his gaze flickers to me. Something unreadable flashes across his features before he schools his expression, a familiar mask sliding into place. "What is it?" I ask, my voice small.

He smiles, but it doesn't reach his eyes. "It was just a lot," he replies, voice steady but rough. His calm delivery would convince anyone else, but I know him too well. Still, his performance is impeccable.

"Are you okay?" he asks, his tone soft, tender.

I nod, though the tightness in my chest lingers. His concern feels genuine, yet I can't shake the sense he's carrying something too heavy to share.

"I believe so," I whisper, though the weight between us remains. Finn studies me for a moment longer before leaning in and pressing a gentle kiss to my lips.

When he pulls back, his eyes search mine, and his voice is steady but full of conviction. "You will be okay," he reassures me. The tension in his shoulders doesn't ease, but his warmth lingers, grounding me.

The group exchange glances, unease still thick in the air. Bran's bravado falters, and even Callan's usual gruffness is replaced with a rare quiet. It's Casey who finally speaks, his voice steady despite the tension. "If what I just saw is any sign that what they say is to be trusted..."

Amelia's eyes soften at the question, her shoulders relaxing just slightly. "You need to get past your grievances between one another." Amelia looks between Callan and Finn, and then Bran and Casey. "If you remain at odds, you've no chance. And second... prepare. There's a storm coming, and it'll test every one of you."

Mannie turns toward Callan. "The blade of eternal light, forged in Gorias, holds the essence of fire itself, said to banish even the darkest shadow. Only a warrior of unyielding courage can wield it."

Bran and Casey exchange glances. Mannie continues, "The Cauldron of Plenty, resting in Murias, provides not just sustenance, but rejuvenation. It is a vessel of life, granting strength to those in need. Its discovery depends on unity and unwavering loyalty."

Finally, Mannie looks at Finn. "The Spear of Lugh, kept in Findias. It is said that no battle fought with it will end in defeat. It chooses its bearer only in the presence of profound purpose."

I look at each one of the men I trust the most with a fondness. "You all saw your task then—that we must now part ways?"

They nod, tension lingering in their stances, but resolve flickers beneath the unease.

"Triona, will you share all that you saw?" Mannie presses.

I nod and begin. "Casey and Bran must journey together, their task bound to the unity and loyalty required to claim the Cauldron of Plenty. It's not a simple prize to be taken. It demands qualities that the two of you possess. Casey's steadfast loyalty and grounded strength balance Bran's quick thinking and adaptability."

I continue. "Meanwhile, Callan, Finn, and I will travel toward the Hill of Tara to awaken The Stone of Fál, as its roar will determine the course of all that follows. These paths are intertwined, yet separate, demanding that we trust not only in ourselves but in the bonds that tie us together."

Casey shifts uncomfortably, glancing at me. "I'm not too fond of leavin' ye." His tone is clipped, his jaw tight as though he's holding back. I offer him a small smile, trying to ease the tension.

Bran crosses his arms, his expression hardening. "You're stuck with me, Casey, so let's just hope we don't kill each other on the way." His voice carries a sharp edge, barely masking his frustration.

"What's with the two of you?" I ask, suspicion creeping into my tone. They lock eyes briefly, tension thick between them, but neither answer.

Bran mutters under his breath, his voice flat and laced with irritation, "Nothing."

Casey's shoulders stiffen, and he exhales sharply through his nose. "Aye, nothin' to it," he states, his tone brusque, refusing to meet my gaze.

Mannie steps forward, his expression solemn. "The path ahead will be fraught with trials that reach beyond the limits of flesh and spirit. Each step you take will unravel truths that may shatter even the strongest of hearts. Forces older than memory, darker than shadow, will rise to oppose you, fearing what you might become."

Finn's grip on my hand tightens, his gaze flickering between Mannie and me. "If that's the case, then she willnae face it alone. None of us will let that happen."

Bran smirks, though his eyes carry a flicker of concern. "Aye, we're in this together. On that, I can agree."

Deidre speaks from her position in the room. "Strength will come not just from the bonds you've already formed, but from those yet to be made—alliances forged in adversity and friendships built through trials. Trust that these connections will guide you when the path grows darkest. Trust in one another."

Mannie nods. "Together, united by bonds forged in fire, in blood, and some even in silence; you may yet find the power to prevail over the forces that seek to undo you."

Finn

I'm resolved to make good on my promise to mend things with Callan, especially in light of all we've uncovered in these past days. There is too much at stake for us to remain divided, and any further delay would only deepen the rift.

The revelations from Mannie and Amelia have laid bare what we may come to face. Alone, we will falter, but together, we may yet succeed. It is a humbling realisation, one that steels my determination. If Callan and I cannot reconcile, it will be more than just our bond that suffers; it could spell ruin for us all.

I find Callan in the stables. The soft, rhythmic sound of a brush moving over a horse's coat greets me as I step inside.

As I watch him now, I notice something I've been too blind to see since coming home: how different he looks and acts. There's a hardness about him, anger simmering beneath the surface that has only intensified in my absence. I should have considered that before I did what I did.

The unease from earlier still lingers in the air. At last, I clear my throat. "Have you calmed down enough to talk like civilised humans? Or do I need to brace for another fight?"

Callan stiffens but doesn't turn. "Depends," he mutters, his tone clipped. "Have ye come to tell me it was all in jest?" He finally looks at me, his gaze sharp but less volatile than it was before. "My sister, Finn? Ye've got a rare nerve, I'll grant ye that."

I square my shoulders, keeping my voice steady. "Go on, Callan. Get it all out. I'll take yer anger. I'll take it because I know I deserve some of it."

The tension thickens between us. I gesture toward the open doors. "If ye'd rather settle this with fists, let us step outside. Perhaps that will help you find reason?"

Callan's eyes narrow, his fists already clenched, and he gives a sharp nod in return. "Aye, Finn. Perhaps that's exactly what I need."

We step into the night; the chill doing little to quell the heat of our unresolved words. The brittle leaves beneath our boots crunch in the stillness as we move away from the stable, the open air before us becoming an unspoken battleground. Callan halts, turning to face me fully. His expression is a tempest of anger, frustration, and something deeper—a worry he cannot quite mask.

"D'ye even understand what it means if ye muck this up?" he asks, his voice low but laden with emotion.

"Aye," I say firmly, my gaze unwavering. "More than you might think. I've thought of little else, Callan."

Without a word, we strip off our shirts, down to our trousers, each movement deliberate and tense.

"Why risk everything for her? She is my blood, and if ye hurt her, there's no forgiveness."

"I willnae harm her, Cal," I affirm, voice calm and controlled. "That ye'd even suggest I could be so lowly cuts deep. You know me better than that. "

Callan lets out a bitter laugh. He shakes his head, his eyes boring into mine. "Do I? Ye've been keeping this to yerself, letting me walk around like a fool while ye've been nursing these feelings for my sister. It feels as though ye've betrayed me."

"It is no betrayal," I say, stepping closer, my hands open and unthreatening. "I did not seek this, Callan. I did not choose it. But I refuse to continue denying what I feel."

The two of us begin to circle each other, tension crackling in the air. Our movements are sharp, eyes locked as though waiting for the other to strike first.

Callan's expression hardens, his anger flaring anew. "And puttin' on this farce just to bed my sister is worth our friendship?"

Callan throws a testing jab, his fist cutting through the air just shy of my shoulder. I shift to the side, my fist snapping out in a feint that sends Callan stepping back.

"In honesty," I reply, my tone steady. "I've never wanted to strike you more than I do right now. I'm not Marcus, and that ye'd dare to compare us confirms ye're not in your right mind. Triona is not some possession of yers. If you would be so daft as to hate me because I dared to *love* yer sister, then I would accept the expiry of the friendship." I throw my arms wide. "There's naught left to hide. No secret left unturned. What about the ones you so deftly hide?"

Callan's eyes narrow, indignation flashing. "Ye dinnae ken why I keep half of what I've had to, Finn. Secrets are a burden, but sometimes they're the only way to protect the people ye care about."

With a sharp motion, Callan lunges forward, his fist connecting solidly with my jaw, the impact cracking through the tense air like thunder. I stagger back a step and reach to wipe a trace of blood from the corner of my mouth. The sting from Callan's punch lingers, but my willpower remains unshaken.

"And I kept this one to myself even as it tore me apart. I spent countless days believin' that I was only a hindrance to her. That she deserved a better man than I could ever be. But she showed me otherwise; she *chose* me. Made me see I belong beside her, not behind her. Triona is as much mine as I am hers, and for her sake, you must make peace with it. No other man alive will *ever* love her the way I do. I'll spend every breath of my existence proving the depth of my faithfulness to her, and to anyone who dares to question it."

I pivot sharply, my fist driving into Callan's midsection with precision, the blow forcing the air from his lungs. He staggers but recovers, regains footing, and swings back in a wide arc that I deftly evade. I counter with a sharp uppercut that connects cleanly with his jaw; the impact leaving us both momentarily breathless as we steady ourselves for the next blow.

The sharp edge of his anger dulls into something heavier as he swipes a hand across his bruised jaw, still smarting from my last punch. His gaze lingers, a mix of frustration and reluctant deference. "Lovin' her means puttin' her first, Finn. Always. Are ye ready for that? She deserves the best, and I willnae stand by and let her settle for less. I made that vow to my parents."

"I've never been more certain of anything in my life, Callan. Puttin' her first is the only way I know how to live. Every choice I've made, every damn thing I've done, has been for her. No one will ever love her as completely, as fiercely, or as endlessly as I do." I don't hesitate, driving forward with another sharp blow that connects with Callan's jaw. The impact drives him back a step, his balance wavering before he falls to the ground.

As I stand poised for his reaction, the sound of rushing footsteps breaks through the tension. Triona, Casey, and Bran appear, their faces a mixture of shock and consternation.

Triona's voice is sharp as she calls out, "What are the two of you doing?"

Just as she opens her mouth to say more, Callan and I speak in unison, our voices resolute and firm. "This is between us."

She crosses her arms tightly over her chest, glaring at both of us as if daring us to explain ourselves. I try not to notice the way the motion pushes her breasts together, and yet, a flicker of heat runs through me, causing my cock to stir in my trousers. I attempt to will it away as Triona's eyes sear into me.

Bran places a hand gently on her shoulder to draw her attention. "I think they're trying to work something out—they both seem to need this," he mumbles, his voice tinged with understanding.

Triona's eyes snap to Bran, her tone sharp. "Says the man who won't *work out* whatever the hell it is that's got you and Casey at odds with one another."

She looks between all four of us, exasperation clear in every gesture. "You are the reason for this species' downfall—you know that, right?"

"*You?*" Casey asks.

"Bloody daft foolish men," Triona mutters, throwing her hands in the air as she turns and stalks off, leaving us standing there in stunned silence.

Even as she disappears from view, her words still biting, I can't shake the way my yearning for her refuses to fade. If anything, her anger only stokes the desire inside me. There's something intoxicating about that fire in her eyes, the way it challenges me, dares me to tame it. All I want is to replace her fury with something far more consuming.

I move to follow her, but Casey holds out a hand. "Just... finish whatever this shite is before you come inside." Casey turns and strides after Triona.

"Callan, consider this," Bran says, fixing him with a serious look. "The man refused to talk about his feelings, but even I knew he was mad about Triona before I'd met her. Never once laid with or looked at another woman. That kind of devotion—it should count for a whole fucking lot. Think about that before you continue throwing punches." Without another word, he turns and heads back inside, leaving Callan and me alone under the fading light.

Callan rubs his jaw, still aching from my last hit. "Ye fight like someone with something to prove." His voice softens, but a weight lingers in his words. He meets my gaze, a flicker of something deeper crosses his features. He pushes to stand. "If ye love her the way ye say, then ye better give her all that ye've got, Finn. Every bit of strength, every piece of yer soul. And if there ever comes a day when it costs ye everything, ye'd better be ready to pay that price."

I don't hesitate at all. "I give my life to her, Cal. I've known it for longer than I care to admit. If it ever comes to that, I'll gladly pay the price—everything I have, and more."

As Callan nods, a reluctant understanding settles in his eyes. He takes a step closer, his hand reaching out to clap my shoulder. The gesture says more than words ever could. "Prove it, Finn." At that familiar phrase, I feel the tension in my chest loosen. I'll carry this challenge with me as a promise—to her, to myself, and to him.

33

THE LULL BEFORE THE ROAR

Triona
Saturday, 7 June 1823
Port of Lisbon

The afternoon stretches beneath a sky streaked with fading light, a storm brewing on the horizon. A charged stillness hangs in the air as we gather at the harbour's edge, the briny tang of the sea cutting through the crisp chill. It feels fitting—this quiet unrest—as we prepare to say our goodbyes.

Bran leans casually against a wooden post, his arms crossed, trying to project an air of nonchalance that doesn't quite reach his eyes. Casey stands a few paces away, hands on his hips, his jaw clenched in what I can only describe as reluctant acceptance.

Finn is unusually quiet, standing beside me, his shoulders stiff. His gaze remains fixed on the ship that rocks gently in the water—a vessel unlike any I have ever seen. Even in the last rays of daylight, it glows. Every line of its design is perfect, from the pristine sails to the gleaming brass fittings.

Tonn Glas is etched into the side. It looks more like a vessel of legend than one meant to ferry Bran and Casey across treacherous waters.

The ship across the dock leaves much to be desired. The contrast between the two vessels couldn't be more striking. *Cairn's Shadow* seems to bear the weight of every storm she's faced, a testament to resilience rather than grandeur, or so one would hope.

Mannie steps forward, his chiseled features bearing an almost ethereal allure. His tailored coat clings perfectly to his broad shoulders, exuding an effortless confidence. "There she lies," he intones. "*Tonn Glas*. She'll carry Bran, Casey, and me to Killybegs."

Casey whistles low, eyes sweeping over the vessel with something between awe and wariness. "She's bonnie," he mutters. "Seen nothin' like her before."

Mannie smiles knowingly, the echo of pride in his expression. "She is a wonder. *Tonn Glas* is not merely a ship. She is born of the ocean's breath and moulded by hands that understand its depths. Treat her well, for she carries not just your hopes but the whispers of tides older than memory."

Bran tilts his head, skepticism creeping into his expression. "Are we talking about a ship or a woman?"

Mannie chuckles. "In some ways, they are one and the same."

Bran huffs, crossing his arms. "All right, but seriously—what are you saying? Are we talking about a ship that can think for itself?"

Mannie's eyes glint with amusement. "In a manner of speaking, she lives as the sea lives, bound to its will. Through me, she feels the currents and the winds. Disrespect her, and you will find yourselves at odds with more than waves—you will meet with the ancient forces that cradle and consume."

Bran raises a skeptical brow but says nothing, while Casey lets out a low, exasperated snort. "Brilliant," he mutters, his tone dripping with sarcasm. "Just what we needed—an ocean full of temperamental gods. Cannae wait."

Amelia steps forward, her voice calm but firm. "This isn't a journey you're meant to enjoy, Casey. It's one you're meant to endure—and to succeed at. Unity will be your greatest weapon."

I step closer, unable to keep the worry from my voice. "I want your word. I want to know they'll be safe with you."

Mannie's gaze softens as it lands on me. "Safe? That word holds little weight upon the open sea. The waters are no sanctuary; they are a mirror, reflecting truths both cruel and kind. Whether they emerge unscathed depends not on fortune but on the strength of their hearts and the bonds they hold. The sea reveals all, and it has no mercy for deceit. But... I give you my word, Little One, that I will not harm any you hold dear. I will guide them as best I can, as I have guided others before them. Yet know this—even my hand cannot shield them from the tides of destiny."

Casey turns to me, his expression softening. "We'll make it back, Triona. Ye've my word."

I nod, swallowing hard against the lump in my throat. "That's all I ask."

"I will keep this one in line," Bran says, jerking his thumb toward Casey.

Casey rolls his eyes. "Let's hope *Tonn Glas* likes ye more than I do." But then his expression softens, and before I can react, he steps forward and pulls me into a tight hug. "Take care of yerself, Triona," he whispers, his voice thick with emotion. "We'll be together again in no time."

I cling to him for a moment, fighting back tears. "Better be," I manage, my voice breaking. "I'm counting on you to keep Bran out of trouble as well."

Casey chuckles, ruffling my hair like he did when we were younger. "Aye, I'll do my best, but we both ken how troublesome that tongue of his can be."

With that, he strides off, leaving just Bran, Finn, and me. Bran smirks, stepping closer. "Oh, come now, Triona. You know I'm the perfect blend of charm and wisdom."

I roll my eyes, but when he pulls me into a hug, it's warm, genuine. His voice drops to something softer. "Don't worry about us. We'll look out for each other. And when we're back, we'll have one hell of a story to tell."

"I'll hold you to it."

Before he can turn away, I grab his collar in a firm grip, pulling him just close enough to hear the steel in my voice. "Whatever's between you and my brother—if he gets hurt over it, you'll regret it."

For a moment, Bran's smirk falters, his expression caught between amusement and something heavier—a flicker of doubt, maybe even guilt. But it's gone just as quickly, replaced with that effortless charm.

"Message received, Triona," he murmurs, pressing a hand to his chest in mock sincerity. "I'll be a perfect angel—not a hair on his head out of place."

I loosen my grip on his collar, but my glare lingers just long enough to drive my point home. Finn steps to my side without hesitation, his arm locking around my waist in a firm, grounding hold. There's an unmistakable possessiveness in the way he pulls me closer—as if he's making a statement all his own.

"Aye, I'd listen to her," Finn says, his voice carrying a low, steady warning. "She's not one to make idle threats."

Bran chuckles, his grin widening. "Oh, I hear her. Loud and clear. Didn't realise she had *you* so well in hand already."

I glance up to find Finn smirking—the kind of smirk that sends warmth curling through my stomach.

"I'm smart enough to know who's really in charge." Finn's tone is light, but the wicked gleam in his eyes suggests otherwise. Then, as if repaying Bran for every over shared experience he's never wanted to hear, he smirks and adds, "She's got me *well* in hand. Has a hold on me in ways ye'd never understand. Uses that sinful little mouth of hers to work me over until I'm on my knees for her—shakin', desperate, wrecked. She's got this way of wrappin' her lips around me, draggin' her tongue so slow it's *torture*, makin' me beg without a single—"

"Oh, for fuck's sake—" Bran interjects. "Keep your filth to yourself."

Then adds with a dramatic shudder, "I'll admit you're a fine enough looking man, but thinking about how poor Triona has to suffer through a roll in the sheets with you? I'll carry that horror to my grave."

Finn, unbothered, grabs my chin, his smirk downright sinful as his fingers tilt my face toward his. Then, instead of the quick, teasing kiss I expect, he presses a slow, deliberate kiss to my lips.

Warm. Deep. Possessive. A kiss meant to prove a bloody point and stake a claim.

Bran makes a noise, something between a groan and a prayer. "Oh, come on."

Finn finally pulls away from the kiss, his breath still warm against my lips. I let the moment linger, then arch a brow, letting a slow smirk spread across my lips. "You're awfully smug for a man who couldn't form a coherent sentence last night."

His chuckle is dark and full of promise.

Bran shifts uncomfortably. "Are you two quite done?"

Finn exudes the smugness of a man who knows he's won. With calculating cruelty, he adds, "Now, dinnae think too hard about all that when you get lonely on Tonn Glas. Ye've got a long trip ahead."

Bran levels him with an unimpressed stare. "Aye, real mature of you."

Finn leans in and brushes a light kiss against my cheek, his lips warm and fleeting.

Bran clears his throat, clearly trying to regain control of the conversation. "I wasn't prepared for you to lack all shame. Were you always this way, or is this torment just for me?"

His voice carries a mix of discomfort and humour, and it catches me so off guard that a small laugh escapes me. "That was him holding back. He is rather lewd-mouthed in the bedroom."

At that, Bran lets out a genuine laugh. "Guess I taught him well," he says with cocksure demure.

"No, Finn has an attitude all his own," I say smoothly, casting him a sideways glance. "Nothing he could have been taught." At that, he turns his head just enough to look at me, and the second our eyes meet, heat curls low in my belly.

His gaze is pure desire—dark, heavy-lidded, the kind of look that sets a woman's resolve on fire. His smirk is slow, deliberate, and the sly curve of his lips makes my pulse stutter. He doesn't have to say a word—*that look alone* is enough to remind me of every sinful thing he's done to me. The way he's touched me, claimed me, memorised every way I come undone beneath him. It's a silent promise, a reminder, and a challenge all at once.

We let the silence stretch, then I tilt my head, my smirk widening. "I'm certain you are the furthest thing from his mind in the bedroom."

Bran clears his throat loudly. "Aye, well, if you two are done making eyes like you intend to ravish the other on the spot, I'd like to formally request to *un-hear* this entire conversation." Finn chuckles—low, dark.

"Request denied. Ye're hearin' every bit of it, Mums."

"Why are you still standing here?" I ask through a giggle.

Bran throws his hands up, exasperated. "I don't *know!* I suppose I thought it was better than standing alone, but then I also kept waiting for it to *stop*—and it hasn't."

Like a bell tolling Bran's salvation, Casey's unmistakable, full-bellied cackle erupts across the dock—loud, sharp, and cutting clean through the surrounding chatter.

Bran seizes the opportunity, voice a little too eager. "Ah, would you listen to that? Casey's found something far more entertaining than whatever this is." He spins on his heel, marching toward the others without another word.

Finn watches him go, still smirking. "Think we broke him. He's willingly goin' over to stand near Casey."

I exhale, crossing my arms as I glance between them. "Aye, well, I hope they get over whatever the hell happened between them. It's miserable watching them act like this."

I chew my lip, mulling over a nagging thought in my head. "I think it was over a lassie."

Finn's smirk falters, just slightly.

I continue, voice thoughtful. "The morning after the party, I saw a girl sneaking out of Bran's room. Looked like she was in a hurry. Thought nothin' of it at the time, but now..." I trail off, glancing back toward them.

"Only... she left the room just as Amelia and I were walking past, which caused a bit of a scene in and of itself."

Finn raises an eyebrow, his interest sharpening just a fraction, but he says nothing, waiting for me to go on.

I pause for dramatic effect, my voice quieter now. "Amelia and I had a *front-row seat* to Bran's cock standing at full attention—no shame whatsoever at being caught."

Finn lets out a sharp bark of laughter, shaking his head. "That lad is beyond saving."

I exhale, shaking my head slightly as the memory comes back clearer. "And then, as we're all standing there, the door to Casey's room flies open, and Finn..."

I meet his gaze, my voice quieter now, thoughtful. "I can't remember the last time I saw such rage in Casey's eyes."

Finn's expression barely shifts—but I see it. That flicker of something, just for a moment, before he smooths it over. A quick flash of realisation, of calculation, before his mask falls perfectly back into place.

I narrow my eyes. "What was that look about?"

Finn exhales through his nose, shaking his head slightly. "They'll work it out. If not for the betterment of internal peace, then for the mission. Bran is many things, but he'd never jeopardise the safety or well-bein' of others."

I study him, suspicion creeping into my voice. "Finn... do you maybe know something you're not telling me?"

He looks at me then, really looks at me—his gaze searching mine for a long, quiet moment.

Then he huffs a breath, shaking his head. "I love you with all that I am, but please dinnae make me tell you."

I tilt my head, lips twitching. "Not even if I put my mouth on your—"

Finn groans, cutting me off as his fingers curl around my waist, tugging me flush against him. "*Caitríona.*"

I let out a small gasp. "My full name?" Then, with a resigned sigh, I relent. "Fine, fine."

"I'll make it up to you, mo ghrá." Before I can react, his hands slide lower, gripping my rear with possessive intent—then a sharp smack lands, sending a jolt through me. A startled gasp escapes my lips, my breath hitching as warmth blooms where his touch lingers.

"Finn!" I hiss, my face burning as I glance around.

He only chuckles, the sound curling through my stomach like heat licking at embers. He takes my hand, tugging me forward with easy confidence, and we walk over to join the others.

As we step into their midst, the familiar hum of conversation dwindles, and the weight of this fleeting unity settles in, unspoken but deeply felt.

I take one last look at those that we must part from—Bran's charming demeanour, Casey's radiant smile, Amelia's quiet strength, Deidre's gentle wisdom, even Mannie and the undeniable flair that amuses those around him. Each of them leaves an imprint that will linger long after the horizon swallows them from view.

"Well, this is it, then," Bran says with an unconvincing smile. "Don't miss us too much."

As Casey and Bran board their ship, Finn, Callan, and I are guided toward Cairn's Shadow. "Now, I don't want to be rude, but are you sure that's seaworthy? Looks like it's held together with wishful thinking," Bran shouts as he pauses on the gangplank.

Casey smirks, pointing toward Tonn Glas with exaggerated pride. "I think it's fair to say we were dealt a better hand. Our ship looks as if it could carry the gods themselves, while yers might not make it out of the harbour."

"It's not about the look of a ship, but the crew who sails her." Callan grits out.

Finn raises a brow, shooting Bran a pointed look. "And I'd rather have an old boat than a cocky crew, so maybe keep yer gloatin' in check till ye've proved yerselves."

I grin, cutting in before Bran can respond. "Oh, come now boys. You can admit, Cairn's Shadow looks like she's seen more rough nights than an old doxy."

Bran bursts out laughing. "See? Even Triona agrees. You should consider adding a few extra dinghies for when you find yourselves in need."

Finn shakes his head, turning toward me with a raised brow. "I think ye've been spendin' too much time with Bran. He's rubbing off on ye."

One by one, we climb the gangplank, each step feeling heavier than the last. I pause at the top, glancing back at Deidre and Amelia. The wind catches Amelia's hair, framing her face in a halo of sunlight. She lifts a hand in a silent farewell, and I mimic the gesture before turning away.

As *Tonn Glas* pulls away from the harbour, her shimmering hull gliding through the water as if it's part of the sea itself, I feel the weight of our singular group becoming two.

I can't help but glance around Cairn's Shadow to occupy my thoughts. The aged vessel creaks as we step aboard. Her wood, weathered and darkened by countless voyages, tells the story of a ship that has seen too much yet refuses to yield. Patches cover the sails in places, and the frayed ropes look ready to give way at the slightest gust. A faint smell of salt and mildew lingers in the surrounding air.

The disparity between vessels is grim—one ship a legend, the other a test of endurance. I stand beside Finn, gripping his arm as both ships begin their journeys onward, and I can't shake the feeling that this is the start of something none of us are truly prepared for.

Callan lets out a low whistle, his brow arching as we take in our surroundings. "This is it?" he asks, his tone laced with skepticism.

The man leading us, a grizzled sailor with a weathered face, grunts. "Aye, she's a tough old girl, but she'll see you where you're bound—so long as you mind her well. Cross her wrong, and the sea'll be takin' what's rightfully hers."

As the ship glides further from the shore, I can't help but steal one last glance down at the dock, needing to see Amelia and Deidre's faces one last time. Only Amelia remains, standing alone, watching.

Her lips move, and I catch the faint impression of *be brave* dancing across them.

The water between us is calm but vast, reflecting the sky's shifting hues—a perfect mirror of light and shadow. We now exist in separate worlds.

Callan stands close—near enough to be present, but not so much that he intrudes on our space. His gaze stays fixed forward, shoulders rigid, his presence a quiet yet imposing force.

Finn stands beside me, his hand wrapped firmly around mine, his thumb tracing slow, steady circles against my skin. Though he doesn't speak, I can feel the tension radiating from him, see it in the way his gaze lingers on the open sea.

Whatever it is feels heavy enough to leave a crack in his composure. I shift closer, my shoulder brushing his arm, offering silent reassurance. We've always found strength in each other, and I hope he feels it now.

He exhales softly, the sound almost lost to the wind, but I catch it. When he finally turns to me, his dark eyes meet mine. There's so much there—so much love, fear, and unspoken promise that it steals the air from my lungs. Without a word, he leans in, resting his forehead gently against mine, the world narrowing to just the two of us.

When he pulls back, his hand remains firmly in mine, and he turns his gaze forward, toward the endless expanse of sea stretching into the unknown. The shadows on his face are still there, but so is the fire—the quiet resolve that burns stronger because we're together.

The toughened sailor from before returns. "Come now. Mistress Curran made it so each of you would have a proper cabin to your name, far better than you might have expected when you first boarded. She's got her charms where it matters."

Finn and I exchange uncertain glances before stepping cautiously below deck. The dimly lit corridor leads us to the cabins, and I push open the door to inspect the space. Relief washes over me as I take in the surprisingly tidy quarters. The bed looks sturdy, the bedding clean, and a faint scent of lavender lingers in the air, as if someone had taken care to make the rooms welcoming. There's even a wooden tub for washing; a rare indulgence aboard the confines of a ship.

"Well, this is a sight better than expected," Callan mutters, his tension easing as he peaks into my living space before moving ahead to his own. Finn's guarded expression softens as he steps into my assigned room, his eyes scanning the surroundings.

He leans lazily against the bedframe, though there's nothing idle about the way his gaze darkens as it drags over me. A wicked smirk tugs at the corner of his lips. "You know I'm not sleepin' alone, aye?"

"Why, Mr MacGregor," I purr, stepping through the door, each movement slow, deliberate. "Are you inviting yourself into a ladies' quarters? How *very* shameless of you!"

Without a word, I reach back, grasping the door and easing it shut, the soft click echoing in the quiet cabin. I bite my lip, my eyes glinting with mischief as I slowly unlatch my cloak, letting it slide from my shoulders.

He makes a low, rough sound in his throat—a sound that speaks of hunger, of want. He does not move away from the bedframe. He waits for me to come to him.

Then his voice dips, husky and unrepentant, meant for my ears alone. "Two weeks at sea. Two weeks of you all to myself in this cabin. And I mean to make *every damned second* count."

My lips curve into a slow, seductive smile. I saunter forward, letting my hips sway, watching the way his eyes flick down, how his breath deepens just slightly, how his hands clench at his sides as if he's already holding himself back.

His eyes darken, and I catch the faint blush creeping up his neck and into his cheeks as I lean up on my toes, my lips brushing his ear. In a voice low and sultry, I whisper, "After I've had a bath, I want to find myself on top as you savour me..."

He exhales sharply, spurring me further. "And then..." I let my fingers graze down his chest, featherlight, like a whisper of what's to come. "I want to see how far down my throat your cock will go."

Finn's composure cracks as he grips the edge of the bed frame so hard that the wood creaks. "Gods help me, Triona," he rasps, his voice rough, trembling with need.

But restraint is not what I want from him tonight. What either of us needs.

His hands are on me before I can draw another breath, his grip firm as he hoists me up with an ease that makes my stomach flip.

His strength is effortless. In a single stride, he moves us to the bed, falling back onto it with me cradled against him. The motion is seamless, his hold unrelenting, and when I find myself straddling his lap, on instinct, the need to press the most intimate part of me to him cannot be ignored.

The hardness beneath me is unmistakable, and when I shift, when I roll my hips against him just slightly, Finn swears low and filthy, his grip tightening at my waist.

"Ye're a wicked, wicked woman," he mutters, voice thick with desire.

"Aye, but I'm *your* wicked woman."

His chest rises and falls beneath me, his gaze near feral as he reaches up, tangling his fingers in my hair, drawing me down until our foreheads nearly touch.

"Tonight," he breathes, "I will worship every inch of you, until you cannae remember where you end and I begin."

And I will let him. I will give myself to him completely—

To lose myself entirely in him; in the cadence of his breath, in the strength of his arms that feel more like home than any place ever could, and in the way his gaze claims me as though I am the sole light in his world.

I ache to claim and be claimed, to leave a mark so indelible that even the stars themselves will sing of it for ages to come. Finnis MacGregor is not merely my love; he is the air I breathe, the pulse in my veins, and the light that pierces shadow.

It is here, entangled in his warmth, that I acknowledge my soul is no longer mine alone but bound irrevocably to his, as if the stars themselves conspired to make us whole.

Part 8 – A Heavy Toll

34

MATRON OF SECRETS

Triona

Saturday, 21 June 1823

Nearing North Wall Quay, Dublin, Ireland

J ust as Finn promised, we spent the last fourteen days tangled in each other's arms, discovering all the ways we could please one another.

As the days blurred into nights, the reality of our world faded into the background, overtaken by the way we had become so profoundly imbedded into each other. Within the walls of our cabin, we were infinite, unstoppable, and utterly consumed by one another. The lavender-scented air in our quarters felt sacred, a haven that only welcomed us.

I didn't care what waited on the other side of the door. Not until the bell tolled, followed by the cry of "*Land ho!*"—which broke me from my reverie.

The faint light of dawn seeps through the edges of the cabin window, casting a soft glow over the small space. I've been awake for some time, nestled against Finn's bare chest. His

444

heartbeat is steady beneath my palm, a rhythm that soothes and ignites in equal measure. The warmth of his skin against mine feels right.

Careful not to wake him, I let my gaze roam his face. In sleep, he is unguarded, his brow smooth, his lips parted just slightly, his dark hair a tousled mess against the pillow. The soft glow of morning catches in the strands, and I can't help myself.

I reach out, brushing my fingers along his jawline, memorising him, savouring him. *How had I lived without this? Without him?*

It feels as if the universe has finally corrected itself, placing me where I'm meant to be—wrapped in his arms, with him always.

A slow, sleepy grin tugs at Finn's lips, and without even opening his eyes, he murmurs, "How long are you plannin' on watchin' me sleep, lass?"

His voice is low, warm, laced with that playful charm that never fails to make my heart flutter.

I smile, my fingers still tracing his jaw. "Perhaps until the sun sets again," I tease. "You're far too handsome for me to look away from."

His grin widens, and one eye cracks open, golden flecks glinting in the early light. "Good," he whispers, his voice still thick with sleep. "It's all the distraction I need."

I furrow my brow, confused. "What dis—"

Before I can finish, Finn flips the blankets away in one smooth motion, the cool air hitting my bare skin just as he flips us, pinning me beneath him with effortless ease.

A startled gasp leaves me, but protest dies on my lips as his weight settles above me, strong arms bracketing my head, his mischievous golden gaze locking onto mine.

"Now tell me," he murmurs, as his lips descend to the hollow of my throat, warm and unhurried, as though he has nothing but time.

"What were you thinkin' while you were starin' at me?"

His breath brushes against my skin, each exhale a whisper of heat, his lips dragging lower—teasing, tormenting—until every nerve in my body is strung tight, attuned to him and nothing else.

I part my legs, welcoming him in, a silent invitation he doesn't hesitate to accept. His body sinks between mine, the thick, throbbing heat of him lingering above where I need him. It's torture, the way he idles, the way I can feel every inch of him pulsing, teasing, taunting, keeping me on the edge of madness.

My body tightens, hips tilting, searching for more, but his grip is firm, his control absolute. A slow, aching fire builds deep in my core, desperate, insatiable, but he doesn't move, doesn't give me the friction I crave. He holds me there, making me feel every agonizing second of it, drowning me in the unbearable, dripping need he's so effortlessly set ablaze.

He *wants* me to beg for it.

My breath hitches as his mouth drags along my collarbone, down to the tops of my breasts, lingering just to hear me gasp.

"The truth?" I manage, my voice trembling slightly. "It feels as though I loved you before I ever took my first breath."

Finn stills, his lips hovering just above my skin, his breath warm against me.

"Aye?" he whispers, his voice thick with something deeper than desire.

I moan in response, already arching into him, already aching for more.

"As if a long forgotten part of me has carried you for so long that I can't truly recall a time when you were not mine, and I was not yours."

"Mmm," the low, approving groan rumbles from him, vibrating against my skin as his mouth closes over the delicate flesh around my nipple.

"Repeat yerself," he commands, his tone rich with playfulness and intensity, his words a silken threat against my already fevered skin.

When I don't respond quickly enough, he nips at my flesh, dragging a startled shriek from me that quickly melts into laughter.

The sound seems to ignite something in him, his grin widening as his lips trail back up to the sensitive hollow of my neck. "I'll have it from you," he murmurs, his tone teasing yet insistent. "Even if I have to tease—", he presses a kiss to my skin, "it out—", his tongue circles around the peak of my nipple "of you."

Then, with deliberate care, he takes my sensitive bud into his mouth and sucks tenderly, each pull sending waves of pleasure rippling through me.

"*Finn...*" His name escapes my lips in a shallow moan as he continues his sensual assault. I melt against the hard planes of his body, my hands sliding up his muscled chest to loop around his neck.

"I need you," I breathe out.

His eyes soften as they meet mine, filled with both tenderness and conflict.

"Say it..." he demands, eyes searching mine with an intensity that strips me bare.

I don't hesitate this time.

"I am yours."

The words tremble from my lips, a vow sealed in the quiet of morning, spoken only for him.

And suddenly, there is nothing else—no past, no fears, no world beyond this bed. Only Finn, only us, lost in a dance as old as time but utterly unique to the two of us. Passion surges through me with every beat of his heart against mine.

I am his.

I am his.

I. Am. His.

"Perfect," he murmurs, the words spilling out like a prayer, voice thick with awe and something far greater than lust. His fingers trail down my already nude body, leaving a path of fire in their wake. As his fingers trace the curvature of my waist, he stops to stare into my eyes.

"I love the feel of you," he rasps, his voice low and rough with need. "But the colour that enters yer cheeks the moment I do this..." he says, as he runs the pad of his finger right over my clit. "This colour cannae be replicated."

I can only whimper in response, my hips undulating shamelessly, seeking more of his touch. He obliges, sinking one thick finger, then two, into my tight sheath. I clench around him, my inner muscles fluttering wildly as he strokes me from within.

Stars burst behind my eyelids as he works me higher, his fingers pumping, his thumb circling around my most sensitive pleasure point. The pressure builds, coiling tighter and tighter, until I am balanced on a razor's edge.

"That's it," he encourages, his voice tightened with his own barely restrained desire. "Let go for me. Let me feel you come undone."

I shatter with a keening cry, my release crashing over me in waves of ecstasy. He works me through it, his fingers never ceasing their skillful ministrations until the last tremors of my climax fade away.

As the haze recedes, a spark of desire reignites. I shift in Finn's embrace, straddling his muscular thighs as I capture his lips in a searing kiss. My fingers tangle in his dark, wavy locks, tugging gently as I deepen the kiss. He groans into my mouth, his large hands gripping my hips possessively.

"Your turn," I purr, just before tugging his bottom lip between my teeth before releasing it with a wicked smile. My nails rake lightly down his chest as I roll my hips, teasing, tempting. A feral noise rumbles in his throat, and my pulse spikes when his grip tightens possessively around my waist.

"Tri," he says, his burr thickening with desire. "You undo me. I cannae think straight for wantin' you."

His cock pulses between us, heated and demanding. I roll against him, savouring the way his breath stutters, his muscles tightening under my touch. I want to drive him wild, to watch him lose control the way he watched me.

"I love you, Triona. From the moment I first saw you, and long past the time I take my final breath."

Tears prick at my eyes, his words striking deep, an anchor tethering me to this moment. I suck in a breath, steadying myself as I brush my lips over his. "And I you. Not just in this moment, not just in this life—but in all the ones that come after."

His arms tighten around me, but I refuse to let him take control. I push him back, guiding him onto his elbows, my body pressing him down. His muscles flex beneath me, a struggle between instinct and surrender, but I don't give him the choice. My nails scrape down his chest, leaving a burning trail in their wake.

A deep groan rumbles from his throat. His head tips back against the bed, lips part, and breaths come out ragged. His jaw is tight, the veins in his neck straining as if he's barely holding himself together—and gods above, the sight of him like this, undone and desperate, makes me ache with power.

I thread my fingers through his hair, gripping tight as I pull his face close—close enough to feel his breath hitch, to taste the anticipation lingering between us. My mouth hovers just above his, the barest brush of a tease.

"Hands off," I murmur.

Then I drag my tongue along the sharp line of his jaw, slow and claiming, savouring the tremble that rips through his body beneath mine.

"You don't move them... you don't touch me," I whisper against his skin, "unless I say so."

He surges forward, mouth angling to claim mine in a kiss, but I pull back just in time, a wicked smile tugging at my lips.

"Ah, ah..." I murmur, voice like velvet and fire. "Hands and lips... off limits."

The denial lands like a lash. He lets out a primal sound—half growl, half moan—and the sheer depth of it sends a jolt through me. My nipples tighten in response, betraying just how much his desperation is feeding my own.

I press my lips to his ear, my breath a wicked caress. "Now tell me," I breathe, "what you want. What you need. What you *crave*."

His voice rasps against my skin. "I want you to ride me, mo ghrá. Take me deep, stretch yerself around me, make me feel the squeeze of that perfect cunt until I'm lost in you. I want to feel you drench me, want you to squeeze me so tight I cannae think of anythin' but how good it feels to be buried inside you."

I shift, placing both of my hands on his outstretched thighs. I press my slick heat against his length, teasing him as I roll my hips, savouring the tortured groan that rumbles from his throat. "I love when you take me," I murmur, voice thick with need. "When you fill me until I'm stretched tight around you. Until I'm drenched and ruined for anything but this."

I feel crazed, driven by a need so consuming that it eclipses all sense of propriety. "I want your cock to fill me until I can scarcely breathe."

His breath shudders out of him. His eyes are dark—molten heat and restraint—watching me like a man on the edge.

"Aye," he grits, his voice rough and nearly feral. "And I'm hangin' by a bloody thread." His brogue thicker now, like it's unravelling with him.

I roll my hips again, deliberately slow, dragging myself across the thick length of him with enough friction to draw a low, tortured groan from his throat. His hips jerk, seeking more, but I lift myself just enough to deny him.

"Ye're testin' my patience, you wicked little minx. Do that again and I'll have you on your back before you can finish another sentence."

I let out a soft laugh, pleased by the way his control slips beneath my hips. "Easy, there," I whisper, dragging my nails lightly down his chest. "I'm just sitting here..."

"Triona," he growls, my name a warning, a plea, a reminder that he's seconds away from snapping

But I don't relent.

Instead, I shift again—rolling my hips with more pressure this time, slow but devastating, and his breath catches violently. The muscles in his thighs twitch under me.

"You're shaking," I whisper. "So close to breaking. I can feel it."

His hands twitch, trembling with restraint, and I see him bite down on a curse.

"I want you," he growls, like the effort to hold himself still is fraying at the edges.

I pause, heart stammering beneath the intensity of his gaze. There's something unholy in it—wild and reverent, all-consuming.

I reach for his face, brushing my thumb across his cheekbone, and press soft kisses along his jaw. Then I lean in, my mouth barely grazing the shell of his ear.

"Let go," I whisper, then softly nip at his earlobe and neck. "You can touch me now."

He moves in a flash, gripping my waist to pull me up as he aligns himself. The thick, aching length of him sliding through my slickness, teasing me, tormenting me. My breath hitches as I feel the broad head press against my entrance, a delicious, torturous pressure.

As he pushes inside, a moan escapes my lips at the exquisite stretch, the delicious fullness felt by him sheathing himself to the hilt inside my aching quim.

"Tri," he growls, desire thick in his voice. "Ye're a vision. A goddess made flesh."

I lift my hips eagerly, driving down onto him and taking him to the limit of my body's pleasure. We both cry out at the exquisite sensation, his length stretching and filling me in a way that blurs my senses.

With a sensual rhythm, I move, rolling my hips in a motion that has us both gasping with pleasure. Finn's hands roam my body, caressing my breasts and tweaking my sensitive nipples, sending sparks of desire racing through my veins. I lean forward, bracing my hands on his broad chest as I ride him harder, faster, chasing the building ecstasy.

"Gods, Triona," he grunts, his voice thick, his hips surging upward as he thrusts harder, deeper. "Ye're takin' me so beautifully—squeezin' me like you never want to let me go. Like you were made for this... made for me."

I gasp as he lifts me slightly, nearly pulling me off him before slamming me back down, burying himself inside me again with a force that sends waves of pleasure crashing through me. My nails rake over his broad shoulders as I cling to him, frantic, overwhelmed.

Each thrust sends shockwaves of bliss radiating through my core, the friction exquisite, the heat unbearable. My peak is rising fast, the pressure coiling, winding tighter, tighter—

"Don't stop," I beg, my voice breaking on a moan. "Finn, I'm so close..."

"Ride me, Triona," he commands, his fingers biting into my hips as he takes control, driving into me with a fervour that makes my vision blur. "Take yer pleasure from me. Drench my cock."

Our bodies move in perfect synchronisation, our passion reaching new heights with each thrust. His hand finds its way between us and he creates an even more intense rhythm that only he knows how to master. Circling my swollen clit with knowing fingers, he drives me closer and closer to the edge of pure euphoria.

His mouth claims mine in a punishing kiss, swallowing my cries as his hips piston faster, rougher, claiming me in every way imaginable. I shatter with a wail, my release flooding through me in violent, breathtaking waves, my body clenching around him as I convulse in his grasp.

"Triona!" he roars, his rhythm stuttering, his thrusts turning frantic. A ragged shout tears from his throat as he jerks inside me, his seed spilling deep, filling me with his heat as he groans against my lips.

We collapse together, a tangle of limbs and sweat-slicked skin, our bodies still trembling with the aftermath. My heart races, my breath uneven, my soul alight with something more than just passion—something infinite.

"You were made for me," he murmurs, his voice hoarse, sated. "Just as I was made for you."

In his arms, I am remade—body, heart, and soul.

I take a deep breath, smoothing my hands down the snug fighting leathers that are just as beautiful now as the day they were when I last wore them. Gifted to me by one of the best men I will ever have had the privilege of knowing. I feel the weight of his love and his belief in me settles over my shoulders like armour. It takes all my strength not to let my emotions show as I step onto the deck.

Finn's eyes soften when he sees me, and he nods, approval glimmering in his gaze. Callan's voice is soft when he speaks. "They look right on ye, lass." His words strike something deep within me, and I nod, unable to communicate past the lump in my throat.

Finn and Callan have changed into finer clothing. Finn's usually rough attire has been replaced with a tailored coat and clean, dark trousers, while Callan wears a sharp waistcoat over his shirt, its deep green fabric catching the light. They both look uncharacteristically polished, the effort clearly made to ensure we can blend in if necessary.

I can't help but smirk as I turn to Callan. "You know, you'd find a wife easily enough if you dressed like that more often."

Callan snorts, rolling his eyes but not denying it. "Aye, and deal with the headaches that come with it? Absolutely not."

Then I glance at Finn, my smirk widening. "I might just have to carry a beating stick around with me. You look *ravishing*."

Callan groans, running a hand over his face. "Please feckin' don't."

Finn smirks, mischief dancing in his eyes. "Lucky for you, my heart's already claimed by a doe-eyed beauty with the most irresistible lips. Stands about, oh, yay high—" he gestures toward me, a playful glint in his gaze. "Have you seen her? Impossible to miss—she's absolutely breathtaking."

Before I can even muster a response, my cheeks burn at his words, and I feel my heart stutter. A giddy warmth swells in my chest, and I whisper, "You're impossible." Finn's smirk deepens. Ignoring Callan's exaggerated groan, he steps closer, cups my face with both hands, and pulls me into a deep, searing kiss. His lips claim mine with a warmth that sends heat rushing through me.

The ship creaks and groans as it eases into the bustling harbour at North Wall Quay in Dublin, pulling me from that kiss. Finn kisses the tip of my nose before pulling me by the hand to the rail of the ship. The salty tang of the sea blends with the earthy aroma of the city. I lean over the railing, my braid whipping in the wind as scan the docks for a familiar face. Finn stands close behind me, his hand resting instinctively near the hilt of his sword, while Callan keeps his usual brooding silence, his sharp eyes darting through the crowd below.

"See anything, Doe?" Finn asks, his voice low and steady, though his knuckles whiten slightly on the rail.

"What, no *Little*?" I say with a mock pout.

He chuckles as he pushes my lip in with a pointer finger. "That would be the part you catch—ye're not so little anymore."

His voice dips in a way that sends heat curling low in my belly. My breath stills as his fingers trail from my lip, down my throat, pausing just at the hollow above my collarbone. He leans in, his breath warm against my ear.

"Ye've done things to me that only a woman would do, mo ghràdh. And I've touched you in ways that left my hands burned into yer skin. Made you tremble, beg, and whisper my name like it was a prayer." His thumb sweeps over the spot, his voice turning husky. "And you still think ye're little?"

A shiver runs through me, my pulse hammering against his touch. I should step away, I should say something sharp and teasing, but his words have taken root. My fingers twitch at my sides, aching to reach for him.

He smirks, watching me unravel. "Aye, I thought not." He presses a lingering kiss to the side of my neck before pulling away. The moment lingers between us, charged and unspoken, before I force myself to turn, my attention shifting to the world beyond us.

"I see nothing out of sorts," I murmur breathlessly, trying to take my mind off the heat coursing through me as I narrow my eyes against the morning sun. The docks pulse with life—fishmongers calling out their wares, sailors maneuvering crates of goods, and children weaving through the bustle with peals of laughter. Yet amidst the ceaseless movement, no eyes linger on us, no furtive glances give away our presence—a quiet uncertainty that is neither reassuring nor foreboding.

The gangplank is lowered with a resounding thud, and we descend, our boots clattering against the wooden boards. I adjust my cloak, the rich fabric a subtle marker of my status, while Finn's eyes remain vigilant, scanning every movement around us. Callan brings up the rear, his imposing presence a silent warning to anyone considering mischief.

Just as we reach the bottom of the gangplank, a figure emerges from the crowd. Unlike the rugged sailors and harried merchants, this person is immaculate. The woman's fair hair cascades down her back, her dark eyes glow with an inner light that resembles amber when the sun reflects off the surface.

The cloak draped around her shoulders is a deep violet hue, striking against the surrounding scenery, and clasped together by a silver raven.

"Lady Triona," the woman says, her voice warm yet commanding, like the earth itself speaking in quiet authority. It carries the weight of ages, yet holds an undertone of nurturing comfort. "I have long waited for this day."

"You have me at a disadvantage," I reply, my tone guarded. "You know my name, but I don't believe we've been introduced."

She laughs, the sound light and melodic, yet it carries a gravity that seems to echo through the air. "I would not expect your memory to hold the face of one you met as an infant," she says, her gaze softening with a hint of something deeper—affection, perhaps, or nostalgia. "But I have not forgotten you. I am Dana," she continues, inclining her head slightly. "And how you have grown, Triona. You look so much like your parents—your father's strength and your mother's grace are both in you."

Before I can respond, Callan steps forward, his brows knitting tightly. "Ye'll forgive me if I'm not keen to trust a stranger at their word," he challenges, his tone edged with suspicion.

"Callan," Finn says, his voice steady but firm, "trust her judgment." He glances at me, his gaze softening. "She guides us. We follow."

His faith in me doesn't just uplift me—it gives me a profound sense of freedom, a validation I didn't realise I craved. Gratitude swells inside me, confirming what I've always known: Finn will *always* be my strongest ally. One I can rely on no matter where this path takes us.

Callan exhales slowly, but the tension in his shoulders doesn't fully leave. His eyes vacillate between Finn and me, filled with a hesitation I recognise well. It's not distrust—it's the burden of someone who's carried too much for too long.

I step closer, placing a gentle hand on his upper chest. "It's okay if you need more time to catch up to how Finn feels," I say genuinely.

Callan's gaze softens, and his hand lifts to cover mine, his grip gentle. "I'm already there," he assures. "I ken ye're wiser than I'll ever be. I do trust ye, Triona. I'll work on showin' ye that."

He squeezes my hand lightly, and for a moment, I feel the weight of his pain lift, replaced by something stronger—hope.

"My, my," Dana purrs, her voice like velvet, rich and sinuous. "Warriors, these two are indeed," she intones, her dark eyes glinting with wicked amusement. Her lips curve into a slow smile, the kind that promises secrets untold. "You would marvel at the art of balancing such forces. Two men, working each with rigour and grace, at once. The push, the pull, the rhythm... it is a symphony of power, my darlings, one I conduct with flawless precision."

My cheeks flush hot, as something primal stirs in my chest. The possessiveness surges, untamed and undeniable. I reach for Finn's hand, my fingers curling firmly around his. "Finn is accounted for, and you'd do well by yourself to remember that," I say, the declaration vibrating with finality.

Dana's expression is one of mischievous fulfilment. "Ah," she murmurs, a knowing smile tugging at her lips. "As I suspected. It is as it should be."

She laughs, her tone silky and unapologetic. "Excuse my playfulness. Word from Mannie suggested it would be delightful to stir the two of you. I see he was not wrong." The mention of Mannie's name sends a jolt through me, my shock clear in the way my hand tightens on Finn's.

Her tone shifts to something close to awe. "He was also correct when he spoke of your fiery spirit. How it shapes you, strengthens you, and readies you."

"Ready for what?"

"Perhaps this is a conversation best continued somewhere more private. Where truths can breathe freely, yes?"

"You know Mannie?"

Dana's laughter ripples through the air, a melody that seems to both charm and unnerve. Heads turn, captivated by her presence. "Someone had to teach him how to weave threads of fate. And what a student he was." Her gaze lands on me, sharp and seeing. "But I see he has left the most tangled knot for you to unravel."

35

BARED BENEATH THE STARS

Triona

"**C**ome on, then. I have already sent for the horses."

Dana doesn't wait for a reply. Her violet cloak sweeps behind her as she steps gracefully into the bustling streets.

"Good luck with that," I mutter. "There's no way Shadow's going to—"

But as I glance back, the words catch in my throat.

Shadow is, to my utter disbelief, standing calmly at the end of the dock, reins held loosely by a young man. He's tall, lean, with striking features that carry the unmistakable resemblance of Eamon and Saoirse—long, copper-toned hair and a smirk that borders on knowing. His fingers move with quiet confidence as he strokes Shadow's neck, and the stallion—my impossible, stubborn stallion—actually leans into the touch.

My jaw drops. "That beastly wee bastard. He's acting downright obedient," I mutter under my breath.

Callan snorts behind me, a rare laugh rumbling in his chest. "I've officially seen it all."

Finn chuckles beside him, then leans in, his breath warm against my ear. "Should I be worried he didnae even take to me that quickly?"

I blink at him, then glance back at Shadow—who's still nuzzling into the stranger's touch like an overgrown lapdog. "Honestly?" I say, deadpan. "I'm not even sure."

Finn hums, feigning offense. "Come now, before I develop a complex."

"I wouldn't dwell on it," I say, nudging him with my elbow. "You're still doing better than most."

We fall into step, weaving our way through the throngs of merchants and sailors to catch up to Dana. The noise of the docks fades as Dana leads us down narrower, quieter lanes, the cobblestones uneven beneath our feet.

We arrive at a modest-looking tavern tucked far from the bustling principal streets. Its weathered sign swings faintly in the breeze, creaking on rusted hinges. Despite its unassuming exterior, there's an air of mystery about the place, as though it has seen secrets unfold within its walls.

Dana pushes the door open with a light touch, revealing a modest interior, lit primarily by a low-burning hearth casting flickering shadows across the room.

"This will suffice," she says, her voice low and resonant. "Come, Triona. There is much to discuss, and time is not on our side."

Once inside, I take a moment to admire Dana. The light of the hearth catches her features in a way that makes her seem otherworldly. Up close, she is breathtaking—youthful beauty that's sharp and undeniable. There is a warmth to her presence, something that feels like home, like safety, yet it is paired with an undeniable authority. It is that quality, that quiet power, that reminds me of Mannie. The same timelessness woven from the same thread.

"I trust, since you made landing in Dublin, that word of what lies ahead befell your ears—that you must journey beneath the Hill of Tara to collect the Stone of Fál."

Her tone is layered with both command and care. "The path within is no gentle road, but it will reveal what must be seen."

Then her gaze settles on me with solemn finality. "This charge falls to you and Finn... alone."

She turns to Callan, tone softening. "You will stay behind. You're not meant to walk this path—not yet."

Callan stiffens, his jaw tightening with restrained protest. "Why?" he demands, his voice rough but not unkind.

Dana steps closer to him, placing a hand on his shoulder. "The mound recognises only those tied to its power. It is not a question of worth, but of design. The magic within allows those chosen by the tome itself. The stone has *chosen* Triona, and she has *chosen* Finn. So they are tied to the stone in ways you are not."

Dana pauses, allowing reasoning to take root. "Let me explain the intricacies of our world," she begins, her tone warm yet firm. "Magic is not something to be taken lightly, nor is it limitless. It is drawn from the primal forces of nature, woven into the fabric of reality by the great celestial bodies—the Sun, the Moon, the Stars, and the Sea. These forces provide a constant flow of power, but only those attuned to their rhythms can access it."

She shifts closer. "There are five primary schools of magic, each bound to a different source. Solar Magic channels the Sun's radiance, granting healing and empowerment. Lunar Magic draws from the Moon's phases, controlling water and dreams. Stellar Magic harnesses the power of the stars, allowing for prophecy and celestial communication. Oceanic Magic calls upon the ocean's currents, granting adaptability and the power of transformation. And finally, Primordial Magic—the rarest and most powerful of all—harnesses the full breadth of the natural world, drawing from all four elemental forces in perfect balance."

"Only three in all of history have ever wielded it," Dana continues, her voice quiet but resolute. "It is not a gift that can be learned, nor is it simply inherited. To command Elemental Magic requires more than skill—it demands an unbreakable bond with every force of nature, an innate harmony with the world itself. Those who possess it do not merely use magic; they *are* magic."

Dana's gaze sweeps over us, measuring our understanding before she continues. "Each school of magic follows distinct rituals, symbols, and traditions, guided by divine patrons among the Tuatha Dé Danann. The land itself reflects this connection—each region of Ireland is attuned to a specific type of magic, governed by its respective deity."

She pauses, letting the knowledge settle. "To wield magic, one must either be born with it, like the Tuatha Dé Danann, gifted it by one who already commands its power, or wield it through an object imbued with magic. But know this—magic is not a force to be used recklessly. It demands understanding, reverence, and, above all, balance."

Her expression grows eerie. "But there are forces—dark, greedy forces—that seek to steal magic. When magic is stolen or approached without welcome, it twists. It corrupts. The mound's magic is conscious. It is the oldest and strongest form of magic. Alive since the beginning of time. It knows when it is not respected, and it does not take kindly to those who attempt to approach without invitation or purpose. That is why this path is not yours to walk, my son. It's for your safety... and for theirs."

Callan bites down on his bottom lip, his arms crossed tightly over his chest. His fingers flex against his upper arms, tension rippling through him as his gaze darts to me, then to Finn, and back to Dana, hesitation clear. "So, ye're saying that if I tried..."

"It would reject you," Dana says simply. "And that rejection often comes at a heavy price. This is why there are those who wish to harm Triona. If they can control her, they could force her to act against her will, allowing them to take what they want from her. She has not yet fully come into her powers—she is weak, susceptible, easily manipulated."

"It is why Triona and Finn must do this alone. Your role is no less important. You are the one who will protect them from what waits beyond the mound. Protect the entry, guard the connection. That is your strength, and it is enough."

A cold knot forms in my stomach as I listen. My voice comes out quieter than I intend. "How can you all be so sure that I have been chosen for this?" I ask. "What if you're wrong? What if I don't have this ability? Or worse—what if the magic rejects me?"

Dana meets my gaze, steady and unwavering. "You will feel the draw, Triona," she says. "Before you ever reach for it, before you even think of using it, you will know. It will call to you."

Dana's gaze softens. "I know the trials you have all faced. What happened has shaped you, but it has also brought you here, with people at your side—people who would never wish you harm, who speak no falsities, and who will not abandon you in times of need."

I see understanding on Callan's face. Though reluctant, he nods slowly, his shoulders easing. "If it's for them, I'll stay behind."

She turns back to Finn and me, her voice gaining that divine resonance once more. "Inside, you will face what lies in your hearts and emerge stronger for it. The Stone will answer only to those who prove themselves worthy."

Dana reaches into the folds of her cloak and pulls out a rolled parchment tied with a thin, silver cord. She hands it to Finn, her expression solemn. "This map will guide you. It shows the path to the Hill of Tara, where you must enter, and where you will emerge. Study it carefully, for there will be no turning back once inside."

Dana's gaze darkens, though her voice remains steady. "The magic within the mound does not suffer hesitation. Once you enter, you must complete the journey, or it will reject you entirely. If that happens... the consequences will not be kind."

The weight of what lies ahead settles heavily on my shoulders. Yet, as I glance at Finn, his determination doesn't falter. His persistent presence, his quiet strength, radiates something abiding.

"What exactly is it inside me that makes this my task? And how do we know what I'm meant to find is truly there?" The words taste unpleasant, as if voicing them gives life to fear.

Dana's expression is brimming with warmth, the kind often given maternally. "To have you here now is a gift from the gods themselves... because no one like you has been born in over four thousand years," she states.

"Your soul carries a spark of the divine—a connection to the old magic that has not existed in millennia. The Hill of Tara is not just a destination for you; it is a part of you, Triona. What lies within the mound has rested for all that time, but do not mistake its dormancy for weakness. The power within has never once faltered; no less powerful than the day it was hidden away. It is time for you to claim, shape, and wield it to protect others once more."

Dana lifts her hand and gently touches the centre of my chest, just above my heart. "I know, for you and so many others, you must see and feel for the truth to ring. The Stone will only awaken for one whose soul mirrors its origin," she says gingerly. "And when you step before it, it will know you, and you will feel its significance. That is how we prove it. No test, no trick—only truth. If you are who *I* believe you are, the Stone will answer."

As I turn her words over in my mind, I turn my gaze to Finn, who is studying the map. He glances at me, then at Dana.

"What's wrong?" I ask, stepping closer.

He hesitates, then says slowly, "I can... read each of these words."

Dana looks at Finn with a gleam in her eye. "Of course you can," she says softly. "It is written in the tongue of the old ones—Gaeilge in its purest form. Before men's destruction ever touched it."

Finn looks at the map again, his jaw tightening as he processes her words. "I've never spoken it a day in my life. How...?"

Dana's smile is faint but knowing. "The same spark that calls Triona to the Stone of Fál burns within you. It connects you to the truths hidden in this language—truths older than words themselves."

I look at the map, its symbols shimmering faintly, but nothing registers. "I cannot read it."

Dana's expression remains serene. "I cannot say what gifts will or will not awaken in you, Triona. Magic chooses its own time."

I meet Finn's eyes and smile tenderly. "See? I needed you all along. You were always meant to be here by my side."

"Hard to argue with that," he murmurs, his voice laced with a heat that feels poised to stoke my desire for him. "And yet, it's me who's grateful—you saved me from myself that day in my bedroom, when I thought I was beyond savin'."

I reach out and place a hand on his upper arm, giving it a light squeeze, feeling the warmth and strength beneath my fingers. The sharp intensity of his gaze gives way to something tender.

From behind us, Callan clears his throat. "Suppose it's a good thing I didnae impede savin' the world," he mutters, his eyes snapping briefly to mine.

Before I can respond, Finn—without even looking at him—says, "Our love isnae fragile. You never stood a chance. 'Sides, it was nothin' a few good punches couldnae fix."

I swat him lightly on the chest, and he huffs a quiet laugh, the sound curling low in his throat. When I glance over at Callan, his arms are crossed, posture stiff as ever—but there's a small smile teasing the corners of his mouth. The apology is there, clear in his eyes, even if it never makes it to his lips.

With a deep breath, I turn back to Dana, ready to receive whatever comes next.

She steps closer, her violet cloak sweeping around her. She gestures for Finn to lay the map down on the table, and points toward a narrow path leading away from the tavern. "The way to Tara begins here," she says, pointing to a road leading inland going northwest.

"Just beyond the last farms of County Dublin. You'll follow the old way that winds toward Navan—keep to it past the rise at Skryne, and you'll see Tara greet you from the land like a crown."

Her finger drifts along the path, then pauses over a faint marking.

"The door to the mound answers only to the sun," she continues. "It must be approached at the precise moment—no sooner, no later. When the sun strikes the threshold at its peak angle, it will reveal itself to those it deems worthy."

Dana straightens, her dark eyes locking onto each of us. "The journey will take ten to twelve hours... *on foot*," she says, her voice firm but warm. "You'll need to leave much behind to move as quickly—and as quietly—as possible. There are paths that will help you avoid unnecessary attention, but time is not on your side. Stay together, and remember—magic does not favour hesitation."

The thought of leaving our horses behind—entrusting them to practical strangers—twists in my chest. Shadow is more than just a horse—he's mine. Stubborn, temperamental, half-wild... but mine.

"My—Shadow..." I murmur, voice low. "He's not one to take kindly to strangers. He'll hate being left behind."

Dana's lips curl into a faint, knowing smile. "I have dealt with my fair share of beasts, Triona. He will be well cared for. Focus on the path ahead—he will be waiting for you when the time comes."

Something stirs in my gut—not dread, but instinct. A quiet knowing, like the world is whispering, they're safe. They'll be here when we all come back.

I nod slowly, though it costs me.

We pause at the edge of the tavern courtyard, where the three of them wait—Meara shifting her weight anxiously, Aisling flicking her tail, Shadow standing uncharacteristically still.

Without a word, Callan steps forward and presses his forehead to Meara's, his hand brushing her mane. Finn runs a palm along Aisling's neck, murmuring something low and private into her ear. She nudges him in response, her breath puffing warm and soft against his cheek.

I approach Shadow last. His ears flick toward me before I say a word, and when I reach out, he leans into my touch like he knows exactly what this is. I press my forehead gently to his, fingers curling into his thick mane.

"Be good," I whisper. "Don't scare the poor lad too badly."

He huffs, almost like he understands, and my heart aches with the force of it.

We leave the tavern behind, taking only what we can carry on our person. The street outside is near empty, the hush complete but for our footsteps tapping against worn cobblestones. The silence feels foreboding, broken only by the faint rustle of Dana's cloak as she leads the way forward, to the trail's edge.

She turns to face us. "This is where I leave you," she says, her voice low and sonorous.

"As you draw nearer to Tara, you'll find the land grows quiet—no birdsong, no footsteps but your own. No soul in sight. It is best if you part ways with them before that point and wait just beyond Tara's reach. When Triona has done what is necessary, and returned whole, you need to be there waiting for her."

She pauses, waiting for Callan's silent agreement. He nods, and she continues.

"For millennia, many have been tempted to claim the power inside. None were worthy. Many become twisted by the magic's wrath, their essence reshaped into what they fear most. Some become shadows of their former selves, cursed to guard the mound they sought to plunder. Others..." Her voice lowers to a hush. "Others were claimed by the earth itself. Their torment endless. Their cries are now only wind among the stones."

A beat of silence.

"You will hear their whispers and warnings... it is best that you ignore them. Trust in yourselves, and in each other. The path ahead is yours to walk, but know this: you are not alone. What you carry—who you are—will guide you to the answers you seek."

The bustling chaos of the Dublin docks fades behind us as we leave the city, its shouts and clamour dissolving into the distant hum of trade and sea breeze. Callan follows some distance back, his stance protective. Though Dana said we'd walk alone soon enough, for now he shadows us in silence. I'm grateful for his presence, brief though it may be.

The air feels fresh out here—cooler, sharper, laden with a heaviness that defies explanation. I glance back at the distant sprawl of Dublin, where trade and humanity thrive. It feels almost like a memory now, something too loud and bright to belong to this hushed, ancient road.

I turn to Finn, who has the map unfurled once again. He traces the symbols with a light fingertip, the arcane lines shimmering in the low light.

"It says we should keep northwest," he mutters, half to himself, "and cross the river at the shallows." He glances up, brow knitted in concentration. "We should stop near

Dunshaughlin tonight. Then reach the Hill of Tara by early light tomorrow." Our silence is the answer he seeks.

We fall into step beside one another, our strides matching as the world narrows to the path ahead.

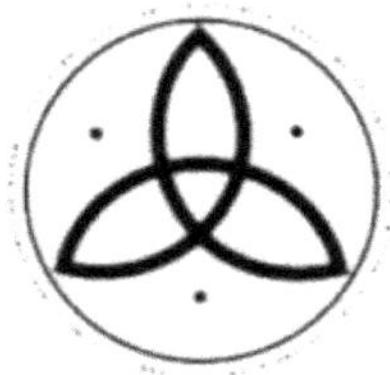

We haven't spoken in some time, but the silence is easy. Companionable. The kind that doesn't press, doesn't need to be filled.

The hush around us deepens, wrapping the world in stillness, and a warm glow stirs in my chest. It feels as if I am following a thread that's always existed, one that now tugs me forward. I can finally fully feel the pull.

"I can feel it," I murmur. "The pull. Faint at first... but it's growing."

Callan's footsteps slow behind us. "So, it is real," he says, voice low, cautious. "And we can confirm that now."

I nod. "Aye. No question."

He exhales through his nose, tension bristling in the sound. "Then the two of ye should go ahead."

We pause, turning toward him. His eyes sweep the horizon, as if reading something in the air that the rest of us cannot see. A strange stillness settles around us—thick, expectant.

"I can feel the unrest settlin' into me," he mutters. "Like the ground's turned restless beneath our feet. I think we've reached the point where I need to part—per Dana's word."

My heart twists at the thought of leaving him behind. But there's no fear in his expression—only calm resolve. His jaw is set, his gaze unflinching. He's already accepted what must be done.

"I'll be fine," he says, reading the worry on my face. "Keep yer heads on. I'll be there to greet ye when ye're done. Aye?"

Before I can respond, Finn steps forward, his expression firm. "Callan, can we talk? Just the two of us."

Callan's brows furrow, but he nods and gestures to the side of the path.

Finn leans close to me, his voice a muted whisper. "I want to say one last thing to Callan now that things have settled between us." Before stepping away, he presses a gentle kiss to my cheek, his touch warm and reassuring.

He follows Callan, and they stop just out of earshot. From where I stand, their low voices are a murmur against the backdrop of rustling leaves.

Turning my attention to the beautiful countryside greenery around us, I let my eyes wander over the rolling hills and clusters of wildflowers swaying in the breeze. The distant hum of a stream blends with the low cadence of their voices, offering a tranquil contrast to the tension of the moment. I try to focus on the serenity of the landscape, giving the men their privacy, but a small shout from Callan has me whipping back around.

I catch a flash of something on Callan's face—a raw emotion that vanishes the instant his eyes meet mine, replaced by his usual composed demeanour. Callan places both arms on Finn's shoulders, his grip firm and steady. I quickly turn back around, determined to offer them privacy once more, and walk a little farther out of earshot, letting the greenery pull my focus again.

Callan eventually calls out for me, his voice carrying a warmth that draws me back. "Triona," he says, his tone softer than I'd expected. I turn in time for him to throw his arms around me and give me a hug.

"Stay safe, aye?" he murmurs against my hair.

"I will if you will," I reply, my voice steadier than I feel. I give him an equally commanding hug back, holding on tightly for a moment before stepping back to meet his steady gaze.

Callan looks past me to Finn, his eyes lingering a moment too long. Finn steps forward and holds out his arm. Callan hesitates for a fraction of a second, then clasps him firmly by the forearm. Their grips tighten, and Callan leans in slightly. "Ye watch yerself in there," he says, his voice low and strained, the words carrying a depth that makes my chest tighten.

Finn's jaw sets, his voice steady. "I will. I promise."

"Ye're one of the best men I ken, Finn."

Callan's gaze doesn't waver, but something shifts beneath it—like stone groaning beneath pressure, silent but undeniable. He inclines his head once, solemn and spare, and releases Finn's arm with a grip that lingers—not in hesitation, but in farewell.

He straightens. For a breath, he studies us both with a stillness that hums, as though he's sealing the moment in the marrow of his bones.

Then, without a word, he turns. The fading light carves shadows along his back as he walks, each step quieter than the last until only the curve of his silhouette remains, swallowed by the dusk.

Finn and I watch him go, the sound of his boots on the dirt fading into the stillness. I feel an ache in my chest, but Finn steps closer, his hand brushing against mine. "He'll be all right," he says smoothly.

"We should make camp for the night," Finn murmurs, his voice low, sure, yet threaded with something more tender than command. His gaze lifts to the sky, where the first stars begin to blink into being.

"If it all changes tomorrow," he pauses, as though shaping the next words with care, "then I want this night with you. One more, beneath the stars, where I learned what it meant to love you. I want to hold you here until dawn—no past, no future. Just this."

His words don't simply land in my chest—they settle like stone in the riverbed, anchoring me against the current of all that's unknown. I nod, unable to speak, and let him take my hand.

When we stop, Finn kneels to gather kindling with practiced ease, each motion quiet and sure. I busy myself with the tent, my hands working more from memory than thought.

When I return to his side, the tension in his shoulders eases. He glances back at me, eyes unreadable for a beat, before a faint, wistful smile tugs at the corner of his mouth. With the fire crackling low and the tent secured, Finn lays a cloak beside the flame, then lowers himself and pats the space beside him—an invitation not just to sit, but to stay.

As I settle, the sky opens above, vast and endless, the stars painting stories in the dark. Finn's arm slips around me, drawing me closer until I can feel the steady rise and fall of his chest, a rhythm that steadies my racing heart. He leans his head slightly against mine, and for a long moment, we sit in silence, the pressure of tomorrow dulled.

"I dinnae want this night to end," he admits, his voice barely more than breath. His words carry the raw honesty of someone who knows time is fleeting.

I turn to look at him, the firelight catching in his eyes, and I see something there that makes my throat tighten—a depth of feeling that goes beyond words.

"Then let's make it ours," I say, resting my hand over his. He smiles, and it's a small, fragile thing, but it's enough.

Finn leans in, his lips brushing mine with a tenderness that steals the breath from my lungs. The fire crackles softly beside us, its warmth a quiet echo to the heat building between our bodies. His arms gather me close, strong and sure, as he shifts over me—his hands moving with aching care, tracing the lines of my face, my neck, my shoulders.

Above us, the stars seem to shimmer brighter, as if stirred by the gravity of this moment. Their distant light pulses in time with our breaths, silent witnesses to the quiet unravelling of something sacred. Finn's touch is reverent, almost worshipful—as though he's committing me to memory, reading every sigh, every soft gasp like scripture.

I match him beat for beat, threading my fingers through his hair and pulling him closer, needing the press of him, the weight of this closeness. If time is only lending us this fleeting sliver of forever, then I'll anchor us here—together, in this breathless now.

Suddenly, Finn rises, his strong arms wrapping around me as he lifts me with effortless grace. He says nothing—he doesn't have to. The firelight casts gold and shadow across the canvas of the tent as he carries me inside.

He sets me down with gentle adoration, as though I'm something sacred, then leans in, his breath brushing my ear. "Tonight," he murmurs, voice low and rough, "ye're not wearin' a thing. Just you and me, bared beneath these stars."

I pull him closer, ready to lose myself completely in the safety of his embrace, in the fleeting forever of this night.

A soft chuckle escapes me as I glance at the canvas overhead. "We're not *technically* beneath the stars."

Finn flashes me a wicked grin. "Aye, well—I'd rather not risk some poor bastard glimpsin' you and losin' my head. I'm not in the habit of sharin' what's mine."

My breath hitches at the possessive edge in his voice, at the way he says *mine*. I lean up, catch his bottom lip gently between my teeth, and give it a playful tug before murmuring against his mouth, "Good. Because I've no intention of being anyone else's."

There are no words between us now, only the unspoken promises carried in every glance, every caress.

The sounds that rise between us are music born of heat and reverence—his low bellows of pleasure, answer the breathless whimpers he draws from my lips. They clash and mingle in the tent's hush, raw and unfiltered—masculine hunger and feminine surrender, strength and softness entwined.

Each time I gasp, he answers with a growl. Each moan he tears from me becomes a vow he returns in sound alone—rough, reverent, and wrecked with need. The deeper I draw him in, the deeper he falls, until we're no longer two voices, but one song—aching and beautiful and divine in the way only love can be.

Together, we let the rest of the world fall away, leaving only the sky, the stars, and the love that has bound us long before we knew to name it.

36

HEART IN THE DARK

Finn
Sunday, 22 June 1823
Dunshaughlin, Ireland

Morning arrives with a softness that feels at odds with the intensity of the night before. Pale sunlight filters through the thin canvas of our tent, casting warm, muted shapes across Triona's sleeping features. She lies curled on her side, her hair cascading over the blanket, her breathing steady and calm.

I take a moment to study her—the way her lashes rest against her cheeks, the subtle curve of her lips, the peaceful expression that softens her face. She looks so serene that I almost thank the gods above for granting us this delicate slice of time.

Eventually, I shift away, careful not to wake her. A chill lingers in the air, and gooseflesh rises along my skin as I step into the morning hush. The clearing is wrapped in stillness, broken only by distant birdsong and the soft whisper of leaves overhead.

The fire has dwindled to a whisper, its ashes faintly glowing. I kneel beside it, feeding kindling into the embers, coaxing the flame back to life. The warmth creeps over my hands, a welcome anchor in this quiet moment before the world begins again.

Behind me, there's the soft rustle of the tent's flap. I turn to see Triona emerging, her hair tousled from sleep, eyes still heavy-lidded. She offers me a small, wry smile that sends a gentle warmth through my chest.

She settles beside me, stretching her arms overhead with a low groan. "Morning," she murmurs, her voice soft and husky.

"Mornin'." My gaze shifts to the sky, which has lightened into a pale, cloudless blue. "We should get moving soon if we're to make Tara by midday."

She nods, her expression turning serious as she follows my line of sight. For a moment, we sit in comfortable silence, the weight of our task palpable. Then, with a quiet exhale, I lean in to press a tender kiss to her temple. Wordlessly, we pack away what's left of our camp.

After a quick breakfast of dried fruit and bread, I unfurl the map again. The shimmering symbols trace a winding path northwest through low-lying hills and gentle farmland.

There's something different about this land—an ancient hush that seems to listen. Stones, old trees, even the faint winding streams we occasionally follow: they all carry an agelessness, as though the ground itself holds memory. With every step, an odd sense of belonging coils in my gut, whispering that we're moving toward a place meant for us.

Beside me, Triona strides with determined purpose. I steal another glance at the map, unsettled by how naturally I can read it—the symbols speaking to me in a language I never formally learned. As if sensing my thoughts, Triona meets my gaze, her brow creasing with concern.

"You all right?" she asks quietly.

I offer a small smile. "I suppose I am. Just... marvellin' at everything."

She exhales a soft laugh. "We're both far from the people we were a week ago, let alone a month ago, aye?"

"Aye," I echo, letting that single word convey more than a string of sentences ever could.

As the sun stretches its golden fingers across the land, the world around us shifts—rolling fields give way to a wide sweep of low hills, each one rising and falling in gentle succession until they cradle a singular rise in the distance.

The Hill of Tara.

It doesn't tower like a mountain, nor cut the sky with jagged stone. It simply rests—majestic in its quiet, ancient in its bearing. As if the land bent to cradle it, shaped not by violence but by time itself.

Something tightens in my chest at the sight—a stirring both timeworn and strangely personal. It's as though the hill is calling forth memories I can't quite name. The wind sweeping across the hilltop grazes my cheeks with a cool touch, smelling of sun-warmed grasses and distant rain. I realise I've slowed, and beside me, Triona has stopped as well.

"There it is," I murmur, the words nearly stolen by the breeze.

She inhales softly. "The pull is strong," she says, her voice touched with awe. "Just as Dana described…"

The silence between us deepens. Not empty but full—of meaning, of memory, of whatever fate we're walking into.

At the base of the hill, a solitary stone stands—weatherworn, half-swallowed by the earth, but unmistakably deliberate. It hums, faintly. Not sound, exactly, but sensation. A resonance that vibrates through the soles of my boots, syncing to something buried in my bones.

I reach for Triona's hand. She doesn't hesitate. Our fingers intertwine, steadying and sure, as we crest the last gentle rise. And there—hidden until now by slope and shadow—waits the archway.

It isn't perched atop the hill as I'd imagined. It's etched into the side, nearly erased by time. Overgrown with moss, heather, and the creeping ivy of centuries, it might've remained hidden to anyone not drawn by the quiet summons of whatever slumbers within.

Together, we clear it away. Fingers creep through the damp moss, peeling it back in swaths. The stone beneath is cool and dark, patterned in lines we can barely decipher. When my hand brushes a smooth curve of etched spiral, I flinch—not from pain, but from a sudden pulse that travels up my arm.

A spark—not fire, not pain, but energy. Ancient and alive.

My breath snags. I jerk back slightly, eyes widening. Before I can say a word, I glance at Triona.

She's already looking at me.

Her hand is still pressed to the stone, and the shimmer in her eyes says she felt it too.

For a moment, we just stare at each other—unspoken bewilderment hanging between us like breath in cold air.

"Did that feel like…" I trail off.

She nods, slow and sure. "Aye. Like it… knew us."

We continue clearing, more deliberate now. Careful not to damage even a scrap of moss that might be more than it seems. The more we reveal, the clearer it becomes—the archway isn't just stone. It's carved in the shape of something familiar.

Braided spirals and knotted loops form its arch. Its lines glint faintly with gold-veined quartz, now catching the early morning sun in fleeting sparks of light.

"A crown," Triona murmurs, her voice barely audible. "Just as Dana said."

My throat goes dry.

She's right.

Not a threshold—an invitation. Not a passage—but a coronation. The mound doesn't just hold power. The archway shaped not like a door, but like a circlet.

It demands it be claimed—curved and knotted like a crown of woven stone, hidden in plain sight.

Ancient symbols curl along the lintel, etched deep into the stone—knots and spirals that almost writhe if you stare too long.

Triona steps closer, her breath quick. "Dana said we had to time it perfectly," she says, her voice thin with awe. "When the sun strikes just right."

The pull to the archway is exactly as Dana described. Not physical, but undeniable.

"And we'll need to speak the correct words to breathe life into it," I say aloud, more to myself than to her.

Her green eyes meet mine, and there's a steadfast determination in her eyes that gives me hope that this day will end in her victory.

We stand shoulder to shoulder before the archway. The hum in the air intensifies—no longer faint, but present, pulsing like a heartbeat beneath the earth.

Shapes that were once meaningless to my eyes now shimmer with clarity, forming words not written in any language I was ever taught—but one I somehow know all the same. They rise in my mind, unbidden. Ancient syllables spoken in the tongue of those who walked long before us. Words meant for me. Me alone.

I know what I must say.

My throat tightens. This is not mere speech—it is invocation.

And before us, the crown glows.

The path shall open thrice each day,
A path that once kept me locked away.
The first for hope, the second for might,
The third to reflect in the fading light.
Put to the test for strengths I possessed,
The same three you once named in me.

I speak the words aloud, etched across the stone in curling script.

Beside me, Triona huffs out air. "Three times a day?"

I nod, my gaze never leaving the softly pulsing arch. "Hope, might, reflection," I murmur. "They aren't just virtues... they're times of the day. Dawn for hope, zenith for might, and dusk for reflection."

She studies the ancient markings, brow furrowed. "But who's it referring to?" she asks. "Who speaks those words? Who passed those tests?"

We fall into silence, combing through every myth and whispered tale we've ever heard. The ones recited at hearths. The ones half-remembered in dreams.

Her lips part slightly as something clicks into place.

"Lugh," she breathes.

I turn toward her, caught off guard by the certainty in her tone.

"The God of the Sun," she says, eyes wide. "They called him master of all arts. The *shining* one. The champion who possessed every skill, and had to *prove* himself worthy of entry into their realm. Dana said the magic would respond to what is old... to what is *true*."

And suddenly, it all fits.

The sun. The timing. The trial.

"Aye," I murmur, the truth settling deep in my chest. "Lugh."

The archway pulses again—stronger now, as though the hill itself has heard and recognised its maker. The ancient lines shimmer faintly, not in response to force, but to understanding. To memory.

"Could it be—" she hesitates, voice lowering. "Could it be that a *god* laid this path with their own hands? And why? What purpose would drive such *power* to sleep?"

I shake my head slowly, not in doubt—but with certainty. "I dinnae ken, but I believe you're right. This magic... it moves with the sun itself. If it's as old as they said it is—if it's as old as it *feels*—then aye... I'd believe a god built it."

"Maybe it guards more than power? Maybe it guards what was once sacred," I say softly, "placed inside—something loved—left waitin' for the soul who once held it to return."

A hush settles between us, heavy with thought.

"I guess we'll find out soon enough..." I mutter. "The second moment draws near."

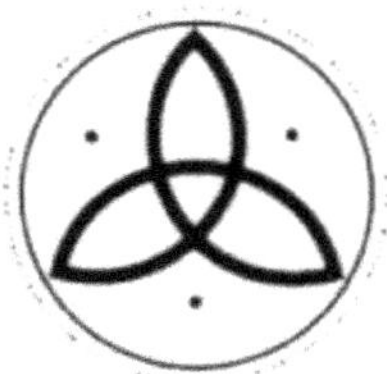

Only half an hour passes as the sunlight climbs steadily, warming the air and shrinking the surrounding shadows. As the sunlight reaches its zenith, a glowing inscription emerges below the first one, its letters pulsing faintly, as if alive. Triona gasps as the unfamiliar words appear:

A bond with whom remains unbroken, even by death's blade?

I read it aloud for her. The air hums with anticipation, the question hanging between us like the stillness before a storm. Triona's lips part, her voice soft. "A bond with a... soulmate?"

"*Anam Cara*," I say, surprised still by my ability to speak a language I've never learned. Triona repeats the words.

I read the second inscription that appears on the other side of the archway:

To the earth, give sacrifice true,
Only together shall the way open for you.

"It wants a word and a physical sacrifice..." Without hesitation at my declaration, she draws a dagger from her belt, its blade glinting faintly in the shifting light. Her hand trembles slightly as she grips the hilt, but her resolve is clear. I pull my dagger free as well, and we press the edges to our palms. A sharp sting cuts through the stillness, followed by the warmth of blood pooling in my hand.

Together, we step forward and press our palms to the stone. The mingling of our blood traces faint, glowing paths along the carvings. The hum deepens, a vibration reverberating through the earth itself.

We speak the answer together, our voices steady and sure.

"*Anam Cara.*"

The carvings ignite in a cascade of golden light, each glowing with an intensity that makes us shield our eyes. The light spills across the stones, painting the surrounding grass in hues of amber and gold. Shadows dance wildly on the hill's slopes, and Triona's face is bathed in the glow, her expression caught between awe and determination. The radiance pulses like the heartbeat of the earth itself. The ground beneath the arch trembles, and a soft gust of wind rushes past us, carrying the faint scent of something archaic.

The archway shudders, and slowly, impossibly, the stone shifts. The carvings twist and realign, forming a new pattern, and the once-solid entrance splits down the middle, revealing a dark passage beyond. A low, resonant hum emanates from the corridor, inviting yet foreboding. The air inside feels different—thicker, older.

I glance at Triona. She stands frozen, her eyes wide and bright as she stares into the passage. "It worked," she breathes, her voice barely audible.

I nod, swallowing the lump in my throat. "Aye. It did."

As we approach, warmth radiates from the doorway like a living presence. The golden light fades into a soft glow that illuminates the first few feet of the corridor. Beyond it lies only darkness, dense and impenetrable. The threshold's glow holds it at bay, a lingering line of magic dividing the day from whatever ancient gloom lies inside.

I look at her—*really* look at her—as her fingers tighten around mine. "Are you ready?"

She smiles, though it's faint and forced. "With you? Always."

Emotions upsurge in my chest—fear, determination, a tremor of anticipation. I think of Callan, waiting behind, determined to guard us from any threat that might strike from the outside. I think of Dana's words, of the spark she claims I carry. Whatever waits beyond, there's no turning back now.

We step forward together.

The air shifts immediately, cool and damp, carrying with it the faintest whisper of voices—too soft to make out, but unmistakably there.

Behind us, the stone groans.

Light shrinks to a sliver, then disappears entirely as the entrance seals with a deep, resonant thud. The sound rolls through the ground like the toll of a long-forgotten bell. A low vibration hums beneath our feet, settling into my bones.

Then silence. Thick. Final.

The path ahead is dark, and it belongs to us alone.

37

FINAL TOLL

Finn

The atmosphere within the mound consumes me. As I cross the threshold, silence folds inward, cool and dense, pressing against my senses until I feel hollowed out by it. The moment I step inside, something takes hold—a surge of sensation that crashes like a wave. My vision dips, then swells. For the briefest flicker, I see not my own hands, but someone else's: broader, sun-browned, brushing along these same walls centuries ago.

Voices echo along the edges of my hearing, indistinct but beckoning. The air pricks across my skin like static. Beside me, Triona stiffens. I feel her fingers tighten around mine. Neither of us speaks.

The corridor before us breathes with age. Stalactites descend from the ceiling, glistening with collected moisture, surfaces adorned with veins of luminescent quartz and streaks of pale malachite. Water drips in measured intervals, pooling in shallow basins carved into the stone floor.

Swirling patterns etched into the stone seem to shift when I look too long, curling like smoke. My heartbeat pounds in my ears, and somewhere beyond the stone, I feel—not a presence, but a memory. Not mine. Not fully.

Triona inhales sharply. I squeeze her hand. We move together, our steps soft and steady. The air thickens as we descend. The carvings glow faintly, pulsing in rhythm with something I cannot name. Blue, then green, then gold—like sunlight bleeding through water. The deeper we go, the more the energy folds in, like a tide pressing from all sides.

A whisper rises.

Not heard.

Felt.

My name—not *Finn*, but something older.

The corridor arcs downward. Moisture clings to the walls, and faint chanting slithers through the stone, voices overlapping. The further we walk, the more the map shifts in my hand. Lines glisten, moving like veins, guiding us forward as if remembering the path rather than revealing it.

As we round a bend, a draft rises from the depths of the mound, invading my senses with the scent of damp earth and ancient stone. My pulse speeds up as realisation dawns—we are no longer bound by mortal constraints.

We are being watched. Not by eyes, but by the very shape of the place.

I press forward, one hand clutching the map and the other never letting go of Triona's. She trembles beside me, her breaths uneven and shallow.

"Finn... if I fail—"

"There's not a chance that happens," I answer, my voice firm, leaving no room for doubt. I release her hand only briefly, turning to face her fully. My fingers trail to her cheek, warm against the coolness of the chamber, compelling her gaze to mine. My voice lowers, calm and unwavering. "Ye're not alone in this, Triona."

For a moment, she surrenders to the reassurance, leaning into my touch. Then, summoning the remnants of her courage, she surges onward. A ripple distorts the air before her, the walls themselves responding to her movement. A low-frequency hum reverberates, its resonance settling deep within me.

The temperature plunges as we advance, the impact of each step reverberating against the damp stone floor. Faint rivulets of water trickle along the walls, catching the residual light of the carvings that have thus far guided us. Unease coils within me, an instinctual warning gnawing at my resolve. The path beckons, yet it does so with the promise of something neither seen nor understood.

"It's too quiet," Triona whispers, her voice a fragile thread against the silence.

My breath stalls as we step around a slight bend—an entrance framed by two imposing stone pillars, their jagged curvature reminiscent of gaping fangs.

"Stay close," I murmur, my voice tempered and firm. Triona doesn't need to be told twice; her fingers tighten around mine, and we step into the consuming shadows together.

The walls press in, the passage narrowing until it barely accommodates two bodies abreast. Overhead, the ceiling vanishes into darkness, and the omnipresent hum of magic mutates into a deep, rhythmic resonance. It mimics a heartbeat—steady, ancient, immutable.

As we venture deeper, each corner reveals more of the same endless stone. The map's glowing lines guide us still, shifting subtly, as though adapting to the labyrinth. A prickle of unease runs down my spine as I notice the carvings have ceased. The once-etched walls are now smooth, featureless, their absence unsettling in its stark finality.

"Finn," Triona breathes, her voice laced with apprehension. I follow her line of sight—and freeze. The passage ends into a vast circular chamber, its walls lined with jagged stone spires. The entire space looks untouched by time, as though it has been sealed away from the world since its creation. The air is thick with an omnipresent sentience that feels woven into the very fabric of the stone.

There is only one way forward—through this chamber. Our only way out.

At the centre, atop a raised dais, a singular coffin dominates the space. It's hewn from black obsidian, the surface etched with grooves that glisten faintly in the dim light. An aura of condensed energy surrounds it, permeating the air with an unspoken warning.

To its right stands a solitary stone pillar, taller than me, its surface smooth except for a single jagged inscription that twists down its length. My eyes catch the words.

Recognition slams into me, unbidden.

These words—I have seen them before. Not in the waking world, but in the vision that has haunted me since the moment Mannie placed it into my mind.

The significance is now irrefutable.

My throat tightens as I step toward the monolithic pillar, its very presence exuding an almost otherworldly pull.

Resting atop is an artifact unlike any other—a sphere of flawless peridot, its luminescent core pulsing in synchrony with the chamber's resonance. The gentle oscillation of light refracts across the walls, a silent beacon embedded within the sanctum.

I have seen this.

I have *walked* this.

But not as myself. In dreams, in visions, always as someone else—someone who carved these lines—laid that stone to rest. A figure draped in sunlight, grief trailing behind like a shadow.

Triona steps forward, her gaze flashing between me and the weathered stone.

"What does it say?" she asks, her voice edged with anticipation.

"A great power lies within," I answer, keeping my voice steady as I pull a linen from my bag. "Something ancient... and waiting reclamation." Another lie rolling off my tongue with ease.

"What is this place?" Triona whispers, her voice trembling, steeped in awe. Her gaze flits between the coffin and the glowing artifact. "It doesn't feel real," she adds, her words hushed, as though afraid to disturb the sanctity of the room.

"It is real," I affirm. The low hum beneath our feet deepens, resonating within our bones. "And *aware*."

She takes a hesitant step forward, eyes locked on the black coffin at the centre of the dais. Her voice wavers. "Do you think..."

I turn to her fully, meeting her gaze without flinching. "We both know what this place is... and what's likely restin' in that coffin."

My fingers hesitate as I reach for the peridot sphere. Carefully, I enshroud it in the linen, veiling its radiance. I wait, expecting something to happen—a shift in the chamber, a surge of power, anything—but only the steady hum continues, vibrating faintly through the air.

I ensure the artifact is securely wrapped, its glow now imperceptible. Turning to Triona, I hand it to her with a resolute expression. "You need to keep it bundled until you get to Uisneach Hill.... Standing precisely where it tells you." I say, my voice firm. She nods, clutching it close. The chamber seems to breathe around us, watching silently as we prepare to leave.

The air shifts—subtle, but unmistakable. My pulse quickens as an unseen presence brushes against my senses, like a shadow stirring in the dark.

And then, a figure steps into the chamber from within the shadowy depths of the cave. The dim, shifting light catches on the green hue of his hair. His features are sharp as carved glass, angular and ageless.

"The concern with breaking a seal," he says, his voice smooth and venomous, "is that one must mend what is sullied. Otherwise you... well, I suppose I need not speak of consequences to you, being as apparent as they are."

His attire is as peculiar as his presence—intricate gold trim lines his cloak, its flowing layers resembling something torn from the pages of a centuries-old legend. The fabric bears arcane patterns and gilded accents, their craftsmanship hinting at power long forgotten. A gold-belted sash cinches his waist, and ornate bracers clink faintly as his arms cross.

The malevolent curve of his lips and piercing green eyes burn with a cold intensity, promising no mercy.

His echoing steps create an aura of silent menace, as though the very air around him bends to his will. He says nothing, waiting silently. I instinctively move in front of Triona, hands reaching to my sides as I pull both daggers free in one fluid motion. I grip them tightly, squaring my stance, ready for whatever comes next.

"Keep yer eyes off her," I growl, daring him to challenge me. The smirk on his face widens, but he does not shift his gaze.

"Who are ye?" I demand, my tone even despite the storm building in my chest.

An unsettling smirk tugs at the corner of his mouth. He remains silent, watching us with the patient menace of a predator savouring the moment before the pounce.

The air between us grows heavier with each passing second. A shuffle in Triona's step seems to embolden him. With calculated ease, he reveals a dark, jagged blade that appears to swallow the faint light around it. The air grows colder, the hum of magic shifting into a low, ominous thrum.

"I am Indech," he says smoothly. His eyes rest lazily on the weapon in his hand, and a dark chuckle escapes his lips. "Are you familiar with items such as this?" he asks, holding the blade aloft as though presenting a prize.

He tilts the blade, letting its dark surface glint faintly in the dim light. "A Void Dagger. Forged in the depths of chaos itself. It does more than cut—it severs the threads of magic, rends the shield of gods, and leaves even immortals to bleed in silence."

His mocking laugh echoes in the chamber as he continues, "No, you would not, living the *filthy* mortal lives you have been living. Ignorant of the powers that shape your fragile world."

His sneer deepens as he watches our reactions, the weight of his words sinking in. Before we even have a chance to question how he knows who we are, he lunges toward me—blade in hand, a jagged extension of his hostility. The weapon gleams with a sickly shimmer, its edge pulsing faintly with some corrupted magic.

I react on instinct, twisting just in time to avoid a strike that would have gutted me. The force of his swing rips through the air, sending a shockwave that rattles the cavern walls.

I parry with a flurry of swift strikes, my daggers flashing, but Indech moves like liquid shadow, moving through my attacks with inhuman grace. Sparks fly as steel clashes against the cursed blade, each impact sending tremors through my arms. The dagger seems to leave behind an unnatural void, the sense of magic draining with every swing.

He lunges again, vicious and precise. I roll back, landing in a crouch, only to find him already there. He twists mid-air, aiming the Void Dagger straight for my ribs. I barely bring both blades up in time, catching his strike in a cross-block. The impact reverberates through my arms and knocks me backward, boots scraping against stone as I fight to remain standing.

"Stop!" Triona's voice cuts through the clash of steel, trembling with urgency.

I glance toward her—but she's already in motion.

She throws herself between us without hesitation, driven by instinct more than strategy. Her blade comes up to parry, but Indech is faster. Too fast.

His blade, meant for me, catches her instead. The cursed dagger slips past her defence, slicing deep through her thigh with a sickening hiss. She crumples with a strangled gasp, blood pooling fast as she hits the ground.

A sharp, searing agony lances through my chest from sheer, unrelenting fear. Every fibre of my being screams to strike, to end him now, to drive my daggers into his heart and carve him apart for what he's done. My grip tightens around my weapons, fingers aching with the force of my fury. The need to kill him surges through me like wildfire, violent and consuming. Triona, bleeding, gasping, needs me now.

Indech halts, and his amusement flickers into something sharper—alarm.

His eyes burn with rage, and he steps back as if trying to regain control of himself. "Foolish girl," he hisses. "You are not meant to die yet." His hands tremble slightly as he tightens his grip on the dagger, but his focus wavers.

Seizing the moment, I explode forward, twisting my body as I launch one of my daggers straight at his chest as every muscle screams for vengeance. He dodges at the last second, but it grazes his shoulder, drawing dark ichor instead of blood. Snarling, he retaliates, his strikes becoming more feral, more desperate. I duck and weave, dodging deadly arcs of his cursed blade until I find an opening. With a burst of speed, I drive my remaining dagger into his sternum.

His eyes widen in shock as the blade sinks deep, the hum of the Void Dagger faltering as his grip weakens. He stumbles backward, the green light in his eyes dimming.

Wasting no time, I sweep Triona into my arms, her blood soaking into my tunic as I carry her. She clings to me with surprising strength. "Hold on," I murmur, my voice a mix of desperation and determination.

I turn toward the exit, my heart pounding as I navigate the uneven path. The chamber seems to shudder behind us, the faint hum of magic fading into silence. Then, a sound breaks through the stillness—the sickening, wet drag of steel being wrenched from flesh. I hear Indech struggling, and reality crashes down on me like a tidal wave—my attempt to kill him failed. He's still got fight left in him. This isn't over.

A cold certainty settles in my chest. There's only one choice now. I push forward, each step carrying me deeper into the only decision that matters now—saving her, no matter the cost.

I push forward, Triona's weight heavy in my arms as her blood drips steadily onto the stone floor. The path narrows before widening again, leading us to another door—smaller but equally foreboding. The surface shimmers faintly, etched with glowing patterns that seem to pulse in time with the hum of the artefact still clutched tightly in her arms.

"It's sealed," I mutter, glancing at the faint outline of symbols. I shift Triona, leaning her against the wall for a moment as I reach for the intricate carvings. The moment my hand brushes the surface, it flares with light, the glow briefly illuminating the chamber. Then, with a low groan, the door slides open, revealing the tunnel beyond.

The faint glimmer of hope I felt reaching the exit vanishes as I see the gate—a towering iron barrier that looms like a fortress wall. Its massive, interlocking bars are wrought from iron and reinforced with glowing runes, pulsating faintly with an energy that suggests ancient fortification. I set Triona down once more as I assess what's in front of me. My eyes dart to the lever mechanism mounted on the wall nearby, a counterweighted system meant to lift the gate from the inside.

I can hear Triona's ragged breaths behind me, and every second we linger feels like a lifetime. The lever groans faintly when I tug it, but the rusted chain anchoring the counterweight barely shifts.

I spot a weak point—a chain-link that's almost worn through. My stomach knots as I realise there's likely only one chance to get this gate open before the weak link snaps entirely. I remove Triona's daggers, to replace the ones I lost, and brace myself.

Sliding one dagger into the weakened link, I wedge the other against the lever for clout. My muscles burn as I push with everything I have, the sound of groaning metal filling the air. With a final, desperate kick, the chain snaps, the mechanism screeching in protest as the gate jolts upward just enough to leave a narrow gap. The finality of the decision hits me like a blow, but I don't let myself stop.

"Come on," I whisper, sweeping Triona into my arms. Her blood-soaked leg dangles and her head lolls weakly against my chest. I position her carefully, angling her through the gap with everything I have.

My chest tightens as I watch her hit the ground harder than I wanted, her body crumpling into the dirt. The sound is gut-wrenching, and a sharp pang of guilt pierces through me. For a moment, I can't breathe, my vision blurring with panic. Relief washes over me when I see her stir, weak but aware. Then I spot Callan running toward us, his face twisting into pure terror as his eyes lock onto Triona's bloodied leg, and the exhaustion etched into her features.

His panicked voice cuts through the heavy air. "What happened?" He looks up briefly, terror clear. I watch as he assesses her wounds—eyes widening at the severity—eyes flitting between her pale face and blood pooling at her leg. I force myself to stay rooted, to give him the space to act without my panic clouding the moment.

"A man named Indech followed us in. The defensive barrier at the entrance failed to hold," I say, my voice deliberate and sharp, each word carrying the weight of urgency. My chest seethes with a fury that is only intensified as I witness the dawning comprehension of his expression.

"The weapon responsible for that—he called it a Void Dagger," I continue, my tone tightening. "He said it severs magic. Callan, his intent was never to end her life but to claim her. Take her from here now. I believe he's alive... and he willnae be far behind." Callan wavers, his expression hovering between understanding and hesitation as he considers my position.

"Finn... please tell me ye aren't going through with this," he says, with much vacillation in his face.

"We both understood the cost, Cal."

Then I hear it—the metallic groan of the gate above. The chain, weakened and strained, shudders violently, its links trembling under the weight.

Snap.

The sound is deafening in the still air.

Part 9 – Let Inner Strength Unchain with Might

38

WHEN LIGHT FADES

Triona

Sunday, 22 June 1823

County Meath, Ireland

Formerly Province of Mide: Seat of the High Kings

A distant shout claws at my senses, dragging me back to the brutal, suffocating reality around me. My body trembles under the weight of blood loss, and my mind teeters between panic and disorientation. The wound on my thigh throbs mercilessly, a searing reminder of the dagger's cruel gift. Blood pools beneath me, mixing with the cold sweat, as black spots pepper the edges of my sight.

I force my gaze downward, sickened by the deep gash that refuses to close, an open wound that might as well be an open door to death. When I try to lift my head, the world rocks, a cruel mockery of the hope I once held.

Shapes coalesce in front of me. Callan is there, kneeling at my side, his face etched with a rare and terrifying panic.

Finn's voice cuts through the fog that clouds my thoughts, deliberate and sharp, each word weighted with urgency. "A man named Indech followed us in. The defensive barrier at the entrance failed to hold." The fury in his voice is palpable, a seething anger that intensifies as he continues.

"The weapon responsible for that—he called it a Void Dagger. He said it severs magic," Finn continues, his voice tightening as though the words themselves burn. "Callan, his intent was never to end her life but to claim her. Take her from here now. I believe he's alive... and he willnae be far behind."

Callan falters, his face a conflicted mask of understanding and hesitation as he weighs Finn's warning. "Finn... please tell me ye aren't goin' through with this."

"We both understood the cost, Cal."

A metallic groan roars to life from somewhere I can't see, followed by a violent shuddering. The sound reverberates through the air, sharp and sudden, but I can't place its source.

Callan curses under his breath before tearing his shirt off. His calloused hands work with raw desperation, turning the fabric into a makeshift bandage. He presses it against my wound, and I bite back a cry as fire shoots through my leg. His lips move, urgency dripping from every word, but I can't make sense of them. They're muffled, garbled—like hearing through water.

"Triona..." Callan's voice finally breaks through, hoarse and desperate.

"Cal..." My voice is a ghost, trembling and faint. "It was so much... it was so wrong. All of it..."

My mind claws for coherence, but panic surges in my chest, drowning out reason. "Finn—" I try to finish, but my words crumble as I look around frantically.

Where is he?

The absence of him at my side is deeply troubling. I can hear his voice cutting through the chaos like a lifeline, but it's not enough. I push weakly against Callan's hands, my limbs shaking with the effort to move, to stand, to find him.

"Where is he?" I croak, the words a desperate plea.

"Stop, Tri!" Callan snaps, gripping my shoulders to still me. "Ye're losin' blood—ye cannae move!" But his words barely register. I claw at the dirt, searching wildly, my eyes darting through the haze.

Then—there, I see him. Finn. On the wrong side of the gate.

"Finn." The whisper escapes my lips, the world narrowing to the scene before me.

Something primal rips from my throat, a sound born of sheer terror and disbelief. My limbs move of their own accord, feebly pushing Callan away with the desperation of a dying woman. I collapse forward, barely catching myself before my face hits the ground.

My arms shake with the effort to push myself up and drag myself toward the gate. My leg screams in protest. The pain is unbearable, a fire that swallows everything, but it doesn't matter. Not now. My breath comes in frantic, shallow bursts as I claw at the dirt beneath me, inching closer to him.

"Tri, stop." Callan's command pierces the air, but it's distant, far away, a flicker of sound muted by the abyss that's swallowing me whole.

I reach the gate, my fingers trembling as I curl around the cold metal and pull myself up. I press against it, my chest heaving as my vision sways. I claw at the bars, helplessly trying to find any weakness, any way through—but the gate stands solid, unyielding.

"No," I whisper, the word barely audible, my breath rattling in my chest. "No, no, this can't be..."

Behind me, Callan attempts to remove me, but I muster as much effort as I can to elbow him in the sternum, which seems to halt his efforts. "Ye stubborn wee brat." He rasps out past his pain as his voice cracks with something close to panic.

I don't care. Nothing matters anymore but getting to Finn.

"Finn..." The whisper escapes me like a prayer, a final breath of hope.

He looks up, and I see it. His face is streaked with blood and dirt. His knuckles are raw and bleeding. But it's his eyes that stop my heart—they're *empty*, hollow with something I can't name.

"*Mo chridhe*," His voice is softer than the world I'm trapped in. "You have to listen to me."

I can't breathe. His words echo, a faint echo of something worse than death.

"What happened?" I moan, the question a plea, a sob in disguise. My chest cracks open with the weight of it. "Finn, *why...*"

Finn's hands grip the wrought iron bars of the gate, his knuckles white from the strain.

"Doe, you have to leave," he pleads, his voice trembling despite his effort to remain steady. "You have to leave with Callan... stop fighting him. Stop fighting *this*."

But I can't stop.

I lean against the cold, unforgiving metal of the gate, gasping for air, chest heaving with the effort to stay upright.

"No," I whisper, my voice trembling with desperation. "No, this can't..."

Behind me, Callan's presence looms over me. "Tri, stop bein' so bloody stubborn," he roars, his voice cracking with uncharacteristic emotion.

But I don't care. I don't care about the pain, or the blood, or that my body is failing me.

Because Finn is on the other side. And I'll tear the world apart if I have to... to bring him back to me.

I turn to look back at Callan, my body shaking under the weight of pain and fear. His usual confidence is gone. A body laden with trepidation betrays the man who's always been unshakable in the face of danger. It sends a chill down my spine. I know the next few minutes will require his cooperation. I can't do this alone.

Right now, I've never felt more useless.

All the years I'd spent training, the sweat, the bruises, the countless hours honing my strength—every bit is utterly pointless when it matters most. My body refuses to cooperate, my strength sapped by blood loss and the overwhelming tide of emotions crashing over me.

Callan's eyes flit past me, lingering over my shoulder. His hesitation ignites a fury in me, hot and searing. How dare he waste precious seconds when Finn is trapped, when everything is falling apart?

"Callan, help me!" I wail, the desperation in my voice sharp enough to cut through the air. "Finn is stuck—"

"Tri, stop it now!"

The command slams into me like a blow. At Finn's shout, I whip my head back around. The look in his eyes stills the breath in my lungs. There's something there—a faint, haunting shimmer of silver pooling in the corners of his gaze, a warning of something I don't want to name.

"This was the only way," he says, his voice low and resolute.

My mind rebels against his words, my head shaking vehemently in denial. I grip the cold iron bars tighter, using the last threads of strength in my failing body to fight against the reality they're trying to sell me.

"No," I choke out, the word thick with determination and panic. "We'll find a way—like we always do."

He presses himself closer to the bars, his expression softening despite the storm raging in his eyes. "Tri..."

"Stop," I whisper, tears blurring my vision as my voice cracks. "Don't... Don't you *dare*."

Finn doesn't respond, not with words. Instead, he reaches his hand through the bars, palm outstretched toward me. "Come here."

I hesitate, the raw vulnerability in his voice slicing through me, but I refuse to move. My pride, my fear, my refusal to believe this moment could end in anything but both of us walking away together, keeps me rooted. I shake my head stubbornly.

But Finn doesn't *let* me refuse.

He grabs my hand and intertwines his fingers with mine. His touch sends a jolt through me, a familiar warmth that's both comforting and devastating.

"I will not hear another word until you are on this side with me, and we are well away from this hellhole." I try to rip my hand from his, but there's no force behind it. I have nothing left to give. My body is spent, my strength drained to nothing but the quivering embers of willpower.

Callan's approach is cautious, slow, as if I were a wounded animal liable to lash out at any moment. I look to find his expression taut with something too close to pity.

My heart hammers as I glare at him, my fury igniting anew. "Do not look at me like that," I spit through gritted teeth. "We're getting him out of there, Callan. Help me, damn you!"

But when he speaks, his tone isn't the booming, commanding one I expect. It's quiet. Controlled.

"Triona," he says, his voice pleading. "Please, listen to him."

A bitter scoff escapes my lips, sharp and jagged, and I hiss when his hand comes to rest lightly on my back.

"Don't touch me," I snap, my words venomous and unfiltered.

For a moment, Callan's jaw tightens, but then, with a heavy exhale, he steps back. His shoulders slump, the fight draining from him as he meets my glare one last time before looking away.

I turn back to Finn, my breaths coming in ragged gasps. "This isn't over," I whisper, clinging to the bars as if sheer force of will could tear them apart. "I swear to you, Finn, this isn't over."

"This was the only way," Finn repeats, slower this time.

My gaze darts between him and Callan. "When did you decide to do something so foolish?"

"When Mannie showed me that yer success here ended in my death... and again when I saw the dagger tear through yer flesh," he mutters, his voice thick with restrained emotion.

Callan adds in a strained whisper, "It should have been me."

Finn's head snaps toward him. "No," he says firmly, his gaze piercing as it shifts back to me. "This was written before we ever drew breath."

The weight of the prophecy lingers in the air between us. Finn's expression hardens with a resigned clarity, and his next words strike me like lightning.

"I *was* always meant to be here. To protect you, as I swore I would. I never made a promise to you I didnae intend to keep."

A sob tears free from my throat as I shake my head, gripping the bars between us as if I could break the universe itself to undo this moment. "No," I cry, my voice breaking. "You are *so much more* than *this*. More than all the things they've summed you up to be. And you *know* that, Finn. This was not your destiny."

His hand tightens around mine, his touch grounding me even as my world falls apart.

"I would die a thousand deaths for you, Triona," he says, with a faint smile on his lips. "I would stare death in the face again and again if it meant ye'd live, free and whole."

"Finn—"

"We dinnae have long," he interrupts, urgency creeping into his tone. He glances over his shoulder, and I can almost feel the shadows closing in. "He's not dead, Triona. You *have* to leave."

"I can't!" My voice is raw, shredded by emotion. "How can I be without you? You are the reason I still breathe, Finn. You *just* became mine."

I'm fighting against time itself, desperate to hold on to every fleeting second, to keep my grip on the man who is my everything.

"Triona," Finn says softly, his voice trembling as he cups my hand tighter, his thumb brushing over my knuckles. "If there's one thing you must know—it's that I've never belonged to prophecy, or fate, or anyone else. *Only you.*"

Each breath scrapes like glass through my chest. Air shouldn't hurt—but it does.

"You live for more than me," he whispers. "You live for others—for the world that still needs you. Our love story will outlive us both, I promise you that. Love like ours..." His voice falters. Tears fall in quiet trails. "Love like ours is rare. And it's infinite."

"Finn..." I breathe.

"Just for a moment," I whisper, voice trembling, "let me pretend I can keep you. Selfishly. Let me pretend this world doesn't exist. Just us. One memory."

He lets out a breath of a laugh—soft, shaky, still somehow warm. "One memory? To sum up every day I've spent with you these seven years?"

I chuckle weakly; the sound cracked with sorrow. "You were always good at the impossible."

His smile deepens, bittersweet and aching. He brings my hand to his lips and kisses it softly, reverently. "Then how about one for the future?"

Callan moves beside me. His hand rests on my back—solid and steady—and for once, I don't push him away.

"Callan," Finn says, barely louder than a breath. "Give me the bag."

Callan hands him a small leather pouch. Finn cradles it carefully, fingers brushing over the worn edge. His eyes lock with mine—and the world stills.

"The last of my dreams."

With trembling fingers, he lifts a ring from the pouch and slides it onto my finger, the cool metal sending a shiver through me. A sharp breath slips past my lips, and for a moment, the world narrows to just him—his voice, his touch, his unwavering gaze.

Forged from silver, its intricate ivy design winding along the band like a living thing. At its heart, an emerald glimmers, catching the light even in the shadow of despair. It's as if the ring itself holds a piece of his soul, crafted with a love that defies time.

If I thought my heart had been breaking before, it now feels as though it's shattered entirely, the pieces piercing every part of me.

"It was yer mother's," he whispers, his voice full of equal parts affection and sorrow.

With shaky hands, I bring the ring closer; the inscription etched into the band catching my eye. As I read the words aloud, my breath falters.

"Éire go Brách."

Ireland to the end of time.

A sob breaks free, uncontainable and raw.

I shut my eyes tightly, as if by doing so, I can stop the flood of emotions threatening to drown me.

"My love for you does not end in death," his voice remains steady despite the tears glistening on his cheeks. "I would die a thousand times over for you."

His voice gains a rushed urgency, as though he's racing against time itself to tell me everything he's held back.

"The only thing I'd change about these past seven years—every precious moment I've had with you—is not tellin' you this sooner. I should have told you years ago. I should have told you every day."

Before I can respond, his hand glides into my hair, his fingers threading through it with a tenderness that unravels me further, and he pulls my lips to his.

His kiss is everything—a collision of desperation and passion, of love and finality. It's hungry, consuming, a kiss that demands to be remembered for a lifetime. I feel his heartbreak, his devotion, and his unwavering resolve in every movement, and I cling to him as though I can hold him here, keep him from slipping away.

When he finally breaks the kiss, he brings his forehead to rest against mine. Our breaths mingle as tears stream down both our faces.

"I'll wait," he declares. "At the entrance to the Otherworld. I would've been honoured to be yer husband in this life."

He draws back just enough to meet my gaze. His hands cradle either side of my face, thumbs brushing away tears.

"Next time," he says, voice cracking. "Next time, I'll do it right. Ye'll be mine. And I'll be yers."

"You already are," I whisper, my voice trembling. "You ruined me, as you said you would."

His lips quirk into the faintest smile, bittersweet and full of longing.

"A piece of me will die here today if I lose you," I breathe. "I would never be the same. I could never belong to another. And I refuse—" my voice gains an edge, his grip on me tightening momentarily. "I refuse to truly accept a world without you in it. You are the last whisper in my consciousness. Nothing can replace you, Finn. Nothing ever could."

"You have much to do before yer last day," he says, his tone soft but resolute.

He presses a kiss to my lips. And this one, this one feels like a goodbye. The final nail in the coffin.

Nothing in me cares about what lay ahead—the days and weeks to come, the turmoil, the suffering of others. There is no room left in my body to care about anything but the devastating truth that my heart is being ripped away. The pieces of me that remain are hollow, fragile, and I feel as though I might collapse under the weight of it all.

Callan's hand, steady and strong, is the only reason I can still stand. My legs waver beneath me, my thoughts a disjointed mess, and I can't summon the will to fight against the pull of despair. If Finn is leaving me—if his fate is to be sealed here—then I will happily die in this place, knowing I won't have to live a moment without him.

Behind me, I feel Callan stir. I hear him take a deep breath before speaking. "Ye have my thanks," he says, his tone steady despite the emotion thick in his throat. "For everything. But most importantly, for lovin' my sister."

Callan smiles as a single tear rolls down his face.

Finn and Callan grip each other's forearms, a gesture that carries the weight of everything left unspoken between them.

Finn's eyes lock onto mine with an intensity that steals the air from my lungs. "*I love you*," he says, each word heavier than the last. "We will never part."

Callan tugs at my arm, his grip firm but careful. "Now, Triona," he urges, his tone sharpening with the desperation of the moment as a shadow emerges behind Finn, a form solidifying and closing in. My heart seizes in panic, and I instinctively tighten my grip on Finn's hand.

"I can't—" My voice breaks, each word a struggle as my breaths grow shallow. "I can't leave you. I don't care if I fall—if I fall right now..." My knees buckle slightly, my vision swimming in and out of focus.

Finn's gaze softens, his love for me written in every line of his face. He turns to Callan, his voice a low command. "Take her from here."

"No!" I gasp, my legs refusing to move as the weight of the moment crushes me.

Callan's arms wrap around my waist, his strength far outmatching my failing resolve, and he tosses me over his shoulder.

I let out a scream as he begins to run.

Finn stands firm, hand moving to the hilt of his sword, drawing it with the precision of a man prepared to fight until the bitter end.

Before turning, he raises two fingers to his lips, kissing them softly, and gestures them toward me.

Then, without hesitation, he faces the oncoming threat, and I can do nothing but watch in helpless horror. He fights valiantly, his movements swift and precise.

"Finn!" The scream shreds my throat. I pound my fists into Callan's back—uselessly, like trying to dam a river with my bare hands. Time slows, each second stretching into an eternity as my body weakens further, my grip on this life slipping away.

"Look away," Callan begs, voice cracking. "Gods, Triona, look away!"

I can't. Tears well in my eyes as I choke out, "Not while he still draws breath, Cal... don't leave him... please." My voice trembles with desperate sorrow as I cling to consciousness by a thread, my gaze fixed on Finn.

Through what feels like the eyes of another, I see it—see him as a blade buries itself in his chest—the steel glinting cruelly as it exits through where the tattoo of the stag lay on his back.

Finn staggers but keeps his grip on the sword, forcing Indech back with a desperate thrust. For a heartbeat, I dare to hope—but then Indech wrenches the blade free, and scarlet blooms across Finn's shirt in a pattern too cruelly beautiful for this nightmare.

He lifts his gaze to find me in the chaos. A tired smile ghosts over his lips—tender, resigned. In that final, silent moment, he mouths something I know intimately and irrevocably: *'I love you.'*

And then he collapses.

Something inside me shatters. A sound erupts from my throat—not a scream, not a sob—something inhuman. I feel an indescribable pain that destroys a person from the inside out.

Darkness threatens to steal our final moments—the press of his lips against my fingers, the mingling warmth of his body with the fading embers of my own, and those whispered words, as soft as a sigh from the Otherworld: *"We will never part."*

But the world is too cruel a place to hold such solace.

The last thing I know is the taste of iron on my tongue, the burn of tears in my throat, and the faint press of the ring against my chest—unbreakable, even as I break.

Then, the world is gone, taking Finn with it.

39

THE STRENGTH TO STAND

Callan

Monday, 23 June 1823

County Meath, Ireland

Formerly Province of Mide: Seat of the High Kings

Triona hasn't spoken since she woke—since the blood loss and exhaustion nearly took her.

The image of her bleeding, the wound on her leg pouring out as Finn had me drag her away, haunts me. It's replaying endlessly in my mind, but I know it'll haunt her in ways I could never understand. He died for us—for her. And I let it happen.

I can still hear her screaming his name, still see the blood draining from her face as she struggled to stay conscious—until she wasn't. She was out for hours, long enough I thought I'd lose her. I stayed up all night, and all bloody day, watching her chest rise and fall, praying it wouldn't stop.

But like before, somehow, the wound on her leg healed too fast—far too fast for the injury Finn swore was made by a blade imbued with magic.

When she finally woke... there wasn't even panic in her eyes. Just this hollow stillness. She looked down, touched the bandage on her leg like she had to check the wound was real. Then she looked around—searching for him. That's when reality set in, and silent tears came.

And I couldn't take it. The guilt, the agony—I had to step outside before it crushed me.

Now, hours later, I want to bridge the gap. Before I lose her.

I step cautiously into the long-forgotten cottage. My footsteps barely make a sound on the worn wooden floor as I study her.

Her tawny brown hair hangs in limp strands around her face, her green eyes duller than I've ever seen them; absent is the warmth that normally lights up a room. The spark that has always danced there is extinguished, replaced with a void so deep it chills me.

"Tri," I croak, my voice rough and broken. She winces at her name, refusing to look up at me with those lifeless eyes. Eyes that are fixed on the Stone of Fál, bundled in her palm.

"You knew," she whispers, the accusation sharp as a blade. Though her voice is barely audible, I feel the weight of it all the same.

I hesitate, unsure of what to say, unsure how to fix this. I join her on the floor, close enough that I can feel her warmth, but far enough not to intrude.

"You *knew* what he was going to do, and you didn't tell me," she accuses, her voice louder now, though still trembling. I still don't respond—I can't. What could I possibly say to make this better? To make it right. To undo the damage.

"You knew I was walking out of there without him. You knew he wasn't coming back, and you didn't tell me," she spits, her voice shaking with rage. "You let me walk into Tara thinking we had a chance." Her head snaps to me, her eyes finally meeting mine, and all I see is fury and despair there, like a storm raging in her soul.

"I couldnae tell ye, Tri." I whisper, my voice barely more than a breath. It feels like the words are strangling me as they leave my throat, guilt and sorrow twisting together until I can hardly tell them apart. My heart aches, but hers—it's shattered. And focusing on her pain, on her grief, is far easier than facing my own.

"There was no other way," I say, my voice low. "That's what he told me—right before we parted. '*A soul for a soul.*'"

Her face twists in disgust, but I see it—the moment she recognises the truth in those words. That was the prophecy, and the truth of what Finn had seen written on a pillar in some hazy vision. Five words that changed that course of our lives forever. Words he prepared to make true. Words he made me swear I'd honour.

His death was the cost.

Ignoring me, she presses on, her frustration spilling over. "Why didn't you tell me, Callan?" Her voice cracks with despair and accusation. "I deserved to know. I deserved to fight for him." The hurt in her voice hits me like a physical blow; filled with malice. Just an abyss of grief that's threatening to swallow her whole.

"Because if I had told ye," my voice is quiet but firm, "ye'd have stopped him. And he had to do this."

Quickly moving from where she lay, to a seated position, she starts, voice trembling, "You're right. I would have tried to stop him. I would've fought for him. I would have... I would've done something." She bites her lip to stop the quivering, failing miserably. "But you robbed me of that. You didn't even give me the chance."

My fists clench, my nails biting into my palms, but it's nothing compared to the agony in her voice—the same anguish that's tearing me apart from the inside out. My breath shudders, my chest tight, and before I can stop myself, the words rip free.

"Do ye think I wanted this?" My voice cracks, rising despite the burn in my throat. "Do ye think I wanted to send him to his death while I stood outside, helpless, waitin' for the inevitable? Do ye think I wanted to let ye believe he'd come home—to watch hope flicker in yer eyes when I kent the truth all along? Do ye think I wanted to watch ye shatter and ken there's not a damn thing I can do to put ye back together?"

The silence that follows is deafening, thick with the weight of everything we've lost. My breath comes hard and fast, but it's nothing compared to the way my chest feels—like I've ripped it open, like I've bared every wound I never wanted her to see.

"I didnae tell ye 'cause I couldnae risk ye throwin' yerself into a fight ye'd not walk away from. I had to protect ye."

"Protect me? You consider this protection? I could have made a difference!" She shouts, the dam inside her shattering. "I could've... we could've found another way. He was right there, Callan. He was right there, and you left him!"

"There was no other way!" I say, voice breaking, pools of silver dancing in my eyes, hating how raw I sound. "Finn believed in something bigger than himself—bigger than all of us. And now we have to believe in it, too."

"No!" Her voice cracks, raw and broken. "He did it for this bloody stone!" She hurls it across the room. It bounces off the wall and hits the floor with a force great enough to shatter the board upon impact. The light that shines through the linen it's wrapped in flickers and dims. Almost as if it senses its distance from Triona.

"I want to hate you." Her voice is raw, breaking apart. My stomach tightens, a sharp, twisting pain—because I know she means it. "I want to hate you so much, Callan. You knew I was walking out of there without him."

My countenance falls, revealing the turmoil within. I feel broken—more broken than I've ever been; even in the wake of our parents' passing.

"I'm sorry," I whisper, voice barely a breath in the stillness. "I'm truly sorry, Tri. But I couldnae let ye go, too."

"It should have been me." She chokes out, wiping furiously at her tears.

"Dinnae say that." My voice comes out sharper than I intend, my eyes narrowing with sudden anger. "Ye dinnae get to give up because he's gone. D'ye think he did this for ye to shatter? So ye could throw yerself into the same darkness and stop fightin'?"

She flinches, as if my words are blades pressing into already-open wounds. "I don't know how to keep going on without him, to draw breath in a world devoid of him," she whispers, voice hollow. "I don't know how to bear the weight of being the one he left behind."

"I can see what Finn meant to ye." My throat tightens, burning with the words I don't know how to say. My fingers tremble before I reach out, steadying them at the last moment. She takes my hand, and that fragile connection is enough to keep me from breaking completely.

I draw in a shaky breath, forcing the rest out.

"But ye have to get through this," I say softly. "Ye have to try. I'm not goin' anywhere, and if ye can endure this, we'll come out the other side—together. Scream at me. Hate me if it helps. Strike me if it eases the pain."

She doesn't speak, but her grip tightens, and it's enough.

I press on, voice rougher now, heavier.

"From the moment Ma and Da brought ye into Connemara, I kent I'd shield ye with my life. For nineteen years, Triona, my only purpose has been keepin' ye safe—makin' sure ye were standin' here, right now, whole. I dinnae ken what happens next," I admit, eyes burning, "but I'll be yer shield. I'll give ye strength, just like ye've done for me all these years."

A long silence stretches between us. I almost leave it there—but my heart won't let me.

"Ye're the blessin' that made our family whole," I murmur. "Ye filled our home with light—a light guidin' all of us."

I pause, catching her narrowed gaze as she finally glances up. The emotion there is sharp—uncertain. I clear my throat, suddenly awkward under the weight of my own words.

"What I'm tryin' to say is... the love Ma and Da had for ye—it's the same love I carry. I've just been too blind to show it right."

Without a second thought, she crashes into my arms, allowing me to shoulder some of the unbearable pain. I hold her as she weeps. I hold her through the sobbing and wailing. And as I hold her, I allow myself to grieve.

For the first time since our parents' deaths, I let the pain course through me—grief for the hand fate has dealt us, for all that we've lost, and all that we are yet to lose.

With my head bowed to the top of hers, I murmur, "I dinnae expect ye to forgive me now. I'll carry the weight for the rest of my life, but I'll *never* regret my decision to choose ye."

We sit in silence, the world outside fading away, swathed in our shared sorrow.

"Cal," she finally whispers, her voice so fragile it nearly shatters me. "I feel as if the broken shards inside of me will never heal... and I'll fail everyone because of this misery."

I hold her tighter, my voice soft in her ear. "Ye're not broken, Triona. Ye're hurtin', but it'll heal enough. Yer strength isn't lost. And I'll be right here, no matter what."

She shakes her head against my chest, then chokes out, "I don't believe this will ever heal... and I wish Finn hadn't loved me."

My grip tightens instinctively, fear lacing through me at the rawness of her confession. "And I wish I hadn't loved him."

"Ye dinnae mean that," I murmur, though deep down I know the pain makes her believe it. It makes me terrified to take my eyes off her, afraid of what she might do if the weight becomes too much.

"By the sounds of it, Finn's love for ye was inevitable," I say quietly. "I was a fool for how I acted when I found out."

She doesn't respond—only cries harder. Her tears fall in steady streams, each one cutting deeper into both of us.

"He loved ye more than anythin', Tri. It'd been right in front of my face for years, and I was too blind to see it. He made this choice so ye could live—so *we all* could. And I promise, the time he spent lovin' ye was worth the sacrifice."

She nods, finally accepting the truth, even as the tears keep falling.

"I know," she whispers. "But knowing that doesn't make it hurt any less."

I hook a finger under her chin and gently drag her gaze up to meet mine. Her emerald eyes are clouded with a sorrow too deep for words.

"Ye're stronger than ye think, Triona. I believe in ye. Every step forward is a step toward healin', no matter how small."

She nods again, but it feels hollow. She pushes off my chest, gaze falling back to the ground as if the weight of her grief has dragged her back down.

"Cal?" she breathes, voice stretched so thin it barely holds.

"Aye?" I reply, my heart aching to feel her presence steady once more.

"I'm sorry."

I close my eyes, swallowing the lump in my throat. Somehow needing to hear those words. "I ken, but ye dinnae have to be."

"You lost him, too."

"Aye," I say, and it's all I can manage.

Because I lost more than Finn.

I lost the last part of me that believed I can keep anyone safe.

It's easier to focus on her pain than face the truth of my failure—facing the fact that I let my greatest friend walk into death's arms. It doesn't matter that he chose it. I'll always believe I should have fought harder. Should have done more.

"I don't hate you." She admits, her words a quiet vow amidst the storm of her emotions.

"I ken that, too." I answer, wishing I could offer more comfort. There are no words to fix this, no way to make her feel whole again.

For now, all I can do is help her survive this. To convince her to finish what was set in motion. To keep moving. To make his sacrifice count. To live for others when she feels too beaten to live for herself.

One breath at a time. One heartbeat after another.

She believes she is lost forever. But I have seen her rise from ruin before. And when she stands again—

Gods help anyone who tries to stop her.

40

Upon the Ivory Seat, She Reigns

Callan

Tuesday, 24 June 1823

County Meath, Ireland

Formerly Province of Mide: Seat of the High Kings

The cottage feels like a tomb, its walls pressing in with the weight of everything left unsaid. The Stone of Fál sits in my pack now, its light muted but constant, like a heartbeat I can't escape. The faint hum of its power fills the silence between us, an unwelcome reminder of what has been lost to bring it here.

Triona is seated on the floor, her back against the cracked wooden wall, her knees drawn to her chest. Her hands tremble as she grips the edges of her sleeves, the movement subtle but telling.

I kneel a few paces from her, close enough to offer support but not so near as to crowd her. "Tri," I begin softly, "we cannae stay here."

Her fingers tighten until her knuckles turn white. Her gaze doesn't waver from the splintered floorboards beneath her.

"Let them come. Let them see what it means to stand against someone who has nothing left to lose."

I freeze, my hand falling from the hilt of my sword. My head snaps toward her, and I know my eyes are blazing. "Dinnae be daft, Triona."

Her glare hardens. "Daft? For wanting to stop running? For standing up for myself?" Her voice rises, echoing in the enclosed space. "You think I should just keep running forever? That I should keep cowering while they destroy everything? The only thing we haven't tried is to stop running and fight back."

I move closer, my towering frame casting her in shadow, my expression thunderous. "Aye, if it keeps ye alive, I do. I'm not about to let ye throw yerself into the wolves' den because ye're too bloody stubborn to listen."

She screams and turns to meet my heated gaze. "You think this is about being stubborn? I want their *blood*, Callan!" Her shout echoes through the enclosed space, and for a fleeting moment, I swear I see the colour of her eyes change.

I grip the hilt of my sword tighter, my voice cutting through the air like steel. "Wantin' their blood willnae bring back what ye've lost, Triona."

"You think I haven't felt the weight of it every second since I opened my eyes?" she shoots back, her voice shaking.

I move closer still, my voice dropping to a dangerous, biting growl. "Then act like it, Triona. Being angry doesnae make ye invincible. And if ye die because of some daft need to prove yerself, the rest of us die with ye. Think that's strength? That's not fightin' back—that's surrenderin' to the anger they've already put inside."

I take a deep breath in and wait a beat before speaking again.

"Where is this comin' from, Triona?"

Her throat tightens, and she looks away, blinking against the sting of tears.

"If none of you had ever known me, you'd all still be safe back in Keiss where you belong—living happily, without this prophecy, without this chaos. Don't you see?" Her voice cracks, thick with emotion. "I'm not just carrying destruction, Callan. *I am* destruction."

She shakes her head, a bitter laugh escaping through the ache. "Everywhere I go, lives are torn apart—and it doesn't stop. Not for me. Not for anyone."

Her eyes are brimming with anguish. "It's me who's ruined everything—for you, for Casey, for everyone. You'd all be better off if I just walked away. Disappeared. Let the storm follow *only* me."

I shoot out my hand, gripping her arm—not rough, but firm enough to make her look at me. "Dinnae say that," I hiss. "Dinnae *ever* say that."

My voice cracks with the weight of it.

"Think ye've got nothin' left to lose? Fine. But I still have *ye* left to lose—and I'll be damned if I let ye sit here and do this. To me. To *us*."

She looks away from me. I release her arm, only to cup her chin, forcing her to meet my eyes.

"Ye're not carryin' this alone," I murmur. "Each of us has a part to play in this—and that's not yer fault. Stop lettin' those demons creep in and convince ye the world's better off without ye. Because it isn't. It never will be."

I swallow hard, my thumb brushing her cheek.

"Before yer birthday, I thought I had nothin' but duty. Nothin' but a fight I didnae understand. But ye... gave me somethin' worth fightin' for. Ye gave me purpose, Tri."

Her eyes glisten, but I press on.

"Ye think everything ye touch ends in ruin... but ye dinnae see what it's done to me. Without ye, I'd still be driftin'. It was *ye* who reminded me what it means to have hope."

I pause, my voice breaking at the edge.

"Dinnae take that away from us now."

Her hands fall limply to her sides, and for a moment, she looks utterly lost. Then, with a deep, shuddering breath, she lifts her gaze to meet mine. "I'm scared, Cal," she whispers. "I'm so scared of what comes next."

I take her hand in mine. "Aye," I say softly. "So am I. But we dinnae have to face it alone."

We sit there for a moment longer, the strange hum from the stone filling the silence. Then, slowly, she nods. It's a small motion, tentative and fragile, but it's enough.

"I am eternally grateful that you did not give up on me. For believing in me." Her voice wavers and she gives a weak, self-deprecating smile. "And I appreciate you for dealing with me when I'm like this. When I'm sad one minute, out for blood the next, and just utterly miserable in between." She takes a shuddering breath and straightens her shoulders. "Just give me a moment to shake this off... then we can go."

I nod, releasing her hand and rising to my feet.

I step outside, the chill wind biting at my skin as I lean against the weathered door-frame. The grey light of dawn breaks over the hills. The clouds are thin, revealing slivers of pale blue sky. I draw in a deep breath, letting the cold air fill my lungs, and try to tamp down my grief.

When Triona stalks out a short while later, she looks steadier, even with a face streaked with tears. Her hands tremble as she adjusts her cloak, pulling it tight against the wind. Her gaze finds mine and I see a flicker of something I haven't seen since Tara—resolve.

Her lips press into a thin line. "For Ma and Da. Robert and Sarah... and Finn," she murmurs, as if trying to summon strength from the words.

"For family," I answer.

We start down the narrow path, our steps uncertain but forward-moving. The wind tugs at us, carrying with it the scent of rain and earth.

For now, the pain still claws at us. But with each step, I can feel something shift—a small, almost imperceptible change. Not healing, not yet, but the first stirrings of what might one day become the strength to try.

We walk together, the weight of the Stone balanced between us, its faint glow a beacon in the storm. The path is long, and the end uncertain, but we walk it anyway.

For Finn. For each other. For the future *I* believe in.

Triona

The road to Uisneach Hill stretches before us like a punishment I've no choice but to endure. Every step feels as if I'm taken further from Finn, from the place where he died, and closer to a future I don't know how to face. Callan walks beside me, quiet and steady, his presence a constant reminder of what I've lost.

The Stone of Fál pulses faintly in his pack, its light piercing the corner of my vision. I hate it. And yet, I can't seem to stop staring at it, as though it holds the answers to questions I'm too afraid to ask.

The first day passes in a haze. I remember very little beyond the sound of our footsteps and the icy wind biting at my cheeks. Callan doesn't push me to talk, and I'm grateful for it. There's nothing to say that hasn't already been screamed or sobbed into the walls of that cursed cottage.

By the time we stop for the night, my legs ache, and my chest feels like it's caving in. Callan builds a fire, the flames flickering weakly against the encroaching darkness. I sit on the opposite side, staring into the embers until my eyes burn. When I finally close them, all I see is Finn's face.

His bright smile, and his golden-brown eyes.

If I let myself think of him only in the quiet of night, as my body descends into slumber, maybe I can have him in my dreams every night.

Maybe then I won't ever forget the way he looked at me—as if I was the centre of his entire being.

The second day is worse. Rain starts early, soaking us through and turning the dirt paths into rivers of mud. My cloak clings to me, heavy and uncomfortable, but I can't bring myself to complain. What's the point? Callan slows his pace to match mine, though

I can tell he wants to move faster. The air between us is thick, and it feels as if he's waiting for me to break.

I don't. I can't.

By midday, the rain finally lets up. We find a stream to refill our waterskins, and light a fire to dry our clothes, best we can.

I kneel at the water's edge, my fingers trembling as I scoop the icy water into my hands. It's cold enough to sting, but I let it drip over my face, hoping it will wash away the numbness clinging to me like a second skin. It doesn't.

"We're getting closer," I mumble. "I can feel the same pull I felt before."

"I follow yer lead," he says. His words are quiet but firm, as if they're meant to anchor me. "I'm here. Every step of the way."

I want to tell him to stop, to leave me in my misery and let me crumble. But some small, stubborn part of me—the part Finn loved—won't let me. So I nod, wiping my face with the back of my hand.

My body is heavy with exhaustion, but it's nothing compared to the weight on my chest. Every time I think I can't take another step, I hear Finn's voice in the back of my mind, urging me on. *Keep going, Triona. Don't stop now.*

By the third day, I feel like a spectre, drifting through the world without truly belonging to it. The land shifts around us—the hills rising steeper, the air turning sharp with cold. The paths grow rougher, winding through jagged outcrops and narrow valleys, each step heavier than the last.

As the sun dips low on the horizon, Uisneach Hill emerges—a faint shadow against the fiery sky. A breath stutters in my chest, and for a moment, something stirs deep inside me. Not hope. Not yet. But something close to it.

"Almost there?" Callan asks.

I glance at him, his face tired but resolute, and nod. "Almost."

The final climb is brutal. The wind howls around us, tearing at my cloak and stinging my skin. I can feel The Stone's pulse quickening as we near the summit. It feels alive, its energy humming in my chest, mingling with my grief in a way that makes me want to scream. But I press on, one step at a time, until we reach the top.

The view alone is enough to quiet some of the unrest in me. It's a wild, vast, and untamed sort of beauty.

Land stretches out in every direction, bathed in the golden light of the setting sun. The Stone is nearly blinding now. Even tucked away in Callan's pack, its brilliance slices through the cold air like a blade of firelight, defiant against the dusk.

I stand there, staring out at the horizon. Callan steps beside me and gently takes my arm, turning me around with quiet purpose.

"There," he murmurs, nodding toward a patch of grass just beyond the crest of the hill.

I follow his gaze—and see them.

Callan's voice is barely more than a whisper. "The hill became a place of reverence," he says, reciting the words as if they were etched into him, "where violets bloomed year-round as a reminder of her sacrifice and endurin' protection."

The line hits hard—one we heard our mother recite, over and over, until it was part of us.

I glance at Callan—and see his eyes shine with the same unshed tears burning in mine. "That story—*all* this time. She told it like a legend, like a bedtime tale, and we never realised..."

I stare fondly at the spot and grin for the first time in what feels like weeks. "If Ma were here... if she could see this... she'd be in absolute awe." He just nods, jaw tight, tears clinging stubbornly to his lashes.

I take a step forward, the ground firm beneath my boots—but it feels like stepping into another world. The hum of The Stone grows louder, resonating through my chest.

Finn's voice echoes in my mind, as clear as if he were standing beside me: *"...keep it bundled until you get to Uisneach Hill... Standing precisely where it tells you."*

"This is it," I murmur, mindlessly. My hands tremble at my sides, and my heart pounds so hard it feels as if it might tear free from my chest.

"Are ye sure?" Callan asks, his brow furrowing as his eyes flick to the horizon and back to me, voice barely more than a breath, strained with uncertainty.

I nod, though the certainty I feel isn't entirely my own. It's as if the hill itself is speaking to me, whispering truths buried so deeply I can't yet grasp them.

"I'm sure," I whisper, though my voice sounds distant to my own ears.

Callan kneels, setting the pack down on the grass with deliberate care. He pulls out The Stone, and its glow swells, golden and warm and impossibly bright. For a moment, he just stares at it, then looks at me.

"Here," he says, holding it out, his hands steady.

With trembling hands, I take it. Heat blooms through my fingers, and a surge of power sends shivers cascading down my spine. The linen wrapping is old and soft, but as I pull it away, a sudden surge of light bursts through the fabric. I gasp, nearly dropping it as the power within it grows stronger, more insistent.

The moment the last fold of linen falls away, the world shifts.

The ground beneath my feet quakes. The Stone glows brighter than the sun, its light spreading out in waves that roll across the hilltop and beyond. I hear Callan shout my name, but a low, resonant hum that seems to come from everywhere and nowhere all at once drowns his voice out.

And then it happens.

The light surges, shooting skyward like a pillar of fire. Somewhere on the edges of my awareness, I sense Callan being hurled away, but I can't focus on him—not when the energy courses through me, crackling through every vein like a living storm.

I rise, weightless, lifted by the sheer force surrounding me. The light grows impossibly bright, as though I've become the sun itself—searing and freezing in the same breath, too vast to hold, too powerful to resist.

Memories that aren't mine flood my mind—visions of a land steeped in golden light, where forests breathe magic, where rivers sing and mountains pulse like beating hearts. Faces I don't know but somehow recognise come into focus—too many, too fast.

And then—one among them is vastly different. A presence. A love so deep it aches, its weight pressing into my chest. But the face remains shrouded, just beyond reach, slipping through my grasp like mist.

Voices rise all around me—pressed, layered, not from one place, but *everywhere*. They don't call me Caitríona.

They call me something else—something older.

Ériu.

The name booms through the air like thunder. It echoes through bone and blood, not spoken to me, but *claimed by me*.

It's not just a name.

It's a memory. A legacy. A *homecoming*.

The name belongs to me.

My heart hammers. The world around me blurs as the memories surge deeper—rising, roaring—pulling me beneath like a tide too strong to resist.

And I don't fight it because somewhere inside, I remember what it means to be *her*.

I see myself standing on this very hill, my hair flowing in the wind, my hands raised as the land itself responds to my command. The sky darkens, and the earth splits beneath my feet, a fissure of light bursting forth. I feel the power in my veins, ancient and endless, as I give myself to The Stone—*my* stone.

The Soul Stone of Fál.

My voice carries an incantation, the words that bind my soul to the earth, sealing it away to save the land from destruction.

And then, four thousand years later, here I am. A fragment of myself, broken and mortal, standing in the place where I once sacrificed everything.

The light fades, and I collapse forward onto my hands, breath ragged. My body pulses with a strange power—both heavier and lighter, as if something inside me has been reforged. When I lift my head, I find Callan staring, eyes wide with disbelief. Blood streaks his face, his lower lip split. A jolt runs through me. The blast must have thrown him.

"Triona," he says, his voice frantic, "yer eyes... they were glowin' a purple hue like nothin' I've ever seen. And yer hair... it went silver."

I blink at him, trying to process his words, but there's no time.

Movement interrupts my thoughts in the distance. Three figures are approaching, their shapes growing clearer with every passing second.

I force myself to my feet, my legs trembling beneath me, and shake off Callan's attempt to help with a sharp gesture.

"Ah, finally," says the one in the middle, his voice a cryptic blend of weariness and amusement. "I wondered if you would ever touch Lia Fál. Millennia... Millennia spent waiting for this moment. Can you feel it yet? The echoes of an age long past, the weight of it pressing against your soul?"

I don't think—I just run, a snarl rising in my throat as rage takes over.

The three figures falter, surprise flashing across their faces—but they brace for the blow. It doesn't matter.

I lunge at the man in the centre, slamming him to the ground with every ounce of strength I have. Straddling him, I press my hand to his throat, power crackling through me—wild, untamed, and searing. He swallows hard beneath my grip, his wide eyes filled with fear... and recognition.

"Finn was right about *you*," I hiss, my voice shaking with fury as I lean in. "We trusted you. You led us to Tara... and I *lost* him."

They walked here as if the world belongs to them. As if they didn't help tear mine apart.

Mannie.

Dana.

...And the bloody maiden.

Mannie lets out a laugh, low and almost mocking, as he effortlessly pushes me off him. I stumble back on my hands, rage bubbling at the surface as he stands up, rubbing at his throat.

Callan is at my side before I've fully caught myself. He doesn't ask—he *checks*. Quick once-over, then he turns on Mannie.

"Piss off," he snaps, the words rough and thick with rage.

"I suppose I might have earned that, had I truly betrayed you," he says, his tone calm but edged with something dangerous. "Though I must admit, I am quite curious to see the extent of your power at its peak. You have only brushed the edge of your strength, Little One. At your height? I doubt I would still be on my feet."

I stagger to my feet, my breathing ragged as anger courses through me. "Where are my brother and Bran?" The question bursts from me, sharp and demanding, overriding my fury for a moment. "What have you done with them?"

Mannie's smirk falters, replaced by an expression of faint exasperation. "They are safe," he says, his tone clipped. "I assure you, Little One, we have no intention of harming them. In fact, they had a far less... *eventful* journey than you."

Callan steps closer to me, his body tense as he glares at Mannie. "Safe where? Ye better not be lyin'."

Mannie sighs. "I swore when you asked, my dear Triona, that no harm would befall those you cherish."

My voice breaks as I give way to my rising temper. "I *trusted* you! You *lied*—Finn was hurt!"

Power burns beneath my skin, curling through my limbs like fire seeking release.

His voice drops, calmer now. "I made a vow not to harm them. That vow was iron then, and it remains so now. Now, if you are finished baring your teeth at me, there are matters of far greater consequence to address."

The fury roils tighter in my chest, coiling hot and alive. His calm doesn't soothe—it infuriates. My hands glow, faint at first, then brighter, pulsing with the same light that surged through me when the Stone's power first awakened. I don't hide it. Let him see what I've become.

But Mannie doesn't flinch. He watches me with something else entirely—awe.

"You are a wonder," he breathes.

Then his expression shifts, solemn and unguarded. A man—no, something far older—stepping out from behind the curtain of myth.

"I am sorry," he says quietly, "for what happened to Finn."

Something in his voice makes me falter—not enough to cool the fire in my blood, but enough to make me *listen*.

"I know that kind of loss," he continues, each word carved from some old grief. "I once had a wife. Children, too. All of them gone now—lost to time, to war, to fate. It burrows deep, Triona. Deeper than anyone expects. And once it is in you... it never truly leaves."

My hands lower, the glow dimming—but only for a heartbeat.

I take a step forward, fists clenched, the air around me humming with restrained power. "Tell me the truth," I grit out. "*What* the hell are you—and *why* are you here? How did you know I'd be here?"

Mannie studies me with an unsettling calm before speaking. "You must by now understand who you are, aye?" He pauses, then suddenly throws his hands around his head in a theatrical display of frustration. "Surely you saw the memories, felt the echoes of who you *were*?"

I narrow my eyes, refusing to respond.

He tilts his head, the corner of his mouth twitching with something close to amusement. "I suppose I should make this simpler for you."

A faint glimmer of mischief dances in his eyes. "Though I am not *technically* a Sí uaisle, and Rhiannon is not a Keeper. Titles can be... limiting. But they help paint the picture, do they not?"

He gestures to his left. "Dana here is the goddess Danu, mother of the Tuatha Dé Danann."

Then, turning toward the third figure, his tone shifts—just slightly—softening with something almost fond. "And she is Rhiannon, the maiden goddess."

His posture straightens.

"And I," he says, voice low but commanding, "am Manannán mac Lir. God of the Seas. Gatekeeper of Tír na nÓg."

He looks directly at me now. The authority in his voice doesn't waver, but it carries something gentler beneath it. Something familiar.

"Your guide, Little One—though it seems you've forgotten even the sound of my name."

A fresh wave of memories surges through me. They come unbidden, vivid yet fragmented, flashing in my mind like firelight on water. I see their faces faintly, not as they are now but as they once were—timeless, radiant, and filled with an otherworldly power.

Manannán's laughter, wild and boundless. Danu's serene, knowing gaze. Rhiannon's fierce determination, sharp as a blade.

They are familiar—*achingly* familiar—etched into the deepest part of me, though I still can't grasp how or why. The memories swirl, tugging at me like a current, pulling me deeper into a past I can barely comprehend.

Dizziness roots itself in my spine, spreading fast. The world around me tilts—sky and earth blurring together—and I drop to my knees in the grass.

Callan is at my side in a flash. I barely register the way his arm steadies me, one hand braced between my shoulder blades, grounding me as everything else spins.

"Triona," he says, voice low, demanding. "Look at me. Breathe."

But I can't. The air feels thick as the burden of memories press down. My hands sink into the soil as if the earth itself might hold me together.

Dana steps forward and crouches in front of me, her movements slow and deliberate, as if approaching a skittish animal. "Triona," she whispers, her voice a blend of calm and urgency, "you have lived a mortal's life, but the truth of who you are is timeless."

She leans in, eyes searching mine. "Please—let us explain."

To my surprise, Callan doesn't interject. He doesn't pull me back or demand answers. He simply follows my lead—even in my disoriented state—his steady presence a silent shield beside me.

I hesitate as I stare into her calm, ancient eyes. Something in her presence quiets the storm raging inside me, if only slightly. I nod stiffly, allowing her nearness, though my body remains tense, ready to strike again if necessary.

The words tumble out of me before I can stop them. "How are you even here? Why are you here? And what is going on?"

Mannie straightens with a sigh. "It is unwise to remain here for much longer," he says, his tone measured but teetering on forceful. "There will be time for answers, but not here. It is pertinent that we make haste with our departure."

My jaw tightens, suspicion warring with the faint flicker of understanding beginning to stir within me. "What makes you believe I'll ever go anywhere with you? You refuse to answer most of my questions."

Mannie's smirk fades into something more solemn, his eyes narrowing as the moment stretches.

Dana remains crouched in front of me, her posture steady but not without strain. There's a tightness in her jaw now, barely concealed beneath her calm.

Rhiannon's gaze flicks between Callan and me—less gentle now, more calculating. Measuring. As if deciding whether I'm still a threat.

My breath slows. Not steady, but no longer ragged. The storm in my chest quiets just enough for me to lift my head... and hold Mannie's eyes.

"Triona," Dana says gently.

My gaze shifts to her, drawn by the quiet strength in her voice—light, lilting, like something carried on the wind.

"We know what you have lost far more deeply than you may ever understand. But there is more at stake than grief or vengeance. This land—the very essence of you—depends on your strength to endure. Without you, the delicate balance we have fought to preserve for millennia will crumble."

I glare at her. "Don't talk to me about balance. When the people I love are dead because of this cursed stone and the lies that led us to Tara." My voice cracks, but I don't care. "Why should I trust you?"

Callan's presence grounds me. I catch the way his hand hovers near the hilt of his sword, his muscles taut with tension. "Aye," he growls. "Why should she? Much of what we've seen since leavin' home is betrayal and bloodshed. Tell me why this isnae just more of the same."

Mannie's gaze flicks to Callan, his smirk returning, but it's more subdued this time—less mocking, more measured. "You do not trust us. Fair enough." His tone is calm, almost resigned. "But the rifts growing in this land will not wait for your grief to settle or your rage to burn out. Every moment you delay allows chaos to creep closer. Do you truly believe Finn would have wanted you to stop here, to falter now?"

"Don't," I hiss, my voice low and venomous. "Don't you *dare* speak his name. Don't use him to make a point."

Mannie nods slowly, as though he expected my reaction. "Perhaps it feels right to hate me for what has happened. For what it cost you to reach this point, but hate changes nothing, Little One. The task before you remains, as it has for ages untold."

My fists unclench, though I'm still trembling. The words hit something deep inside me, something I can't name or ignore. "If I'm so important," I murmur, "why didn't you come sooner? Why didn't you stop this before it all fell apart?"

Rhiannon speaks at last, her voice calm and unflinching. "Even gods walk within boundaries laid by hands older than time. Mortal lives are threads we cannot untangle, not until the bindings fray and fall. It was you, Ériu, who severed the cords that bound you to silence. Only then could we come."

"Who was strong enough to keep people out for over four thousand years? Who could put up all those barriers?" I ask.

"Who but Lugh, son of the sun, could weave such barriers? He, whose strength outmatched even the tides and winds, locked you away where no shadow could reach. But what became of him, none can say. Since that day, his light has not graced the earth, and the echoes of his steps have fallen silent."

A sudden, jagged ache lances through me at her words. My breath hitches, stolen by a weight I can't name—a memory not yet whole. Finn's face flares in my mind, bright and aching. Rhiannon's voice echoes behind it, the sound curving like a blade through everything I thought I understood.

"You called him... you called Finn *child of the sun,*" I whisper, my voice raw, the phrase striking something deep in my chest like a memory flaring to life. A flash of warmth, a golden field, laughter that felt older than time—gone in a blink, but the ache it leaves behind is sharp and sudden. "When you came to me at the tavern, you said that. Why did you call him that?"

Rhiannon tilts her head, her expression unreadable. "It is a title passed down through many lifetimes. Finn was blessed with a strength that bends the world without breaking it—and carries knowledge born of more than one life."

Callan speaks quietly beside me. "He always felt like an old soul," he says, a touch of fondness in his voice.

I glance at him. He reaches for my hand and grips it firmly. There's a silent question in his eyes.

Slowly, I nod. "I feel the truth in their words," I murmur, voice hoarse. "I wish I could explain how I *know* it—how I can *feel* it in my bones..."

Callan squeezes my hand, cutting me off before I can spiral further. I look up, startled by the intensity in his eyes.

His voice softens, but his grip doesn't. "Where ye go, I go."

I take a shaky breath, then look at Mannie.

"If this is a trap... if you're lying to me..."

Mannie lifts his hands in mock surrender. "There is no trap set to fool you. But if I lie," he adds, his gaze sharpening, "you shall certainly have the power to make me regret it."

The corner of my mouth twitches—a fleeting, bitter smile. "You can count on it. If you need me as badly as you're suggesting you do, I won't hesitate."

I glance between Mannie, Dana, and Rhiannon, their expressions unreadable but unrelenting.

"I ask again...where are you urging me to follow you to?"

The wind rises, lashing my hair across my face—but I don't flinch.

Mannie's smirk fades into something quieter. His gaze locks with mine, heavy with meaning, and something in it twists deep in my gut.

He glances once at Dana. Then at Rhiannon. Wordless understanding passes between them before he finally speaks.

"To the edge of Tír na nÓg," he says. "To the stronghold where it began... and where it must end."

Mannie's gaze turns thoughtful, and he lowers into a crouch before me. His voice drops to a near whisper. "Little One," he murmurs, "I forget how much you truly missed—how much time has passed between lives."

He exhales softly, a breath that feels like the turning of a page.

"We are here to take you *home*."

EPILOGUE

The world had narrowed to a dim haze of light and shadow. Blood slicked his hands, sticky and warm as he pressed them to the wound on his chest. It wasn't enough—he wasn't enough. He felt the life leaking out of himself, the edges of his vision blurred as the stars above danced and flickered like distant ghosts.

Thoughts trailed to the woman he loved more than anything else in existence.

She was the best parts of every season. A soft spring fog curling over the green-stitched mountains. The shimmer of sunlight skimming warm ocean waters in summer. The scent of autumn—rich, earthy, golden—carried on a wind that always felt like home. The hushed crunch of muffled snow under the weight of a boot.

The brightest star in the night sky—distant, radiant, and the last thing he wanted to see before everything went still.

She was all of it. Every moment that ever made life feel like something worth holding onto.

Her face burned in his mind. Not the way she looked when she smiled at him, though he'd spent a thousand nights memorising that.

And then wonderful memories went dark. This was different—her expression when she realised the truth. That he wouldn't be there when it mattered most. He'd failed her, and the thought was hollowing.

The pain in his chest was worse than the blade that had been plunged through him. It wasn't just the agony of the wound—it was the weight of failure crushing him. How could he leave her like this? Unprotected, vulnerable, while the world he had fought so hard to shield her from continued to close in?

The guilt was unbearable. He wanted to cry out, to fight against the darkness pulling him under, but the truth loomed large: he *had* failed. And nothing, not even the gods, could change that now.

He tried to move, but his body refused. His breaths were shallow, each one more ragged than the last. Around him, the world seemed to quiet. The chaos of the fight faded, leaving only the whisper of the wind and the faint hum of something he couldn't name.

Then, he saw someone, or felt them rather, and the world around him grew so cold it burned.

A figure stepped into view, cloaked in shadow, the edges of their form shimmering as if they didn't belong to this world. Their voice was low and resonant, a sound that sent a chill down his spine even as warmth still somehow flooded through him, though it wouldn't be long before it left him for good.

Her dark gown trailed across the ground like smoke, and her pale hands glimmered faintly in the moonlight. The edges of her figure shimmered, as if she were carved from the night itself. Her face was obscured beneath a black hood, but her eyes—gods, her eyes—shone like twin shards of frost.

"So, this is he who resists the end." Her voice was quiet, smooth as silk, but it carried a weight that felt like a blade pressed to his throat. "What binds you to a life already undone?" She knelt beside him, her movements unnaturally fluid, like a predator deciding when to strike.

He tried to speak, to ask her what she wanted, but the words wouldn't come.

She leaned closer, her shadow spilling across his face. Her gloved hand brushed his cheek, a touch both searing and icy.

"You fought with the strength of a living mortal," she murmured, her voice almost tender. "But all things turn to their end, and your time has come."

Her fingers lingered near his chest, pulling at something deeper than flesh—something ancient, as though she sought more than his life alone.

"A shame," she said, tilting her head as if she could see through him. "So much of her is written on your soul, so much of your heart beats only for her. Much remains that you would have done for her."

Her name screamed in his mind, but his lips wouldn't form the word.

"Did you see the betrayal before it struck? I watched as the two of them stood over you—Indech and the other did not linger to savour your fall. Too caught in a sick and twisted celebration, I suppose."

"I find it curious you breathe, yet not by your own will. Much of that has to do with her. You are... different this time. You once let memory break you, but you stand taller now. I had dared to hope." The old crone sighed, a sound that felt heavy with something close to pity. "Either way... she shall mourn you. That will be enough."

'Enough for what?' he wanted to shout as it burned in his chest. Was it enough for her to grieve him? To remember him in fleeting moments and shadows, as the world demanded she move forward without him?

He wasn't ready to be a memory. He wasn't ready to be forgotten. But what choice did he have? If this was truly the end, then what remained of him belonged to her, even if only in the spaces he left behind. His chest tightened as her hand pressed lightly against his skin. A cold so deep it felt endless poured through him, dragging him into the dark.

And then she paused.

The hand stilled, and her head tilted again, as if listening to something distant. Her eyes narrowed beneath the hood, and for a single heartbeat, the surrounding silence roared like a storm.

"No," she said, her tone calm but edged with finality, as though addressing a force unseen. "Not yet."

The shadows coiled tighter around her, and though her face was hidden, he felt her smile.

"Eternal rest shall wait," she whispered, rising to her full, towering height. "Soon, the river will carry you to peace, and the weight of this world will no longer burden you."

He tried to speak, to beg for healing, but the sound that tore from his throat was raw and agonised. There was no mercy present in what touched him.

And then, light—brighter than bright—erupted around them, blinding and searing. It consumed everything, swallowing shadow and flame alike, until there was nothing left but silence.

GLOSSARY & KEY TERMS OF THE VIOLET RAVEN

T he world of *The Violet Raven* is steeped in history, myth, and unyielding loyalty. Here are the terms, phrases, and figures that hold significance in this tale. While not required to enjoy the story, they offer deeper insight into the legends whispered across the land.

WORD	TYPE	DESCRIPTION/ MEANING
A leanbh/ Ah LAHN-uv	Irish Phrase	My child/ Dear child
Abhartach/ Ow-ar-tach	Figure/ Person/ Creature	Legendary figure in Irish folklore, often referred to as an early vampire-like creature
Amergin/ AH-vur-gin	Figure/ Person/ Creature	Prominent figure in Irish mythology
An gortóidh sé thú?/ Ahn GOR-toh-eeh shay hoo	Old Gaeilge (Irish) Phrase	Will he hurt you?
Anam Cara/ AH-num SHERK	Old Gaeilge (Irish) Phrase	Soulmate
Até não haver dúvida nenhuma de quem é que você pertence/ ah-TEH now ah-VEHP DOO-vee-dah neh-NYOO-mah djee kang eh kee voh-SEH pehr-TEN-seh	Portuguese Phrase	Until there's no doubt who you belong to
Bairn/ Bay-urn	Scottish Term	Baby/child
Balor/ BAL-or	Figure/ Person/ Creature	Fearsome giant and king of the Fomorians

Word	Type	Description/ Meaning
Bampots	Scottish Slang	Foolish, eccentric, crazy
Bán Sídhe/ Bawn shee	Gaeilge (Irish) Phrase	Fairy woman, white woman, banshee
Bawbag	Scottish Slang	Scrotum, idiot, fool
Beag gráinneog/ Byug GRAWN-yohg	Gaeilge (Irish) Term	Little Hedgehog
Bevvy	Scottish Slang	Alcohol
Boak	Scottish Slang	Throw Up
Bodhrán/ Baw-rawn	Item	Traditional Irish frame drum
Boggin	Scottish Slang	Stinky or dirty
Bogle/ Bow-gl	Figure/ Person/ Creature	Supernatural spirit
Brehon/ BREE-huhn	Celtic Term	Refers to a historical judge
Bugger	Slang Term	Term of endearment/ mild Insult, a curse word, mischievous people, troublemakers

Word	Type	Description/ Meaning
Cannae/ CAN-nee	Scottish Slang	Cannot
Casa da Prímula/ KAH-zah dah PREE-moo-lah	Portuguese Phrase	House of the primrose
Cèilidh/ Kay-lee	Celebration	Social gathering that features music, dancing, storytelling, and sometimes poetry
Chief Ollam/ OH-lav	Irish Term	Refers to the highest-ranking poet or scholar in ancient Irish society
Cosain í, onóraigh í/ KUS-inn ee, uh-NOH-ree ee	Gaeilge (Irish) Phrase	Defend/protect her, honour her
Couldnae/ could nee	Scottish Slang	Could Not/ Couldn't
Crony	Scottish Slang	Companion
Daft	Scottish Slang	Scottish slang term used affectionately (or sometimes teasingly) to refer to someone as a bit silly, foolish, or absent-minded

WORD	TYPE	DESCRIPTION/ MEANING
Dagda/ DAH-guh	Figure/ Person/ Creature	One of the most powerful and important deities in Irish mythology
Danu/ DAH-noo	Figure/ Person/ Creature	Prominent figure in Irish mythology and is considered a primordial goddess and mother figure
Dealan-dé/ JAL-an JAY	Gaelic (Scottish) Term	Butterfly
Didnae/ DID-nee	Scottish Slang	Did not/ Didn't
Dinnae/ DIN-nee	Scottish Slang	Do not/ Don't
Disnae/ DIZ-nuh	Scottish Slang	Does Not/ Doesn't
Divan	Item	A backless, armless couch
Dram	Scottish Slang	Small measure of whisky, though it can sometimes mean a small drink of any alcohol
Dublin (Baile Átha Cliath)	Location	The beating heart of Irish identity, literature, music, and political history

Word	Type	Description/ Meaning
Dullahan/ DOO-luh-han	Figure/ Person/ Creature	Figure from Irish mythology, often depicted as a headless horseman riding a black steed
Éber Donn/ AY-ver Dunn	Figure/ Person/ Creature	Figure in Irish mythology recognized as the eldest son of Míl Espáine, the legendary ancestor of the Irish people
Éire/ Ay-ruh	Gaeilge (Irish) Term/ Name	Derivative of Ériu, means Ireland
Éireann/ AIR-un	Name	
Ériu/ Air-yoo	Figure/ Person/ Creature	Goddess from Irish mythology who is considered the matron goddess of Ireland
Falias/ FAH-lee-ass	Location	One of the Four Great Cities of the Tuatha Dé Danann
Feckless	Scottish Slang	Weak, incompetent
Findias/ FIN-dee-us	Location	One of the Four Great Cities of the Tuatha Dé Danann

Word	Type	Description/ Meaning
Fomóire (Fomorians)/ Foe-MOHR-yeh	Figure/ Person/ Creature	Evil supernatural race in Irish mythology. Means underworld beings.
Fomorians (Fomóire)/ Fo-MORE-ee-uns	Figure/ Person/ Creature	Evil supernatural race in Irish mythology
Foreshots	Item	The first vapors that boil off during the distillation of an alcoholic liquid
Gaugers/ GOW-jers	Figure/ Person/ Creature	Excise officers or tax collectors in Ireland and Scotland
Geggie/ GEG-ee	Scottish Slang	Mouth
Gobbin'/ GOB-in	Scottish Slang	Fool, an idiot, or a clumsy person
Gobshite/ GOB-shyte	Slang Term	Annoying, menace
Golspie/ GOL-spee	Location	A Coastal Village in Scotland
Gorias/ GOR-ee-as	Location	One of the Four Great Cities of the Tuatha Dé Danann
Groonies	Scottish Slang	Bad guys

Word	Type	Description/ Meaning
Hasnae/ HAZ-nay	Scottish Slang	Head
High Kings	Figure/ Person/ Creature	In Irish history and mythology, the High King of Ireland was the supreme ruler over the various provinces and kingdoms of Ireland
Highland Clearances	Historical Event	
Hispania/ His-PAHN-yah	Location	What Iberia/Spain/Portugal used to be called
Huv'nae	Scottish Slang	Haven't
Informers	Figure/ Person/ Creature	Someone who secretly provides information to authorities, often about rebels, criminals, or political movements
Inis Fáil/ In-ish fawl	Gaeilge (Irish) Term	Island of Destiny, poetic and mythical name for Ireland
Irish Gaelic (Gaeilge)/ GAYL-guh	Language	The Irish Language

Word	Type	Description/ Meaning
Isnae/ IZ-nay	Scottish Slang	Isn't/ Is not
Jacobite	Figure/ Person/ Creature	
Keiss/ Keess	Location	Small coastal village in Caithness, Scotland (Originally inhabited by the Sinclair Clan)
Ken	Scottish Slang	Know
Kent	Scottish Slang	Knew
Killybegs/ Kill-ee-begs	Location	Coastal town in County Donegal, Ireland, known for its thriving fishing industry
Lá Bealtaine/ Law BYAL-tin-eh	Celebration	Ancient Celtic festival marking the start of summer, celebrated May 1. Celebrates Ériu, the goddess of fertility of the land
Laudanum/ LAW-duh-num	Item	Alcoholic solution containing morphine, prepared from opium and formerly used as a narcotic painkiller
Leite creme/ Lay-tuh KREH-muh	Item	Portuguese Dessert similar to crème brûlée.

Word	Type	Description/ Meaning
Lia Fáil/ Lee-ah Fawl	Item	One of the legendary Four Treasures of the Tuatha Dé Danann
Lugh Lámhfhada/ LOOG Law-va-da	Figure/ Person/ Creature	Lugh was a rather famous demigod. Lámhfhada means "of the Long Arm," referring to Lugh's skill with his spear or reach in battle in Irish mythology. The "mh" in Irish Gaelic creates a "v" sound, and "fh" is often silent.
Mac Cuill, Mac Cecht, and Mac Greine/ Mock Coo-il, Mock Kecht, Mock Gray-neh	Figure/ Person/ Creature	Three kings of Ireland at the time of the Milesian invasion and played a key role in the transition of power from the Tuatha Dé Danann to the Milesians
Manannán mac Lir/ Muh-NAN-awn mak Leer	Figure/ Person/ Creature	Son of the Sea
Míl Espáine/ Meel Es-pawn-yeh	Figure/ Person/ Creature	Soldier of Spain
Milesians/ Mil-ee-zhuns	Figure/ Person/ Creature	Legendary group in Irish mythology who are said to be the ancestors of the Irish people

Word	Type	Description/ Meaning
Mo chridhe/ Muh kree-yuh	Gaelic (Scottish) Term	My heart
Mo chroí/ Muh khree	Gaelic (Scottish) Term	My heart/ my love
Mo ghrá/ Muh ghrah	Gaeilge (Irish) Term	My love
Mo ghràdh/ Muh graw	Gaelic (Scottish) Term	My love
Mo luaidh/ Muh LOO-ee	Gaelic (Scottish) Term	My darling
Mo nighean bheag/ Muh NEE-uhn vek	Gaelic (Scottish) Term	My little girl
Murias/ MUR-ee-us	Location	One of the Four Great Cities of the Tuatha Dé Danann
Nae/ Nay	Scottish Slang	No
Needna/ NEED-nuh	Scottish Slang	Need not/ Needn't
Nighean/ NEE-uhn	Gaelic (Scottish) Term	Daughter
Otherworld	Location	In Irish Mythology, it's where Gods reside

Word	Type	Description/ Meaning
Piuthar/ PYOO-uhr	Gaelic (Scottish) Term	Sister
Por todos os santos/ Poor TOH-dooz ooz SAHN-toosh	Portuguese Phrase	By all the saints
Province of Mide/ Mee-th	Location	The Fifth Province of Ancient Ireland
Quero ver tudo—cada tremor, cada suspiro/ KEH-roo vehr TOO-doo — KAH-dah treh-MOHR, KAH-dah soos-PEE-roo	Portuguese Phrase	I want to see everything—every tremble, every sigh
Sap	Irish Slang	Stupid person
Scáthfhóilt/ Skawfolt	Gaeilge (Irish) Phrase	Shadow mane
Scottish Gaelic (Gàidhlig)/ GAH-lik	Language	The Scottish Language
Scud	Scottish Slang	Naked
Shouldna/ SHOOD-nuh	Scottish Slang	Should Not/ Shouldn't
Sí uaisle/ Shee oo-ash-leh	Gaeilge (Irish) Term	Noble fae
Sídhe/ Shee	Gaeilge (Irish) Term	Fairy

Word	Type	Description/ Meaning
Slàinte mhòr/ Slan-ja-vore	Gaelic (Scottish) Term	Good health, but doubles as a Jacobite toast.
Sliotar/ Slit-er	Item	Small, hard ball used in the traditional Irish sport of hurling
Stone of Fál/ Fawl	Item	Located on the Hill of Tara in County Meath, Ireland, it served as the coronation stone for the High Kings of Ireland. According to legend, when the rightful king placed his feet upon it, the stone would emit a roar, signifying his legitimate claim to the throne.
Tagann aimsir ar cách, toilteanach nó ainneonach/ TAH-gun AM-sheer air kawkh, TULL-chun-ukh noh AN-yoh-nukh	Gaeilge (Irish) Phrase	Time comes for everyone, willing or not
Tão apertada... tão boa, meu amor/ Tah-ow ah-pehr-TAH-dah... tah-ow BOH-ah, meh-ooh ah-MOHr	Portuguese Phrase	So tight... so good, my love

WORD	TYPE	DESCRIPTION/ MEANING
Tír na nÓg/ Teer na Nohg	Location	Land of the young, Otherworldly realm in Irish Mythology
Tonn Glas/ TON GLASS	Gaeilge (Irish) Term	Green wave
Tonnag/ TON-ak	Clothing Item	Woolen shawl or cloak
Tuatha Dé Danann/ Too-ah-ha Day Dah-nuhn	Figure/ Person/ Creature	"People of the Goddess Danu" or "Tribe of the Goddess Danu."
Uisneach Hill/ ISH-nock Hill	Location	Regarded as the geographical and symbolic center of Ireland
Wasna/ WAZ-nuh	Scottish Slang	Was not/Wasn't
Waterskin	Item	Portable container made from animal hide or other materials, used to carry water
Willnae/ WILL-nay	Scottish Slang	Will not/ Won't
Wouldnae/ WUD-nay	Scottish Slang	Would not/ Wouldn't
Wurnae/ WUR-nee	Scottish Slang	Were not/ Weren't